The Pledge of Allegiance

I pledge allegiance to the Flag

of the United States of America,

and to the Republic

for which it stands,

one Nation under God, indivisible,

with liberty and justice for all.

HARCOURT HORIZONS

United States History: Beginnings

Harcourt
SCHOOL PUBLISHERS

Orlando   Austin   New York   San Diego   Toronto   London

Visit *The Learning Site!*
www.harcourtschool.com

HARCOURT HORIZONS

UNITED STATES HISTORY: BEGINNINGS

General Editor

Dr. Michael J. Berson
Associate Professor
Social Science Education
University of South Florida
Tampa, Florida

Contributing Authors

Dr. Robert P. Green, Jr.
Professor
School of Education
Clemson University
Clemson, South Carolina

Dr. Thomas M. McGowan
Chairperson and Professor
Center for Curriculum and Instruction
University of Nebraska
Lincoln, Nebraska

Dr. Linda Kerrigan Salvucci
Associate Professor
Department of History
Trinity University
San Antonio, Texas

Series Consultants

Dr. Robert Bednarz
Professor
Department of Geography
Texas A&M University
College Station, Texas

Dr. Asa Grant Hilliard III
Fuller E. Callaway Professor
  of Urban Education
Georgia State University
Atlanta, Georgia

Dr. Thomas M. McGowan
Chairperson and Professor
Center for Curriculum and Instruction
University of Nebraska
Lincoln, Nebraska

Dr. John J. Patrick
Professor of Education
Indiana University
Bloomington, Indiana

Dr. Philip VanFossen
Associate Professor,
  Social Studies Education,
  and Associate Director,
  Purdue Center for Economic Education
Purdue University
West Lafayette, Indiana

Dr. Hallie Kay Yopp
Professor
Department of Elementary, Bilingual, and
  Reading Education
California State University, Fullerton
Fullerton, California

Content Reviewers

United States Geography

Dr. Phillip Bacon
Professor Emeritus
Geography and Anthropology
University of Houston
Houston, Texas

Native Americans and European Exploration

Dr. Susan Deans-Smith
Associate Professor
Department of History
University of Texas at Austin
Austin, Texas

Dr. John Jeffries Martin
Professor
Department of History
Trinity University
San Antonio, Texas

Richard Nichols
President
Richard Nichols and Associates
Fairview, New Mexico

Early Settlement and the American Revolution

Dr. John W. Johnson
Professor and Head
Department of History
University of Northern Iowa
Cedar Falls, Iowa

Dr. John P. Kaminski
Director, Center for the Study of
  the American Constitution
Department of History
University of Wisconsin
Madison, Wisconsin

Dr. Elizabeth Mancke
Associate Professor of History
Department of History
University of Akron
Akron, Ohio

The Constitution and United States Government

Dr. James M. Banner, Jr.
Historian
Washington, D.C.

Carol Egbo
Social Studies Consultant
Waterford Schools
Waterford, Michigan

Dr. John P. Kaminski
Director, Center for the Study of
 the American Constitution
Department of History
University of Wisconsin
Madison, Wisconsin

Dr. John J. Patrick
Professor of Education
Indiana University
Bloomington, Indiana

The National Period and Westward Expansion

Dr. Ross Frank
Professor
Department of Ethnic Studies
University of California at San Diego
La Jolla, California

Civil War and Reconstruction

Dr. Judith Giesburg
Assistant Professor
Department of History
Northern Arizona University
Flagstaff, Arizona

The United States in the Twentieth Century

Dr. Carol McKibben
Visiting Professor
Monterey Institute of International Studies
Monterey, California

Dr. Albert Raboteau
Henry W. Putnam Professor
Department of Religion
Princeton University
Princeton, New Jersey

Classroom Reviewers

Kathleen Arseneau
Teacher
St. Matthew's School
Kalispell, Montana

Sharalyn Barkley
Teacher
Dougherty County School District
Albany, Georgia

Lounelle M. Beecher
Social Studies/Foreign Language
 Coordinator
William Robinson Curriculum Center
Augusta, Georgia

Portia F. Bohannon-Ramsey
Teacher and Social Studies Chair
James E. McDade Classical School
Chicago, Illinois

Mary Ann Coe
Teacher
Lenox Elementary School
Portland, Oregon

Katherine Dalton
Teacher
Breckinridge Elementary School
Fincastle, Virginia

Lucille Ferragamo
Teacher
A. C. Whelan Elementary School
Revere, Massachusetts

Brenda Gesst
Teacher
Bethel Elementary School
Clover, South Carolina

Barbara Haack
Teacher
Perkins Academy
Des Moines, Iowa

Kimberly Hillman
Teacher
Council Traditional Magnet School
Mobile, Alabama

Margaret Kennedy
Teacher
Jason Lee Elementary School
Portland, Oregon

Karen Little
Teacher
Hubbertville School
Fayettville, Alabama

Cindy Merchant
Teacher
Denver Place School
Wilmington, Ohio

Barbara Motzer
Teacher
General Wayne Elementary School
Malvern, Pennsylvania

Maps
researched and prepared by

Readers
written and designed by

Take a Field Trip
video tour segments provided by

Copyright © 2005 by Harcourt, Inc.

All rights reserved. No part of this publication may be reproduced or transmitted in any form or by any means, electronic or mechanical, including photocopy, recording, or any information storage and retrieval system, without permission in writing from the publisher.

Requests for permission to make copies of any part of the work should be mailed to:

School Permissions and Copyrights
Harcourt, Inc.
6277 Sea Harbor Drive
Orlando, Florida 32887-6777
Fax: 407-345-2418

HARCOURT and the Harcourt Logo are trademarks of Harcourt, Inc., registered in the United States of America and/or other jurisdictions. TIME FOR KIDS and the red border are registered trademarks of Time Inc. Used under license. Copyright © by Time Inc. All rights reserved.

Acknowledgments appear in the back of this book.

Printed in the United States of America

ISBN 0-15-339643-1

4 5 6 7 8 9 10 048 13 12 11 10 09 08 07 06

Contents

xvi	Reading Your Textbook
A1	**Atlas**
A2	**Map and Globe Skills** Read a Map
A18	Geography Terms
1	**Introduction**
2	Why History Matters
4	**Reading Skills** Compare Primary and Secondary Sources
6	Why Geography Matters
8	Why Economics Matters
9	Why Civics and Government Matter
10	Why Culture and Society Matter

UNIT 1 · The Land and Early People

- 11 **Unit 1 Introduction**
- 12 **Unit 1 Preview**
- 14 **Start with a Poem**
  "If We Should Travel" by Joseph Bruchac

17 Chapter 1 Our Country's Geography

- **Main Idea and Details**
- 18 **Lesson 1** The Land and Natural Regions
- 24 🌐 **Map and Globe Skills**
  Use Elevation Maps
- 26 **Lesson 2** Bodies of Water
- 33 **Lesson 3** The Climate and Vegetation Regions
- 40 **Lesson 4** Using the Land
- 44 **Lesson 5** Where People Live and Work
- 50 🌐 **Map and Globe Skills**
  Use Latitude and Longitude
- 52 **Chapter 1 Review and Test Preparation**

55 Chapter 2 The Earliest Americans

- **Compare and Contrast**
- 56 **Lesson 1** The First Americans
- 60 📊 **Chart and Graph Skills**
  Read Time Lines
- 62 **Lesson 2** Ancient Indians
- 68 🌐 **Map and Globe Skills**
  Use a Cultural Map
- 70 **Lesson 3** The Desert Southwest
- 74 **Examine Primary Sources**
  Native American Pottery
- 76 **Lesson 4** The Northwest Coast and the Arctic
- 81 **Lesson 5** The Plains
- 86 **Lesson 6** The Eastern Woodlands
- 91 🇺🇸 **Citizenship Skills**
  Resolve Conflict
- 92 **Chapter 2 Review and Test Preparation**
- 94 **Visit**
  The Hopi Nation

96 Unit 1 Review and Test Preparation
- 98 **Unit Activities**

v

UNIT 2

Time of Encounters

- 99   Unit 2 Introduction
- 100   Unit 2 Preview
- 102   **Start with a Story**
  "San Salvador" from *The World in 1492* by Jamake Highwater

105   Chapter 3   A Time of Exploration

 Sequence

- 106   Lesson 1   The World in the 1400s
- 112   **Map and Globe Skills** Follow Routes on a Map
- 114   Lesson 2   Background to European Exploration
- 120   **Reading Skills** Identify Causes and Their Effects
- 121   Lesson 3   Europeans Explore the World
- 127   Lesson 4   The Spanish Conquerors
- 134   **Examine Primary Sources** Conquistador Armor
- 136   Lesson 5   Search for the Northwest Passage
- 140   Chapter 3 Review and Test Preparation

143   Chapter 4   European Settlement

 Categorize

- 144   Lesson 1   New Spain
- 150   Lesson 2   New France
- 156   Lesson 3   The English in the Americas
- 160   Lesson 4   The Jamestown Colony
- 165   **Citizenship Skills** Solve a Problem
- 166   Lesson 5   The Plymouth Colony
- 171   **Chart and Graph Skills** Compare Tables to Classify Information
- 172   Chapter 4 Review and Test Preparation
- 174   **Visit** The Mission San Diego de Alcalá

- 176   **Unit 2 Review and Test Preparation**
- 178   Unit Activities

UNIT 3

The English Colonies

- 179 **Unit 3 Introduction**
- 180 **Unit 3 Preview**
- 182 **Start with a Journal**
  Stranded at Plimoth Plantation, 1626
  words and woodcuts by Gary Bowen

- 187 ## Chapter 5 The New England Colonies
   Summarize
- 188 Lesson 1 The Massachusetts Bay Colony
- 194 Lesson 2 New Ideas, New Colonies
- 200 Lesson 3 New England's Economy
- 205 **Chart and Graph Skills**
  Use a Line Graph
- 206 **Chapter 5 Review and Test Preparation**

- 209 ## Chapter 6 The Middle Atlantic Colonies
   Make Inferences
- 210 Lesson 1 The Breadbasket Colonies
- 216 **Examine Primary Sources**
  Great Awakening Sermons
- 218 Lesson 2 Colonial Philadelphia
- 223 **Chart and Graph Skills**
  Use a Circle Graph
- 224 Lesson 3 Moving West
- 228 **Chapter 6 Review and Test Preparation**

- 231 ## Chapter 7 The Southern Colonies
   Generalize
- 232 Lesson 1 Settlement of the South
- 240 **Reading Skills**
  Tell Fact from Opinion
- 241 Lesson 2 Southern Plantations
- 246 **Map and Globe Skills**
  Read a Resource and Product Map
- 248 Lesson 3 Southern Cities
- 252 **Chapter 7 Review and Test Preparation**
- 254 **Visit**
  Colonial Williamsburg

256 Unit 3 Review and Test Preparation
258 Unit Activities

UNIT 4

The American Revolution

259 Unit 4 Introduction
260 Unit 4 Preview
262 Start with a Song
"Yankee Doodle" Traditional Song

267 Chapter 8 Uniting the Colonies

 Cause and Effect

268 Lesson 1 The French and Indian War Begins
273 Lesson 2 Britain Wins North America
278 Map and Globe Skills
Compare Historical Maps
280 Lesson 3 Colonists Speak Out
286 Reading Skills
Determine Point of View
288 Lesson 4 The Road to War
293 Lesson 5 The Second Continental Congress
298 Chapter 8 Review and Test Preparation

301 Chapter 9 The Revolutionary War

 Sequence

302 Lesson 1 Independence Is Declared
308 Lesson 2 Americans and the Revolution
313 Citizenship Skills
Make a Decision
314 Lesson 3 Fighting the Revolutionary War
320 Examine Primary Sources
Washington's Mess Chest
322 Lesson 4 Independence Is Won
330 Chart and Graph Skills
Compare Graphs
332 Chapter 9 Review and Test Preparation
334 Visit
The Freedom Trail

336 Unit 4 Review and Test Preparation
338 Unit Activities

viii

UNIT 5 — A New Nation

- **339** Unit 5 Introduction
- **340** Unit 5 Preview
- **342** Start with a Story
  Shh! We're Writing the Constitution by Jean Fritz pictures by Tomie dePaola

345 Chapter 10 The Constitution

Summarize

- **346** Lesson 1 The Confederation Period
- **351** Lesson 2 The Constitutional Convention
- **358** Lesson 3 Three Branches of Government
- **364** Chart and Graph Skills
  Read a Flow Chart
- **366** Lesson 4 Approval and the Bill of Rights
- **373** Citizenship Skills
  Act as a Responsible Citizen
- **374** Lesson 5 The New Government Begins
- **380** Chapter 10 Review and Test Preparation

383 Chapter 11 The Nation Grows

Draw Conclusions

- **384** Lesson 1 The Louisiana Purchase
- **389** Lesson 2 The War of 1812
- **395** Lesson 3 The Age of Jackson
- **400** Examine Primary Sources
  Audubon's Paintings
- **402** Lesson 4 From Ocean to Ocean
- **410** Map and Globe Skills
  Identify Changing Borders
- **412** Lesson 5 An Industrial Revolution
- **420** Chapter 11 Review and Test Preparation
- **422** Visit
  Old Ironsides

424 Unit 5 Review and Test Preparation
- **426** Unit Activities

UNIT 6

Civil War Times

- **427** Unit 6 Introduction
- **428** Unit 6 Preview
- **430** **Start with a Journal**
  All for the Union: The Civil War Diary and Letters of Elisha Hunt Rhodes
  edited by Robert H. Rhodes

- **435** ## Chapter 12 The Nation Divided
   Categorize
- **436** Lesson 1 Regional Disagreements
- **442** **Reading Skills**
  Identify Frame of Reference
- **444** Lesson 2 Slavery and Freedom
- **450** Lesson 3 The Union Breaks Apart
- **456** **Map and Globe Skills**
  Compare Maps with Different Scales
- **458** Lesson 4 Civil War
- **465** Lesson 5 The Road to Union Victory
- **472** Chapter 12 Review and Test Preparation

- **475** ## Chapter 13 The Nation Reunited
   Point of View
- **476** Lesson 1 Reconstruction
- **481** Lesson 2 The South After the War
- **486** Lesson 3 Settling the Last Frontier
- **492** **Chart and Graph Skills**
  Use a Climograph
- **494** Lesson 4 The Rise of New Industries
- **500** **Examine Primary Sources**
  Edison's Inventions
- **502** Lesson 5 A Changing People
- **508** Chapter 13 Review and Test Preparation
- **510** **Visit**
  The Gettysburg National Military Park

- **512** ## Unit 6 Review and Test Preparation
- **514** Unit Activities

· UNIT ·
7

From Past to Present

515 Unit 7 Introduction
516 Unit 7 Preview
518 Start with a Story
The Eagle Has Landed edited by William J. Bennett
illustrated by Michael Hague

523 Chapter 14 Changes in the United States

 Predict an Outcome

524 Lesson 1 New Ideas and New Inventions
532 **Map and Globe Skills**
Use a Time Zone Map
534 Lesson 2 People on the Move
542 **Chart and Graph Skills**
Use a Cartogram
544 Lesson 3 Society Changes
552 Lesson 4 A United Country
560 **Citizenship Skills**
Identify Political Symbols
562 Chapter 14 Review and Test Preparation

565 Chapter 15 Becoming a World Power

 Fact and Opinion

566 Lesson 1 The United States Grows
574 **Map and Globe Skills**
Compare Map Projections
576 Lesson 2 Defending Democracy
584 **Examine Primary Sources**
Editorial Cartoons
586 Lesson 3 A World Superpower
594 **Citizenship Skills**
Make Economic Choices
596 Chapter 15 Review and Test Preparation
598 Visit
Ellis Island

600 Unit 7 Review and Test Preparation
602 Unit Activities

xi

Reference

R2 Almanac
- R2 Facts About the States
- R6 Facts About the Western Hemisphere
- R8 Facts About the Presidents

R11 American Documents
- R11 The Declaration of Independence
- R15 The Constitution of the United States of America
- R36 The National Anthem
- R37 The Pledge of Allegiance

R38 Biographical Dictionary

R47 Gazetteer

R56 Glossary

R65 Index

Features You Can Use

Skills

CHART AND GRAPH SKILLS
- 60 Read Time Lines
- 171 Compare Tables to Classify Information
- 205 Use a Line Graph
- 223 Use a Circle Graph
- 330 Compare Graphs
- 364 Read a Flow Chart
- 492 Use a Climograph
- 542 Use a Cartogram

CITIZENSHIP SKILLS
- 91 Resolve Conflict
- 165 Solve a Problem
- 313 Make a Decision
- 373 Act as a Responsible Citizen
- 560 Identify Political Symbols
- 594 Make Economic Choices

MAP AND GLOBE SKILLS
- A2 Read a Map
- 24 Use Elevation Maps
- 50 Use Latitude and Longitude
- 68 Use a Cultural Map
- 112 Follow Routes on a Map
- 246 Read a Resource and Product Map
- 278 Compare Historical Maps
- 410 Identify Changing Borders
- 456 Compare Maps with Different Scales
- 532 Use a Time Zone Map
- 574 Compare Map Projections

READING SKILLS
- 4 Compare Primary and Secondary Sources
- 120 Identify Causes and Their Effects
- 240 Tell Fact from Opinion
- 286 Determine Point of View
- 442 Identify Frame of Reference

Citizenship

DEMOCRATIC VALUES
- 89 The Common Good
- 163 Representative Government
- 214 Justice
- 290 The Right to Privacy
- 548 Individual Rights
- 555 Citizen Participation

POINTS OF VIEW
- 124 An Unknown Land?
- 281 Taxes
- 368 For or Against the Bill of Rights
- 453 Union or Secession

Music and Literature
- 14 "If We Should Travel" by Joseph Bruchac
- 102 "San Salvador" from *The World in 1492* by Jamake Highwater
- 182 *Stranded at Plimoth Plantation, 1626* words and woodcuts by Gary Bowen
- 262 "Yankee Doodle" Traditional Song
- 342 *Shh! We're Writing the Constitution* by Jean Fritz pictures by Tomie dePaola
- 393 "The Star-Spangled Banner" by Francis Scott Key
- 430 *All for the Union: The Civil War Diary and Letters of Elisha Hunt Rhodes* edited by Robert H. Rhodes
- 518 *The Eagle Has Landed* edited by William J. Bennett illustrated by Michael Hague

Primary Sources

EXAMINE PRIMARY SOURCES
- 74 Native American Pottery
- 134 Conquistador Armor
- 216 Great Awakening Sermons
- 320 Washington's Mess Chest
- 400 Audubon's Paintings
- 500 Edison's Inventions
- 584 Editorial Cartoons

AMERICAN DOCUMENTS
- 167 Mayflower Compact
- 468 The Gettysburg Address
- 556 The American's Creed
- R11 The Declaration of Independence
- R15 The Constitution of the United States of America
- R36 The National Anthem
- R37 The Pledge of Allegiance

ANALYZE PRIMARY SOURCES
- 84 A Calendar Robe
- 158 John White's Map
- 282 Stamp Act Protest
- 304 The Declaration of Independence
- 440 Kansas–Nebraska Act Flyer
- 535 An Immigrant Passport

Biography
- 30 Samuel Langhorne Clemens
- 72 Luci Tapahonso
- 118 Ahmad Ibn Majid
- 145 Bartolomé de Las Casas
- 237 James Oglethorpe
- 244 Olaudah Equiano
- 270 George Washington
- 289 Samuel Adams
- 296 Phillis Wheatley
- 303 Thomas Jefferson
- 312 Thayendanegea
- 317 Haym Salomon
- 352 James Madison
- 376 Benjamin Banneker
- 405 Narcissa Prentiss Whitman
- 461 Robert E. Lee
- 463 Clara Barton
- 479 Edmund G. Ross
- 505 Hiram L. Fong
- 530 Louis Armstrong
- 549 Booker T. Washington
- 549 W.E.B. Du Bois

Geography
- 47 The Center of Population
- 133 Conquest of the Incas
- 233 St. Marys City
- 249 Charles Town
- 284 Boston
- 408 Marshall Gold Discovery State Historic Park
- 490 Little Bighorn Battlefield

Heritage
- 79 Family Heritage
- 123 Columbus Day
- 155 The French Quarter
- 168 Thanksgiving Day
- 306 Independence Day
- 393 "The Star-Spangled Banner"
- 471 Memorial Day
- 482 Juneteenth
- 553 Flag Day
- 569 Hula Dance

Science and Technology
- 117 Navigational Tools
- 419 Cast-Steel Plow
- 466 The *H. L. Hunley*
- 528 Early Motion Pictures

Charts, Graphs, and Diagrams

- **A18** Geography Terms
- **13** United States Population
- **24** Reading Contour Lines
- **28** The Water Cycle
- **34** The Rain Shadow
- **35** The Change of Seasons
- **49** The Ten Largest Cities in the United States
- **71** Pueblo
- **77** Making a Dugout
- **101** First Explorers to the Americas, 1492–1542
- **116** The Caravel
- **120** Causes and Effects
- **146** Castillo de San Marcos
- **160** Jamestown
- **171** Table A: European Settlements in the Americas
- **171** Table B: European Settlements in the Americas
- **181** The 13 Colonies
- **190** A New England Town
- **205** Colonial Exports to England, 1700–1750
- **223** Population of the 13 Colonies, 1750
- **226** Frontier Life
- **242** A Southern Plantation
- **261** Population of the 13 Colonies, 1750
- **283** Colonial Imports from Britain, 1764–1768
- **294** The Battle of Bunker Hill
- **313** Decisions for the Colonists
- **324** The Battle of Yorktown
- **331** Exports to Main Trading Partners, 1790
- **331** Chief Colonial Exports, 1790
- **331** Colonial Exports to Britain, 1760–1790
- **341** Population of the 10 Largest Cities in the United States, 1850
- **353** Travel Times
- **354** Federal System of Government
- **362** Checks and Balances
- **365** How a Bill Becomes a Law
- **369** Constitution Ratification Vote
- **376** Washington, D.C.
- **397** Voter Participation, 1824–1840
- **413** A Canal Lock
- **417** A Textile Mill
- **429** United States Foreign-Born Population, 1860–1920
- **445** Southern Slaveholders in 1860
- **448** African Americans in the United States, 1800–1860
- **454** Fort Sumter Prior to the Civil War
- **459** Advantages in the Civil War
- **493** Climograph: Omaha, Nebraska
- **493** Climograph: Philadelphia, Pennsylvania
- **494** Transcontinental Railroad
- **496** Steel Production, 1865–1900
- **497** Oil Production, 1865–1900
- **504** Immigration to the United States, 1871–1910
- **517** Miles Traveled by Type of Transportation, 1940–Present
- **525** Ford's Factory
- **526** Automobile Sales, 1920–1929
- **543** Population Cartogram of the Western United States
- **546** Labor Union Membership, 1898–1920
- **555** Voter Turnout in Presidential Elections, 1952–2000

Maps

- **A2** The United States with Grid
- **A4** World: Political
- **A6** World: Physical
- **A8** Western Hemisphere: Political
- **A9** Western Hemisphere: Physical
- **A10** United States: Overview
- **A12** United States: Political
- **A14** United States: Physical
- **A16** Canada
- **A17** Mexico
- **12** North America
- **20** Landforms of North America
- **25** Elevations of the United States
- **27** Oceans and Continents
- **29** Major Bodies of Water in the United States
- **36** Climate Regions of the United States
- **38** Vegetation of the United States
- **42** Land Use and Resources of the United States
- **45** Regions of the United States
- **47** The Center of Population
- **50** Latitude and Longitude
- **51** United States Latitude and Longitude
- **57** Land Routes of Early People
- **65** Ancient Cultures of North America
- **69** Early Cultures of North America
- **89** Iroquois Nation
- **97** Great Plains
- **100** Early European Settlements
- **108** Major Cities of the 1400s
- **113** Routes of Marco Polo, 1271–1295
- **119** Routes of Dias and da Gama
- **122** Voyages of Columbus
- **125** Routes of Caboto, Vespucci, Balboa, and Magellan
- **126** Line of Demarcation
- **129** Conquistadors in North America
- **133** Pizarro's Route
- **138** Routes of Cartier and Hudson
- **149** Major Missions of New Spain
- **151** Routes of Champlain, 1603–1615
- **153** Routes of Marquette and Joliet and La Salle
- **154** New France, 1760s
- **157** Drake's Voyage Around the World 1577–1580
- **177** Route of Cabeza de Vaca, 1528
- **180** Colonial America, 1750
- **189** Massachusetts Bay Colony
- **197** New England Colonies
- **202** Colonial Trade Routes
- **211** Dutch and Swedish Colonies, 1654
- **212** Middle Atlantic Colonies
- **219** Center City, Philadelphia
- **225** English Colonists Move West
- **233** St. Marys City
- **234** Southern Colonies
- **238** Thirteen English Colonies
- **247** Colonial Products
- **249** Charles Town
- **257** Colonial Products: Middle Atlantic Colonies
- **260** Colonial America, 1775
- **269** North America in 1754
- **274** The French and Indian War, 1754–1763
- **279** Map A: North America Before the French and Indian War
- **279** Map B: North America After the French and Indian War
- **284** Boston
- **291** Lexington and Concord
- **323** Major Battles of the Revolution
- **329** North America in 1783
- **337** Land Claims in 1763
- **337** Land Claims in 1783
- **340** The United States, 1783–1853
- **349** The Northwest Territory, 1785
- **353** Routes to the Philadelphia Convention, 1787
- **369** Ratification of the Constitution
- **385** The Louisiana Purchase
- **391** Major Battles of the War of 1812
- **398** The Trail of Tears
- **404** Texas Independence, 1835–1836
- **406** Trails to the West

408 Marshall Gold Discovery State Historic Park
411 The Growth of the United States
415 Transportation in the East, 1850
425 Texas, 1821–1845
428 The Nation Divided, 1861
438 The Missouri Compromise, 1820
439 Compromise of 1850
440 Kansas–Nebraska Act
446 The Underground Railroad
456 Map A: Fort Sumter
457 Map B: Fort Sumter
460 The Union and the Confederacy
470 Major Battles of the Civil War
488 Cattle Trails
489 Settlers Move West, 1870–1890
490 Little Bighorn Battlefield
498 Industry in the United States, 1890s
513 South Carolina Coast, 1861
516 The United States, 2001
533 Time Zones of the United States
538 United States, 1900
540 The Sun Belt of the United States
542 The Western United States
545 United States National Parks
570 United States Possessions, 1900
572 The Panama Canal
574 Map A: Western Hemisphere
575 Map B: Western Hemisphere
577 World War I
580 World War II
588 NATO Countries, 2002

Time Lines

Unit 1 Preview Time Line, **12**
Horizontal Time Line, **60**
Vertical Time Line, **61**
Chapter 2, Lesson Summary Time Line, **67**
Unit 1 Summary Time Line, **96**
Unit 2 Preview Time Line, **100**
Chapter 3, Lesson Summary Time Lines, **111, 119, 126, 133, 139**
Chapter 3 Summary Time Line, **140**
Chapter 4, Lesson Summary Time Lines, **149, 155, 159, 164, 170**
Chapter 4 Summary Time Line, **172**
Unit 2 Summary Time Line, **176**
Unit 3 Preview Time Line, **180**
Chapter 5, Lesson Summary Time Lines, **193, 199, 204**
Chapter 5 Summary Time Line, **206**
Chapter 6, Lesson Summary Time Lines, **215, 222**
Chapter 6 Summary Time Line, **228**
Chapter 7, Lesson Summary Time Lines, **239, 251**
Chapter 7 Summary Time Line, **252**
Unit 3 Summary Time Line, **256**
Unit 4 Preview Time Line, **260**
Chapter 8, Lesson Summary Time Lines, **272, 277, 285, 292, 297**
Chapter 8 Summary Time Line, **298**
Chapter 9, Lesson Summary Time Lines, **307, 319, 329**
Chapter 9 Summary Time Line, **332**
Unit 4 Summary Time Line, **336**
Unit 5 Preview Time Line, **340**
Chapter 10, Lesson Summary Time Lines, **350, 357, 372, 379**
Chapter 10 Summary Time Line, **380**
Chapter 11, Lesson Summary Time Lines, **388, 394, 399, 409, 419**
Chapter 11 Summary Time Line, **420**
Unit 5 Summary Time Line, **424**
Unit 6 Preview Time Line, **428**
Chapter 12, Lesson Summary Time Lines, **441, 449, 455, 464, 471**
Chapter 12 Summary Time Line, **472**
Chapter 13, Lesson Summary Time Lines, **480, 485, 491, 499, 507**
Chapter 13 Summary Time Line, **508**
Unit 6 Summary Time Line, **512**
Unit 7 Preview Time Line, **516**
Chapter 14, Lesson Summary Time Lines, **531, 541, 551, 559**
Chapter 14 Summary Time Line, **562**
Chapter 15, Lesson Summary Time Lines, **573, 583, 593**
Chapter 15 Summary Time Line, **596**
Unit 7 Summary Time Line, **600**

Reading Your Textbook

Getting Started

Your textbook is divided into eight units.

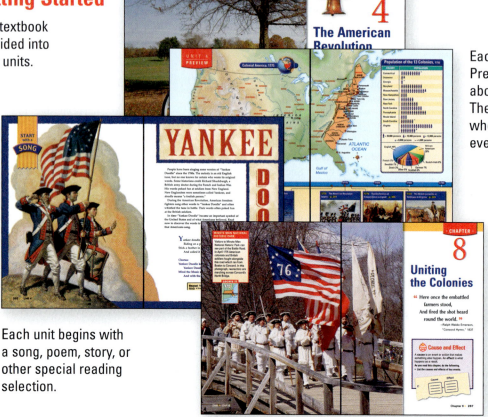

Each unit has a Unit Preview that gives facts about important events. The Preview also shows where and when those events took place.

Each unit begins with a song, poem, story, or other special reading selection.

Each unit is divided into chapters, and each chapter is divided into lessons.

The Parts of a Lesson

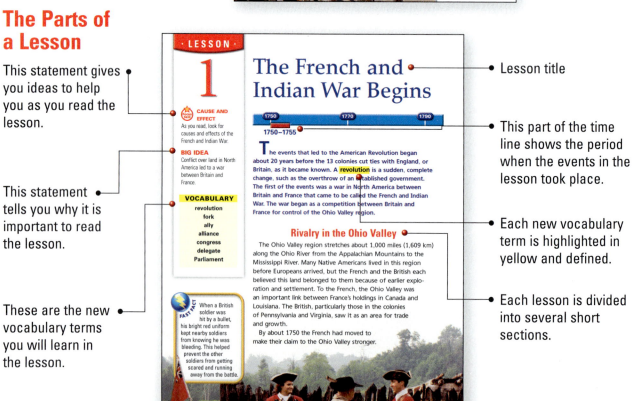

This statement gives you ideas to help you as you read the lesson.

This statement tells you why it is important to read the lesson.

These are the new vocabulary terms you will learn in the lesson.

Lesson title

This part of the time line shows the period when the events in the lesson took place.

Each new vocabulary term is highlighted in yellow and defined.

Each lesson is divided into several short sections.

xvi

Each lesson, like each chapter and each unit, ends with a review. There may be a Summary Time Line that shows the order of the events covered in the lesson. Questions and a performance activity help you check your understanding of the lesson.

Each short section ends with a REVIEW question that will help you check whether you understand what you have read. Be sure to answer this question before you continue reading the lesson.

Skills

Your textbook has lessons that will help you build your reading, citizenship, chart and graph, and map and globe skills.

You will be able to practice and apply the skills you learn.

This statement tells you why it is important to learn the skill.

xvii

Special Features

The feature called Examine Primary Sources shows you ways to learn about different kinds of objects and documents.

The Visit feature lets you "visit" many interesting places.

Atlas

The Atlas provides maps and a list of geography terms with illustrations.

For Your Reference

At the back of your textbook, you will find the reference tools listed below.

- Almanac
- American Documents
- Biographical Dictionary
- Gazetteer
- Glossary
- Index

You can use these tools to look up words and to find information about people, places, and other topics.

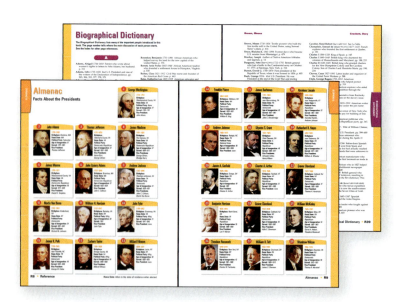

xviii

Atlas

 Map and Globe Skills
A2 READ A MAP

The World
A4 POLITICAL
A6 PHYSICAL

Western Hemisphere
A8 POLITICAL
A9 PHYSICAL

United States
A10 OVERVIEW
A12 POLITICAL
A14 PHYSICAL

Canada
A16 POLITICAL/PHYSICAL

Mexico
A17 POLITICAL/PHYSICAL

Geography Terms
A18

A1

SKILLS: Read a Map

VOCABULARY

map title	grid system	compass rose
map key	locator	cardinal directions
inset map	map scale	intermediate directions

▶ WHY IT MATTERS

Maps provide many kinds of information about the world around you. Knowing how to read maps is an important social studies skill.

▶ WHAT YOU NEED TO KNOW

A map is a drawing that shows all of or part of the Earth on a flat surface. Mapmakers add certain features to most of the maps they draw.

- A **map title** tells the subject of the map. It may also identify the kind of map.
  - Political maps show cities, states, and countries.
  - Physical maps show kinds of land and bodies of water.
  - Historical maps show parts of the world as they were in the past.

- A **map key**, or legend, explains the symbols used on a map. Symbols may be colors, patterns, lines, or other special marks.

- An **inset map** is a small map within a larger map.

Mapmakers sometimes need to show places marked on the map in greater detail or places that are beyond the area shown on the map. Find Alaska and Hawaii on the map of the United States on pages A10–A11. This map shows the location of those two states in relation to the rest of the country.

The United States

A2

Now find Alaska and Hawaii on the map below. To show this much detail for these states and the rest of the country on one map, the map would have to be much larger. Instead, Alaska and Hawaii are each shown in a separate **inset map**, or a small map within a larger map.

To help people find places on a map, mapmakers sometimes add lines that cross each other to form a pattern of squares called a **grid system**. Look at the map of the United States below. Around the grid are letters and numbers. The columns, which run up and down, have numbers. The rows, which run left and right, have letters. Each square on the map can be identified by its letter and number. For example, the top row of squares in the map includes square A1, square A2, and square A3.

▶ **PRACTICE THE SKILL**

Use the map of the United States to answer the following questions.

1. What city can be found in square D3?
2. In which direction would you travel to go from Montgomery, Alabama, to Richmond, Virginia?
3. About how many miles is it from Richmond, Virginia, to Albany, New York?
4. Which two oceans border Alaska?

▶ **APPLY WHAT YOU LEARNED**

Choose one of the maps in the Atlas. With a partner, identify the parts of the map and discuss what the map tells you. Ask each other questions that can be answered by reading the map.

- A **locator** is a small map or picture of a globe that shows where the place on the main map is located.

- A **map scale** compares a distance on the map to a distance in the real world. It helps you find the real distance between places on a map.

- A **compass rose**, or direction marker, shows directions.
  - The **cardinal directions**, or main directions, are north, south, east, and west.
  - The **intermediate directions**, or directions between the cardinal directions, are northeast, northwest, southeast, and southwest.

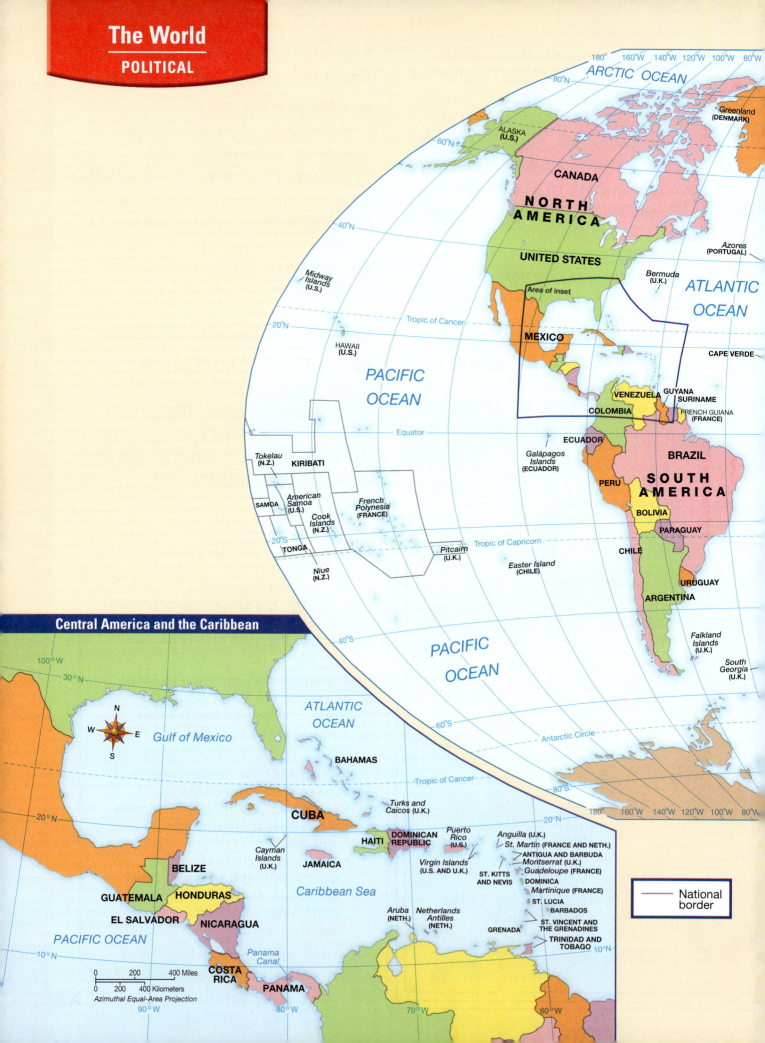

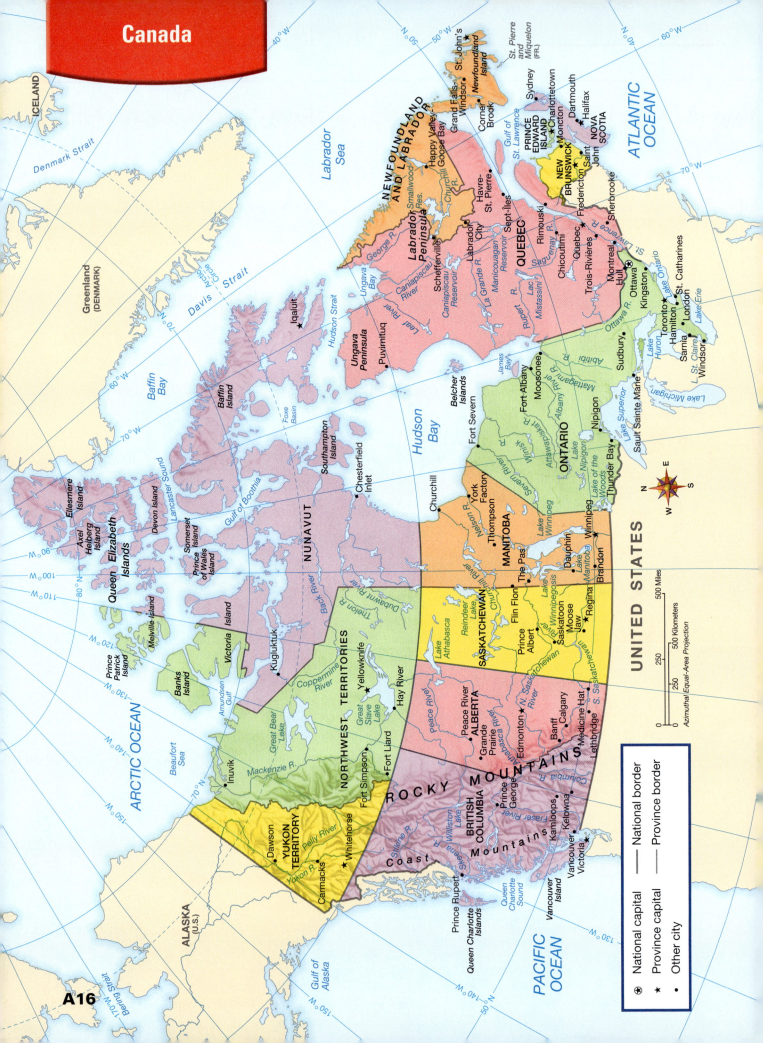

Geography Terms

1. **basin** bowl-shaped area of land surrounded by higher land
2. **bay** an inlet of the sea or some other body of water, usually smaller than a gulf
3. **bluff** high, steep face of rock or earth
4. **canyon** deep, narrow valley with steep sides
5. **cape** point of land that extends into water
6. **cataract** large waterfall
7. **channel** deepest part of a body of water
8. **cliff** high, steep face of rock or earth
9. **coast** land along a sea or ocean
10. **coastal plain** area of flat land along a sea or ocean
11. **delta** triangle-shaped area of land at the mouth of a river
12. **desert** dry land with few plants
13. **dune** hill of sand piled up by the wind
14. **fall line** area along which rivers form waterfalls or rapids as the rivers drop to lower land
15. **floodplain** flat land that is near the edges of a river and is formed by silt deposited by floods
16. **foothills** hilly area at the base of a mountain
17. **glacier** large ice mass that moves slowly down a mountain or across land
18. **gulf** part of a sea or ocean extending into the land, usually larger than a bay
19. **hill** land that rises above the land around it
20. **inlet** any area of water extending into the land from a larger body of water
21. **island** land that has water on all sides
22. **isthmus** narrow strip of land connecting two larger areas of land
23. **lagoon** body of shallow water
24. **lake** body of water with land on all sides
25. **marsh** lowland with moist soil and tall grasses

26	**mesa**	flat-topped mountain with steep sides
27	**mountain**	highest kind of land
28	**mountain pass**	gap between mountains
29	**mountain range**	row of mountains
30	**mouth of river**	place where a river empties into another body of water
31	**oasis**	area of water and fertile land in a desert
32	**ocean**	body of salt water larger than a sea
33	**peak**	top of a mountain
34	**peninsula**	land that is almost completely surrounded by water
35	**plain**	area of flat or gently rolling low land
36	**plateau**	area of high, mostly flat land
37	**reef**	ridge of sand, rock, or coral that lies at or near the surface of a sea or ocean
38	**river**	large stream of water that flows across the land
39	**riverbank**	land along a river
40	**savanna**	area of grassland and scattered trees
41	**sea**	body of salt water smaller than an ocean
42	**sea level**	the level of the surface of an ocean or a sea
43	**slope**	side of a hill or mountain
44	**source of river**	place where a river begins
45	**strait**	narrow channel of water connecting two larger bodies of water
46	**swamp**	area of low, wet land with trees
47	**timberline**	line on a mountain above which it is too cold for trees to grow
48	**tributary**	stream or river that flows into a larger stream or river
49	**valley**	low land between hills or mountains
50	**volcano**	opening in the earth, often raised, through which lava, rock, ashes, and gases are forced out
51	**waterfall**	steep drop from a high place to a lower place in a stream or river

Introduction

"**The history of every country begins with the heart of a man or a woman**"

—Willa Cather, *O Pioneers!*, 1913

Learning About Our Country

This year in social studies, you will be studying the United States, past and present. You will learn about past events and the places where those events occurred. You will also read about people who helped shape our country. You will see how people have worked together to meet their needs and wants and to govern themselves. You will learn what it means to be a citizen of the United States.

Why History Matters

VOCABULARY
history   oral history   historical empathy   analyze
chronology   point of view   frame of reference

Studying **history**, or what happened in the past, helps you see how the past and the present are linked. Studying history also helps you understand how the events of today may be linked to the future. As you learn to recognize these links, you will begin to think more like a historian, a person who studies the past.

Measuring Time

One way historians see connections in history is by studying the order in which events happened. The order of events is called their **chronology** (kruh•NAH•luh•jee). By looking at the chronology of events, historians can learn how the past is connected to the present.

Finding Evidence

Historians study the past by looking for clues in the objects and documents that people have left behind. They read journal entries, newspaper articles, and other writings by people who experienced past events. They also listen to or read records of oral histories. An **oral history** is a story of an event or an experience told aloud by a person who did not have a written language or who did not write down what happened. Historians also look at photographs, films, and artwork. By examining such clues, historians can piece together what took place in the past and can better explain why they think events happened as they did.

In the past and the present, many people from other countries have chosen to immigrate to the United States.

In the past, many immigrants to the United States arrived by boat at Ellis Island in New York. The letters and diaries and oral histories of the immigrants tell much about their adventures.

Identifying Points of View

Historians examine people's points of view. A person's **point of view** is how he or she sees things. It can depend on whether that person is old or young, a man or a woman, rich or poor. A point of view is also shaped by a person's background and experiences. People with different points of view may see the same event differently.

Historians learn about the times and places in which people lived. They study how scientific discoveries and new ways of doing things affected people's lives. In that way, historians can understand earlier people's actions and feelings. This understanding is called **historical empathy** (EM•puh•thee).

Understanding Frames of Reference

Historians also work hard to understand people's **frames of reference**. A frame of reference includes where people were when an event took place and what part they took in it. Historians must be careful not to judge the actions of people in the past based on the way people of today would act.

Drawing Conclusions

Many events in history are connected to other events. To **analyze** an event, historians look closely at how the parts of it connect with one another and how the event is connected to other events. Analyzing an event allows historians to draw conclusions about how and why it happened.

REVIEW Why is it important to study history?

This display at Ellis Island shows a few of the people who arrived there. Immigrants to the United States have many different backgrounds and experiences. This may lead them to have different points of view.

Immigrants wait at Ellis Island. Historians use photographs like this one to draw conclusions about early United States immigration.

Introduction ■ 3

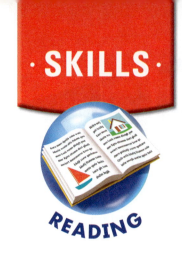

SKILLS · Compare Primary and Secondary Sources

VOCABULARY
primary source
secondary source

▶ WHY IT MATTERS

To know what really happened in the past, you need to find proof. You can do this by studying and comparing two kinds of sources—primary sources and secondary sources.

▶ WHAT YOU NEED TO KNOW

Primary sources are the records made by people who saw or took part in an event. These people may have written down their thoughts in a journal, or they may have told their story in a letter or a poem. They may have made a speech, produced a film, taken a photograph, or painted a picture. Primary sources may also be objects or official documents that give information about the time in which they were made or written. A primary source gives people of today a direct link to a past event.

This photograph **A**, letter **B**, and pen and ink bottle **C** are all examples of primary sources from the time of the Civil War.

4 ■ Introduction

A **secondary source** is not a direct link to an event. It is a record of the event written by someone who was not there at the time. A magazine article, newspaper story, or book written by someone who only heard about or read about the event is a secondary source. So is an object made at a later time.

Some sources can be either primary or secondary, depending on how the event is reported. A newspaper might print the exact words of a person who saw the event take place. It might also print an article about the event, written by a reporter who was not there. Oral histories, textbooks, and online resources can also be either primary or secondary sources.

▶ PRACTICE THE SKILL

Look at the photographs of objects and printed materials that give information about the American Civil War. Then answer these questions.

1. How are items A and F alike and different?
2. What kind of information might be found in item B but not in item D?
3. Why might secondary sources D and E also be considered primary sources?

▶ APPLY WHAT YOU LEARNED

Look through your textbook for examples of primary and secondary sources. Explain to a classmate what makes each source you selected a primary source or a secondary source.

This newspaper **D**, Civil War Web site **E**, and recent photograph of people dressed as Civil War soldiers **F** are secondary sources.

Introduction • 5

READING SKILLS

Why Geography Matters

VOCABULARY			
geography	physical feature	modify	region
location	human feature	adapt	

Every event you will read about in this book has a setting, and part of the setting is the place where the event happened. Learning about places is an important part of **geography**—the study of Earth's surface and the way people use it. People who study geography are called geographers.

The Five Themes of Geography

Geographers often speak of five main themes when they study a place. You will find that most of the maps in this book focus on one of these themes. Keeping these themes in mind as you read will help you think like a geographer.

Location
Everything on Earth has its own **location**—the place where it can be found.

Human-Environment Interactions
Humans and their surroundings interact, or affect each other. People's activities may **modify**, or change, the environment. The environment may affect people, causing them to **adapt**, or adjust, to their surroundings.

Place
Every location has features that make it different from all other locations. **Physical features** are formed by nature. **Human features** are created by people.

Movement
Each day, people in different parts of the country and around the world exchange products and ideas.

Regions
Areas of Earth that share features that make them different from other areas are called **regions**. A region can be described by its physical features or human features.

Essential Elements of Geography

Geographers also use six other topics when they study a place. These six topics are called the six essential elements of geography. Thinking about them will help you understand the world around you.

• GEOGRAPHY •

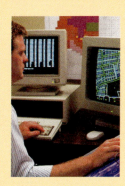

The World in Spatial Terms
Geographers use maps and other kinds of information to study relationships among people and places. They want to know why things are located where they are.

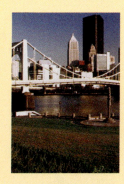

Human Systems
People's activities include where they settle, how they earn a living, and the laws they make. All of these help shape Earth's surface.

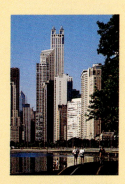

Places and Regions
People are linked to the places and regions in which they live. Places and regions have both physical and human features.

Environment and Society
People's activities often affect the environment, and the environment affects people's activities.

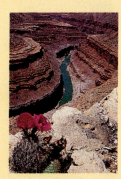

Physical Systems
Physical processes, such as wind and rain, shape Earth's surface. Living things interact with physical features to create and change environments.

The Uses of Geography
Knowing how to use maps, globes, and other geography tools helps people in their everyday lives.

REVIEW What is geography?

Why Economics Matters

VOCABULARY
economy
economics

Have you ever earned money for doing chores? Did you use the money to buy something you needed or wanted? When you do these things, you are taking part in the economy. An **economy** is the way people of a state, a region, or a country use resources to meet their needs. The study of how people do this is called **economics**.

In this book you will read about how people in the past made, bought, sold, and traded goods to meet their needs. You will learn how the economy of the United States changed over time to become one in which businesses are free to sell many kinds of goods and services.

REVIEW How are resources important to a country's economy?

Farmland (above) is just one of the many resources people use to meet their needs. Paper money and coins (top right) are used in the economy to buy and sell goods. Children as well as adults find it wise to save money for the future (bottom right).

8 ■ Introduction

Why Civics and Government Matter

VOCABULARY
civics civic participation government

"Ask not what your country can do for you; ask what you can do for your country." When President John F. Kennedy said these words in 1961, he was talking about another key area of social studies—civics. **Civics** is the study of citizenship. In this textbook you will read about the rights and responsibilities of citizens of the United States. You will also learn about the importance of **civic participation**. Civic participation is being concerned with and involved in issues related to your community, state, or country or the entire world.

In the United States, citizens have an important part in making government work. A **government** is a system of leaders and laws that helps people live together in their community, state, or country. It protects citizens and settles disagreements among them. In this book you will read about the people and events that shaped government in the past. You will also find out how government works today.

REVIEW How is civics different from government?

The Constitution of the United States (below left) and the United States Capitol building (below right) are both symbols of American government.

Why Culture and Society Matter

VOCABULARY
culture   heritage
society

In this book you will read about people of the past who helped shape the present. You will learn about their customs and beliefs, their families and communities, and the ways they made a living. All these things make up a **culture**, or way of life.

Each human group, or **society**, has a culture. This book will help you discover the many cultures of our country, both now and in the past. You will also learn about our country's **heritage**, or culture that has come from the past and continues today.

REVIEW How are the terms *culture* and *society* related?

The photograph above gives a glimpse of Mexican culture within the United States. The photograph below shows the many different heritages of the students in a Gary, Indiana, classroom of long ago.

The Land and Early People

GEORGIA CONNECTION

A Cheyenne shield, 1860–1868

Paria Canyon, Vermillion Cliffs National Monument, Arizona

UNIT 1

The Land and Early People

" And the People came to live in the Northern Mountains and on the Plains, in the Western Hills and on the Seacoasts, in the Southern Deserts and in the Canyons. "

—Simon Ortiz, *The People Shall Continue,* 1977

Preview the Content

Scan the pictures in each chapter and lesson. Use them to create a list of topics you will learn about in Unit 1.

Preview the Vocabulary

Word Meanings Write what you think each word below means and why. Use the Glossary to check your answers.

WORD	POSSIBLE MEANING	WHY
savanna		
tepee		
wampum		

Unit 1 ■ 11

Facts About United States Geography

PHYSICAL FEATURE	LOCATION
Largest Gorge	Grand Canyon, Nevada/Arizona
Largest Freshwater Lake	Lake Superior
Deepest Lake	Crater Lake, Oregon
Longest River	Mississippi River
Highest Mountain	Mount McKinley, Alaska
Lowest Point	Death Valley, California
Largest Cave	Mammoth Cave, Kentucky

United States Population

Two out of ten people live in rural, or country, areas.

Eight out of ten people live in or near cities.

4,000 years ago — **PRESENT**

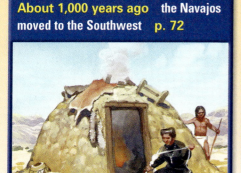

About 1,000 years ago the Navajos moved to the Southwest p. 72

By 800 years ago more than 30,000 people lived in Cahokia p. 66

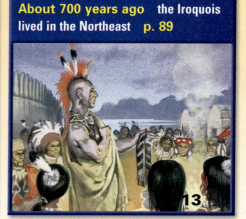

About 700 years ago the Iroquois lived in the Northeast p. 89

START with a POEM

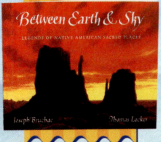

IF WE SHOULD TRAVEL
by Joseph Bruchac

Many people use poems, songs, or stories to tell about important events and people in their past. Some of these stories are legends. A legend is a story handed down by a group of people over time. Some legends tell about brave or heroic people. Others try to explain the origins of animals, plants, and physical features found in the world.

If we should travel
far to the South,
there in the land
of mountains and mist,
we might hear the story
of how Earth was first shaped.

Water Beetle came out
to see if it was ready,
but the ground was
still as wet as a swamp,
too soft for anyone to stand.

Great Buzzard said, "I will help dry the land."
He began to fly close above the new Earth.
Where his wings came down,
valleys were formed,
and where his wings lifted,
hills rose up through the mist.

So the many rolling valleys and hills
of that place called the Great Smokies
came into being there.
And so it is that the Cherokee people,
aware of how this land was given,
know that the Earth is a sacred gift
we all must respect and share.

Analyze the Literature

1. What is the author describing in the poem?

2. Explain why people use poems, songs, and stories to explain the world around them.

READ A BOOK

START THE UNIT PROJECT

A Multimedia Presentation
Work with your classmates to create a multimedia presentation about the landforms and early people of the United States. As you study the unit, write down the landforms you read about and tell how early people used the natural resources around them.

USE TECHNOLOGY

Visit The Learning Site at **www.harcourtschool.com** for additional activities, primary sources, and other resources to use in this unit.

GRAND TETON NATIONAL PARK

The Grand Teton Mountain Range is located in the Cowboy State of Wyoming. In this photograph, the Snake River winds its way near the mountains. Twelve peaks in the mountain range reach above 12,000 feet (4 km).

LOCATE IT

Grand Teton National Park
Snake R.
WYOMING

CHAPTER 1

Our Country's Geography

" O beautiful for spacious skies,
For amber waves of grain,
For purple mountain majesties
Above the fruited plain! "
—from the poem "America the Beautiful"
by Katharine Lee Bates, 1893

Main Idea and Details

The **main idea** is the most important idea in a passage. The **details** give more information that supports the main idea.

As you read this chapter, list the main ideas and details.

- List the main ideas.
- Under each main idea, list the supporting details.

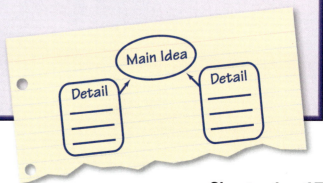

Chapter 1 ▪ 17

LESSON 1

Land and Regions

MAIN IDEA AND DETAILS
As you read, identify main ideas and details about land and regions in the United States.

BIG IDEA
The United States can be divided into regions based on different kinds of land.

VOCABULARY
landform
mountain range
piedmont
sea level
plateau
basin
volcano

In 1893 the poet Katharine Lee Bates saw the Rocky Mountains for the first time. She was in Colorado on a tour. "One day some of the other teachers and I decided to go on a trip to 14,000-foot (4,267-m) Pikes Peak," she later wrote. "We hired a prairie wagon. Near the top we had to leave the wagon and go the rest of the way on mules. I was very tired. But when I saw the view, I felt great joy. All the wonder of America seemed displayed there, with the sea-like expanse." By the time she left Colorado, Bates had written the opening lines to her poem "America the Beautiful." Her poem later became a well-known song when it was set to music.

Landform Regions

The United States is more than a land of beauty. It is also a land of many different places. To better study the land of the United States, geographers often divide it into landform regions. A landform region is a region that has similar landforms throughout. Landforms are physical features on the Earth's surface, such as plains, mountains, hills, and valleys. Each landform is unique because of its shape and the way it came to be made.

All of the United States, except for the island state of Hawaii, is in North America. North America is one

LOCATE IT
COLORADO
Colorado Springs
Pikes Peak

18 • Unit 1

of the Earth's seven continents, or largest areas of land. In addition to sharing the continent of North America, the United States shares landform regions with its neighbors, Canada and Mexico.

REVIEW What details explain landform regions? **MAIN IDEA AND DETAILS**

America's Largest Mountains

The two largest mountain ranges in the United States are the Appalachian (ap•uh•LAY•chee•uhn) Mountains and the Rocky Mountains. A **mountain range** is a group of connected mountains. The Appalachians cover much of the eastern United States. They stretch all the way from central Alabama to southeastern Canada. The Rocky Mountains cover much of the western United States. They extend north from Mexico through Canada and into Alaska.

Most scientists believe the Appalachian Mountains were formed more than 250 million years ago. Over time the mountains' peaks have been worn down. The highest peaks in the Appalachians are less than 7,000 feet (2,134 m) tall.

Most of the mountain peaks in the Appalachians are less than 3,500 feet (1,067 m) tall.

A large part of the Appalachians is made up of a series of ridges and valleys that run next to each other. Among these ridges are the Blue Ridge, Catskill, Pocono, and White Mountains. The area of high land on the eastern side of the Appalachians is called the Piedmont (PEED•mahnt). A **piedmont** is an area at or near the foot of a mountain. The Piedmont begins in New Jersey and stretches as far south as Alabama.

Pikes Peak (center) is one of many peaks that make up the Rocky Mountains.

FAST FACT Pikes Peak was named for explorer Zebulon Pike. Because he did not have enough supplies, Pike was unable to climb to the top of the mountain he first saw in 1806. Today people can reach the top by using a highway or a mountain railway.

Chapter 1 ■ 19

Landforms of North America

Regions North America is made up of several landform regions.

> What mountain region lies to the east of the Mississippi River?

Many scientists believe that most of the Rocky Mountains were formed more than 30 million years ago. Like the Appalachians, the Rocky Mountain Range is so large that it is made up of smaller ranges. Each range is separated from another by high plains and valleys.

Unlike the peaks of the Appalachians, the peaks of the Rockies appear sharp and jagged. They are also much higher because they are newer and have not been worn down by wind and water for as long a time. More than 50 peaks in Colorado alone are higher than 14,000 feet (4,267 m). Because the Rockies are so high, many of the peaks are covered with snow all year.

REVIEW What mountain range covers much of the eastern United States? the western United States?

Regions of Plains

The two largest landform regions in the United States are plains—the Coastal Plain and the Interior Plains. A coastal plain is low, mostly flat land that lies along an ocean or another large body of water. The Coastal Plain stretches inland from the Atlantic Ocean and the Gulf of Mexico. The Interior Plains, also called the Interior Lowlands, extend across most of the center of the United States. The word *interior* means "the inside or inner part."

The Coastal Plain region begins along the Atlantic Ocean in Massachusetts. There it is only a narrow strip of land no more than 10 miles (16 km) wide. It gets wider—hundreds of miles wider—farther south toward Florida. From Florida the Coastal Plain extends west along the Gulf of Mexico into Texas and eastern Mexico. The land of the Coastal Plain region lies close to sea level and gradually rises inland. **Sea level** is the level of the surface of the oceans. It is used as a starting point in measuring the height and depth of landforms. Another, smaller coastal plain, the Arctic Coastal Plain, lies in northern Canada and Alaska.

The very large Interior Plains region stretches across the middle of North America, from the Appalachian Mountains in the east to the Rocky Mountains in the west. It extends north from Mexico, across the United States, and into Canada. In the eastern part of the Interior Plains, often called the Central Plains, the land is mostly flat to rolling with areas of forests to the east and grasslands to the west. Farther to the west, however, the land becomes much flatter and rises to meet the base of the Rocky Mountains. This western part of the Interior Plains is called the Great Plains. The Great Plains stretch from southern Texas into Canada.

While most of the land between the Appalachians and the Rockies is plains, there are areas with other kinds of landforms. To the north of the Interior Plains is the Canadian Shield. This rocky, horseshoe-shaped region wraps around Hudson Bay. There are hundreds of lakes in this region. In other places, such as the Black Hills of South Dakota and the Ozark Plateau (pla•TOH) in Missouri and Arkansas, the land rises very sharply to an area of hills and small mountains. A **plateau** is a broad area of high, mostly flat land.

REVIEW How is the location of the Coastal Plain different from that of the Interior Plains?

This wheat field in Kansas is a part of the miles and miles of flat land that makes up the Great Plains.

A Region of Basins, Ranges, and Plateaus

Between the Rocky Mountains and other mountain ranges farther west is a large area sometimes called the Intermountain Region. *Intermountain* means "between the mountains." Part of this land is the Great Basin, which includes Nevada and parts of five neighboring states. A **basin** is low, bowl-shaped land with higher ground all around it. At the southwestern edge of the Great Basin lies the lowest point on the continent of North America. Part of Death Valley in California lies more than 280 feet (85 m) below sea level.

Because the Intermountain Region has areas of low and high land, it is often called the Basin and Range Region. Not only basins and mountain ranges but other landforms mark this region. These include plateaus and canyons. The two largest plateaus in the region are the Columbia Plateau to the northwest of the Great Basin and the Colorado Plateau to the southeast.

The Grand Canyon, one of the world's natural wonders, cuts across part of the Colorado Plateau. Carved by the Colorado River over thousands of years, it extends 280 miles (451 km) through Arizona. It is up to 18 miles (29 km) wide and about a mile (1.6 km) deep.

REVIEW What kinds of landforms are found in the Intermountain Region?

More Mountains and Valleys

Lying west of the Intermountain Region and stretching to the Pacific Ocean is the Pacific Mountains and Valleys region. This region extends north from Mexico to Canada and Alaska. It is made up mainly of separate mountain ranges and a series of valleys between those mountain ranges.

On the eastern edge of the Pacific Mountains and Valleys region is the Sierra Nevada (see•AIR•ah neh•VAH•dah). *Sierra Nevada* is Spanish for "Snowy Mountain Range." The Sierra Nevada runs almost the length of California. Other mountains lie north of the Sierra Nevada. These are the Cascade Range in northern California, Oregon, and Washington, and the Coast Mountains in Canada. These ranges include some volcanoes. A **volcano** is an

Death Valley is about 140 miles (225 km) long and about 5 to 15 miles (8 to 24 km) wide.

LOCATE IT
Death Valley National Park
Sacramento
San Francisco
CALIFORNIA
Los Angeles

opening in the Earth through which hot lava, gases, ash, and rocks may pour out. When this happens, a volcano is erupting. Sometimes the lava and ash build up to form a mountain.

Farther north, in Alaska, is the Alaska Range. It has the highest mountain peak in North America, Mount McKinley. The peak, which is sometimes called by its Native American name, Denali (duh•NAH•lee), is 20,320 feet (6,194 m) high. *Denali* means "The Great One" or "The High One." The peak was first climbed in 1913.

Beside the Pacific Ocean in California, Oregon, and Washington are the Coast Ranges. These low mountains give much of the Pacific Coast a rocky, rugged look. At many places these mountains drop sharply into the ocean. Unlike the Atlantic Coast, the Pacific Coast has very little flat land along its coast.

Sandwiched between the Coast Ranges, the Sierra Nevada, and the Cascade Range are three large, fertile valleys. The largest is the more than 400-mile (644-km) long Central Valley in California. The others are the Puget Sound Lowland in Washington and the Willamette (wuh•LA•muht) Valley in Oregon.

REVIEW What region extends north from Mexico to Canada and Alaska?

In Big Sur, California, steep cliffs have formed where the Coast Ranges meet the Pacific Ocean.

LESSON 1 REVIEW

 MAIN IDEA AND DETAILS What region extends across most of the center of the United States?

❶ **BIG IDEA** What are the major kinds of land that determine the landform regions of the United States?

❷ **VOCABULARY** Write a paragraph that includes the terms **mountain range**, **piedmont**, and **sea level**.

❸ **GEOGRAPHY** How do the Appalachian Mountains differ from the Rocky Mountains?

❹ **GEOGRAPHY** What are the two largest landform regions in the United States?

❺ **CRITICAL THINKING—Analysis** How might the similarities and differences of the land in different parts of your state affect how people live there?

 PERFORMANCE—Draw a Map Draw a map of the United States that shows the main landform regions. Describe and label each region, and list some of the region's main physical features. Share your map with a classmate.

Chapter 1 ■ 23

SKILLS: Use Elevation Maps

VOCABULARY
elevation
contour line

▶ WHY IT MATTERS

Different maps provide different kinds of information. If you want to know how high or how low the land is, you need to use an elevation (eh•luh•VAY•shuhn) map. **Elevation** is the height of the land in relation to sea level.

▶ WHAT YOU NEED TO KNOW

The elevation of land is measured from sea level, usually in feet or meters. The elevation of land at sea level is 0 feet (0 m). Find sea level on Drawing A. The lines on this drawing of a mountain are contour lines. A **contour line** connects all points of equal elevation. Find the contour line for 13,120 feet (4,000 m) on Drawing A. This line connects all the points on the mountain that are 13,120 feet (4,000 m) above sea level.

Drawing B shows the hill as you look down on it from above. On the steeper side of the hill, the contour lines are closer together. On the sloping side of the hill, the lines are farther apart.

On Drawing C, color is added between the contour lines. A key is used instead of labels. The key for Drawing C shows that every place shown in green is between sea level and 655 feet (200 m). The border between green and yellow on the map is a contour line for 655 feet (200 m). The borders between the other colors are also contour lines.

Reading Contour Lines

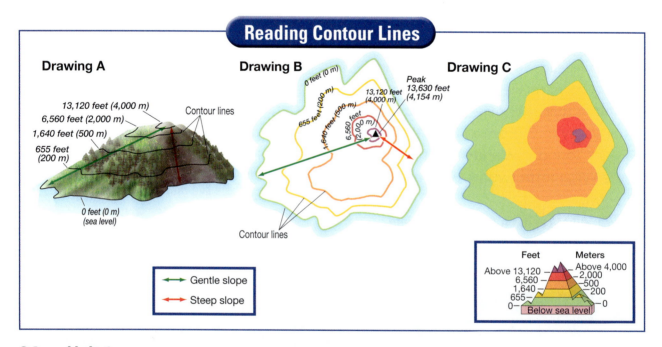

24 ▪ Unit 1

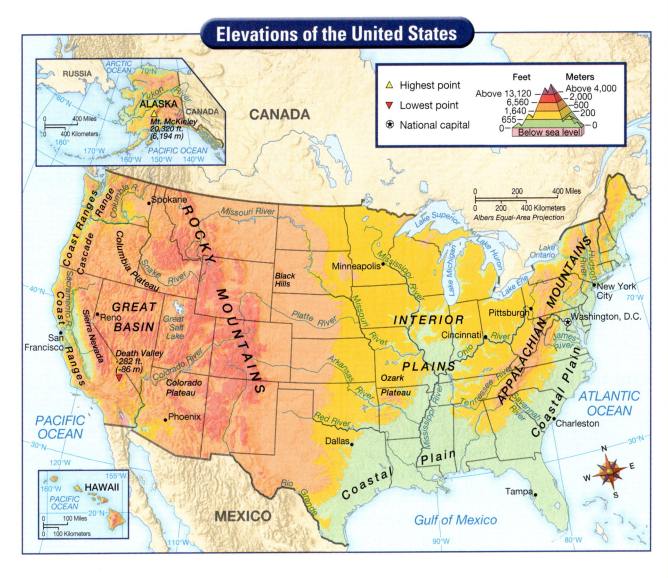

Most elevation maps use only a few important contour lines, with colors added between the lines. Look at the elevation map of the United States on this page. The map does not show exact elevations. Instead, the key shows the range of elevation that each color stands for. On this map, green is used for land in the range between sea level and 655 feet (200 m).

PRACTICE THE SKILL

Use the map to answer the following questions.

1. Find the Coastal Plain on the map. What is the elevation of the land around Dallas, Texas?
2. What range of elevations is shown by the color red?
3. Which city has a higher elevation: Reno, Nevada, or Tampa, Florida?

APPLY WHAT YOU LEARNED

Lay a ruler across the map on this page to connect any two cities. Describe the elevation of the land you would cross if you were to travel by car from one city to the other. Compare your description with that of a classmate.

Practice your map and globe skills with the **GeoSkills CD-ROM**.

Chapter 1 ▪ 25

LESSON 2

Bodies of Water

MAIN IDEA AND DETAILS
As you read, look for details that give information about each kind of body of water.

BIG IDEA
There are different kinds of bodies of water.

VOCABULARY
current
tide
inlet
sound
tributary
drainage basin
fall line

Bodies of water are important to life in the United States. Oceans help connect the United States to other countries of the world. Lakes and rivers provide fresh water for wildlife and, in many places, for people and their farms, factories, and cities. Large lakes and rivers also provide important transportation routes within the United States. Like landforms, bodies of water have different shapes and sizes.

Oceans

The largest bodies of water on Earth are the four oceans. From largest to smallest, they are the Pacific Ocean, the Atlantic Ocean, the Indian Ocean, and the Arctic Ocean. The Pacific Ocean alone covers nearly one-third of the Earth's surface, an area larger than all the continents put together.

These four oceans hold most of the Earth's water. They also separate most of the Earth's seven continents. From largest to smallest, these continents are Asia, Africa, North America, South America, Antarctica, Europe, and Australia. Geographers sometimes group Europe and Asia together and call them Eurasia (yu•RAY•zhuh).

Oceans form a natural boundary for a large part of the United States. On the northern coast of Alaska is the Arctic Ocean. On the eastern coast of the United States is the Atlantic Ocean. On the western coast and surrounding Hawaii is the Pacific Ocean.

Oceans move in the form of waves and currents. A **current** is that part of a body of water

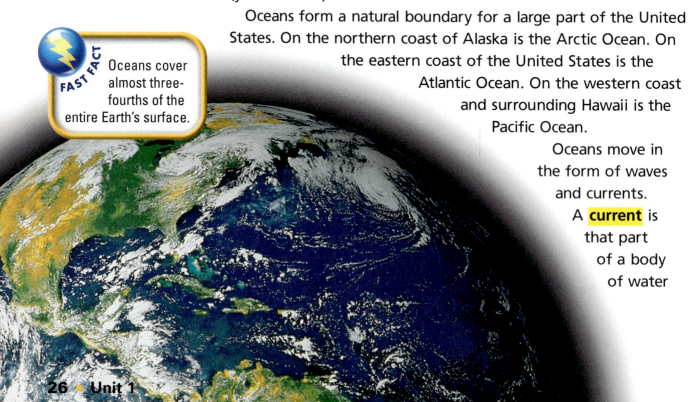
FAST FACT Oceans cover almost three-fourths of the entire Earth's surface.

26 • Unit 1

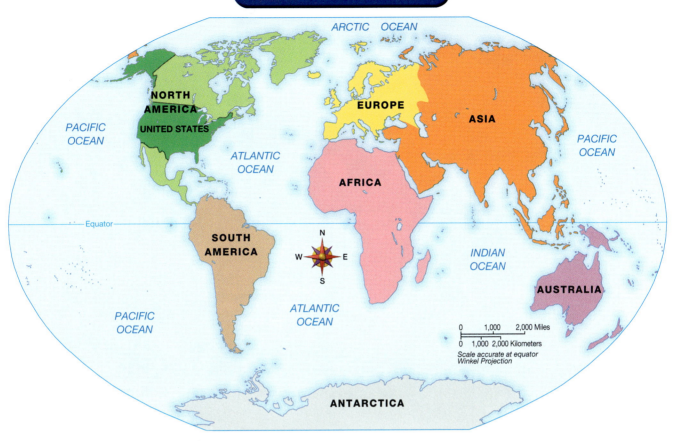

Oceans and Continents

Movement Oceans separate most of the continents.
➤ What ocean separates North America and Africa?

flowing in a certain direction. Ocean currents are caused mainly by the Earth's wind patterns.

Ocean water also moves in the form of tides. **Tides** are the regular rise and fall of an ocean and of the bodies of water connected to it. When the tide is high, some of the low-lying land near the ocean is covered with water.

REVIEW What is the main cause of ocean currents?

Gulfs, Bays, and Inlets

Hundreds of inlets along the Coastal Plain help define the shape of the United States. An **inlet** is any area of water extending into the land from a larger body of water. The largest of these inlets are called gulfs. The largest gulf bordering the United States is the Gulf of Mexico. Several states in the southeastern United States border this gulf. Another large gulf, the Gulf of Alaska, lies south of Alaska, along the Pacific Coast.

Hundreds of bays also shape the coastline. Many large bays provide harbors where ships can safely dock.

Most of the largest bays and other inlets in the United States are found along the Atlantic and Gulf Coasts. On the Atlantic Coast these include Chesapeake Bay between Maryland and Virginia, Delaware Bay between Delaware and New Jersey, and Albemarle (AL•buh•marl) Sound in North Carolina.

Chapter 1 ■ 27

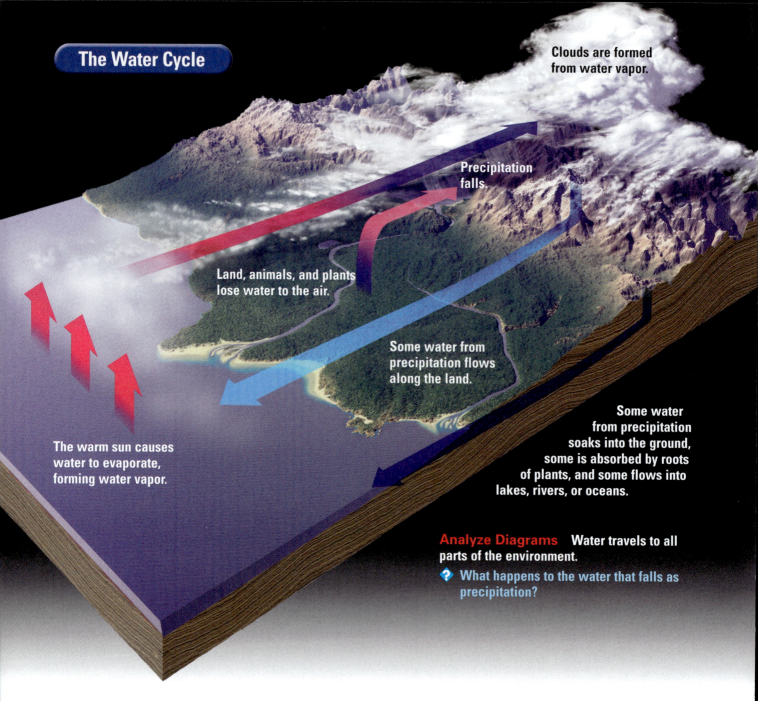

The Water Cycle

Clouds are formed from water vapor.

Precipitation falls.

Land, animals, and plants lose water to the air.

Some water from precipitation flows along the land.

The warm sun causes water to evaporate, forming water vapor.

Some water from precipitation soaks into the ground, some is absorbed by roots of plants, and some flows into lakes, rivers, or oceans.

Analyze Diagrams Water travels to all parts of the environment.
- What happens to the water that falls as precipitation?

A **sound** is a long inlet that often separates offshore islands from the mainland.

Other large bays and inlets are found along the Gulf Coast. The largest of these are Tampa Bay in Florida, Mobile Bay in Alabama, and Galveston Bay in Texas. The largest bays and inlets on the Pacific Coast include San Francisco Bay near San Francisco, California, and Puget Sound in Washington State.

REVIEW What large bays can be found along the Gulf of Mexico?

Lakes

North America has more lakes than any other continent. The largest lakes in North America are together known as the Great Lakes. They are located along the border between the United States and Canada. These five lakes—Superior, Michigan, Huron, Erie, and Ontario—are among the world's largest freshwater lakes.

One-fifth of all the fresh water on Earth is found in the Great Lakes, and

Lake Superior is the world's largest freshwater lake. It covers about 31,800 square miles (82,362 sq km), an area almost the size of South Carolina. Today the Great Lakes and the rivers connected to them form an important inland waterway for ships. This waterway links the Middle West region of the United States to the Atlantic Ocean. Other large freshwater lakes in the United States include Lake Okeechobee (oh•kuh•CHOH•bee) in Florida and Lake Tahoe on the California–Nevada border.

Most lakes in the United States are made up of fresh water, but the Great Salt Lake in Utah is as salty as any sea or ocean. Some people even consider it to be a sea—an inland body of salt water. Although freshwater streams feed the Great Salt Lake, they carry small amounts of salt. Because the lake lies in the Great Basin, surrounded by higher ground, the water coming into the lake has no way to escape.

Over time, as water evaporates, salt is left behind. As a result, the lake is so salty that no fish can live in its water.

REVIEW Which five lakes form the Great Lakes? **MAIN IDEA AND DETAILS**

GEOGRAPHY THEME

Location Lake Michigan is the only Great Lake that is completely in the United States.

♦ What states border Lake Michigan?

Major Bodies of Water in the United States

· BIOGRAPHY ·

Samuel Langhorne Clemens
1835–1910

Character Trait: Individualism

As a young man Samuel Clemens began his career by writing short, humorous stories for his brother's newspaper. At age 21 Clemens stopped writing for a while and took a job aboard a steamboat that traveled the Mississippi River. Clemens learned to guide a steamboat through the winding channels of the river and became a steamboat pilot. He traveled the Mississippi River for almost four years before ending his career as a pilot in 1861.

Clemens used his experiences to write about life along the Mississippi in his novels *The Adventures of Tom Sawyer* and *The Adventures of Huckleberry Finn* and in his autobiography, *Life on the Mississippi*. He wrote these books under his pen name, Mark Twain. The name Mark Twain comes from a term steamboat pilots used on the Mississippi. It meant that the river was at least 12 feet (about 4 m) deep, which was a safe depth for steamboats.

MULTIMEDIA BIOGRAPHIES
Visit The Learning Site at
www.harcourtschool.com
to learn about other famous people.

The Mississippi River System

Rivers are bodies of fresh, moving water. Every river begins at a source and ends at a mouth, where it empties its water into an ocean or another body of water. As a river crosses the land, it may be joined by other streams or rivers. A stream or a river that flows into a larger stream or river is called a **tributary**. Tributaries are also called branches. Together, a river and its tributaries make up a river system.

River systems drain, or carry water away from, the land around them. The land drained by a river system is its

The Mississippi River drains all or parts of 31 states including Minnesota. Many people in these states depend on the river.

LOCATE IT

Minneapolis
MINNESOTA
Mississippi River

drainage basin. When a river is long, its drainage basin can be quite large. The Mississippi River, along with its largest tributaries—the Arkansas, Illinois, Missouri, Ohio, and Red Rivers—creates a gigantic drainage basin in the middle of North America. The mighty Mississippi and its tributaries drain most of the land between the Appalachian and Rocky Mountains.

The Mississippi River's source is Lake Itasca (eye•TAS•kuh) in Minnesota. From there the river flows more than 2,300 miles (3,701 km) south to the Gulf of Mexico.

REVIEW What is a drainage basin?

Rivers East of the Appalachians

Many rivers cross the Coastal Plain and flow into the Atlantic Ocean. They include the Delaware, Hudson, James, Potomac, Roanoke, Savannah, and Susquehanna (suhs•kwuh•HAN•uh) Rivers. All of these rivers, or their tributaries, begin in the Appalachian Mountains.

Many cities in the United States have grown near where these rivers flow into ocean inlets. Philadelphia, for example, was built along the Delaware River near where it flows into Delaware Bay. New York City was built at the mouth of the Hudson River. Baltimore was built where the Patapsco River empties into Chesapeake Bay.

Cities such as Richmond and Raleigh were built farther inland on rivers where the Coastal Plain meets the Piedmont. These cities lie along the Fall Line. A **fall line** is a place where the elevation of the land drops sharply, causing rivers to form waterfalls or rapids. Cities grew along the Fall Line because people used the fast-moving water there to power machines in factories.

REVIEW Where is the source of many rivers in the eastern United States?

The Delaware River passes through the Kittatinny Mountains of Pennsylvania.

Chapter 1 ■ 31

The Pecos, Chama, and Puerco Rivers are some of the tributaries that flow into the Rio Grande.

Rivers in the West

An imaginary line runs north and south along the highest points of the Rocky Mountains. This line is called the Continental Divide. It divides the major river systems of North America into those that flow into the Gulf of Mexico and the Atlantic Ocean and those that flow into the Pacific Ocean. Western rivers that begin east of the Continental Divide empty into the Mississippi River or the Gulf of Mexico to reach the Atlantic Ocean. Rivers that begin west of the Continental Divide empty into the Pacific Ocean.

Many western rivers flow from sources on the eastern side of the Continental Divide. The largest of these include the Missouri and Arkansas Rivers and the Rio Grande. The Rio Grande forms part of the border between the United States and Mexico. In Mexico the river is known as the Río Bravo.

The major rivers on the western side of the Continental Divide include the Sacramento, San Joaquin (wah•KEEN), and Columbia Rivers. Another important western river is the Colorado. The Colorado River flows from the Rocky Mountains across the Colorado Plateau to Arizona before it empties into the Gulf of California in Mexico. The river passes through three national parks.

REVIEW What river forms part of the border between the United States and Mexico?

LESSON 2 REVIEW

 MAIN IDEA AND DETAILS What are the largest bodies of water on Earth?

❶ **BIG IDEA** Identify the major bodies of water in the United States.

❷ **VOCABULARY** Write a couple of sentences that explain how the terms **tributary** and **drainage basin** are related.

❸ **HISTORY** Why did many cities grow along the Fall Line?

❹ **CRITICAL THINKING—Synthesize** Why do you think it is important to have a waterway that links the states in the Middle West to the Atlantic Ocean?

 PERFORMANCE—Draw a Poster Find out what river is located nearest to where you live. Make a poster showing the river and its surrounding landforms. Label nearby cities and any tributaries the river may have. Share your poster with the class.

Climate and Vegetation Regions

· LESSON ·

3

 MAIN IDEA AND DETAILS
As you read, look for main ideas about climate and vegetation.

BIG IDEA
The United States can be divided into regions based on different kinds of climate and vegetation.

VOCABULARY
climate
natural vegetation
rain shadow
humidity
drought
arid
tundra
prairie
savanna

At any time or place on Earth, the weather may change—sometimes quickly or violently. Weather is the day-to-day conditions in a place. **Climate** is the kind of weather a place has most often, year after year. The climate of a place can affect what people wear, what kinds of activities they do, and how they earn their living. Few countries in the world have as many different kinds of climate as the United States.

Climate and **natural vegetation**, or the plant life that grows naturally in a place, are closely related. The different climates in the United States influence the kinds of vegetation found in different parts of our country.

Factors Affecting Climate

The climate of a place depends partly on its distance from the equator. Usually, the closer a place is to the equator, the warmer it is. For example, average temperatures between Maine and Florida can vary greatly, especially in winter. That is because places closer to the equator, like Florida, receive more direct sunlight than places farther away. This causes higher average temperatures. Generally, the farther a place is from the equator, the cooler it is.

In places with high elevations, some mountains can have snow year-round.

Chapter 1 ■ 33

Distance from oceans and other large bodies of water also affects climate. Water heats and cools more slowly than land does. Near the ocean, temperatures are usually not as hot in summer and not as cold in winter as they would be inland. The ocean often helps warm the land in winter and cool it in summer.

Ocean currents can also affect climate. The currents carry cold water from the North Pole and the South Pole toward the equator, and warm water from the equator toward the poles. The Gulf Stream, which carries warm water northward along the east coast of the United States, helps make winters there less cold than places farther inland. The California Current, which flows along the west coast of the United States, brings cold water southward from the Arctic Ocean. It helps keep places along the west coast cool in the summer.

Elevation affects climate, too. Places in the mountains are usually much cooler than places where the elevation of the land is closer to sea level. Temperatures drop about 3°F (about 2°C) for every 1,000 feet (305 m) above sea level. Because elevation can affect the temperature so greatly, even the tops of high mountains in tropical Hawaii are sometimes covered with snow.

Where a place is located on a continent can affect climate in other ways. In the West, mountain ranges such as the Sierra Nevada and the Rocky Mountains act like huge walls. When streams of air meet the mountains, they are forced to rise. As air rises, it cools. Because cool air cannot hold as much moisture as warm air, rain

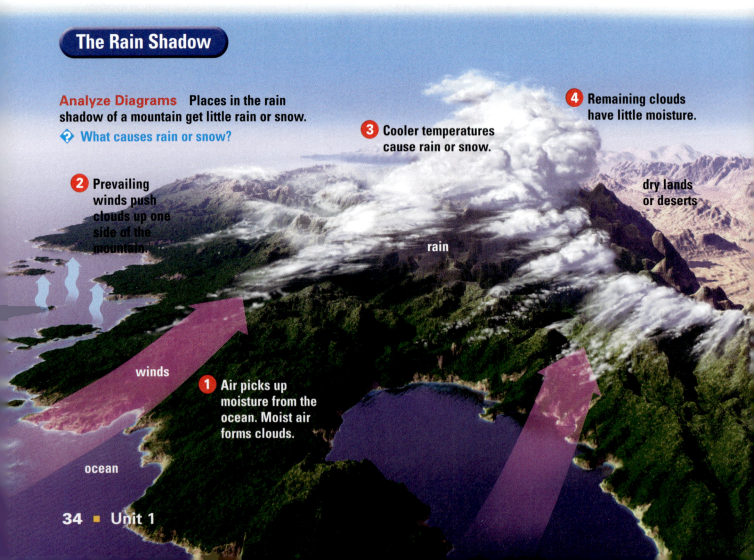

The Rain Shadow

Analyze Diagrams Places in the rain shadow of a mountain get little rain or snow.
❓ **What causes rain or snow?**

1. Air picks up moisture from the ocean. Moist air forms clouds.
2. Prevailing winds push clouds up one side of the mountain.
3. Cooler temperatures cause rain or snow.
4. Remaining clouds have little moisture.

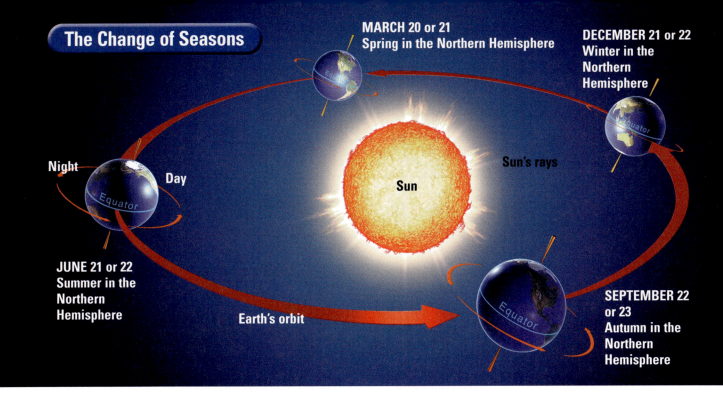

The Change of Seasons

MARCH 20 or 21
Spring in the Northern Hemisphere

DECEMBER 21 or 22
Winter in the Northern Hemisphere

JUNE 21 or 22
Summer in the Northern Hemisphere

Earth's orbit

SEPTEMBER 22 or 23
Autumn in the Northern Hemisphere

Analyze Diagrams   As the Earth moves around the sun, the seasons change.
◆ How does the rotation of the Earth also cause night and day?

or snow falls on the mountains' western slopes. As the air begins to slide down the eastern side of the mountains, it gets warmer. The warm air can hold more moisture. As a result, places on the eastern sides of the mountains get little precipitation. They lie in the **rain shadow**, or on the drier side of a mountain.

Not having mountains can affect the climate almost as much as having them, but in a different way. Because there is no large mountain range in the central part of the United States to block the flow of air, bitter-cold air masses can move rapidly out of Canada across the plains. Called northers because they come from the north, these large, cold air masses can bring freezing temperatures to places as far south as the states of Texas and Florida.

REVIEW   What factors affect the climate of a place?

Climate Regions

The Earth's orbit around the sun causes changes in seasons—summer, autumn, winter, and spring. These changes are not noticeable in all 11 climate regions of the United States. Almost every season is cold in the *polar climate* and *subpolar climate regions* of Alaska. Almost every season is warm in the *tropical wet climate* region of Hawaii and the *tropical wet and dry climate* region in South Florida.

The *continental climate* region covers the northeast quarter of the United States. This region usually has four very different seasons, including a hot, wet summer and a cold winter. Most of the southeast quarter of the United States is in the *humid subtropical climate* region. This region also has four seasons, but its winters are milder and its summers are hotter than in the continental climate region.

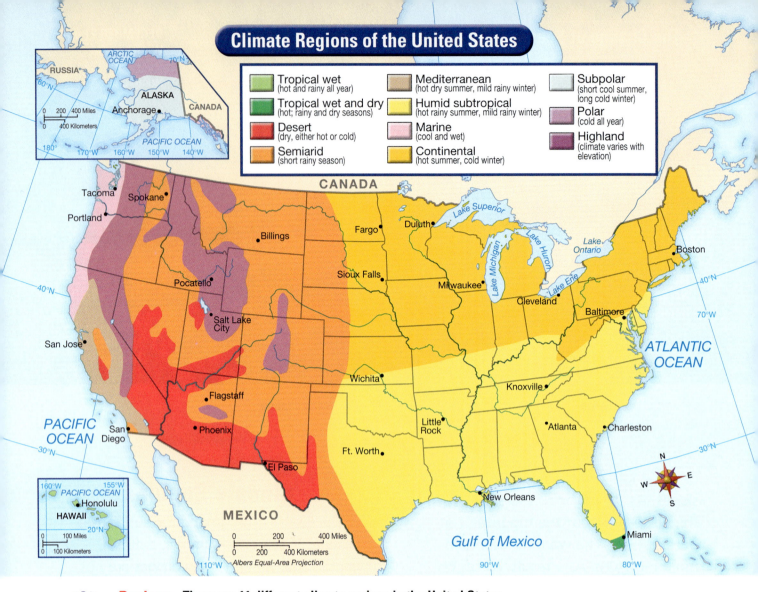

Regions There are 11 different climate regions in the United States.

In what climate region is your state located?

For most of the year, places in the humid subtropical region experience plenty of precipitation and high humidity. **Humidity** is the amount of moisture in the air. Like most other climate regions, however, this region does experience droughts (DROWTS). A **drought** is a long period with little or no rain.

Because the western United States is much more mountainous than the eastern part of the country, the climate varies more from place to place. The *semiarid climate* region covers much of the West. In this region the climate is hot and **arid**, or dry, for most of the year with only a short rainy season. The writer Michael Grant once described the semiarid region with the words "hot, dry, wind, cold, sleet, thunder, puddles, drama." The "drama" was Grant's way to describe the huge thunderstorms that often form in the region during the spring and fall. These storms can drop hail that can damage crops as well as automobiles, roofs, and windows.

Mountainous areas in the western United States have a *highland climate*.

In those areas, climate varies with elevation. Places at higher elevations have very cold winters with lots of snow.

The *desert climate* region covers a large part of the southwestern United States. Places with desert climates receive, on average, less than 10 inches (25 cm) of precipitation per year. The desert climate region receives little precipitation because much of it lies in the rain shadow of the western mountains. The land is part of a much larger desert region called the North American Desert, which extends southward into Mexico.

Most of the land near the Pacific Coast has one of two climates, a *marine climate* or a *Mediterranean* (meh•duh•tuh•RAY•nee•uhn) *climate*. A cool and wet marine climate can be found on the northern Pacific Coast west of the Cascade Mountains and is greatly affected by its location near the Pacific Ocean. The Mediterranean climate in central and southern California provides for long, sunny summers and mild, wet winters. This climate is called Mediterranean because it is very similar to the climate of some European countries located on the Mediterranean Sea.

REVIEW What details help explain the desert climate in the southwestern United States? MAIN IDEA AND DETAILS

Vegetation Regions

The Earth is covered with different kinds of natural vegetation. The natural vegetation that grows in a place varies depending on whether the soil there is sand, clay, or loam. These are the three main kinds of soil. The natural vegetation also varies because of temperature and precipitation. In fact, the amount of precipitation in a place is the single most important factor affecting where different kinds of natural vegetation will grow.

Most of the United States can be divided into four main vegetation regions. These are forest, grassland, desert, and tundra. Tundra regions are found far to the north and high on mountains. A **tundra** is a cold, dry region where trees cannot grow.

The forest vegetation region is found in much of the eastern United States. Across the northern Coastal Plain, the Appalachian Mountains, and much of the Central Plains, forests have mostly evergreens, such as cedar and pine, and broadleaf trees, such as oak, ash, and birch. While evergreens stay green all year round, broadleaf trees change color in autumn and drop their leaves in winter.

Sequoias are some of the world's tallest trees.

Chapter 1 ▪ 37

Regions Most of the nation can be divided into five vegetation regions.

❓ What vegetation region can be found on both the east and west coasts of the United States?

Forests of evergreen pines and broadleaf oaks cover much of the southern Coastal Plain and the Gulf Coast.

Forests also cover areas of the western United States. In western Washington and Oregon and in northern California, rainfall amounts are often greater than 80 inches (203 cm) per year. Redwoods and giant sequoias, which are some of the world's oldest trees, grow in the forests there.

Trees need lots of water, but grasses can survive in much drier areas. The largest grassland region in the United States stretches across the middle of the country. It includes the western part of the Central Plains and all of the Great Plains. This part of the Central Plains is sometimes called a tall-grass prairie. A **prairie** is an area of flat or rolling land covered mostly by grasses and wildflowers. Left to grow, the grasses on this prairie would become as tall as people! Mostly short grasses cover the drier Great Plains. The land there has almost no trees and few rivers.

38 ■ Unit 1

As a result, it often looks the same, mile after mile.

Another vegetation region—savanna—is generally found between areas of grasslands and forests. A savanna is a kind of grassland that has areas with some trees. These trees are scattered, and the land is mostly covered with shrubs and bushes.

Only plants that can grow in a dry climate can grow in deserts. These plants include short grasses, low bushes, and cactuses. Cactuses store water in their thick stems so that they can survive until rain falls. A shrublike tree known as mesquite (muh•SKEET) sends its long roots 70 feet (21 m) into the ground to find water.

Small, hardy plants such as mosses, lichens (LY•kuhnz), herbs, and low shrubs grow in tundra regions. Tundra regions are covered by snow more than half the year. Yet there is not enough water for trees to grow because the water in the soil is frozen year-round.

There are two kinds of tundra regions. They are arctic and alpine. Arctic tundras lie near the Arctic Ocean. The only arctic tundra region in the United States is in northern Alaska. Alpine tundras can be found on mountains with elevations that make it too cold for trees to grow.

REVIEW What four main vegetation regions cover most of the United States?

LESSON 3 REVIEW

MAIN IDEA AND DETAILS In which climate region do people experience heavy precipitation, high humidity, and droughts?

1 BIG IDEA What are the main climate and vegetation regions found in the United States?

2 VOCABULARY Write a description of a savanna region.

3 GEOGRAPHY What are some kinds of plants that grow in the desert?

4 CRITICAL THINKING—Analyze How are winter weather in the continental climate region and winter weather in the humid subtropical climate region different?

PERFORMANCE—Write a Poem Write a poem about the climate and vegetation of the region in which you live. Share your poem with classmates.

Caribou and sheep feed on the plants that grow in the tundra.

LESSON 4

Using the Land

MAIN IDEA AND DETAILS

As you read, look for the main idea about land use.

BIG IDEA

People use the land and its resources to meet their needs, and people change their environment.

VOCABULARY

natural resource
modify
fertilizer
irrigation
nonrenewable
renewable
erosion
land use

The United States has many natural resources. A **natural resource** is something found in nature that people can use. Natural resources include soil, water, minerals, and plants.

Different physical environments and the natural resources found there affect the way people live. At the same time, people and their activities also affect their environment. Personal interests affect the way people use the resources in different places and regions.

People and the Environment

The environment affects the activities of many people. It affects not only the kinds of activities people take part in for recreation, but also how they earn a living. That is because people often do work related to the resources around them.

People throughout time have used the land and its resources to meet their needs. However, not all resources are spread out equally around the Earth. Not every place has enough of every resource it needs. To meet their needs or to do their jobs, people must often **modify**, or change, their environment. People modify their environments based on how they value and use the Earth's resources.

Many people agree that water is one of the most important natural resources. Without it, crops would not grow and people could not live. To make sure they have enough water, people sometimes modify their environment by digging wells in the ground. They also build dams across rivers and streams. These dams form reservoirs (REH•zuh•vwarz) behind them. Both people and industries use the water stored in those reservoirs. Dams help make electricity, too. Water from large reservoirs can be used to turn large machines called generators, which make electricity. This hydroelectric power is an important source of electricity in many parts of the country.

This builder is modifying the environment.

40 • Unit 1

Some natural resources are difficult to find. To reach coal and mineral resources such as copper, gold, and silver, people dig huge mines into the Earth's surface. To reach oil and natural gas resources, they must drill wells deep into the ground or down into the ocean floor.

Soil is another important natural resource. Without fertile soil, the United States could not grow food to feed its people or to sell to other countries. Before people can plant crops, however, they must often plow or disk the land to prepare it for planting. They may also add fertilizers. **Fertilizer** is material added to the soil to make it more fertile.

Many places in the United States have fertile soil, but sometimes the land is too dry for crops to grow well. Farmers in those areas have modified their environment by using irrigation. **Irrigation** is the use of canals, ditches, or pipes to move water to dry areas. With irrigation, many desert regions have been turned into productive farmland.

When people modify the environment for one purpose, they often change it in other ways. For example, if too much water is pumped from the ground for irrigation, then the amount of underground water available for other uses decreases. Once nonrenewable resources, such as minerals and fuels, are used up, there will be none left for future use. **Nonrenewable** means that a resource cannot be made again by nature or people. However, as people use these resources, they often find ways to use them more efficiently. They may also discover new resources to take their place.

Sometimes the results of changes to the environment may not be seen for years. At one time, forests covered almost all of the eastern United States. One early traveler told of spending "day after day among the trees of a hundred feet high, without a glimpse of the surrounding country." Over time, however, people cut down many of those trees and some of the forests disappeared.

People modify the environment when they lay pipes and build highways.

Chapter 1 ■ 41

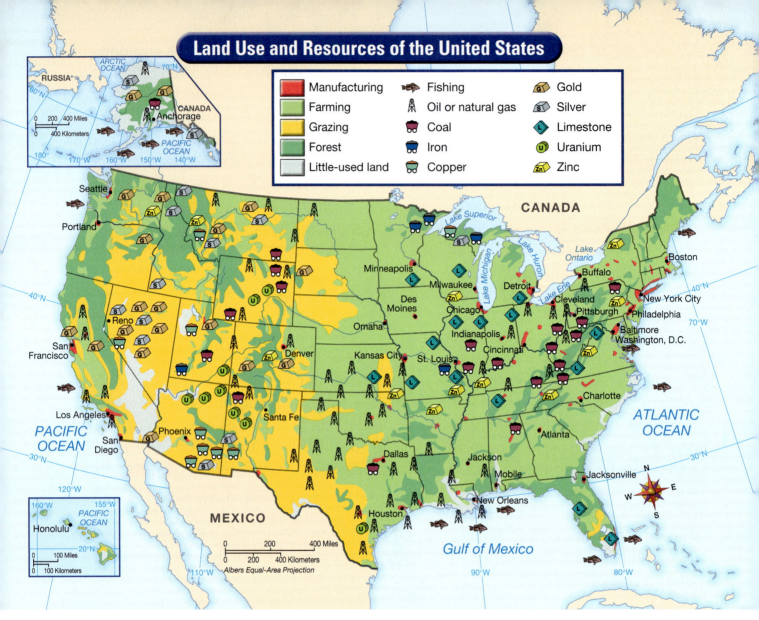

Human-Environment Interactions People in the United States use the land in many ways.

 Where is most of the land used for grazing?

In the past, many people thought that our supply of natural resources would last forever. However, Americans came to understand that the Earth does not have an endless supply of trees. People began planting new trees to replace the ones they cut down. They understood that trees are a renewable resource. **Renewable** means that a resource can be made again by nature or by people.

When people first plowed the grasslands of the Interior Plains, the topsoil—the fertile top layer of soil—was as deep as 16 inches (41 cm). Now, in many places, only 6 to 8 inches (15 to 20 cm) of topsoil are left. Plowing the land can speed up the process of erosion. **Erosion** is the wearing away of the Earth's surface, usually by wind and rain. Over time, people came to understand that they had to take action to protect soil and other natural resources.

REVIEW How do people modify their environment? **MAIN IDEA AND DETAILS**

42 ■ Unit 1

Patterns of Land Use

People use the Earth's surface in a variety of ways. They divide it into nations, states, and other government units. They build communities, transportation systems, and businesses on it. They also gather natural resources from it. Some of the land is owned by the public, and some of it belongs to private property owners. People buy and sell the land and make laws to decide how it can be used.

In every place on Earth, landforms and climate influence land use, or how most of the land in a place is used. In the United States, about half of the land is used as farmland. Most farming takes place on the Coastal Plain, on the Interior Plains, and in the large valleys in the western part of the country. In those regions, the land is fertile and there is enough water for crops to grow. In more arid regions, most of the land is used for grazing cattle, sheep, and horses.

Forests cover about one-third of the land in the United States. The largest forests are found in mountain regions, along the Great Lakes, or on the Coastal Plain. Much of the mining in the United States also takes place in mountain regions, although mining may take place wherever there are ore or fuel deposits.

Cities also occupy large areas of the United States. There, most of the land is used for housing, transportation, and businesses. In cities, most people work in service industries, such as banking, education, or health care. Most manufacturing also takes place on land in or near cities.

REVIEW What factors influence land use?

This worker has a job in manufacturing. She is building computers.

 MAIN IDEA AND DETAILS What are the two types of natural resources?

1. **BIG IDEA** What are two ways that people use the land in the United States?
2. **VOCABULARY** Explain why the use of fertilizers and irrigation are examples of how people modify their environment.
3. **GEOGRAPHY** Why do people dig wells or lay pipes that take water to dry places?
4. **GEOGRAPHY** What might people discover as they use resources?
5. **CRITICAL THINKING—Synthesize** How do the natural resources found in your community affect the way you live?

 PERFORMANCE—Write a Paragraph Use sources from the Internet and the library to research land use in your state. Then write a paragraph describing the different ways the land is used.

· LESSON ·

5

Where People Live and Work

 MAIN IDEA AND DETAILS
As you read, find the main ideas about people's activities.

BIG IDEA
People live and work in various regions.

VOCABULARY
relative location
political region
economic region
cultural region
population region
urban
suburban
rural
crossroads
metropolitan area

Regions can be based on physical features, such as landforms, climate, and vegetation. But people can define a region by using just about any feature. Because the United States is such a large country with so many differences, some states have different kinds of regions.

Regions of the United States

To make it easier to talk about different areas of the country, people often group the 50 states into four large regions—the Northeast, the South, the Middle West, and the West. Each of these regions is based on its relative location in the United States. The **relative location** of a place is where it is, compared to one or more other places on the Earth. For example, the relative location of the Northeast region is in the northeastern part of the country.

The states in each of these regions are alike in many ways. In addition to being in the same part of the country, they often have the same kinds of landforms, climate, and natural resources. Because of that, the people who live there often earn their living in ways that are alike. The states in each region may also share a history and culture.

REVIEW What are the four large regions of the United States?

Newfane, Vermont, is typical of the small towns located in the Northeast.

44 ▪ Unit 1

Regions of the United States

Regions People often divide the United States into four regions based on location.

◆ In which region is your state located?

Regions Based on People's Activities

Regions can also be based on patterns of human activity. Patterns of human activity include such factors as how people move from place to place and make settlements. These patterns also include how people work together to meet their needs and how they divide and share the land. Regions based on people's activities often form and change over time as people move and adopt new ways of living.

One kind of region based on patterns of human activity is a political region. A **political region** is a region in which people share a government and have the same leaders. Nations, states, counties, and cities are all political regions. Each political region has an exact boundary either set by law or agreed upon by the people in the neighboring areas. If people cannot agree on where a boundary is, conflict often results.

Other kinds of regions, known as **economic regions**, are based on the work people do or the products they make. In agricultural regions many people are farmers or ranchers. In manufacturing regions many people work in factories.

Another region based on human activity is a **cultural region**, a region based on culture. In a cultural region the main group of people who live there share customs and beliefs. The region may be based on the religion that most of the people follow or the language they speak.

Still another kind of region that is based on people is a population region. A **population region** is one based on where people live. Today, about three-fourths of the people in the United States live in **urban**, or city, regions. In urban regions many people live close together in cities.

Almost every large city has suburbs, or smaller cities and towns around it.

Chapter 1 ■ 45

People who live in these **suburban** regions often work in the larger city nearby. Other people live in **rural**, or country, regions. Homes in rural regions are built farther apart, and people there often have to travel farther to go to school or work or to go shopping.

REVIEW What are the four kinds of regions that are based on people's activities?

Patterns of Settlement

Geographic factors, such as landforms, bodies of water, and climate, usually affect where people settle. Through most of human history, people have tended to settle in areas where the soil is fertile and good for farming. People have also settled where there is enough fresh water to meet their needs. Having waterways and other transportation routes nearby has always been important, too.

Geographic factors have also discouraged people from settling in areas. Most people have avoided settling in deserts, tundras, or high, mountainous areas. That is because building shelters, finding food and water, and meeting other basic human needs are more difficult in those areas. Today, however, people use tools and inventions to modify their environments and make living in some of those areas possible. In fact, some of the fastest-growing cities in the United States are in desert regions of the West.

When more and more people settle in a particular place, they tend to cluster, or group together, near harbors or crossroads. In the past, a **crossroads** was a place where two roads or railroads crossed and people met to buy and sell goods, communicate, and rest. Today, it is any place that connects people, goods, and ideas. A crossroads may be a shopping center or a business park.

Other people may create settlements that are more spread out. These settlements are often found along major rivers, roads, or railroads or along a coast. Wherever people settle, their settlements become part of the physical environment. Settlements change the land on which they are built, and they are in turn changed by the land.

REVIEW What details support the main idea that geographic factors influence where people settle? **MAIN IDEA AND DETAILS**

New York Harbor has helped to make New York City a busy crossroads.

• GEOGRAPHY •

The Center of Population
Understanding Human Systems

Since the beginning of our nation, the center of population has gradually moved westward. A nation's center of population is the place within that nation where there are an equal number of people living to the north, south, east, and west. The center of population in the United States has shifted westward because over time people have moved farther west to settle the land and seek new opportunities. In 1790 the center of population was near Baltimore, Maryland. Today it is located at a point southwest of St. Louis, Missouri.

Types of Settlement

Settlements of many sizes can be found in the United States and around the world. Some are made up of single houses scattered far apart across the landscape. Others are clusters of houses neatly arranged in villages or towns. Still others are crowded cities. About half of all the people in the world live in cities.

Cities are the largest and the most crowded type of settlement. Together, a large city and its surrounding suburbs make up that city's **metropolitan area**.

Some metropolitan areas are so large that they stretch across state borders. The largest metropolitan area in the United States, the New York City metropolitan area, stretches across parts of three states.

Settlements also differ in how they are arranged and how they are used. The way settlements are arranged often depends on the background of the people who settled there or the leaders who planned the community. For example, many communities in the Northeast are built around a town square or common.

Many early settlers there were from England, where they used this kind of area to graze their farm animals.

The ways people organize their settlements reflect not only their past and their economic activities but also their culture and the way they govern themselves. If you flew over the Middle West in an airplane, for example, you could see that many places there were planned using a grid system. The roads are mostly straight, framing large, square plots of land. If you flew over parts of the West, however, you might see towns that are laid out a different way because of the culture of the people who first settled there. Many of the towns in the West were first settled by people from Spain and from Mexico, and other countries in Latin America. Like many towns in Latin America, some of the towns in the southwestern United States have a central plaza with a church surrounded by buildings that are made of stone or a clay-and-straw mixture known as adobe (ah•DOH•bee).

REVIEW What are the largest types of settlements?

The Location of American Cities

In the 1700s most people in our country lived in rural regions. At that time there were only 24 cities in the whole country. The biggest of these were port cities along the Atlantic Ocean.

Over time, new cities developed. Many grew up along the Mississippi River or its tributaries or along the shores of the Great Lakes. Other cities developed along railroad lines that were being built to connect different parts of the country. New cities also developed along the Pacific and Gulf Coasts.

Improvements in farm machinery, new methods of farming, and the growth of manufacturing encouraged people to move to cities. With new tools and new ways of growing food, farmers could produce more. That meant that not as many farmers were needed. Many people also moved to cities to find work in manufacturing and in other businesses.

Other factors have also caused the population to move from one area to another. Sometimes the importance of an industry

Santa Fe, the capital of New Mexico, is the oldest capital city in the United States. The buildings in Santa Fe reflect the city's heritage.

LOCATE IT
Santa Fe
NEW MEXICO

48 ■ Unit 1

changes, and people may leave a place to get a job with a growing industry. For example, when oil was discovered in Texas, many people from across the country moved there to take jobs in the oil industry. People moving to the United States from other countries have also affected population in different areas of the country. They continue to do so today.

Today, most of the largest cities in the United States continue to be found near a coast, along rivers or the shores of the Great Lakes, or on other major transportation routes. In fact, the five largest cities in the country—New York City, Los Angeles, Chicago, Houston, and Philadelphia—are all located within 50 miles (80 km) of a coast or one of the Great Lakes.

Location also played a role in the selection of some cities as capitals. Often these cities were chosen because they were located near the central part of a state or country. Some state capitals were chosen because they were among the largest cities in their states or were located near the coast or near a major transportation route.

The Ten Largest Cities in the United States

CITY	POPULATION
New York City, NY	8,008,278
Los Angeles, CA	3,694,820
Chicago, IL	2,896,016
Houston, TX	1,953,631
Philadelphia, PA	1,517,550
Phoenix, AZ	1,321,045
San Diego, CA	1,223,400
Dallas, TX	1,188,580
San Antonio, TX	1,144,646
Detroit, MI	951,270

Analyze Tables Three of the country's largest cities are in the state of Texas.
◆ Which city has a larger population—Dallas or San Antonio?

At the time the site for our nation's capital was chosen, there were only 13 states. The capital, Washington, D.C., was built about halfway between the northernmost and southernmost states.

REVIEW Where are most of the largest cities in the United States?

LESSON 5 REVIEW

MAIN IDEA AND DETAILS What features describe a political region?

❶ **BIG IDEA** Describe regions in the United States that are based on human activity.

❷ **VOCABULARY** Explain in a sentence or two how the terms **urban** and **suburban** are related.

❸ **ECONOMICS** In what kind of region based on people's activities would a community of farmers live?

❹ **CRITICAL THINKING—Analyze** Why do you think that people tend to live near crossroads?

PERFORMANCE—Make a Brochure Work with a partner to make a brochure about your community. Include information about the types of settlements there and the activities people do. Take the brochure home and share it with family members.

SKILLS · Use Latitude and Longitude

VOCABULARY
absolute location · parallel · meridian
line of latitude · line of longitude · prime meridian

▶ WHY IT MATTERS

Lines of latitude and lines of longitude help you describe the **absolute location**, or exact location, of any place on Earth.

▶ WHAT YOU NEED TO KNOW

Mapmakers use a system of imaginary lines to form a grid system on maps and globes. The lines that run east and west are the **lines of latitude**. Lines of latitude are also called **parallels** (PAR•uh•lelz). This is because they are parallel, or always the same distance from each other.

Lines of latitude are measured in degrees north and south of the equator, which is labeled 0°, or *zero degrees*. The parallels north of the equator are marked N for *north latitude*. This means that they are in the Northern Hemisphere. The parallels south of the equator are marked S for *south latitude*. This means they are in the Southern Hemisphere.

The lines that run north and south on a map or globe are the **lines of longitude**, or **meridians**. Each meridian runs from the North Pole to the South Pole. Unlike parallels, which never meet, meridians meet at the poles.

Meridians are numbered in much the same way that parallels are numbered. The meridian marked 0° is called the **prime meridian**. Lines of longitude to the west of the prime meridian are marked W for *west longitude*. They are in the Western Hemisphere. The meridians to

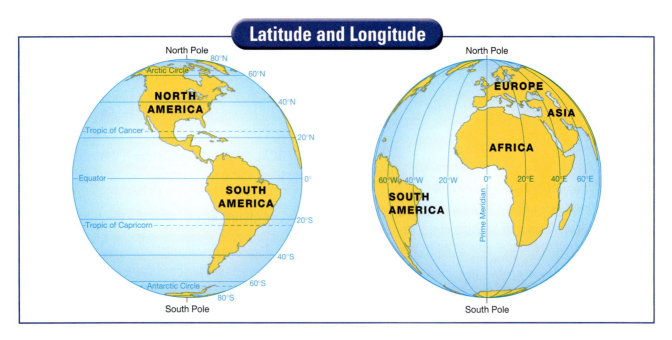

Latitude and Longitude

the east of the prime meridian are marked *E* for *east longitude*. They are in the Eastern Hemisphere.

▶ PRACTICE THE SKILL

The map above, which shows the locations of state capitals in the United States, uses crossing lines of latitude and longitude to describe absolute location. On this map every fifth parallel is shown and every fifth meridian is shown.

At the left-hand side of the map, find 40°N. At the bottom, find 90°W. Use your fingers to trace these lines to the point where they cross. Springfield, Illinois, is not far from this point. So you can say that Springfield is near 40°N, 90°W.

Now use the map to answer these questions.

1. What line of latitude is closest to Tallahassee, Florida?
2. What line of longitude is closest to Santa Fe, New Mexico?
3. Which location is farther north—50°N, 80°W or 30°N, 90°W?

▶ APPLY WHAT YOU LEARNED

Use latitude and longitude to describe the location of your state's capital city. Write a paragraph to descibe how you found the capital's location.

Practice your map and globe skills with the **GeoSkills CD-ROM**.

Chapter 1 ▪ 51

• CHAPTER •

1 Review and Test Preparation

Focus Skill: Main Idea and Details

Copy the following graphic organizer onto a separate sheet of paper. Use the information you have learned to identify supporting details in this chapter about regions of the United States.

Regions of the United States
Main Idea

Detail
1. _____

The United States can be divided into regions.

Detail
2. _____

THINK & WRITE

Write a Letter Imagine that you are traveling across the country, from New York City in New York to San Francisco in California. Write a letter to a friend that describes how the climate changes as you travel from east to west.

Write a Compare and Contrast Report Write a report about the mountains in the United States. In your report, compare and contrast the mountains in the eastern United States with those in the western United States.

USE VOCABULARY

Identify the term that correctly matches each definition.

landform (p. 18)
inlet (p. 27)
rain shadow (p. 35)
fertilizer (p. 41)
relative location (p. 44)

1. where a place is, compared to other places
2. physical feature on Earth's surface
3. material added to soil to make it more fertile
4. any area of water that extends into the land from a larger body of water
5. the dry side of a mountain

RECALL FACTS

Answer these questions.

6. What group of lakes makes up the world's largest freshwater lakes?
7. What do river systems do?
8. What is the Continental Divide?
9. How do people today modify their environment?
10. How does erosion change the land?

Write the letter of the best choice.

11. Which of the following vegetation regions has low bushes and cactuses?
    A forest
    B grassland
    C desert
    D prairie

12. Cultural regions can be based on all of the following except—
    F the religion that people follow.
    G the language people speak.
    H the work that people do.
    J the customs of the people.

THINK CRITICALLY

13. What types of regions are based on people's activities?
14. What are some ways the land is used in the United States?

APPLY SKILLS

Use Elevation Maps
Use the map of the United States on page 25 to answer these questions.

15. How would you describe the land in the Great Basin?
16. What is the highest elevation in the Interior Plains?
17. Which mountain range has a higher elevation, the Rocky Mountains or the Appalachian Mountains?

Use Longitude and Latitude
Use the Latitude and Longitude map on page 51 to answer these questions.

18. What capital cities are located closest to 45°N?
19. Which is farther north, a city at 40°N, 85°W or a city at 35°N, 80°W?
20. What city is located closest to 40°N, 120°W?
21. What is the location of Denver, Colorado?

Chapter 1 ■ 53

CHAPTER 2

The Earliest Americans

" It is from this land that we obtained the timber and stone for our homes and kivas. "
—Hopi, quoted by Alvin M. Josephy, Jr. in *500 Nations*, 1994

MESA VERDE NATIONAL PARK

For more than 700 years, from A.D. 600 to A.D. 1300, many Native American peoples made their homes in the area that is today Mesa Verde National Park. These early Americans built sturdy stone villages carved directly into the canyon walls. This photograph shows the Cliff Palace in winter.

LOCATE IT

COLORADO

Mesa Verde National Park

Compare and Contrast

Focus Skill

To **compare** two things is to find how they are alike. To **contrast** is to find how they are different.

As you read this chapter, compare and contrast.
- Compare and contrast information about the Native American tribes in what is now the United States.

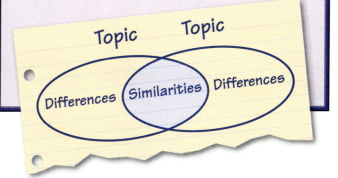

Chapter 2 ■ 55

LESSON 1

The First Americans

 COMPARE AND CONTRAST
As you read, compare and contrast facts about groups of early people.

BIG IDEA
People may have first come to live in North and South America.

VOCABULARY
glacier
migration
theory
archaeologist
artifact
descendant
origin story
ancestor

The history of the United States of America begins long before there was a United States. It begins with the first people in North America many thousands of years ago. At that time, however, the continent was a far different place from what it is today.

At different times in its past, the Earth has experienced long periods of freezing cold. During these periods, known as the Ice Ages, the Earth's climate became so cold that huge, slow-moving sheets of ice called glaciers formed. These glaciers covered large parts of the Earth. So much of the Earth's water was trapped in glaciers that the level of the oceans dropped. At several different times this caused a "bridge" of dry land to appear between the continents of Asia and North America.

The Land Bridge Story

Scientists gave the name Beringia (buh•RIN•gee•uh) to this land bridge between Asia and North America. It was named for the Bering Strait, a narrow body of water that now separates Siberia, in present-day Russia, from Alaska. Some scientists believe that between 12,000 and 40,000 years ago, hunting groups from Asia began traveling across the Beringia land bridge.

FAST FACT
During the Ice Ages so much water was trapped in glaciers that the water level in the oceans dropped as much as 350 feet (107 m).

56 ▪ Unit 1

This migration, or movement of people, probably took place very slowly, with groups traveling only a few miles in an entire lifetime. Finally, after thousands of years, Asian hunters reached what is today Alaska. However, they and the animals they hunted could go no farther. Huge glaciers blocked their path.

About 12,000 years ago, the climate began to get warmer. Some of the glaciers started to melt. As a result, the oceans began to rise. Once again water covered Beringia. At the same time, a narrow path opened between two melting glaciers that covered what is now Canada.

The animals followed the path between the glaciers, and the hunters followed the animals. Slowly the hunters made their way farther into the Americas—North America and South America. These people became the first Americans.

REVIEW According to the land bridge story, why did the hunters make their way into the Americas?

New Discoveries

The land bridge story is one theory, or possible explanation, for when and how the first Americans arrived in the Americas. Scientists, however, continue to ask if the first Americans could have been here earlier, and if they could have come by some other means.

The scientists who study the cultures of people who lived long ago are known as archaeologists (ar•kee•AH•luh•jists). In recent years archaeologists have made discoveries that seem to support an "early arrival" theory. According to this theory, Beringia appeared during an earlier Ice Age.

Movement According to the land bridge story, it took thousands of years for people to spread out over North and South America.

◆ About how many miles is it from Asia to the tip of South America?

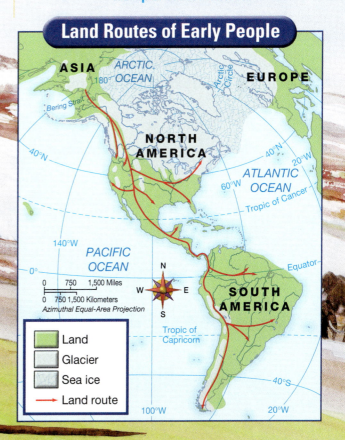

Land Routes of Early People

Chapter 2 • 57

One of the most important discoveries that supports the early arrival theory was made at a dig, or an archaeological site, located in southwestern Pennsylvania. This site, known as the Meadowcroft Rock Shelter, appears to have been an Ice Age campsite. Archaeologists discovered **artifacts**, or objects made by early people, at the site. Most of the artifacts are 14,000 to 15,000 years old. A few are more than 19,000 years old.

Discoveries in South America also support the early arrival theory. In Monte Verde (MOHN•tay VAIR•day), Chile, archaeologists uncovered artifacts, animal bones, and even a child's footprint. This evidence, or proof, shows that people were there at least 13,000 years ago. In Brazil human-made stone chips were found that may be 30,000 years old.

Other discoveries, in California and Peru, support the theory that the first Americans did not cross the land bridge at all. Instead, they may have traveled to the Americas in boats. Some may have actually crossed the Pacific Ocean. On San Miguel Island, about 25 miles (40 km) off the coast of California, archaeologists found evidence that people lived there about 13,000 years ago. Archaeologists know that these people used oceangoing boats because they ate fish that could be caught only far from shore. In Peru archaeologists found two 12,000-year-old sites whose residents also ate foods only found in the deep ocean.

REVIEW How is the land bridge story different from recent discoveries in California and Peru?
COMPARE AND CONTRAST

Origin Stories

There are also people today who believe that the first Americans did not come from Asia or anywhere else. Many present-day Native Americans, or American Indians, the descendants of the first Americans, believe that their people have always lived in the Americas. A **descendant** is a person's child, grandchild, or later relative.

All Native American peoples use stories to tell about important events and people in their past. Some of these stories tell

Many archaeologists believe that these tools (above) found in Pennsylvania, and the cave paintings (left) at Pedra Furada, Brazil, are proof that people arrived in the Americas earlier than previously thought.

Native American storytellers, like this one, share stories of the past with young people.

about the origins, or beginnings, of Native American people. Such stories are called **origin stories**. Like the Creation story in the Bible, some Native American origin stories explain how the world was made. The Blackfoot people, for example, tell a story of Old Man the Creator. According to the story, he made the animals and plants and formed the prairies and mountains.

The Hurons tell an origin story that begins when water covered the Earth. According to the story, land was formed from a tiny bit of soil taken from the claws of a turtle. The turtle had picked up the soil from the bottom of the ocean. Because of this story and others like it, some Native Americans use the name Turtle Island to describe the Americas.

No one knows exactly when the first Americans arrived. However, it was so long ago that the descendants of the first Americans have no stories of distant homelands where their **ancestors**, or early family members, once lived. They tell only stories of the Americas.

REVIEW What do Native American origin stories tell?

LESSON 1 REVIEW

 COMPARE AND CONTRAST How do Native Americans' views on how they arrived in the Americas differ from archaeologists' views?

1 BIG IDEA By what ways may early people have arrived in the Americas?

2 VOCABULARY What is a **theory**?

3 HISTORY How did the artifacts found at Meadowcroft Rock Shelter change many archaeologists' theories?

4 CULTURE Why do many Native Americans believe that their people have always lived in the Americas?

5 CRITICAL THINKING—Evaluate Why do people disagree about when and how the first Americans came to the Americas?

 PERFORMANCE—Make a Chart With a classmate, make a chart that compares the points of view on how people first came to the Americas.

Chapter 2 ■ 59

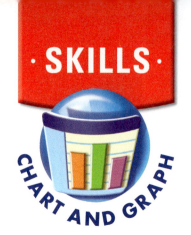

SKILLS · Chart and Graph

Read Time Lines

VOCABULARY

time line
decade
century
millennium

▶ WHY IT MATTERS

An easy way to see relationships among events in history is to look at a **time line**. A time line is a diagram that shows events that took place during a certain period of time. Like a calendar, a time line can help you understand the order of the events and the amounts of time between events.

▶ WHAT YOU NEED TO KNOW

A time line looks like a ruler marked in dates instead of inches. Like inches marked on a ruler, the dates on a time line are equally spaced. However, not all time lines look the same or are read in the same way. Most time lines run horizontally, or across the page. But some run vertically, or down the page. Horizontal time lines, like the one shown below, are read from left to right. The earliest date is on the left end of the time line, and the most recent date is on the right end. The time line on page 61 is a vertical time line. It is read from top to bottom. The earliest date is at the top of the time line, and the most recent date is at the bottom.

Time lines can show events that took place during any period of time. Some time lines show events that took place over a **decade**, or a period of 10 years. Others show events that took place over a **century**, or a period of 100 years. Both a decade and centuries are shown on the horizontal time line below. Some time lines even show events that took place over a **millennium**, or a period of a thousand years. A millennium is shown on the vertical time line on page 61.

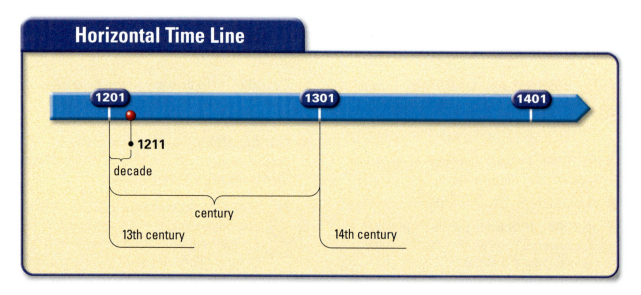

Horizontal Time Line

60 ▪ Unit 1

The vertical time line here shows dates from the ancient past to today. Notice the letters B.C. and A.D. in the middle of the time line. Many people today identify years by whether they took place before or after the birth of Jesus Christ. The years before the birth of Christ are labeled B.C., which stands for "before Christ." Years after the birth of Christ are labeled A.D. This stands for the Latin words *Anno Domini*, which mean "in the year of the Lord."

An event that happened in 100 B.C. took place 100 years before the birth of Christ. An event that happened in A.D. 100 took place 100 years after the birth of Christ. Because every year in modern times is A.D., these letters are often not needed.

You may also see the letters B.C.E. or C.E. with dates. The abbreviation B.C.E. stands for "before the Common Era." It is sometimes used instead of B.C. The abbreviation C.E., which stands for "Common Era," is sometimes used in place of A.D.

▶ PRACTICE THE SKILL

Use the horizontal time line on page 60 to answer the following questions.

1. How many centuries are shown on the time line?
2. What were the first and last years of the thirteenth century?

Use the vertical time line on this page to answer the following questions.

3. How many millenniums are shown on this time line?
4. Which year came earlier, 1000 B.C. or A.D. 500?

▶ APPLY WHAT YOU LEARNED

Make a time line that shows the twentieth and twenty-first centuries. Label the first and last years of both centuries and the year you were born. Mark some other important events for you in the past and in the future. Display your time line in the classroom.

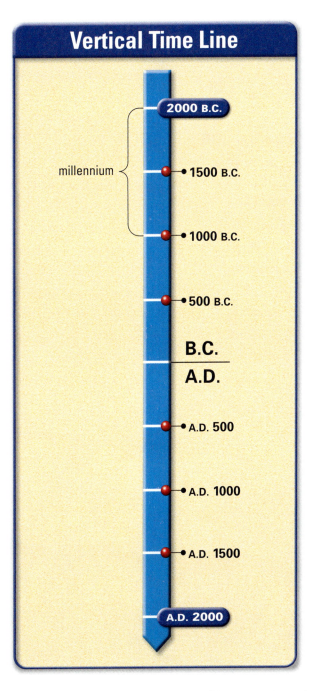

Chapter 2 ■ 61

LESSON 2

Ancient Indians

10,000 years ago – 600 years ago

 COMPARE AND CONTRAST

As you read, compare and contrast different cultures among the ancient Indians.

BIG IDEA
Changes in the environment caused the ancient Indians' ways of life to change.

VOCABULARY
nomad
technology
extinct
agriculture
tribe
civilization
class
slavery
pueblo

In many ways, the story of the first Americans, or ancient Indians, is filled with mystery. Just when archaeologists think they have some answers, they find new evidence that creates new questions. One thing, however, is known for certain. For many generations, the ancient Indians and their descendants slowly moved throughout the Americas. They settled in different regions and developed many different ways of life.

Hunters and Gatherers

After the last Ice Age, the climate of North America remained mostly cool and humid. Rich vegetation provided food for very large animals, including horses and camels. Giant mastodons and mammoths also roamed the vast grasslands and forests. Mastodons and mammoths looked like huge, hairy elephants. They stood 14 feet (4 m) tall, had tusks up to 14 feet (4 m) long, and weighed as much as 10,000 pounds (4,536 kg).

Many of the ancient Indians depended on these giant animals in order to survive. They ate the meat and used the fur, skins, and bones to make clothing, shelter, and tools. Daily life for these ancient Indians was spent mostly tracking and hunting

62 • Unit 1

the animals and gathering fruits and nuts for food along the way. These people were mostly **nomads**, or wanderers who had no settled home. They built shelters in caves or in tents made from animal skins. The ancient Indians lived and hunted together in small groups or in families.

Compared to the animals they hunted, the ancient Indians were small and weak. Over time, however, they had learned to sharpen stones into spear points and tie them to wooden poles.

Some hunters also made and used clubs and axes with stone blades. From time to time, different groups of ancient Indians invented new tools or weapons. One such important weapon was the atlatl (AHT•lah•tuhl), or spear-thrower.

At about the same time the atlatl was invented, another early inventor had found a way to make a spear point by a process scientists call flaking. Using a bone or a stone, the early inventor knocked off flakes, or small thin chips, from flint or another kind of stone. The inventor continued to flake the stone until a sharp point was formed. The point was then hollowed out and fastened tightly to a spear. These new spear points were razor-sharp, making them the best weapons early hunters had ever had.

A Clovis point

These delicate yet deadly spear points are called Clovis points. They are named after the town of Clovis, New Mexico, where archaeologists first found them. Similar points have been found in places ranging from Alaska to the Andes Mountains, in South America.

The atlatl and Clovis points were two improvements in technology by ancient Indians. **Technology** is the use of scientific knowledge or tools to make or do something. These inventions were just as important to the ancient Indians as computers are to many people today.

REVIEW Why were Clovis points important to ancient Indians?

The ancient Indians moved from place to place to follow the animals they hunted.

Chapter 2 • 63

Early farmers may have ground corn into flour by using a grinding stone (left) and may have stored kernels in containers like this one (above).

A Time of Change

Over thousands of years the environment of North America slowly changed. The climate became warmer and drier. As a result, much of the vegetation the giant animals ate could no longer grow. This may be one reason the giant animals became **extinct** (ik•STINGT), or died out. By about 10,000 years ago, most of them had disappeared from North America.

Life no longer centered around the hunting of giant animals. People began to fish and to hunt more of the smaller animals, such as deer and rabbits. To hunt them, the ancient Indians developed new hunting tools, such as the bow and arrow.

The ancient Indians also began to eat a greater variety of plants. In time they learned where certain plants grew best. They learned at what time of the year nuts, berries, and other plant parts became ripe. Each season the people traveled to places where they could gather food and hunt.

As the ancient Indians gathered more food than they could use at a time, they found ways to store the extra food. They made storage containers from reeds, vines, or strips of wood. Later, people learned to make storage containers out of other materials, such as clay.

Over time some ancient Indians changed their way of life even more. Some took the first steps toward producing their own food. They planted seeds and grew food crops. This was the beginning of **agriculture**, or farming.

Agriculture started at different times in different parts of the world. Ancient Indians in Mexico, however, were among the first to develop agriculture in North America. Some of the earliest farmers lived in the Tehuacán (tay•wah•KAHN) Valley in central Mexico. The early farmers of the valley grew at least 12 kinds of corn, as well as avocados, squash, and beans. Maize (MAYZ), or corn, became the most important crop for many ancient Indians living in North America.

Farming changed the lives of many of the ancient Indian groups. By about 5,000 years ago, some were building stronger homes and had started villages. Some groups also formed what are now called tribes. **Tribe** is a term often used to describe a group of Native Americans who share a language and customs. Over time each tribe came to have its own culture. A tribe's culture set it apart from other tribes.

REVIEW How did the life of nomads compare to the life of farmers?
COMPARE AND CONTRAST

Early Civilizations

Having turned to a more settled way of life, some ancient Indian groups began to develop civilizations. A **civilization** is a culture that usually has cities and well-developed forms of government, religion, and learning. Among the most ancient American civilizations were the Olmecs (AHL•meks), the Maya (MY•ah), the Mound Builders, and the Anasazi (ah•nuh•SAH•zee).

From about 1500 B.C. to A.D. 300, the Olmecs lived in what is now southeastern Mexico. They developed their own calendar, number system, and form of writing. Because later groups learned so much from them, the Olmec culture came to be known as the "mother civilization" of the Americas. The Olmecs shared their ideas through trade with other groups.

One of these groups was the Maya, who lived south of the Olmecs. The Maya began to develop around 500 B.C. Building on what the Olmecs had done, the Maya slowly created their own civilization. They built more than 100 stone cities. Each city had its own ruler and government. Tikal, in what is now Guatemala, was the largest.

Like the Olmecs, the Maya were divided into social **classes**. Depending on what the people of a certain class did to make a living, its members were treated with different amounts of respect. At the top were the Mayan priests.

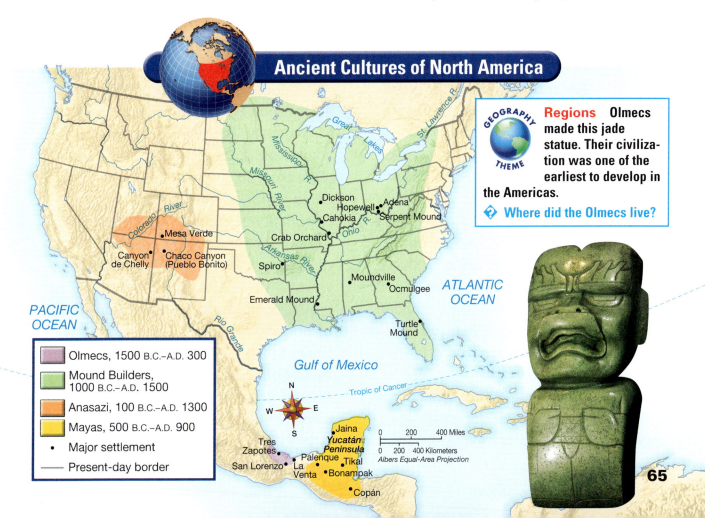

Ancient Cultures of North America

Regions Olmecs made this jade statue. Their civilization was one of the earliest to develop in the Americas.

◆ Where did the Olmecs live?

- Olmecs, 1500 B.C.–A.D. 300
- Mound Builders, 1000 B.C.–A.D. 1500
- Anasazi, 100 B.C.–A.D. 1300
- Mayas, 500 B.C.–A.D. 900
- • Major settlement
- — Present-day border

65

Then came the people from important families. Below them were the traders and craftspeople, the farmers, and finally the slaves. **Slavery** is the practice of holding people against their will and making them carry out orders. In Mayan society most slaves were people accused of crimes.

While cultures developed in Central America, other ancient civilizations grew in what is today the eastern half of the United States. These people became known as the Mound Builders because of the earthen mounds they built as burial sites or as places of worship.

The earliest of the Mound Builders were the Adenas (uh•DEE•nuhz), who lived in the Ohio River valley from about 1000 B.C. to A.D. 200. One of the most famous Adena mounds, Serpent Mound, is about 1,330 feet (405 m) long. When you look at it from the air, you can see that it forms the shape of a snake.

Around 300 B.C. a larger mound-building civilization known as the Hopewells developed in the central part of what is now the United States. The culture of the Hopewells was the strongest in the region for nearly 500 years. Hopewell goods and ideas spread far and wide through trade.

The greatest mound-building civilization was that of the Mississippian culture. It developed in the Mississippi River valley about A.D. 700. The Mississippians lived in hundreds of towns and several large cities. The largest Mississippian city was near where East St. Louis, Illinois, stands today. By A.D. 1200 more than 30,000 people lived in this city, called Cahokia (kuh•HOH•kee•uh).

From about 100 B.C. to A.D. 1300, the Anasazi, or "Ancient People," built a civilization in what is today the southwestern United States. They lived in groups of houses built next to or on top of one another, like apartment houses today. Spanish explorers later described these homes as pueblos (PWEH•blohz). **Pueblo** is the Spanish word for "village." Most pueblos were built on top of mesas, or high, flat-topped hills. Others were

Cahokia (left) had 85 mounds in all. One mound, now called Monk's Mound, stood 100 feet (30 m) high and covered 16 acres. People today can climb steps to reach the top of this mound (above).

built into the sides of high cliffs. The largest was Pueblo Bonito (boh•NEE•toh) in present-day New Mexico.

Over hundreds of years, the Anasazi and other early civilizations in North America gave way to new cultures and new civilizations. By about A.D. 1400, hundreds of different tribes of Native Americans lived throughout North America. North America was a land of great diversity—a land of many different peoples and cultures.

REVIEW Which early civilization lived in what is now the eastern United States?

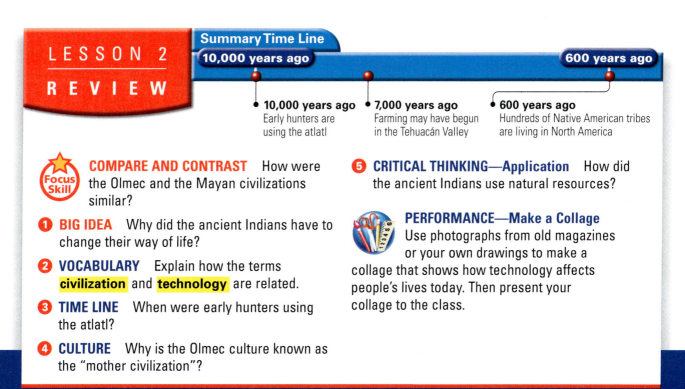

LESSON 2 REVIEW

Summary Time Line

- 10,000 years ago — Early hunters are using the atlatl
- 7,000 years ago — Farming may have begun in the Tehuacán Valley
- 600 years ago — Hundreds of Native American tribes are living in North America

COMPARE AND CONTRAST How were the Olmec and the Mayan civilizations similar?

1. **BIG IDEA** Why did the ancient Indians have to change their way of life?
2. **VOCABULARY** Explain how the terms **civilization** and **technology** are related.
3. **TIME LINE** When were early hunters using the atlatl?
4. **CULTURE** Why is the Olmec culture known as the "mother civilization"?
5. **CRITICAL THINKING—Application** How did the ancient Indians use natural resources?

PERFORMANCE—Make a Collage Use photographs from old magazines or your own drawings to make a collage that shows how technology affects people's lives today. Then present your collage to the class.

Chapter 2 ■ 67

SKILLS · Use a Cultural Map

VOCABULARY
generalization

This butterfly was made by a Crow Indian.

▶ WHY IT MATTERS

Some maps give you a general picture of the cultures of the people living in different regions. Maps showing cultural regions often use colors or symbols for places where most of the people speak a certain language or follow a certain way of life. Knowing about cultural regions can help you understand more about people and where they live.

▶ WHAT YOU NEED TO KNOW

Learning about the general picture of a place can help you make generalizations. A **generalization** is a statement that summarizes groups of facts and shows relationships among them. A generalization tells what is true most of the time.

The map on page 69 shows the early Native American cultural regions of North America. Each of the 11 regions is based on the unique location, landforms, climate, and vegetation that affected the cultures and traditions of Native Americans.

Within each cultural region are labels giving the names of some of the Native American tribes that lived there. The map also includes present-day state borders so you can better understand where these early cultures were located.

▶ PRACTICE THE SKILL

Use the following questions as a guide for making generalizations about the early cultures of North America.

1. Identify the color that covers most of the eastern half of what is today the United States. What generalization can you make about the way of life of the people who lived there?
2. Which three cultural regions included parts of present-day Oregon?
3. What generalizations can you make about early Native American cultures in the present-day states of New Mexico, Nevada, and Florida?

▶ APPLY WHAT YOU LEARNED

Draw a cultural map of present-day North America based on the main languages spoken. Gather information for your map by using books or Internet sources. Use colors to show where different languages are generally spoken today. Have a classmate use your map to make generalizations about the cultures of North America.

 Practice your map and globe skills with the **GeoSkills CD-ROM**.

68 ▪ Unit 1

LESSON 3

COMPARE AND CONTRAST

As you read, compare and contrast groups in the Southwest.

BIG IDEA
The way of life of Indian peoples of the Southwest was affected by the dry environment.

VOCABULARY
adapt
staple
surplus
ceremony
hogan

The Desert Southwest

The Southwest, with its rocky mesas, deep canyons, steep cliffs, and rugged mountains, is a challenging place to live, even today. Intense heat during the day can be followed by bitter cold at night. Weeks can go by without a drop of rain or snow. However, in summer, a sudden storm can bring so much rain that floods occur. It is difficult to survive in such a land. The many peoples who lived in the Southwest were able to **adapt**, or fit their ways of living to the land and its resources. By adapting to their environment, they found ways not only to survive but even to live well in the desert region.

The Pueblo Peoples

To the peoples of the Southwest, the expression "up the ladder and down the ladder" meant "to enter a house." Like their Anasazi ancestors, many peoples of the Southwest lived in pueblos. To enter a home or to reach other levels of the pueblo, people went "up the ladder and down the ladder." In time all of the tribes who lived in pueblos, including the Hopis (HOH•peez), the Zunis (ZOO•neez), and others, became known as the Pueblo peoples.

The Pueblo peoples built their homes mostly from resources they could find nearby. Some made their pueblos out of adobe. Others, such as the Hopis and the Zunis, built their pueblos from stones held together with mud. Some wood was used to build the roofs of the pueblos, but there are very few trees in the desert. Pueblo Indians had to travel long distances into the mountains to find pine and juniper trees from which they could make wooden beams. Here is how Charlotte and David Yue describe life in an early Hopi pueblo in their book *The Pueblo*.

"Pueblo families lived in one room, but most of the daily activities were out of doors. Their homes were used mainly for sleeping and for being sheltered from bad weather. The terrace was an outdoor kitchen and sitting room. The women went up

Pueblo families helped their children learn the names of the kachinas (kuh•CHEE•nuhz) by giving them kachina figures.

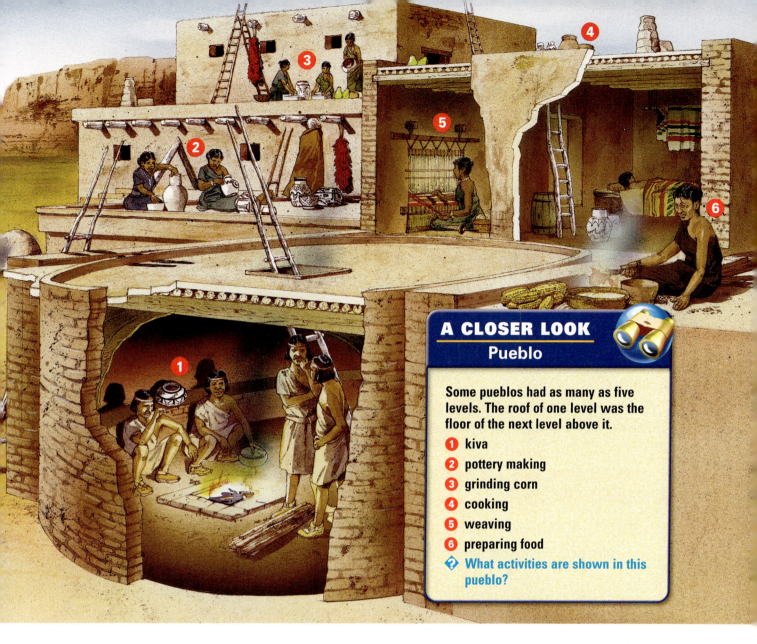

A CLOSER LOOK
Pueblo

Some pueblos had as many as five levels. The roof of one level was the floor of the next level above it.
1. kiva
2. pottery making
3. grinding corn
4. cooking
5. weaving
6. preparing food

❓ What activities are shown in this pueblo?

and down ladders to outside ovens on the terrace or down to the ground. The outdoor drying racks had to be tended, and baskets and pottery were often worked on outside."

The land of the Southwest also affected how the Pueblo Indians hunted and grew food. The **staple**, or main, foods of the Pueblos were corn, beans, and squash. As it was for most Native American groups, the most important of these was corn. The Pueblos also grew cotton, from which they made blankets and clothing. To grow these crops in the dry climate, the Pueblos depended on water from rain and underground springs, which they used to irrigate the land. While the men tended the crops, the women spent hours each day grinding corn into meal, using smooth, flat stones. Part of every home was filled with containers of corn and cornmeal. A food **surplus**, or an amount more than what is needed, meant survival during times of drought.

The Hopis and other Pueblo peoples believed in gods of the sun, rain, and Earth. Spirits called kachinas (kuh•CHEE•nuhz) were an important part of the Hopis' religion.

Chapter 2 ■ 71

The Hopis believed that kachinas visit the world of living people once a year and enter the bodies of kachina dancers. The kachina dancers were men who wore painted masks and dressed to look like the kachinas. Kachina dancers took part in many Hopi ceremonies. A **ceremony** is a series of actions performed during a special event, such as a religious service. Some of these ceremonies were held in special underground rooms called kivas (KEE•vuhz), and others were held in large meeting places outside. Today many Hopis continue to perform their traditional dances, some with kachina masks and some without.

REVIEW What kinds of natural resources did the Pueblo peoples use to build their homes?

Desert Newcomers

Not all of the people of the Southwest were Pueblo Indians. Before moving to the Southwest, peoples such as the Navajos (NA•vuh•hohz) lived mainly as nomads. They traveled in groups of families and did not have a formal leader.

The Navajos began moving into the Southwest about A.D. 1025. They settled in an area known today as the Four Corners. This is the place where the corners of the states of Arizona, Colorado, New Mexico, and Utah meet. The Navajo people still live in the Four Corners area today.

Some of this land was also Hopi land. In time the Navajos began learning Hopi ways of life. Soon they, too, were growing crops and making cotton clothing as the Hopis did.

In this land, the Navajos built shelters called hogans (HOH•gahnz). A **hogan** was usually cone-shaped. It was built by covering a log frame with bark and mud.

Rather than building their hogans close together, the Navajos built them in small, family-sized groups miles apart from one another.

REVIEW How did Navajo shelters contrast to those of the Hopis?
COMPARE AND CONTRAST

• BIOGRAPHY •

Luci Tapahonso 1953–
Character Trait: Loyalty

Luci Tapahonso's writings help keep the Navajo culture alive. Tapahonso is the Navajo author of six books of poetry and short stories. She was born in Shiprock, New Mexico, and started writing poetry at the age of 9. She uses both the Navajo and the English languages in her writings, which are often about the landscape of the Southwest and the history of her people.

MULTIMEDIA BIOGRAPHIES
Visit The Learning Site at
www.harcourtschool.com
to learn about other famous people.

GO ONLINE

72 • Unit 1

Navajo Beliefs

The Navajos believed in gods they called the Holy People. Some gods, such as the Earth Mother, were kind. Others, such as the sun god, could cause crops to dry up. The Navajos believed that they needed to honor the gods so that the gods would not use their powers against the people.

The Navajos honored their gods in ceremonies. Navajo ceremonies were led by religious leaders and healers called medicine people. Medicine people called upon the gods to protect the Navajos' families, homes, and crops or to cure the sick. In healing ceremonies medicine people made sandpaintings, also called dry paintings, that were believed to help heal people. First, the medicine person created a pattern of symbols on the ground, using colored sand. Then, the sick person sat or lay on the sandpainting while the medicine person held a ceremony that the Navajos believed would help the sick person feel healing powers. The painting was always rubbed away after the ceremony.

REVIEW What is a medicine person?

Today some sandpaintings are preserved. This one was made by Michael Tsosie.

The desert lands of Monument Valley are part of the Navajo lands.

LOCATE IT
UTAH
ARIZONA
Monument Valley Tribal Park

LESSON 3 REVIEW

COMPARE AND CONTRAST In what ways were the Navajos different from the Hopis?

1. **BIG IDEA** How did the dryness of the environment affect the Indian people of the Southwest?

2. **VOCABULARY** Use the term ceremony in a sentence to describe Hopi customs.

3. **HISTORY** Why was it important to the Pueblo peoples to store food?

4. **CRITICAL THINKING—Evaluate** How do you think the Navajos' way of life affected their need for a formal leader?

 PERFORMANCE—Make a Graphic Organizer Using the information in the lesson, make a graphic organizer about the way of life of the Hopis. Then use your organizer to write a story about them.

EXAMINE PRIMARY SOURCES

Native American Pottery

For hundreds of years, pottery-making has been an important part of Native American cultures. Over time, products such as metal pans, glassware, and imported ceramics have changed the way traditional pottery is made and changed its uses. However, the designs and decoration of pottery continue to reflect themes that are important to Native American cultures.

This present-day potter makes pottery in the Native American tradition.

FROM THE PHILBROOK ART CENTER, THE MAXWELL MUSEUM OF ANTHROPOLOGY, AND THE NATIONAL MUSEUM OF AMERICAN HISTORY AT THE SMITHSONIAN INSTITUTION

1990

This traditionally styled Pueblo seed pot shows contemporary images of the space shuttle and an astronaut.

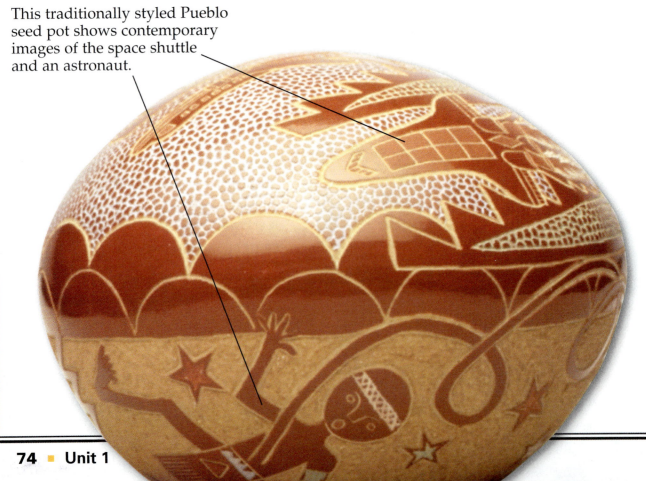

Analyze the Primary Source

1. How do you think these pots are similarly decorated? How are their decorations different?
2. What differences do you see in the pottery of different time periods? How do you think each vessel would be used today?

About 1300
The paints used to decorate pots were made from plants.

About 1000
Bowls like this may have been used to store grain.

Middle 1800s
Jars like this were made for storing food and water. By the late 1800s, however, glass jars were often used instead.

ACTIVITY

Compare and Contrast Make a list of uses that you might have for a clay pot. Then select designs that you would like to show on your pot. Use your information to draw a picture showing what your pot will look like. Share your drawing with your classmates. How are your pottery designs alike? How are they different?

RESEARCH

 Visit The Learning Site at www.harcourtschool.com to research other primary sources.

LESSON 4

The Northwest Coast and the Arctic

COMPARE AND CONTRAST
As you read, compare and contrast ways of life in the Northwest.

BIG IDEA
The environment of the Northwest Coast and Arctic regions made life different for the peoples who lived there.

VOCABULARY
dugout
barter
potlatch
clan
pit house
harpoon
totem pole

The Indians of the Northwest Coast and the Arctic lived in a place that was very different from the deserts of the Southwest. The Northwest Coast is a strip of land that stretches along the Pacific Ocean from northern California to Alaska. Nestled between the ocean and rugged mountains, it is a land of rivers and forests filled with fish and game. The Arctic region is much colder, and the land is frozen for most of the year.

River Traders

Along the Northwest Coast there was little agriculture. But there were plenty of fish, especially salmon. There were also plenty of deer, bears, and other animals. Therefore, instead of growing their own food, the Indians of the Northwest Coast met their need for food by fishing, hunting, and gathering plants. The enormous trees that grew in the forests provided them with wood for boats, houses, and tools.

If the Indians of the Northwest Coast needed items they could not make, they could get them through trade. Although the region's mountains made overland travel difficult, people could travel long distances on its waterways. In fact, the Columbia River became the "highway" of the Northwest. People used it to travel from place to place in wooden dugouts. A **dugout** is a boat made from a large, hollowed-out log.

One of the greatest trading centers located on the Columbia River was called The Dalles (DALZ). People would travel hundreds of miles to trade there. Dozens of tribes, some speaking languages as different from each other as English is from Chinese, took part in the trading through the mild summer months.

REVIEW What was one of the greatest trading centers on the Columbia River?

The people of the Northwest Coast traveled from place to place in dugouts.

76 ▪ Unit 1

The Chinooks made people pay them for the right to travel on the Columbia River.

The Chinooks

The best-known traders among the Northwest Coast Indians were the Chinooks (shih•NUKS). The Chinooks, who lived at the mouth of the Columbia River, controlled the river from the coast all the way to The Dalles—about 200 miles (322 km) upstream.

Because many tribes gathered at The Dalles to trade, the different languages they spoke made communication difficult. To help solve the problem, the Chinooks developed a language for trading. It was made up of Chinook words and words borrowed from other languages. This language made it easier for people of different tribes to talk to each other and to **barter**, or exchange goods. People traded dried fish, shells, furs, whale products, seal oil, cedar, dugouts, masks, jewelry, baskets, copper, and even prisoners.

Wealth was important to the people of the Northwest Coast. Tribes often attacked one another to gain wealth and, in turn, respect. Prisoners, a sign of wealth, were frequently taken as slaves during the many wars.

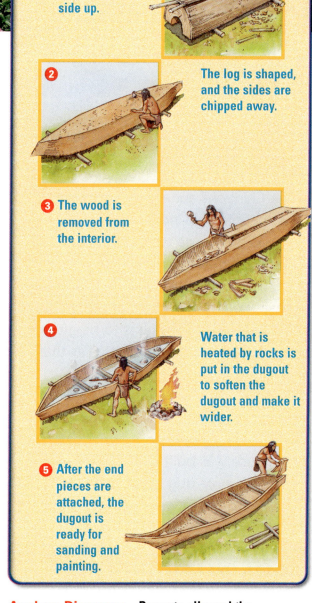

Making a Dugout

1. A cedar log is split lengthwise and turned round-side up.
2. The log is shaped, and the sides are chipped away.
3. The wood is removed from the interior.
4. Water that is heated by rocks is put in the dugout to soften the dugout and make it wider.
5. After the end pieces are attached, the dugout is ready for sanding and painting.

Analyze Diagrams Dugouts allowed the Northwest Coast Indians to travel on the many rivers in the region.

❖ How were the dugouts made wider?

Chapter 2 ■ 77

During a whale hunt the chief harpooner showed his respect for the huge animal by singing a special song, promising to give the whale gifts if it allowed itself to be killed.

The Chinooks and other Northwest Coast people held **potlatches** to show their wealth. These were celebrations with feasting and dancing. During a potlatch, the hosts gave away gifts as a sign of their wealth. Members of some clans spent years preparing gifts to be given away. A **clan** is a group of families that are related to one another.

Chinook villages were made up of rows of long wooden houses. The houses were built of boards and had no windows. Each house was built so that part of it was over a hole dug in the earth and some of its rooms were partially underground. Such a house is called a **pit house**.

In each house lived several families belonging to the same clan. Each clan was headed by its oldest member. The Chinooks traced their clans through the mother's family line. The people of the clan had the same mother, grandmother, or great-grandmother.

REVIEW What were potlatches?

The Makahs and the Kwakiutls

Most peoples of the Northwest found plenty of food in rivers and nearby coastal waters. Salmon and other fish and whales were in good supply. The Makahs (mah•KAWZ), who lived in what is now the state of Washington, were one of the many coastal peoples who built dugouts to hunt whales at sea. Some other coastal tribes, such as the Kwakiutls (KWAH•kee•oo•tuhlz), captured whales only if they became stranded on the shore. The Kwakiutls lived north of the Makahs on what is now Vancouver Island and western Canada.

Whale hunts were very important to the Makahs. Makah whale hunters often spent months preparing for a whale hunt. They fasted and prayed to their gods to favor them. They made new wooden **harpoons**—long spears with sharp shell points. They repaired their canoes and paddles. Made of wood, their canoes were 6 feet (about 2 m) wide and carried up to 60 people. They were built to travel over the open ocean. However, they still could be tipped over by an angry whale.

Imagine one group of whale hunters setting out to sea. The chief harpooner leads the hunters. Once they get close enough to the whale, the chief harpooner throws his harpoon. The whale is hit! Sealskin floats tied to the harpoon line make it difficult for the whale to dive down into the water and escape. Harpooners from nearby canoes throw their weapons, too. When the whale dies, the hunters start towing it to shore.

It takes hours of paddling for the hunters to reach their village. Wooden houses line the narrow beach between the water and the forest. Outside each house stands a tall wooden post called a **totem pole**. Each totem pole is carved with shapes of people and animals.

Some of the best woodcarvers in the Northwest Coast were the Kwakiutls. Like the Makahs, the Kwakiutls lived in wooden houses along the shore. Some houses were huge, up to 60 feet (18 m) long. Like others in the region, the Kwakiutls ate plants, shellfish, salmon, elk, and deer. They also held the most lavish potlatches of all the Northwest Coast Indians.

REVIEW How do the whale-hunting methods of the Makah and Kwakiutls compare?
COMPARE AND CONTRAST

The carvings on a totem pole show a family's history and importance.

• HERITAGE •

Family Heritage

Different Indian tribes in North America celebrated their identity in different ways. Groups on the Northwest Coast passed on their family and tribal histories through expertly carved and painted masks and totem poles. Masks were used in elaborate dances and ceremonies to act out stories of important events in the Indians' lives, such as births, deaths, and marriages. Totem poles were used to represent their ancestors and to tell the history of their people.

These Inuit sisters are wearing traditional dress.

The Inuit

The native peoples of the Arctic lived mostly north and east of the Northwest Coast Indians. Among them were the Inuit, who first settled in the harsh environment of the Arctic region of present-day northern Alaska and Canada only about 4,000 years ago. Since much of this land was frozen tundra, it was much too cold for farming. The early Inuit, like the early Northwest Coast Indians, got most of their food and made most of their clothing, shelters, and tools from the animals they hunted. Although resources were scarce in the Arctic, the Inuit developed the skills necessary to survive in a land of ice and snow.

To survive in the harsh environment, the Inuit had to be skilled hunters and fishers. They hunted seal, walrus, and caribou. They used the meat for food, the bones for tools, and the skins for clothing. Like the Makahs, the Inuit along the Alaskan coast hunted whales.

The Inuit made many kinds of shelters. Some built igloos—dwellings made of ice—in which they lived during the winter months. Igloos were made from large blocks of ice stacked into a dome shape. A hole in the top allowed the smoke from cooking fires to escape, and blocks of clear ice served as windows. During the summer the Inuit lived in tents made of animal skins. Other Inuit lived in tents and huts year-round.

REVIEW How did the Inuit use the environment to meet their needs?

LESSON 4 REVIEW

 COMPARE AND CONTRAST In what ways were the Makahs and the Kwakiutls similar?

① **BIG IDEA** How was life in the Northwest Coast region different from life in other regions?

② **VOCABULARY** Use the term **barter** in a paragraph about trade on the Northwest Coast.

③ **CULTURE** Who was the head of a Chinook clan?

④ **HISTORY** Why did the Makahs build canoes that could travel on the open ocean?

⑤ **CRITICAL THINKING—Synthesize** What do you think the Northwest Coast Indians learned from each other by trading at The Dalles?

 PERFORMANCE—Write a Description Using facts from the lesson, write a paragraph that describes what life was like for the Indians of the Northwest Coast or the Arctic. Then read your paragraph to a classmate.

The Plains

Millions of buffalo, or American bison, as scientists call them, once roamed the grassy lands of the Interior Plains. These hairy, cowlike beasts moved in huge herds made up of thousands of animals. The herds were so large that they were said to blacken the horizon. To the Plains Indians, who lived on the Interior Plains between the Mississippi River and the Rocky Mountains, the buffalo were second only to water as the region's most important resource.

Life on the Plains

Imagine a Native American hunting party coming upon a herd of buffalo. Wearing animal skins as disguises, the hunters creep into position around some of the buffalo. At a signal, the hunters all shout together. The frightened buffalo run, and the hunters drive them toward a steep cliff. The buffalo fall over the cliff and are killed.

Most of the women of the tribe were not hunters. Their job was to skin the buffalo and prepare them for many uses. Some of the meat was eaten right away. The rest was dried and saved for winter or a time when there were no buffalo nearby to hunt. Dried meat, which people today call jerky, can be kept for many months.

LESSON 5

COMPARE AND CONTRAST
As you read, compare and contrast the lives of the Plains Indians.

BIG IDEA
The Plains Indians used natural resources to live in their environment.

VOCABULARY
lodge
sod
tepee
travois

This painting by George Catlin shows two hunters hiding under wolf skins.

The Plains Indians used every part of the buffalo they hunted. They made clothing, blankets, and moccasins from the skins. They carried water in bags made from the stomachs. They twisted the hair into cord. They made needles and other tools from the bones and horns.

REVIEW What did the peoples of the plains make from buffalo skins?

Farmers and Hunters

Among the many Plains Indians who lived on the tall-grass prairies of the Interior Plains were the Mandans, Pawnees, Wichitas (WICH•ih•tawz), and some bands, or groups, of Sioux (SOO). These groups lived mostly in the eastern part of the Plains cultural region. They were both farmers and hunters. They farmed the rich land in the valleys along rivers such as the Missouri, Mississippi, and Platte. They also hunted deer, elk, and buffalo.

These people lived in villages made up of circular houses called **lodges**. Each lodge was built over a shallow pit. On the northern prairies of the Interior Plains, the lodges were covered with sod. **Sod** is earth cut into blocks or mats and held together by the grass and its roots. Because these houses were covered with earth, they are often called earth lodges. On the southern prairies, the earth lodges were covered with grass or animal skins.

Each earth lodge was home to several families. Sometimes as many as 60 people, plus their dogs, lived in one lodge. Each family had its own bed or beds next to the outer wall. In the center of the earth lodge was a shared fireplace under a hole in the roof for letting out smoke. The earth lodge was warm, and it protected the people during the cold winters.

Buffalo were a very important resource to the Indians of the western Plains. Buffalo hides were used to make much of their clothing, such as dresses and moccasins (right).

This painting by Karl Bodmer shows the Mandan lodges and the boats the Mandans used. To make the boats, they stretched buffalo skins around a wooden frame.

About twice a year the villages on the prairies emptied, as men, women, and children took part in a great buffalo hunt. The people walked for several days from their villages in the river valleys and forests to the grassy hunting areas.

When they were not hunting, the Indians on the prairies farmed. Their farms were small—more like gardens than farms. Their crops were mainly beans, corn, squash, and sunflowers. The farmers often traded their crops for goods that other tribes brought to them. Some of the villages along the Missouri River became trade centers for Native Americans from faraway places. The present-day site of Pierre (PIR), South Dakota, for example, was once the capital of the Arikara (uh•RIK•uh•ruh) Indian nation and a center for trade for more than 400 years.

REVIEW How did types of lodges differ?
COMPARE AND CONTRAST

The Great Plains Nomads

Many of the people who lived on the Great Plains, the western part of the Plains cultural region, did not farm or live in villages. Groups such as the Crows, the Cheyennes (shy•ANZ), the Kiowas (KY•uh•wuhz), and the Comanches (kuh•MAN•cheez) were nomads. They moved from place to place because they followed herds of buffalo. They did not grow crops because the flat grasslands on which they roamed had no rich river valleys. The roots of the short grass were so tough that it was almost impossible to break the soil with a digging stick.

Although these nomads had no permanent dwellings, they claimed certain areas as their own hunting lands. They followed specific routes within their lands. These routes usually depended on the movement of the herds of buffalo.

Chapter 2 ■ 83

A Calendar Robe

Analyze Primary Sources

Many Plains Indians kept the history of their tribe on what is now called a calendar robe. Each year leaders met to decide what event should be recorded on the robe. The drawings of the events could be read from left to right, right to left, or outward in a spiral from the center. This calendar robe was drawn by a Dakota Indian named Lone Dog. It covers the period 1800–1871.

1. 1837–1838: A successful elk hunt was held.
2. 1840–1841: The Dakotas and the Cheyennes made peace.
3. 1845–1846: Buffalo meat was plentiful.

❖ Why is it important to record historical events?

They depended on the buffalo as one of their most important resources. Houses, clothing, food, and even fuel for fire came from the buffalo. For fuel they used dried buffalo droppings, called chips.

Because the nomads had no permanent home, they built shelters that were easy to move. One kind was a cone-shaped tent called a **tepee** (TEE•pee). The nomads set wooden poles in a circle and tied them together at the top. They covered the poles with buffalo skins, leaving a hole at the top to let out the smoke from their fires.

Wood was hard to find because few trees grew on the Great Plains. The early Native Americans made double use of their wooden tepee poles by turning them into a kind of carrier called a **travois** (truh•VOY). A travois was made up of two poles fastened to a harness on a dog. Goods were carried on a skin tied between the poles.

In the Plains Indian way of life, each person was equal in the group. No one person was born more important than anyone else. Any man could become chief by proving himself a good hunter and a good leader of people. He was chief because his people chose and trusted him.

Women were responsible for sewing buffalo hides together to make tepee coverings. They also set up the tepees. Tepees were usually set up so that the entrance faced east. This kept the strong western winds on the Great Plains from blowing inside.

In some nomadic tribes, members who did not follow the ways of their group were free to live on their own. Sometimes a leader and his followers would start a new group. In this way, one tribe often had many subgroups. Each subgroup was made up of families who worked together.

REVIEW How could a man become chief of a Plains Indian tribe?

LESSON 5 REVIEW

COMPARE AND CONTRAST How were the Great Plains nomads different from the Indians who lived along the rivers in the eastern part of the Interior Plains?

1. **BIG IDEA** How did the peoples of the Plains use natural resources to live in their environment?

2. **VOCABULARY** Write a sentence that compares and contrasts a **lodge** and a **tepee**.

3. **GEOGRAPHY** What were the two most important resources to the Plains Indians?

4. **CULTURE** How did the Plains Indians divide the work that went into a buffalo hunt?

5. **CRITICAL THINKING—Analyze** How did the way of life of the Plains Indians affect the type of shelters they built?

PERFORMANCE—Do Research Use library resources or the Internet to find more information about the Plains Indians. Then report your findings to the class.

Chapter 2 ■ 85

· LESSON ·

6

The Eastern Woodlands

COMPARE AND CONTRAST

As you read, compare and contrast ways of life in the Eastern Woodlands.

BIG IDEA
Read to find out how the people of the Eastern Woodlands shared similar ways of life even though they spoke different languages and had different governments.

VOCABULARY
palisade
slash-and-burn
wigwam
wampum
longhouse
confederation
council

The cultural region known as the Eastern Woodlands covers most of the present-day United States east of the Mississippi River. Its name comes from the dense forests that once blanketed the land and that were the region's main natural resource. In some places, it was said, the forests were so thick with trees in the Eastern Woodlands that only a little sunlight could reach the ground.

Life in the Eastern Woodlands

The people of the Eastern Woodlands had many uses for trees. They used trees and tree bark to make canoes and shelters. Some trees even provided food. Nuts came from trees such as the walnut, the hickory, and the American chestnut. In the northern part of the Eastern Woodlands, maple sugar was made from the sap of maple trees.

Eastern Woodlands people were farmers, gatherers, and hunters. However, the Eastern Woodlands was a huge region of great diversity. In the northeastern part of the Woodlands, where the soil was rocky and there were many mountains, the people did more gathering and hunting than farming.

FAST FACT The sugar maple tree of the northeastern part of North America is one of the most valuable trees on the continent. Its sap is used to make maple syrup, and the wood is used for lumber.

The rich forests of the northeastern United States were home to the Eastern Woodlands people.

86 ■ Unit 1

The people of the Eastern Woodlands used resources like deer hides and clay to make storage containers, such as this bag (left) and this pot (right).

In southern areas, the soil and climate were better for growing crops. In their fields, the Eastern Woodlands people raised corn, beans, squash, and other plants.

Because they farmed and got enough food where they lived, the Eastern Woodlands people settled in villages. The villages often included a community building for meetings and ceremonies. Surrounding many villages was a wall, called a **palisade**, made of sharpened tree trunks. The palisade was built to protect the village from enemies and wild animals. The farm fields were located outside the palisade.

The Eastern Woodlands people made clearings in the forests for their fields. They cleared the land by cutting away a circle of bark on selected trees in the fall. By spring the tree was dead. With the leaves gone, the sun shone through the branches to the ground. Among the dead trees, the Woodlands people planted crops. After a year or two the dead trees were burned. After several more years, a field might be completely cleared. This method of clearing fields and growing crops is called **slash-and-burn** agriculture.

Some people in the Eastern Woodlands used fish as fertilizer. Others did not. Without fertilizer a field wore out in about ten years and no longer grew good crops. As a result some peoples had to move to new places, build new villages, and start clearing new fields.

Although Eastern Woodlands people raised much of their food, they also gathered and hunted. They gathered nuts, berries, wild fruits, greens, and shellfish. They caught fish and hunted beavers, porcupines, deer, and birds. They also hunted to get animal skins for clothing. Furry beaver and bear skins made warm robes, capes, and blankets. Scraped and tanned deer hides made soft buckskin for lighter clothing.

The peoples of the northeastern part of the Eastern Woodlands included two main language groups, the Algonquian (al•GAHN•kwee•uhn) and the Iroquoian (ir•uh•KWOY•uhn). Most of the Native Americans who spoke the Algonquian languages lived on the Coastal Plain. Most of the Iroquoian people, or Iroquois (IR•uh•kwoy), lived farther inland.

REVIEW How did the lives of different Eastern Woodlands people compare and contrast?
COMPARE AND CONTRAST

The Algonquians

Among the Algonquian tribes were peoples such as the Delawares, Wampanoags (wam•puh•NOH•agz), and Powhatans (pow•uh•TANZ), who lived along the Coastal Plain. Some of the Algonquian tribes lived farther inland, around the Great Lakes. These tribes included peoples such as the Algonkins (al•GAHN•kuhnz), the Chippewas (CHIP•uh•wahz), and the Miamis.

Each Algonquian tribe had anywhere from 1 to 20 villages. In most villages, 10 to 20 round, bark-covered shelters called **wigwams** were grouped around a village common. Most Algonquian tribes built their villages along the banks of rivers or streams. Some were built where two rivers or streams met. In wetland areas, villages were built on high ground to keep them safe from flooding.

The Algonquian peoples built birchbark canoes to fish in the rivers and along the coast. They used animal bones and wood to make fishing tools, such as hooks, lines, and fishing traps. Fish was a very important food source in winter, when crops would not grow. Near the coast, many tribes also made strings of beads that were cut from seashells. These beads, which they called **wampum** (WAHM•puhm), were used to keep records and send messages to other tribes. Algonquian peoples sometimes gave belts of wampum beads as gifts or in exchange for bartered goods.

Many Algonquian tribes had leaders who governed groups of villages. These villages traded together and helped one another during times of war. Other Algonquian peoples had two chiefs. One chief ruled during times of peace. The other chief ruled during times of war. Some tribes had a third leader, who was in charge of religious ceremonies.

REVIEW What were some of the uses of wampum?

This scene (below) shows an Algonquian village. The shirt (right) was worn by an Algonquian chief.

88 ■ Unit 1

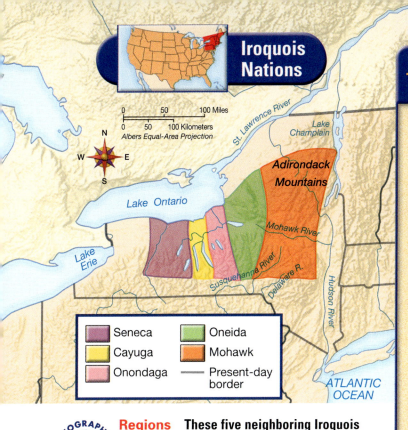

Regions These five neighboring Iroquois nations shared a government.

? How did the locations of the tribes help make working together so important?

DEMOCRATIC VALUES
The Common Good

The leaders of the five Iroquois nations agreed to stop fighting and unite so that together they could defend their lands against attacks from others. They recognized that they had more to gain by working together for the common good than by continuing to fight one another. The people worked together for the good of their village. To make it easier for the village to meet its needs, the work was usually divided among different workers. Some members of the village might have worked at making pots, while others made arrow points. Like the people of the Iroquois League, people living in the United States today often work together for the common good of all the citizens.

Analyze the Value

1. Why was it important for the Iroquois to work together as one?
2. **Make It Relevant** Identify some examples of people who are working for the common good of your school. Then write a paragraph that explains why their work is important.

The Iroquois

Like the Algonquians, the Iroquois were not one tribe but a group of tribes that lived near each other and spoke a common language. Five of the largest Iroquois tribes were the Senecas (SEN•uh•kuhz), Cayugas (ky•YOO•guhz), Onondagas (aw•nuhn•DAG•uhz), Oneidas (oh•NY•duhz), and Mohawks. These tribes, known as the Five Nations, were the most common groups in what is now upstate New York and the Lake Ontario region of Canada.

Also like the Algonquians, the Iroquois tribes farmed and lived in villages. The Iroquois lived in dwellings called longhouses. A **longhouse** was a long wooden building in which several related Iroquois families lived together. It was made of elm bark and had a large entrance at each end.

The longhouse was also a symbol for the Iroquois. Just as several families shared a longhouse, the five largest Iroquois tribes shared a government. It became known as the Iroquois League and acted as a **confederation** (kuhn•feh•duh•RAY•shuhn), or a loose group of governments working together. In *The Law of the Great Peace*, the Iroquois described the League. "Five arrows shall be bound together very strong and each arrow shall represent one nation each. As the five arrows are strongly bound this shall symbolize [represent] the complete union of the nations."

Chapter 2 ■ 89

This computer-generated picture shows what an Iroquois village may have looked like.

Each tribe in the League governed itself. However, matters that were important to all of the tribes, such as war and trade, were decided by the Great Council. A **council** is a group that makes laws.

For many years before the League came into being, the Iroquois had fought with each other and with neighboring tribes. The fighting often began over land.

In one Iroquois legend, a man named Deganawida (deh•gahn•uh•WIH•duh) spoke out against the fighting. He said that the Iroquois must come together "by taking hold of each other's hands so firmly and forming a circle so strong that if a tree should fall upon it, it could not shake nor break it . . ."

A Mohawk leader named Hiawatha (hy•uh•WAH•thuh) shared Deganawida's hopes for peace. Hiawatha visited each of the Iroquois tribes, asking for an end to the fighting. The tribes finally agreed to work together in the Iroquois League.

REVIEW What was the Iroquois League?

LESSON 6 REVIEW

COMPARE AND CONTRAST In what ways were the Algonquians and the Iroquois different?

1 BIG IDEA What ways of life did the peoples of the Eastern Woodlands share?

2 VOCABULARY Use the terms **confederation** and **council** in a report about the Iroquois.

3 GEOGRAPHY Why was fish an important food source in winter for the Algonquian peoples?

4 CULTURE Why did the Iroquois form the Iroquois League?

5 CRITICAL THINKING—Analyze How was the Iroquois longhouse a symbol of the Iroquois League?

PERFORMANCE—Deliver a Speech Write and deliver a speech to persuade Iroquois leaders to join the Iroquois League. Be sure to include the benefits of working together.

SKILLS · Resolve Conflict

VOCABULARY
compromise
resolve

▶ WHY IT MATTERS

The Iroquois resolved the conflicts over land by forming the Iroquois League. In forming the Iroquois League, it is likely that the different tribes had to compromise to reach an agreement. You **compromise** when you give up some of what you want in order to reach an agreement. Knowing how to compromise gives you another way to **resolve**, or settle, conflicts.

▶ WHAT YOU NEED TO KNOW

Here are some steps that can help you resolve conflicts through compromise.

Step 1 Tell the other person clearly what you want.

Step 2 Decide which of the things you want are most important to you.

Step 3 Present a plan for a possible compromise, and listen to the other person's plan.

Step 4 Talk about any differences in the two plans.

Step 5 Present another plan, this time giving up one of the things that is important to you.

Step 6 Continue talking until the two of you agree on a plan. If either of you becomes angry, take a break and calm down.

Step 7 Plan a compromise so that it will work for a long time.

▶ PRACTICE THE SKILL

Think of a disagreement that your class or your community might be facing. Form groups to discuss it. Using the steps listed in this skill, vote on a compromise plan.

▶ APPLY WHAT YOU LEARNED

With your classmates, choose an issue that you do not all agree on. Form sides and discuss the issue, using the steps in What You Need to Know.

This staff was used to list the members of the Iroquois League. The pegs in the staff stood for each tribe's representatives.

CHAPTER 2 Review and Test Preparation

Focus Skill: Compare and Contrast

Copy the following graphic organizer onto a separate sheet of paper. Use the information you have learned to compare and contrast life for the Plains and the Northwest Coast Indians.

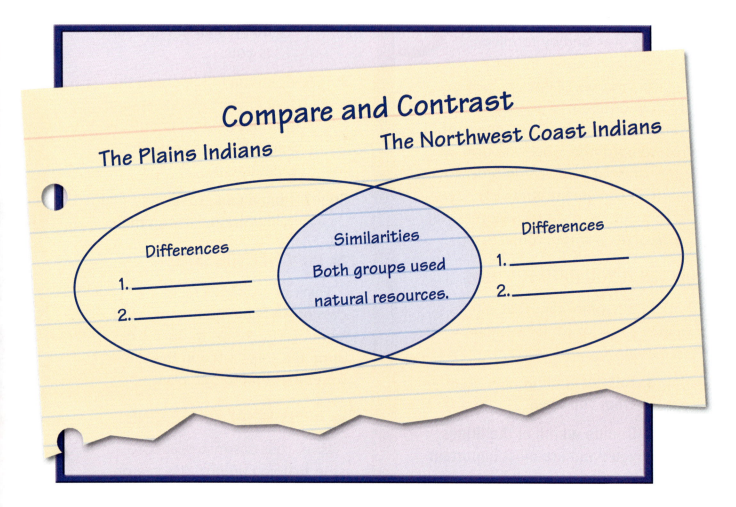

THINK & WRITE

Write an Article Imagine that you are one of the archaeologists that uncovered artifacts at the Meadowcroft Rock Shelter in Pennsylvania. Write an article that explains why this evidence supports the early arrival theory.

Write a Journal Entry Suppose that you are an early traveler on the Columbia River. Write a journal entry about your journey as you travel to The Dalles. Describe your experiences as you travel the river and at the trading center.

USE VOCABULARY

Use each of the following terms in a sentence that will help explain its meaning.

archaeologist (p. 57)
technology (p. 63)
civilization (p. 65)
adapt (p. 70)
barter (p. 77)
travois (p. 85)
confederation (p. 89)

RECALL FACTS

Answer these questions.

1. What connected the continents of Asia and North America long ago?
2. Why were the ancient Indians nomads?
3. How did changes in the environment affect the way of life of the ancient Indians?
4. How were the Olmecs and the Maya divided?
5. What was the purpose of Navajo sandpaintings?

Write the letter of the best choice.

6. The Pueblo peoples modified their environment by—
   A traveling long distances to gather wood.
   B irrigating land for farming.
   C storing food in containers.
   D making kachinas.

7. One of the most important resources for the Plains Indians was—
   F the forest.
   G the buffalo.
   H the river.
   J the whale.

8. The Iroquois tried to make peace by—
   A forming a confederation.
   B leaving the Eastern Woodlands.
   C building a longhouse.
   D building palisades around the villages.

THINK CRITICALLY

9. How did the environment affect the ways of life of people across North America?
10. How is North America a place of great diversity today?

APPLY SKILLS

Read Time Lines
Use the time lines on pages 60–61 to answer the following questions.

11. Between which years did the fourteenth century take place?
12. Which year was earlier, 200 B.C. or A.D. 2000?

Use a Cultural Map
Use the map on page 69 to answer the following questions.

13. What is the largest cultural region in North America?
14. Do you think more people relied on fishing in the Northwest Coast or in the Plains?

Resolve Conflict

15. Think of an issue that you and a friend disagree about. Make a list of the steps that you might follow to resolve the conflict. Include a compromise that could resolve the conflict.

VISIT THE Hopi Nation

GET READY

The Hopi Nation is made up of 12 villages. The villages are located at the tops and at the bases of three mesas in northeastern Arizona. Many Hopis still follow their traditional way of life. They perform Kachina ceremonies, produce traditional craft work, and farm the land as they have done for hundreds of years. On a visit to the Hopi Nation, you can learn about Hopi culture and see examples of how Hopis keep their traditions alive.

WHAT TO SEE

Visitors to the Hopi Nation may have the chance to see a Kachina ceremony. The Kachina dances express prayers for rain, health, and bountiful harvests.

LOCATE IT

ARIZONA — Hopi Nation

94 ■ Unit 1

This young girl is dressed for the Butterfly Dance, which celebrates the harvest.

Hopi artists create jewelry, baskets, and pottery. They use patterns and styles that have been passed down from generation to generation.

TAKE A FIELD TRIP

A VIRTUAL TOUR
Visit The Learning Site at **www.harcourtschool.com** to take virtual tours of other cultures.

A VIDEO TOUR
Check your media center or classroom library for a videotape tour of the Hopi Nation.

Unit 1 ■ 95

UNIT 1 Review and Test Preparation

VISUAL SUMMARY

Write a News Story Imagine that you are a news reporter. Your job is to review the Visual Summary below and choose one of the events to write a news story about. Tell when and where the event took place and its importance.

USE VOCABULARY

Use the words from the list to complete the sentences below.

sea level (p. 21)
tributary (p. 30)
nonrenewable (p. 41)

1. A resource that cannot be made again by nature or people is called ____.
2. The land of the Coastal Plain region lies close to ____.
3. A stream or river that flows into a larger stream or river is called a ____.

RECALL FACTS

Answer these questions.

4. Name the seven continents, from largest to smallest.
5. Why are oceans, lakes, and rivers important to life in the United States?
6. What are the similarities between the desert and tundra regions of the United States?
7. Which of these ancient cultures developed first?
   A Anasazi
   B Olmec
   C Mound Builder
   D Maya
8. Which groups of Native Americans call the Northwest Coast and the Arctic home?
   F Hopis, Zunis, Chinooks
   G Comanches, Kiowas, Cheyennes
   H Chinooks, Makahs, Inuit
   J Maya, Olmecs, Makahs

Visual Summary

12,000 years ago — 8,000 years ago

About 10,000 years ago ancient Indians hunted large animals p. 62

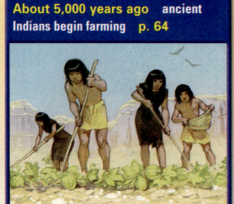

About 5,000 years ago ancient Indians begin farming p. 64

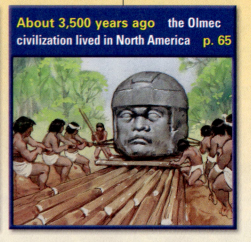

About 3,500 years ago the Olmec civilization lived in North America p. 65

96

9 Navajo religious ceremonies are led by a religious leader known as a—
A totem pole.
B kachina.
C kiva.
D medicine person.

THINK CRITICALLY

10 Why do you think there are different ideas as to how people may have come to live in North and South America?

11 What role do you think farming had in the development of civilizations in North and South America? Explain.

12 Do you think the Iroquois Nations could have survived without the Iroquois League? Why or why not?

APPLY SKILLS

Use Longitude and Latitude
Use the map of the Great Plains region on this page to answer the following questions.

13 Which location is farther north, 35°N, 100°W or 45°N, 95°W?

14 What line of latitude is closest to the border of North and South Dakota?

15 What state capital is located closest to 40°N, 105°W?

Great Plains

4,000 years ago — PRESENT

About 1,000 years ago the Navajos moved to the Southwest p. 72

By 800 years ago more than 30,000 people lived in Cahokia p. 66

About 700 years ago the Iroquois lived in the Northeast p. 89

Unit Activities

Visit The Learning Site at www.harcourtschool.com for additional activities.

Draw a Map

In a group, work together to draw a map of the United States. Include the present-day borders of all 50 states. Using a different color to represent each of these regions—the Desert Southwest, the Northwest Coast and Arctic, the Plains, and the Eastern Woodlands—divide your map into sections. Label each section with the names of the Native American tribes that lived in that region.

Write a Short Story

Imagine that you are a member of an ancient Indian tribe living in North America. Write a short story explaining what your everyday life is like. Include the kind of food you eat, the clothing you wear, and what type of shelter you live in.

VISIT YOUR LIBRARY

- ***Squish! A Wetland Walk*** by Nancy Luenn. Atheneum.

- ***Anasazi*** by Leonard Everett Fisher. Simon & Schuster.

- ***Earth Always Endures: Native American Poems.*** Edited by Neil Philip and Edward S. Curtis. Viking.

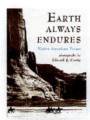

COMPLETE THE UNIT PROJECT

A Multimedia Presentation Work with a group of classmates to complete the unit project—a multimedia presentation. Decide on a topic and what information you want to include. Next, create a variety of visual and written aids to help your group present information from the unit. Invite students from other classes to see your presentation.

Time of Encounters

GEORGIA CONNECTION

A compass, 1570

GEORGIA CONNECTION

ENCOUNTERS IN GEORGIA

Europeans began exploring Georgia in the 1520s. Spanish explorer Pedro de Quejos (PAY•dro day KAY•hohs) explored the Georgia coast and the barrier islands nearby. In 1540 Hernando de Soto (er•NAHN•doh day SOH•toh) led an expedition through Georgia. De Soto and other Spanish explorers were often not friendly toward the Native Americans in Georgia.

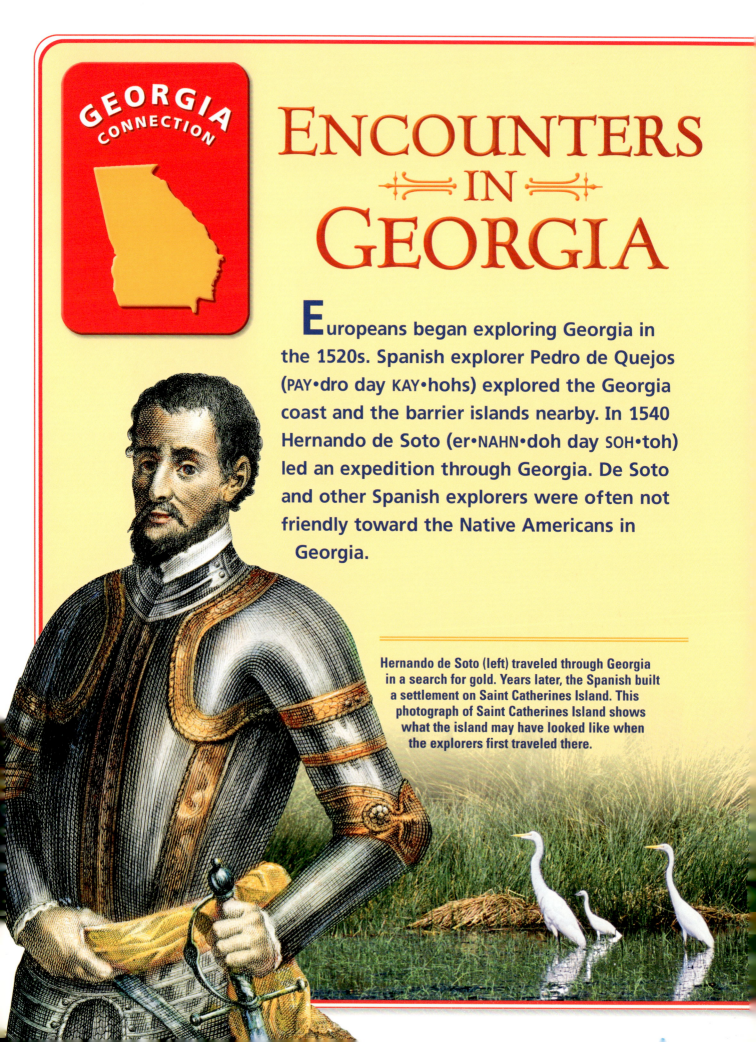

Hernando de Soto (left) traveled through Georgia in a search for gold. Years later, the Spanish built a settlement on Saint Catherines Island. This photograph of Saint Catherines Island shows what the island may have looked like when the explorers first traveled there.

In 1566 Pedro Menéndez de Avilés (PAY•droh muh•NEN•dez day ah•vee•LAYS) met with a group of Native Georgians from Saint Catherines Island. They agreed to let him build a fort on the island. Soon the Spanish built missions along the Georgia coast to protect their land in what is now Georgia. Missions are small religious settlements. One of these missions was Santa Catalina, on Saint Catherines Island. The people who worked in the mission, or missionaries, wanted the Native Georgians to become Catholic and be loyal to the king of Spain.

Some Native Georgians enjoyed living in the Santa Catalina mission. Missionaries protected them and taught them new skills. But many Native Georgians were forced to work on the mission farm against their will. Many grew angry and decided to fight the missionaries. The church was burned to the ground, and the mission was abandoned. In 1604 the Santa Catalina mission was again settled by missionaries. It remained a mission until the English arrived in the 1670s.

This Spanish gold bead was found near Saint Catherines Island.

★ CRCT ★ TEST PREP

❶ The first Spanish explorer to explore Georgia was
A Hernando de Soto.
B Pedro de Quejos.
C Pedro Menéndez de Avilés.
D Christopher Columbus.

❷ Why did the Spanish build missions in Georgia?
A to give Native Georgians a place to live
B to farm the land and ship food to Spain
C to protect their land
D to give their missionaries a place to live

❸ What happened when the Native Georgians fought the missionaries at Santa Catalina?
A The church was burned.
B Native Georgians got more land.
C The missionaries hired workers.
D The missionaries built a second mission.

Trunk Bay, United States Virgin Islands

UNIT 2

Time of Encounters

> " I saw so many islands I could not count them all... "
>
> —Christopher Columbus, November 14, 1492

Preview the Content

Skim the unit. When you have finished, answer the following— *Who* and *What* is the unit about? *Where* are the places you will learn about? *When* did the events happen? *Why* are these events important? Make a graphic organizer and fill in your responses.

Who →	Germany, other European Nations, Japan, the United States
What →	World War II
Where →	Europe and in the Pacific
When →	1940s
Why →	to preserve democracy

Preview the Vocabulary

Related Words Use the Glossary to look up the vocabulary words below. What do these words have in common?

colony   hacienda   presidio   mission

Unit 2 ■ 99

UNIT 2 PREVIEW

Early European Settlements

PACIFIC OCEAN

NORTH AMERICA

NEW SPAIN
- Mexico City (1522)

Legend:
- French
- Spanish
- ● Settlement
- FOX Name of Native American tribe
- — Present-day border

0 250 500 Miles
0 250 500 Kilometers
Lambert Equal-Area Projection

Key Events

| 1200 | 1300 | 1400 |

1275 Marco Polo reaches China p. 109

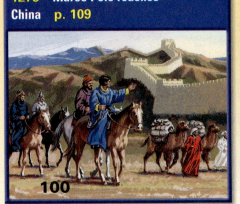

1492 Christopher Columbus lands at San Salvador p. 122

1498 Vasco Da Gama reaches India by sea p. 118

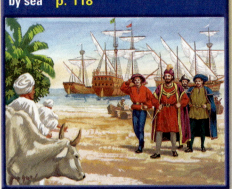

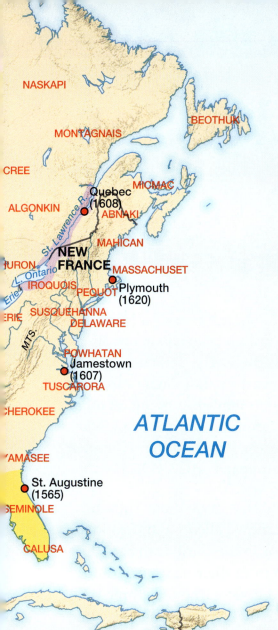

First Explorers to the Americas, 1492–1542

COUNTRY	EXPLORER	DATES OF EXPLORATION	AREA EXPLORED
Spain	Christopher Columbus	1492	Caribbean
England	Giovanni Caboto	1497	Newfoundland
Spain	Amerigo Vespucci	1499–1501	eastern South America
Portugal	Pedro Alvarez Cabral	1500	Brazil
Spain	Vasco Núñez de Balboa	1513	Isthmus of Panama
Spain	Juan Ponce de León	1513	Puerto Rico and Florida
Spain	Ferdinand Magellan	1519–1522	Brazil, eastern South America
Spain	Hernando Cortés	1519–1536	Mexico, California
France	Giovanni da Verrazano	1524	northeast North America
Spain	Panfilo de Narvaez	1528	Gulf of Mexico
Spain	Álvar Núñez Cabeza de Vaca	1528–1536	Texas, New Mexico, Mexico
Spain	Francisco Pizarro	1531–1535	western South America
France	Jacques Cartier	1534–1541	eastern Canada
Spain	Hernando de Soto	1539–1542	southeastern North America
Spain	Francisco Vásquez de Coronado	1540–1542	southwestern North America
Spain	Juan Rodriguez Cabrillo	1542	California

1500 — 1600 — 1700

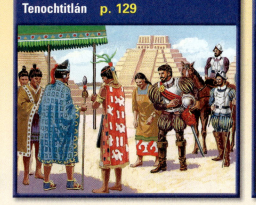

1519 Hernando Cortés arrives in Tenochtitlán p. 129

1607 English colonists settle Jamestown p. 161

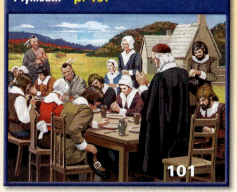

1620 English colonists settle Plymouth p. 167

101

START with a STORY

San Salvador

from *The World in 1492* • by Jamake Highwater

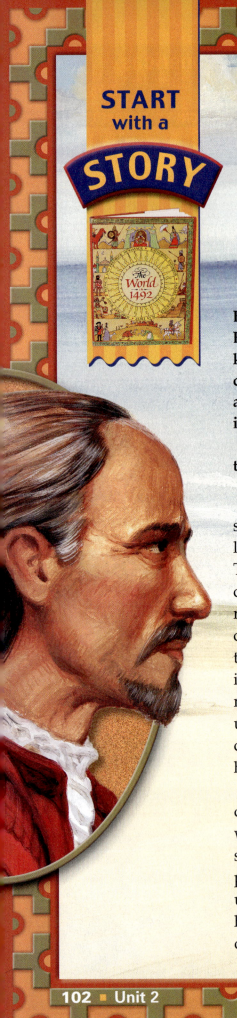

San Salvador is among the many tropical islands of the Bahamas, off the coast of Florida. Before the arrival of the Europeans, who gave the island its present-day name, people known as the Tainos (TY·nohz) lived there. The Tainos grew crops in the warm climate. They hunted small animals and birds, and they fished. They also traded with the tribes living on other islands and in other coastal regions around the Caribbean Sea.

Nothing in their experience, however, prepared them for what they saw one day in the year the Europeans called 1492.

On that morning of October 12, 1492, a miraculous sight is seen by the people of a little island, now called High Cay, that lies just off the coast of San Salvador in the Caribbean Sea. There in the twilight, as they climb from their hammocks and come out of their palm-leaf-covered houses, they see three moving islands that gradually make their way across the water, coming out of the great unknown and moving ever closer to the astonished people on the shore. In the first light, the floating islands give birth to small rafts that float away from their mothers and drift toward the beach, carrying the most unbelievable creatures. They look like people made of bright colors. Their faces are covered with bushy hair, as if they are holding squirrels in their mouths.

Despite the strangeness of these creatures, the people are delighted and astounded to see them, and they run toward the water to greet them. At close range, the people realize that the strangers from the sea look like real men, except they have very pale faces covered with bunches of curly hair. They are terribly ugly and have a dreadful smell of spoiled milk. Yet they seem harmless, despite the strange gray and black weapons they carry. The people smile happily when the strangers admire their spears made of reeds and the lovely little ornaments of gold they wear on their ears and nostrils. The people cannot understand why the yellow metal is so fascinating to them. To make them happy, they bring their strange guests many gifts—green parrots and bundles of precious cotton—in return for which they are given beautiful colored beads and small bells that make a delightful sound. These strangers, who completely hide themselves behind clothing, seem ill at ease with the nakedness of the people of the island, who do not cover their handsome bodies except for lavish painted designs of black, white and red.

Then a man with a scarlet chest steps forward and tries to talk to the people, though he does not know how to speak properly and can only make strange noises and wave his arms in the air. Despite this strange behavior, the people smile at him respectfully. Hoping to teach him how to speak, they gesture across the landscape, and they tell the scarlet man that their island is called Guanahani. He seems to understand. Then the man points to himself and repeatedly tells the people his name. At this the people of the island begin to laugh. For this stranger has a most peculiar name!

Christopher Columbus.

Analyze the Literature

1. Why do you think the Tainos were so surprised by the Europeans?

2. Write about how Columbus may have viewed the Tainos.

READ A BOOK

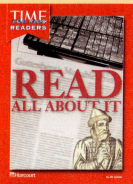

START THE UNIT PROJECT

An Exploration Map With your classmates, create a map that shows the exploration of North America. As you read, take notes about the key explorers and the routes they traveled. Your notes will help you decide which routes to show on your map.

USE TECHNOLOGY

Visit The Learning Site at www.harcourtschool.com for additional activities, primary sources, and other resources to use in this unit.

Unit 2 ■ 103

CHAPTER 3

A Time of Exploration

REENACTMENT OF COLUMBUS'S SHIPS

On October 12, 1492, Christopher Columbus first saw Guanahani Island. The next days would mark the start of a period that would forever change the world. Today, the island that Columbus renamed San Salvador continues to attract visitors to its shores.

LOCATE IT

BAHAMAS

San Salvador

" *Lumbre! Tierra!* "

(Light! Land!)

—Pedro Yzquierdo, member of Columbus's first expedition to America, midnight, October 11, 1492

Focus Skill: Sequence

A **sequence** is the order in which one event comes after another.

As you read the chapter, do the following.

- Put events related to exploration in the correct sequence.

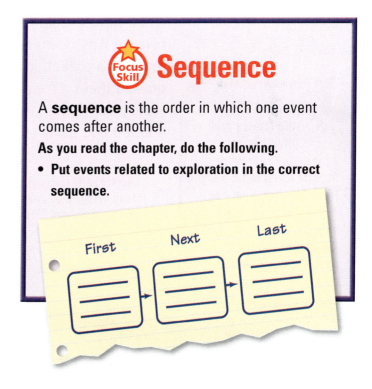

Chapter 3 ■ 105

LESSON 1

The World in the 1400s

1400–1500

SEQUENCE
As you read, look for the sequence of events that led to exploration.

BIG IDEA
The world's cultures became connected in the 1400s.

VOCABULARY
encounter
empire
monarch
Renaissance
compass
city-state

When the Tainos welcomed Christopher Columbus in 1492, almost 500 years had passed since the last **encounter**, or meeting, between Europeans and Native Americans. In about A.D. 1000, Leif Ericson led a group of people known as Vikings to North America. The Vikings were from what is today the country of Norway, but they did not stay long, and they met few people. The memory of their visit soon faded. As a result, Native Americans knew nothing about Europe.

In the 1400s Europeans knew nothing about the Americas and very little about the rest of the world. That was beginning to change, however, as new trade routes connected Europe with parts of Asia and Africa.

The Americas

Long before Columbus arrived in the Americas, some groups of Native Americans had established powerful empires. An **empire** is a collection of lands ruled by the nation that conquered them. One of the largest and richest of these empires was ruled by the Incas of South America. Their empire covered about 3,000 miles (4,828 km) of the western coast of South

 FAST FACT
Legend says that the Aztecs built their capital where they saw what they believed to be a sign from the gods—an eagle with a snake in its mouth, sitting on a cactus. Today the eagle with the snake appears on the Mexican flag.

Analyze Illustrations The Aztecs built causeways, or land bridges, to connect the island capital of Tenochtitlán to the mainland. They also built pyramids (right).
◆ How would having water on all sides of the capital help keep it safe from attacks?

America, including parts of what are now the countries of Ecuador, Peru, Bolivia, Chile, and Argentina.

The Incas expanded their empire by using force to take over other peoples' land. In time, they ruled as many as 12 million people, most of whom lived in villages along the coast, in the Andes Mountains, and in the rain forests along the Amazon River. The Incas' capital city was Cuzco (KOOS•koh), in what is now Peru.

A system of roads connected Cuzco to all areas of the Inca Empire. In fact, two major roads—one along the coast and one through the Andes Mountains—ran the length of the empire. These roads led to great cities whose grand buildings were made of stones. These stones were cut by hand to fit together. This way of building can still be seen today in the ruins of the Inca city of Machu Picchu (MAH•choo PEEK•choo).

The Incas kept records on groups of colored, knotted strings known as quipus (KEE•pooz). The different-colored knots stood for words or ideas. For example, a knot made from yellow string represented the word *gold.* A knot made from white string stood for *peace.* Although archaeologists have found many quipus, most of what is known about the Incas was written down by Spanish explorers after they arrived in the Americas.

North of the Incas lived the Mexicas, a tribe later known as the Aztecs. For many years the Aztecs moved from place to place in search of food. In about A.D. 1200 they began to settle in the Valley of Mexico, in the central part of present-day Mexico. By the late 1400s the Aztecs had taken control of much of central and southern Mexico. They ruled over a huge empire that covered about 200,000 square miles (518,000 sq km) and included more than 5 million people.

The Aztecs built their capital city, Tenochtitlán (tay•nawch•teet•LAHN), on two islands in the middle of Lake Texcoco (tays•KOH•koh). Today Mexico City, the capital of Mexico, stands on this same spot.

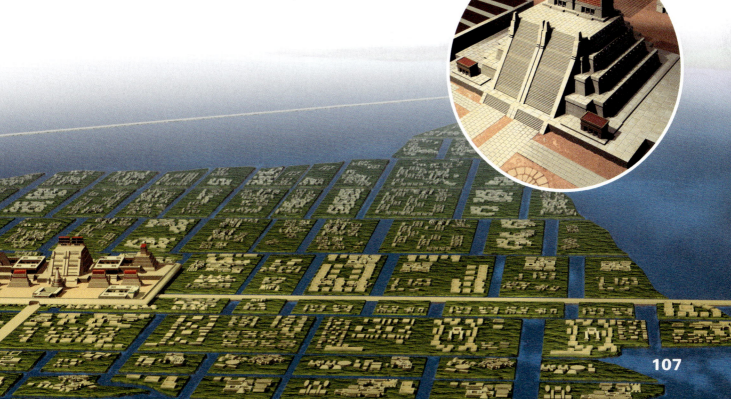

Major Cities of the 1400s

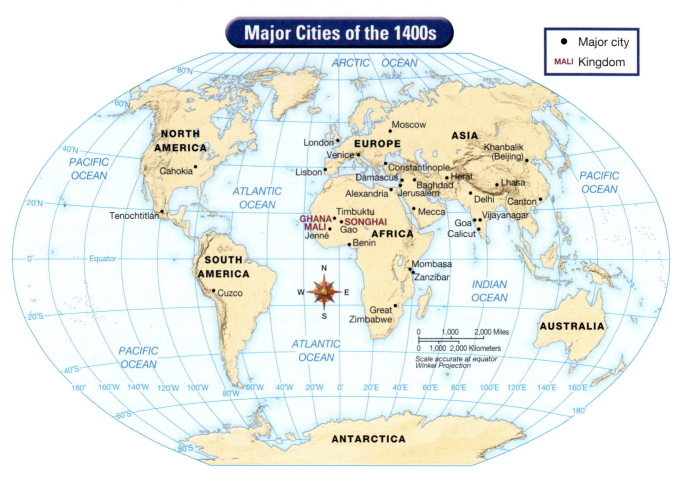

Location In the early 1400s most people knew little or nothing about cities on other continents.

◆ What major cities were located in North America?

In the very center of Tenochtitlán, huge flat-topped pyramids rose toward the sky. On top of the pyramids stood the great stone temples that were built to honor the Aztecs' gods. Past the temples was a large, open area where a daily market was held.

The Aztecs recorded information by using pictures of objects and symbols to represent words and syllables. They used these pictures and symbols to make calendars and keep records. This system of communication made the Aztec Empire one of the most advanced civilizations in the Americas at that time.

REVIEW How did the Incas expand their empire?

Europe

In the 1400s many changes were taking place in Europe. In earlier times, almost all of Europe had been divided into many small land areas, each owned by a different noble. Over time, some of these separate land areas had been joined to form countries. Portugal, Spain, France, England, and other European countries were now ruled by **monarchs**, or kings and queens.

Europeans at this time were making big improvements in science and technology. With this new knowledge, they entered into an age of thought, learning, art, and science. This period lasted through the

108 ■ Unit 2

1400s and 1500s and was known as the **Renaissance** (REH•nuh•SAHNS). *Renaissance* is a French word meaning "rebirth." During this time people were eager to explore unknown lands.

Knowledge of the Renaissance spread with the help of Johannes Gutenberg. In about 1450 he invented a new way to print books that was easier and less costly. As a result, more books were printed. In addition to the Bible, one of the most popular books of the Renaissance was *The Travels of Marco Polo.* Written almost 200 years earlier, this book described what the traveler from Venice, Italy, had seen on his journey to Asia in the late 1200s. When he was just 17 years old, Marco Polo, his father, Nicolò Polo, and his uncle, Maffeo Polo, set out to explore Asia. Four years later the Polos reached Cathay, as China was then called. They also traveled to the Indies, the islands off the China coast, as well as to Myanmar (Burma), India, and Southwest Asia.

The Polos were impressed by everything they saw, especially in China. They were amazed by Chinese inventions such as gunpowder and the **compass**—an instrument for finding direction. They also held paper money for the first time and saw the palace of Kublai Khan (KOO•bluh KAHN), China's ruler.

As Europeans read Marco Polo's accounts, they became interested in the lands he had visited. They wanted to share in the great wealth he described and buy Asian goods such as silks and spices. Soon, traders from Europe were traveling the long, difficult land routes that connected Europe and Asia.

REVIEW To which countries did Marco Polo and Nicolò Polo travel? **SEQUENCE**

Asia

Some Asian countries began to explore the world by sailing the oceans. The Chinese ruler Yong Le (YUHNG LEH) paid for the ocean voyages of Admiral Zheng He (JUHNG HUH). Zheng He made at least seven voyages between 1405 and 1433.

Zheng He (far right) and his crew made many ocean voyages for the Chinese emperor on junks like this one (below).

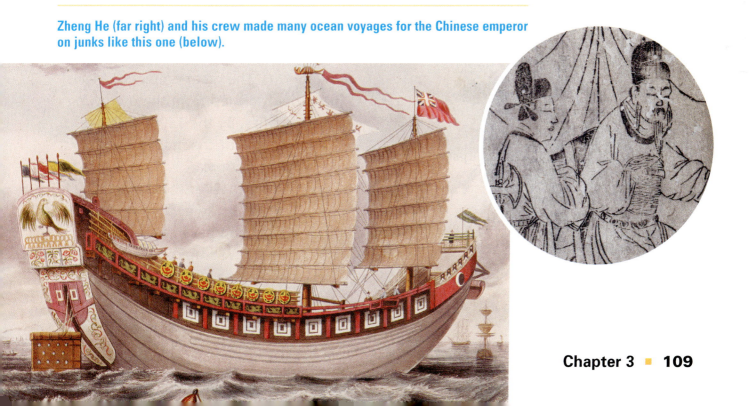

Chapter 3 ■ 109

Timbuktu became a center of learning as well as a trading center.

The admiral and his crews sailed in junks, Chinese wooden boats with four-sided sails. Zheng He sailed to Southeast Asia and to present-day Sri Lanka (SREE LAHNG•kuh). He also visited several ports along the Persian Gulf, the Red Sea, and the eastern coast of Africa.

After Yong Le's death, new Chinese rulers decided to keep China apart from other civilizations. They stopped all ocean voyages and limited trading outside of China's borders. They later ordered that the records of Zheng He's voyages be destroyed.

While China moved to limit its contact with the rest of the world, other places in Asia, such as India, Korea, and Japan, continued to develop trading centers. In the southern part of India, Vijayanagar (vih•juh•yuh•NUH•ger) became an important trading center for Asian and European countries. It was also known for its art, writing, and buildings.

REVIEW How did China limit its contact with other countries?

Africa

For centuries, groups in Africa traded with one another. In time, African trading centers grew. As early as the eighth century, Ghana in western Africa had become a great African empire. Ghana had grown from just a small town into a grand walled city with palaces and busy market centers. The capital of Ghana was Kumbi Saleh (koom•BY sah•LAY), a large market center that stood in what is now a desert region of Senegal.

In the 1100s, the powerful trading centers of Ghana began to move east to the cities of Gao (GOW), Timbuktu (tim•buhk•TOO), and Jenné (jeh•NAY). The great empire of Mali (MAH•lee) formed from these growing market cities. By the 1300s Mali had become one of the most powerful empires in Africa.

In the 1400s these market centers broke away from Mali rule. Gao became the head of a new empire known as Songhay (SAWNG•hy).

A Chinese vase traded in Africa.

110 ■ Unit 2

Benin was known for its brass and bronze sculptures. This statue was made in the 1500s.

The Songhay Empire controlled many of the market cities. This gave the Soninkes (sawn•IN•kayz), the people of Songhay, control of much of the trade across the Sahara to the north where they traded gold for European goods.

One of the best-known leaders of the Soninkes was Sunni Ali. He ruled from 1464 to 1492. Under his rule the Songhay Empire stretched more than 1,000 miles (1,609 km). Sunni Ali also encouraged more trade, which helped Songhay remain a strong empire until the end of the 1500s.

Also in western Africa was the kingdom of Benin. Benin was located in what is now southern Nigeria, near the mouth of the Niger River. Benin was an artistic center where sculptors carved ivory and worked with brass and bronze.

On the eastern coast of Africa, groups of people called the Swahili (swah•HEE•lee) lived in several city-states. A **city-state** included a city and the surrounding area. These city-states grew from the trading centers that Arab settlers had started at ports along the coast. Trade centered around gold and ivory, which were exchanged for goods from China, India, and Southwest Asia.

REVIEW How did Emperor Sunni Ali keep Songhay a strong empire?

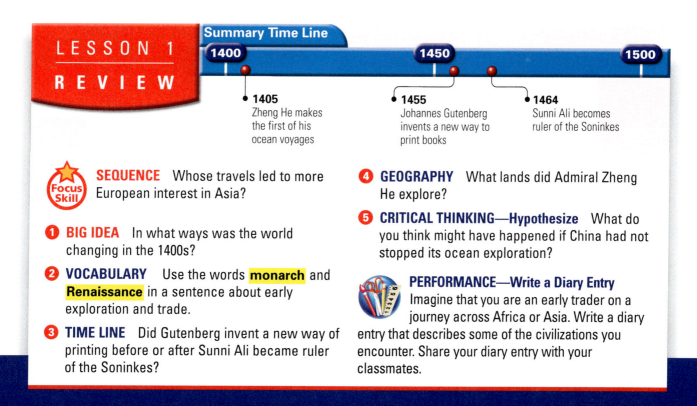

LESSON 1 REVIEW

Summary Time Line

- 1405 — Zheng He makes the first of his ocean voyages
- 1455 — Johannes Gutenberg invents a new way to print books
- 1464 — Sunni Ali becomes ruler of the Soninkes

SEQUENCE Whose travels led to more European interest in Asia?

❶ **BIG IDEA** In what ways was the world changing in the 1400s?

❷ **VOCABULARY** Use the words **monarch** and **Renaissance** in a sentence about early exploration and trade.

❸ **TIME LINE** Did Gutenberg invent a new way of printing before or after Sunni Ali became ruler of the Soninkes?

❹ **GEOGRAPHY** What lands did Admiral Zheng He explore?

❺ **CRITICAL THINKING—Hypothesize** What do you think might have happened if China had not stopped its ocean exploration?

PERFORMANCE—Write a Diary Entry Imagine that you are an early trader on a journey across Africa or Asia. Write a diary entry that describes some of the civilizations you encounter. Share your diary entry with your classmates.

SKILLS: Follow Routes on a Map

VOCABULARY
historical map

▶ WHY IT MATTERS

Marco Polo's book *The Travels of Marco Polo* inspired other Europeans to go to Asia. You can learn more about Marco Polo, and about other people and events, by using historical maps. A **historical map** gives information about a place as it was in the past. It may show where a historical event took place. It may show where cities or towns were once located. It may also show the routes that people followed as they traveled from one place to another. Knowing how to follow a route on a historical map can help you better understand the past and gather information about it.

▶ WHAT YOU NEED TO KNOW

The map on page 113 shows the routes followed by Marco Polo on his journey to and around Asia. Notice on the map key that the colored arrows represent the different routes he used during his adventure. These include the route to China, the route to Pagan, and the route back to Venice. The map also shows the lands and cities he visited along these routes. The dates of his journey are included in the map title.

▶ PRACTICE THE SKILL

Look at the map key to learn about the routes Marco Polo used during his exploration of Asia. Use the information provided on the map to answer the following questions about Marco Polo's journey.

1. What color shows the route Marco Polo followed to China?

Marco Polo wrote about Asia in The Travels of Marco Polo. *This copy was printed in 1577.*

112 ▪ Unit 2

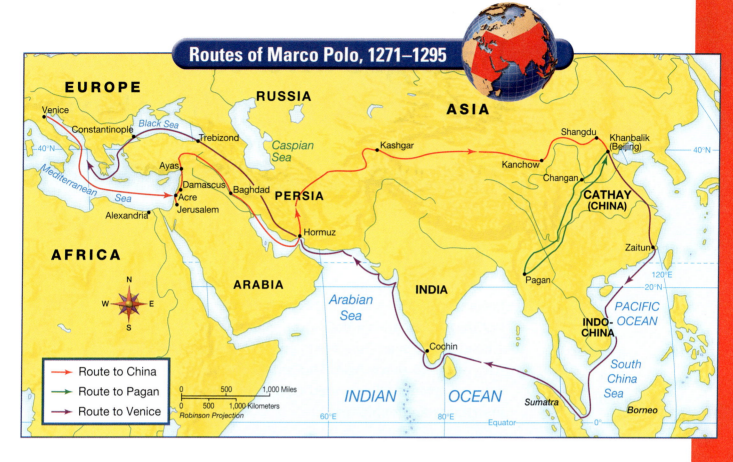

2. What lands did he visit on his way to China?
3. What lands did he visit on his way home to Venice?
4. What geographic features did Marco Polo come across on his journey to China?
5. What geographic features did Marco Polo come across on his journey back to Venice?

APPLY WHAT YOU LEARNED

Imagine that the ruler of Italy has given you money to explore Asia. Like Marco Polo, you will begin your journey from Venice. Draw a map like the one on this page. Show the routes you would take on your expedition to Asia and the lands you would visit along the way. Use a map key to explain what the symbols on your map stand for. You can use both land and sea routes to get to and from Asia.

Practice your map and globe skills with the **GeoSkills CD-ROM**.

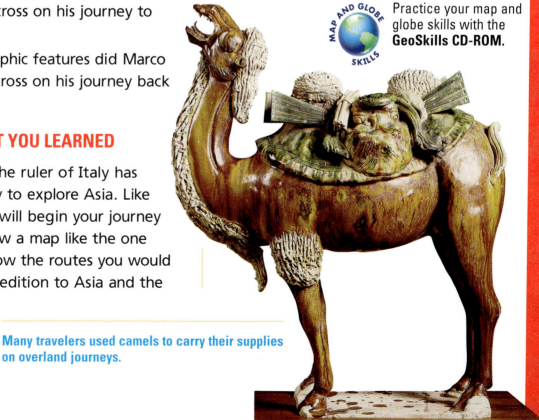

Many travelers used camels to carry their supplies on overland journeys.

· LESSON ·

2

Background to European Exploration

SEQUENCE
As you read, look for the sequence of events that led to new trade routes.

BIG IDEA
The Portuguese wanted to find a water route to Asia.

VOCABULARY
profit
navigation
cartographer
astrolabe
caravel
expedition

1200 — 1475 — 1700
1450–1500

During the Renaissance, the overland trade routes between Europe and Asia became dangerous because of fighting between religious groups in Europe and Asia. As a result, European merchants and explorers looked for less risky ways to reach Asia. This led to the development of better ways of travel and provided new opportunities for European merchants and explorers.

An End to East-West Trade

For hundreds of years Europeans carried on a busy trade with people from Asia. To get goods from China and other places in Asia, merchants set off on the ancient Silk Road. The Silk Road, also known as the Silk Route, was not really a road, but a group of overland trade routes between China and Italy.

The Silk Road stretched over the mountains and deserts of Asia, so travel was often difficult and slow. Instead of going all the way to the Far East, as the Europeans called Asia, most European merchants traveled only part of the way. They went to trading cities in North Africa and in Southwest Asia, which the Europeans called the Middle East. The major trading cities included Alexandria (a•lig•ZAN•dree•uh) in North Africa and Baghdad (BAG•dad) and Constantinople (kahn•stant•uhn•OH•puhl) in Southwest Asia. There, European merchants exchanged their goods for goods that had been brought there from Asia.

Items such as silk (left), Chinese bank notes (center), and containers of tea leaves (right) were all traded along the Silk Road.

114 • Unit 2

These people are traveling on what was once a part of the Silk Road.

The Asian goods that Europeans wanted most included gold, jewels, silks, perfumes, and spices. Spices such as pepper, cloves, cinnamon, and nutmeg were used to help add flavor to food and keep it fresh.

Asian goods were usually expensive because Europeans could not easily get them. Europeans, however, were willing to pay high prices to have them. As a result, merchants made huge profits from selling these goods. A **profit** is money left over after the goods and the costs of getting them have been paid for.

European merchants continued to enjoy these huge profits until 1453, when trade with Asia was suddenly stopped. In that year the Turks, a people from a land called the Ottoman Empire in the Middle East, captured the important trading city of Constantinople. This gave the Turks control of the Middle East, and they closed the trade routes to Asia. Now there was no way for Europeans to get Asian goods.

REVIEW What sequence of events stopped Asian trade?

SEQUENCE

Portugal Leads the Way

By the time the city of Constantinople was captured, Portugal's monarch, King John I, had already decided to spend as much money as needed to find a new route to Asia. King John asked his son Henry to direct the country's search for a water route to Asia. Prince Henry soon set up a school for training sailors in navigation (na•vuh•GAY•shuhn). **Navigation** is the skill of controlling the course of a ship.

Prince Henry started his school at Sagres (SAH•gresh), a town on the southwestern tip of Europe. There he brought together sailors, shipbuilders, and **cartographers** (kar•TAH•gruh•ferz), or mapmakers. The cartographers drew up new, more accurate maps. Many were based on information from the journals of early travelers.

Prince Henry also hired people who helped improve two important navigation tools—the compass and the astrolabe (AS•truh•layb).

Prince Henry later became known as Henry the Navigator.

Chapter 3 ■ 115

An **astrolabe** is an instrument used to calculate the positions of the sun, moon, and stars. The astrolabe helped sailors find their location by using the position of the sun or the North Star.

Sailors at Prince Henry's school learned how to sail a new kind of ship, the **caravel**. This ship used square or triangular sails to travel long distances quickly. It also was able to survive heavy seas. Since the caravel was easier to sail and could carry more cargo than older types of ships, it was the preferred ship for ocean exploration.

Prince Henry believed that the most direct way to reach Asia from Europe by sea would be to go south around Africa and then sail east across the Indian Ocean. Under his direction, dozens of Portuguese ships made their way down Africa's west coast. Altogether, Henry organized more than 50 voyages, but he did not go on any of them. For this reason he is sometimes called "the explorer who stayed at home."

A CLOSER LOOK
The Caravel

Many sailors in the 1400s used caravels to travel long distances.
1. side view
2. captain's cabin
3. hold
4. crow's nest
5. main mast
6. main deck
7. ship's boat

❓ Where do you think food and other supplies were kept?

• SCIENCE AND TECHNOLOGY •

Navigational Tools

In the 1400s sailors used the compass and the astrolabe to help determine their location at sea. In the 1700s, however, they used more advanced instruments, such as the sextant and the chronometer, to help find a ship's position. The sextant was used to determine the altitude, or the height above the horizon, of the sun or stars. The chronometer (kruh•NAHM•uh•ter) kept very accurate time. It was used to measure the positions of certain stars based on the time. Today, radar and other electronic systems have replaced these tools.

An astrolabe

Chapter 3 ■ 117

· BIOGRAPHY ·

Ahmad Ibn Majid
1432–1500

Character Trait: Inventiveness

Ahmad Ibn Majid (AH•mahd IH•bihn ma•JEED) was born in what is today the United Arab Emirates. He learned navigation skills, geography, astronomy, and Arabic literature at an early age.

In 1498, Majid helped Vasco da Gama sail around the Cape of Good Hope and on to India. He is considered by many to be a great contributor to the study of navigation.

MULTIMEDIA BIOGRAPHIES
Visit The Learning Site at
www.harcourtschool.com
to learn about other famous people.

GO ONLINE

As the Portuguese explored the western coast of Africa, they found new markets where they could trade European goods for nuts, fruits, and gold. They also discovered that they could trade their goods for slaves. Like Native Americans and other groups throughout history, Africans had long used prisoners of war as slaves. Traders from Portugal saw that they could make money by buying slaves in Africa and taking them to Europe to be sold as servants. By 1460 Portuguese traders were buying about 800 slaves from African traders each year.

REVIEW How did Prince Henry contribute to ocean exploration?

Dias and Da Gama

After Prince Henry's death, the Portuguese continued to explore the west coast of Africa. King John II of Portugal ordered Bartolomeu Dias (DEE•ahsh) to sail to the southern tip of Africa. The king wanted to know for sure that ships could reach Asia by sailing around Africa. Earlier **expeditions**, or journeys of exploration, had failed because of the rough ocean currents along the southern coast of Africa.

Dias commanded a fleet of three ships. In 1488 the ships reached southern Africa, and a storm blew them out to sea. When the winds died down and the sky cleared, Dias realized that the storm had blown the ships around to the east coast of the continent. He and his crew had become the first Europeans to sail around the southern tip of Africa!

On their way back around the tip of Africa, Dias sighted what is now called the Cape of Good Hope. Some historians believe that Dias originally named it the Cape of Storms but that King John later renamed it the Cape of Good Hope. To King John the discovery of the cape meant that a sea route to India would soon be found.

Almost ten years later Vasco da Gama (dah GA•muh) reached India. He sailed around the Cape of Good Hope with four

FAST FACT
Vasco da Gama returned to Portugal in 1499 with Indian spices and jewels. The sale of the items brought 60 times what the trip had cost!

ships. He brought back to Portugal perfumes, silks, spices, and other goods that he had traded for in India. The expedition returned to Lisbon, Portugal's capital, in September 1499. Many of da Gama's crew, however, did not survive the long voyage. Of the 170 crew members who started the voyage, only 55 lived to return home.

As a reward for his successful expedition, da Gama was given the title Admiral of the Sea of India. His voyage opened the Cape Route to India and led to the regular sailing of ships between Europe and Asia. The trade that resulted helped Portugal become wealthier and more powerful. It also spread Portuguese influence and culture to Africa and Asia. Portugal quickly became one of the most important trading powers in the Indian Ocean.

REVIEW What led to the regular sailing of ships from Europe to Asia?

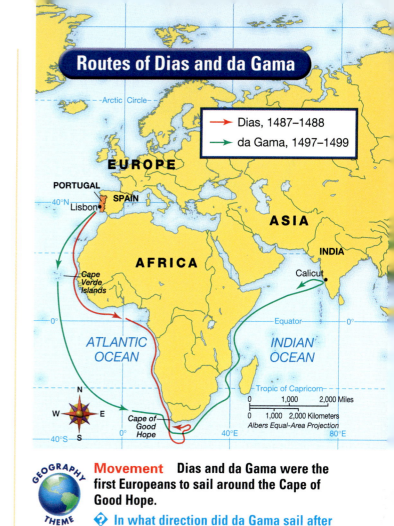

Movement Dias and da Gama were the first Europeans to sail around the Cape of Good Hope.

◆ In what direction did da Gama sail after he sailed around the Cape of Good Hope?

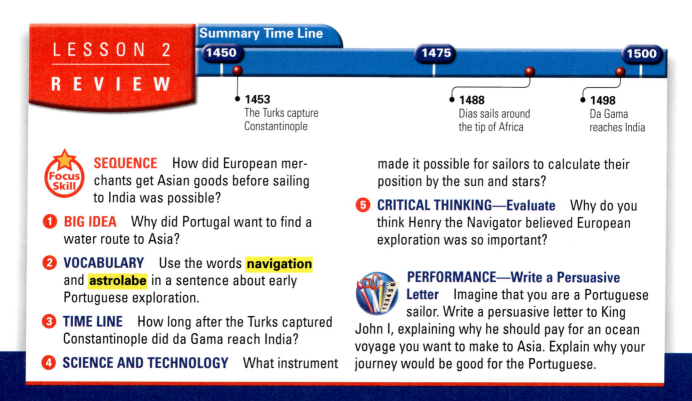

LESSON 2 REVIEW

Summary Time Line
- 1453 The Turks capture Constantinople
- 1488 Dias sails around the tip of Africa
- 1498 Da Gama reaches India

SEQUENCE How did European merchants get Asian goods before sailing to India was possible?

1. **BIG IDEA** Why did Portugal want to find a water route to Asia?

2. **VOCABULARY** Use the words **navigation** and **astrolabe** in a sentence about early Portuguese exploration.

3. **TIME LINE** How long after the Turks captured Constantinople did da Gama reach India?

4. **SCIENCE AND TECHNOLOGY** What instrument made it possible for sailors to calculate their position by the sun and stars?

5. **CRITICAL THINKING—Evaluate** Why do you think Henry the Navigator believed European exploration was so important?

PERFORMANCE—Write a Persuasive Letter Imagine that you are a Portuguese sailor. Write a persuasive letter to King John I, explaining why he should pay for an ocean voyage you want to make to Asia. Explain why your journey would be good for the Portuguese.

Chapter 3 ■ 119

SKILLS: Identify Causes and Their Effects

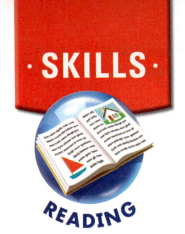

VOCABULARY
cause   effect

▶ WHY IT MATTERS

To find the links between events in history, you need to identify cause-and-effect relationships. A **cause** is an event or action that makes something else happen. An **effect** is what happens as a result of that event or action. Knowing about causes and effects can help you predict likely outcomes so that you can make more thoughtful decisions.

▶ WHAT YOU NEED TO KNOW

Events in history can have more than one effect. You can use these steps to help you identify the causes and the effects of events.

Step 1 Look for the effects.

Step 2 Look for the causes of those effects.

Step 3 Think about how the causes relate to the effects.

▶ PRACTICE THE SKILL

The following cause-and-effect chart lists the effects of the Turks taking over Constantinople and closing the trade routes between Europe and Asia. Use the chart to answer these questions.

1. The capture of what city caused Europeans to begin searching for water routes to Asia?

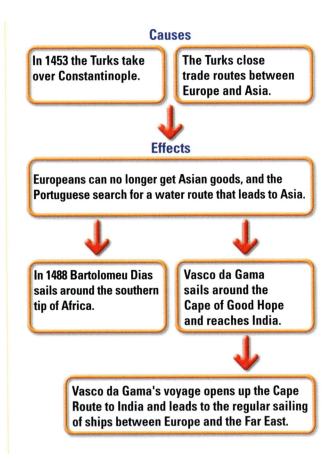

2. What was the immediate effect of the Turks closing these trade routes?

3. Name an event that took place as a result of da Gama sailing around the Cape of Good Hope to India.

▶ APPLY WHAT YOU LEARNED

Look through pages 114–119 of your textbook, and identify at least two other cause-and-effect relationships in this lesson. Then share your findings with a classmate.

Europeans Explore the World

1200 — 1475 — 1700
1482–1522

LESSON 3

 SEQUENCE
As you read, look for the sequence of events that led to European exploration.

BIG IDEA
The Europeans attempted to find a western route to Asia.

VOCABULARY
claim
isthmus
demarcation
treaty

Portugal and other European countries, such as Spain, Denmark, England, Holland, and France, were determined to find new and faster water routes to Asia. These nations also hoped to **claim**, or declare they owned, new lands in the hope of building their empires and discovering new riches.

Christopher Columbus

Born and raised in Italy, Christopher Columbus had sailed to all parts of the world that were known to Europeans, including the Mediterranean Sea, England and the European coast, the Canary Islands, and the coast of Africa. He was fascinated by the stories he had heard of the wealth in Asia, especially in China and on the islands of Southeast Asia, then a part of what was known as the Indies.

For years Columbus had worked on a plan to reach Asia by sailing west across the Ocean Sea, as the Atlantic Ocean was then known. He believed that sailing west was a more direct route to Asia than going around Africa. Columbus first took his plan to the king of Portugal in 1482. The Portuguese king turned him down. Three years later, in 1485, Columbus asked Spain's monarchs, King Ferdinand and Queen Isabella, to support his plan.

At the time, Spain's monarchs were more interested in life at home than in paying for an ocean expedition. Ferdinand and Isabella believed that Spain could be united as a nation only if all its people were Catholic. Their plan to make Spain all Catholic was called the Reconquista (ray•kohn•KEES•tah), or Reconquest.

Christopher Columbus was determined to reach Asia by sailing west across the Ocean Sea.

Chapter 3 ■ 121

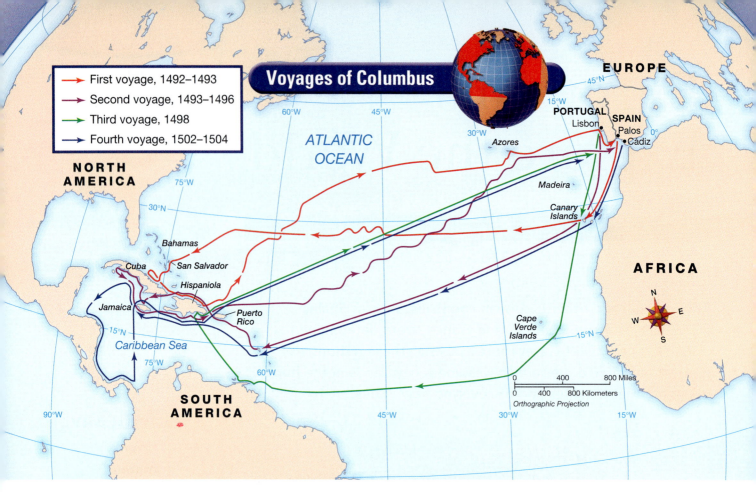

 Movement The King and Queen of Spain declared Columbus Admiral of the Ocean Sea and governor of any lands he discovered.

◆ In which voyage did Columbus reach the islands off the coast of South America?

By 1492 the Spanish monarchs had forced the Muslims, who would not become Catholic, out of Spain. They also forced all Jewish people to leave Spain.

When Spain was united under one religion, Columbus again asked Ferdinand and Isabella to support his expedition. He promised the monarchs great wealth and new lands. Columbus also said that he would take the Catholic religion to the people of Asia. The king and queen agreed to support his plan.

On August 3, 1492, Columbus and a crew of nearly 90 sailors set forth on three ships—the *Niña* (NEEN•yuh), the *Pinta* (PEEN•tuh), and the *Santa María*. On October 12 they anchored off an island that Columbus named San Salvador, which in Spanish means "Holy Savior." He claimed the island for Spain.

Columbus believed he had reached Asia and was now in the Indies. For this reason he called the people of the island Indians. The name West Indies is still used to refer to the islands Columbus visited in the Caribbean Sea.

News of Columbus's voyage stirred an excitement to explore. Columbus himself made three more voyages to the "new world." Today, his arrival in the Americas is remembered in many cities in the United States on Columbus Day.

REVIEW What sequence of events led to Columbus's expedition? **SEQUENCE**

An Unknown Continent

Soon after Columbus's first voyage, most European monarchs wanted to send ships across the Atlantic to China and the Indies. In 1497 the king of England paid an Italian sailor named Giovanni Caboto (kah•BOH•toh) to lead an expedition.

Caboto's course across the Atlantic Ocean was far north of Columbus's course. Many believe that Caboto reached the coast of present-day Newfoundland, a part of Canada. When Caboto returned to England, he said he had found Cathay, and it was a place so rich in fish that a person could simply lower baskets into the water and draw them up filled with fish. Caboto became a hero. In England he was given the English name John Cabot.

Not everyone believed that Columbus had found the Indies or that Caboto had found Cathay. Amerigo Vespucci (veh•SPOO•chee) of Italy was one who had doubts. In 1499 Vespucci sailed to a place just south of where Columbus had landed. Two years later Vespucci sailed on an expedition down the coast of South America.

Vespucci looked for signs that he had reached Asia, but he could find none. Something else did not make sense. Years earlier he had studied the work of Ptolemy (TAH•luh•mee), an astronomer in ancient Egypt, and had learned that Earth was larger and Asia was smaller than most people had thought. If Asia were as far east as Columbus claimed, it would cover half the Earth.

Vespucci came to realize that he, Columbus, and Caboto had found an unknown continent. In 1507 a mapmaker named Martin Waldseemüller (VAHLT•zay•mool•er) published a world map that included this unknown continent. He named the new lands for Amerigo Vespucci, calling them America.

The first to prove Vespucci's idea was the Spaniard Vasco Núñez de Balboa (NOON•yays day bahl•BOH•uh), who crossed the Isthmus of Panama in 1513. An **isthmus** (IS•muhs) is a narrow strip of land that connects two larger land areas.

• Heritage •

Columbus Day

The first Columbus Day celebration was held in 1792, when New York City celebrated the three-hundredth anniversary of Columbus's landing at San Salvador. Columbus Day became a legal federal holiday in 1971. It is celebrated on the second Monday in October. Today, many cities and organizations hold parades and banquets to honor this early explorer.

Many cities, like Chicago, hold parades to celebrate Columbus Day.

POINTS OF VIEW
An Unknown Land?

CHRISTOPHER COLUMBUS, from a letter he wrote to his friend Doña Juana de Torres in 1500

❝I should be judged as a captain who went from Spain to the Indies . . .❞

AMERIGO VESPUCCI, from a letter to his friend Lorenzo Medici announcing the discovery of a new continent

❝Those new regions [America] which we found and explored with the fleet . . . we may rightly call a New World . . . a continent more densely peopled and abounding in animals than our Europe or Asia, or Africa . . .❞

Analyze the Viewpoints
1. What view about his discovery did each explorer hold?
2. **Make It Relevant** Look at the Letters to the Editor section of your newspaper. Find two letters that express different viewpoints about the same topic. Then write a paragraph that summarizes each viewpoint.

First Voyage Around the World

In 1522 a Spanish expedition headed by the Portuguese explorer Ferdinand Magellan (muh•JEH•luhn) also proved Vespucci was correct. That same expedition proved that Columbus's dream was possible and that Europeans could reach Asia by sailing west. First, however, the explorers had to sail around the Americas. That proved to be a long and dangerous task.

Magellan set sail from Spain in September 1519, in command of about 250 sailors on five ships. He sailed to what is now Brazil and then south along South America's eastern coast. For many months he sailed up rivers into the middle of the continent, hoping to find a river that would lead to the ocean on the other side. However, he never did, and each time he had to sail back down the rivers, to the coast. As the ships fought their way through huge, pounding waves and against howling winds, one ship and many of its crew were lost.

Finally, in the fall of 1520, the rest of Magellan's ships sailed through what is now called the Strait of Magellan, near the southern tip of South America. The sailors found themselves in the same ocean that Balboa had seen. Magellan named it Pacific, which means

The Isthmus of Panama connects the continents known today as North America and South America. Balboa's explorers landed on the east coast of the isthmus and marched west. They eventually reached a huge, unfamiliar ocean known today as the Pacific Ocean.

REVIEW Why was Amerigo Vespucci's discovery important? **SEQUENCE**

When Vasco Núñez de Balboa crossed the Isthmus of Panama he proved that Vespucci was right about an unknown continent.

"peaceful," because it seemed so still and quiet compared with the Atlantic.

For more than three months, the ships sailed across the Pacific Ocean toward Asia. The voyage around the world was full of hardship—disease, shipwreck, and hunger. Four of the ships were lost. The small amount of food that was left quickly spoiled, and there was no place to stop for fresh food. Many sailors died of hunger and illness. Magellan himself was killed in the spring of 1521 during a battle with the people of one of the Philippine Islands in Southeast Asia.

Despite the terrible losses, the last of Magellan's ships, with just 18 sailors aboard, finally made it around the world. In September 1522, the *Victoria* limped into the Spanish port of Seville.

REVIEW What did Ferdinand Magellan and his crew prove?

Spain Challenges Portugal

In the early days of European exploration, explorers always claimed the lands they visited for the country they represented. Sometimes more than one country claimed the same land. Spain and Portugal often disagreed about the ownership of the lands they had been exploring. Since the monarchs of both nations were Catholic, they asked Pope Alexander VI to settle their argument.

Movement Caboto, Vespucci, Balboa, and Magellan were among the first Europeans to sail across the Atlantic.

♦ Where did Vespucci sail in 1501–1502?

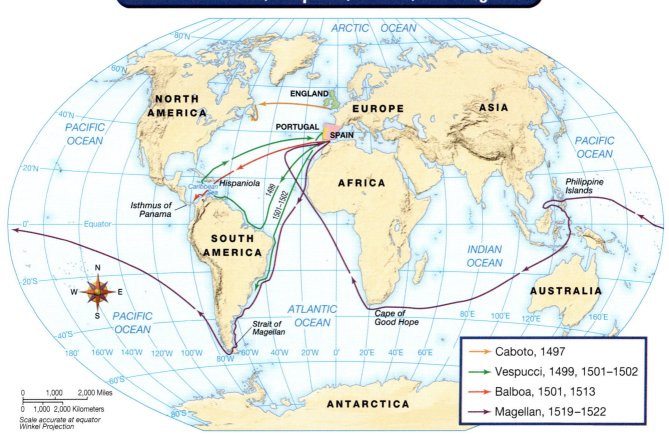

Chapter 3 ▪ 125

The pope is the leader of the Catholic Church.

In 1493 the pope drew on a map a line of **demarcation**, or a line that marks a boundary. The line divided the world as he knew it. Portugal had the right to all lands east of the line. Spain got all lands west of the line. This included both North America and South America.

A year later, in 1494, Portugal and Spain signed the Treaty of Tordesillas (tawr•day•SEE•yahs). A **treaty** is an agreement between nations about peace, trade, or other matters. This treaty moved the Pope's line of demarcation farther west, allowing Portuguese explorer Pedro Álvares Cabral (kuh•BRAHL) to claim Brazil for Portugal when his expedition landed there in 1500. Spain claimed the rest of the Americas.

REVIEW What role did the pope play in settling the argument over land ownership?

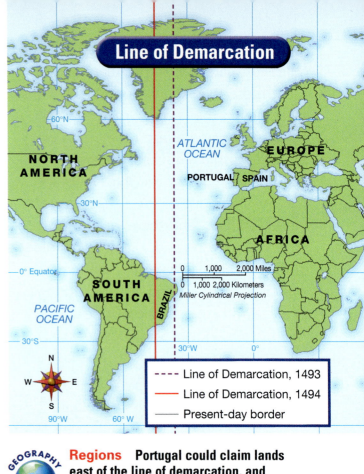

Regions Portugal could claim lands east of the line of demarcation, and Spain could claim lands west of the line.

◆ Who would be able to claim an island off the coast of Africa?

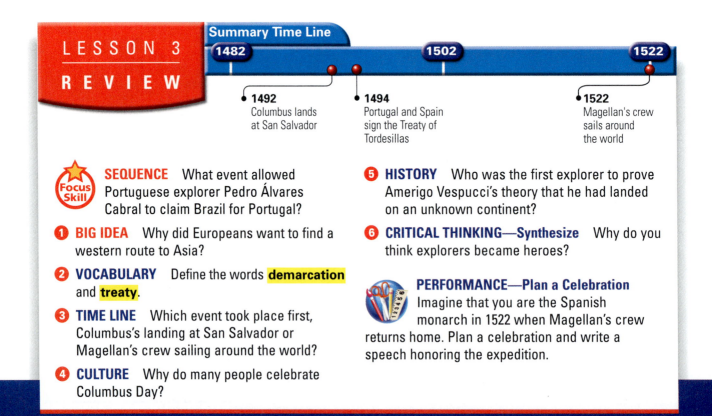

LESSON 3 REVIEW

Summary Time Line
- 1492 Columbus lands at San Salvador
- 1494 Portugal and Spain sign the Treaty of Tordesillas
- 1522 Magellan's crew sails around the world

SEQUENCE What event allowed Portuguese explorer Pedro Álvares Cabral to claim Brazil for Portugal?

❶ **BIG IDEA** Why did Europeans want to find a western route to Asia?

❷ **VOCABULARY** Define the words **demarcation** and **treaty**.

❸ **TIME LINE** Which event took place first, Columbus's landing at San Salvador or Magellan's crew sailing around the world?

❹ **CULTURE** Why do many people celebrate Columbus Day?

❺ **HISTORY** Who was the first explorer to prove Amerigo Vespucci's theory that he had landed on an unknown continent?

❻ **CRITICAL THINKING—Synthesize** Why do you think explorers became heroes?

PERFORMANCE—Plan a Celebration Imagine that you are the Spanish monarch in 1522 when Magellan's crew returns home. Plan a celebration and write a speech honoring the expedition.

The Spanish Conquerors

1200 — 1475 — 1700
1505–1545

· LESSON ·
4

 SEQUENCE
As you read, look for the sequence of events that led to Spanish exploration.

BIG IDEA
The desire for wealth led to exploration of the Americas by Europeans.

VOCABULARY
grant
conquistador
desertion

Once Spain had claim to the Americas, explorers and soldiers from Spain soon sailed there. Some wanted to serve their country and win fame. Some dreamed of becoming rich through a series of trades known today as the Columbian Exchange. Others wanted to change the beliefs of Native Americans, or convert them, to Christianity. To encourage the explorers, the Spanish king offered grants to those who would lead expeditions. A **grant** is a sum of money or other payment given for a particular reason.

The explorers and soldiers eventually pushed deep into North America and South America. Along the way they conquered many of the native peoples who were already living there. Among the Europeans, these explorers and soldiers came to be known as **conquistadors** (kahn•KEES•tuh•dawrz), or "conquerors."

Juan Ponce de León

By 1508 the island of Hispaniola (ees•pah•NYOH•lah), in the Caribbean, had become the center from which the Spanish directed their conquest of the Americas. Today, Hispaniola is made up of the countries of Haiti and the Dominican Republic. From Hispaniola, the conquistadors soon conquered Puerto Rico, Jamaica, and Cuba. Eager to add to their growing empire, Spain's rulers urged the conquistadors to go farther. One of the first to do so was Juan Ponce de León (POHN•say day lay•OHN).

Ponce de León had sailed with Christopher Columbus on his second voyage and had later helped take over Puerto Rico.

Juan Ponce de León was the first conquistador known to arrive in Florida.

From the Native Americans who lived there, Ponce de León had heard about an island to the north called Bimini (BIH•muh•nee). Legend says he also may have heard about a special spring on the island. This "Fountain of Youth" was said to have water that made old people young again!

In 1513 Ponce de León set out to find Bimini. Instead, he landed on the mainland of North America in what is now the state of Florida. He claimed the land for Spain and named it *La Florida*, Spanish for "flowery." To the Spanish, La Florida came to refer to all of what is now the Southeast United States. Though Ponce de León never found a fountain of youth, he was the first Spanish explorer to set foot on territory that became part of the United States.

REVIEW When Ponce de León discovered Florida, what was he really looking for?

This Aztec pendant is made of gold.

Cortés in Mexico

Ponce de León never found the great riches he was looking for, but the dramatic fight for what is today Mexico would bring Spain a great deal of wealth. Spain's fight for Mexico began in 1519 when the Spanish sent Hernando Cortés, a Spanish noble, on an expedition to find gold in the land of the Aztecs.

Cortés had heard stories about the great wealth of the Aztec Empire. Before setting out from Cuba, Cortés told his soldiers,

> **We are waging a just and good war which will bring us fame. . . . If you do not abandon me, as I shall not abandon you, I shall make you the richest men who ever crossed the seas.**

In the spring of 1519, Cortés landed on the east coast of Mexico with more than

This painting shows the meeting of Motecuhzoma (left) and Cortés (right). Malintzin (next to Cortés) helped translate for the conquistadors.

Movement Many conquistadors set out to the Americas in search of gold and other riches.

◆ Which conquistador traveled through part of what is now Texas?

650 soldiers and 16 horses—the first horses in the Americas for thousands of years. Nearby he founded the settlement of Veracruz (vair•ah•KROOS). To make turning back impossible, Cortés destroyed all but the one ship he sent back to Cuba. He then led a march from the coast, over the mountains, and into the Valley of Mexico. After several months, the expedition reached the Aztec capital of Tenochtitlán. There the Spaniards saw the treasures they were seeking.

Along the way, the Spanish had been joined by groups of Indians who were unhappy with Aztec rule. They gave food to the Spanish and even agreed to help them fight the Aztecs. Yet perhaps the greatest help to Cortés came from the Aztecs' belief in a god named Quetzalcoatl (ket•zahl•KOH•ah•tuhl). According to legend, this god had sailed away years before but had promised to return. The Aztecs believed that the light-skinned Quetzalcoatl would one day return to rule his people. Thinking that Cortés might be Quetzalcoatl, Motecuhzoma (maw•tay•kwah•SOH•mah), the Aztec emperor, welcomed Cortés and offered him housing and gifts of gold.

Chapter 3 ◾ 129

Cortés, however, took Motecuhzoma prisoner. He hoped to rule the Aztecs by capturing their king.

When fighting broke out, Motecuhzoma tried to stop it by speaking to his people. While he was talking, someone threw a stone at him. The stone struck Motecuhzoma in the head, and the injury soon killed him. The Spanish were forced to leave Tenochtitlán, but only after heavy fighting. Half of Cortés's soldiers died.

Cortés and his expedition found safety with the Indians who had helped them earlier. The next year, in 1521, Cortés returned to Tenochtitlán to capture the Aztec treasures. With the help of the Indians, the Spanish tore down the Aztec temples and destroyed the great city. Cortés believed that only by destroying the city would he be able to break the power of the Aztecs. On the ruins of the Aztec capital, the conquistadors built Mexico City, which was officially recognized by Spain in 1522. Mexico City later became the capital of Spain's new empire in the Americas.

REVIEW What did Cortés do after founding the settlement of Veracruz? **SEQUENCE**

This ceramic figure is of an Aztec eagle warrior.

Pánfilo de Narváez

Following the success in Mexico, Spain once again turned its attention to Florida. In 1528 Pánfilo de Narváez (PAHN•fee•loh day nar•VAH•ays) led another Spanish expedition there. The purpose of Narváez's expedition was to conquer all the lands along the Gulf of Mexico.

Narváez and his ships arrived near Tampa Bay, on the west coast of Florida, in April 1528. He went ashore with a landing party of 300 soldiers and 40 horses. Narváez decided that this group would travel north over land. The remaining crew and the ships, which carried most of the food and supplies, would sail north and meet the landing party at a certain harbor. This decision proved to be a terrible mistake.

Although the ships' crews searched the Gulf Coast for nearly a year, they did not find the harbor or the members of the landing party. Meanwhile, when Narváez and the landing party reached the place where they expected to find the ships, the ships were not there. Tired and hungry, the 242 survivors in the landing party decided to build small rafts and sail along the Gulf Coast until they reached Spanish lands in Mexico.

Having built their rafts by splitting pine trees into thick boards and sewing together their shirts to make sails, the survivors set sail on the Gulf of Mexico. After 31 days at sea, their rafts were wrecked in a storm off the coast of what is now Texas. The 80 men who reached shore set out to walk to Mexico City, however poor health and lack of food killed all but four of them.

REVIEW What was the purpose of Pánfilo de Narváez's expedition?

130 ▪ Unit 2

Golden Cities

In 1536 the four survivors from the Narváez expedition arrived in Mexico City. They were three Spanish explorers, including Álvar Núñez Cabeza de Vaca (kah•BAY•sah day VAH•kah), and an African named Estevanico (es•tay•vahn•EE•koh), also called Esteban (es•TAY•bahn). Cabeza de Vaca told the survivors' story to Spanish leaders in Mexico City. He explained that during their long overland journey from the Texas coast to Mexico City, they had met Native Americans along the way who told them about seven cities rich in gold, silver, and jewels. The Spanish listened to the story with great interest.

In 1539 the Spanish leaders sent Esteban and a priest named Marcos de Niza (day NEE•sah) on an expedition to see if the story about the Seven Cities of Gold was in fact true. During the expedition, Esteban was killed by a group of Zuni Indians after he approached the Zuni pueblo. De Niza, however, returned safely, saying he had seen a golden city during his travels.

After hearing about de Niza's expedition, Francisco Vásquez de Coronado (kawr•oh•NAH•doh) set out in 1540 with more than 300 Spaniards, several Africans, and more than 1,000 American Indians to find the seven cities. The expedition traveled through lands that are now parts of Arizona, New Mexico, Texas, Oklahoma, and Kansas. They marched through the Zuni town of Hawikuh (hah•we•KOO) and other Pueblo Indian towns, but they did not find any trace of the Seven Cities of Gold. Terribly disappointed, Coronado began the long journey home. The route he took would later become the Santa Fe Trail, one of the most traveled overland trade routes in North America before the time of the railroad.

Coronado arrived back in Mexico City in June 1542. Only 100 of his party returned. Many had died. Others had run away.

Cabeza de Vaca, Esteban, and two others were the only survivors of the Narváez expedition to North America.

Many historians believe that men from a scouting party of the Francisco Coronado expedition were the first Europeans to see the Grand Canyon and the Colorado River.

Although Coronado failed to find any riches, he had explored vast areas of New Spain and claimed lands in what is now the southwestern United States for Spain.

REVIEW Why were the Spanish leaders interested in finding the seven cities?

De Soto in the Southeast

At about the same time that Coronado was planning his expedition, another Spanish conquistador, Hernando de Soto (day SOH•toh), was beginning one in what is now the Southeast United States. In May of 1539 de Soto and more than 600 soldiers landed near Tampa Bay. From there, they traveled north and reached what is now Georgia. Finding no gold, they moved on through parts of South Carolina and North Carolina, crossed the Smoky Mountains of Tennessee, and turned south into Alabama.

De Soto and his soldiers met many Native American peoples during this expedition. These encounters often ended in brutal battles. One of the worst took place in Alabama. There the Spanish fought the Mobile people, who were led by Tuscalusa (tuhs•kuh•LOO•suh). A Spanish soldier who witnessed the battle wrote later that the number of Native Americans killed may have been as high as 11,000. The Spanish lost most of their supplies during the fighting. Because of this, de Soto's army was soon reduced in size by starvation and **desertions**, as soldiers ran away to save themselves.

De Soto and those who remained marched on, reaching the banks of the Mississippi River in May 1541. They were the first

De Soto brought these bells to trade for Native American goods.

132 ■ Unit 2

GEOGRAPHY

Conquest of the Incas
Understanding Places and Regions

In 1531 Francisco Pizarro and a group of 180 soldiers explored the west coast of South America. They went in search of the riches of the Inca Empire. For months they traveled the Andes Mountains collecting gold and riches from the Native Americans they encountered. Pizarro later met with the Inca emperor, Atahuallpa (ah•tah•WAHL•pah). When Atahuallpa refused to accept Christianity and to accept the king of Spain as his ruler, Pizarro captured him and later had him killed. The Spanish then conquered the Inca Empire.

Europeans to see the great river. The Spanish built rafts to cross it and continued their search for gold on the other side of the river in what is now Arkansas and Louisiana. Then in May 1542 de Soto died of fever. The soldiers buried their leader in the Mississippi River to hide his death from the Native Americans. Then they made their way to Mexico.

Although de Soto and his soldiers found no gold, de Soto claimed for Spain much of the land his expedition had explored. The Spanish had now claimed all of what is today the Southeast United States.

REVIEW How did the battle against the Mobile people hurt de Soto's army?

LESSON 4 REVIEW

Summary Time Line

- 1513 Ponce de León claims Florida for Spain
- 1521 Cortés conquers Tenochtitlán
- 1540 Coronado sets out to find the Seven Cities of Gold
- 1541 De Soto reaches the Mississippi River

SEQUENCE Which event happened first, the fall of Tenochtitlán or Coronado's search for the seven golden cities?

1. **BIG IDEA** How did a desire to find gold and riches affect early exploration in the Americas?

2. **VOCABULARY** Use the word **grant** in a sentence about Spanish exploration.

3. **TIME LINE** Which was claimed by the Spanish first, Florida or the Mississippi River?

4. **HISTORY** What decision by the Narváez expedition proved to be a terrible mistake?

5. **CRITICAL THINKING—Analyze** Why did the Spanish build the settlement of Mexico City?

PERFORMANCE—Draw a Map Using the maps in the lesson as a guide, draw a map that shows all early Spanish expeditions in the Americas.

EXAMINE PRIMARY SOURCES

Conquistador Armor

Like most other soldiers, Spanish conquistadors wore suits of armor to protect themselves in battle. The armor, called plate armor, was made of large pieces of steel. The armor was often designed to cover and protect the entire body. Some armor-makers, or armorers, made very decorative armor that they engraved with special designs or scenes. Although the armor was a highly effective means of protection, it was very heavy, weighing up to 60 pounds (27 kg), and very hot. It was also expensive. A full suit of armor would sometimes cost as much as an entire farm!

This portrait of Hernando Cortés shows that he wore the armor of Spanish nobility.

FROM THE NATIONAL MUSEUM OF ARMS AND ARMOUR AND THE HIGGINS ARMORY

In the 1400s a Spanish conquistador wore this helmet.

Helmets were styled in various ways. Their function, however, was always the same—to protect the people's heads.

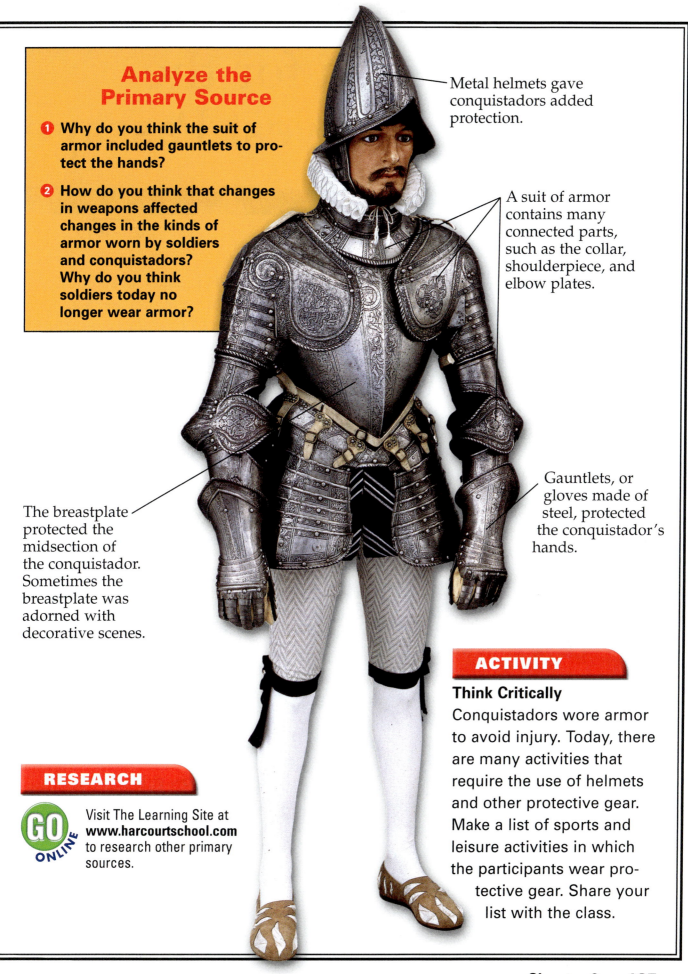

Analyze the Primary Source

1. Why do you think the suit of armor included gauntlets to protect the hands?

2. How do you think that changes in weapons affected changes in the kinds of armor worn by soldiers and conquistadors? Why do you think soldiers today no longer wear armor?

Metal helmets gave conquistadors added protection.

A suit of armor contains many connected parts, such as the collar, shoulderpiece, and elbow plates.

Gauntlets, or gloves made of steel, protected the conquistador's hands.

The breastplate protected the midsection of the conquistador. Sometimes the breastplate was adorned with decorative scenes.

RESEARCH

Visit The Learning Site at www.harcourtschool.com to research other primary sources.

ACTIVITY

Think Critically
Conquistadors wore armor to avoid injury. Today, there are many activities that require the use of helmets and other protective gear. Make a list of sports and leisure activities in which the participants wear protective gear. Share your list with the class.

Chapter 3 ■ 135

LESSON 5

Search for the Northwest Passage

1200 — 1475 — 1700
1520–1610

 SEQUENCE
As you read, look for the sequence of events that led to the exploration of what is today Canada and the northeast United States.

BIG IDEA
Some explorers searched for a northern route to Asia.

VOCABULARY
Northwest Passage
estuary
rapid
company
mutiny

In the 1500s Spain became the richest nation in Europe due to its conquests. Spanish ships sailed from Mexico and South America with their treasure chests full of gold and silver. Other countries in Europe believed that if they could find a new trade route to Asia, they might also gain such wealth. The route followed by Ferdinand Magellan around South America to Asia was long and difficult. Other European explorers looked for what they called the **Northwest Passage**, a waterway along the north coast of North America connecting the Atlantic Ocean and the Pacific Ocean. The search for such a route between Europe and Asia began in the early 1500s.

Verrazano Leads the Way

The French king Francis I was one of the many European rulers who wanted to find a Northwest Passage through North America. In 1524 he sent an Italian, Giovanni da Verrazano (ver•uh•ZAH•noh), to find it. The king gave Verrazano ships, sailors, food, and other supplies. Verrazano set sail for North America in January 1524 on his ship, the *Dauphine* (doh•FEEN). A few months later he reached what is now the Cape Fear River on the North Carolina coast. After sailing farther north, Verrazano saw that only a narrow strip of land—perhaps a mile wide—lay between the Atlantic Ocean and another great body of water to the west.

Giovanni da Verrazano (top) sailed the *Dauphine* (left) into what is now New York Bay.

He thought that body of water might be the Pacific Ocean. It was actually what we call today the Pamlico (PAM•lih•koh) Sound. From Pamlico Sound, Verrazano sailed northward along the Atlantic coast to what is now New York Bay.

Verrazano sailed into the bay and landed the *Dauphine* on the north end of present-day Staten Island. He was given a warm welcome by the native people, who had never had contact with a European before. Verrazano developed a strong friendship with these Native Americans and described them in his report to King Francis I.

> 66 These people are the most beautiful and have the most civil customs we have seen on this voyage. They are taller than we are. They are of a bronze color and some tend to whiteness, others to a tawny color. The face is clear-cut, the hair is long and black, and they take great care to decorate it . . . 99

From New York Bay Verrazano sailed as far north as present-day Nova Scotia before returning to France. He made two more voyages to the Americas to try to find a water route to Asia. On these voyages, he searched the coastlines of North America and South America and still found no passage.

REVIEW What sequence of events led Verrazano to look for a Northwest Passage?

SEQUENCE

Cartier Moves Inland

Ten years after Verrazano sailed into New York Bay, a French navigator named Jacques Cartier (ZHAHK kar•TYAY) also tried to find the Northwest Passage for France. Between 1534 and 1541, Cartier made three voyages and claimed land for France in North America.

In 1534 King Francis I sent Cartier to North America to search for gold and other valuable metals. The explorer left France with two ships to search the northern Atlantic coast. On this first voyage, he sailed up the estuary of the St. Lawrence River. An **estuary** is the wide mouth of a river where the ocean tide flows in. He landed on the Gaspé (ga•SPAY) Peninsula and claimed the land for France.

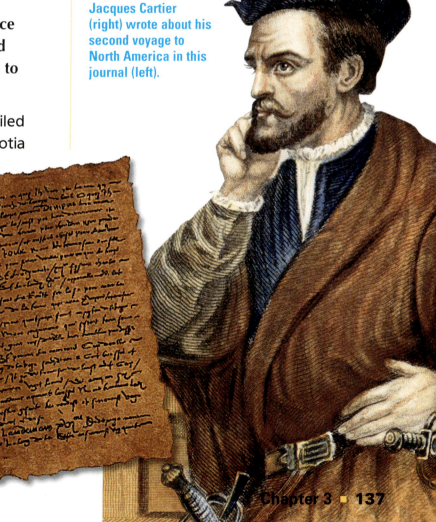

Jacques Cartier (right) wrote about his second voyage to North America in this journal (left).

Chapter 3 ▪ 137

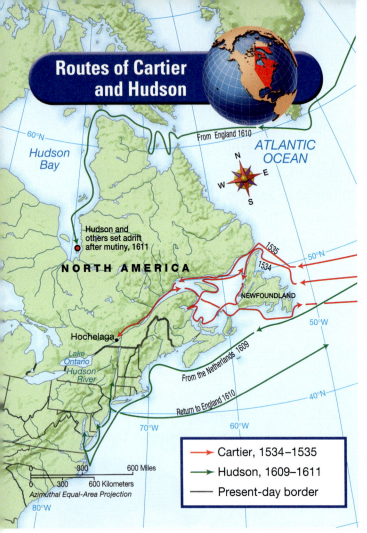

Routes of Cartier and Hudson

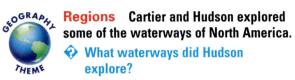

Regions Cartier and Hudson explored some of the waterways of North America.
♦ What waterways did Hudson explore?

During this expedition, Cartier was told by a group of Iroquois that jewels and metals could be found farther northwest. The French became friendly with the Iroquois and gave them gifts. When Cartier left to return to France, he carried a supply of corn that was given to him by the Iroquois. The corn was well received by northern Europeans, many of whom had never seen this vegetable before.

The following year, on his second voyage, Cartier became the first European to reach the inland of what is now Canada. He sailed up the St. Lawrence River, hoping to find a water route through the continent. But his hopes disappeared when he came upon great rapids. No boat could travel through the fast-moving water. The expedition was forced to turn back. It had gone as far as what is now Montreal (mahn•tree•AWL), where a Huron Indian village called Hochelaga (hah•shuh•LA•guh) was located.

Cartier made a third journey in 1541, but he was never able to find the Northwest Passage. He sailed up the St. Lawrence near to what is now Quebec City. Some of his men remained there and built a camp while Cartier and the others searched for gold. They traveled even farther west but found nothing. Cartier returned to the camp and eventually returned to France.

REVIEW What stopped Cartier from searching for a water route through the North American continent?

The Voyages of Henry Hudson

After Verrazano and Cartier, other Europeans continued to look for the Northwest Passage. Henry Hudson, an English sea captain, was one of them. In 1608, on his first expedition, he reached an island east of Greenland. He then sailed farther north by way of the Arctic Ocean but failed to find the Northwest Passage. The following year Hudson searched by way of the Barents Sea, an arm of the Arctic Ocean.

For his third voyage, Hudson had been hired by the Dutch East India Company to find the Northwest Passage. The company, or business, gave him a ship, the *Half Moon*, and a crew of about 20 sailors. They set sail in 1609 for the Arctic

138 ■ Unit 2

Ocean, but his crew soon **mutinied**, or rebelled. Hudson was forced to head south along the North American coast.

Hudson's journey led him to the coast of Maine, where members of the crew went ashore. They fished and traded with the Native Americans and soon went south to the Delaware and Chesapeake Bays. Hudson then sailed north to the mouth of the Hudson River. He spent a month exploring the river, which he named for himself. Hudson's voyage gave the Dutch rulers in Holland control of the whole Hudson River valley.

In 1610 Hudson set out on his final search for the Northwest Passage. This time he was sailing for an English company. On this voyage Hudson reached the bay that also carries his name—Hudson Bay.

He spent three months exploring the huge bay, located in east central Canada, north of present-day Ontario and Quebec. By November his ship was frozen in the

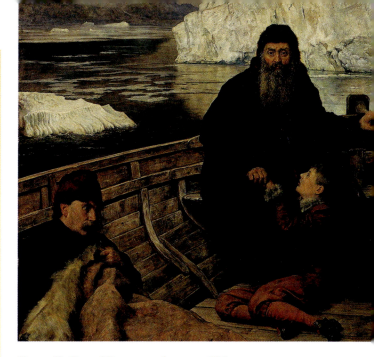

Henry Hudson, his son, and some of his crew were set adrift on Hudson Bay.

ice, and after a cold winter and much suffering, his crew again mutinied. They put Hudson, his son, and seven others into a small boat and left them drifting on the bay. They were never seen again.

REVIEW What area of North America did Henry Hudson claim for the Dutch?

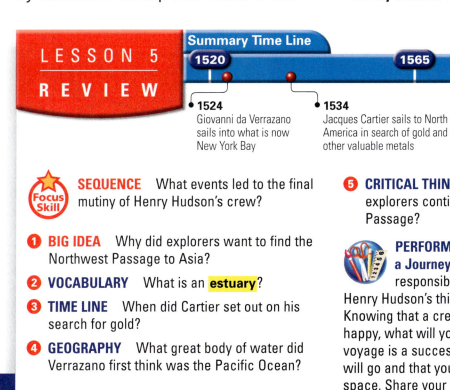

LESSON 5 REVIEW

Summary Time Line

- **1524** Giovanni da Verrazano sails into what is now New York Bay
- **1534** Jacques Cartier sails to North America in search of gold and other valuable metals
- **1611** Henry Hudson is set adrift on Hudson Bay while searching for the Northwest Passage

SEQUENCE What events led to the final mutiny of Henry Hudson's crew?

1 BIG IDEA Why did explorers want to find the Northwest Passage to Asia?

2 VOCABULARY What is an **estuary**?

3 TIME LINE When did Cartier set out on his search for gold?

4 GEOGRAPHY What great body of water did Verrazano first think was the Pacific Ocean?

5 CRITICAL THINKING—Evaluate Why did explorers continue to search for the Northwest Passage?

 **PERFORMANCE—Write a "Packing for a Journey" List** Imagine that you are responsible for getting the supplies for Henry Hudson's third voyage to Hudson Bay. Knowing that a crew might mutiny if they are not happy, what will you put on the list to make sure the voyage is a success? Consider where the expedition will go and that you have a limited amount of cargo space. Share your list with your classmates.

CHAPTER 3

Review and Test Preparation

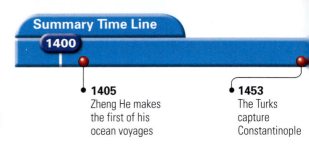

Summary Time Line

- **1405** Zheng He makes the first of his ocean voyages
- **1453** The Turks capture Constantinople

 **Sequence**

Copy the following graphic organizer onto a separate sheet of paper. Use the information you have learned to show that you understand the sequence of some of the key events that encouraged exploration and led to the discovery of the Americas.

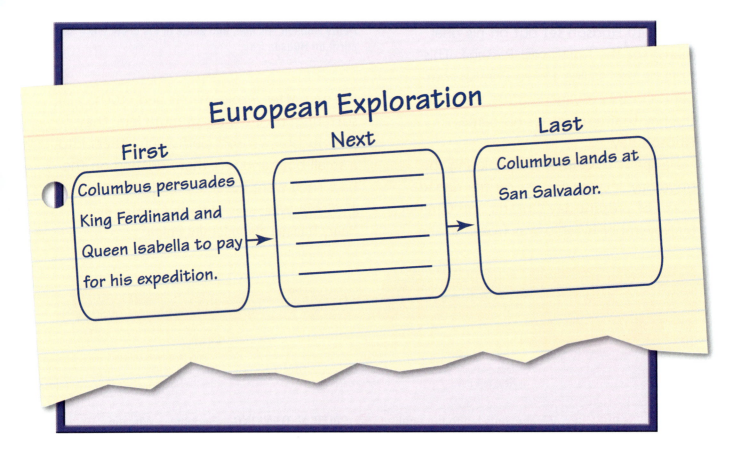

European Exploration

First: Columbus persuades King Ferdinand and Queen Isabella to pay for his expedition.

Next: _____

Last: Columbus lands at San Salvador.

THINK & WRITE

Write a Letter Imagine that you are Prince Henry of Portugal and that you have set up your navigation school in Sagres, Portugal. Write a letter to your father, King John I, describing how you are successfully training sailors to find new ocean routes to Asia.

Write a News Story Suppose that you are a Spanish newspaper reporter who has been sent along with Hernando Cortés's expedition to write about the Aztec Empire. Write a short newspaper article in which you describe the Aztecs and their culture.

1492 Columbus lands at San Salvador
1498 Da Gama reaches India
1541 De Soto reaches the Mississippi River
1608 Hudson sails to find the Northwest Passage

USE THE TIME LINE

Use the chapter summary time line to answer these questions.

1. What happened first, the Turks' capture of Constantinople or Zheng He's voyages?
2. How many years after Columbus landed at San Salvador did de Soto reach the Mississippi River?

USE VOCABULARY

Identify the term that correctly matches each definition.

empire (p. 106)
astrolabe (p. 116)
claim (p. 121)
grant (p. 127)
estuary (p. 137)

3. to declare you own
4. a collection of lands ruled by the nation that conquered them
5. the wide mouth of a river where the ocean tide flows in
6. a sum of money or other payment given for a particular reason
7. an instrument used to calculate the positions of the sun, moon, and stars

RECALL FACTS

Answer these questions.

8. Why did King John I of Portugal decide to spend as much money as needed on ocean exploration?
9. How did Balboa prove Amerigo Vespucci's theory that Columbus had landed on an unknown continent?
10. Why did the Aztecs welcome Cortés with gifts of gold?

Write the letter of the best choice.

11. Prince Henry helped Portugal lead the way in ocean exploration by—
    A giving explorers money.
    B encouraging people to read Marco Polo's book.
    C setting up a school for training sailors in navigation.
    D inventing the astrolabe.

12. Hernando Cortés was sent to Mexico to—
    F convert the Indians to Catholicism.
    G make maps.
    H build a city.
    J find gold.

THINK CRITICALLY

13. How did trade play an important role in the growth of exploration?
14. How might history have been different if the Turks had not captured Constantinople in 1453?

APPLY SKILLS

Follow Routes on a Map
Use the map on page 113 to answer the following questions.

15. What city did Marco Polo visit after visiting Baghdad?
16. What two cities on the Black Sea did Polo visit on his way back to Venice?

Identify Causes and Their Effects

17. Think again about the Northwest Passage. Draw a cause-and-effect chart similar to the one on page 120. Show the causes that led to the French exploration of North America.

Chapter 3 ■ 141

CHAPTER 4

European Settlement

> " . . . the front and vanguard of all my West Indies . . . the most important of them all—and the most coveted by my enemies. "
>
> —King Philip IV of Spain, 1645, on the importance of Puerto Rico to Spain

Categorize

To **categorize** information is to classify, or to arrange, the data into similar groups so that it is easier to understand and compare.

As you read this chapter, categorize information about the European settlement.

- Classify what you read into the following categories: people, settlements, and events.

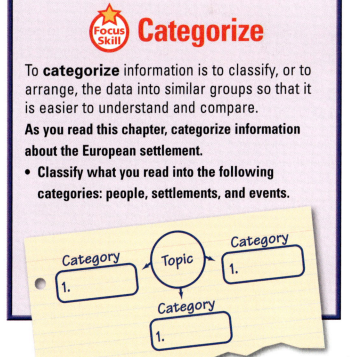

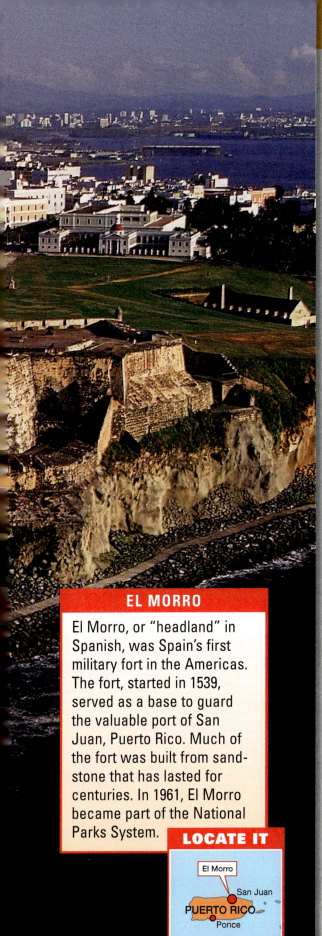

EL MORRO

El Morro, or "headland" in Spanish, was Spain's first military fort in the Americas. The fort, started in 1539, served as a base to guard the valuable port of San Juan, Puerto Rico. Much of the fort was built from sandstone that has lasted for centuries. In 1961, El Morro became part of the National Parks System.

LOCATE IT

Chapter 4 ■ 143

· LESSON ·

1

New Spain

1200 — 1475 — 1700

1500–1600

 CATEGORIZE

As you read, categorize different types of Spanish settlements in the Americas.

BIG IDEA
The early Spanish settled in the Americas.

VOCABULARY

colony
colonist
buffer zone
borderlands
presidio
permanent
hacienda
self-sufficient
missionary
mission

By the 1500s several European nations had sent explorers to claim land in the Americas. Often more than one country claimed the same land because an explorer had no way of knowing that another explorer had already claimed it. In those days of exploration, people claimed the land and moved on, leaving no one to protect the claim.

Over time, Spain decided it needed to protect its claims in the Americas. To protect the land in its growing empire and govern the people there, Spain formed colonies. A **colony** is a land ruled by another country. The colony of New Spain was formed in 1535, with most of its land in Mexico and its capital at Mexico City. New Spain included mostly the Spanish lands north of the Isthmus of Panama and the many islands of the Caribbean Sea.

Building New Spain

At first very few Spanish people settled in New Spain. Many of those who did were conquistadors. After news spread of the discovery of gold, silver, and other treasures, however, many colonists came to seek their fortunes. The people who go to live in a colony are called **colonists**.

FAST FACT   These irregularly shaped gold doubloons were called cobs, meaning "cut of the bar."

Many of the colonists worked in the gold and silver mines. Others brought oxen and plows to work the land and horses to ride. They brought cattle and sheep, fruit trees, grain, and vegetable seeds. Over time, the Spanish began to build cities, and tens of thousands more colonists came to live in them.

The Spanish colonists needed many workers to grow their crops, to mine gold and silver, and to build and provide services in their cities. So they made slaves of the American Indian peoples they had conquered.

144 ▪ Unit 2

• BIOGRAPHY •

Bartolomé de Las Casas 1474–1566
Character Trait: Respect

Bartolomé de Las Casas was one of the first Europeans to work to improve the treatment of American Indian workers. He became known as the Apostle to the Indians and wrote many essays questioning the Spanish colonists' treatment of the enslaved Indians.

Las Casas became bishop of Chiapas in Mexico in 1544. In 1547 he returned to Spain, where he continued to work for better treatment of the Indians until his death in 1566.

MULTIMEDIA BIOGRAPHIES
Visit The Learning Site at www.harcourtschool.com to learn about other famous people.

American Indians were forced to mine gold and silver for the Spanish (left).

Thousands of Indians had already died fighting the conquistadors. Now thousands more died of hunger, overwork, and disease. The diseases the settlers unknowingly brought from Europe, such as measles, influenza, and smallpox, sometimes killed whole tribes.

In time, some colonists grew concerned about the cruel treatment of the Indians. One such colonist was Bartolomé de Las Casas (bar•toh•loh•MAY day lahs KAH•sahs). Las Casas settled on the island of Hispaniola in 1502 and became a successful plantation owner.

Las Casas used American Indians as enslaved workers, but came to believe that making the Indians slaves was wrong. In 1509 he freed his slaves and began to work to get better treatment for them. Las Casas spoke out so strongly that the king of Spain, Charles I, agreed to pass laws to protect the Indians. In 1550 the king ordered that the Spanish could no longer enslave the Indians. These orders, however, were not always carried out.

As more Indians died, the number of Indian workers fell sharply. The colonists now looked for other workers. They began to bring Africans to the colony as slaves. Even Bartolomé de Las Casas thought that Africans could be used to do the work. It was an idea he came to regret. Soon Africans were working under the same terrible conditions that the Indians had worked under.

REVIEW Why did the Spanish colonists need many workers?

The Spanish Borderlands

As other European countries started colonies in North America, Spain believed it needed to protect its own. To do so, the Spanish created a buffer zone. A **buffer zone** is an area of land that serves as a barrier. The buffer zone north of New Spain came to be known as the **borderlands**. The borderlands stretched across what are today northern Mexico and the southern United States from Florida to California.

Spanish soldiers led the way into the borderlands, where they built **presidios** (pray•SEE•dee•ohz), or forts, and places for the settlers to live. In 1565 Pedro Menéndez de Avilés (may•NAYN•days day ah•vee•LAYS) and 1,500 soldiers, sailors, and settlers set sail from Spain. After several ships were lost in storms, the surviving members of the expedition reached the location of present-day St. Augustine, Florida. There they built the first **permanent**, or long-lasting, European settlement in what is now the United States.

Analyze Diagrams Once the coquina was brought to St. Augustine from a nearby island, workers shaped it into blocks.
◆ How did workers transport heavy materials?

LOCATE IT
Castillo de San Marcos
Tallahassee
FLORIDA

FAST FACT
The Castillo de San Marcos is the only early Spanish structure in Florida to survive to the present. It survived mostly because it was made from coquina.

146 ■ Unit 2

In 1672, after years of attacks by European pirates and American Indian raiders, the queen of Spain sent money to pay for the building of a strong stone fort. Workers built the fort with coquina (koh•KEE•nuh), a type of stone formed of broken seashells. After 23 years of work, the Castillo (kah•STEE•yoh) de San Marcos, as the presidio was called, was strong enough to protect Spanish settlers from any attackers. It was one of a line of hundreds of presidios stretching from Florida to California that protected the colonists in New Spain.

REVIEW Why did the Spanish build the Castillo de San Marcos in St. Augustine?

Ranches and Haciendas

The Spanish realized that gold and silver were hard to find in the borderlands. They also knew that in many places the land was so hot and dry "that even the cactus pads appeared to be toasted." But settlers moved there anyway. They often traded for things they needed with Indian tribes who lived in the borderlands. In many cases, trade with Indian tribes was mutually beneficial, or good for both groups. For example, settlers in what is now the southwestern United States traded with the Pueblos for corn and pottery. In return, the Pueblos got tools and other goods they needed.

The Spanish—and the animals they brought with them—changed life for many of the Indians living in the borderlands. Horses, long extinct in the Americas, once again roamed the land. The Plains Indians learned to tame horses and use them in hunting and in war. In what today is the southwestern United States, the Navajos learned to raise sheep. They also began weaving sheep's wool into clothing and blankets.

Some ranchers in the borderlands of northern Mexico built large estates called **haciendas** (ah•see•EN•dahs). There they raised cattle and sheep by the thousands. In what are now Texas and California, cattle were the most important kind of livestock. Ranchers who lived on the haciendas raised their own livestock, grew their own crops, and made most of what they needed to live. These **self-sufficient**, or self-supporting, communities began to grow far from the markets of Mexico City and the other large cities of New Spain.

REVIEW How can you categorize the ways animals changed life for the Indians?
CATEGORIZE

Chapter 4 ▪ 147

Missions

Spain's main interest in settling the borderlands was to protect its empire and to expand its economy. However, the Spanish king also said he wanted to "bring the people of that land to our Holy Catholic faith." To do this, missionaries were sent to turn the American Indians into Catholics as well as loyal Spanish subjects. A **missionary** is a person sent by a church to teach its religion.

The first successful missionaries in the borderlands were the Franciscans, members of a Catholic religious order. They built **missions**, or small religious settlements, in what are now the states of Georgia, Florida, Texas, New Mexico, Arizona, and California. Their first mission was Nombre de Dios (NOHM•bray day DEE•ohs), or "Name of God." It was built near St. Augustine as the first in a chain of missions that would eventually connect the Atlantic and Pacific coasts. On the Pacific coast of New Spain, a Franciscan priest named Junípero Serra (hoo•NEE•pay•roh SEH•rah) later helped build a string of 9 missions in California.

When missionaries came to the borderlands, the missions they built included ranch and farm buildings as well as churches. Some of the missions were built near Indian villages. In other places, Indians settled around the missions.

The coming of the missions changed the way many Indians lived and worked. It also changed something more important to the Indians—the way they worshipped. While many Indians kept to their traditional religions, others became Catholics.

At first some of the Native Americans welcomed living at the missions. Like the missionaries, they were learning new ways. The missionaries and soldiers also protected them from enemies. Problems developed, however. Many Indians had to work on mission farms and ranches

Father Junípero Serra (below right) founded the mission of San Carlos Borromeo del Rio Carmelo (below left) in 1770. It was the second of nine missions started by Father Serra along what is now the California coast.

LOCATE IT
Mission San Carlos Borromeo del Rio Carmelo
CALIFORNIA

against their will. Some missionaries also treated the Indians cruelly.

Some Indians fought back. They destroyed churches and other mission buildings. To protect its missions, the Spanish government built roads linking them with nearby presidios. This road system was called *El Camino Real* (el kah•MEE•noh ray•AHL), or "The Royal Road." One road stretched for more than 600 miles (966 km) from San Diego to Sonoma in what is today California.

The government of New Spain, and later the Mexican government, continued to build missions in the borderlands until the 1830s. Many cities in the western and southwestern areas of the United States—such as San Antonio, Texas, and San Diego, California, began as missions.

REVIEW Why did the Spanish send missionaries to the borderlands?

Movement El Camino Real connected most of the missions and presidios in New Spain.

◆ How did this system of roads help the Spanish missionaries?

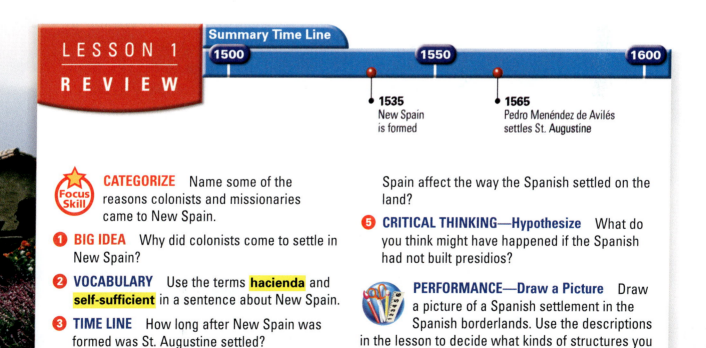

LESSON 1 REVIEW

Summary Time Line
1500 — 1535 New Spain is formed — 1550 — 1565 Pedro Menéndez de Avilés settles St. Augustine — 1600

CATEGORIZE Name some of the reasons colonists and missionaries came to New Spain.

① **BIG IDEA** Why did colonists come to settle in New Spain?

② **VOCABULARY** Use the terms **hacienda** and **self-sufficient** in a sentence about New Spain.

③ **TIME LINE** How long after New Spain was formed was St. Augustine settled?

④ **GEOGRAPHY** How did the location of New Spain affect the way the Spanish settled on the land?

⑤ **CRITICAL THINKING—Hypothesize** What do you think might have happened if the Spanish had not built presidios?

PERFORMANCE—Draw a Picture Draw a picture of a Spanish settlement in the Spanish borderlands. Use the descriptions in the lesson to decide what kinds of structures you want to draw.

Chapter 4 ■ 149

LESSON 2

New France

1200 — 1475 — 1700
1600–1700

CATEGORIZE
As you read, categorize different types of French settlements in North America.

BIG IDEA
The presence of the French grew in North America.

VOCABULARY
civil war
royal colony
proprietary colony
proprietor
plantation

While the Spanish were growing rich in New Spain, the French were making their own claims in what is today Canada and the northeastern United States. They found good fishing waters along the coast, and farther inland they began to trade with the Native Americans. They traded for a good that became nearly as valuable in Europe as gold—fur.

French Settlement in North America

The fur trade between the French and the American Indians grew following Jacques Cartier's trips up the St. Lawrence River. Cartier had begun to trade with the Huron Indians. The Hurons were as eager for European goods as the French were for furs. Trade between the French and the Hurons was voluntary, or agreed upon by both groups.

By 1600, trade with the Indians was important for many Europeans, especially for French merchants. Knowing this, the French king, Henry IV, said that any merchant who wanted to trade in furs had to build a colony in North America.

French merchants jumped at the chance to get rich from the fur trade. Several of them formed a company to start a colony. In 1603 the company sent a cartographer named

Europeans (below) traded items, such as glass beads (left), for beaver furs.

150 • Unit 2

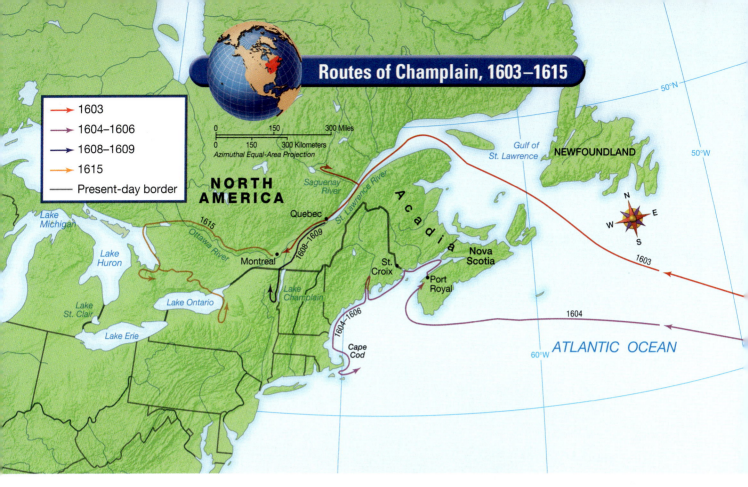

Movement Champlain explored inland waterways in North America.

♦ In what waterway did Champlain travel to reach Quebec?

Samuel de Champlain (sham•PLAYN) to North America to map the places where beavers were found.

Champlain explored the forests of what is now eastern Canada, which he called New France. When he returned to Europe, Champlain's reports made more people want to go there. He himself went again.

For the next five years, Champlain explored the lands along the St. Lawrence River. He also built a settlement on the St. Lawrence River at a place that the Hurons called *kebec*. In 1608 Kebec became Quebec (kwih•BEK), the first important French settlement in North America.

REVIEW Which areas did the French explore?
CATEGORIZE

The Growth of New France

The early French settlements grew very slowly. One reason for this slow growth was trouble in France. In the early 1600s, civil war kept many people from leaving France. A **civil war** is a war between two groups in the same country.

In North America, English and Dutch colonists began settling the southern coast of New France. Soon disagreements over the fur trade broke out among the French, the English, and the Dutch, as well as between the Iroquois and the Hurons. By the 1660s the French fur trade was nearly destroyed, and the French hold in North America was crumbling.

Chapter 4 ■ 151

The French used birchbark canoes to explore the waterways of New France.

Hoping to rebuild the French empire in North America, King Louis XIV made New France a royal colony. A **royal colony** is ruled directly by a monarch. Louis XIV appointed leaders to live in New France to help him govern. The leader of these officials was called the governor-general.

In 1672 King Louis XIV appointed Count de Frontenac (FRAHN•tuh•nak) governor-general of New France. Frontenac encouraged exploration of the lands west of Quebec and Montreal. These lands were not easy to reach, however. Rapids and shallow waters prevented French ships from traveling very far inland. To travel the rivers, the French had to learn from their Native American trading partners how to build and use birchbark canoes. These boats could navigate in very shallow water. They also could be carried around waterfalls and rapids or overland between rivers.

The Native Americans often spoke of a great river to the west, larger than all the others. The Algonkins called it the *Mississippi*, which means "Father of Waters." Ever since the days of Jacques Cartier, the French had hoped to find the Northwest Passage through North America. Frontenac believed the Mississippi River might be that route.

REVIEW Why was New France made a royal colony?

Exploring the Mississippi

In 1673 Governor-General de Frontenac sent an expedition to explore the rivers and lakes that he hoped would lead them to the Mississippi River. One member of the expedition was Jacques Marquette (mahr•KET), a Catholic missionary who spoke several Indian languages. The other members were Louis Joliet (zhohl•YAY), a fur trader and explorer, and five other adventurers.

The explorers set out from northern Lake Michigan in two birchbark canoes.

This painting by George Catlin shows La Salle and his expedition entering the Mississippi River.

In 1712 the king made Louisiana a **proprietary colony** (pruh•PRY•uh•ter•ee). This meant that the king gave ownership of the land to one person and allowed that person to rule it. In 1717 John Law, a Scottish banker, became Louisiana's **proprietor**, or owner. Law formed a company to build more towns and to start farms. More settlers came, and Louisiana finally started to grow. In 1718 the town of New Orleans was founded, and four years later it became Louisiana's capital.

Despite Law's efforts, the colony still needed workers—especially on the large farms called **plantations**. Many settlers began to bring in Africans to do the work as slaves.

Louisiana, like the rest of New France, failed to attract enough people for it to do well. By 1754 only about 55,000 French colonists lived in the area that stretched from the St. Lawrence River to the Gulf of Mexico. That same year, more than 1,200,000 English colonists lived in North America.

REVIEW Why was it difficult to settle in Louisiana?

• HERITAGE •

The French Quarter

In downtown New Orleans the French Quarter is the oldest historic area in the city. The French Quarter was named in honor of the French colonists who first lived there in the 1700s. Many people in New Orleans trace their ancestors to the first French settlers of the area.

Many streets in the French Quarter have French names.

LESSON 2 REVIEW

Summary Time Line
- 1608 Quebec is founded
- 1673 Jacques Marquette and Louis Joliet explore the Mississippi River
- 1682 Sieur de la Salle claims Louisiana for the French

 CATEGORIZE Name some French explorers who helped expand New France.

1 BIG IDEA How did Henry IV get merchants to build colonies in North America?

2 VOCABULARY Explain the difference between a **royal colony** and a **proprietary colony**.

3 TIME LINE When was Quebec founded?

4 HISTORY Why was the Marquette and Joliet expedition important to the French?

5 CRITICAL THINKING—Analyze What were the economic reasons behind the exploration and settlement of New France?

 PERFORMANCE—Make a Poster Suppose that you are a French citizen who is asked by the French government to get people to settle in New France. Make a poster that persuades people to move to New France. Use words and pictures in your poster to show people the benefits of moving to New France. Compare your poster with those of your classmates.

Chapter 4 ■ 155

LESSON 3

The English in the Americas

1550–1600

 CATEGORIZE
As you read, categorize different English settlements in North America.

BIG IDEA
The English began to explore and start colonies in North America.

VOCABULARY
sea dog
raw material
armada

The English had been sailing to North America since John Cabot made his first voyage there in 1497. Unlike the Spanish or the French, most of the English who first came to North America did not come in search of gold or the riches of the fur trade. Instead, they came mostly for the rich fishing found at the Grand Banks, off the coast of Newfoundland. However, by the late 1500s, the English rulers began taking more of an interest in the Americas.

England Challenges Spain

England saw that Spain had become very wealthy as a result of its colonies in the Americas. Its gold and silver mines and the sale of products from its ranches in the Americas had filled Spain's treasury. England was not as wealthy as Spain, but it did have fast ships and skilled ocean sailors. At first the English sailors went to catch fish in the Grand Banks. Then they went to capture Spanish treasure ships.

England's queen, Elizabeth I, encouraged English sea captains to attack Spanish treasure ships carrying riches to Spain. English merchants and sea captains used their own money to build ships, hoping to capture Spanish treasure. When they succeeded, they had money to build more ships. The commanders of these English warships were known as **sea dogs**. They were pirates, but Queen Elizabeth protected them

Sailing in the *Golden Hind,* Drake captured a Spanish treasure ship.

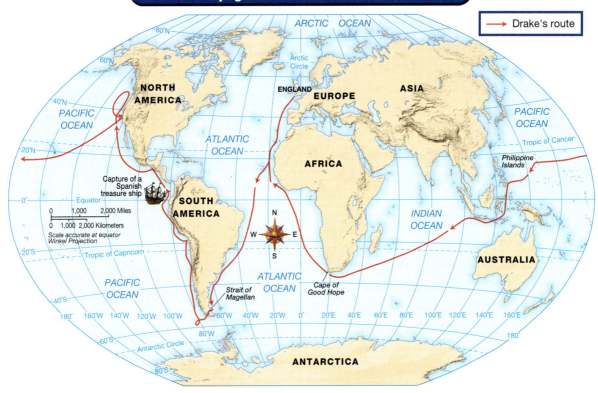

Drake's Voyage Around the World, 1577–1580

Movement Before sailing back to England, Drake may have sailed as far north as Vancouver Island, Canada.

Which ocean did Drake cross to reach Asia?

because they shared their wealth with the government.

England's best-known sea dog was Francis Drake. In 1577 Drake started his most famous voyage. He sailed through the Strait of Magellan at the southern tip of South America to the Pacific Ocean. Off the western coast of South America, he captured a Spanish treasure ship so loaded with riches that it took the crew four days to transfer all the gold and boxes of jewels to Drake's ship.

Worried that Spanish warships would come after him, Drake decided not to follow the same route home. Instead, he continued north along the Pacific coast of North America. He stopped near San Francisco Bay in what is now California and claimed the land for England. Drake eventually returned to England by sailing westward. In doing so, Drake and his men became the second crew to sail around the world. Upon Drake's return, Queen Elizabeth made him a knight, and he became known as Sir Francis Drake.

REVIEW Why did Queen Elizabeth I protect the English pirates known as sea dogs?

When Drake returned to England, he was made a knight.

Chapter 4 ■ 157

England Starts a Colony

The treasure captured by sea dogs increased England's wealth. With that wealth, England built a strong navy and became a powerful country. At that time, Europe's most powerful countries had colonies. So in 1584 Queen Elizabeth gave Sir Walter Raleigh (RAW•lee) permission to set up England's first colony in North America.

Raleigh sent two sea captains, Philip Amadas and Arthur Barlowe, to explore the Atlantic coast to find a good place for a settlement. Upon their return, Barlowe told Raleigh that they had "found such plenty" in what is now North Carolina. The good news led Raleigh to set up his colony there. He named the area that he chose Virginia. He hoped the colony would provide lumber and other raw materials for England. A **raw material** is a resource that can be used to make a product.

Raleigh sent about 100 colonists to North America but did not go himself.

In the late summer of 1585, the colonists landed on an island, which the Hatteras Indians called Roanoke (ROH•uh•nohk), just off the coast. Under the leadership of Ralph Lane, the colony's governor, the colonists built a fort and several houses, but they stayed on Roanoke Island less than a year.

The ship that had brought the colonists to Roanoke Island sailed back to England for more food and supplies. By spring, however, it had not returned. Food ran low, and the colonists wanted to go home. So when Sir Francis Drake visited the colonists, they went back to England on his ship.

REVIEW What did Raleigh hope to gain from the colony on Roanoke Island?
CATEGORIZE

The Lost Colony

In 1587 Sir Walter Raleigh sent a second group of colonists to settle a colony in Virginia. This time Raleigh chose John White to be their governor.

John White's Map

Analyze Primary Sources

This map drawn by John White shows the eastern region of North America.
1. Florida
2. Sir Walter Raleigh's coat of arms
3. Virginia
4. a compass rose
5. measurements that may have indicated longitude
6. English ships

♦ Why do you think ships are shown along the coastline?

158 • Unit 2

The English colonists reached Roanoke Island in July. They quickly rebuilt the fort and repaired the old houses and built new ones. However, they arrived too late in the year to plant crops. White decided to return to England for food and other supplies.

When White reached England, he wanted to gather supplies and return quickly to his family, but he could not get a ship. England was at war with Spain and needed all of its ships for battle. Three years later, after English ships had defeated Spain's **armada**, or a fleet of warships, John White returned to Roanoke—only to find everyone gone. All that was left were some of his books with the covers torn off, maps ruined by rain, and armor covered with rust.

White did make a puzzling discovery. He found the letters *CRO* carved on a tree and the word *CROATOAN* carved on a wooden post. No trace, however, was ever found of the Roanoke Island settlers. Some people believe they went to live with the Croatoan Indians, who later became known as the Lumbees. Many Lumbee Indians today have the same English last names as the missing colonists from the "lost colony."

When John White returned to Roanoke Island, he found that the settlers were gone and that the word *CROATOAN* had been carved into a post.

REVIEW Why did John White return to England?

LESSON 3 REVIEW

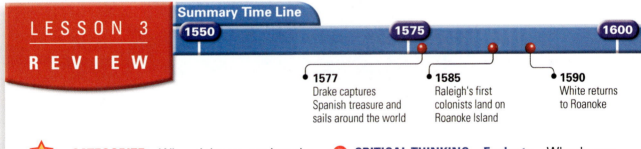

Summary Time Line

- 1577 Drake captures Spanish treasure and sails around the world
- 1585 Raleigh's first colonists land on Roanoke Island
- 1590 White returns to Roanoke

 CATEGORIZE Who might you put into the category of "English pirate"?

1. **BIG IDEA** Why did the English begin to settle in North America?

2. **VOCABULARY** Define the terms **sea dog** and **raw material**.

3. **TIME LINE** In what year did Raleigh's first colonists land on Roanoke Island?

4. **HISTORY** Where did the English first set up a colony?

5. **CRITICAL THINKING—Evaluate** Why do you think it would be important that the English colonists reached Roanoke Island in time to plant crops?

 PERFORMANCE—Write a Journal Entry Imagine that you are John White. Write a journal entry describing why you decided to leave your family and go back to England to get supplies for the colonists. Then write another journal entry about returning three years later to find everyone missing. Describe what you think may have happened to them. Share your journal entries with your classmates.

Chapter 4 ■ 159

LESSON 4

The Jamestown Colony

1200 — 1475 — 1700
1600–1625

 CATEGORIZE
As you read, categorize different events in the history of Jamestown.

BIG IDEA
The English settlers overcame many hardships to make the Virginia Colony of Jamestown a success.

VOCABULARY
stock
prosperity
cash crop
legislature
burgess
authority

Although English settlements at Roanoke Island had failed, the idea of settling an English colony in North America lived on. A group of English merchants decided to try again. To establish a new colony in Virginia, they needed permission from England's monarch. The English believed that the king or queen controlled all land claimed by England. With the permission of King James I, the merchants organized the Virginia Company. The aim of these merchants was to make money by starting trading posts in Virginia. Despite the company's plans, however, most of the colonists went to look for gold.

FAST FACT
By the end of the first year at Jamestown, over half of the colonists had died.

LOCATE IT
Virginia — James R. — Jamestown

160 • Unit 2

The Founding of Jamestown

The Virginia Company was owned by many people. Each owner had given money to organize the company. In return, each one had received **stock**, or a share of ownership, in the company. The owners hoped that over time the company would make a profit. If it did, each stock owner would make money.

In the spring of 1607, three ships sent by the Virginia Company sailed into the deep bay now called Chesapeake Bay. The 105 men and boys aboard sailed up a river that they named the James River to honor their king. They chose a spot along the shore and began to build a settlement they called Jamestown.

The location of Jamestown turned out to be a poor choice for a settlement. The land was wet and full of disease-carrying mosquitoes. The water in the wells that the colonists dug was foul, or bad.

Many of the colonists were not used to working with their hands, and they did not know how to farm or fish in this new land. They had come to Virginia to get rich, and they were so busy searching for gold that no one bothered to plant or gather food. As a result, the second winter became known as the "starving time." One survivor later wrote, "Our men were destroyed with cruel diseases, . . . burning fevers, and by wars."

Jamestown might have become another lost colony, like the earlier settlement at Roanoke, if it had not had a strong leader like Captain John Smith. Smith was a soldier, an explorer, and a writer. Smith made an important rule for the colonists: Anyone who did not work did not eat. The colonists were soon very busy planting gardens and building shelters.

A CLOSER LOOK
Jamestown

This drawing shows what Jamestown may have looked like in the early 1600s. The first settlers built the fort. As more settlers came, additional homes were built outside the fort.

1. pasture
2. crops
3. artillery
4. James River
5. fort
6. common
7. church

Why do you think the colonists built Jamestown near the James River?

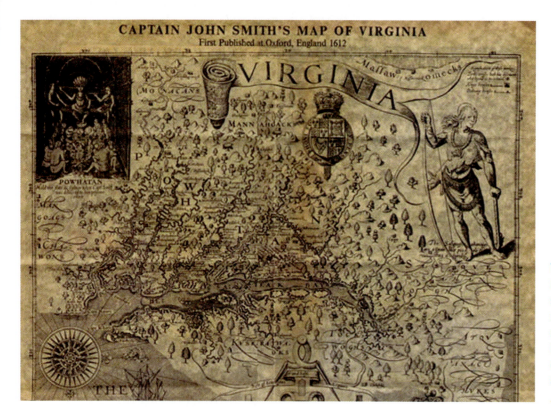

This map, drawn by Captain John Smith, shows the locations of the Virginia Colony and the Powhatan Confederacy. The chief of the Powhatans is also shown (top left).

They also put up fences to protect the settlement from attack by Indians.

During this time, more than 30 tribes of Eastern Woodlands Indians lived in Virginia. Most were members of a confederation known as the Powhatan (pow•uh•TAN) Confederacy. Its members were united under one main chief. When the Jamestown colonists heard this, they gave the name *Powhatan* to all the member tribes, as well as to their chief. The way the colonists behaved toward the Powhatans—seizing their crops for food—put them in constant danger of attack.

One day, while in the countryside around Jamestown, Captain Smith was captured by the Powhatans. A legend says that the chief ordered Captain Smith to be put to death but that the chief's daughter, Pocahontas (poh•kuh•HAHN•tuhs), saved his life. It is not known whether this story is true or not, but it is known that fighting continued between the colonists and the Powhatan Confederacy. Jamestown remained a dangerous place to live.

REVIEW How did Captain John Smith help the colonists at Jamestown? **CATEGORIZE**

This portrait of Pocahontas shows her wearing English clothing.

Prosperity and Growth

Despite Jamestown's troubles, the colony survived. In time, it prospered, or did well. This prosperity, or economic success, began when the colonists finally found the "gold" they had hoped would make them rich. Their "gold" was not a precious metal but a crop called tobacco.

A Jamestown leader named John Rolfe experimented with various kinds of tobacco and ways of drying it. By 1613 Rolfe had developed a kind of tobacco that the English liked. The colonists at Jamestown were soon growing tobacco as a **cash crop**, or a crop that people raise to sell rather than to use themselves. The Virginia Company sold its tobacco all over Europe and made huge profits.

Jamestown saw even more success when the Virginia Company began to give land to those who stayed in the colony seven years. Until then, there had been no private ownership of land. Everyone was supposed to work for the benefit of the company. After receiving land of their own, the colonists worked harder. Now individual colonists, as well as the company, enjoyed prosperity.

Most of the early colonists had planned to make money in Virginia and return to England. To encourage people to settle permanently, the company allowed the first women to become colonists in 1619.

The first Africans also arrived that year. They came as free laborers paid to work in the tobacco fields. As more workers were needed, more Africans were brought to the colony. Instead of paying these workers, however, colonial leaders enslaved them. Later, all Africans arriving in Virginia were made slaves.

By 1619 Virginia had more than 1,000 colonists. With so many people, the colony needed laws to keep order. The Virginia Company said that the English in the colony would live under English laws and have the same rights as the people living in England. One of these was the right to set up a lawmaking assembly, or legislature. A **legislature** is the branch of a government that makes laws.

Virginia's legislature, called the House of Burgesses (BUHR•juhs•iz), first met in 1619. A **burgess** is a representative who is chosen by and speaks for other people. The Virginia House of Burgesses was the first legislature in the English colonies.

REVIEW What was the House of Burgesses?

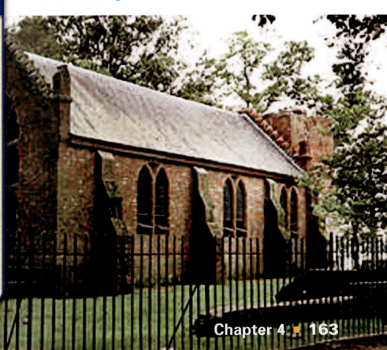

The House of Burgesses met in the Jamestown church. The tower from the original church is part of this building.

DEMOCRATIC VALUES
Representative Government

CITIZENSHIP

The House of Burgesses was modeled after the English Parliament. Burgesses would meet once a year with the royal governor to make local laws and decide on taxes. These representatives were wealthy landowners who were elected by the people to speak for them. Electing leaders to make decisions continues to be an important right that Americans have today.

Analyze the Value
1. What was the House of Burgesses modeled after?
2. **Make It Relevant** Identify a present-day example of representative government.

Chapter 4 ■ 163

The End of Company Control

King James I

For the Virginia Colony to continue to prosper, the settlers had to grow and sell more and more tobacco. This meant that they needed to clear more land to grow it. As a result, the Indians of the Powhatan Confederacy lost much of the land they had used for hunting and farming. In 1622 the Powhatans attacked and killed more than 340 colonists. Having lost nearly one-third of their people, the Virginia colonists fought back in an all-out war. They defeated the Powhatans and took over their remaining lands.

After the fighting ended, King James took away the charter of the Virginia Company and made Virginia a royal colony. The king, rather than business people, now held direct control over the colony.

The king knew that he ruled from too far away to look after all of Virginia's concerns and problems. As a result, he appointed a royal governor to represent him. The royal governor of Virginia shared ruling authority with the House of Burgesses. **Authority** is the right to control and make decisions. The king instructed the royal governor to meet with the burgesses "once a year or oftener."

REVIEW Who did King James appoint to represent him in Virginia?

LESSON 4 REVIEW

Summary Time Line
1600 — 1625

- 1607 English colonists land at Jamestown
- 1613 John Rolfe develops a profitable tobacco crop
- 1619 House of Burgesses meets for the first time

CATEGORIZE In what category would you put John Smith and John Rolfe?

1 BIG IDEA Why did the English continue to try to settle an English colony in North America despite the hardships?

2 VOCABULARY Use the words **legislature** and **burgess** in a sentence about Jamestown.

3 TIME LINE Which happened first, John Rolfe developing a profitable tobacco crop or the House of Burgesses meeting for the first time?

4 ECONOMICS What important contribution did John Rolfe make to the Virginia Colony?

5 CRITICAL THINKING—Evaluate How did the success of the Virginia Colony lead to the development of the House of Burgesses?

PERFORMANCE—Write a Letter Expressing Your Opinion Imagine that you are a Jamestown colonist. Write a letter to Captain John Smith expressing your opinion about his leadership abilities. Do you approve or disapprove of his rule?

SKILLS: Solve a Problem

▶ WHY IT MATTERS

People everywhere face problems at one time or another. Many people face more than one problem at the same time. Think about a problem you have faced recently. Were you able to solve it? Did you wish you could have found a better way to solve the problem? Knowing how to solve problems is a skill that you will use all your life.

▶ WHAT YOU NEED TO KNOW

Here are some steps you can use to help you solve a problem.

Step 1 Identify the problem.

Step 2 Gather information.

Step 3 Think of and list possible options.

Step 4 Consider advantages and disadvantages of possible options.

Step 5 Choose the best solution.

Step 6 Try your solution.

Step 7 Think about how well your solution helps solve the problem.

▶ PRACTICE THE SKILL

You have read about the problems that made life in Jamestown difficult. Colonists did not have enough food, and they were often attacked by Indians. Captain John Smith wanted to solve these problems. Think again about the problems Captain Smith saw and the way he tried to solve them.

1. What problems did Captain Smith see in Jamestown?
2. What did Captain Smith decide was a good way to solve the problems?
3. How did Captain Smith carry out his solution?
4. How did Captain Smith's solution help solve the colonists' problems?
5. Do you think Captain Smith's solution was the best way to solve these problems?

▶ APPLY WHAT YOU LEARNED

Identify a problem in your community or school. Use the steps shown to write a plan for solving the problem. What solution did you choose? Why do you think that your solution will help solve the problem?

Captain John Smith

Chapter 4 ▪ 165

LESSON 5

The Plymouth Colony

1200 — 1475 — 1700

1600–1700

 CATEGORIZE

As you read, categorize reasons for the settlement of the Plymouth Colony.

BIG IDEA

The desire for religious freedom led to the colonization of the Plymouth Colony.

VOCABULARY

pilgrim
compact
self-rule
majority rule

Tobacco profits and the private ownership of land led more English settlers to North America. So did a book written by Captain John Smith after he explored the Atlantic coast in 1614. In *A Description of New England*, published in 1616, Smith mapped the coastline, described its landscape, and named the region that today includes the states of Connecticut, Maine, Massachusetts, New Hampshire, Rhode Island, and Vermont.

The Mayflower Compact

Among those who read Smith's description of New England was a group of English people who were living in Holland. They were known as Separatists, because they had left, or separated from, the Church of England. At the time, everyone in England had to belong to the Church of England. Those who refused were not safe. In 1608 the Separatists had moved to Holland, where they could follow their own religion freely.

In Holland the Separatists had religious freedom, but they soon worried that their children would not learn English ways. So they decided to go to the Americas, where they would live among English colonists and still be able to follow their own religion. In time, these Separatists came to be known as Pilgrims. A **pilgrim** is a person who makes a journey for religious reasons.

Early in 1620 a group in England invited the Pilgrims to join them in their journey to North America. The Virginia Company agreed to pay for the colonists' voyage. In return, the colonists would send the company furs, fish, and lumber.

Items such as this beaver-fur hat and these eyeglasses were worn by settlers on the *Mayflower*.

166 ■ Unit 2

The Mayflower Compact

In the name of God, Amen. We, whose names are underwritten, the loyal subjects of our dread sovereign Lord, King James, by the grace of God, of Great Britain, France, and Ireland, King, defender of the faith, etc.

Having undertaken for the Glory of God, and Advancement of the Christian Faith, and the Honour of our King and Country, a voyage to plant the first colony in the northern Parts of Virginia; do by these Presents, solemnly and mutually in the Presence of God and of one another, covenant [enter into an agreement] and combine ourselves together into a civil Body Politick, for our better Ordering and Preservation, and Furtherance of the Ends aforesaid; And by Virtue hereof to enact, constitute, and frame, such just and equal Laws, Ordinances, Acts, Constitutions, and Offices, from time to time, as shall be thought most meet [proper] and convenient for the General good of the Colony; unto which we promise all due Submission and Obedience.

In witness whereof we have hereunder subscribed our names at Cape Cod the eleventh of November, in the year of the reign of our sovereign Lord, King James of England, France, and Ireland the eighteenth, and of Scotland the fifty-fourth. Anno Domini, 1620.

On a cold day late in 1620, a ship called the *Mayflower* set sail for North America. It carried 101 passengers, including Captain Miles Standish, who had been hired as the new colony's military leader. Fewer than half of the passengers on the *Mayflower* were Pilgrims. Some of them were servants and workers hired by the Virginia Company to help build the new colony.

The *Mayflower* had a long and troubled journey. Violent storms drove the ship off course, and the Pilgrims ended up far north of the lands governed by the Virginia Company. They had reached Cape Cod in what is now Massachusetts.

The people had landed in a place without a government. To keep order, all the men aboard the *Mayflower* signed an agreement, or compact. This agreement became known as the Mayflower Compact. The signers agreed that "just and equal laws" would be made for the common good of the colony and promised to obey these laws. In other words, they would govern themselves.

At a time when monarchs ruled, **self-rule**, or governing oneself, was a very new idea. The Mayflower Compact gave everyone who signed it the right to share in the making of laws. It also recognized the right of the majority to rule. **Majority rule** means that more than half of the people have to agree for a decision to be made. The Mayflower Compact was the first example of self-rule and majority rule in the English colonies.

REVIEW What is self-rule?

• HERITAGE •

Thanksgiving Day

In the fall of 1621, the Pilgrims gathered their first harvest. William Bradford, governor of Plymouth Colony, decided they should have a celebration so that the people could "rejoice together" to give thanks to God. He invited the neighboring Wampanoag Indians to join the Pilgrims for a festival that lasted for three days.

This is what many people today think of as the first Thanksgiving. Some people think the first European Thanksgiving in the Americas took place in 1598, when Spanish settlers gave thanks for safely reaching the Rio Grande.

Thanksgiving became a national holiday in 1863, when President Abraham Lincoln declared the last Thursday in November as "a day of thanksgiving and praise to our beneficent Father."

LOCATE IT

Boston
MASSACHUSETTS
Plymouth Colony

Plymouth Colony

For more than four weeks, Captain Miles Standish and the colonists explored what is now Massachusetts Bay, looking for a suitable place to settle. Finally, on December 25, 1620, they chose a place near Cape Cod with a harbor, open fields nearby, and fresh water. John Smith had called it Plymouth. William Bradford, one of the Pilgrim leaders, described the scene that day. "Being thus arrived in a good harbor, and brought safe to land, they fell upon their knees and blessed the God of Heaven, who had brought them over the vast and furious ocean, and delivered them from all the perils and miseries thereof, again to set their feet on the firm and stable earth, their proper element."

The first winter was hard for the colonists. The weather was cold, and there was not enough food. Many people became ill, and about half of them died. Help, however, came in the spring, when a Native American who spoke English walked into their settlement.

"Welcome, Englishmen," the Indian said. He was an Abenaki (AH•beh•nah•kee) Indian named Samoset who had been visiting the neighboring Wampanoags (wam•puh•NOH•agz). Samoset had learned English from sailors who fished along the Atlantic coast.

Several days later Samoset returned to Plymouth with a Wampanoag who spoke English better than he did. This was Tisquantum, or Squanto, as the English called him. Years before, Tisquantum had been taken and sold as a slave in Spain. He had escaped and spent several years in England before returning to his homeland.

Tisquantum stayed with the Plymouth colonists, showing them where to fish and how to plant squash, pumpkins, and corn. Because resources were so scarce, the Pilgrims chose to live in peace with the Wampanoags, who were led by their chief, Massasoit (ma•suh•SOYT). Both groups benefited from sharing. However, as more English colonists came to settle in Massachusetts, the situation changed. Many new colonists were not friendly toward the Indians and settled on more of their lands. Over time, the quarrels between the Wampanoags and the colonists grew into terrible wars.

REVIEW How would you categorize the first winter at Plymouth? **CATEGORIZE**

Plymouth Colony Prospers

When the Plymouth colonists first arrived, there was very little food available. To help, the colony's leaders decided that the harvest would be divided equally among the families and there would be no private ownership of land. Some settlers thought this system was unfair.

People today can visit this re-creation of the Plymouth Colony (below) in Massachusetts. Actors there take on colonial roles in which they chop wood (right), sew (far right), and plant crops (bottom right).

In 1623 the colonial leaders divided the land among the colonists. The result was the same as it had been at Jamestown—the people worked harder when they owned the land. However, the idea of community sharing remained strong. Large areas of land in Plymouth were set aside for common use.

The Plymouth colonists, including the Pilgrims, began to prosper with their fishing, farming, and fur trading. As new colonists arrived, the earlier ones had extra goods ready to sell or trade. They sold or traded milk, meat, fruit, and vegetables to the newcomers.

William Bradford was a governor of the Plymouth Colony.

Colonists like William Bradford provided the strong, steady leadership that kept the community alive. Bradford fought for the religious ideals of Plymouth's founders and kept the colony separate from any neighboring settlements. Bradford was so popular with the colonists that he was reelected governor of Plymouth 30 times! After a hard beginning, Plymouth continued to prosper. In 1691 Plymouth became a part of the Massachusetts Bay Colony, a larger colony that was formed later.

REVIEW What helped the Plymouth colonists prosper?

LESSON 5 REVIEW

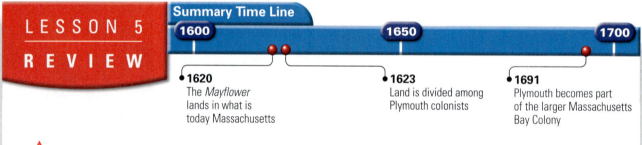

Summary Time Line

- **1620** The *Mayflower* lands in what is today Massachusetts
- **1623** Land is divided among Plymouth colonists
- **1691** Plymouth becomes part of the larger Massachusetts Bay Colony

CATEGORIZE What were the names of some of the Indians who had contact with the first Plymouth colonists?

1 BIG IDEA Why did many settlers come to the Plymouth Colony?

2 VOCABULARY Describe the difference between **self-rule** and **majority rule**.

3 TIME LINE When did Plymouth become part of the Massachusetts Bay Colony?

4 CIVICS AND GOVERNMENT Describe the Mayflower Compact and tell why you think it would serve as a model for later documents.

5 CRITICAL THINKING—Hypothesize What do you think might have happened if Tisquantum had not helped the Pilgrims?

PERFORMANCE—Write a List of Questions Write a list of questions you might ask people who want to join you in starting a colony. As you write the questions, think about the personal qualities and skills people need in order to start a successful colony. Compare your questions with those of your classmates.

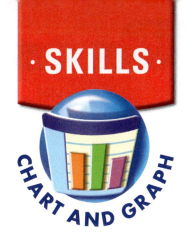

SKILLS · CHART AND GRAPH

Compare Tables to Classify Information

VOCABULARY
classify

▶ WHY IT MATTERS

Information can be easier to find if you **classify**, or group it. Knowing how to classify information can make facts easier to find.

▶ WHAT YOU NEED TO KNOW

When you read about European settlement in the Americas, you were given a lot of information. You learned where, when, and why the Spanish, French, and English set up colonies. This and other information can be classified by using a table.

The tables below classify information about European settlement in the Americas in two different ways. In Table A, the settlements are classified according to when they were founded. Table B gives the same information as Table A, but the information is classified according to what countries founded the settlements.

▶ PRACTICE THE SKILL

Use the tables below to answer the following questions.

1. Which table makes it easier to find out when the first European settlement in the Americas was founded?
2. Which table makes it easier to find out the number of settlements founded by the French?
3. When was Roanoke founded? Explain which table you used.

▶ APPLY WHAT YOU LEARNED

Make a table to show information about European explorers. Choose some headings under which to classify the information by topic. Then compare your table with a classmate's table.

Table A: European Settlements in the Americas

DATE FOUNDED	SETTLEMENT	COUNTRY
1521	Mexico City	Spain
1565	St. Augustine	Spain
1585	Fort Raleigh (Roanoke)	England
1607	Jamestown	England
1608	Quebec	France
1620	Plymouth	England

Table B: European Settlements in the Americas

COUNTRY	SETTLEMENT	DATE FOUNDED
England	Fort Raleigh (Roanoke)	1585
England	Jamestown	1607
England	Plymouth	1620
France	Quebec	1608
Spain	Mexico City	1521
Spain	St. Augustine	1565

Chapter 4 ■ 171

CHAPTER 4

Review and Test Preparation

Summary Time Line

1500 — 1550

• **1535** The colony of New Spain is formed

Focus Skill: Categorize

Copy the following graphic organizer onto a separate sheet of paper. Use the information you have learned to categorize people and settlements with the countries they are associated with.

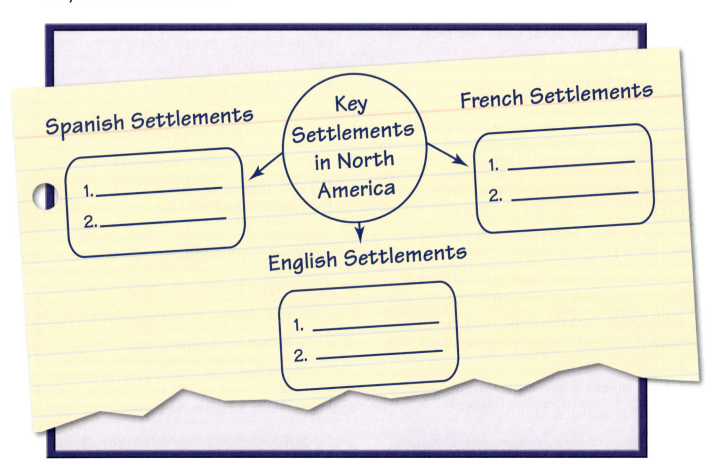

THINK & WRITE

Write a Classroom Compact The Mayflower Compact set up rules designed to help the Plymouth settlers. Write a classroom compact that lists rules for your class. Explain how this compact will benefit the members of your class.

Write a Letter Imagine that the year is 1620 and you have just moved to the Plymouth Colony with your family. Write a letter to a friend in England about your new life. Describe your new environment and the challenges you and your family face.

- 1565 St. Augustine is settled
- 1600
- 1607 Jamestown is founded
- 1608 Quebec is founded
- 1620 The Pilgrims establish the Plymouth Colony
- 1650
- 1673 Marquette and Joliet explore the Mississippi River
- 1682 La Salle claims Louisiana
- 1700

USE THE TIME LINE

Use the chapter summary time line to answer these questions.

1. When was the Jamestown Colony founded?
2. Was St. Augustine settled before Quebec?

USE VOCABULARY

Identify the term that correctly matches each definition.

colony (p. 144)
proprietor (p. 155)
burgess (p. 163)
compact (p. 167)

3. an owner
4. a representative who speaks for other people
5. a signed agreement
6. a settlement ruled by another country

RECALL FACTS

Answer these questions.

7. What group of people did Bartolomé de Las Casas work to protect?
8. What early problems did the Jamestown colonists face?
9. How was the government of a royal colony different from that of a proprietary colony?

Write the letter of the best choice.

10. The forts built by Spanish soldiers were known as—
    A haciendas.
    B plantations.
    C presidios.
    D missions.

11. After leaders of the Plymouth Colony divided the land among the colonists—
    F many people starved.
    G people stopped immigrating to Plymouth.
    H people lost their sense of community.
    J people worked harder and the colony began to prosper.

THINK CRITICALLY

12. Why do you think problems developed between Native Americans and Spanish missionaries?
13. How do you think English pirates such as Francis Drake would have been treated by Queen Elizabeth I if they had not shared their wealth?

APPLY SKILLS

Solve a Problem

14. Imagine that you are a Jamestown colonist in 1622. What ideas would you offer to solve the problems between the colonists and the Powhatan Indians?

Compare Tables to Classify Information

15. Choose a lesson from this chapter and make a table about the explorers discussed in that lesson. Make sure to list the places the explorers visited and the dates of their travels. Compare your table to a classmate's table.

VISIT
The Mission San Diego de Alcalá

GET READY

High on a hill overlooking the city of San Diego, California, sits the Mission San Diego de Alcalá. It was the first in a string of 21 missions that stretched across the Spanish borderlands of California. San Diego de Alcalá was founded by Father Junípero Serra on July 16, 1769. In time, the city of San Diego grew around the mission. Today, many people visit to learn about mission life hundreds of years ago. At San Diego de Alcalá, you can see artifacts that belonged to Native Americans, early Spanish settlers, soldiers, and missionaries. Experience life in another time as you walk where they once walked.

LOCATE IT

San Diego
CALIFORNIA

WHAT TO SEE

Visitors can spend time in the mission's scenic gardens.

A statue of Father Junípero Serra stands on the mission grounds.

People still attend church services at the Mission San Diego de Alcalá.

This songbook, on display at the mission, was used more than 200 years ago.

TAKE A FIELD TRIP

A VIRTUAL TOUR
Visit The Learning Site at www.harcourtschool.com to find virtual tours of historic sites in the United States.

A VIDEO TOUR
Check your media center or classroom library for a videotape tour of the Mission San Diego de Alcalá.

Unit 2 • 175

UNIT 2 Review and Test Preparation

VISUAL SUMMARY

Write a Journal Entry Choose one of the events shown below. Write a journal entry from the perspective of a person present at one of the events.

USE VOCABULARY

Use each of the following words in a sentence about exploration.

1. **compass** (p. 109)
2. **claim** (p. 121)
3. **Northwest Passage** (p. 136)
4. **missionary** (p. 148)

RECALL FACTS

Answer these questions.

5. Why did Prince Henry set up a school for navigators?
6. What Native American group was one of the first to trade furs with the French?
7. How did the Jamestown Colony finally achieve prosperity?

Write the letter of the best choice.

8. The Inca Empire covered thousands of miles on the western coast of—
   A Europe.
   B Asia.
   C South America.
   D Africa.

9. One of the first Spanish explorers to journey through what is now the state of Texas was—
   F Hernando Cortés.
   G Álvar Núñez Cabeza de Vaca.
   H Juan Ponce de León.
   J Hernando de Soto.

10. Sieur de la Salle set out to find—
    A the Northwest Passage.
    B the mouth of the Mississippi River.
    C El Dorado.
    D the Fountain of Youth.

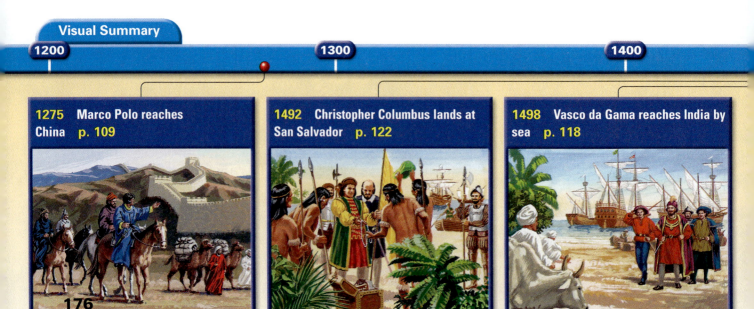

Visual Summary

1200 — 1300 — 1400

1275 Marco Polo reaches China p. 109

1492 Christopher Columbus lands at San Salvador p. 122

1498 Vasco da Gama reaches India by sea p. 118

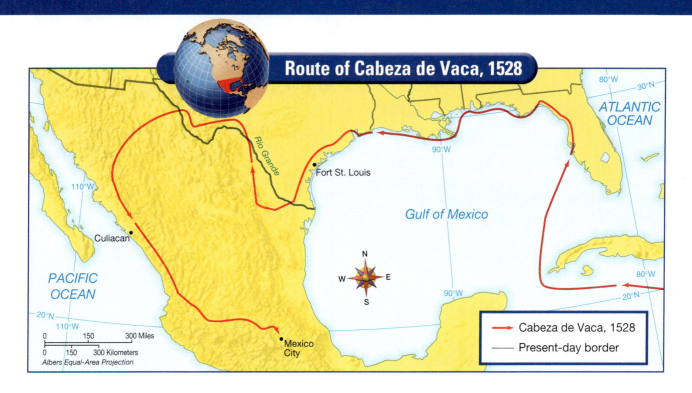

11. The Mayflower Compact allowed the colonists to—
   F govern themselves.
   G trade.
   H grow tobacco.
   J join the Virginia Company.

THINK CRITICALLY

12. Why do you think *The Travels of Marco Polo* was such a popular book?

13. Do you think Francisco Vasquez de Coronado's 1540 expedition was a success or a failure? Explain.

APPLY SKILLS

Follow Routes on a Map

Use the map on this page to answer the following questions.

14. For the most part, did Cabeza de Vaca travel east or west on his expedition?

15. Where did Cabeza de Vaca end his expedition?

16. How many times did Cabeza de Vaca cross the Rio Grande on his way to Mexico City?

1519 Hernando Cortés arrives in Tenochtitlán p. 129

1607 English colonists settle Jamestown p. 161

1620 English colonists settle Plymouth p. 167

Unit Activities

Visit The Learning Site at www.harcourtschool.com for additional activities.

Conduct an Interview

Work with a classmate to select an explorer from the unit and research information about the explorer. Write a list of questions to ask the explorer during an interview. Then take turns role-playing the explorer and the interviewer.

Make a Display

Work in a group to create a chart titled *Daily Life in America*. Your chart should feature Spanish missions, French settlements, and the Jamestown and Plymouth Colonies. For each settlement or colony, list the location, climate, foods available, and buildings. To illustrate the chart, draw pictures, cut them out of magazines, or print them out from the Internet.

VISIT YOUR LIBRARY

- ***If You Were There in 1492*** by Barbara Brenner. Macmillan.

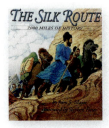

- ***The Silk Route: 7,000 Miles of History*** by John S. Major. HarperCollins.

- ***The History News: Explorers*** by Michael Johnstone. Candlewick.

COMPLETE THE UNIT PROJECT

An Exploration Map Work with a group of your classmates to complete the unit project—a map that shows exploration of North America. Decide which key explorers' routes you want to include on your map. Start by drawing a map of North America on posterboard. Then draw the routes of the explorers you have chosen. Use a different color for each route. Also label each route with the correct explorer's name and the dates of the exploration.

The English Colonies

GEORGIA CONNECTION

Quaker gift to a Native American

GEORGIA CONNECTION

Colonial Savannah

James Oglethorpe and a group of more than 100 settlers came from Britain to found the colony of Georgia in 1733. At the time, Spain, France, and Britain all claimed what became the Georgia Colony. Oglethorpe hoped that setting up a British colony would strengthen Britain's claim to the land.

This early engraving of Savannah shows mountains in the background even though no mountains are visible from the city.

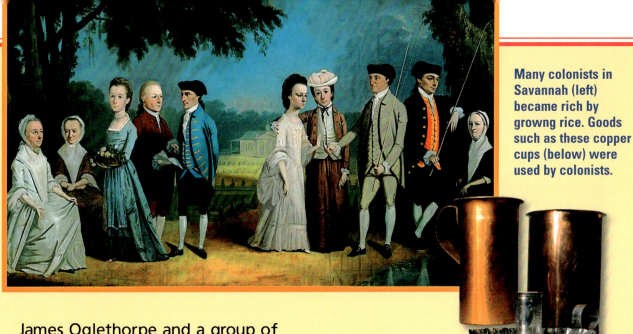

Many colonists in Savannah (left) became rich by growng rice. Goods such as these copper cups (below) were used by colonists.

James Oglethorpe and a group of settlers landed on a high bank above the Savannah River. The first settlement Oglethorpe founded was the city of Savannah. Savannah is often called the first planned city in the United States. Oglethorpe laid out the city in a grid so that squares made up the downtown area. Originally, there were 24 squares in Oglethorpe's plan. Houses, churches, and businesses were built around each square. The squares were used as meeting places and centers of business. Each family was given a plot of land.

At first, the colonists tried to produce silk. However, mulberry trees, which are needed to produce silk, did not grow well in Georgia's climate. Farmers around Savannah found that cotton and rice grew well in Georgia soil. In time, rice became the main crop. Farmers relied on the port at Savannah to ship both rice and cotton. Colonists also shipped wood products from Georgia's forests. The port at Savannah became one of the busiest ports in the British colonies.

★ CRCT ★ TEST PREP

1 What was the author's purpose in writing this passage?
  A to describe colonial Savannah
  B to explain silk production
  C to encourage people to visit Savannah
  D to tell about James Oglethorpe

2 Why did Oglethorpe lay out Savannah in squares?
  A to make places easy to find
  B to make it different from other cities
  C to create community meeting places and business centers
  D to help colonists plant vegetable gardens in the squares

3 What was NOT shipped from Savannah's port?
  A rice
  B silk
  C cotton
  D wood products

The home of William Penn, Pennsbury Manor, Pennsylvania

The English Colonies

"Any government is free to the people under it where the laws rule and the people are a party to the laws."

—William Penn, Frame of Government of Pennsylvania, 1682

Preview the Content

Scan the unit. Then make a K-W-L chart. First, write what you have learned about the 13 colonies. Next, write what you would like to know about them. As you read, fill in details.

Preview the Vocabulary

Synonyms Synonyms are words with similar meanings. Look in the unit to find vocabulary words you can match to the synonyms below. Then use each word in a sentence.

SYNONYM	VOCABULARY WORD	SENTENCE
1. setting up 2. shelter 3. army	charter	

The 13 Colonies

COLONY	LOCATION	DATE FOUNDED
Massachusetts	New England Colony	1630
Connecticut	New England Colony	1636
Rhode Island	New England Colony	1647
New Hampshire	New England Colony	1680
Delaware	Middle Atlantic Colony	1638
New Jersey	Middle Atlantic Colony	1664
New York	Middle Atlantic Colony	1664
Pennsylvania	Middle Atlantic Colony	1681
Virginia	Southern Colony	1607
Maryland	Southern Colony	1632
North Carolina	Southern Colony	1663
South Carolina	Southern Colony	1712
Georgia	Southern Colony	1733

1750

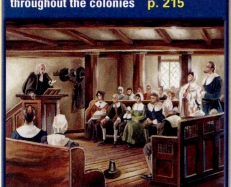

1730s The Great Awakening spreads throughout the colonies p. 215

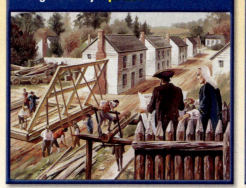

1733 James Oglethorpe settles the Georgia Colony p. 236

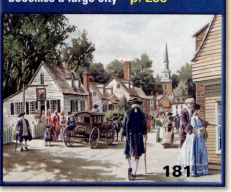

1750s Williamsburg, Virginia becomes a large city p. 238

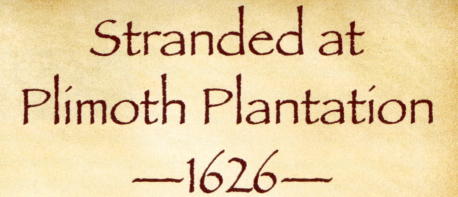

Stranded at Plimoth Plantation
—1626—

words and woodcuts by Gary Bowen

On October 12, 1626, a ship bound for the Jamestown colony set sail from England. The actual name of the ship is unknown, but the Pilgrims called it the *Sparrowhawk*. On November 6, the ship crashed in the fog along the New England coast near the Pilgrim colony at Plimoth Plantation, known today as Plymouth, Massachusetts. Rescued by the colonists, the ship's passengers remained stranded there for nine months until another ship arrived to take them to Jamestown. The following is a fictional journal based on the wreck of the *Sparrowhawk*. The writer is one of the passengers, 13-year-old Christopher Sears. After being rescued, Sears stayed with the family of William Brewster, a Pilgrim church leader. Also living with the Brewsters at that time was another boy, Richard More, whose parents had died during the first years of the Pilgrim colony. The entries from Sears's fictional journal, accompanied by woodcut engravings, tell what life was like in the early New England colonies. Read now about Christopher Sears's experiences at Plimoth Plantation.

November 24, 1626

His worship the Governor [William Bradford] met at the fort this afternoon with all of us who crossed on the *Sparrowhawk*. He told us that 21 other ships have arrived in Plimoth in six years, and said it may be months before another anchors again.

We are to earn our board by working for the families with whom we reside. Our labors are to be reported weekly to Captain Sibsey or Master Fells.

I am happy that Richard lives and works here, too. When he was six years old, he came over on the *Mayflower* with two brothers and a sister who did not survive their first year here. Richard says they had been told their mother and father died, but he does not remember their illnesses or any funeral service. He says his parents did not like each other.

My knee aches and I am cold because my garments are not warm enough for this climate.

December 23, 1626

Governor Bradford talked with me today and showed me the notes that he has been keeping since he arrived in 1620. He commended me for recording my experiences here and said that I am participating in a "great event, which is the founding of God's community."

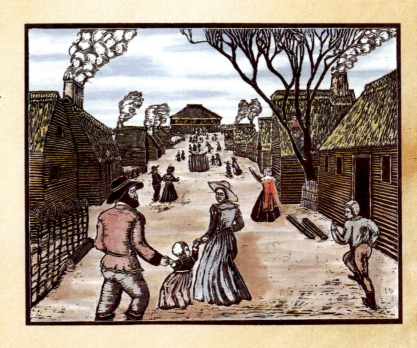

His Worship suggested that I make larger woodcuts and consider using color. The physician gave me these mixtures.

December 30, 1626

I was measured for new woolen breeches as my old ones are too small. The Mistress plans to sew them from fabric that once was her skirt. She will re-dye the cloth with agrimony roots and nutshells because all textiles are imported and are difficult to come by here.

It is surprising that I have seen no spinning wheels or looms in Plimoth since they are so common in England.

January 23, 1627

Master Brewster will include me in his tutoring of Richard, Oceanus Hopkins (who was born aboard the *Mayflower*), and Peregrine White, who Master Brewster says is the first Anglo-Saxon born in New England.

We had cold eel pie in a <u>coffin</u> for dinner.

coffin a pastry crust

February 3, 1627

I am happy that my schooling continues.

Each evening Master Brewster works with me on herb lore, farming, reading, and scriptures. He says the Plimoth people are more learned than in most English villages, as all parents must educate their children, even if that requires tutoring in another home.

March 3, 1627

I was with a group of men organized by the Governor, cutting timbers in the forest.

Indians approached us, wanting to trade some furs, three turkeys, and a deer for grain. His Worship agreed to the barter, and the Indians will receive a bushel of corn.

April 5, 1627

I carried in 24 buckets of springwater to heat. Each member of the Brewster household had a bath today. It felt good to wash.

Love [the Brewster's son] cautioned me that it is unhealthy to have more than three or four baths a year because, if done too often, all the body's natural protection against disease is washed away.

Tomorrow we will be fishing for herring, which is plentiful this month and next.

June 1, 1627

Because Master Brewster predicts rainy weather is coming, we worked doubly hard to sow our seeds for peas, beans, wheat, rye, barley, and turkey corn. Not all families have planted their crops yet.

Mistress Priscilla Alden gave birth to baby John. Master John Alden, her husband, was very pleased.

Love prepared mussels again.

July 1, 1627

The weather has been hot and dry and our garden has suffered. Richard and I carried buckets of water to give the crops a drink.

Since there is no rain in sight, we plan to cut a field of grain tomorrow. After it is turned over to dry thoroughly in the sun, we will stack the barley in the shape of cones.

I boiled seawater to replenish the Brewsters' salt supply.

Love says I am growing like a weed!

August 18, 1627

Today when we returned from the Indian settlement, I learned that two barks had arrived from Jamestown to transport the *Sparrowhawk* passengers to Virginia. For me it was not a welcome sight.

August 22, 1627

Since the ship will depart Thursday at sunrise, tomorrow will be my last full day here.

I feel very sad.

Analyze the Literature

1. How did people at Plimoth Plantation get goods that they needed?

2. Compare Christopher Sears's daily activities with your own. How are they alike and how are they different?

READ A BOOK

START THE UNIT PROJECT

A Book on Colonial America
With your classmates, create a book on the 13 colonies. As you read, take notes about why different colonies were started, key people, economic practices, and how the colonies were governed. These notes will help you decide what to include in your book.

USE TECHNOLOGY

Visit The Learning Site at **www.harcourtschool.com** for additional activities, primary sources, and other resources to use in this unit.

A NEW ENGLAND CHURCH

Religion was the center of life for most early New England colonists. As a result, nearly every town had its own church, or meetinghouse. A town's church was usually among the first major structures built. In the case of Thetford Hill, Vermont, the building of the meetinghouse marked the beginning of the village itself.

LOCATE IT

VERMONT — Thetford Hill

CHAPTER 5

The New England Colonies

"The New Englanders are a people of God...."
—Cotton Mather,
Wonders of the Invisible World, 1693

Summarize

When you **summarize,** you tell a shortened version of what you have just read.

After you read this chapter, summarize what you learned.

- Identify the main topic of each lesson.
- Use the key facts to summarize what you read.

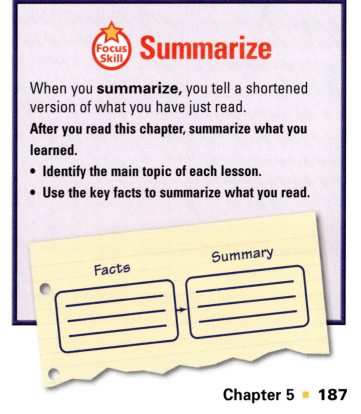

LESSON 1

The Massachusetts Bay Colony

 SUMMARIZE

As you read, summarize facts about the Massachusetts Bay Colony.

BIG IDEA

A group of English colonists, called Puritans, founded the Massachusetts Bay Colony.

VOCABULARY

Puritan
charter
common
specialize
town meeting
public office

1625 — 1750

1625–1645

Less than ten years after the Pilgrims founded Plymouth, another group of religious settlers founded an English colony in North America. Like the Pilgrims, these settlers disagreed with many practices of the Anglicans (AN•glik•anz), or members of the Church of England. Unlike the Pilgrims, however, they did not want to separate from the church. They wanted to change some religious practices in order to make the church more "pure." For this reason, they were called **Puritans**. The Puritans set up a community in North America so they could make money and live by their Christian ideas.

A City on a Hill

In 1628 a group of Puritans joined other people in England to form the New England Company. That year King Charles I granted the company a charter. A **charter** is an official paper in which certain rights are given by a government to a person or business. The king's charter allowed the Puritans to settle in the region Captain John Smith had named New England.

In 1628 John Endecott led the first group of Puritans to sail to New England. There they built a settlement named Salem on a bay they called Massachusetts Bay. The word *Massachusetts* means "at the big hill" in the Algonquian language. The following year the company became the Massachusetts Bay Company, and the king granted a new charter.

 FAST FACT

Salem was the Puritans' first settlement in the Massachusetts Bay area. Its name comes from the Hebrew word *shalom*, which means "peace."

King Charles I is shown in the top left corner of the Massachusetts Bay Company Charter.

188 • Unit 3

Massachusetts Bay Colony

 Location In 1630 John Winthrop (far right) led more than 700 Puritans to Massachusetts Bay. They soon settled on the Massachusetts coast north of Plymouth.

♦ Why do you think most of the settlements in Massachusetts were located near the coast?

In 1630 John Winthrop brought a second and much larger group of Puritans from England to settle along Massachusetts Bay. Winthrop served as the governor of the Massachusetts Bay Colony. In fact, he would serve as governor of the colony several times during the next 20 years. In that time more than 20,000 newcomers, mostly Puritans, settled in the colony.

Winthrop said that Puritan cities should be models for Christian living.

> ❝For we must consider that we shall be as a city upon a hill. The eyes of all people are upon us....❞

The Puritans hoped that all their communities would become models for good living. They built new villages, many of which were near Boston.

In 1637 Winthrop worked at forming a confederation among the people of New England. He believed a confederation would help them better defend themselves in case they were attacked by nearby Indian groups or by the Dutch, who had started settlements to the south of New England. Winthrop became the first president of the confederation when it was formed in 1643.

REVIEW What did John Winthrop accomplish as leader of the Puritans? **SUMMARIZE**

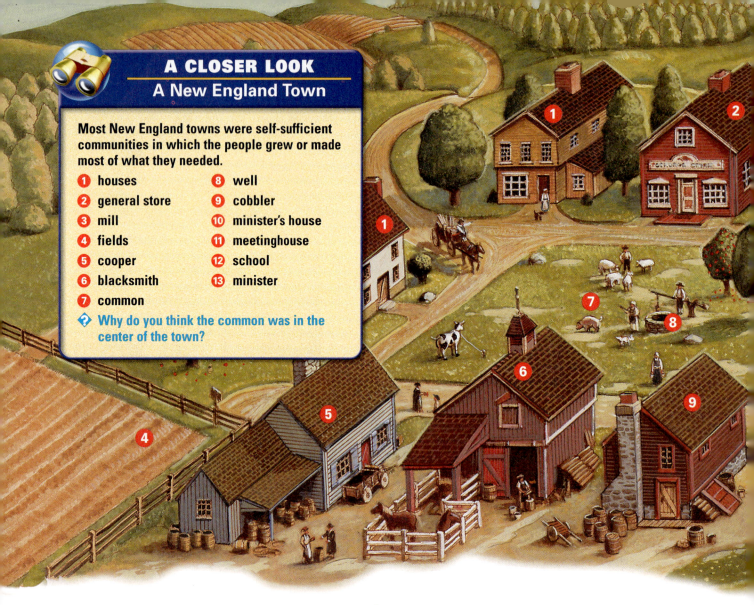

A CLOSER LOOK
A New England Town

Most New England towns were self-sufficient communities in which the people grew or made most of what they needed.

1. houses
2. general store
3. mill
4. fields
5. cooper
6. blacksmith
7. common
8. well
9. cobbler
10. minister's house
11. meetinghouse
12. school
13. minister

❓ Why do you think the common was in the center of the town?

A Puritan Village

At the center of each Puritan village was the **common**, or village green. This was a parklike area shared by all the villagers and used for grazing their animals. At one end of the common was the church, called the meetinghouse. Houses and other buildings lined the other sides of the common.

In time, other buildings that might be found around the common were a general store, a sawmill, and a blacksmith shop. Blacksmithing is one particular craft in which a person in a village may have specialized. To **specialize** is to become skilled at one kind of job.

A blacksmith might make nails for a neighbor. In exchange, the neighbor might make barrels for the blacksmith. Specialization allowed the colonists to be more productive. It also made them more dependent on each other as they bartered for goods.

Another building that might be found near the common was a school. Schools were important because the Puritans wanted every person to be able to read the Bible. At first, Puritan children went to schools that were run by women in their homes. Later, villagers began to build schools after the Puritans passed a law stating that every village of 50 families or more must have a school.

Puritan schools were the first community schools in the English colonies. Some of these schools still exist. They include Boston Latin School, which was founded in 1635, and Harvard College, now Harvard University, which was founded in 1636. Harvard was the first college in England's North American colonies.

The small size of a Puritan village made people feel they belonged to a community and made it easier for them to help each other. Village life also made it easier for church ministers to keep their authority in the village. The duty of the minister was to make sure people lived their lives in ways that the Puritan leaders thought were right.

REVIEW How did the small size of villages help the Puritans?

The Meetinghouse

The meetinghouse was at the center of village life because it was where church services were held. The most important part of the Puritan church service was the minister's sermon, or his explanation of the Bible's teachings. The sermon often lasted for several hours. The whole service lasted for most of the day, with a break for a meal at noon.

The meetinghouse was also where the Puritans conducted all town business. Everyone in the town could attend a **town meeting**, but only men who owned property could vote. They voted on laws and on matters that affected the whole community. At first, a man had to be a member of the Puritan church to vote. By the end of the 1600s, however, any man who owned property could vote.

Each year at a town meeting, some people were elected to **public offices**, or jobs for the community. Offices in a Puritan town included constable, town crier, digger of graves, drummer, sweeper of the meetinghouse, and fence viewer. The constable was in charge of maintaining order and keeping the peace. The town crier walked around and called out important news and other announcements. The fence viewer made sure that the fences around the crops were kept in good repair.

A town meeting held in Haverhill, Massachusetts, once elected a man to run a ferry across the Merrimack River. He could not charge passengers any price he wanted, however. The town meeting set the charges.

REVIEW What were some of the public offices that the Puritans could be elected to?

Home and Farm Life

The main room of a Puritan home contained a large fireplace, where a fire was always kept burning. All cooking was done in the fireplace. Baking was done in a small oven inside the fireplace. Most food was roasted over the fire or simmered in large iron kettles hung in the fireplace. Kettles were also used to heat water for cooking and washing.

Women and girls spent many hours preparing food for the rest of the family. They used churns to turn cream into butter. They dried and preserved fruits. They pickled cabbages and other vegetables grown in the gardens they tended. Pickled vegetables could be eaten throughout the cold, hard winter.

The women and girls also made all the clothing for the family. Sometimes pieces of worn-out clothing were used to make

This reenactment shows how Puritan women prepared meals.

This scene shows a New England farm.

new clothing and patchwork quilts for bedding. Nothing useful went to waste.

Puritan farmers grew corn, rye, barley, and wheat. They traded some of these crops for sugar from English colonists on the Caribbean islands. Farmers also grew pumpkins and other kinds of squash among the corn. This method of farming was first used by the Wampanoag Indians.

The Puritans also raised cattle, hogs, and sheep as sources of food, leather, and wool. They made their own tools from wood and their own shoes from leather. They also wore warm clothing from sheep's wool.

Life was difficult for the early Puritans, but children still found time for leisure activities. Because of the Puritans' religious beliefs, children were not allowed to have many toys. Instead, they played games and read religious books.

REVIEW What kinds of crops were grown on New England farms?

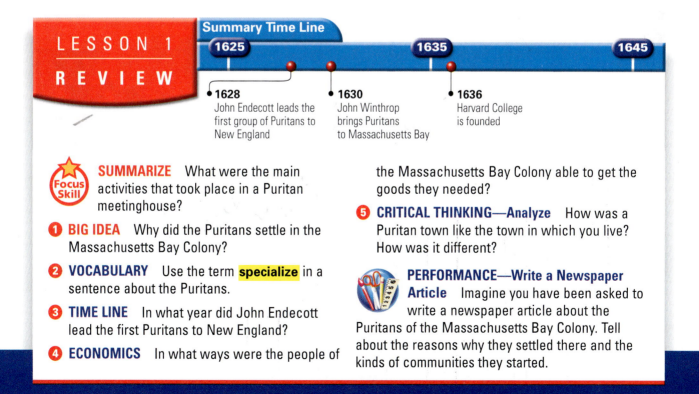

LESSON 1 REVIEW

Summary Time Line

- 1628 John Endecott leads the first group of Puritans to New England
- 1630 John Winthrop brings Puritans to Massachusetts Bay
- 1636 Harvard College is founded

SUMMARIZE What were the main activities that took place in a Puritan meetinghouse?

1. **BIG IDEA** Why did the Puritans settle in the Massachusetts Bay Colony?
2. **VOCABULARY** Use the term **specialize** in a sentence about the Puritans.
3. **TIME LINE** In what year did John Endecott lead the first Puritans to New England?
4. **ECONOMICS** In what ways were the people of the Massachusetts Bay Colony able to get the goods they needed?
5. **CRITICAL THINKING—Analyze** How was a Puritan town like the town in which you live? How was it different?

PERFORMANCE—Write a Newspaper Article Imagine you have been asked to write a newspaper article about the Puritans of the Massachusetts Bay Colony. Tell about the reasons why they settled there and the kinds of communities they started.

Chapter 5 ■ 193

LESSON 2

New Ideas, New Colonies

1625 — 1630–1680 — 1750

Focus Skill: SUMMARIZE
As you read, summarize the ways in which people expanded the ideas of freedom of speech and freedom of religion.

BIG IDEA
Events led some Massachusetts Bay colonists to form new colonies nearby.

VOCABULARY
expel
consent
sedition
fundamental
frontier

The lives of the Puritans in the Massachusetts Bay Colony centered around religion. In fact, religion was so important to the Puritans that they expected all newcomers to follow the Puritans' beliefs. They did not welcome people whose ideas were different from theirs. When the Puritan leaders disapproved of someone's ideas, they sent that person back to England or to another English colony. Some colonists who left the Massachusetts Bay Colony started new colonies nearby.

Roger Williams and Rhode Island

In 1631 Roger Williams and his family arrived in the Massachusetts Bay Colony from England. They settled in the village of Salem, where Roger Williams became a minister.

Roger Williams lived with the Narragansett Indians before starting a settlement he called Providence.

194

Williams was a popular minister because he and many people in Salem shared the same beliefs. They believed that their church should be separate from the colonial government and free from the rule of the Church of England. They also believed that people should not be punished if their beliefs were different from those of the Puritan leaders.

Roger Williams often stated his beliefs in his sermons and in letters that he wrote to Governor John Winthrop. Before long his ideas became unpopular with other ministers and with Winthrop. In 1635 the Puritan leaders voted to **expel** him, or to force him to leave. This meant that he was no longer allowed to live in the Massachusetts Bay Colony.

From Salem, Williams and his family fled beyond the border of the colony south to Narragansett (nar•uh•GAN•suht) Bay. There they received food and protection from the Narragansett Indians. In 1636 many of Williams' followers also left Salem and joined him. He bought land from the Narragansetts and founded a settlement he called Providence. It later became the capital of the present-day state of Rhode Island.

Williams set up a government based on the **consent**, or agreement, of the settlers. The new government of what would later become the Rhode Island Colony gave its people the freedom to follow any religion they chose.

REVIEW What did Roger Williams accomplish after he left the Massachusetts Bay Colony?

Anne Hutchinson on Trial

Not long after the Puritan leaders expelled Roger Williams from the Massachusetts Bay Colony, they faced

Anne Hutchinson was put on trial for causing people to work against the government.

other challenges to their leadership. One such challenge came from a colonist named Anne Marbury Hutchinson.

Hutchinson and her husband, William, moved to North America in 1634. They settled in Boston and attended church services there. Hutchinson soon began to question the authority of the Puritan ministers and their teachings. Her strong and spirited personality attracted many followers. She started holding her own religious meetings at home and stated her own beliefs during these services.

The Puritan leaders said Hutchinson was "a woman not fit for our society." In 1637 they brought her to trial.

Chapter 5 ■ 195

This painting by Fredric Edwin Church shows Thomas Hooker and his followers arriving in what became Hartford.

She stood trial before a Puritan court on charges of **sedition**, or the use of speech or behavior that causes people to work against a government. She was found guilty, and the Puritan leaders ordered her to leave the colony. A year later they also expelled her from the Puritan church.

With her family and many followers, Anne Hutchinson moved to Narragansett Bay. There they founded a settlement on an island near Providence. Hutchinson's settlement later united with the one founded by Roger Williams under the charter that formed the Rhode Island Colony.

REVIEW What were some of Anne Hutchinson's accomplishments?

SUMMARIZE

Connecticut

Other settlers also left the Massachusetts Bay Colony, but not for religious reasons. They wanted to leave the rocky fields of Massachusetts to find better farmland. By the early 1630s people began moving into the fertile Connecticut River valley. The first permanent settlement, Windsor, was founded in the river valley in 1633. It was soon followed by the Wethersfield settlement.

Most early Connecticut settlers came to find better farmland, but many also came in search of religious freedom. The best-known of these settlers was a minister named Thomas Hooker.

Thomas Hooker

Hooker had left the Massachusetts Bay Colony because he did not like the way the colony's Puritan leaders tried to influence the lives of the colonists. Hooker thought that a colony's government should be based on what its people wanted, not on what its leaders wanted. Many of Hooker's followers went with him to the Connecticut River valley, where they founded the settlement of Hartford. Hartford, along with Windsor and Wethersfield, united in 1636 to become the Connecticut Colony. The name *Connecticut* comes from the Mohegan (moh•HEE•guhn) Indian word *quinnitukqut*, which means "at the long tidal river."

In 1638 Hooker preached a sermon calling for a government that would be based on the consent of the people. In 1639 the Connecticut Colony adopted Hooker's idea in the form of the Fundamental Orders. The word **fundamental** means "basic." The Fundamental Orders were the first written plan of government in North America. They allowed Connecticut's voters—all landowning male colonists—to elect their leaders.

REVIEW Why did Thomas Hooker leave the Massachusetts Bay Colony?

New Hampshire

The Connecticut River valley was not the only place where Massachusetts Bay colonists went in search of more fertile land and greater economic opportunity. Some settlers moved north of the Merrimack River into what is now New Hampshire in search of these things.

The earliest permanent settlements in New Hampshire were started in the 1620s. In 1623 David Thomson founded

Location Most towns in the New England Colonies were located near a body of water.

❓ Which two rivers ran through parts of New Hampshire and Massachusetts?

the first settlement near the mouth of the Piscataqua (pi•SKA•tuh•kwaw) River. In 1630 the settlement moved to a site near a thick growth of trees and wild berries. The settlers cut down the trees and shipped them as lumber to England. The settlement was renamed Strawberry Banke. Today it is the city of Portsmouth. In 1679 the town of Strawberry Banke and other settlements in the area were united under a charter from King Charles II as the New Hampshire Colony.

REVIEW Why did some settlers move north into what is now New Hampshire?

Chapter 5 • 197

Metacomet (left) led the Wampanoags in the fight to keep their lands. Some historians believe this club (below) was Metacomet's.

Indian Wars

As settlers moved beyond the Massachusetts Bay Colony, they tried to keep peace with the region's many Indian groups. In the Connecticut River valley, however, fighting broke out between the colonists and the Pequots (PEE•kwahts). The Pequots wanted to stop the colonists from taking over Indian lands. With the help of some soldiers from the Massachusetts Bay Colony, the Connecticut settlers defeated the Pequots in the 1630s. The conflict became known as the Pequot War.

Most of the disagreements between the Native Americans and the settlers were over land ownership. The Wampanoags, Narragansetts, Mohegans, Podunks (POH•duhnks), and Nipmucs (NIP•muhks) felt that no one could "own" land. When they "sold" land to the settlers, they thought they were agreeing to share it. The English, however, expected the Indians to leave the land when they sold it.

In 1675 bad feelings between the Indians and the settlers started an all-out war. The settlers called it King Philip's War. Metacomet, known to the English as King Philip, was the leader of the Wampanoags.

After the Indian wars settlers moved into areas like northern New Hampshire.

Metacomet was also the son of Massasoit, who years earlier had helped the Pilgrims.

The war began when the Indians attacked and destroyed the town of Swansea. To get back at the Indians, the English settlers destroyed a nearby Indian settlement and took the Indians' lands. The war quickly spread as far north as present-day Maine and as far south as Connecticut. Both sides suffered terrible losses in the fighting. At least 3,000 Indians, including Metacomet, died. Among the colonists, 1 out of every 16 men of military age died.

As a result of King Philip's War, some Native American tribes were forced off their lands and very few Indians remained along the eastern coast of New England. Because many of the Indians had left, waves of settlers began pushing farther north up the Connecticut River valley into the Berkshire Hills in what is now western Massachusetts. Others moved even farther north into areas of present-day Vermont, northern New Hampshire, and Maine. The frontier was being pushed farther west as well. A **frontier** is land that lies beyond settled areas. The New England frontier separated the land settled by Europeans from the land lived on by Native Americans.

Buckets like this were often used by settlers who lived on the frontier.

REVIEW What started King Philip's War?

LESSON 2 REVIEW

Summary Time Line

1630 — 1655 — 1680

- 1635 Roger Williams is expelled from the Massachusetts Bay Colony
- 1637 Anne Hutchinson is brought to trial
- 1639 The Connecticut Colony adopts the Fundamental Orders
- 1675 King Philip's War begins

 SUMMARIZE Why did Massachusetts Bay colonists settle Connecticut and New Hampshire?

1 BIG IDEA What led some Massachusetts Bay colonists to form new colonies nearby?

2 VOCABULARY Write a sentence about Roger Williams, using the words **expel** and **consent**.

3 TIME LINE When was Anne Hutchinson brought to trial?

4 HISTORY What were the effects of King Philip's War?

5 CRITICAL THINKING—Evaluate Do you think the beliefs of leaders such as Roger Williams, Anne Hutchinson, and Thomas Hooker helped bring positive changes to the New England Colonies? Explain your answer.

 PERFORMANCE—Write a Letter Imagine that you are a follower of Thomas Hooker who has just moved to the settlement of Hartford. Write a letter to a friend in England that explains why Hooker disagreed with the leaders of the Massachusetts Bay Colony.

Chapter 5 • 199

· LESSON ·
3
New England's Economy

SUMMARIZE
As you read, summarize facts about New England's economic successes.

BIG IDEA
New England's economy depended mostly on resources found in the ocean and in the forests.

VOCABULARY
industry
export
import
triangular trade route
naval store

1625 — 1750
1700–1750

As time passed, life in New England became less difficult. Many people, especially those who lived in the coastal towns, had to struggle less to make a living. By the 1700s the great-grandchildren of the early colonists lived much more comfortable lives. This prosperity, or economic success, was based mainly on the sea and the region's dense forests. Many colonists in New England had built successful fishing, whaling, trading, and ship-building industries. An **industry** includes all the businesses that make one kind of product or provide one kind of service.

Fishing and Whaling

Many coastal towns in the New England Colonies prospered because of good fishing in the ocean waters. Because New Englanders could catch more fish than they needed, they had a surplus. The surplus catch could be dried and then sold or traded to people in Europe or to other English colonists in the West Indies.

The town of New Bedford, in Massachusetts, prospered in the 1700s because some of its settlers began catching whales in addition to hunting. Colonial whalers used methods brought from England. They launched small rowboats from beaches and hunted for whales in the waters not far from the shore. Once they captured a whale, they killed it and towed it to shore. The whalers then cut up and boiled the whale's blubber, or fat, to obtain oil.

FAST FACT
In one year, during the peak of colonial whaling, at least 350 whale-hunting ships sailed from colonial ports.

Oil made from whale blubber was used to fuel lamps.

New Englanders fished and hunted whales in the waters of the Grand Banks, near Newfoundland, and off the Greenland coast.

Oil made from whale blubber was very popular at that time because it burned brightly without an unpleasant odor. One lamp filled with burning whale oil gave as much light as, and much less smoke than, three candles.

So many New England whalers hunted close to shore that after a while the number of whales in those waters started to decline. As a result, the New England whalers began hunting in bigger ships and sailed farther out into the ocean. As the years passed, whaling trips became longer and longer. Some whaling ships left their home ports on ocean voyages that lasted for several months or even years.

REVIEW What industries helped New England coastal towns prosper?

Trading

In addition to fishing and whaling, many New England fortunes were made in trade. Ships owned by New England merchants carried trade goods to and from ports in the Caribbean, southern Europe, and England.

Many ships owned by the colonial merchants followed a direct trade route between the New England ports and England. They followed this route because the English government insisted. It wanted the colonists to send their **exports**, or goods leaving a country, only to England or to other English colonies. The English government also expected the colonists to buy only English-made **imports**, or goods brought into a country.

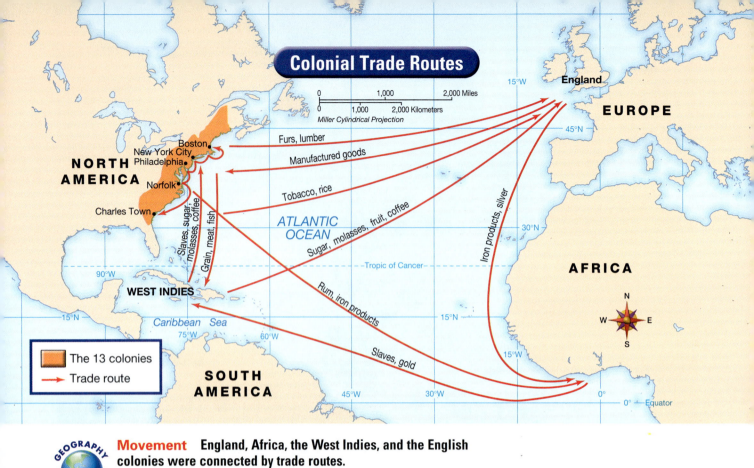

Movement England, Africa, the West Indies, and the English colonies were connected by trade routes.

> What goods did the colonies get from England?

Along this direct trade route, colonial ships from ports such as Boston and New Haven, in Connecticut, and Newport, in Rhode Island, carried exports of furs, lumber, and dried fish to England. The ships returned to the colonies with imports of tea and spices, as well as manufactured goods, such as buttons, cloth, and shoes.

Other New England trading ships followed what came to be known as **triangular trade routes**. These routes connected England, the English colonies in North America, and the west coast of Africa. They formed great imaginary triangles on the Atlantic Ocean. Trading ships carried goods from England and raw materials from the English colonies and the West Indies. Slave ships also carried enslaved people from central and western Africa. These people were used as workers in the English colonies. During this time, millions of enslaved Africans were forced to voyage across the Atlantic Ocean. The voyage across the Atlantic Ocean from Africa to the West Indies came to be known as the Middle Passage.

Barrels were used to ship goods.

The Africans suffered greatly on the slave ships. Many of them died during the Middle Passage. Their long voyage in overcrowded ships with cramped quarters was part of a large and cruel slave trade business. During the 1700s some of the people in the colonies became alarmed by the cruelty of the slave trade. Later, some of the New England colonists began to form groups that worked to end slavery.

REVIEW What were the triangular trade routes? **SUMMARIZE**

Shipbuilding

Fishing, whaling, and trading encouraged the shipbuilding industry in New England. The forests of New England provided the raw materials needed for building ships in colonial times. Logs cut in inland forests were floated down rivers to the coastal towns. There, skilled craftworkers used the logs to produce **naval stores**, the products that were used to build and repair ships. Workers used oak trees to make planks, or thick boards, for shaping ships' hulls. They used tall pines to make the masts. Pine trees also provided tar and turpentine to make pitch, a coating that is used to seal the wood and to help make a ship watertight.

Workers called coopers used wood to make barrels and casks. A cooper was a regular member of a merchant ship's crew. It was the cooper's responsibility to put together and repair barrels and casks for the long ocean voyages. Merchants used barrels to store grain, dried fish, salted meats, and other foods they traded. Casks held molasses, whale oil, and other liquids.

By the late 1700s nearly one-third of all the ships sailing under the English flag were built in the New England Colonies.

This harbor scene shows the city of Portsmouth, New Hampshire in the 1700s. Portsmouth was one of the busy ports in the New England Colonies.

This painting by Ashley Bowen, a sailor, shows a newly built ship ready to be launched.

One reason was the low cost of building ships there. Ships that were built in New England cost merchants only half of what they might have to pay for them in Europe. The shipbuilding industry contributed greatly to the growth and prosperity of many coastal towns in the New England Colonies. Some of these towns became cities. By 1750 more than 15,000 people lived in Boston. It was one of the largest cities in the North American colonies.

REVIEW In what ways did people in the shipbuilding industry earn a living?

LESSON 3 REVIEW

Summary Time Line

1700 — 1725 — 1750

- **1700s** The triangular trade routes connect England, the English colonies in North America, and the west coast of Africa
- **1750** With more than 15,000 people, Boston becomes one of the largest cities in the North American colonies

SUMMARIZE How did industries in New England help its economy prosper?

1. **BIG IDEA** In what ways did New England's economy depend on the ocean and the forests?
2. **VOCABULARY** Use the terms **export** and **import** to explain the **triangular trade routes**.
3. **TIME LINE** What happened by 1750?
4. **ECONOMICS** Why did the shipbuilding industry grow?
5. **CRITICAL THINKING—Analyze** How was colonial whaling similar to the whaling done by the Makah Indians, whom you read about in Chapter 2? How was it different?

PERFORMANCE—Draw a Poster Draw a poster that shows the products that New England colonists made from the resources found in the ocean and in the forests. Label the products, and indicate each product's connection to the ocean or the forests. Share your poster with the class.

SKILLS: Use a Line Graph

VOCABULARY
line graph

▶ WHY IT MATTERS

Soon there were 13 English colonies along the Atlantic Coast. The value of exports that these colonies sent away to England changed during the years from 1700 to 1750. The numbers that show how the value of these exports changed are very large. These numbers are easier to understand if they are placed on a line graph. A **line graph** is a graph that uses a line to show changes over time.

▶ WHAT YOU NEED TO KNOW

This line graph shows the changes in the value of colonial exports to England from 1700 to 1750. The numbers along the left side of the graph show the value of colonial exports. Across the bottom of the graph are years. As you read the red line from left to right, you see how the value changed.

▶ PRACTICE THE SKILL

Use this line graph to answer the following questions.

1. Find the year 1700 at the bottom of the graph. Move your finger up from that date until you reach the red dot. Then move your finger left to the value numbers. Your finger will be a little below 500,000, so you will need to estimate the value. To *estimate* is to make a close guess. The value of the exports was worth about 375,000 English pounds in 1700. Pounds are the name of the English currency.

2. Now find 1740 at the bottom of the graph. Repeat the process. About how many pounds was the value of exports in that year?

3. Look at the red line on the graph. How did the value of exports change?

▶ APPLY WHAT YOU LEARNED

On this graph notice that the value of exports decreased between 1700 and 1710. What factors could have caused the value to decrease during those years?

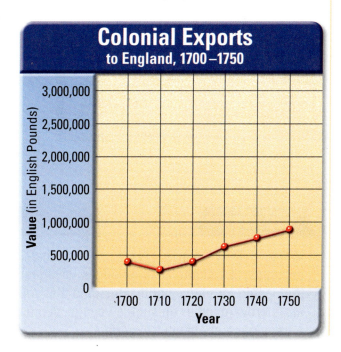

CHAPTER 5

Review and Test Preparation

Summary Time Line

- **1628** The first group of Puritans arrives in New England
- **1635** Roger Williams is expelled from the Massachusetts Bay Colony
- **1637** Anne Hutchinson is brought to trial

Focus Skill: Summarize

Copy the following graphic organizer onto a separate sheet of paper. Use the information you have learned to summarize facts about the Massachusetts Bay Colony.

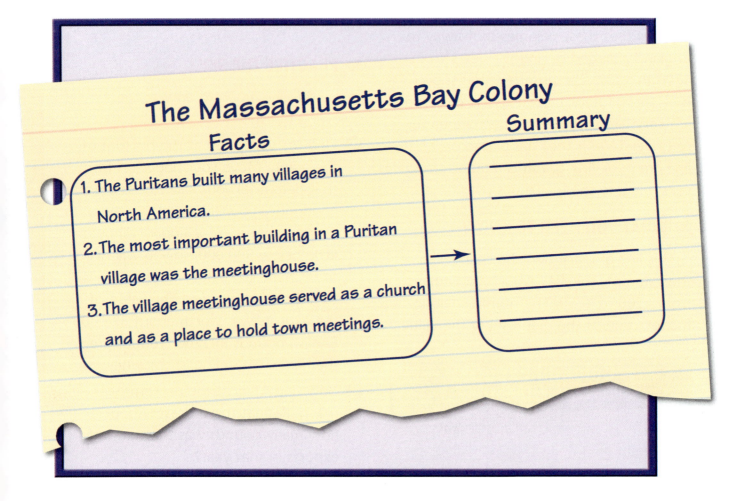

The Massachusetts Bay Colony

Facts:
1. The Puritans built many villages in North America.
2. The most important building in a Puritan village was the meetinghouse.
3. The village meetinghouse served as a church and as a place to hold town meetings.

THINK & WRITE

Write a Folktale Every New England town had several public-office jobs. These jobs included constable, town crier, and fence viewer. Write a folktale about a person who held one of these jobs.

Write a Travelogue New England whaling ships sometimes went on ocean voyages that lasted for many months. Imagine that you are a crew member on such a voyage. Write a travelogue about your experiences.

| 1675 | 1700 | 1725 | 1750 |

- **1639** The Fundamental Orders are adopted by the Connecticut Colony
- **1675** King Philip's War begins
- **1750** Boston becomes one of the largest cities in North America

USE THE TIME LINE

Use the chapter summary time line to answer these questions.

1. When did the first group of Puritans arrive in New England?
2. When did King Philip's War begin?

USE VOCABULARY

Use a term from this list to complete each of the following sentences.

town meeting (p. 192)
consent (p. 195)
sedition (p. 196)
industry (p. 200)
naval stores (p. 203)

3. The government of Providence was based on the ____ of the settlers.
4. The ____ was where public officers were elected.
5. Anne Hutchinson was brought to trial on charges of ____.
6. A major ____ in New England was shipbuilding.
7. Logs from New England forests were used to produce ____.

RECALL FACTS

Answer these questions.

8. What group of settlers set up the first community schools in the New England Colonies?
9. What were some of the results of King Philip's War?
10. Why was New England a good location for the shipbuilding industry?

Write the letter of the best choice.

11. Problems developed between the New England colonists and Native Americans because—
    A the colonists forced Native Americans to work on their farms.
    B Native Americans refused to trade furs with the colonists.
    C the two groups had different understandings of land ownership.
    D Native Americans never offered the colonists any help.

12. The New England colonists used whale blubber to make—
    F tar.
    G turpentine.
    H molasses.
    J lamp oil.

THINK CRITICALLY

13. Compare the system of government of the Connecticut Colony to that of the Massachusetts Bay Colony.
14. How might history have been different if King Philip's War had not taken place?

APPLY SKILLS

Use a Line Graph

15. Look in newspapers or magazines for a line graph that shows a trend. Cut out the graph and tape it to a sheet of paper. Below the graph, identify the trend shown. How does the trend change over time?

Chapter 5 ■ 207

LANCASTER COUNTY

Many early immigrants settled in Pennsylvania because of its rich farmland. Today, areas such as Lancaster County continue to produce a variety of crops. Among the Amish and Mennonite families who make their homes here, many live and work in the same manner as their eighteenth century ancestors.

LOCATE IT

PENNSYLVANIA

Lancaster County

CHAPTER 6

The Middle Atlantic Colonies

> " The Fields, most beautiful, yield such Crops of Wheat, And other things most excellent to eat. "
> —Richard Frame, *A Short Description of Pennsylvania,* 1692

Make Inferences

When you make an **inference,** you use facts and your own experiences to come to a conclusion.

As you read this chapter, be sure to do the following.

- List facts about the Middle Atlantic Colonies. Then list information from your own experiences.
- Use the lists to make inferences.

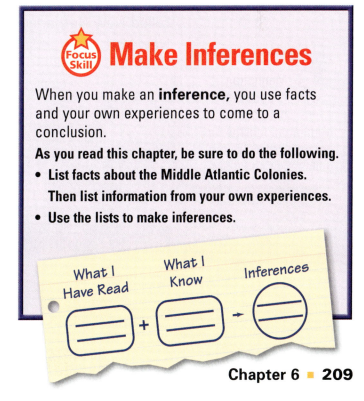

What I Have Read + What I Know → Inferences

Chapter 6 ■ 209

LESSON 1

Breadbasket Colonies

1625 – 1750
1625–1700

 MAKE INFERENCES
As you read, make inferences about people, places, and events in the Middle Atlantic Colonies.

BIG IDEA
The Middle Atlantic Colonies attracted people of many different cultures and religions.

VOCABULARY
refuge
trial by jury
justice
farm produce
Great Awakening

While the Puritans were building settlements in New England, other settlers were establishing colonies to the south. This region, which included present-day New York, New Jersey, Delaware, and Pennsylvania, came to be known as the Middle Atlantic Colonies.

The first settlers in the Middle Atlantic region discovered that when the land was cleared of trees and rocks, it was good for farming. The climate was also good for growing crops. The summers were long, and the amount of rain each year was just right for crops such as wheat, corn, and rye. In fact, the Middle Atlantic Colonies produced so many crops used in making bread that they came to be called the "breadbasket" colonies. The region's rich resources attracted people from many European countries and people of various religions.

New Netherland

Not long after the English started colonies in North America, the Dutch began to build settlements in their own colony, called New Netherland. They settled in parts of what are today New York, New Jersey, and Delaware. The Dutch came to the

FAST FACT Manhattan Island was bought from the Manhattan Indians for goods worth 60 Dutch guilders, or about $24.

area because the explorer Henry Hudson had claimed it for their country, Holland, in 1609.

A few years after Hudson's visit, the New Netherland Company established several trading posts in the Hudson River valley. In 1621 the Dutch West India Company took control of trade in the area. The first Dutch settlers arrived three years later. Some were sent to a fort on the Delaware River, and others sailed to a fort on the Hudson River.

In 1626 the Dutch began building a fort and laying out a town on Manhattan Island in New York Bay. They called the settlement New Amsterdam. In that same year Peter Minuit (MIN•yuh•wuht), one of the directors of the New Netherland Colony, bought Manhattan Island from the Manhattan Indians. During the next few years, New Amsterdam grew and became the capital of New Netherland. The Dutch built other settlements that would one day become Brooklyn, Kingston, Rensselaer (ren•suh•LIR), and Schenectady (skuh•NEK•tuh•dee), New York.

The Dutch welcomed settlers to New Amsterdam from many countries. People from Belgium, Denmark, France, Italy, and Spain all made their homes there. Among these newcomers was the first group of Jews to settle in North America. However, the Jews in New Amsterdam did not have many of the same rights as Christian colonists had. Under Dutch rule, Jews could not work at certain jobs and could not freely practice their religion.

REVIEW Where did the Dutch first settle in North America?

GEOGRAPHY THEME

Place New Amsterdam was the capital of New Netherland. The Dutch and Swedish colonies eventually became English colonies.

◆ What natural resources do you think the colonists used?

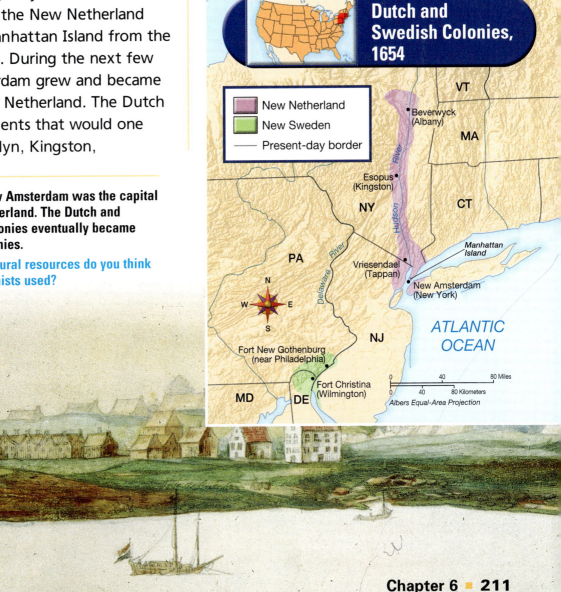

Dutch and Swedish Colonies, 1654

Middle Atlantic Colonies

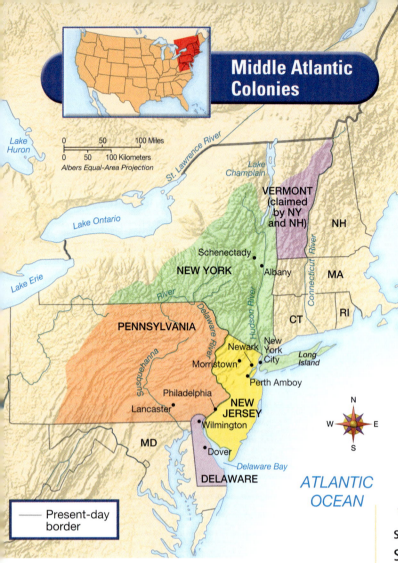

Regions Many towns in the Middle Atlantic Colonies were located near waterways.

◆ What were some of the waterways in the Middle Atlantic Colonies?

New Netherland Becomes New York

In 1646 the Dutch West India Company appointed Peter Stuyvesant (STY•vuh•suhnt) as director general of New Netherland. When Stuyvesant arrived in New Amsterdam the following year, he found New Netherland in trouble. The government was having problems. The settlers were fighting over land with the neighboring Delaware and Wappinger (WAHP•ihn•jer) Indians and with other European colonists. Not long after he arrived, however, Stuyvesant helped resolve the conflicts over land.

Stuyvesant's strong way of ruling helped solve some problems, but it created new problems between him and the colonists. The colonists wanted more voice in their government, which Stuyvesant would not allow. Despite such disagreements, the colony prospered under Stuyvesant's leadership. He expanded New Netherland into what is now New Jersey. Then he pushed south into what is now Delaware, taking over the small colony of New Sweden in 1655. Swedish settlers had founded the colony in 1638. It was chiefly a group of trading posts built around Fort Christina, where today Wilmington, Delaware, stands.

Even though the population of New Netherland remained small, the English still thought that the Dutch colony prevented their own colonies from expanding. This was one reason King Charles II of England declared war on Holland. The king then told his brother, James, the Duke of York, that he could have the Dutch colonies if he could seize them.

Peter Stuyvesant

This Quaker meetinghouse was located in New Jersey. Chests (above) like this one could often be found in Quaker homes.

In 1664 English warships sailed into the harbor at New Amsterdam. Stuyvesant tried to get the Dutch settlers to fight the English, but they refused. Stuyvesant had to give up the colony. The English split up New Netherland, giving it the present-day names of New Jersey and New York. New York City grew from the Dutch capital, New Amsterdam.

REVIEW What were some of Peter Stuyvesant's accomplishments?

New Jersey

Not long after the English divided New Netherland, the Duke of York gave New Jersey and part of New York to John Berkeley and George Carteret. The two offered to sell the land at low prices to anyone in England willing to settle in North America. The offer attracted many settlers to New Jersey. Among them were numerous members of the Society of Friends, a religious group also known as the Quakers. In 1674 a group of Quakers led by Edward Byllinge bought Berkeley's share of New Jersey. They started the first colony in North America founded by Quakers.

The Quakers believe that all people are equal and basically good. Because they think that violence is always wrong, they refuse to carry guns or to fight. They also believe in solving all problems peacefully. In England, Quakers often were treated poorly because of their beliefs, particularly their refusal to fight for the king. In New Jersey, they hoped to find a **refuge**, or safe place, where they could live and worship as they pleased.

REVIEW Why did many Quakers refuse to fight for the English King?
MAKE INFERENCES

Pennsylvania and Delaware

While New Jersey was being sold to groups of Quakers, King Charles II gave a charter to William Penn, who had become a Quaker. The charter made Penn the proprietor, or owner, of what is now Pennsylvania. The English king granted him the region because the king owed a debt to Penn's father. Penn wanted to call his new colony *Sylvania*, which means "woods." King Charles asked that the land be named Pennsylvania.

Chapter 6 ■ 213

DEMOCRATIC VALUES
Justice

In his Frame of Government of Pennsylvania, William Penn included the idea that all citizens of the Pennsylvania Colony were to be treated equally by the law.

Penn's Frame of Government guaranteed everyone the right to a trial by jury. This right was important because it allowed a group of citizens, instead of a single judge, to decide whether or not someone had broken the law. This method is a more democratic way of making this kind of decision. It gives decision-making control to the people. In most countries there was no right to trial by jury.

Today the United States government upholds the idea of equal justice for all. All people in the United States have the right to a fair trial and to equal treatment under the law.

Analyze the Value

1. How did Penn make sure people in the colony would be treated equally under the law?
2. **Make It Relevant** Imagine that a student in your school has been accused of breaking a school rule. With some classmates, decide whether one person or a group should determine whether the student really broke the rule.

William Penn with Indian leaders

The new name, which means "Penn's woods," honored William's father.

Before coming to Pennsylvania, William Penn planned his colony's government. In 1682 he wrote a document called the Frame of Government of Pennsylvania. It provided for a legislature called the General Assembly to make the laws for the colony. Penn's Frame of Government also provided for the citizens of Pennsylvania to have freedom of speech, freedom of worship, and trial by jury. **Trial by jury** guarantees a person accused of breaking the law the right to be tried by a jury of fellow citizens.

When Penn arrived in Pennsylvania, he met with many of the leaders of the local Delaware Indian tribes. He paid them for most of the land King Charles II had given him. A legend says that Penn and Tamenend (TAM•uh•nehnd), a chief of the Delaware people, exchanged wampum belts as a sign of friendship. Indian leaders came to respect Penn and believed he was their friend. Penn had said, "Let them have justice, and you win them." Penn also ensured that his colonists were ruled with **justice**, or fairness.

Penn also became the owner of what is now Delaware. When colonists in Delaware asked for their own general assembly, Penn granted it to them. The first Delaware General Assembly met in 1704.

REVIEW What did the right of trial by jury guarantee a person?

Market Towns

Most people in the Middle Atlantic Colonies made their living by farming. Because the soil was fertile and the land was not too mountainous, many were able to develop large farms. On these farms they were able to grow enough food to feed their families and also have a surplus.

Farmers depended on market towns as places to trade their livestock and their surplus **farm produce**—grains, fruits, and vegetables—for goods and services. Market towns became a common sight throughout the Middle Atlantic Colonies.

In most market towns a general store sold goods, such as tools, cloth, shoes, stockings, and buttons. Near the general store there was often the shop of a cobbler, who made and repaired shoes. Nearby there was also a gristmill, where grain was ground into flour and meal, and a sawmill, where logs were sawed into lumber.

Unlike the New England Colonies, the Middle Atlantic Colonies welcomed people of different religions. Towns in these colonies often had more than one kind of church. A Presbyterian church, for example, might be only a block away from a Methodist church and a Quaker meetinghouse.

Interest in religion led to the **Great Awakening**, a movement that called for a rebirth of religious ways of life. This way of thinking quickly spread through other English colonies during the 1730s and 1740s.

Wheat was traded in market towns.

REVIEW What kinds of goods were bought and sold in market towns?

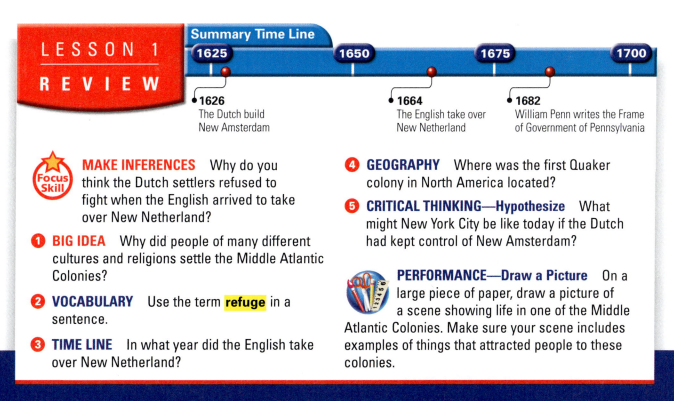

LESSON 1 REVIEW

Summary Time Line

- 1626 — The Dutch build New Amsterdam
- 1664 — The English take over New Netherland
- 1682 — William Penn writes the Frame of Government of Pennsylvania

MAKE INFERENCES Why do you think the Dutch settlers refused to fight when the English arrived to take over New Netherland?

1. **BIG IDEA** Why did people of many different cultures and religions settle the Middle Atlantic Colonies?

2. **VOCABULARY** Use the term **refuge** in a sentence.

3. **TIME LINE** In what year did the English take over New Netherland?

4. **GEOGRAPHY** Where was the first Quaker colony in North America located?

5. **CRITICAL THINKING—Hypothesize** What might New York City be like today if the Dutch had kept control of New Amsterdam?

PERFORMANCE—Draw a Picture On a large piece of paper, draw a picture of a scene showing life in one of the Middle Atlantic Colonies. Make sure your scene includes examples of things that attracted people to these colonies.

Chapter 6 ■ 215

Examine Primary Sources

Great Awakening Sermons

In the 1730s and 1740s, The Great Awakening swept the English-speaking world. The Great Awakening was a revival, or rebirth, of the importance of religion in people's lives. In the colonies of North America, it was led at first by a minister named George Whitefield. He traveled from Maine to Georgia preaching sermons. Whitefield and The Great Awakening were not popular with all people. In the end, however, The Great Awakening contributed to a new sense of unity among all the English colonists.

FROM THE LIBRARY OF CONGRESS ONLINE EXHIBIT "RELIGION AND FOUNDING OF THE AMERICAN REPUBLIC"

George Whitefield used this collapsible field pulpit for open-air preaching.

George Whitefield

Many sermons delivered by the preachers of the Great Awakening were later published as books.

Analyze the Primary Source

1. In which colonies did Gilbert Tennent and Jonathan Edwards live?
2. When and where were the original sermons delivered?
3. When and where were the sermons published as books?
4. Who printed Tennent's sermon?

Gilbert Tennent

Jonathan Edwards

ACTIVITY

Write to Explain Make a list of the kinds of things that people might learn from sermons. Then use your list to help you write a paragraph about why you think sermons were important to the people in the colonies.

RESEARCH

Visit The Learning Site at www.harcourtschool.com to research other primary sources.

Chapter 6 ■ 217

LESSON 2

Colonial Philadelphia

1625 — 1750
1700–1750

MAKE INFERENCES
As you read, make inferences about people, places, and events in Philadelphia.

BIG IDEA
Philadelphia became the Pennsylvania Colony's main port.

VOCABULARY
township
immigrant
militia
almanac

As proprietor of the Pennsylvania Colony, William Penn planned not only its government but also its settlements. One of them, Philadelphia, became the largest and wealthiest city in all the English colonies of North America. By 1770 it had more than 28,000 people—a small population by today's city standards but very large for that time.

Early Colonial Days

William Penn named his colony's chief city Philadelphia, a word meaning "brotherly love" in Greek. Like all of Pennsylvania, Philadelphia was founded on the idea that people of diverse backgrounds could get along with each other. That idea was reflected in the layout of most of the colony's settlements. Penn wanted to divide his colony into townships. Each **township**, or area of land, would be 5,000 acres—a space large enough for ten families. Land belonging to individual families would be carved out of the township in giant pie-like slices. Penn wanted settlers to build their homes at the tips of the slices so that every family would be within walking distance of one another and of whatever church they chose to build.

Philadelphia grew to become one of the largest cities in the English colonies.

William Penn had a different layout in mind for Philadelphia, his colony's most important town. It covered a strip of land between the Schuylkill (SKOO•kuhl) River on the west and the Delaware River on the east. Early drawings of one plan looked like a checkerboard, with straight streets laid out in great squares. Public parks added open spaces to the city that Penn called "a green country town."

Philadelphia's location near good land and waterways contributed to growth in shipping and trading. During the 1700s Philadelphia developed into one of the busiest ports in the English colonies. By 1710 it had become the largest city in the colonies. Chief among its exports were farm products such as wheat, corn, rye, hemp, and flax. Imports consisted mostly of manufactured goods from England, which were then sent all over the Middle Atlantic Colonies.

REVIEW What did William Penn accomplish as leader of the Pennsylvania Colony?

The People of Philadelphia

Philadelphia soon became the main port in Pennsylvania for receiving not only imports but also immigrants. An **immigrant** is a person who comes into a country to make a new home there. According to Reverend William Smith, Philadelphians in the 1700s were "a people, thrown together from various quarters of the world, differing in all things—language, manners and sentiment [attitude]."

The largest group in Philadelphia was made up of English and Welsh Quakers.

Place As shown on this present-day map of Center City (right), the checkerboard pattern of William Penn's city plan can still be seen.

◆ What rivers form the east and west boundaries of Center City?

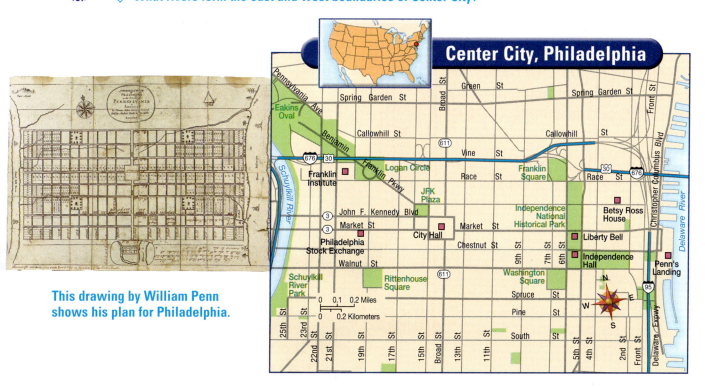

This drawing by William Penn shows his plan for Philadelphia.

Chapter 6 ■ 219

Some advertisements (below) on playing cards encouraged settlers to move to the colonies. The two cards below show people buying and settling land. The scene (left) shows a farm in Pennsylvania.

They had arrived with William Penn. Later, Irish Catholics, German Lutherans, and Jews from many countries arrived. Free Africans came, too.

Some immigrants came to Philadelphia to find refuge from war and famine, or shortage of food, in their homelands. Many sought religious freedom. Others came because Philadelphia quickly gained a reputation for offering economic opportunity. Immigrants arriving in the city included farmers and skilled workers, such as bakers, blacksmiths, butchers, carpenters, shoemakers, and tailors. They set up their own shops, selling goods and services in Philadelphia and in other Pennsylvania settlements nearby.

One of the largest groups of immigrants to arrive in Philadelphia came from what is now Germany. The Germans brought with them many of their customs and traditions, including barn raising. First, a farmer dug his barn's foundation and prepared a frame made of lumber. He then invited his friends and neighbors and their families to help raise the frame into place. To feed all the people, the families prepared huge meals.

German immigrant gunmakers developed the long-barrel gun called the Pennsylvania rifle. In the 1700s it was the most accurate rifle in the world. It was particularly valued on the frontier, where accurate weapons were needed for hunting. German craftworkers also designed a deep-bellied wagon known as the Conestoga. Conestoga wagons were larger than regular wagons and were first used mainly by farmers to carry produce to market.

Scotch-Irish settlers also came to Pennsylvania. These were people from Scotland who had settled in northern Ireland in the 1600s.

When a visitor from England first saw Conestogas, he called them "huge moving houses."

The Union Fire Company was, according to Benjamin Franklin (left), the first group of firefighters he organized. After Franklin raised money to build a hospital, others were soon built (right).

Many of them and their descendants came to the English colonies. Like other immigrants to Pennsylvania, they entered the colony through the port of Philadelphia. Then they moved into the hilly frontier areas located near the Appalachian Mountains.

REVIEW Why did so many immigrants choose to come to Philadelphia?
 MAKE INFERENCES

Benjamin Franklin and His City

The story of Benjamin Franklin's rise to wealth and fame matches colonial Philadelphia's rise to become one of the most prosperous cities in the English colonies. As a citizen, Franklin left a strong mark on the growing city. He organized the first trained firefighting company in the 13 colonies and the first fire insurance company. He worked to have Philadelphia's streets paved and lit at night. He raised money to help build the first hospital in Philadelphia. He also organized a **militia**, or volunteer army, to protect Philadelphia and the frontier settlements.

As a scientist, Franklin is best known for his experiments with electricity. It is believed that he proved that lightning is a form of electricity by tying a metal key to the string on his childhood kite and flying the kite in a thunderstorm. Using what he learned from his experiments, Franklin invented the lightning rod. A lightning rod is a straight, thin bar of metal attached to the top of a house or barn. It conducts, or guides, lightning into the ground. As a result, the building will not be damaged if it is struck. Until the invention of the lightning rod, buildings struck by lightning were likely to burst into flames.

Benjamin Franklin's interest in learning included the education of others. He even helped establish the first library in the colonies which people could subscribe to.

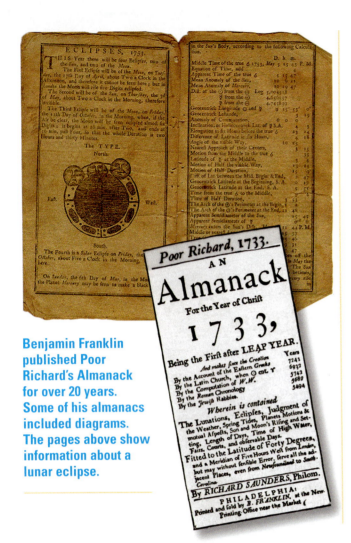

Benjamin Franklin published Poor Richard's Almanack for over 20 years. Some of his almanacs included diagrams. The pages above show information about a lunar eclipse.

Colonists could borrow books after paying a small fee to become a member of the library. As a result, people seeking knowledge did not have to pay much money. Franklin's opinions on education were used, too, when a school called the Philadelphia Academy was founded.

As a printer, Benjamin Franklin helped make Philadelphia a major publishing center in the English colonies. In 1729 he started printing a newspaper, the *Pennsylvania Gazette*. In 1732 he began publishing *Poor Richard's Almanack*. An almanac is a book issued only once each year. Franklin's had a calendar and a yearly weather forecast, which helped farmers know the best time to plant crops. It also had stories, jokes, and witty sayings, such as "Early to bed and early to rise, makes a man healthy, wealthy, and wise."

REVIEW What were some of Benjamin Franklin's contributions as a scientist and inventor?

LESSON 2 REVIEW

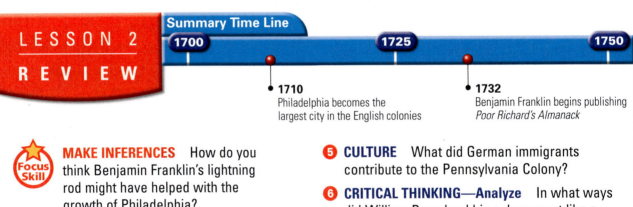

Summary Time Line

- 1710 Philadelphia becomes the largest city in the English colonies
- 1732 Benjamin Franklin begins publishing *Poor Richard's Almanack*

MAKE INFERENCES How do you think Benjamin Franklin's lightning rod might have helped with the growth of Philadelphia?

1. **BIG IDEA** Why did Philadelphia become the Pennsylvania Colony's main port?

2. **VOCABULARY** Use the term immigrant in a sentence to describe why some people settled in Philadelphia.

3. **TIME LINE** When did Philadelphia become the largest city in the English colonies?

4. **ECONOMICS** What were some of Philadelphia's chief exports?

5. **CULTURE** What did German immigrants contribute to the Pennsylvania Colony?

6. **CRITICAL THINKING—Analyze** In what ways did William Penn lead his colony most like a leader in the United States today?

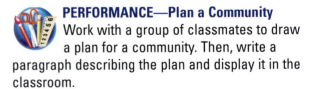

PERFORMANCE—Plan a Community Work with a group of classmates to draw a plan for a community. Then, write a paragraph describing the plan and display it in the classroom.

SKILLS: Use a Circle Graph

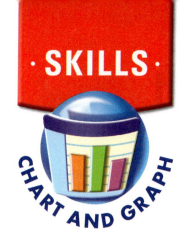

VOCABULARY
circle graph

▶ WHY IT MATTERS

Suppose you want to show in a simple, clear way how the population of the 13 colonies was divided between the New England, Middle Atlantic, and Southern Colonies. One way to show the information is by making a **circle graph**. A circle graph is sometimes called a pie graph because it is round and is divided into pieces, or parts, like a pie is.

▶ WHAT YOU NEED TO KNOW

The circle graph below shows the population of the 13 English colonies in the year 1750. The graph's parts are the colonial regions that made up the population.

A percent, shown by the symbol % in the graph, is given to each part of the graph. A percent is one-hundredth of something. For example, if you cut a pie into 100 pieces, those 100 pieces together equal the whole pie, or 100 percent (100%) of it. Fifty pieces would be one-half of the pie, or 50% of it. Ten pieces would be one-tenth of the pie, or 10% of it. Each piece would be one-hundredth, or 1%, of the pie.

▶ PRACTICE THE SKILL

Use the circle graph to answer the following questions.

1. In which region did the largest part of the population in the 13 colonies live in 1750?
2. What percent of the total population did the region with the largest population make up?
3. What percent of the total population did the Middle Atlantic Colonies make up?
4. What percent was made up by the New England Colonies?

▶ APPLY WHAT YOU LEARNED

Use information from the circle graph to write a paragraph about the different colonial regions in the 13 colonies. Compare the population sizes of the regions.

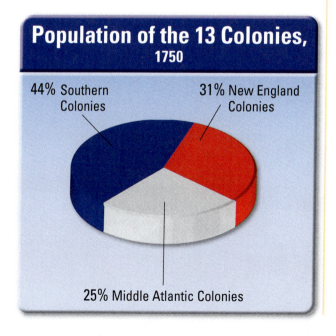

Population of the 13 Colonies, 1750
- 44% Southern Colonies
- 31% New England Colonies
- 25% Middle Atlantic Colonies

Chapter 6

LESSON 3

Moving West

 MAKE INFERENCES
As you read, make inferences about people, places, and events in the new western lands.

BIG IDEA
Colonists faced many challenges as they settled on lands farther west.

VOCABULARY
backcountry
loft

Settlers from Pennsylvania, especially the Germans and the Scotch-Irish, were among the first to settle farther inland, away from the Atlantic coast. There they claimed what they saw as open land, even though American Indians lived there. They hoped to make a piece of the frontier into a farm, where they could build a house and raise a family. They felt that moving to the frontier would give them a chance for a better life.

The Great Wagon Road

In the early 1700s most cities, towns, farms, and plantations in the 13 English colonies were located near the coast, in the Coastal Plain region. At that time, few colonists had settled in the Piedmont—the land between the Coastal Plain and the Appalachian Mountains. Settlers called this frontier region the **backcountry** because it was beyond, or "in back of," the area settled by Europeans.

The waterfalls in the rivers along the Fall Line and the lack of roads made travel to the backcountry difficult. To get around the waterfalls, settlers had to portage, or carry overland, their boats and supplies. This kind of travel was so difficult that it discouraged many settlers from moving inland.

This forested land in Virginia was once a part of the backcountry.

By the mid-1700s many settlers in the 13 colonies began to settle in areas west of the Coastal Plain. From Pennsylvania large numbers of German and Scotch-Irish immigrants had begun moving into the backcountry of western Virginia, North Carolina, and South Carolina. To get there, the settlers followed an old Indian trail. As more and more settlers used the trail, it became wider and wider. Finally, wagons could travel on it, and it became known as the Great Wagon Road.

From Pennsylvania the Great Wagon Road passed through the Shenandoah Valley of Virginia and along the eastern side of the Blue Ridge Mountains. The land there was hilly, and travel on the road was difficult. "[In places] it was so slippery the horses could not keep their footing but fell . . . to their knees," wrote one early traveler. However, the Great Wagon Road was the only way to get wagons loaded with household goods to the backcountry.

Thousands of people followed the Great Wagon Road to move inland from Pennsylvania. Among them was a young man named Daniel Boone. When Boone was 16 years old, his family followed the Great Wagon Road to settle in the Yadkin Valley in North Carolina. The journey took more than a year. Later, Boone would become a well-known explorer who made new trails that took settlers even farther west.

REVIEW Why was the Great Wagon Road important to the settlement of the frontier?

 MAKE INFERENCES

Movement Thousands of settlers moved to the backcountry to start farms.
◆ By what year had settlers moved the farthest west?

Chapter 6 ■ 225

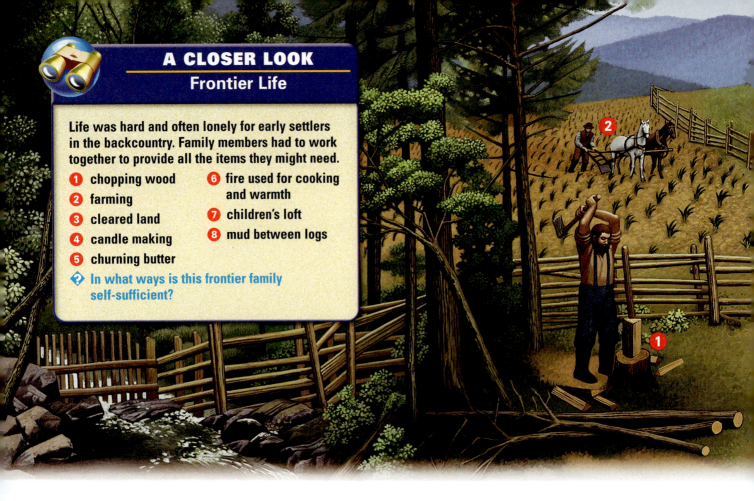

A CLOSER LOOK
Frontier Life

Life was hard and often lonely for early settlers in the backcountry. Family members had to work together to provide all the items they might need.

1. chopping wood
2. farming
3. cleared land
4. candle making
5. churning butter
6. fire used for cooking and warmth
7. children's loft
8. mud between logs

❓ In what ways is this frontier family self-sufficient?

Life in the Backcountry

Most of the people who settled the backcountry lived simply. Their homes were log huts with chimneys made of sticks and mud. Most homes had one room with a dirt floor and no windows. Light came through the open door in the daytime and from the fireplace at night. Families burned wood in the fireplace to cook their food and to keep warm.

At night the adults in a family spread their blankets over piles of dry leaves on the floor. The children slept in the **loft**, a part of the house between the ceiling and the roof. To get up to the loft, they climbed a ladder, which was often just wooden pegs driven into the wall.

A settler named Oliver Johnson remembered sleeping in a loft when he was a child growing up on the frontier. He wrote, "If you slept in the loft, you pulled your head under the covers during a storm. When you got up in the mornin[g], you [would] shake the snow off the covers, grab your shirt and britches [pants] and hop down the ladder to the fireplace, where it was good and warm."

People on the frontier worked hard to get food, hunting in the forests and farming in the clearings. They farmed in the Indian way. They planted corn, beans, and squash all in the same mound of soil. The cornstalks provided a stake for the beans to climb. The squash vines spread out on the ground between the mounds.

As families had done in early New England, frontier families made almost everything they needed. They churned their own butter, dyed their own cloth, and made their own soap and candles. Those who could not do things for themselves, a frontier minister observed

in 1711, would "have but a bad time of it; for help is not to be had at any rate."

Life on the frontier was full of dangers. Families had to protect themselves not only from wild animals but also from possible attacks from Indians or other settlers. Despite these dangers, people still moved farther and farther west. By the mid-1700s, English settlers had crossed the Appalachian Mountains into the Ohio Valley. The land that they moved into was also claimed by France.

REVIEW How did frontier families get the food and goods they needed?

LESSON 3 REVIEW

MAKE INFERENCES What do you think life was like for English settlers in the Ohio Valley if the land they lived on was also being claimed by France?

1 BIG IDEA How did settlers meet the challenges of living on the frontier?

2 VOCABULARY Write a sentence about frontier life, using the terms **backcountry** and **loft**.

3 HISTORY Why did settlers move west?

4 CRITICAL THINKING—Synthesize Why do you think settlers of the backcountry were willing to face the hardships there?

PERFORMANCE—Write a Journal Entry Imagine that you are a settler who has moved to the frontier in the early 1700s. Write a journal entry in which you describe your journey to the backcountry and the building of your new home.

Chapter 6 ■ 227

CHAPTER 6

Review and Test Preparation

Summary Time Line

1624 — The first Dutch settlers arrive in New Netherland

Make Inferences

Copy the following graphic organizer onto a separate sheet of paper. Use the information you have learned to make inferences about the Middle Atlantic Colonies.

Breadbasket Colonies

What I Have Read: The Middle Atlantic Colonies attracted people from many different backgrounds.

What I Know:

Inference:

THINK & WRITE

Write a Wise Saying Benjamin Franklin's *Poor Richard's Almanack* included many wise sayings such as, "If you have time, don't wait for time." Many of these sayings suggested that good behavior is often rewarded. Write a wise saying about the benefits of behaving well.

Write a Song Imagine the year is 1750 and your family is moving to the backcountry. Write a song about your family's journey along the Great Wagon Road. Be sure to describe the changing environment and the difficulties your family must overcome on the journey.

1664 The English take over New Amsterdam

1675

1682 William Penn writes the Frame of Government of Pennsylvania

1700

1710 Philadelphia becomes the largest city in the Middle Atlantic Colonies

1725

1732 Benjamin Franklin begins publishing *Poor Richard's Almanack*

1750

USE THE TIME LINE

Use the chapter summary time line to answer these questions.

1 When did the first Dutch settlers arrive in New Netherland?

2 When did William Penn write the Frame of Government of Pennsylvania?

USE VOCABULARY

For each pair of terms, write a sentence that explains how the terms are related.

3 trial by jury (p. 214), justice (p. 214)

4 township (p. 218), militia (p. 221)

5 backcountry (p. 224), loft (p. 226)

RECALL FACTS

Answer these questions.

6 Why did King Charles II grant William Penn the charter to Pennsylvania?

7 How did German immigrant craftworkers contribute to western settlement?

8 What was the name of the trail followed by settlers moving west from Pennsylvania?

Write the letter of the best choice.

9 The Middle Atlantic Colonies included New York, New Jersey, Pennsylvania, and—
  A Connecticut.
  B Delaware.
  C Massachusetts.
  D Virginia.

10 Farmers in the Middle Atlantic Colonies depended on market towns as places to—
  F meet with local Native American tribes.
  G sell their furs to European merchants.
  H trade their surplus farm produce for goods and services.
  J purchase naval stores.

11 Benjamin Franklin contributed to the education of others by—
  A helping start the Great Awakening.
  B designing the layout for the city of Philadelphia.
  C establishing the first subscription library in the colonies.
  D printing playing cards.

THINK CRITICALLY

12 What do you think was William Penn's greatest accomplishment as proprietor of Pennsylvania?

13 Why do you think Benjamin Franklin took such an active part in community life?

14 What do you think backcountry families did when a family member became sick?

APPLY SKILLS

Use a Circle Graph

15 Look in newspapers, magazines, or on the Internet to find an example of a circle graph. Cut out or print out the graph, and tape it to a sheet of paper. Then write a paragraph about what the graph represents.

Chapter 6 ■ 229

CHESAPEAKE BAY

For hundreds of years the Chesapeake Bay has shaped the history, culture, and economy of Virginia and Maryland. The bay takes its name from the Native American word *Chesepiooc,* meaning "Great Shellfish Bay." Today, more than 15 million people live along its shores.

LOCATE IT

MARYLAND

Hooper Island

CHAPTER 7

The Southern Colonies

" Heaven and earth never agreed to frame a better place for man's habitation. "
—John Smith, on Chesapeake Bay, 1607

Focus Skill: Generalize

When you **generalize,** you summarize a group of facts and show how they are related.

As you read this chapter, make generalizations.
- Identify and list important facts.
- Use the facts to make generalizations about the Southern Colonies.

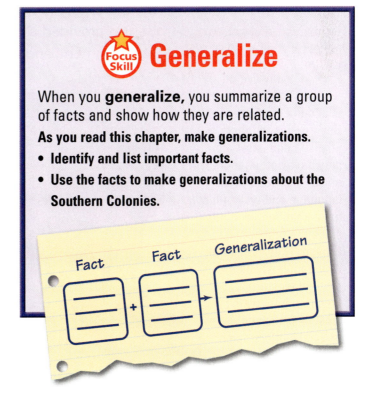

LESSON 1

Settlement of the South

1633–1733

In 1606 the king of England granted the Virginia Company a charter allowing settlement of the Chesapeake Bay region. In 1607 Virginia became the first permanent English colony in North America. By the 1730s the English had settled the remaining colonies in the South—Maryland, North Carolina, South Carolina, and Georgia. With its 13 colonies, the English claimed much of the Atlantic coast of North America from present-day Maine to present-day Georgia.

GENERALIZE
As you read, make generalizations about settlements in the Southern Colonies.

BIG IDEA
Selling crops was important to the success of the Southern Colonies.

VOCABULARY
indentured servant
constitution
indigo
debtor

Maryland

Maryland was founded by the Calverts, a family of wealthy English landowners. The Calverts, who were Catholic, wanted to build a colony in North America that not only made money but also provided a refuge for Catholics. Like English Quakers, Catholics in England could not worship as they wanted.

George Calvert, the first Lord Baltimore, had been a member of the Virginia Company. He had purchased a large amount of land on the large island of Newfoundland, in what is now Canada. His goal had been to establish a colony there, but he found the climate too cold and the soil too rocky. In 1628, with Lady Baltimore,

FAST FACT
The people who today live on Tangier (tan•JIR) Island in Chesapeake Bay are descendants of English colonists, who may have settled there as early as 1686. Their language and way of life have changed very little since the first settlers arrived. They speak the way people speak in parts of western England, from which most of the island's original settlers came.

George Calvert, the first Lord Baltimore

232 ■ Unit 3

GEOGRAPHY

St. Marys City
Understanding Places and Regions

St. Marys City, Maryland, is located near the mouth of the Potomac River. For most of the 1600s the town served as Maryland's first capital. Then the capital was moved to Annapolis, and the town was abandoned. Later the area was used as a tobacco plantation. In the 1970s historians and archaeologists dug up the area on which they thought the town once stood. What they discovered was a town designed in the shape of two triangles that met at a central square.

This painting by Walter Crowe shows St. Marys City in 1685.

he traveled south to the Chesapeake Bay region. There they found a site where the climate was mild and the soil was rich. King Charles I signed the final colonial charter two months after George Calvert died in 1632. The king gave the grant to Cecilius Calvert, George Calvert's oldest son and the second Lord Baltimore. As proprietor, Cecilius Calvert named the new colony Maryland in honor of Queen Henrietta Maria, wife of Charles I.

In 1633 Cecilius Calvert's first group of colonists left England. "I have sent a hopeful colony to Maryland," he wrote. The colonists established Saint Marys, later known as Saint Marys City, not far from the mouth of the Potomac River.

Cecilius Calvert appointed his brother Leonard Calvert as the governor of Maryland. Leonard Calvert had learned about the unfortunate experiences of earlier English colonists, such as those who settled early Roanoke and Jamestown. As a result, he planned ahead and prevented the Maryland colonists from suffering a period of starvation. Calvert also knew that Jamestown was nearby in case the new settlement needed supplies or help.

Chapter 7 ■ 233

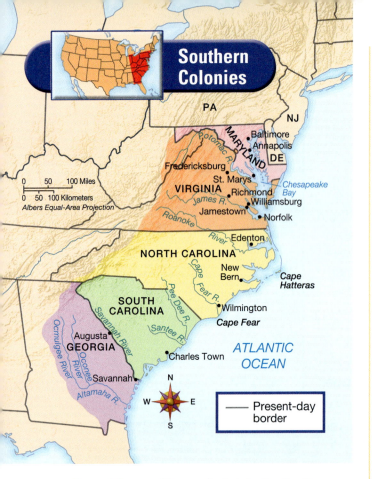

 Place Many colonists in the Southern Colonies started plantations.

◆ Why do you think most of the settlements in the Southern Colonies were located in Virginia?

The Calverts granted some colonists large pieces of land, and these colonists used the land to start tobacco plantations. However, most of the colonists going to Maryland went as indentured servants. An **indentured servant** was a person who agreed to work for another person without pay for a certain length of time in exchange for passage to North America. Most indentured servants were men between the ages of 18 and 22. Many indentured servants were Europeans who wanted to move to the colonies but had little or no money to pay for their travel.

The indentured servants in Maryland fared better than some who went to other colonies to live and work. When their time of service was finished, they were legally free. In addition, colonial leaders helped them start their own farms. They received 50 acres of land, a suit of clothes, an ax, two hoes, and three barrels of corn.

From the beginning Maryland's leaders welcomed settlers of many religions. In 1649 the Maryland assembly, a group that made laws for the colony, passed the Toleration Act. It was the first law in North America to allow all Christians to worship as they pleased. Maryland became known throughout the English colonies for its religious freedom.

REVIEW Why did the Calverts want to build a colony in North America?

The Carolinas

The Southern Colonies of Virginia and Maryland continued to grow during the 1600s. Then in 1663 King Charles II, the son of King Charles I, granted land for another colony, located between Virginia and Spanish Florida. The charter divided the colony, known as Carolina, among eight English nobles, known as the Lords Proprietors.

The Toleration Act allowed all Christians in Maryland to worship as they pleased.

Even before the charter was granted, colonists from Virginia had been building villages and were farming in the northern part of the area that became the Carolina Colony. After 1663, colonists from England and the Caribbean, as well as Huguenots (HYOO•guh•nahts) from France, came to settle there. The Huguenots were Protestants forced to leave their country by the French king because of their different religious beliefs.

One of the first actions the Lords Proprietors took was to set up a government for the colony. They chose a Virginian, William Drummond, to be governor. Then in 1669 the Lords Proprietors wrote a **constitution**, or written plan of government, for the colony. Their plan was called the Fundamental Constitution of Carolina. The plan allowed the colonists to make some laws for themselves, but it kept most of the authority in the hands of the king in England.

The Carolina colonists tried raising different cash crops. The climate was good for agriculture, and the soil was fertile. At first, they planted tobacco, grapes, and cotton, but these crops did not do as well as expected. They had more success in raising cattle and trapping animals for their fur, but they still searched for a cash crop. Only when they "found out the true way of raising and husking rice" did Carolina begin to prosper. The colonists also produced naval stores.

As the population grew, Carolina became more difficult to govern. In 1712 the northern two-thirds of the colony was divided into two colonies, North Carolina and South Carolina. Hilly North Carolina continued to develop as a colony of small farms. In South Carolina, however, landowners on the flat Coastal Plain created larger and larger plantations.

The main cash crop on many of South Carolina's plantations was rice. On drier land, where rice would not grow, landowners found they could grow indigo plants. From these plants they made **indigo**, which is a blue dye. The dye was widely used in the clothmaking process common in the 1700s.

Rice (left) was an important cash crop in the Carolinas. The drawing (below) shows workers in a Carolina rice field.

Indigo became an important cash crop after Eliza Lucas Pinckney, the 17-year-old daughter of a plantation owner, experimented with the plant. Using seeds from the Caribbean, Pinckney spent several years growing different kinds of indigo. By 1744 samples of the dye made from her plants were of excellent quality. Pinckney gave her indigo seeds to neighbors and friends. Within a few years South Carolina plantation owners were selling a million pounds of indigo a year to cloth makers in Europe.

The plantations of South Carolina required many workers, and since there were not enough workers available, many landowners bought enslaved Africans. The coastal settlement of Charles Town, later renamed Charleston, became the most important seaport, social center, and slave market in the Southern Colonies.

REVIEW Which crops were valuable to the Carolina colonists? **GENERALIZE**

Many plantations in South Carolina prospered by growing indigo plants.

Georgia

The southern one-third of what had originally been Carolina was not settled by English colonists until 1733. A year earlier King George II had given James Oglethorpe and 19 partners a charter to settle Georgia, a colony they named for the king. Oglethorpe was an English general and lawmaker. The charter gave Oglethorpe and his partners the right to settle the region between the Savannah and Altamaha Rivers for 21 years.

Oglethorpe and his partners hoped an English colony in Georgia would strengthen England's claim to the land. At the time Spain, France, and England all claimed what became the Georgia Colony.

Oglethorpe also had the idea of bringing over **debtors**—people who were in prison for owing money—to settle the colony. In the 1700s most debtors were imprisoned as punishment for not paying back money. Oglethorpe offered each settler 50 acres of land plus a bonus of 50 acres for every debtor that the settler brought along to help with the work of starting a colony. Those who paid their own way might get up to 500 acres. Oglethorpe hoped that once the debtors were out of prison, they would better themselves through hard work. Settling them in Georgia, he thought, was the answer to this social problem.

In 1733 Oglethorpe and a group of more than 100 settlers established Savannah near the mouth of the Savannah River. During the first year, to keep the colony fairly small, Oglethorpe limited the amount of land a person could own. To avoid conflicts with the Native Americans, he forbade trading with them. He also did not allow slave traders to bring enslaved Africans to the colony. As a result, there were no plantations in Georgia, only small farms.

In 1752 control of Georgia passed from Oglethorpe and his partners back to the king, making it a royal colony. With this change in ownership also came a change to allow slavery. As a result, plantations growing cash crops quickly began to develop, and Georgia landowners began to prosper. Their way of life became similar to that in the other Southern Colonies.

Rice became the most profitable cash crop in the Georgia Colony. Some Georgia planters became so wealthy from growing rice that they were able to own a house in a nearby town in addition to the one they had on the plantation.

REVIEW What did James Oglethorpe accomplish as the leader of the Georgia Colony?

BIOGRAPHY

James Oglethorpe
1696–1785

Character Trait: Kindness

While working as a lawmaker in England, James Oglethorpe found a special cause. He heard that a good friend of his had been sent to prison for not paying his debts. Oglethorpe hurried to the prison but arrived too late. His friend had died of smallpox from the terrible conditions in the prison. Oglethorpe made up his mind then and there to help debtors.

This 1734 engraving (below) of Savannah was used to attract settlers to the Georgia Colony.

MULTIMEDIA BIOGRAPHIES
Visit The Learning Site at
www.harcourtschool.com
to learn about other famous people.

GO ONLINE

Chapter 7 ■ 237

Location The 13 English colonies were located along the Atlantic Coast.

❓ Why do you think Georgia was the last English colony to be founded?

Virginia Grows and Changes

By the 1730s, after all of the other Southern Colonies had been founded, the Virginia Colony continued to grow and change. By 1700 Virginia had become the largest English colony in North America. Because the population continued to grow, more and more settlers moved from the coastal areas of Virginia into the Piedmont, the Great Valley, and the mountains of western Virginia. Settlers from Pennsylvania also continued to move into these areas.

In the 1700s transportation improved throughout the Virginia Colony. It became easier to travel between the coastal areas and the western part of the colony. Indian trails became small roads, over which pack horses carried supplies. These roads soon widened and became wagon roads. Soon there were ferry boats that crossed rivers to transport passengers, livestock, tobacco, and other goods. When the ferries became very busy, the Virginia General Assembly voted to build bridges across some of the rivers. The General Assembly was made up of Virginia's governor, the Governor's Council, and the members of the House of Burgesses.

While more people in Virginia were moving west, changes were also happening along the coast. In 1699, because of fires and other problems in Jamestown, the House of Burgesses moved to the nearby village of Williamsburg, which became the colony's new capital. By the mid-1700s Williamsburg was a large, well-planned city. The city was soon being compared to other important cities of the 13 colonies, such as Boston, New York City, and Philadelphia.

238 ▪ Unit 3

The Governor's House in Williamsburg soon became known as the Governor's Palace.

Williamsburg became the political, social, and cultural center of the Virginia Colony. It was the home of many firsts for the colony. Virginia's first theater was built there in 1716. The colony's first successful printing press was set up there in 1728. Also, the first newspaper in the colony, the *Virginia Gazette*, was started there in 1736. Williamsburg remained Virginia's most important city for much of the 1700s.

REVIEW How did transportation change in the Virginia Colony?

LESSON 1 REVIEW

Summary Time Line

- **1633** Cecilius Calvert's first group of colonists leave England
- **1712** The Carolina colony is divided into two colonies—North Carolina and South Carolina
- **1733** Colonists settle Georgia

GENERALIZE How do you think most people in the Southern Colonies made a living?

1. **BIG IDEA** Why was selling crops for a profit important to the success of the Southern Colonies?

2. **VOCABULARY** Use **indigo** in a sentence to describe the accomplishments of Eliza Lucas Pinckney.

3. **TIME LINE** In what year was the Carolina Colony divided into two colonies?

4. **GEOGRAPHY** What geographic factors led the Calverts to start a colony in Maryland instead of in Newfoundland?

5. **CRITICAL THINKING—Hypothesize** What might have happened if rice and indigo had not grown well in the South Carolina Colony?

PERFORMANCE—Write a Paragraph Find out what kinds of cash crops are grown today in the states that were once the Southern Colonies. Use the Internet and other research tools to write a paragraph about the cash crops in those states. Share your paragraph with your classmates.

SKILLS: Tell Fact from Opinion

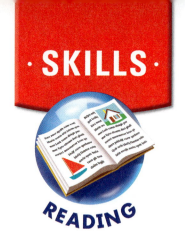

VOCABULARY
fact
opinion

▶ WHY IT MATTERS

Knowing how to tell a fact from an opinion can help you better understand what you hear and read. A **fact** is a statement that can be checked and proved. An **opinion** is a statement that tells what a person thinks or believes.

▶ WHAT YOU NEED TO KNOW

You have read that the Maryland Colony was founded by the Calverts. You could check whether this is a fact by looking in an encyclopedia, in other books, or on the Internet.

Facts often give dates, numbers, and other pieces of information. To tell whether a statement is a fact, ask yourself the following questions.

- Do I know this idea to be true from my own experience?
- Can the idea be proved by testing or other checking?

Other statements in this chapter give opinions. You have read John Smith's opinion about Chesapeake Bay: "Heaven and earth never agreed to frame a better place for man's habitation." There is no way to prove that Chesapeake Bay is a better place than any other place.

An opinion is what a speaker or writer believes. The following clues can help you decide whether a statement is an opinion.

- Look or listen for phrases such as *I think*, *I feel*, and *in my opinion*.
- Watch for words such as *best*, *worst*, *wonderful*, and *terrible*.

Historians can use facts to help them form opinions about the past.

▶ PRACTICE THE SKILL

Decide whether the following statements are facts or opinions.

1. In 1628 George Calvert traveled to the Chesapeake Bay region.
2. Saint Marys was the best settlement in the English colonies.

▶ APPLY WHAT YOU LEARNED

Many people rely on newspapers for information. Look at a recent newspaper. Underline three facts and circle three opinions. Explain how you were able to tell the facts from the opinions.

Southern Plantations

· LESSON · 2

As towns and cities in the 13 English colonies grew, plantations also grew—especially in the Southern Colonies. Plantations became prosperous because plantation owners, known as **planters**, were able to grow large amounts of cash crops, more than on small farms. Planters acquired as much land as they could in order to grow more and more crops to sell.

The Plantation Economy

From the time that the first English colonists settled Jamestown, plantations became important to the economy of the Southern Colonies. As planters learned to grow more cash crops well, such as tobacco, rice, and indigo, they started even more plantations.

The earliest plantations were usually built in the rich soil of the southern tidewater. **Tidewater** is low-lying land along a coast. Waterways in the area made it easy for boats to get crops to market. Crop buyers from England traveled the waterways with English-made goods—shoes, lace, thread, farm tools, and dishes. The planters bartered, or traded, crops for these goods.

Owners of the largest plantations most often sold their cash crops through a broker. A **broker** is a person who is paid to buy and sell for someone else. Planters sent their crops to England together with a list of things they wanted the broker to buy there for them.

GENERALIZE
As you read, make generalizations about life on southern plantations.

BIG IDEA
Southern plantations changed as plantation owners added more and more workers.

VOCABULARY
planter
tidewater
broker
auction
overseer
spiritual
public service

Goods like these buttons (left and below) and this tea caddy (right) were brought to the colonies from England.

Chapter 7 ■ 241

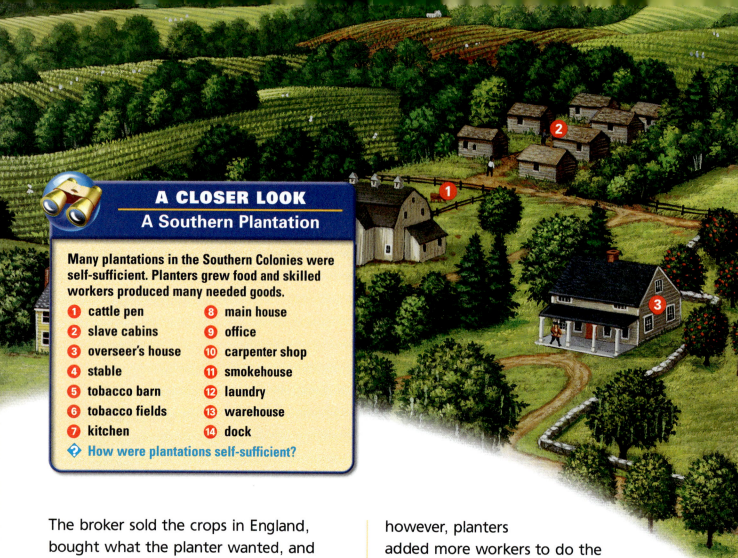

A CLOSER LOOK
A Southern Plantation

Many plantations in the Southern Colonies were self-sufficient. Planters grew food and skilled workers produced many needed goods.

1. cattle pen
2. slave cabins
3. overseer's house
4. stable
5. tobacco barn
6. tobacco fields
7. kitchen
8. main house
9. office
10. carpenter shop
11. smokehouse
12. laundry
13. warehouse
14. dock

❓ How were plantations self-sufficient?

The broker sold the crops in England, bought what the planter wanted, and sent the goods back to the colonies.

To raise more crops, planters had to keep clearing new land. Crops such as tobacco ruined the fertile soil in only a few years. As land wore out near the coast, planters began to move up the rivers to higher land. There they built even larger plantations.

REVIEW Why were the earliest plantations usually built in the southern tidewater?

Plantation Workers

On small farms every member of the family worked long hours. They worked hard, making sure that the crops were planted, harvested, stored, and shipped to market. The same was true for small plantations. As plantations grew in size, however, planters added more workers to do the hard labor. In time, the main job of the planter's family was to watch over the work of others.

Many of the earliest plantation workers came to the colonies in the South as indentured servants. However, not all indentured servants came willingly to the English colonies. Some were sent there by the English courts to work in the colonies to pay for their crimes as a form of punishment. Other indentured servants were people who had been kidnapped and then sold in the colonies against their will.

Among the first indentured servants to be sold in the English colonies were kidnapped Africans. After the mid-1600s, however, traders were bringing thousands of Africans to the English colonies not as

indentured servants but as slaves. Slaves in the colonies were sold like property at an **auction**, or public sale. Unlike indentured servants, slaves were not given their freedom after a certain length of time. They were enslaved for life. Before long, laws were passed in the colonies with a ruling that said that the children of enslaved people were also slaves.

REVIEW Why did some people come to the colonies as indentured servants?

A Slave's Life

There were generally two kinds of slaves—field slaves and house slaves. Field slaves worked hard in the fields, raising cash crops for the planters to sell. Some slave owners hired **overseers** to watch the field slaves as they worked and to punish them if they did not work hard.

• BIOGRAPHY •

Olaudah Equiano   1750?–1797
Character Trait: Courage

Olaudah Equiano (OHL•uh•dah ek•wee•AHN•oh) was 11 years old when he and his sister were kidnapped by slave traders. Later Equiano was separated from his sister when they were sold into slavery to different owners. Equiano's owner showed him some kindness and gave him some education. When Equiano was freed from slavery, he wrote a book about his life. In the book he told about his life in Africa and spoke out against slavery. A group of English people working against slavery used Equiano's book to help with the cause to end slavery.

Olaudah Equiano's book was published in 1789.

MULTIMEDIA BIOGRAPHIES
Visit The Learning Site at
www.harcourtschool.com
to learn about other famous people.

House slaves had more contact with the planter and the planter's family. House slaves often were clothed, fed, and housed better than field slaves. Women who were house slaves did the washing, cooking, cleaning, and sewing for the household. Male house slaves drove carriages, took care of horses, and practiced skills such as carpentry. Children of house slaves were often playmates of the planters' children, at least when they were young.

Slaves were treated well or cruelly depending on their owners. Some planters took pride in being fair and kind to their slaves. There was little protection, however, for slaves who had cruel masters. Slave owners were free to beat, whip, or insult any slave as often as they chose to do so. These slaves looked only to escape or to resist their cruel treatment. "No day ever dawns for the slave, nor is it looked for," one enslaved African later wrote. "For the slave it is all night—all night, forever."

Laws in the colonies forbade slaves to learn to read and write. By the age of 10, most enslaved children were working alongside the adults.

Enslaved people spent very long days working. At night slaves often told stories and sang songs about their homeland. Later, the Christian religion became a source of strength for slaves as they tried to deal with the hardships of slave life. Some slaves expressed their belief in the Christian religion by singing spirituals. **Spirituals** (SPIR•ih•chuh•wuhlz) are religious songs based on Bible stories.

REVIEW Why were spirituals important to slaves? **GENERALIZE**

244 ■ Unit 3

A Planter's Life

Plantations in the South were often far from one another and far from any towns. Weeks or months could go by without visitors and without news about the latest happenings. For this reason, visitors were always welcome.

Because people lived so far apart, there were few schools. Nevertheless, southern planters were among the best-educated people in the 13 English colonies. Some plantations had their own schools for the planters' children, and some hired teachers from Europe. Later, the planters' sons might go to Europe to complete their education. Girls stopped going to school by the age of 12 or 13 because planters' daughters were supposed to learn only basic skills and "to read and sew with their needle."

A planter and his wife were responsible for running a business and for taking care of all the people on the plantation. They had to clothe, feed, and provide medical care not only for their family but for all the members of their household. By the 1740s a large plantation household—family, servants, and slaves—often numbered in the hundreds.

Besides taking care of a plantation, a planter's duties also included public service. **Public service** is doing a job to help the community or society as a whole. Public service for a planter could mean serving as a judge or as a representative in the colonial assembly. Some planters served as advisers to the governor. Some performed all these duties. This tradition of public service may explain why so many planters became leaders in the 13 English colonies.

REVIEW How were children of planters educated?

Girls made samplers, like this one from 1675, to practice their sewing skills.

LESSON 2 REVIEW

 GENERALIZE What was the life of a planter like?

1 BIG IDEA How did southern plantations change as planters added more workers?

2 VOCABULARY Use the terms **planter** and **tidewater** to describe the plantation economy.

3 CULTURE Why were spirituals important to enslaved people?

4 CRITICAL THINKING—Analyze What were the consequences of modifying the land to grow tobacco?

 PERFORMANCE—Write a Diary Entry Suppose that you are living on a plantation in colonial times. Take on a role, and write an entry in a diary to show what a day on the plantation is like. Share your entry with a classmate.

Chapter 7 ■ 245

SKILLS · MAP AND GLOBE

Read a Resource and Product Map

▶ WHY IT MATTERS

A resource and product map can help you make a generalization about a place's economy. A generalization is a statement based on facts. It is used to summarize groups of facts and to show relationships between them. Symbols for resources and products, shown in the map key, tell you where they are found, made, or grown. These symbols can help you make generalizations about the areas shown on a resource and product map.

▶ WHAT YOU NEED TO KNOW

In the map key on the next page, pictures stand for resources found in the 13 colonies and goods produced there. These goods were important not only because they were sold in the 13 colonies but also because they were exported for sale in England. The map shows only some of the most important goods and resources in the colonies.

▶ PRACTICE THE SKILL

Now that you know more about the symbols in the map key, you can use these questions as a guide for making generalizations about the economy of the 13 colonies.

1. What products appear most often on the map in the New England Colonies?
2. What generalization can you make about the kinds of work most people did in the Middle Atlantic Colonies?
3. What generalization can you make about the economy of the Southern Colonies?

▶ APPLY WHAT YOU LEARNED

Look through encyclopedias, atlases, and almanacs to find an example of a resource and product map. Work with a partner to make some generalizations about the economy of the place or places shown on the map.

 Learn more about maps with the **GeoSkills CD-Rom.**

Iron was melted in furnaces like this one (left). Lumber was cut (right) and tobacco was dried (far right) before it was sent to England.

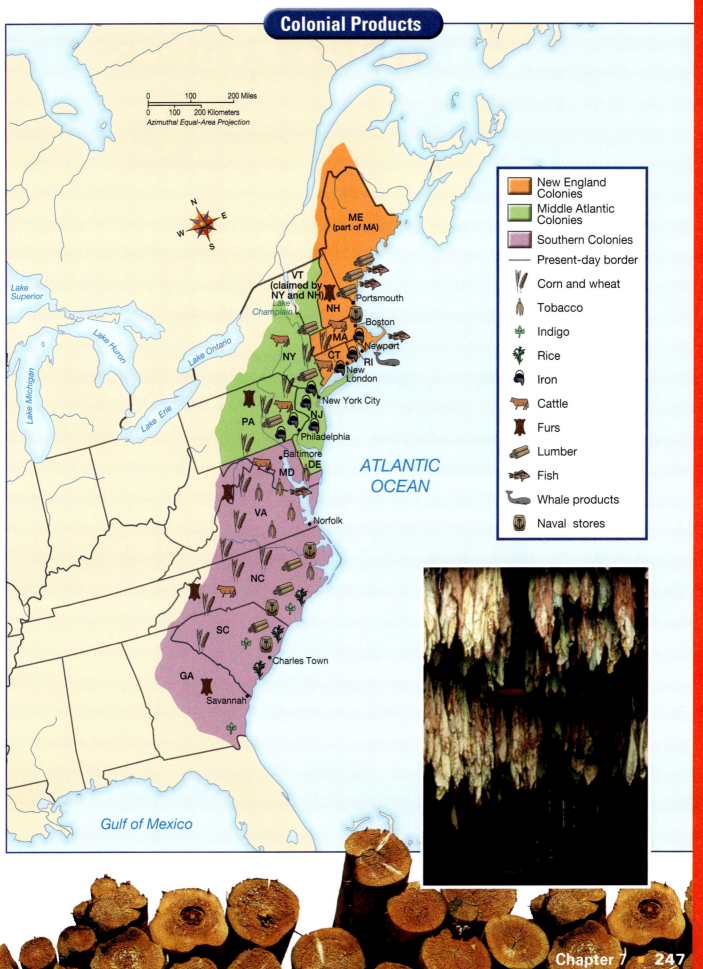

Colonial Products

Chapter 7 • 247

LESSON 3

Southern Cities

1670–1730

GENERALIZE
As you read, make generalizations about the growth of Southern cities.

BIG IDEA
Cities helped the Southern Colonies grow and prosper.

VOCABULARY
apprentice
county seat
county

The Southern Colonies generally had fewer towns and cities than did the Middle Atlantic and New England Colonies. This was because planters and farmers wanted to spread out over as much land as possible. They wanted to use the land to grow crops and were not interested in building towns.

By the mid-1700s, however, some settlements along the Atlantic coast of the Southern Colonies had grown into large towns and even cities. Among these were Charles Town, Wilmington, Norfolk, Baltimore, and Savannah. They all had good harbors, and they grew because of trade. Ships carrying imported goods arrived at these cities. After a few weeks in port, the ships sailed away loaded with exports such as tobacco, rice, and indigo.

Trade Ports

Some settlers who lived inland brought their goods to port cities, where it was easy to find buyers. They sometimes traded their goods for imports that came in on ships from Europe and other places. These imports included tea, coffee, and pepper. Luxury items such as furniture, silverware, and medicine also were imported.

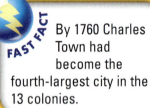

FAST FACT By 1760 Charles Town had become the fourth-largest city in the 13 colonies.

Many people in southern cities worked in the trade business, which helped the cities grow. Other people in the cities worked in other kinds of businesses. Some were fishers, hatmakers, tailors, and printers. Young people learned such jobs by becoming **apprentices**. A child would move in as an apprentice with the family of a skilled worker and help in the family's business for several years. In this way, a young person learned a skill.

REVIEW How did people make a living in southern cities? **GENERALIZE**

Charles Town

Charles Town, South Carolina, became the largest city in the Southern Colonies. In 1688 there were only about 300 people living there. Only 20 years later, in 1708, Charles Town's population had grown to about 6,000 people. An early visitor to the port at Charles Town predicted the city would grow when he said, "There were sixteen ships which had come to trade. The great number of ships will soon make this a busy town."

From 1670 to the mid-1700s, Charles Town was the center of life in South Carolina. During this time most of the people in South Carolina lived in Charles Town or in the area around it. Many residents of Charles Town enjoyed a social life that included dancing, seeing plays, and attending races and concerts.

Merchants and planters had the most power in Charles Town's society. Many wealthy planters in South Carolina lived in Charles Town during the months when insects infested the wetlands on the plantations where rice was grown.

REVIEW Where did most people in South Carolina live between the late 1600s and mid-1700s?

GEOGRAPHY

Charles Town
Understanding Places and Regions

Charles Town was located along the middle of South Carolina's coast where the Ashley and Cooper Rivers joined to form Charles Town Harbor. Until the settling of Georgia in 1733, South Carolina served as a buffer, or shield, between the Spanish in Florida and the other English colonies in North America.

Other Southern Ports

The port city of Wilmington, North Carolina, was started in the 1720s after colonists from South Carolina began moving north along the Atlantic coast to the Cape Fear River. They were looking for fertile soil for establishing plantations. Instead, they found lots of trees. They brought in workers to cut the trees and to build sawmills. They also produced naval stores. From the port at Wilmington, the settlers shipped naval stores and lumber to England as exports.

Wilmington's location on the Cape Fear River helped it prosper. The river is deep enough to be used by large ships, and it flows directly into the Atlantic Ocean. Immigrants also helped Wilmington grow and prosper. They came from other colonies and from many parts of Europe. Some of the town's earliest settlers came from northern Scotland. The first Africans to come to Wilmington were brought as slaves. Eventually, free Africans also lived there. Some were farmers. Others worked as painters, tailors, carpenters, and blacksmiths.

Other coastal towns in the South grew quickly, too. Savannah became the Georgia Colony's chief port. It also served as the capital city of Georgia until the late 1700s. Norfolk, Virginia, grew because it served as a port where tobacco and naval stores were shipped to England. Lumber from North Carolina was also sent to Norfolk to be shipped out to England.

Items like this silver gravy boat could be purchased at a general store.

Baltimore's location near Chesapeake Bay helped it become a busy port city.

Baltimore, Maryland, was founded in 1729 on the Patapsco River, which flows into Chesapeake Bay. It prospered because a port was needed for the growing amounts of grain and tobacco being produced in Maryland and other nearby colonies. It quickly became a major port and a center for shipbuilding. Baltimore's shipyards later became well known for improving the way ships were built.

REVIEW How did immigrants affect the port city of Wilmington, North Carolina?

County Seats

As more people in Southern Colonies moved inland in search of more farmland, some inland towns developed and grew. Most of these towns were county seats. A county seat was the main town for a county, a large part of a colony. Over time, planters and farmers who once used

brokers or brought their crops to trade in coastal cities began to depend more and more on county seats as places to trade.

Several times a year plantation and farm families would pack their bags, dress in their finest clothes, and travel to the county seat. People went to church, held dances, and traded crops for goods there. Some plantation owners bought and sold slaves there. Most county seats had a general store, a courthouse, and a jail. White men who owned land and other property met at the county seat to make laws and to vote for leaders.

REVIEW Why were county seats important to people living on farms and plantations?

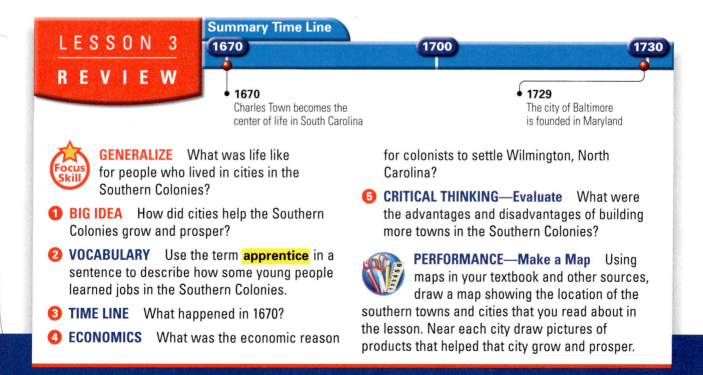

LESSON 3 REVIEW

Summary Time Line
- 1670 — Charles Town becomes the center of life in South Carolina
- 1729 — The city of Baltimore is founded in Maryland

Focus Skill — GENERALIZE What was life like for people who lived in cities in the Southern Colonies?

1. **BIG IDEA** How did cities help the Southern Colonies grow and prosper?
2. **VOCABULARY** Use the term **apprentice** in a sentence to describe how some young people learned jobs in the Southern Colonies.
3. **TIME LINE** What happened in 1670?
4. **ECONOMICS** What was the economic reason for colonists to settle Wilmington, North Carolina?
5. **CRITICAL THINKING—Evaluate** What were the advantages and disadvantages of building more towns in the Southern Colonies?

PERFORMANCE—Make a Map Using maps in your textbook and other sources, draw a map showing the location of the southern towns and cities that you read about in the lesson. Near each city draw pictures of products that helped that city grow and prosper.

Chapter 7 ■ 251

CHAPTER 7
Review and Test Preparation

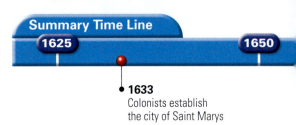

Summary Time Line
1625 — 1650
● **1633** Colonists establish the city of Saint Marys

Focus Skill: Generalize

Copy the following graphic organizer onto a separate sheet of paper. Use the information you have learned to make generalizations about the Southern Colonies.

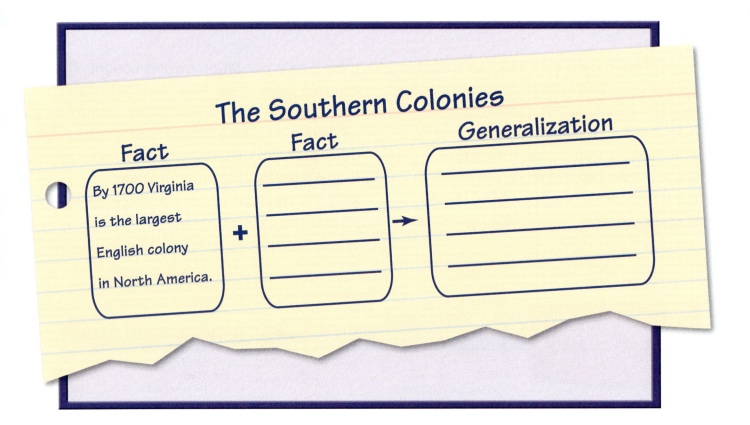

The Southern Colonies

Fact: By 1700 Virginia is the largest English colony in North America. + Fact: _____ → Generalization: _____

THINK & WRITE

Write an Advertisement When a colony was first established, colonial leaders sometimes found it difficult to attract settlers. Write an advertisement for the Georgia Colony, describing the benefits of moving there.

Write a Story During colonial times, young people who wanted to learn a special skill, such as hatmaking or printing, became apprentices. Write a story about a young person who moves in with a skilled worker's family in order to learn a skill.

- **1663** The colony of Carolina is established
- **1712** North and South Carolina are formed
- **1729** The city of Baltimore is founded
- **1733** The settlement of Savannah is established

USE THE TIME LINE

Use the chapter summary time line to answer these questions.

1. When was the Carolina Colony established?
2. Was Baltimore founded before or after Savannah?

USE VOCABULARY

Use a term from this list to complete each of the sentences that follow.

indentured servants (p. 234)

constitution (p. 235)

broker (p. 241)

spirituals (p. 244)

county seat (p. 250)

3. Southern plantation owners often sold their cash crops through a ____.
4. A ____ is a written plan of government.
5. When ____ finished their time of service, they were legally free.
6. Several times a year southern farm families would travel to their local ____.
7. Slaves often sang ____ when they gathered together at night.

RECALL FACTS

Answer these questions.

8. What was the most profitable cash crop produced by the Georgia Colony?
9. Why were there few community schools in the Southern Colonies?
10. How did the location of the city of Wilmington, North Carolina, help it prosper?

Write the letter of the best choice.

11. Planters had to start building their plantations farther up the rivers because—
    A floods often destroyed their homes.
    B their homes were sometimes attacked.
    C crops like tobacco ruined the soil.
    D the English government required it.

12. The largest southern cities were Charles Town, Wilmington, Norfolk and—
    F Boston.
    G Baltimore.
    H Philadelphia.
    J Providence.

THINK CRITICALLY

13. How do you think the demand for indigo affected South Carolina plantation owners?
14. Why were southern waterways important?

APPLY SKILLS

Tell Fact from Opinion

15. Write a news story that includes both facts and opinions. Then exchange stories with a classmate. Find three facts and three opinions in your classmate's story.

Read a Resource and Product Map

Use the map on page 247 to answer these questions.

16. What products appear most often on the map in the Middle Atlantic Colonies?
17. What generalization can you make about the kinds of work most people did in the New England Colonies?

VISIT Colonial Williamsburg

GET READY

Colonial Williamsburg is the restored and rebuilt capital of eighteenth-century Virginia. The town is a living-history museum where you can experience the sights, sounds, and smells of colonial life. You can talk with people in historical costumes who stroll the streets or tend their shops. Guides bring history to life by portraying actual citizens who lived in Williamsburg in the 1700s. In Colonial Williamsburg, history is more than just names and dates. It is the story of people just like you who lived in another time.

WHAT TO SEE

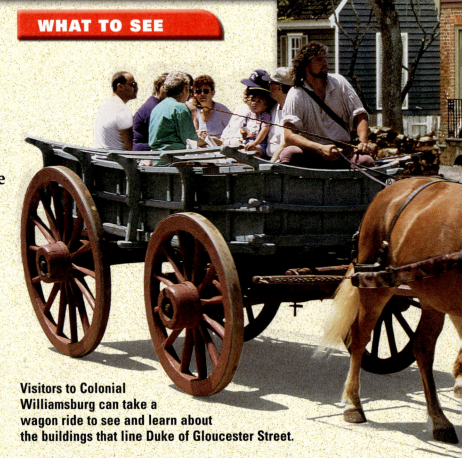

Visitors to Colonial Williamsburg can take a wagon ride to see and learn about the buildings that line Duke of Gloucester Street.

LOCATE IT

Near the James Geddy House, You can take turns at hoop-rolling, stilt-walking, ninepins, and other colonial children's games.

In this shop a violin-maker uses traditional tools to create an instrument.

Milliners (MIH•luh•nehrz) were busy in a time when women's hats were an important part of their outfits. The millinery shop displayed the latest styles in bonnets.

The Capitol is where the Virginia House of Burgesses met to pass laws and debate important issues of the day.

TAKE A FIELD TRIP

GO ONLINE

A VIRTUAL TOUR
Visit The Learning Site at www.harcourtschool.com to take virtual tours of other historic sites.

A VIDEO TOUR
Check your media center or classroom library for a videotape tour of Colonial Williamsburg.

UNIT 3
Review and Test Preparation

VISUAL SUMMARY

Write a Play Choose one of the events shown below. Then write a short play about life in the New England, the Middle Atlantic, or Southern Colonies.

USE VOCABULARY

Identify the term that correctly matches each definition.

public office (p. 192)
militia (p. 221)
debtor (p. 236)
planter (p. 241)

1. a person who was in prison for owing money
2. a person who grew large amounts of cash crops
3. a job for the community
4. a volunteer army

RECALL FACTS

Answer these questions.

5. What kinds of goods did the New England colonists produce from livestock?
6. Why were the Middle Atlantic Colonies also known as the "breadbasket" colonies?

Write the letter of the best choice.

7. Roger Williams received help from—
   A Governor John Winthrop.
   B French fur traders.
   C Dutch merchants.
   D the Narragansett Indians.

8. The triangular trade routes connected England, the English colonies in North America, and the—
   F east coast of South America.
   G west coast of Spain.
   H west coast of Africa.
   J east coast of Mexico.

Visual Summary

1625

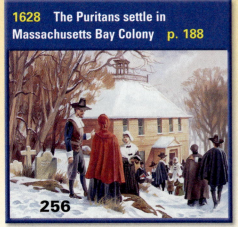

1628 The Puritans settle in Massachusetts Bay Colony p. 188

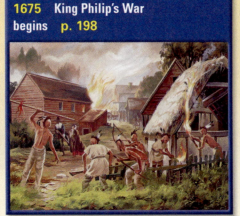

1675 King Philip's War begins p. 198

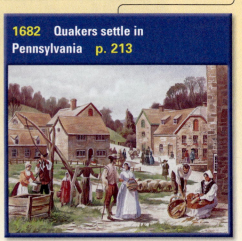

1682 Quakers settle in Pennsylvania p. 213

9 Most people in the Middle Atlantic Colonies earned a living by—
A producing naval stores.
B farming.
C fur trading.
D building ships.

THINK CRITICALLY

10 Why do you think England wanted its colonists to buy only English-made imports?

11 Why do you think the Dutch settlers in New Netherland did not try to fight the English who took over the colony in 1664?

12 Why do you think Virginia was the most important of the 13 colonies to England?

13 How would living on a plantation have been different from living in or near a town?

APPLY SKILLS

Read a Resource and Product Map
Use the map on this page to answer the following questions.

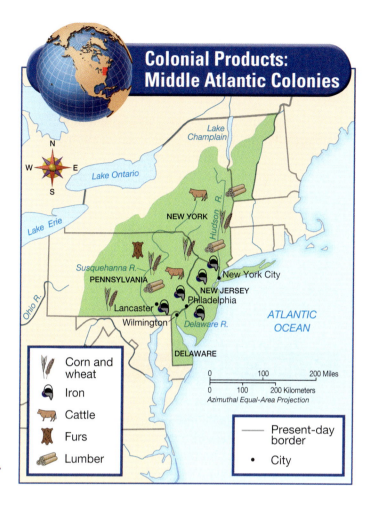

Colonial Products: Middle Atlantic Colonies

14 What products appear most often on the map in the Middle Atlantic Colonies?

15 Which two colonies produced iron?

16 Which two colonies produced lumber?

17 What generalization can you make about the colonies that produced corn and wheat?

18 What generalization can you make about the economy of the Middle Atlantic Colonies?

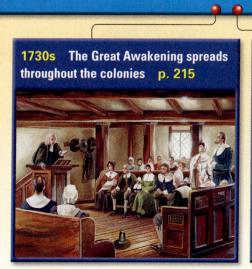

1730s The Great Awakening spreads throughout the colonies p. 215

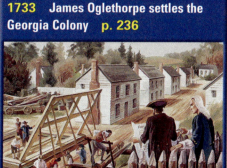

1733 James Oglethorpe settles the Georgia Colony p. 236

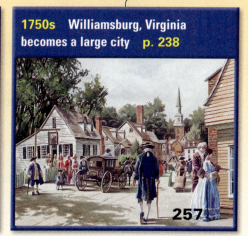

1750s Williamsburg, Virginia becomes a large city p. 238

Unit Activities

Visit The Learning Site at www.harcourtschool.com for additional activities.

Design a Monument

Every colony had individuals who made important contributions to its history, such as Benjamin Franklin in Pennsylvania and Eliza Lucas Pickney in South Carolina. Work in a group to choose an individual from the unit and then design a monument to that person. Your monument can include such things as statues or gardens. Make sure your monument includes something that shows the specific contributions of the person you have chosen.

COMPLETE THE UNIT PROJECT

A Book on Colonial America   Work with a group of your classmates to complete the unit project—a book about colonial America. Review your notes on the New England Colonies, the Middle Atlantic Colonies, and the Southern Colonies. Then write a description of each region. Work together to illustrate your book with both drawings and pictures either cut out of magazines or printed from the Internet. Write captions describing the illustrations and give your book a title. Share your completed book with the rest of the class.

VISIT YOUR LIBRARY

■ *Finding Providence: The Story of Roger Williams* by Avi. HarperCollins.

■ *The Story of William Penn* by Aliki. Simon & Schuster.

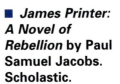

■ *James Printer: A Novel of Rebellion* by Paul Samuel Jacobs. Scholastic.

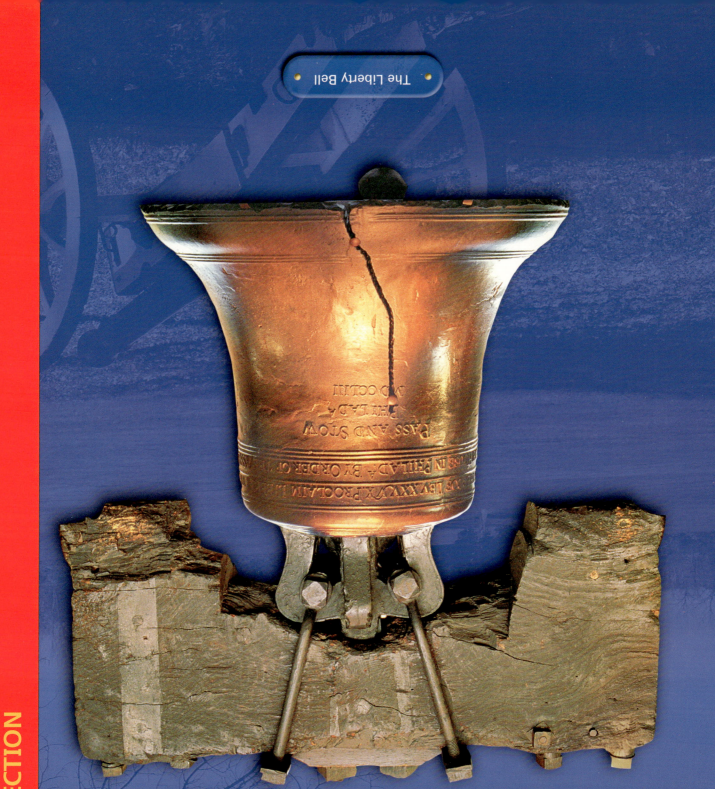

The Liberty Bell

GEORGIA CONNECTION

The American Revolution

Georgia in the Revolutionary War

GEORGIA CONNECTION

In the late 1700s many British colonists grew unhappy with British rule. Some Georgians fought for freedom from Britain, while others worked to create a new government. Some of the battles that took place during the Revolutionary War were fought in Georgia. These battles include the Battle of Brier Creek and the Battle of the Rice Boats.

Revolutionary War Battles in Georgia
- American victory
- British victory

Battles shown on map:
- Thomas Creek 1777
- Fort McIntosh 1777
- Fort Morris 1779
- Battle of the Rice Boats 1776
- Savannah 1778
- Brier Creek 1779
- Augusta 1779
- Fort Galphin 1781
- Kettle Creek 1779

This monument marks the site of the Battle of Kettle Creek.

The Battle of Savannah

General Elijah Clark was a Revolutionary War hero who was victorious over the British at the Battle of Kettle Creek.

Nancy Hart served as a spy for the colonists, getting information on the locations of British troops. She also captured several British soldiers.

Button Gwinnett helped the colonists by working with other colonial leaders to declare their freedom. He also signed the Declaration of Independence. Gwinnett later served as governor of Georgia.

★ CRCT TEST PREP ★

1 Which of the following battles was NOT fought in Georgia?
A Battle of Brier Creek
B Battle of Kettle Creek
C Battle of Saratoga
D Battle of Savannah

2 Who served as governor of Georgia?
A Button Gwinnett
B Elijah Clark
C John Cutler Braddock
D Nancy Hart

3 General Elijah Clark fought in
A the Battle of Savannah.
B the Battle of Kettle Creek.
C the Battle of Brier Creek.
D the Battle of Augusta.

4 Nancy Hart was
A a soldier.
B the commander of a ship.
C the wife of a famous general.
D a spy for the colonists.

Valley Forge National Historical Park, Pennsylvania

UNIT 4

The American Revolution

" By uniting we stand, by dividing we fall. "
—John Dickinson, "The Liberty Song," 1768

Preview the Content

Scan the chapter and lesson titles. Use them to make an outline of the unit. Write down any questions that occur to you about the American Revolution.

Preview the Vocabulary

Multiple Meanings A word can often have several meanings. You may know one meaning but not another. Use the Glossary to look up each of the terms listed below. Then use each term in a sentence.

FORK ⇒ _____   OLIVE BRANCH ⇒ _____

GAP ⇒ _____   PIONEER ⇒ _____

MONOPOLY ⇒ _____   QUARTER ⇒ _____

Unit 4 ■ 259

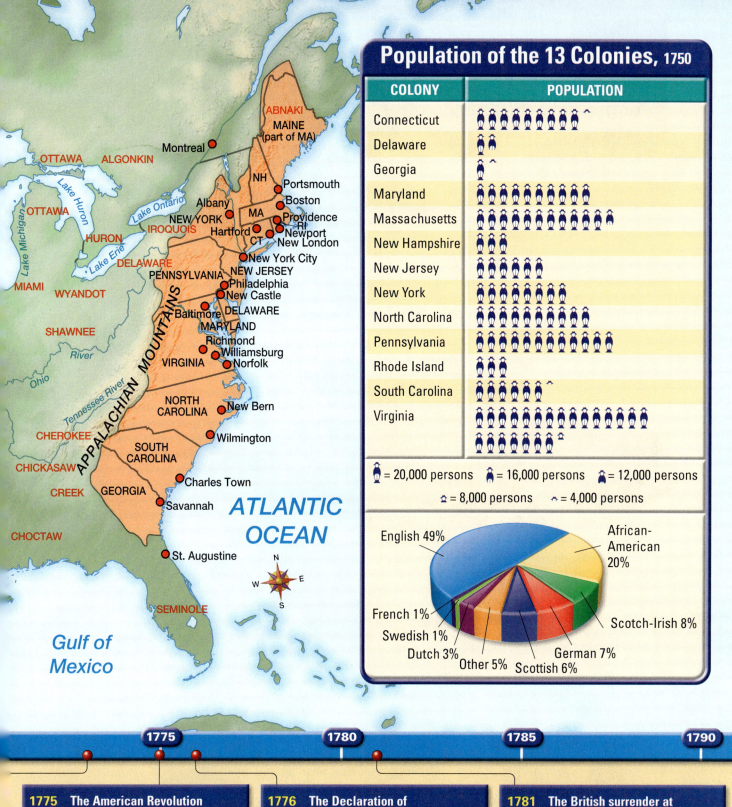

Population of the 13 Colonies, 1750

COLONY	POPULATION
Connecticut	🯅🯅🯅🯅🯅🯅🯅🯅🯅^
Delaware	🯅🯅
Georgia	🯆^
Maryland	🯅🯅🯅🯅🯅🯅🯅
Massachusetts	🯅🯅🯅🯅🯅🯅🯅🯅🯅🯅🯅🯅
New Hampshire	🯅🯅
New Jersey	🯅🯅🯅🯅🯅
New York	🯅🯅🯅🯅🯅🯅🯅
North Carolina	🯅🯅🯅🯅🯅🯅
Pennsylvania	🯅🯅🯅🯅🯅🯅🯅🯅🯅🯅🯅
Rhode Island	🯅🯅
South Carolina	🯅🯅🯅🯅🯅^
Virginia	🯅🯅🯅🯅🯅🯅🯅🯅🯅🯅🯅🯅🯅🯅

🯅 = 20,000 persons   🯅 = 16,000 persons   🯅 = 12,000 persons
🯆 = 8,000 persons   ^ = 4,000 persons

Pie chart: English 49%, African-American 20%, Scotch-Irish 8%, German 7%, Scottish 6%, Other 5%, Dutch 3%, Swedish 1%, French 1%

1775 The American Revolution begins p. 291

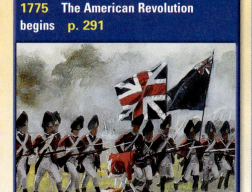

1776 The Declaration of Independence is signed p. 306

1781 The British surrender at Yorktown, in Virginia p. 326

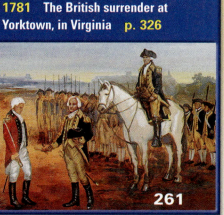

261

START with a SONG

YANKEE DOODLE

People have been singing some version of "Yankee Doodle" since the 1700s. The melody is an old English tune, but no one knows for certain who wrote its original words. Some historians credit Richard Shuckburgh, a British army doctor during the French and Indian War. His words poked fun at soldiers from New England. New Englanders were sometimes called Yankees, and *doodle* means "a foolish person."

During the American Revolution, American freedom fighters sang other words to "Yankee Doodle" and often whistled the tune in battle. Their words often poked fun at the British soldiers.

In time "Yankee Doodle" became an important symbol of the United States and of what Americans believed. Read now to discover the words to a version of "Yankee Doodle" that Americans sang.

Yankee doodle went to town,
    Riding on a pony;
Stuck a feather in his hat
    And called it Macaroni.

Chorus:
Yankee Doodle keep it up,
    Yankee Doodle dandy,
Mind the Music and the step,
    And with the girls be handy.

Macaroni fancy trimming, like gold braid
dandy a fancy young man

Father and I went down to camp,
    Along with Captain Good'in,
And there we saw the men and boys
    As thick as has-ty pud-din'.

And there we saw a thousand men,
    As rich as Squire David;
And what they wasted ev'ry day,
    I wish it could be sav'ed.

And there I saw a little keg,
    Its head all made of leather,
They knocked on it with little sticks,
    To call the folks together.

hasty puddin' a thick cornmeal mush
keg small barrel

And there was Captain Washington
    Upon a slapping stallion,
A-giving orders to his men;
    I guess there was a million.

And the ribbons on his hat,
    They looked so very fine, ah!
I wanted peskily to get
    To give to my Jemima.

And there I saw a swamping gun,
    Large as a log of maple,
Upon a mighty little cart;
    A load for father's cattle.

swamping big or heavy

And every time they fired it off,
    It took a horn of powder;
It made a noise like father's gun,
    Only a nation louder.

The troopers, too, would gallop up
    And fire right in our faces;
It scared me almost half to death
    To see them run such races.

It scared me so I <u>hooked</u> it off,
    Nor stopped, as I remember,
Nor turned about till I got home,
    Locked up in mother's <u>chamber</u>.

hooked to run off quickly
chamber bedroom

Analyze the Literature

1. Why do you think the British and the Americans poked fun at each other?

2. Work with a partner to interpret the meaning of each stanza in "Yankee Doodle." Then share your interpretation with the class.

READ A BOOK

START THE UNIT PROJECT

The History Show With your classmates, plan a history show about the American Revolution. As you read this unit, take notes about the key people and events. Your notes will help you decide which people and events to use in your history show.

USE TECHNOLOGY

Visit The Learning Site at **www.harcourtschool.com** for additional activities, primary sources, and other resources to use in this unit.

Unit 4 • 265

MINUTE MAN NATIONAL HISTORIC PARK

Visitors to Minute Man National Historic Park can see part of the Battle Road. In April 1775 American colonists and British soldiers fought alongside this road which ran from Boston to Concord. In this photograph, reenactors are marching across Concord's North Bridge.

LOCATE IT

Boston, MASSACHUSETTS

CHAPTER 8

Uniting the Colonies

"Here once the embattled farmers stood,
And fired the shot heard round the world."
—Ralph Waldo Emerson,
"Concord Hymn," 1837

Cause and Effect

A **cause** is an event or action that makes something else happen. An **effect** is what happens as a result.

As you read this chapter, do the following.
- List the causes and effects of key events.

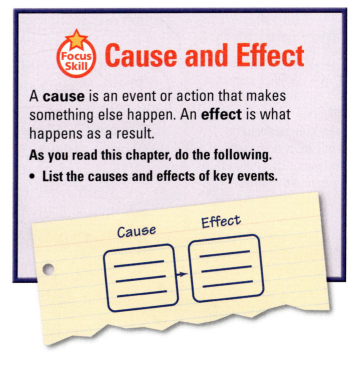

Chapter 8 ■ 267

LESSON 1

The French and Indian War Begins

CAUSE AND EFFECT
As you read, look for causes and effects of the French and Indian War.

BIG IDEA
Conflict over land in North America led to a war between Britain and France.

VOCABULARY
revolution
fork
ally
alliance
congress
delegate
Parliament

FAST FACT
When a British soldier was hit by a bullet, his bright red uniform kept nearby soldiers from knowing he was bleeding. This helped prevent the other soldiers from getting scared and running away from the battle.

1750 — 1770 — 1790
1750–1755

The events that led to the American Revolution began about 20 years before the 13 colonies cut ties with England, or Britain, as it became known. A **revolution** is a sudden, complete change, such as the overthrow of an established government. The first of the events was a war in North America between Britain and France that came to be called the French and Indian War. The war began as a competition between Britain and France for control of the Ohio Valley region.

Rivalry in the Ohio Valley

The Ohio Valley region stretches about 1,000 miles (1,609 km) along the Ohio River from the Appalachian Mountains to the Mississippi River. Many Native Americans lived in this region before Europeans arrived, but the French and the British each believed this land belonged to them because of earlier exploration and settlement. To the French, the Ohio Valley was an important link between France's holdings in Canada and Louisiana. The British, particularly those in the colonies of Pennsylvania and Virginia, saw it as an area for trade and growth.

By about 1750 the French had moved to make their claim to the Ohio Valley stronger.

268 • Unit 4

They sent soldiers into the region to drive out the British traders. They also began building a line of forts near the eastern end of the valley. The British viewed this move as an act of war and took action.

In 1753 Lieutenant (loo•TEH•nuhnt) Governor Robert Dinwiddie of Virginia sent young George Washington, then 21 years old, across the Appalachians to order the French to leave. When the French replied that they intended to stay, Dinwiddie sent a small force of soldiers from Virginia. Their orders were to build a fort at the Forks of the Ohio River, where the city of Pittsburgh, Pennsylvania, now stands. A **fork** is a place where two rivers join to form a third.

The Virginians had barely finished the fort when the French attacked it. The French drove off the Virginians and built a larger fort on that site. They called it Fort Duquesne (doo•KAYN) in honor of the Marquis (mahr•KEE) de Duquesne, the newly appointed governor general of New France. Unaware of the French attack, Dinwiddie sent young George Washington to the Forks of the Ohio River to reinforce the Virginians' fort.

Regions By the 1750s much of North America had been claimed by Europeans.
◆ Which two groups of Europeans claimed land east and west of the Ohio Valley?

A re-creation of the original Fort Necessity can be seen at Fort Necessity National Battlefield near Farmington, Pennsylvania. In this photograph, reenactors take on colonial roles.

Chapter 8 ■ 269

· BIOGRAPHY ·

George Washington   1732–1799
Character Trait: Perseverance

The action at Fort Necessity was the first major event in the military career of George Washington. It was the only time he ever surrendered to an enemy. Washington returned to Williamsburg two weeks later, discouraged about the battle. Instead of blaming him for losing the battle, the colonists praised Washington and his soldiers for their bravery. The colonists would later praise Washington for even braver deeds as he led the colonial army in the Revolutionary War.

MULTIMEDIA BIOGRAPHIES
Visit The Learning Site at www.harcourtschool.com to learn about other famous people.

In April 1754 Washington left Williamsburg with an army of 150 Virginians. On their way to the fort, the Virginians surprised a small group of French soldiers on patrol. Thinking "we might be attacked by considerable forces," Washington later wrote, the Virginians built a makeshift fort that they called Fort Necessity.

Within days a large force of more than 600 French soldiers and 100 of their Indian **allies**, or friends in war, attacked Fort Necessity. Outnumbered, the Virginians surrendered in what turned out to be the opening battle of the French and Indian War. The French let Washington and his soldiers return to Virginia.

REVIEW What caused the British to take action against the French?
CAUSE AND EFFECT

The Albany Plan of Union

As a result of Washington's defeat at Fort Necessity, the British government in London urged its colonial leaders to meet with the Iroquois. The British wanted to be sure of the Iroquois's loyalty in the war against the French. By the mid-1700s both Britain and France had formed alliances with many of the Native American tribes in the Ohio Valley. An **alliance** is a formal agreement among nations, states, groups, or individuals. The Iroquois had become one of Britain's most important Native American allies.

In June and July of 1754, colonial leaders met at Albany, New York, in what was called the Albany Congress. A **congress** is a formal meeting of representatives. Seven colonies sent representatives,

At the time Benjamin Franklin presented his Albany Plan of Union, he was a member of the Pennsylvania Assembly.

or **delegates**, including Benjamin Franklin from Pennsylvania.

Franklin and the others knew that the colonists needed more than Indian allies to defeat the French. The colonies had to be united in the fight against the French. Franklin presented his Albany Plan of Union. It was one of the first proposals for uniting all of the colonies, except for Georgia, under one government.

To get public support for his plan, Benjamin Franklin published the now famous "Join, or Die" cartoon. It first appeared in the *Pennsylvania Gazette,* one of the most widely read newspapers of that time. Franklin based the cartoon's saying on an old tale about snakes. The story said that a snake cut into pieces would come to life again if put back together before sunset.

Franklin wanted the pieces of the snake—the colonies—to come together to survive. However, in 1754, the American colonies were not yet willing to work together for a common goal.

REVIEW What was Benjamin Franklin's role in the Albany Congress?

Braddock's Defeat

As the French and Indian War continued, the British colonists soon knew that they needed more help if they were to win the war. So **Parliament**, the lawmaking body of the British government in London, sent an army to the colonies to help fight the French and their Indian allies. General Edward Braddock commanded the British forces. He invited George Washington along as an adviser.

Braddock's first goal was to capture Fort Duquesne. In April 1755 he and more than 1,800 British and colonial troops began the long march to the fort. Washington later described how the soldiers looked in their bright, colorful uniforms—British red and colonial blue—marching off against the deep green of the forest.

Not far from where Washington and his men had built Fort Necessity, the British met a force of about 900 French and Indian soldiers. For two hours the French and their Indian allies fired at the British from behind trees and boulders.

Benjamin Franklin hoped this simple cartoon would help convince the colonies to approve his Albany Plan of Union. The part of the snake labeled *N.E.* represented the New England Colonies.

General Braddock (above) and his troops panicked when the French and Indians fired on them from behind rocks and trees.

The British, trained to fight in open fields, had never fought an enemy this way. They "broke and ran," Washington later wrote, "as sheep before the hounds." When the battle ended, two-thirds of the British were dead or wounded. Braddock was one of those killed.

Braddock's loss left the British colonists in the Ohio Valley without protection. For the next two years, the French and their Indian allies carried out attacks against those colonists.

REVIEW What was a major cause of General Braddock's loss?

LESSON 1 REVIEW

Summary Time Line

1750 — 1754 Fort Necessity is attacked; Albany Congress meets — 1755 General Braddock is defeated — 1755

Focus Skill — CAUSE AND EFFECT What caused the French and Indian War?

1 BIG IDEA How did conflicts over land lead to a war between Britain and France?

2 VOCABULARY Use the words **congress** and **delegate** in a sentence about the Albany Plan of Union.

3 TIME LINE Which event took place first, General Braddock's defeat or the attack on Fort Necessity?

4 GEOGRAPHY Where was the opening battle fought in the French and Indian War?

5 HISTORY What was George Washington's role in the French and Indian War?

6 CRITICAL THINKING—Analyze Why is the Albany Plan of Union important in American history?

PERFORMANCE—Draw a Cartoon Imagine that you have been asked to draw a cartoon different from the one Franklin published to show support for the Albany Plan of Union. Draw your cartoon and share it with a classmate.

272 ■ Unit 4

Britain Wins North America

1750 — 1770 — 1790
1758–1763

For the first two years of fighting, the French and Indian War had been only a North American conflict. In 1756, however, it became a world war, known as the Seven Years War, with battles fought in Europe and Asia, as well as in North America. To win the war, William Pitt, Britain's new leader of Parliament, decided to focus on North America. He sent more troops and more supplies there and eventually turned the war in Britain's favor.

The British Road to Victory

In 1758 the British captured three French forts—Duquesne at the Forks of the Ohio River, and Louisbourg and Frontenac, in what is now Canada. The following year they took forts at Crown Point, Niagara, and Ticonderoga in present-day New York. The British also attacked French forces near the city of Quebec in Canada. In September 1759 General James Wolfe's British troops defeated French forces under the command of the Marquis de Montcalm on the Plains of Abraham, near Quebec. During the next year, the British closed a circle of troops and ships around French Canada.

· LESSON ·

2

 CAUSE AND EFFECT
As you read, look for causes and effects of the disagreements between British leaders and colonists.

BIG IDEA
Britain refused to allow colonists to settle on its newly won lands.

VOCABULARY
proclamation
bill of rights
pioneer
gap

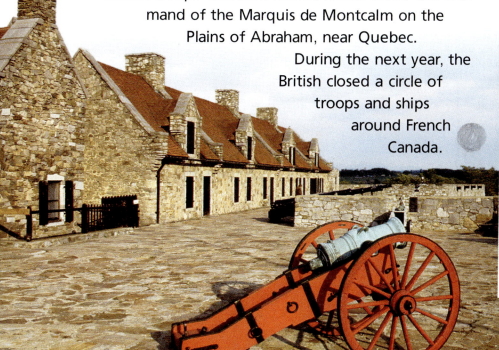

William Pitt's leadership helped the British win many battles against the French, including the one at Fort Ticonderoga (left).

Chapter 8 • 273

Finally, in 1760, after the British captured Montreal, another major French city, the French gave up. Fighting, however, continued in Europe.

In the closing months of the war in North America, Spain joined with France in the fight against the British. Because of its superior sea power, however, Britain defeated Spanish forces in 1762. To make up for Spain's losses in the war, France gave Spain most of Louisiana and part of what is now Florida.

The French and Indian War finally ended in Europe and in North America in 1763, when the French and the British signed a peace treaty in Paris. Under the terms of the Treaty of Paris, France gave most of its lands in present-day Canada to Britain. France also gave up claim to most of the lands between the Appalachian Mountains and the Mississippi River. Also as a result of the Treaty of Paris, Britain received Florida from Spain.

REVIEW What effect did the Treaty of Paris have on Britain? **CAUSE AND EFFECT**

Pontiac's Rebellion

Now that the lands between the Appalachians and the Mississippi were under British control, many colonists began to settle there. The Native Americans who lived there, however, did not welcome these newcomers.

Chief Pontiac (PAHN•tee•ak) of the Ottawa tribe wanted to stop the loss of Indian hunting lands. So Pontiac and other Indian leaders united the tribes of the Great Lakes and Ohio Valley region to fight against the settlers.

In May 1763 Pontiac and his united tribes began attacking British forts in what is now western Pennsylvania, Ohio, Michigan, and Indiana. Most were destroyed. Two of the outposts that survived were Fort Detroit and Fort Pitt, once known as Fort Duquesne.

Pontiac and his forces attacked the forts to get guns and supplies, which in the past they had gotten from the French. However, as winter came, many Indian fighters signed peace treaties with the British and began to return to their homes. Without supplies or soldiers, Pontiac had to give up control of the British forts.

REVIEW What caused Pontiac's Rebellion?

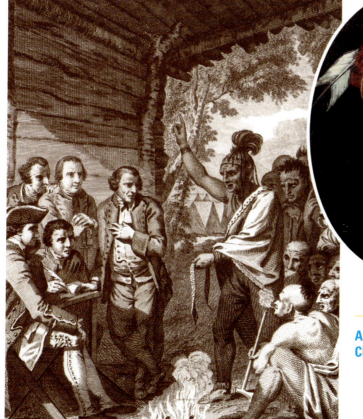

After losing a battle at Bushy Run, in Pennsylvania, Chief Pontiac refused to sign a peace treaty.

Chapter 8 ■ 275

The Proclamation of 1763

Many British leaders in London blamed Pontiac's Rebellion on the backcountry traders and settlers. They believed that these colonists did not have the right to claim or buy land in the region. The British government decided that stopping the westward movement of its colonists was the only way to end the fighting and prevent further trouble. To do this, the British king, George III, issued the Proclamation of 1763. A **proclamation** is an order from a country's leader to its citizens.

The Proclamation of 1763 said that British colonists could not buy land west of the Appalachians from the Indians, hunt on it, or explore it. Settlers already living there were to leave at once. George III said the lands west of the Appalachians were to be used only by the Native Americans. The king hoped the order would prevent more wars between the colonists and the Native Americans.

Indian leaders were pleased that the British king wanted to keep the colonists off their land. The colonists, however, were furious. They felt the proclamation took away their right as British citizens to travel where they wanted. As British citizens, the American colonists had the same rights as British citizens living in Britain. Those rights were listed in the English Bill of Rights which Parliament had created in 1689. A **bill of rights** is a list of rights. The English Bill of Rights said that the government could not take certain rights away from the people.

The colonists grew even more upset when the king ordered British soldiers to remain in North America to protect the newly won lands. The colonists felt this action also took away their rights. They became even angrier when the king gave his colonial governors greater authority over the colonies.

The colonists had not expected these changes. They had hoped to gain more authority to govern themselves. Instead, they now had to obey even stricter laws made by a government far away.

REVIEW What changes took place in the government of the colonies after the French and Indian War?

Americans Continue West

The Proclamation of 1763 did not stop colonial pioneers from continuing their push west into the frontier. A **pioneer** is a person who first settles a new place. Daniel Boone was one of the earliest and best-known colonial pioneers to travel west across the Appalachian Mountains.

During the French and Indian War, Boone met John Finley, a British fur trader. Finley told Boone stories about visiting a wonderful land west of the Appalachians.

Daniel Boone was born in Pennsylvania. At an early age he came to love living in the woods and hunting.

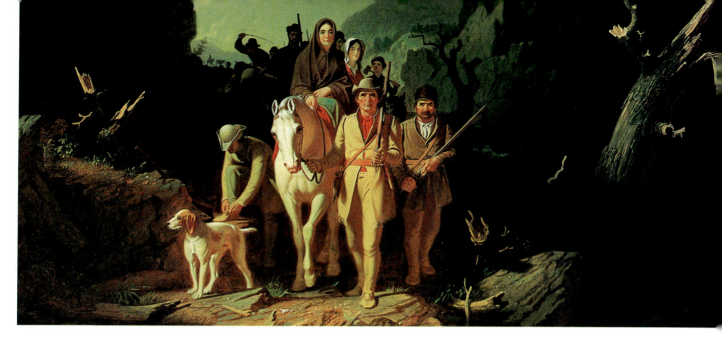

Daniel Boone leads pioneers through the Cumberland Gap in this painting by George Caleb Bingham.

In time, colonists began to call this land Kentucky, which comes from an Indian word for "meadowland."

After the war, Boone tried to reach this land, but he could not find a way over the mountains. In 1769, with Finley's help, Boone found an Indian trail that he followed across the Appalachians through what is now the Cumberland Gap. A **gap** is an opening, or low place, between mountains. The route Boone followed was later widened for wagons and became known as the Wilderness Road.

REVIEW Who was Daniel Boone?

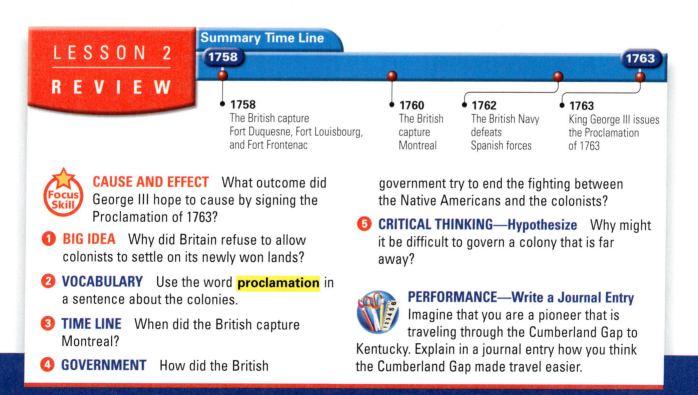

LESSON 2 REVIEW

Summary Time Line 1758 — 1763

- **1758** The British capture Fort Duquesne, Fort Louisbourg, and Fort Frontenac
- **1760** The British capture Montreal
- **1762** The British Navy defeats Spanish forces
- **1763** King George III issues the Proclamation of 1763

CAUSE AND EFFECT What outcome did George III hope to cause by signing the Proclamation of 1763?

1. **BIG IDEA** Why did Britain refuse to allow colonists to settle on its newly won lands?
2. **VOCABULARY** Use the word **proclamation** in a sentence about the colonies.
3. **TIME LINE** When did the British capture Montreal?
4. **GOVERNMENT** How did the British government try to end the fighting between the Native Americans and the colonists?
5. **CRITICAL THINKING—Hypothesize** Why might it be difficult to govern a colony that is far away?

PERFORMANCE—Write a Journal Entry Imagine that you are a pioneer that is traveling through the Cumberland Gap to Kentucky. Explain in a journal entry how you think the Cumberland Gap made travel easier.

Chapter 8 ■ 277

SKILLS · MAP AND GLOBE

Compare Historical Maps

VOCABULARY
hatch lines

▶ WHY IT MATTERS

The Treaty of Paris that officially ended the French and Indian War changed the map of North America. The historical maps on page 279 show the changes. A historical map provides information about a place at a certain time in history. Knowing how to use historical maps can help you learn how borders have changed over time.

▶ WHAT YOU NEED TO KNOW

Colors are important map symbols. Sometimes colors help you tell water from land on a map. Colors on a map can also show you the areas claimed by different cities, states, or countries.

One of the color symbols on Map B has a pattern of stripes that mapmakers call hatch lines. **Hatch lines** on historical maps often show areas claimed by two or more countries. Hatch lines may also show land that has a special purpose.

The map key on Map B tells you that the region shown by hatch lines was claimed by the British. For this reason one of the colors of the hatch lines is the color used for the British. The map key also tells you that the British reserved this land for the Native Americans.

Flags over North America

Spain

France

Russia

Britain

These flags were flown over different parts of North America in the mid-1700s.

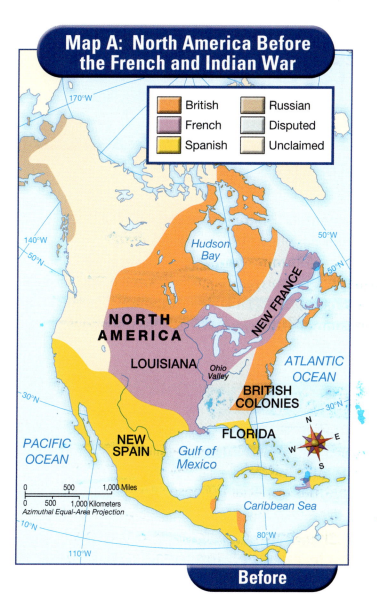

Map A: North America Before the French and Indian War

Before

Map B: North America After the French and Indian War

After

▶ PRACTICE THE SKILL

Look at the map keys to learn what each color represents. Then use the maps to answer these questions.

1. What color is used to show the land claimed by the French? by the British? by the Spanish?
2. After the French and Indian War, which European country claimed the area known as Louisiana?
3. Which European country claimed Florida before the French and Indian War? after the war?

▶ APPLY WHAT YOU LEARNED

Write a paragraph that describes what these historical maps show and explains why historical maps are useful. Share your paragraph with a classmate.

 Practice your map and globe skills with the **GeoSkills CD-ROM**.

Chapter 8 ▪ 279

LESSON 3

Colonists Speak Out

1750 — 1770 — 1790

1764–1770

CAUSE AND EFFECT
As you read, look for causes and effects of the new tax laws in the colonies.

BIG IDEA
Many colonists spoke out against the new tax laws passed by the British Parliament.

VOCABULARY
budget
representation
treason
boycott
declaration
repeal
liberty

As the British Parliament in London discussed its 1764 **budget**, or plan for spending money, British leader George Grenville had a suggestion. He proposed that Parliament pass new laws requiring American colonists to pay more taxes. This extra money would help pay the cost of the French and Indian War. It would also help support the British soldiers stationed in the colonies.

The Sugar Act

Parliament agreed with Grenville and began to pass new tax laws for the colonies. The first of these money-raising laws came to be known as the Sugar Act. Passed in 1764, the Sugar Act added a tax on sugar and other goods coming into the colonies from other places.

Having to pay this new tax angered many colonists. What bothered them even more was that they had had no voice in deciding on this tax law. The king and Parliament taxed the colonists without their consent, or agreement. Many colonists believed that this action violated their rights as British citizens.

One of the first colonial leaders to speak out against the Sugar Act was James Otis of Massachusetts. He called the tax "unjust." Not all colonists agreed. Some sided with the British government. Martin Howard of Rhode Island

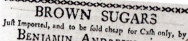

George Grenville urged King George III (left and on British coin) and members of the British Parliament to support new taxes on sugar and other goods.

280 • Unit 4

felt that the colonists should be more grateful to the king and the Parliament than they were. Without British help, Howard reminded them, they might now be under the rule of France or Spain.

REVIEW Why were many colonists angered by the Sugar Act?

The Stamp Act

In 1765, less than a year after the Sugar Act became law, Parliament passed a second tax law for the colonies. The Stamp Act placed a tax on newspapers, almanacs, pamphlets, all kinds of legal documents, insurance policies, licenses, and even playing cards. Each of these items had to have a special stamp on it to show that the tax had been paid. Because Parliament knew that the stamp tax might anger the colonists more than the sugar tax, it hired colonists as tax collectors.

Reaction to the Stamp Act in the colonies was the same as it had been to the Sugar Act. Once again, what really upset many of the colonists was that they had not had a voice in deciding to pass the law. They did not have a voice because they did not have any **representation** in the British Parliament.

POINTS OF VIEW
Taxes

THOMAS WHATELY, a member of the British Parliament

❝ We are not yet recovered from a War undertaken . . . for their [the colonists'] Protection . . . and no Time was ever so seasonable for claiming their Assistance [help]. The Distribution is too unequal, of Benefits only to the colonies, and all of the Burthens [burdens] upon the Mother Country [Britain]. ❞

SAMUEL ADAMS, a member of the Massachusetts legislature

❝ We are told to be quiet when we see that very money which is torn from us by lawless force . . . to feed and pamper a set of infamous wretches [British soldiers and officials] who swarm like the locusts of Egypt. ❞

Analyze the Viewpoints
1. What views about taxes did each person hold?
2. **Make It Relevant** Look at the Letters to the Editor section of your newspaper. Find two letters that express different viewpoints about the same issue. Then write a paragraph that summarizes the viewpoints of each letter.

This leather box held stamps (right) that colonists had to buy to be placed on many printed items.

Chapter 8 ■ 281

No one was acting or speaking for them in London.

James Otis again spoke out. He told a crowd in Boston that they should refuse to pay the stamp tax until they had representation in Parliament. The colonists began repeating his words,

> " No taxation without representation. "

In Virginia, Patrick Henry told his fellow members of the House of Burgesses that they alone should decide what taxes Virginians would pay. Henry said that Parliament did not represent the colonies. The colonies had their own legislatures to represent them.

Members of the House of Burgesses who supported the British government shouted "Treason!" during Patrick Henry's speech. By accusing Henry of **treason**, they were saying that he was working against his government. Henry is said to have answered, "If this be treason, make the most of it!" Although some members protested the decision, the House of Burgesses voted against paying any new taxes Parliament passed unless the colonists gave their consent.

More and more people in the 13 colonies decided not to buy goods that had been stamped. Many colonists also began to **boycott**, or refuse to buy, any British goods. In Boston, women wove their own cloth. Some colonists worked illegally to smuggle tea and other goods

This teapot shows the colonists' unhappiness with the Stamp Act.

Stamp Act Protest

Analyze Primary Sources

This 1765 drawing shows colonists in New Hampshire protesting the Stamp Act.

1. The coffin represents the colonists' wish to see the Stamp Act die.
2. The figure made of straw represents a stamp tax collector.
3. This angry protester prepares to throw a rock at the straw figure.

◆ Why do you think the protesters placed a straw figure high on a pole?

282 ■ Unit 4

from the Netherlands and the Caribbean. In some colonies, people began drinking tea made from the local sassafras trees instead of buying tea from Britain.

Some colonists protested the Stamp Act in more violent ways. They attacked the homes of the stamp tax collectors, breaking windows and stealing property. They beat some tax collectors and chased several out of their cities and towns.

REVIEW What caused many colonists to boycott British goods?
CAUSE AND EFFECT

The Stamp Act Congress

Since the time of the Albany Congress, some colonial leaders such as Benjamin Franklin and James Otis had thought that the colonies should work together. In 1765 Franklin, Otis, and leaders from nine colonies met in New York City to talk about the Stamp Act. This meeting came to be called the Stamp Act Congress.

Members of the Stamp Act Congress talked about the problems the new tax laws caused. For example, people who did not obey the Stamp Act could be tried in special courts without a jury. A British citizen had the right to be tried by a jury of fellow citizens.

British citizens were also considered to be innocent until proven guilty, and their property could not be taken away without just cause. To catch smugglers in the colonies, however, Parliament had passed the Writs of Assistance. These rules allowed British officers to break into any colonist's home or business.

In response, John Dickinson from Pennsylvania proposed that a **declaration**, or official statement, be sent to King

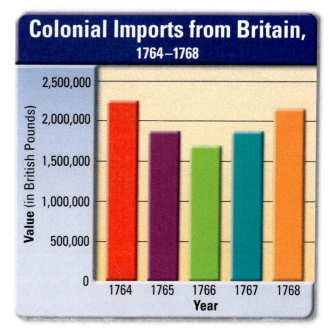

Analyze Graphs After colonists began to boycott British goods in 1765, the value of colonial imports from Britain decreased.

◆ By about how much did the value of colonial imports decrease from 1764 to 1766?

George III. The "Declaration of Rights and Grievances" (GREE•vuhn•suhz) listed the colonists' rights as British citizens. It declared that the British government had no right to tax the colonists without their agreement. Members of the Stamp Act Congress also stated that the use of the special courts took away citizens' rights.

In Britain, merchants began to worry about how the colonists' boycott would affect their businesses. Sales of British goods had decreased by almost half in several colonies, and British merchants who depended on trade with the colonies had already started to lose money. The merchants urged Parliament to **repeal**, or cancel, the Stamp Act.

After much discussion, Parliament repealed the Stamp Act in March 1766. The next year, however, it passed some new laws called the Townshend Acts.

Chapter 8 ■ 283

These laws placed taxes on lead, glass, paint, paper, and tea brought into the colonies. By passing the Townshend Acts, the British government showed it believed that Parliament still had the authority to make laws for the colonists.

REVIEW What did the Declaration of Rights and Grievances state?

GEOGRAPHY

Boston
Understanding Places and Regions

This painting of Boston in 1770 shows the Old State House in the center. At the time it was the headquarters of His Majesty's Custom House. Taxes on trade goods were paid and collected in custom houses located in each port city in the 13 colonies. The Boston Massacre took place just east of the Boston Custom House.

The Boston Massacre

To further show its authority over the colonists, Parliament sent more soldiers to North America. By 1770 there were more than 9,000 British soldiers in the 13 colonies. The British government said that the soldiers were there to protect the western lands won in the French and Indian War. Most of the soldiers, however, were stationed in cities along the Atlantic coast.

Having British soldiers in their cities angered many colonists. They called the soldiers "lobsters," "redcoats," and "bloody-backs," making fun of their bright red uniform jackets. Some soldiers responded to this name-calling by destroying colonial property.

As the anger between the British soldiers and the colonists grew stronger, fights broke out more and more often. Some of the worst fighting took place in Boston on March 5, 1770. In the evening a large crowd gathered near several British soldiers.

Some colonists in the crowd shouted insults at the soldiers and began to throw rocks and snowballs. As the crowd moved forward, the soldiers fired their weapons. Three colonists were killed, and two died later. Among the dead was a former slave named Crispus Attucks (A•tuhks). Many people consider Crispus Attucks the first person to be killed in the struggle for American liberty. **Liberty** means "the freedom of people to make their own laws."

Paul Revere, a Boston silversmith, made an engraving, or picture, showing the soldiers shooting at the colonists. He titled it *The Bloody Massacre*. The word *massacre* (MA•sih•ker) means "the killing of a number of people who cannot defend themselves." The shooting in Boston was not really a massacre, but to this day the event is called the Boston Massacre.

REVIEW What was Crispus Attucks's role in the Boston Massacre?

Crispus Attucks was one of the colonists killed at the Boston Massacre.

LESSON 3 REVIEW

Summary Time Line

- 1764 Sugar Act is passed
- 1765 Stamp Act is passed; Stamp Act Congress meets
- 1766 Stamp Act is repealed
- 1770 Boston Massacre takes place

CAUSE AND EFFECT What caused the Boston Massacre?

1. **BIG IDEA** Why did the new tax laws cause conflict between the colonists and Britain?
2. **VOCABULARY** Use the terms **representation** and **boycott** to describe the colonists' reaction to the Stamp Act.
3. **TIME LINE** How long after the Stamp Act was passed was the law repealed?
4. **ECONOMICS** Why did the British Parliament decide to pass new tax laws for the colonies?
5. **CRITICAL THINKING—Evaluate** Do you think Parliament had the right to tax the colonists? Why or why not?

PERFORMANCE—Make a Poster Imagine that you are a colonist. Make a poster that encourages other colonists to boycott British goods. Tell why you think the tax laws are unfair, and give reasons for the boycott.

Chapter 8 ■ 285

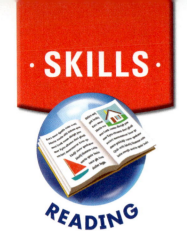

SKILLS

Determine Point of View

VOCABULARY
point of view
bias

▶ WHY IT MATTERS

You can get information from many sources—television, radio, newspapers, reference books, and the Internet. Before you use this information, however, you need to decide if you can trust its reliability.

▶ WHAT YOU NEED TO KNOW

In the study of history, written records and pictures provide important information. They describe or show what happened. Some may show an accurate description from many points of view or from one person's point of view. A person's **point of view** is his or her set of beliefs that have been shaped by factors such as whether that person is old or young, male or female, rich or poor. Some points of view can be supported by fact, but written records and pictures showing a single point of view may bias your thinking. You show **bias** when you favor or oppose someone or something.

To find the point of view in a picture, follow these steps.

Step 1 Identify who made the picture. Did that person see what happened or know about it only from the accounts of others? What appears to be a firsthand account may not be.

This engraving by Paul Revere shows his view of the Boston Massacre.

Step 2 Think about the audience. For whom was this picture meant? The picture's audience may have affected what was drawn and how it was drawn.

Step 3 Check for bias. Watch for clues that show a one-sided view.

Step 4 Compare pictures of the same event, when possible. Comparing sources can give you more balanced information and help you identify bias.

▶ PRACTICE THE SKILL

Drawing B is based on the Boston Massacre as it was described during the trial of the British soldiers who fired at the colonists. John Adams, a lawyer from Boston, was asked by the British government to defend the British soldiers who were arrested for murder. Adams agreed to defend them because he felt the British soldiers deserved a fair trial. He argued that the soldiers had fired their weapons in self-defense. The jury agreed. It found Captain Thomas Preston and six soldiers not guilty. Two of the soldiers were found guilty of a lesser crime.

Drawing A is the engraving of the event made by Paul Revere, a colonist who worked for colonial rights. During the massacre five colonists were killed.

1. In what ways are the drawings alike? How are they different?
2. Which is more likely based on first-hand information?
3. For whom do you think Drawing A was meant? Explain.
4. Does Drawing A show bias? What details in the picture might show Revere's feeling about the British soldiers?
5. For whom do you think Drawing B was meant? Explain.

▶ APPLY WHAT YOU LEARNED

With a partner, preview the pictures in a magazine article. Follow the steps in What You Need to Know to study the pictures more closely. Describe the messages that the pictures convey.

This picture of the Boston Massacre is based on the descriptions given during the trial of the British Soldiers who fired at the colonists.

LESSON 4

The Road to War

1750 — 1770 — 1790
1773–1775

The three years following the Boston Massacre were fairly quiet in the 13 colonies. Some historians have called this time "the calm before the storm." The storm came when Parliament again angered the colonists by passing more laws.

The Boston Tea Party

In 1770 Parliament repealed all of the Townshend Acts except for the tea tax. Soon after, Parliament tried to give a monopoly on tea to the East India Company, Britain's chief tea producer. A **monopoly** is complete control of a product or service in a certain area by a single person or group. This includes control over pricing and competition.

The East India Company was able to sell tea for much cheaper. Colonial merchants could no longer make money in the tea trade. So some colonists decided to boycott tea.

In Pennsylvania, colonists did not allow ships carrying British tea to enter their ports. In Massachusetts, colonists did not want ships loaded with tea to dock at their ports either,

This painting shows one artist's idea of what happened at the Boston Tea Party. The tea leaves in the bottle on the next page are thought to be from this event.

CAUSE AND EFFECT

As you read, look for causes and effects of arguments between the colonists and the British.

BIG IDEA

The colonists began to work together when Parliament passed more laws for the colonies.

VOCABULARY

monopoly
blockade
quarter
intolerable
petition

· BIOGRAPHY ·

Samuel Adams 1722–1803

Character Trait: Citizenship

Samuel Adams, a cousin of John Adams, helped plan the Boston Tea Party. He believed in the use of violence only when all else failed. Since the days of the Sugar Act in 1764, Adams had attempted to get people to work peacefully for their rights through committees and other meetings. In 1772 he set up a committee of correspondence in Boston. Then he got other colonists to do the same. These committees corresponded with, or wrote letters to, one another. In this way news of what was happening in one colony spread quickly to the others.

GO ONLINE — MULTIMEDIA BIOGRAPHIES
Visit The Learning Site at www.harcourtschool.com to learn about other famous people.

---

but the governor, Thomas Hutchinson, gave the order to let the ships dock.

On December 16, 1773, colonists took part in what became known as the Boston Tea Party. That night, members of a group known as the Sons of Liberty boarded the ships. Disguised as Mohawk Indians, they broke open 342 tea chests and dumped the tea into the harbor.

REVIEW How did the colonists respond to the East India Company's unfair advantage in the tea trade?

Intolerable Acts

The Sons of Liberty knew that their actions would anger Parliament. After hearing about the Boston Tea Party, Parliament, now led by Lord Frederick North, passed a new series of laws to punish the colonists of Massachusetts.

The first of these laws was the Boston Port Bill, passed in March 1774. It closed the port of Boston until the colonists paid for the destroyed tea. To enforce the law, Parliament ordered the British navy to blockade Boston Harbor. To **blockade** is to use warships to prevent other ships from entering or leaving a port.

Parliament then passed the Massachusetts Government Act. It stopped the Massachusetts legislature from making laws and banned town meetings not authorized by the governor. To further punish the colonists, the British government ordered them to **quarter** British soldiers, or to feed and provide shelter for them. Some colonists even had to take the soldiers into their homes.

In response, the colonists shouted that these laws were "intolerable acts!" The word **intolerable** means "unacceptable." The Intolerable Acts, as the new laws came to be called, led many colonists to recognize that they had a common enemy.

REVIEW What were some of the Intolerable Acts?

Chapter 8 • 289

The First Continental Congress

Many of the colonists believed that the British government would do anything, even use its army, to make them obey the British laws. So representatives of the colonies decided to meet to discuss ways they might respond to the growing British threat. The first meeting took place in September 1774 at Philadelphia's Carpenters' Hall. Because it was the first of its kind on the North American continent, the meeting was later called the First Continental Congress.

The 56 delegates at the Congress represented the wide range of thought in the colonies. Some wanted to break away from Britain. Others wanted to find a way to get along better with Britain. Following neither extreme, the Congress agreed to develop a statement of rights. The delegates stated these rights in a **petition**, or a signed request, that they sent to Parliament.

In the petition, the Congress said that the colonists had a right to "life, liberty, and property." The Congress also stated that only the colonial legislatures had the authority to make laws "in all cases of taxation and internal polity [government]." The petition concluded by issuing a warning: "We are *for the present* only resolved to pursue . . . peaceable measures."

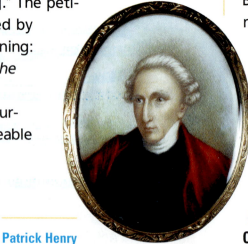

Patrick Henry

DEMOCRATIC VALUES
The Right to Privacy

One of the rights listed in the English Bill of Rights prevented soldiers and other government officials from entering a person's home without the owner's permission or a warrant, or order, from a court of law. As more and more British soldiers were sent to North America, however, the British government needed more places for them to live. Some colonists' homes were seized by British soldiers. These soldiers went into the people's homes and often lived there without the owner's permission.

Today, the right of privacy remains one of the most valued rights in the United States. According to the rights of United States citizens, in most cases government officials must acquire a warrant from a court of law before they can enter a person's home without permission.

Analyze the Value

1. Why did the American colonists believe their rights had been ignored by the British soldiers?
2. **Make It Relevant** Why do you think privacy is an important right for Americans to have?

The Congress set May 10, 1775, as the deadline for Parliament to respond to the petition. If Parliament took no action by then, the Congress would meet again. Before ending the meeting, however, the members of the Continental Congress agreed to stop most trade with Britain.

Meanwhile, in Virginia colonial leaders such as Patrick Henry suggested that the colonists begin preparing for war. He told the House of Burgesses, "I know not what course others may take: but as for me, give me liberty or give me death!"

REVIEW Why did the First Continental Congress meet? **CAUSE AND EFFECT**

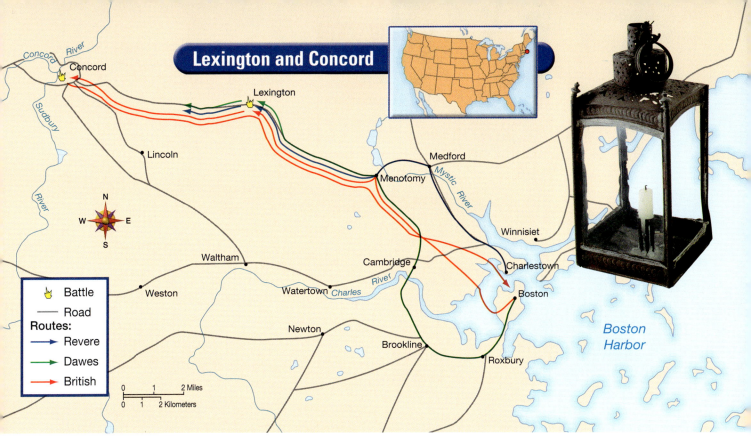

 Movement The battles at Lexington and Concord marked the beginning of a long war between the 13 colonies and Britain. The lantern (above, right) is one of the two lanterns that were hung in a church tower to signal that the British were coming by boat.

❓ What cities did Revere and Dawes ride through to warn of the British approach?

Lexington and Concord

In Massachusetts the colonists responded to the Intolerable Acts by organizing special militia units. They were called Minutemen because they could be ready in a minute to defend Massachusetts.

In April 1775 General Thomas Gage heard that two leaders of the Sons of Liberty, John Hancock and Samuel Adams, were meeting in the village of Lexington. Gage also heard that the Minutemen were storing weapons in Concord, near Lexington. The general ordered 700 British soldiers to find the weapons and arrest Hancock and Adams.

Learning of the general's order, Paul Revere, a member of the Sons of Liberty, rode his horse to Lexington to warn Hancock and Adams. Revere was joined by William Dawes and Samuel Prescott.

A group of men dressed as Minutemen reenact the battle at Concord at Minute Man National Historical Park in Concord, Massachusetts.

Chapter 8 ■ 291

This statue of Paul Revere stands near the Old North Church in Boston, Massachusetts.

They each rode off to Concord to warn the Minutemen that the British were on their way. When the British arrived at Lexington on April 19, 1775, they found that the Minutemen were waiting for them. Shots were fired, and eight of the Minutemen were killed. Several others were wounded.

From Lexington the British marched to Concord. However, the weapons they expected to find had been moved. As they marched back to Boston, the Minutemen fired at the British from the woods and fields beside the road. British losses for the day were 73 killed and 174 wounded. 93 Minutemen were killed or wounded in the fighting.

The fighting at Lexington and Concord marked the beginning of a long, bitter war between Britain and its 13 colonies. To some, it seemed a small battle, but for others it was a world event, a history-making first step in creating the United States of America. The poet Ralph Waldo Emerson would later call the shots fired at Lexington and Concord "the shot heard round the world."

REVIEW Why did the British go to Lexington and Concord?

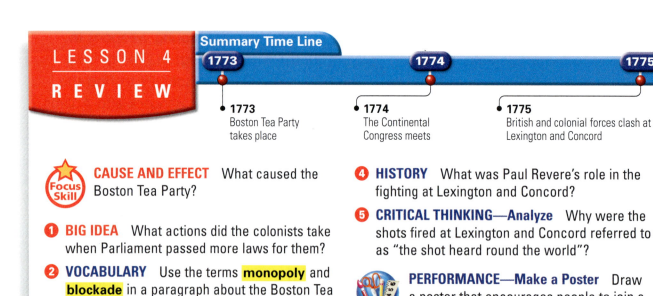

LESSON 4 REVIEW

Summary Time Line

- **1773** Boston Tea Party takes place
- **1774** The Continental Congress meets
- **1775** British and colonial forces clash at Lexington and Concord

CAUSE AND EFFECT What caused the Boston Tea Party?

1 BIG IDEA What actions did the colonists take when Parliament passed more laws for them?

2 VOCABULARY Use the terms **monopoly** and **blockade** in a paragraph about the Boston Tea Party.

3 TIME LINE When was the fighting at Lexington and Concord?

4 HISTORY What was Paul Revere's role in the fighting at Lexington and Concord?

5 CRITICAL THINKING—Analyze Why were the shots fired at Lexington and Concord referred to as "the shot heard round the world"?

PERFORMANCE—Make a Poster Draw a poster that encourages people to join a colonial militia. Use words that you think will convince people to fight for liberty. Share your poster with your classmates.

The Second Continental Congress

LESSON 5

CAUSE AND EFFECT
As you read, look for causes and effects of the Second Continental Congress.

BIG IDEA
Colonial leaders prepared for war with Britain and fought the first major battle of the Revolutionary War.

VOCABULARY
commander in chief
earthwork
olive branch
mercenary

1750 1770 1790
1775

News of the fighting at Lexington and Concord quickly spread throughout the 13 colonies. As a result, the Second Continental Congress was called to meet in Philadelphia on May 10, 1775. Colonial leaders gathered at the Pennsylvania State House to decide what the colonies should do. Only Georgia failed to send representatives.

Hope for Peace, Plan for War

Once again, delegates were divided in their views, or opinions. Some called for war against the British. Others, such as John Dickinson, tried to persuade the group to avoid fighting. Dickinson believed that the "cause of liberty should not be sullied [soiled] by turbulence and tumult [commotion and uproar]." By June, however, the Congress had agreed that the colonies should at least begin to prepare for war.

The first step was for the Congress to form an army. This new "Continental Army" would have full-time, regular soldiers in addition to the part-time militia that each colony already had. The Continental Army was the first united colonial army. It would become the main army that would be assisted by the state militias.

On June 15, 1775, Congress, at the suggestion of John Adams and others, asked George Washington to lead the new Continental Army. Adams suggested Washington because of his "skill and experience as an officer, . . . great talents and universal character." Adams believed that Washington not only understood soldiers but that he knew how to fight a war.

The Second Continental Congress chose George Washington, shown here in his military uniform, to lead the Continental Army.

Chapter 8 ■ 293

The next day Washington humbly accepted the role of commander in chief, the leader of all the military forces.

To supply the Continental Army, the Congress asked each colony to contribute money to pay for guns, bullets, food, and uniforms. The Congress also decided to print its own paper money, which came to be known as Continental currency. The Congress paid the soldiers in bills that they called continentals.

By the time George Washington left Philadelphia to take charge of the Continental Army, which was already in Massachusetts, the first major battle of the Revolutionary War had already been fought. The Battle of Bunker Hill took place near Boston on June 17, 1775.

REVIEW How did the Second Continental Congress prepare for war?

The Battle of Bunker Hill

After the fighting at Lexington and Concord, angry citizens in Massachusetts started to build earthworks, or walls of earth and stone, near Boston. These earthworks would help the colonists defend themselves if there were another battle with the British soldiers.

Meanwhile, Boston had become the only safe place for the British. The Minutemen had taken control of the surrounding countryside. The only way the British could enter or leave Boston was by sea.

After dark on June 16, 1775, some colonists began to build new earthworks on Breed's Hill, across the Charles River from Boston. When General Gage learned of this the next morning, he ordered British ships in the harbor to open fire on the colonists. Gage also sent General William Howe and 2,400 British soldiers to capture Breed's Hill. Shortly after noon,

lines of British soldiers marched up Breed's Hill to the roll of drums. When the British drew close to the earthworks, the 1,600 colonists inside let loose a deadly hail of shot. The fighting was so fierce that, to save bullets, colonial commander Israel Putnam said to his soldiers,

> **"Don't fire until you see the whites of their eyes."**

The colonists drove the British back twice before running out of gun powder. The British finally took the hill but at great cost. More than 1,000 of the 2,400 British soldiers were killed or wounded. About 350 colonists died or were wounded.

The battle at Breed's Hill was misnamed for nearby Bunker Hill. Although the colonists were driven from the field, they were proud of how well they had done. The British had learned that fighting the colonists would not be easy.

REVIEW What was the cause of the Battle of Bunker Hill? **CAUSE AND EFFECT**

A CLOSER LOOK
The Battle of Bunker Hill

The first major battle of the Revolutionary War, the Battle of Bunker Hill, was fought on June 17, 1775. The British won the battle, but they suffered the heaviest losses of the entire war.

1. British forces first landed near Morton's Point and formed battle lines.
2. British forces marched up Breed's Hill to attack the colonists.
3. Colonists fired on the British from behind earthworks on Breed's Hill.

❖ Why do you think the colonists chose to build earthworks on top of Breed's Hill?

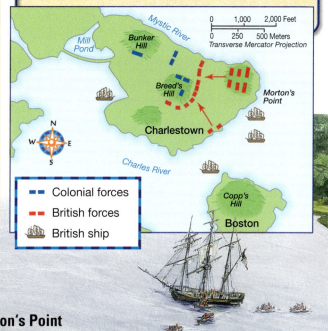

• BIOGRAPHY •

Phillis Wheatley   1753?–1784
Character Trait: Patriotism

Phillis Wheatley was one of the best-known poets of her time. She was born in Africa and brought to Massachusetts as a slave. Unlike most enslaved people, however, Wheatley learned to read and write. She was later freed upon the death of her owner.

Wheatley's poetry was first published in 1770, while she was still a teenager. In October 1775 Wheatley wrote a poem honoring George Washington on his being named commander in chief of the Continental Army.

"Proceed, great chief, and with virtue on thy side,
Thy ev'ry action let the goddess guide.
A crown, a mansion, and a throne that shine,
With gold unfading, Washington! be thine."

MULTIMEDIA BIOGRAPHIES
Visit The Learning Site at www.harcourtschool.com to learn about other famous people.

A Foreign War

Hoping to avoid more fighting, the Second Continental Congress agreed on July 5, 1775, to send another petition to King George III. This petition came to be known as the Olive Branch Petition because it expressed the colonists' desire for a peaceful end to the fighting. The **olive branch** is an ancient symbol of peace.

In London, the Battle of Bunker Hill had further angered British leaders. Lord North advised King George III to think of the fighting in the colonies as a foreign war. On August 23 the king issued a proclamation of rebellion. In it, he promised to use every measure to crush the rebellion and "bring the traitors to justice." As a result, by the time the Olive Branch Petition reached British leaders in London on August 24, it was already a lost cause.

To fight the colonists, the king called for the British army in the colonies to be enlarged. To accomplish this, he ordered the hiring of mercenaries (MER•suhn•air•eez) from Germany. A **mercenary** is a soldier who serves for pay in the military of a foreign government. Many of the German mercenaries were Hessians, from the Hesse region of Germany.

The king also called on Britain's Iroquois and other Native American allies for help. He knew that many Indian tribes hated the colonists for ignoring the Proclamation of 1763 and settling the lands west of the Appalachians. Because of this the king believed that many Native Americans would help the British fight the colonists.

Meanwhile, the Second Continental Congress also prepared for war. In October the Congress created a navy, which at first was nothing more than a few fishing boats. In November the Congress established a marine corps, or "army of the sea." It also set up a committee to seek alliances with various Native American tribes.

Earlier that fall, in September 1775, Georgia had agreed to join the Second Continental Congress and support the Revolutionary War. Many of the delegates could now agree with what Patrick Henry had told them during the First Continental Congress,

> 66 The distinctions between Virginians, Pennsylvanians, New Yorkers are no more. I am not a Virginian, but an American. 99

Finally, the Continental Congress stood for all 13 colonies.

REVIEW How did the Battle of Bunker Hill change Britain's view of the fight with the colonies?

FAST FACT To protect their legs, Hessian soldiers often wore thick leather boots over their regular footgear. These special boots weighed about 12 pounds (5 kg) a pair!

In addition to their leather boots (right), some German mercenaries also wore bright metal helmets like the one shown here.

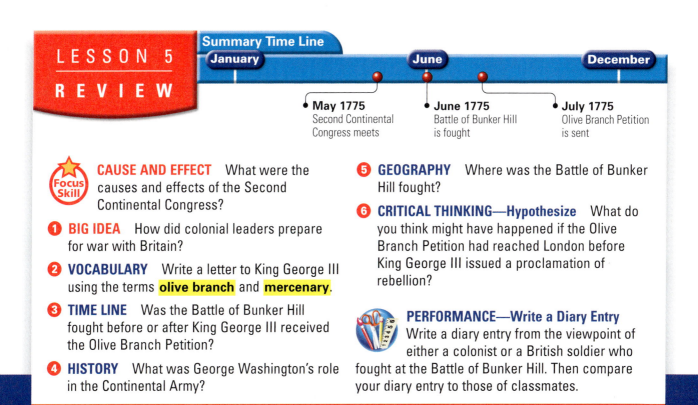

LESSON 5 REVIEW

Summary Time Line

January — May 1775 Second Continental Congress meets — June 1775 Battle of Bunker Hill is fought — June — July 1775 Olive Branch Petition is sent — December

CAUSE AND EFFECT What were the causes and effects of the Second Continental Congress?

1. **BIG IDEA** How did colonial leaders prepare for war with Britain?
2. **VOCABULARY** Write a letter to King George III using the terms **olive branch** and **mercenary**.
3. **TIME LINE** Was the Battle of Bunker Hill fought before or after King George III received the Olive Branch Petition?
4. **HISTORY** What was George Washington's role in the Continental Army?
5. **GEOGRAPHY** Where was the Battle of Bunker Hill fought?
6. **CRITICAL THINKING—Hypothesize** What do you think might have happened if the Olive Branch Petition had reached London before King George III issued a proclamation of rebellion?

PERFORMANCE—Write a Diary Entry Write a diary entry from the viewpoint of either a colonist or a British soldier who fought at the Battle of Bunker Hill. Then compare your diary entry to those of classmates.

CHAPTER 8
Review and Test Preparation

Summary Time Line

1750 — 1755

• 1754 French and Indian War begins; Albany Plan of Union is proposed

Focus Skill: Cause and Effect

Copy the following graphic organizer onto a separate sheet of paper. Use the information you have learned to show that you understand the causes and effects of some of the key events that helped unite the colonies.

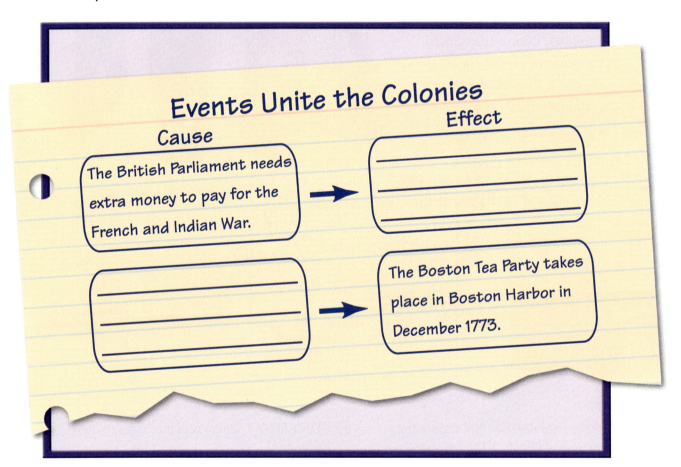

Events Unite the Colonies

Cause: The British Parliament needs extra money to pay for the French and Indian War. → Effect: _____

Cause: _____ → Effect: The Boston Tea Party takes place in Boston Harbor in December 1773.

THINK & WRITE

Write a Persuasive Letter Think about how the Stamp Act Congress asked all colonists to boycott British goods. Write a letter to a delegate of the congress, explaining why you do or do not support the boycott.

Report a News Event Suppose that you are a newspaper reporter who has been asked to write about the fighting at Lexington and Concord. Write a short newspaper article in which you describe the events of April 19, 1775.

Timeline:
- 1760
- 1763 French and Indian War ends
- 1765 Stamp Act Congress
- 1770 Boston Massacre
- 1773 Boston Tea Party
- 1775 Fighting breaks out at Lexington and Concord; Battle of Bunker Hill
- 1780

USE THE TIME LINE

Use the chapter summary time line to answer these questions.

1. When did the French and Indian War begin and end?
2. How many years after the Boston Massacre did the Boston Tea Party take place?

USE VOCABULARY

Identify the term that correctly matches each definition.

- alliance (p. 270)
- budget (p. 280)
- boycott (p. 282)
- monopoly (p. 288)
- mercenary (p. 296)

3. to refuse to buy
4. a soldier who serves for pay in the military of a foreign government
5. a formal agreement among nations, states, groups, or individuals
6. the complete control of a product or service in a certain area by a single person or group
7. a plan for spending money

RECALL FACTS

Answer these questions.

8. The French and Indian War began as a competition for control of what region?
9. How did most colonists react to the Proclamation of 1763?
10. Why was the Wilderness Road important to the pioneers?

Write the letter of the best choice.

11. Colonists were upset about the Stamp Act because—
    A they had no representation in Parliament.
    B it was the second tax law.
    C they had to boycott British goods.
    D many had to work as tax collectors.

12. The Second Continental Congress tried to make peace by—
    F sending a delegate to Britain.
    G sending the Olive Branch Petition.
    H uniting the 13 colonies.
    J refusing to fight for the British.

THINK CRITICALLY

13. How might history have been different if the Albany Plan of Union had been approved by the colonies?
14. Imagine that you are a colonist. Will you speak out against the Sugar Act, or will you side with the British? Explain.

APPLY SKILLS

Compare Historical Maps

15. Use the maps on page 279 to name the countries that received land that was once claimed by the French.

Determine Point of View

16. In a magazine or newspaper, find a photograph showing a recent event. Tell what the photograph shows, and describe the photographer's point of view.

Chapter 8 ■ 299

MORRISTOWN NATIONAL HISTORICAL PARK

During the harsh winter of 1779–1780, no one was sure if the Continental Army would survive to the following spring. That winter in Morristown, New Jersey, George Washington's soldiers suffered many hardships. Many soldiers had to sleep out in the open in the snow until tents arrived and huts were built. Today, visitors can visit the places where these soldiers camped more than 220 years ago.

LOCATE IT

NEW JERSEY — Morristown National Historical Park

CHAPTER 9

The Revolutionary War

" These are the times that try men's souls. "
—Thomas Paine, *The American Crisis*, December 23, 1776

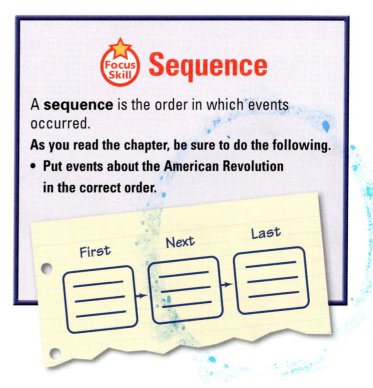

Focus Skill: Sequence

A **sequence** is the order in which events occurred.

As you read the chapter, be sure to do the following.
- Put events about the American Revolution in the correct order.

LESSON 1

Independence Is Declared

1750 — 1770 — 1790

1776–1781

Although the colonies were already at war with Britain, many Americans still believed that their problems with the king and Parliament could be settled. They hoped the British government would change its view and allow them to take part in making laws. By 1776 that thinking began to change.

Common Sense

One of the people who did the most to change public opinion in the colonies was Thomas Paine. **Public opinion** is the point of view held by most people. In January 1776 Paine published a pamphlet, or short book, titled *Common Sense*.

In his pamphlet Paine questioned the right of any king to rule over anyone. Paine wrote that people should rule themselves, "A government of our own is a natural right." Paine called for a revolution, and he challenged the colonists to cut their ties with the British government.

People in the 13 colonies read and talked about *Common Sense*. As a result, many began to urge **independence**. Having

 SEQUENCE
As you read, look for the sequence of events that led to the writing of the Declaration of Independence.

BIG IDEA
The colonists cut ties with the British government and formed their own country.

VOCABULARY
public opinion
independence
allegiance
resolution
preamble
grievance

Thomas Paine argued that the colonies should claim their independence.

FAST FACT Within a few months of being published, over 500,000 copies of *Common Sense* had been sold.

302 ■ Unit 4

· BIOGRAPHY ·

Thomas Jefferson   1743–1826
Character Trait: Individualism

Thomas Jefferson was a very skilled person. He is best known as the chief writer of the Declaration of Independence and later as the third President of the United States. But Jefferson did many other things in his life. He was an eager reader, an inventor, and a student of mathematics, science, agriculture, and architecture. In 1768 he designed his own house, which he called Monticello. Monticello is near Charlottesville, Virginia.

MULTIMEDIA BIOGRAPHIES
Visit The Learning Site at www.harcourtschool.com to learn about other famous people.

---

the freedom to govern themselves was the only way, they said, to have liberty.

Richard Henry Lee of Virginia gave a speech to the delegates of the Second Continental Congress on June 7, 1776. Lee said that the colonies no longer owed **allegiance** (uh·LEE·juhns), or loyalty, to the king. At the end, he suggested a **resolution**, a formal statement of the feelings of a group about an important topic. This resolution read, "Resolved: That these united colonies are, and of right ought to be, free and independent States."

The Congress debated the resolution for a few days, but not all the colonies were ready to vote for independence. They needed more time before taking such a dangerous action. The Congress decided to wait almost a month before calling for a vote.

REVIEW Why did Richard Henry Lee suggest that the colonies become independent?

Writing the Declaration of Independence

The delegates of the Second Continental Congress hoped that the month's wait would help all 13 colonies decide to vote as one in favor of independence. In the meantime, the Congress chose a committee to write the group's view on independence. The committee consisted of Benjamin Franklin of Pennsylvania, John Adams of Massachusetts, Robert R. Livingston of New York, Roger Sherman of Connecticut, and Thomas Jefferson of Virginia.

Thomas Jefferson was a 33-year-old lawyer. He had studied government and had already written about the colonies' problems with British rule.

Jefferson's travel desk holds the first draft of the Declaration of Independence.

The Declaration of Independence

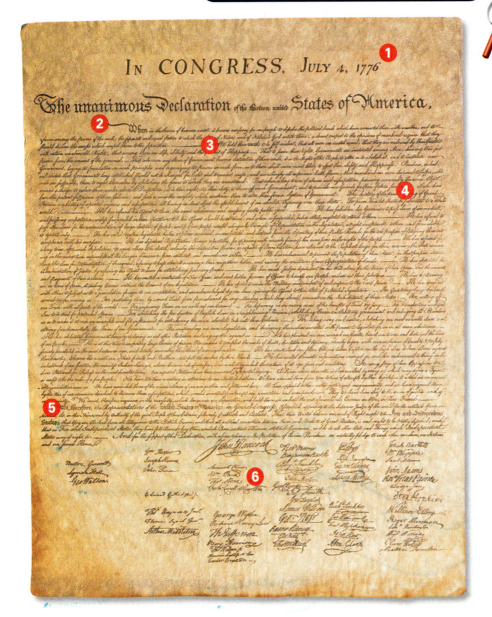

Analyze Primary Sources

The Declaration of Independence includes the idea that a government gets its power from the consent of the people.

1. date
2. Preamble
3. the statement of rights
4. charges against the king
5. statement of independence
6. signers of Declaration

❖ What was included in the Declaration of Independence?

Two years before, Jefferson had written a pamphlet titled *A Summary View of the Rights of British America*. In it he had listed for the First Continental Congress the changes the colonies wanted in their government.

The members of the writing committee added their ideas, but Jefferson did most of the writing. Every evening for about 17 days, he wrote—and rewrote—what became the Declaration of Independence.

Thomas Jefferson planned the Declaration in several parts. In the **preamble**, the first part or introduction, he stated why the Declaration was needed. He said that sometimes a group of people finds that it has no choice but to form a new nation.

In the second part, he described the colonists' main ideas about government. These words have become some of the most famous in United States history.

"We hold these truths to be self-evident, that all men are created equal, that they are endowed [provided] by their Creator with certain unalienable Rights, that among these are Life, Liberty and the pursuit of Happiness."

In the third and largest part of the Declaration, Jefferson listed the colonists' **grievances**, or complaints, against the British king and Parliament. He also listed the ways the colonists had tried to settle their differences peacefully. In the last part of the Declaration, Jefferson wrote that the colonies were free and independent states.

REVIEW What had Thomas Jefferson done two years before he was asked to write the Declaration of Independence? **SEQUENCE**

Approving the Declaration

When he finished writing the Declaration of Independence, Thomas Jefferson gave a draft of it to the whole Congress. On June 28, it was read aloud. For several days it was discussed, and changes were made. Then, on July 2, the delegates returned to vote on Richard Henry Lee's resolution to cut ties with Britain. That morning the resolution was approved. The American colonies now considered themselves free and independent states.

On July 4, 1776, the Congress voted to give its final approval for the Declaration. Delegates of only 12 colonies voted. New York's delegates had not yet received the authority to vote.

John Trumbull's painting of the signing of the Declaration of Independence shows the Second Continental Congress in what is today Independence Hall.

On July 8, 1776, the bell on top of Independence Hall called the citizens of Philadelphia to hear the first public reading of the Declaration of Independence. Many of the members of the Second Continental Congress stood and listened, too, as Colonel John Nixon read the document. The joy shown by the crowd so pleased John Adams that he wrote about it in a letter to his wife, Abigail. Independence Day, he said, should be celebrated "from this time forward for evermore."

By August 2, a formal copy of the Declaration of Independence was ready to be signed by members of the Second Continental Congress. The first to sign it was John Hancock, president of the Congress. He said that he wrote his name large enough so that King George could read it without his glasses. The way he signed the document became so famous that the term *John Hancock* now means "a person's signature."

REVIEW How did the people of Philadelphia react to the first reading of the Declaration of Independence?

Forming a New Government

The work of the Second Continental Congress was not completed with the final approval of the Declaration of Independence. John Hancock organized a second committee to report on how to unite the former colonies into a new country. With independence, a new government had to be formed. Congress chose John Dickinson, of Pennsylvania, to

Independence Hall

• HERITAGE •

Independence Day

The Fourth of July, or Independence Day, is the birthday of the United States of America and a national holiday. The holiday was first celebrated on July 4, 1777, with fireworks and the ringing of the Liberty Bell. Because of a crack that happened in 1846, the Liberty Bell is no longer part of the celebration. Today it is guarded by the National Park Service near Independence Hall in Philadelphia, Pennsylvania.

head the committee to write the plan of government.

Dickinson's committee decided that the new states—the former colonies—should unite into a confederation. This Confederation of the United States of America would bring together the 13 independent states into "a firm league of friendship."

On July 12, 1776, Dickinson presented his committee's report to the Congress. The delegates discussed it off and on for more than a year. They finally approved the plan on November 15, 1777. The first constitution for the new country was called the Articles of Confederation. But the last state did not approve this plan for a central government until March 1, 1781.

Under the Articles, voters of each state elected leaders. These leaders then chose representatives to a national legislature called the Congress of the Confederation. Each state, whether large or small, had one vote in the new Congress. Under the Articles of Confederation, this Congress served as the government of the United States. For eight years, it made laws for the new nation. It led the states during the last years of the Revolutionary War.

John Dickinson helped write the Articles of Confederation.

REVIEW What were the Articles of Confederation?

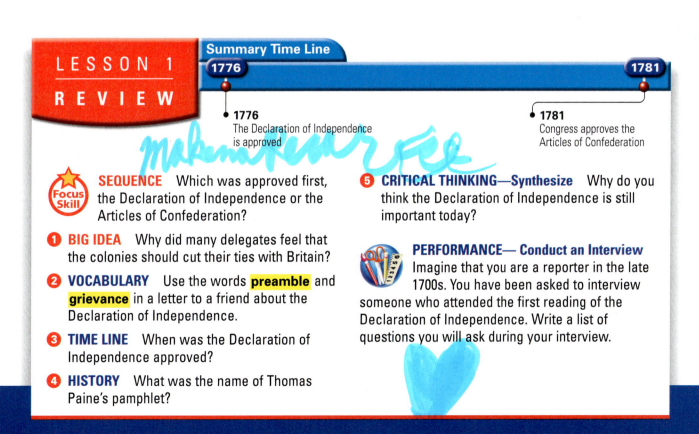

LESSON 1 REVIEW

Summary Time Line

1776 — The Declaration of Independence is approved

1781 — Congress approves the Articles of Confederation

SEQUENCE Which was approved first, the Declaration of Independence or the Articles of Confederation?

1. **BIG IDEA** Why did many delegates feel that the colonies should cut their ties with Britain?
2. **VOCABULARY** Use the words **preamble** and **grievance** in a letter to a friend about the Declaration of Independence.
3. **TIME LINE** When was the Declaration of Independence approved?
4. **HISTORY** What was the name of Thomas Paine's pamphlet?
5. **CRITICAL THINKING—Synthesize** Why do you think the Declaration of Independence is still important today?

PERFORMANCE— Conduct an Interview Imagine that you are a reporter in the late 1700s. You have been asked to interview someone who attended the first reading of the Declaration of Independence. Write a list of questions you will ask during your interview.

Chapter 9 ■ 307

LESSON 2

Americans and the Revolution

The approval of the Declaration of Independence showed that the colonies had united against Britain. But the colonists themselves were not united. Whether to support independence or to remain loyal to the British king was a difficult decision for many Americans.

SEQUENCE
As you read, look for the sequence of events that led to disagreement between Americans.

BIG IDEA
People in the United States had different views about independence.

VOCABULARY
Patriot
Loyalist
neutral
pacifist
regiment

Taking Sides

Many people in the 13 colonies supported independence. They called themselves **Patriots**. Others however, remained loyal to the king and called themselves **Loyalists**, or Tories. Friendships, neighborhoods, and families sometimes were torn apart as people chose to take either the Patriot side or the Loyalist side.

The fighting became as much a civil war, or war between people of the same country, as it was a war with the British. In her book *If You Were There in 1776*, author Barbara Brenner describes life at the time of the Revolution. "If you were part of

Thomas Hutchinson was a governor of the Massachusetts Colony and a Loyalist.

A British flag

308 ■ Unit 4

a Patriot family, you might have been one of the children throwing garbage or stones at the British soldiers. If your family supported the king, you could have been on the receiving end of some serious violence. Your home might have been broken into. Someone you know who was a Tory [Loyalist] could have been tarred and feathered, or ridden on a rail."

Some colonists, however, chose to be **neutral** (NOO•truhl). They took neither side. Those who were neutral were willing to accept whatever the outcome of the war would be.

REVIEW How did colonists view the decision to declare independence from Britain?

Churches and the War

Like other colonists, people in churches were divided on whether they supported the Patriots or the Loyalists or remained neutral. John Peter Muhlenberg, a young Lutheran minister, told his followers in a sermon, "There is a time to pray and a time to fight." Then, before their eyes, he tore off his church robes to show that he was wearing the uniform of a Patriot militia officer. His father, the colonies' Lutheran leader, was shocked. He himself was a Loyalist. The Lutherans, like the people of other church groups, were divided between Patriots and Loyalists.

Taking sides was especially hard for Anglican Church members. The British king was the head of the Anglican Church, as the Church of England was called in the colonies. Many Anglicans in the New England and Middle Atlantic Colonies were loyal to the king. Many of those in the Southern Colonies worked for independence.

Most Congregationalists, members of the largest church group in the New England Colonies, worked for independence. So, too, did many Baptists and northern Presbyterians. Many southern Presbyterians, however, were Loyalists.

Members of the Society of Friends, also called Quakers, would not fight at all.

John Peter Muhlenberg was a Patriot militia officer.

An early United States flag

Chapter 9 ■ 309

Quakers are against all wars because they believe that fighting for any reason is wrong. These **pacifists**, or believers in peaceful settlement of disagreements, wrote pamphlets calling for an end to the war.

REVIEW Why was taking sides especially hard for members of the Anglican Church?

African Americans, Free and Enslaved

At the start of the war, 1 out of every 5 people living in the 13 British colonies was of African descent. Most of these people lived in the Southern Colonies as slaves. African Americans everywhere in the colonies, however, viewed the Declaration of Independence with hope and excitement. It had, after all, stated that "all men are created equal."

Free African Americans were as quick to take sides as many of their white neighbors. Peter Salem was among at least five African Americans who fought at Concord as a Minuteman. A few weeks later he and other African Americans, some free and some enslaved, fought at the Battle of Bunker Hill. Among them was Salem Poor. He won praise for his heroic actions there.

About 5,000 African Americans fought in the Continental Army. Many were promised freedom after the war as a reward for their service. Some were so filled with the idea of freedom, or liberty, that they changed their names. Among the names listed in Continental Army records are Cuff Freedom, Dick Freedom, Ned Freedom, Peter Freedom, Cuff Liberty, and Pomp Liberty.

In November 1775 the royal governor of Virginia also had promised freedom to enslaved African Americans if they ran away from their owners and fought for the British. As a result, he raised a regiment of more than 300 African American soldiers. A **regiment** is a large, organized group of soldiers. These soldiers wore uniforms that had patches reading *Liberty to Slaves*.

REVIEW What sequence of events caused some enslaved African Americans to take sides in the war? **SEQUENCE**

As a young man James Armistead (right) spied on the British army. This proclamation (far right), issued in Virginia, promised freedom to all enslaved people who joined the British army.

310 ▪ Unit 4

Mercy Otis Warren

Sarah Franklin Bache

Abigail Adams

Martha Washington

Women and the War

Many women in the colonies took part in the Patriots' war effort. Some ran farms and businesses. Others, such as Betsy Ross, sewed new American flags for the army. Esther Reed started the Philadelphia Association in 1780 to help the Continental Army. When Reed died, Sarah Franklin Bache (BAYCH), Benjamin Franklin's daughter, took over.

Hundreds of women took part in the fighting. These women, often with children, followed their husbands from battle to battle. In army camps they cooked food and washed clothes. Some nursed the sick and wounded. One woman named Deborah Sampson even dressed herself as a man so she could fight with the Continental Army. Others served as spies.

Some women used their talents to support the Patriot cause. Mercy Otis Warren wrote poems and plays. In her plays Warren often wrote about women heroes in the struggle for freedom in other countries. Later, she wrote a history of the American Revolution, the first by a woman.

Not all women were Patriots, however. There were Loyalist women in every colony. Some of them fought for the British. Many others gave the British food and other supplies.

REVIEW How did women on both sides take part in the war?

People in the Western Lands

Despite the Proclamation of 1763, settlers had continued to move onto the land King George III had reserved for Native Americans. Some Indian groups grew angry about these settlers, but many came to depend on both the Americans and the British as trading partners. The Patriots and the British each hoped that the Indians would take their side or, if not, stay out of the fighting.

Most of the Native American groups had decided to stay out of the fighting.

• BIOGRAPHY •

Thayendanegea, (Joseph Brant)
1742–1807

Character Trait: Self-discipline

Thayendanegea was born in what is now Ohio and as a young man became a friend of British General William Johnson. As a result of that friendship, Thayendanegea attended school in Connecticut, where he became a Christian and took the name Joseph Brant. Until the war Brant had been a missionary in the Ohio Valley. After the war he continued his missionary work among the Native Americans of Canada.

MULTIMEDIA BIOGRAPHIES
Visit The Learning Site www.harcourtschool.com to learn about other famous people.

The loyalties of others, however, were divided, just as they had been during the French and Indian War. Some Iroquois, such as the Mohawk leader Thayendanegea (thay•en•da•NEG•ah), known as Joseph Brant, fought for the British. Others fought for the Patriots.

At first, most Americans on the frontier remained neutral. They wanted to be free of any government—British or American.

After a while their feeling began to change. Although they did not support the Patriot cause, they did want to drive the British out of the western lands. They felt that if they did not help the Patriots drive out the British, the British would probably keep the western lands even if the Americans won the war.

REVIEW Why did many settlers in the western lands decide to help the Patriots?

LESSON 2 REVIEW

 SEQUENCE Were enslaved African Americans given their freedom when they joined the Continental Army or after the war?

1 BIG IDEA Why did Americans have different views about independence?

2 VOCABULARY What was the difference between a Patriot and a Loyalist?

3 HISTORY Which side did most of the Native American groups support?

4 GEOGRAPHY Which side did most of the Americans living on the frontier support?

5 CRITICAL THINKING—Hypothesize How might the war have been different if all Americans had supported the same side?

 PERFORMANCE— Write a Dialogue Write a dialogue that might have taken place between a Patriot and a Loyalist. Be sure to include what their viewpoints on independence might have been. Share this dialogue with a classmate.

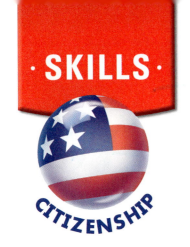

SKILLS · CITIZENSHIP

Make a Decision

VOCABULARY
consequence

▶ WHY IT MATTERS

At the time of the Revolutionary War, colonists had to make many difficult decisions. These decisions often had lasting consequences. A **consequence** is what happens because of an action. The decisions you make can have good or bad consequences. To make a thoughtful decision, you need to think about the consequences before you act.

▶ WHAT YOU NEED TO KNOW

Here are some steps you can use to help you make a thoughtful decision.

Step 1 Know that you have to make a decision.

Step 2 Gather information.

Step 3 Identify choices.

Step 4 Predict consequences and weigh those consequences.

Step 5 Make a choice and take action.

▶ PRACTICE THE SKILL

Imagine that you are living in one of the 13 colonies at the time of the American Revolution. You have to decide whether to join the Patriots, join the Loyalists, or stay neutral. Make thoughtful decisions based on the roles described below. Explain the steps you followed in making each decision.

1. Your family owns a plantation in North Carolina.
2. You are a merchant in Boston.
3. You are a minister in Pennsylvania.
4. You are a settler on the frontier.

▶ APPLY WHAT YOU LEARNED

Think about a decision you made at school this week. What steps did you follow? What choices did you have? What were the consequences of your choices? Do you think your decision was a thoughtful one? Explain.

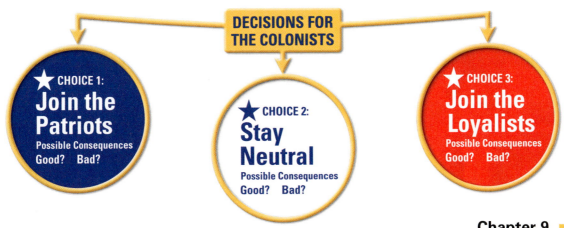

Chapter 9 ▪ 313

LESSON 3

Fighting the Revolutionary War

1750 — 1770 — 1790
1775–1778

 SEQUENCE
As you read, look for the sequence of events that led other countries to send help to the Continental Army.

BIG IDEA
The Continental Army overcame great obstacles to turn the war in its favor.

VOCABULARY
enlist
turning point

George Washington arrived in Massachusetts to meet the Continental Army in July 1775, less than three weeks after the Battle of Bunker Hill. The 14,500 soldiers wore no uniforms—only their everyday clothes. Many had no guns, so they carried spears and axes. With little money and not much training, the Continental Army went to war against one of the most powerful armies in the world, the British army.

Comparing Armies

The soldiers who stood before George Washington that summer day in 1775 had never fought as an army before. Some of them had fought in the French and Indian War, but most had no military experience. Washington quickly had to make rules for the soldiers and get them trained to fight against the British.

Unlike the Continental Army, the British army was made up of professional soldiers. They had the best training and the most experienced officers. But the British had problems, too. It was difficult to fight a war more than 3,000 miles (4,828 km) from home. They often had trouble delivering soldiers and supplies across the Atlantic Ocean.

In the early days of the war, the British army's greater numbers gave it an advantage over the Continental Army. The British had more than

Many soldiers in the Continental Army (left) faced shortages of food and other supplies. British soldiers (right) had the best training.

314 ■ Unit 4

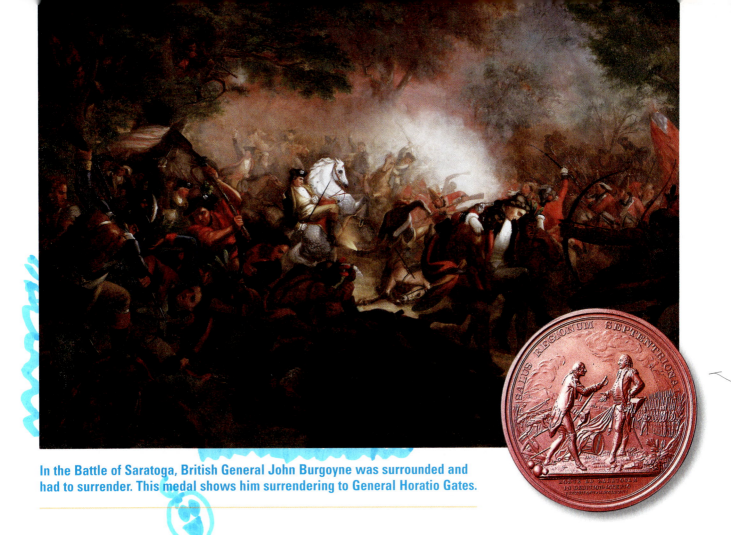

In the Battle of Saratoga, British General John Burgoyne was surrounded and had to surrender. This medal shows him surrendering to General Horatio Gates.

50,000 soldiers in the colonies. General Washington usually had no more than 15,000 soldiers in his army.

REVIEW How was the British army different from the Continental Army?

The War in the North

By the spring of 1776, Washington and his ragged army had moved south from Massachusetts to New York. By the fall the British had defeated the Americans in several battles, including the Battle of Long Island. Now the British were chasing Washington and what was left of the Continental Army.

Most of the Americans **enlisted** in, or joined, the army for almost one year at a time. They might stay that long or longer, or they might not. At harvesttime, some of the Continentals went home to their farms. Washington and the Continentals who stayed with him did their best to keep moving to avoid capture by the British. By winter they had marched through New Jersey to Pennsylvania.

Most of the British army had been sent back to New York for the winter. When Washington learned that the Hessian mercenaries stationed at Trenton, New Jersey, were not prepared for an attack, he decided to move against them. On Christmas Day 1776, Washington and his army crossed the ice-choked Delaware River in boats. By night in freezing weather, the shivering soldiers silently marched toward Trenton. At daybreak the Americans made a surprise attack. More than 900 Hessians were taken as prisoners.

Chapter 9 ■ 315

William B. T. Trego's painting *The March to Valley Forge* shows the hardships Washington (on white horse) and his army faced. This knapsack (right) was carried by one of the soldiers at Valley Forge.

The new year brought more good news for Washington and his army. The best news came in October 1777 with an American victory at Saratoga in New York. There the Americans defeated a British army of more than 5,000 soldiers led by British General John Burgoyne (ber•GOYN). The British plan had called for Burgoyne to move south from Canada, while British General William Howe moved north from Philadelphia. The two armies were to cut the colonies in two. Instead, Howe failed to support Burgoyne, and the British had one of their worst defeats of the war. On October 17, 1777, Burgoyne surrendered his entire army to American General Horatio Gates.

Patriots everywhere were overjoyed at the news. The Battle of Saratoga became a turning point in the war. A **turning point** is a single event that causes important and dramatic change.

REVIEW What sequence of events led to the American victory at the Battle of Saratoga?
 SEQUENCE

Winter at Valley Forge

The Continental Army was encouraged by its victory at Saratoga. But it still faced hardships. In December 1777, General Washington set up headquarters at Valley Forge, Pennsylvania, near Philadelphia. That winter his ragtag Continental Army was almost destroyed by cold and hunger. Many men were ill, and many died.

In these hard times a German soldier named Friedrich von Steuben (vahn SHTOY•buhn) reported to Washington at Valley Forge. Von Steuben was one of many soldiers from other countries who believed in the Patriots' cause and helped them. Two Polish officers, Casimir Pulaski (puh•LAS•kee) and Thaddeus Kosciuszko (kawsh•CHUSH•koh), and the 20-year-old Marquis de Lafayette (lah•fee•ET) from France also supported the Patriots. Washington liked the young Lafayette and immediately gave him important duties.

At Valley Forge, von Steuben's job was to organize and drill the Continental Army so that it could move quickly on command. This would allow it to attack and retreat faster. Von Steuben also taught the American soldiers how to use bayonets. A bayonet is a knifelike weapon attached to a rifle. Bayonets were standard equipment for European soldiers. By the spring of 1778, Washington's soldiers were marching well.

REVIEW Who came to offer help to the Continental Army?

The Marquis de Lafayette, a French noble, was eager to help the Continental Army.

Help from Other Countries

While the Continental Army was at Valley Forge, Benjamin Franklin was in Paris, France. Franklin asked the French leaders for supplies and soldiers. The war had affected the entire American

• BIOGRAPHY •

Haym Salomon   1740–1785
Character Trait: Loyalty

Haym Salomon was a banker who worked for the cause of American freedom. Born in Poland, he came to New York in 1772. When the British captured the city, he stayed there and spied for the Patriots. In 1778 he fled the city with his wife and child and went into business as a banker in Philadelphia. Salomon worked to get money to pay for the Revolution.

MULTIMEDIA BIOGRAPHIES
Visit The Learning Site at www.harcourtschool.com
to learn about other famous people.

Chapter 9 ■ 317

| GEORGE ROGERS CLARK | FRANCIS MARION | JOHN PAUL JONES |

economy. Many businessess had closed and some people did not have enough food to eat. The French listened to Franklin because they wanted the Americans to win and weaken the British. However, they did not feel that the Americans were likely to win.

Franklin talked with the French leaders for months without success. Then news of the American victory at Saratoga reached France. This victory convinced the French to send supplies and soldiers to help the Patriots. After the victory at Saratoga, people from other places helped the Americans, too. Bernardo de Gálvez (GAHL•ves), the governor of Spanish Louisiana, sent guns, food, and money. Later, he led his own soldiers in capturing several British forts. Spanish-born Jorge Farragut (FAIR•uh•guht) fought in the Continental Army and also in the navy.

REVIEW Why did the French decide to help the Patriots?

American Heroes

During the war the Americans cheered as they heard news about the deeds of many brave people from all over the United States. Their acts of courage helped make Americans sure that they could win the war.

In the mountains of the Northeast, Ethan Allen led the Green Mountain Boys. Allen and his soldiers from what is now Vermont won one of the first American victories in the war. They captured Fort Ticonderoga in New York.

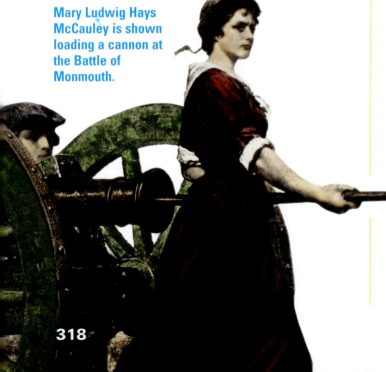

Mary Ludwig Hays McCauley is shown loading a cannon at the Battle of Monmouth.

When General George Washington asked for volunteers to spy on the British in New York City, a young man named Nathan Hale from Connecticut came forward. Dressed as a Dutch schoolteacher, Hale obtained the information Washington needed. As he returned to the American side, the British captured him. According to legend, Hale told the British soldiers before they hanged him, "I only regret that I have but one life to lose for my country."

In the Ohio Valley, George Rogers Clark helped protect the frontier lands claimed by many American settlers as theirs. Leading a small army, he marched through the western lands, defending settlers from attacks by the British and their Indian allies.

From bases in the swamps of South Carolina, Francis Marion led daring raids against the British. The British called him the Swamp Fox because they could never catch him and his soldiers. At sea John Paul Jones, a navy commander, battled larger and better-equipped British ships. In one famous battle in the North Sea near Britain, the British asked Jones to surrender. He replied, "I have not yet begun to fight." Jones kept fighting until the British ship gave up.

This statue of Nathan Hale was built in 1914 to honor him.

Many women also won fame for their bravery during the war. Mary Slocomb joined her husband at the Battle of Moores Creek Bridge in 1776. Mary Ludwig Hays McCauley earned the name Molly Pitcher by carrying water to the troops during the Battle of Monmouth in New Jersey in 1778. When her husband was wounded, she took his place firing the cannons.

REVIEW Who defended settlers in the western lands?

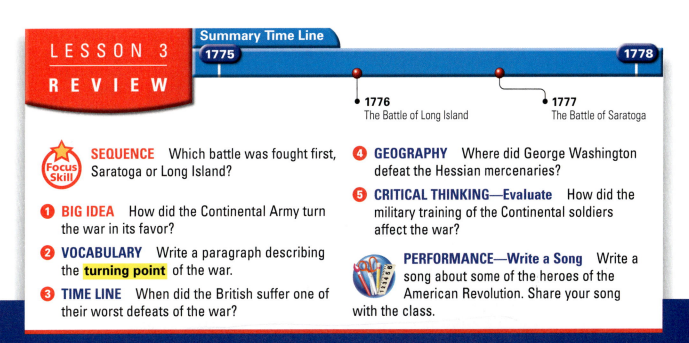

LESSON 3 REVIEW

Summary Time Line
1775 — 1776 The Battle of Long Island — 1777 The Battle of Saratoga — 1778

SEQUENCE Which battle was fought first, Saratoga or Long Island?

1 BIG IDEA How did the Continental Army turn the war in its favor?

2 VOCABULARY Write a paragraph describing the **turning point** of the war.

3 TIME LINE When did the British suffer one of their worst defeats of the war?

4 GEOGRAPHY Where did George Washington defeat the Hessian mercenaries?

5 CRITICAL THINKING—Evaluate How did the military training of the Continental soldiers affect the war?

PERFORMANCE—Write a Song Write a song about some of the heroes of the American Revolution. Share your song with the class.

Chapter 9 ■ 319

EXAMINE PRIMARY SOURCES

Washington's Mess Chest

During much of the Revolutionary War, George Washington and his troops lived in tents or other shelters. To prepare and eat his meals, Washington used this camp kitchen, or mess chest. It was equipped with all the pots, pans, and utensils he needed.

**FROM THE SMITHSONIAN INSTITUTION
NATIONAL MUSEUM OF AMERICAN HISTORY**

Glass storage jars used for storing water or tonics

Kettles used for heating food on the gridiron over an open flame

Kettles stacked inside each other to save space

One of three tin platters used for preparing and serving meals

Lift-out storage bins used for storing dry goods such as breads, flour, or grain

Analyze the Primary Source

1. What do you think went inside the two glass bottles with the pewter tops?

2. What do you think George Washington did with the gridiron? Why did it have collapsible legs?

3. Where might someone today use a chest like this?

ACTIVITY

Compare and Contrast Make a list of items that you might include today in a mess chest. Then draw a picture showing what that mess chest might look like. Use your drawing to explain to classmates how the items you included in your mess chest are similar to and different from the ones in Washington's mess chest.

RESEARCH

Visit The Learning Site at www.harcourtschool.com to research other primary sources.

LESSON 4

Independence Is Won

1750 — 1770 — 1790
1778–1783

 SEQUENCE
As you read, look for the sequence of events that finally led to American independence.

BIG IDEA
The Americans finally won their independence.

VOCABULARY
traitor
negotiate
principle

When the British government learned that the French were helping the Americans, British army leaders shifted the fighting. The British had already captured important cities in the North—Boston, Philadelphia, and New York. They hoped now to defeat the Patriots once and for all. So they concentrated on the South, where there was greater Loyalist support.

The War in the South

In 1778 the British captured Savannah, Georgia. In 1780, they captured the city of Charles Town, later known as Charleston, in South Carolina. From there, they attacked and defeated the Americans at Camden, also in South Carolina. This victory gave the British new hope of quickly defeating the Continental Army and winning the war.

As the British tried to stamp out the fire of independence in one place, they found that it only sprang up in another place. "We fight, get beat, rise, and fight again," General Nathanael Greene wrote. Greene commanded the Continental Army in the Southern Colonies. Under Greene's leadership General Daniel Morgan won the battle at Cowpens, South Carolina, in 1781.

The battle at Cowpens, South Carolina, was a major victory for the Americans. This photograph shows what the battlefield looks like today.

Major Battles of the Revolution

Regions This map shows the major battles of the American Revolution.

❓ In which region did most of the later battles take place?

Early in 1781 Benedict Arnold, a former Continental Army officer, led the British army's attacks on Virginia towns. Arnold was a **traitor**, or someone who acts against his or her country. Earlier, he had given the British the plans to the American fort at West Point, New York, in exchange for money and a high rank in the British army.

Then the British army in South Carolina pushed into North Carolina. There, in March 1781, the Americans suffered a terrible defeat at Guilford Courthouse. The British, however, still could not win the war, because no one city or town was the heart of America.

REVIEW What battle gave the British hope of winning the war?

A CLOSER LOOK
The Battle of Yorktown

The Battle of Yorktown was the last major battle of the Revolutionary War. American and French soldiers surrounded the British, and the fighting lasted for several weeks in September and October 1781. It was a huge victory for the Americans and it helped end the war.

1. French soldiers
2. American officers' headquarters
3. American soldiers
4. field where the British surrendered
5. British earthworks
6. British soldiers
7. Chesapeake Bay
8. French ships
9. British ships
10. York River

❓ Why were the British at a disadvantage in the Battle of Yorktown?

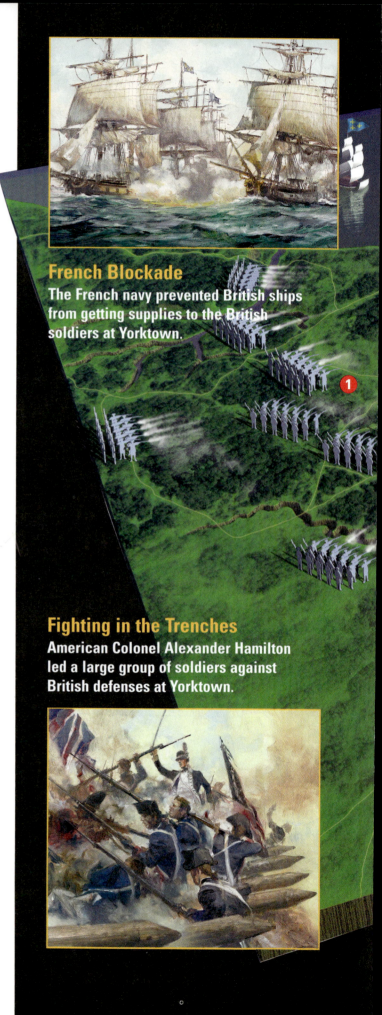

French Blockade
The French navy prevented British ships from getting supplies to the British soldiers at Yorktown.

Fighting in the Trenches
American Colonel Alexander Hamilton led a large group of soldiers against British defenses at Yorktown.

Victory at Yorktown

By late summer of 1781, British General Charles Cornwallis had set up his headquarters at Yorktown, a small Virginia town on Chesapeake Bay. At Yorktown, it was easy for the British ships to land supplies. However, since the town was on the bay, the British could also be surrounded easily. Knowing this, the French and the Americans made a plan to defeat Cornwallis at Yorktown.

The French army joined the Continental Army near New York City and marched south to Virginia in order to surround Yorktown. At the same time, the French navy took control of Chesapeake Bay. Now the British navy could not get supplies to the British army or leave the area. Cornwallis was trapped.

In late September, Cornwallis sent word to his commander in the North. "If you cannot relieve me very soon," he said, "you must be prepared to hear the worst."

Scuttled Ships
Cornwallis ordered his troops to scuttle, or sink, his own ships to block the French navy from attacking Yorktown.

Chapter 9 ■ 325

The painting by John Trumbull shows the British surrender at Yorktown. George Washington is shown in front of the American flag.

The worst happened. Surrounded and under attack for weeks from both land and sea, Cornwallis surrendered. A person who was there wrote, "At two o'clock in the evening Oct. 19th, 1781, the British army, led by General Charles O'Hara, marched out of its lines, with colors cased [flags folded] and drums beating a British march." When the French and American soldiers heard the drums, they stopped their fire. The British soldiers then marched out of Yorktown and laid down their weapons.

In Yorktown a British military band reportedly played a popular tune of the time. It was fittingly called "The World Turned Upside Down." When news of the surrender at Yorktown reached Philadelphia, the Liberty Bell rang out the news of the American victory.

Though fighting dragged on in some places for more than two years, it was clear that the war had been decided at Yorktown in 1781. The Patriots had won after a long, hard fight.

REVIEW What problem did the British face at Yorktown?

The drum was used in the Battle of Yorktown.

The Treaty of Paris

The Battle of Yorktown did not officially end the war. The Treaty of Paris did that. Work on the treaty began in April 1782, when the British and Americans sent representatives to Paris.

There the representatives stated the American terms— that is, what the Americans wanted in the treaty. They wanted the British king and Parliament to accept American independence and to remove all British soldiers from American soil. They also asked that the British pay the Americans whose property had been destroyed in the war.

The British, in turn, asked that Loyalists who chose to remain in the United States be treated fairly. Many Loyalists had fled to Nova Scotia and other parts of Canada and to the Bahamas. Some returned to Britain but were sorry they did. Most of them could not find jobs and soon became very poor. The British government ignored them.

British and American representatives **negotiated**, or talked with one another to work out an agreement. After more than a year of such talks, the representatives signed the Treaty of Paris on September 3, 1783.

The Treaty of Paris officially named the United States of America as a new country and described its borders. The United States reached to Florida on the south. The northern border would be an imaginary line through the Great Lakes. The Mississippi River formed its western border. The Treaty of Paris was just as much a victory as winning at Yorktown had been. Independence was now a fact.

REVIEW What were the American terms of the Treaty of Paris?

Washington's Farewell

Soon after the Treaty of Paris was signed, General Washington and his officers had made their headquarters in New York City. Though joyful about their victory, the American military leaders were sad to say good-bye to one another after the long war.

In early December 1783, Washington and his officers met at Fraunces Tavern in New York City for a farewell dinner.

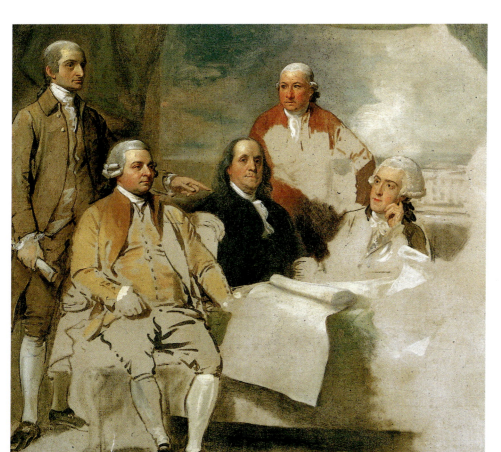

This painting by Benjamin West shows—from left to right—John Jay, John Adams, and Benjamin Franklin negotiating a peace agreement with British representatives in Paris. The negotiations led to the signing of the Treaty of Paris.

At a meeting of Congress in Annapolis, Maryland, George Washington resigns from his position as commander in chief of the Continental Army.

Near the end of the meal, Washington stood up. "With a heart full of love and gratitude, I now take my leave of you," he said. One by one, each man at the dinner went up to say good-bye to the general. Tears streaming down his cheeks, Washington hugged each one. "Such a scene of sorrow and weeping I have never before seen," wrote one of the officers.

After saying his farewells, Washington started home to Virginia. On the way he stopped in Annapolis, Maryland, where Congress was then meeting. He told the representatives that, with peace, his work was done. "Having now finished the work assigned me, I retire from the great theater of action," Washington said. He was leaving public service forever, he thought.

REVIEW What events caused Washington to think his work was done? **SEQUENCE**

Effects of the War

Wars can cause change, and the Revolutionary War was no different. The American states were no longer a source of raw materials and agricultural produce just for Britain, as they had been in colonial times. Dutch, French, Spanish, and Portuguese trading ships soon began leaving American ports loaded with American goods.

After the end of the war, more Americans moved west. From Philadelphia one person wrote, "I can scarcely walk a square without meeting [someone] . . . whose destination is principally [mainly] Ohio and Indiana." Many predicted that by the 1800s most of the people in the United States would be living in the West, which at the time was the region between the Appalachian

328 ■ Unit 4

Mountains and the Mississippi River. Land companies were organized to sell the new lands.

To help defend the new nation's far-reaching borders, leaders later established a regular, full-time army. Since that time a regular army has been added to by the National Guard or the Reserves. To provide leaders for the military, the government established schools to train officers. On July 4, 1802, the United States Military Academy opened at West Point, New York. In 1845 the Naval School, later the United States Naval Academy, opened at Annapolis, Maryland.

The Revolutionary War was not just another war. It was a milestone in human history. The American Revolution became a model for later revolutions, including those in South America. "Government by the consent of the governed" became a guiding principle. A **principle** is a rule that is used in deciding how to act.

REVIEW What effect did the Revolutionary War have on the American economy?

Regions This map shows North America in 1783, after the Treaty of Paris was signed.

❓ What were the boundaries of the United States at that time?

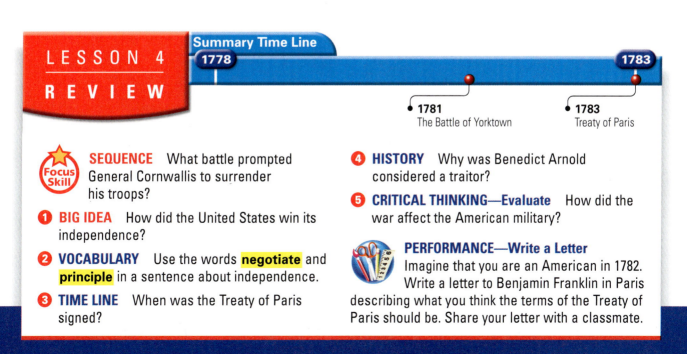

LESSON 4 REVIEW

Summary Time Line
1778 — 1781 The Battle of Yorktown — 1783 Treaty of Paris

SEQUENCE What battle prompted General Cornwallis to surrender his troops?

1. **BIG IDEA** How did the United States win its independence?

2. **VOCABULARY** Use the words **negotiate** and **principle** in a sentence about independence.

3. **TIME LINE** When was the Treaty of Paris signed?

4. **HISTORY** Why was Benedict Arnold considered a traitor?

5. **CRITICAL THINKING—Evaluate** How did the war affect the American military?

PERFORMANCE—Write a Letter
Imagine that you are an American in 1782. Write a letter to Benjamin Franklin in Paris describing what you think the terms of the Treaty of Paris should be. Share your letter with a classmate.

Chapter 9 ■ 329

SKILLS · Compare Graphs

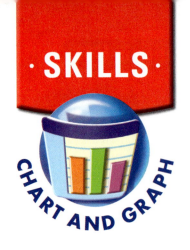

WHY IT MATTERS

Suppose you want to prepare a report on trade during the American Revolution. You want to show a lot of information in a brief, clear way. One way you might do this is by making graphs. Knowing how to read and make different kinds of graphs can help you compare large amounts of information.

WHAT YOU NEED TO KNOW

Different kinds of graphs show information in different ways. A bar graph uses bars and is especially useful for quick comparisons. The bar graph on page 331 shows the chief exports of the United States in 1790. A circle graph can help you make comparisons. The circle graph on page 331 shows the main trading partners of the United States in 1790. A line graph shows change over time. The line graph shows that the amount of goods the Americans exported changed over time.

This map of the world was drawn in the mid-1700s. The exchange table (bottom) was used to compare the values of the many kinds of money that were used in the American colonies.

▶ **PRACTICE THE SKILL**

Compare the information in the bar, circle, and line graphs by answering the following questions. Think about the advantages and disadvantages of each kind of graph.

1. Look at the circle graph. Who were the main trading partners of the United States?
2. Who did the United States export most of its goods to?
3. Did the United States export more goods to Spain or to Portugal?
4. Look at the bar graph. What did the United States export?
5. Did the United States export more corn or more wheat?
6. How much lumber did the United States export?
7. Look at the line graph. How did the amount of exports to Britain change over time?
8. Why do you think the amount of exports to Britain changed over time?

▶ **APPLY WHAT YOU LEARNED**

Use the graphs on this page to write a paragraph summarizing information about trade during the late 1700s. Share your paragraph with a partner, and compare your summaries.

CHAPTER 9

Review and Test Preparation

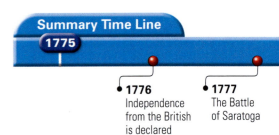

Summary Time Line
- 1775
- 1776 Independence from the British is declared
- 1777 The Battle of Saratoga

 Sequence

Copy the following graphic organizer onto a separate sheet of paper. Use the information you have learned to fill in some events that led to the colonies declaring independence.

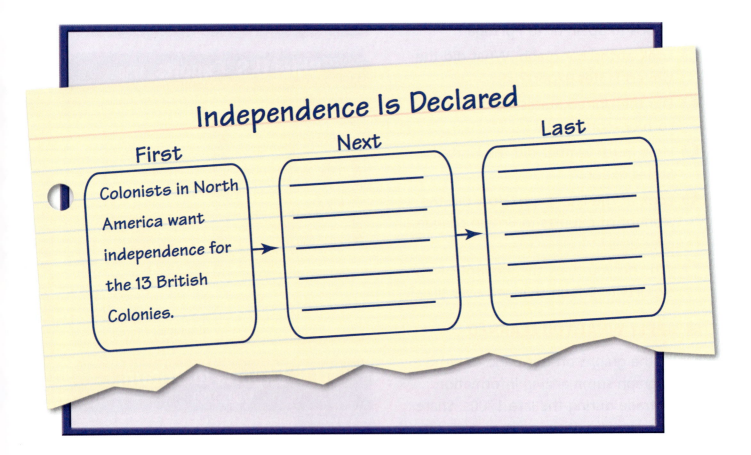

Independence Is Declared

First: Colonists in North America want independence for the 13 British Colonies.

Next: _____

Last: _____

THINK & WRITE

Write a News Story Imagine the year is 1776 and you are a newspaper reporter in Philadelphia. On July 8 you attend the first public reading of the Declaration of Independence. Write a news story about the event and the reactions of those present.

Write a Speech One of the Continental Army's hardest tests was during the winter of 1777. That winter, soldiers who were camped at Valley Forge had to endure extreme cold and hunger. Write a speech to inspire the troops at Valley Forge.

1780

• **1781** The British army is defeated in the Battle of Yorktown

• **1783** The Treaty of Paris is signed

1785

USE THE TIME LINE

Use the chapter summary time line to answer these questions.

1. When did the colonies declare their independence from Britain?
2. Did the Battle of Yorktown take place before or after the Battle of Saratoga?

USE VOCABULARY

Use these terms to write a story about the American Revolution.

public opinion (p. 302), **allegiance** (p. 303)
neutral (p. 309), **enlist** (p. 315),
turning point (p. 316)

RECALL FACTS

Answer these questions.

3. Why was the Declaration of Independence written?
4. How did Mercy Otis Warren contribute to the Patriot cause?
5. What schools were set up by the government to train military officers?

Write the letter of the best choice.

6. Thomas Jefferson's greatest contribution to the American Revolution was—
   A commanding American forces at the Battle of Saratoga.
   B convincing France to support the United States.
   C writing the Declaration of Independence.
   D writing *Common Sense*.

7. The most important effect of the Battle of Saratoga was—
   F France's decision to support the United States.
   G the defeat of more than 900 Hessian mercenaries.
   H the capture of Benedict Arnold.
   J the British army's decision to surrender.

THINK CRITICALLY

8. Why do you think so many people in the colonies read *Common Sense*?
9. What do you think would have happened if American forces had lost the Battle of Saratoga?
10. How did the military training of Continental soldiers affect the war?
11. What do you think was George Washington's greatest contribution to the American Revolution?

APPLY SKILLS

Make a Decision

12. Imagine that the year is 1777 and a friend has asked you to allow your home to be used as a shelter for Patriot soldiers. What steps might you follow to come to a decision?

Compare Graphs

13. Look in an encyclopedia or on the Internet for two population graphs of your state. Make copies of the graphs or print them out. Then write a paragraph explaining the differences between the two.

Chapter 9 ■ 333

VISIT THE Freedom Trail

GET READY

The Freedom Trail is a $2\frac{1}{2}$-mile (4-km) walking trail that weaves its way through the city of Boston. The trail connects landmarks that played an important role in America's struggle for independence. Along the Freedom Trail you can stop at places such as Faneuil Hall, where Bostonians protested British taxation policies. You can also visit the Old North Church, where on April 8, 1775, two lanterns were hung to warn Paul Revere and other colonists of incoming British troops. The Freedom Trail is more than just a path between places. Each stop on the trail tells a story about our nation's independence.

LOCATE IT

Boston, MASSACHUSETTS

WHAT TO SEE

The Freedom Trail is marked by red bricks. It gives visitors the opportunity to follow paths once walked by America's first patriots.

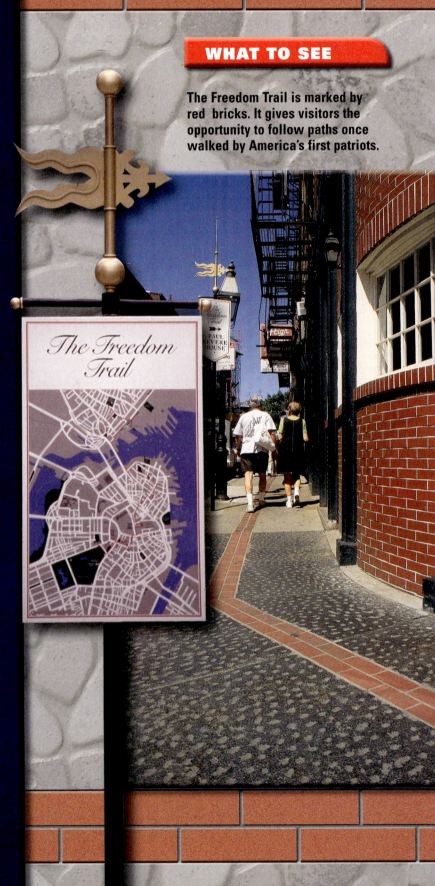

A Freedom Trail Marker

King's Chapel Burying Ground

Faneuil Hall

Bunker Hill Monument

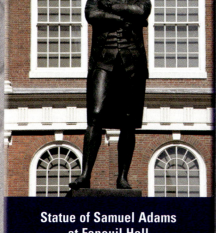
Statue of Samuel Adams at Faneuil Hall

Paul Revere's house

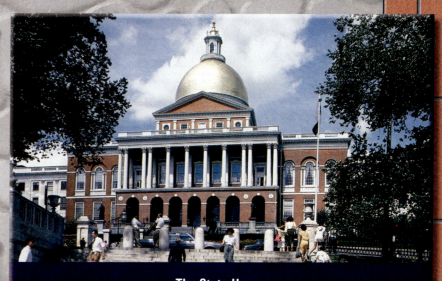
The State House

TAKE A FIELD TRIP

A VIRTUAL TOUR Visit The Learning Site at www.harcourtschool.com to take virtual tours of other historic sites in the United States.

A VIDEO TOUR Check your media center or classroom library for a videotape tour of the Freedom Trail.

Unit 4 ■ 335

UNIT 4 Review and Test Preparation

VISUAL SUMMARY

Write a Paragraph Study the pictures and captions below to help you review Unit 4. Then choose one of the events shown. Write a paragraph that describes what happened and how that event affected the American Revolution.

USE VOCABULARY

For each pair of terms, write a sentence or two that explains how the terms are related.

1. **revolution** (p. 268), **independence** (p. 302)
2. **proclamation** (p. 276), **declaration** (p. 283)
3. **boycott** (p. 282), **blockade** (p. 289)

RECALL FACTS

Answer these questions.

4. What was the Albany Plan of Union?
5. Why did Parliament pass new tax laws for the American colonists after the French and Indian War?

Write the letter of the best choice.

6. The Stamp Act Congress met to—
   A discuss the problems the new tax laws had caused.
   B vote on the Stamp Act.
   C form an American Parliament.
   D choose a new mayor for New York City.

7. What did the British learn from the Battle of Bunker Hill?
   F Earthworks would help them.
   G The colonists had many bullets.
   H The colonists printed their own money.
   J Fighting the colonists would not be easy.

8. Which battle of the American Revolution brought about the end of the war?
   A the Battle of Yorktown
   B the Battle of Moores Creek Bridge
   C the Battle of Saratoga
   D the Battle of Long Island

Visual Summary

1754 The French and Indian War begins p. 269

1765 The Stamp Act is passed p. 281

1773 The Boston Tea Party takes place p. 288

336

THINK CRITICALLY

9. Why do you think the British government believed that it had the right to make the colonists pay taxes?

10. Do you think the British could have avoided war with the colonists? Explain.

11. Why do you think some colonists chose to remain loyal to Britain during the American Revolution?

12. What do you think Nathan Hale meant when he said, "I only regret that I have but one life to lose for my country"?

APPLY SKILLS

Compare Historical Maps
Use the two historical maps on this page to answer the following questions.

13. Which map would you use to determine who claimed the 13 colonies?

14. Which map shows the land that was claimed by both Spain and the United States?

15. What areas shown on the two maps changed very little between 1763 and 1783?

16. Most of the British land that was reserved for Native Americans in 1763 became a part of what country by 1783?

17. Which map would you use to determine the location of the land that was reserved for Native Americans?

18. Who claimed Florida in 1763? in 1783?

1775 The American Revolution begins p. 291

1776 The Declaration of Independence is signed p. 306

1781 The British surrender at Yorktown, in Virginia p. 326

Unit Activities

Visit The Learning Site at www.harcourtschool.com for additional activities.

Create a Time Line

Work in a group to make a large time line to display on a classroom wall. The time line should show either the important events leading up to the American Revolution or the key events that took place during and after the war. Use the time line as you take turns describing each of the events shown.

Honor Your Hero

Choose someone you admire from the American Revolution to be the subject of a poster for a display called Heroes of the American Revolution. Research that person's life, and write a short biography to include on the poster. To illustrate the poster, print out pictures from the Internet or draw your own. Add words or phrases around the pictures, telling what made that person a hero. Present your poster to the class.

VISIT YOUR LIBRARY

■ *The Boston Tea Party* by Laurie A. O'Neill. Troll Associates.

■ *Thomas* by Bonnie Pryor. Morrow Junior Books.

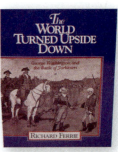

■ *The World Turned Upside Down: George Washington and the Battle of Yorktown* by Richard Ferrie. Holiday House.

COMPLETE THE UNIT PROJECT

The History Show Work with a group of classmates to finish the unit project—a history show about the American Revolution. Decide which key events and people you want to include in your show. Then write a script, create any needed illustrations or costumes, and choose the presenters. Videotape your show and invite other students to watch it, or perform the show "live" for them.

A New Nation

GEORGIA CONNECTION

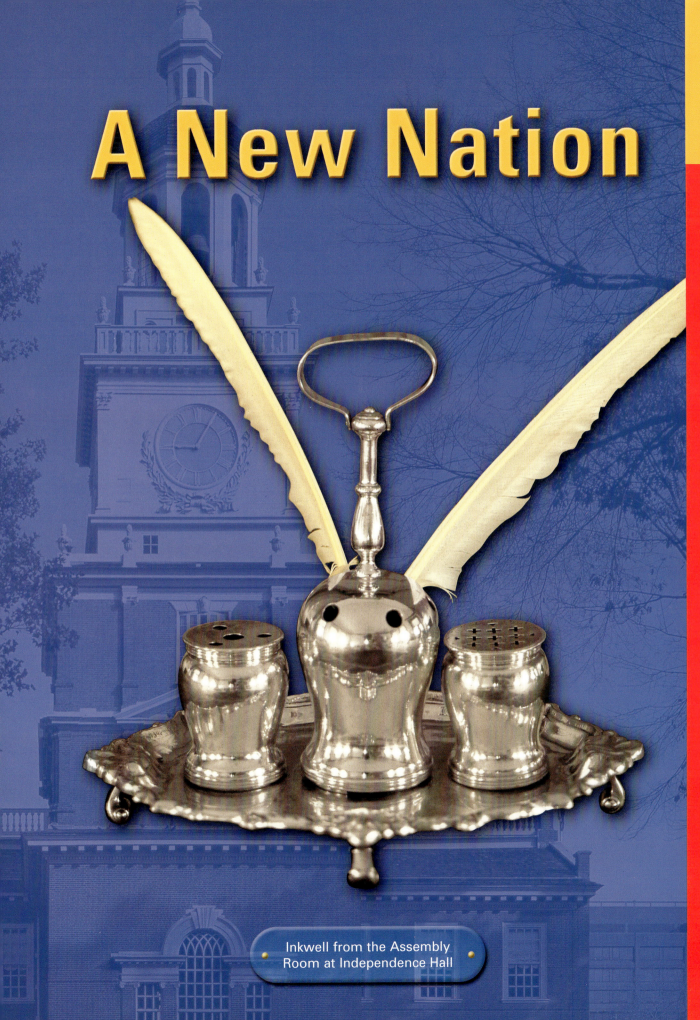

Inkwell from the Assembly Room at Independence Hall

GEORGIA CONNECTION

The Georgia Gold Rush

On January 2, 1788, Georgia became the fourth state and the first southern state to approve the Constitution and enter the Union.

Forty years later, in 1828, settlers discovered gold in Georgia. The discovery brought many people to the Cherokee land where the gold was found. The Georgia legislature started to plan for the removal of the Cherokees. This removal eventually led to the "Trail of Tears." Soldiers forced Native Americans east of the Mississippi to leave their homelands and travel west.

The Treaty of New Echota, signed in 1835, gave President Andrew Jackson the legal right to move the Cherokees west. The Cherokees were forced to walk a great distance to the Indian Territory during the cold winter months.

TRAIL OF TEARS

The New Echota Treaty of 1835 relinquished Cherokee Indian claims to lands east of the Mississippi River. The majority of the Cherokee people considered the treaty fraudulent and refused to leave their homelands in Georgia, Alabama, North Carolina, and Tennessee. 7,000 Federal and State troops were ordered into the Cherokee Nation to forcibly evict the Indians. On May 26, 1838, the roundup began. Over 15,000 Cherokees were forced from their homes at gunpoint and imprisoned in stockades until removal to the west could take place. 2,700 left by boat in June 1838, but, due to many deaths and sickness, removal was suspended until cooler weather. Most of the remaining 13,000 Cherokees left by wagon, horseback, or on foot during October and November, 1838, on an 800 mile route through Tennessee, Kentucky, Illinois, Missouri, and Arkansas. They arrived in what is now eastern Oklahoma during January, February, and March, 1839. Disease, exposure, and starvation may have claimed as many as 4,000 Cherokee lives during the course of capture, imprisonment, and removal. The ordeal has become known as the Trail of Tears.

The Dahlonega Mint produced more than $6.1 million in gold coins by the time of its closing in 1861.

In 1832 the gold rush area was named Lumpkin County. The town of Dahlonega, meaning "yellow money" in the Cherokee language, became the county seat. The population of Dahlonega began to grow. By the height of the gold rush, Dahlonega had 15,000 people.

Due to Dahlonega's success, the national government built a mint, or a place where money is manufactured, in the town. By 1838, the Dahlonega Mint was producing its first coins.

The Georgia gold rush prospered until about 1849, when news of the California gold rush reached the state. Many miners left Georgia for California. Most of the gold mining in Georgia had stopped by 1858.

★ CRCT ★ TEST PREP

❶ Georgia became a state in
  A 1830.
  B 1788.
  C 1828.
  D 1838.

❷ The "Trail of Tears" was
  A the trail that miners followed to find gold.
  B the trail to the California gold rush.
  C the trail that the Cherokees followed west.
  D the trail that led to the Dahlonega Mint.

❸ Why did miners begin leaving Georgia in 1849?
  A to force the Cherokees to leave
  B to join the California gold rush
  C to work at the Dahlonega Mint
  D to follow the "Trail of Tears"

Independence Hall, Philadelphia, Pennsylvania

UNIT 5

A New Nation

" *E pluribus unum* "
(Out of many, one)

—Motto on the Seal of the United States,
adopted on June 20, 1782

Preview the Content
Read the title and the Big Idea for each lesson in the unit. Then use what you have read to make a web for each chapter. Write down words or phrases that will help you identify the main topics to be covered in the unit.

Preview the Vocabulary
Context Clues Context clues are words that can help you figure out the meaning of a word that is unfamiliar. Scan the unit and find the terms **inflation**, **commerce**, and **investor**. Write a sentence explaining how these words relate to one another.

Unit 5 ■ 339

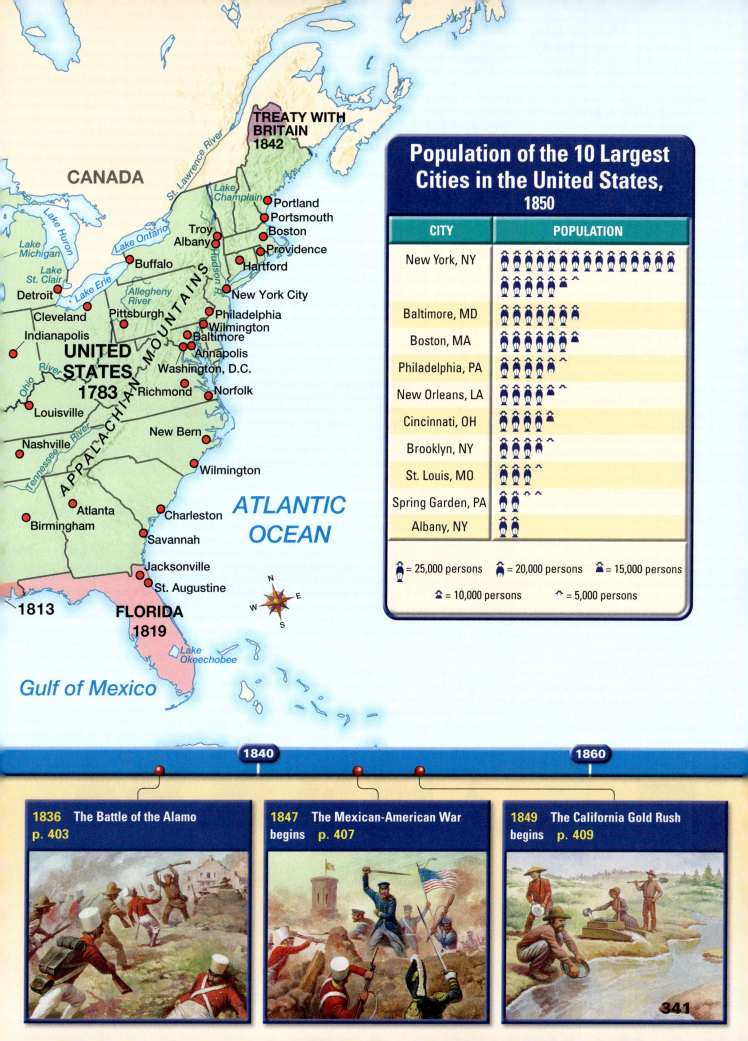

START with a STORY

Shh! We're Writing the Constitution

by Jean Fritz
pictures by Tomie dePaola

The job of turning the 13 former British colonies into a new nation was not an easy one. The biggest problem was getting people to think of themselves as citizens of a country. Until this time most Americans thought of themselves as citizens of their states—Connecticut, Delaware, Georgia, Maryland, Massachusetts, New Hampshire, New Jersey, New York, North Carolina, Pennsylvania, Rhode Island, South Carolina, or Virginia.

☆

After the Revolutionary War most people in America were glad that they were no longer British. Still, they were not ready to call themselves Americans. The last thing they wanted was to become a nation. They were citizens of their own separate states, just as they had always been: each state different, each state proud of its own character, each state quick to poke fun at other states. To Southerners, New Englanders might be "no-account Yankees." To New Englanders, Pennsylvanians might be "lousy Buckskins." But to everyone the states themselves were all

important. "Sovereign states," they called them. They loved the sound of "sovereign" because it meant that they were their own bosses.

George Washington, however, scoffed at the idea of "sovereign states." He knew that the states could not be truly independent for long and survive. Ever since the Declaration of Independence had been signed, people had referred to the country as the United States of America. It was about time, he thought, for them to act and feel united.

Once during the war Washington had decided it would be a good idea if his troops swore allegiance to the United States. As a start, he lined up some troops from New Jersey and asked them to take such an oath. They looked at Washington as if he'd taken leave of his senses. How could they do that? they cried. New Jersey was their country!

So Washington dropped the idea. In time, he hoped, the states would see that they needed to become one nation, united under a strong central government.

But that time would be long in coming.

Analyze the Literature

1. Why was the idea of "sovereign states" important?
2. How was George Washington's point of view about the nation different from that of most other Americans?

READ A BOOK

START THE UNIT PROJECT

A Growing Nation Time Line With your classmates, create an illustrated time line. As you read, make a list of the key events, people, and places you learn about. This list will help you decide which items to include on your time line.

USE TECHNOLOGY

Visit The Learning Site at **www.harcourtschool.com** for additional activities, primary sources, and other resources to use in this unit.

Unit 5 • 343

INDEPENDENCE NATIONAL HISTORIC PARK

Few places in the United States have been home to as many historic events as the Assembly Room of Independence Hall in Philadelphia. In this room, the Declaration of Independence was adopted, the design for the American flag was chosen, and the Constitution was debated and written.

LOCATE IT

PENNSYLVANIA
Philadelphia

CHAPTER 10

The Constitution

" We the people of the United States... "
—Constitution of the United States, Preamble, September 17, 1787

Focus Skill: Summarize

When you **summarize,** you give a shortened version of what you have read.

After you read this chapter, be sure to do the following.
- Summarize the lessons about the Constitution and the early national government.

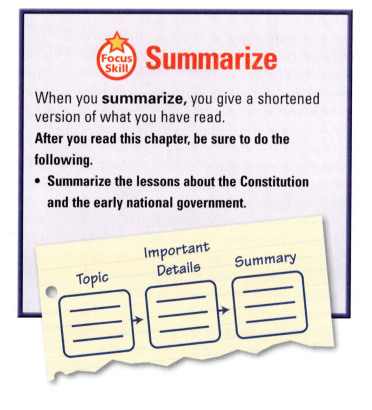

LESSON 1

The Confederation Period

 SUMMARIZE
As you read, summarize the problems and successes of the new nation's first government.

BIG IDEA
The first government of the United States had many problems and successes.

VOCABULARY
republic
inflation
arsenal
territory
ordinance

1780 — 1800 — 1820 — 1840 — 1860

1781–1787

In 1781, before the war with Britain had ended, the 13 former colonies—now independent states—approved the Articles of Confederation. This plan for a central government made the United States of America a republic. A **republic** is a form of government in which people elect representatives to govern the country. People hoped that under the Articles of Confederation, all 13 states could act together as one nation when needed. Under the Articles, however, the central government was weak. It was, as George Washington called it, "a half-starved, limping government."

Problems from the Start

Under the Articles of Confederation, the representatives met in a Congress. However, there often were not enough representatives present to allow Congress to take action. To make an important decision, representatives from at least 9 of the 13 states had to agree. Even when enough representatives were present, the states seldom agreed on anything. No state wanted to be under the control of the other states.

Nassau Hall in New Jersey was once a meeting place for Congress.

FAST FACT Nassau Hall served as the United States capital for three months during the summer of 1783.

Congress printed many paper bills known as Continentals. They had so little value that some Americans used the phrase *not worth a continental* to describe things that were worthless.

The new government had to face other challenges, too. Congress did not have a building of its own, so representatives had to hold meetings in many different cities and states. Also, the Articles limited the powers of the central government. For example, Congress could declare war, make treaties, and borrow money, but it could not collect taxes.

To get some of the money it needed, Congress asked each state to contribute money to help support the central government. Congress could not force the states to pay, though. State leaders could refuse to send money. They could also refuse to pay debts that they owed.

The central government could raise funds by printing and coining money. However, Congress caused inflation by printing too much money. **Inflation** occurs when the value of a government's money falls because there is too much of it. This meant that people needed more money to buy the same goods and services. During this time goods that used to cost two cents cost twenty dollars!

The Articles also stated that Congress could not raise a large army without the permission of the states. State leaders were afraid that a large army could be used to enforce unfair laws. This meant that raising an army to defend the nation against attack was difficult.

REVIEW What happened when Congress tried to print money to raise funds?
 SUMMARIZE

Shays's Rebellion

Economic problems during the 1780s made life difficult for many Americans. Some former soldiers still had not been paid for fighting during the Revolutionary War. Although they were poor, they had to pay high state taxes. To buy tools and seeds for planting, many farmers had to borrow money and go into debt.

Going into debt caused more problems for poor Americans. If people could not pay their debts or their taxes, the courts of some states would take away their farms. In 1786 and 1787, poor farmers protested by refusing to let the courts meet. Some of these protests, such as Shays's Rebellion in Massachusetts, turned violent.

The rebellion was named for Daniel Shays, a captain in the Continental army. During the fall of 1786, some farmers rebelled against the laws of Massachusetts.

Chapter 10 • 347

Shays led the group in attacks against the courthouses. The farmers hoped that they could stop the courts from taking their land. Then, in January 1787, Shays led an attack on a United States arsenal located in Springfield, Massachusetts. An **arsenal** is a building that is used for storing weapons.

The arsenal at Springfield belonged to the central government, but Shays and his group attacked it anyway. Shays declared, "That crowd [the members of Congress] is too weak to act!" Congress did not have an army to defend the arsenal. Instead, the governor of Massachusetts called out state troops to stop Shays. During the fighting, four of Shays's followers died. Soon the rebellion had come to an end.

Shays's Rebellion showed that many Americans were unhappy with the state governments. Under the Articles of Confederation, Congress did not have an army to defend United States property. State governments had to defend their own lands. Americans feared that the states could not stop all the unrest.

REVIEW Why did Daniel Shays and other farmers rebel against the government?

The Western Lands

In spite of such problems, Congress was still responsible for many important decisions. One was about how to divide and govern the nation's new lands west of the Appalachians. In the years after the United States gained its independence, many settlers moved to the

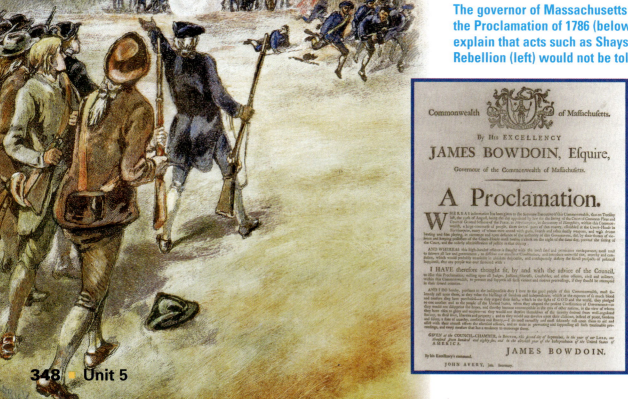

The governor of Massachusetts issued the Proclamation of 1786 (below) to explain that acts such as Shays's Rebellion (left) would not be tolerated.

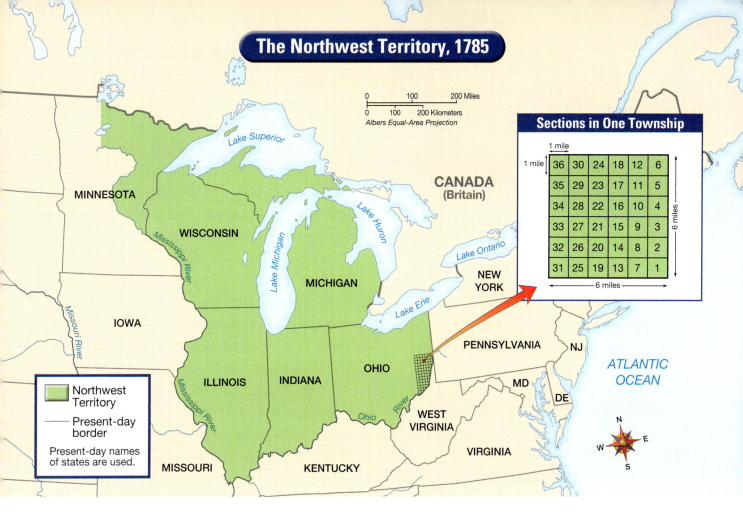

 Regions This map shows how the Northwest Territory was divided into townships with many sections.

❖ How might the township system have helped settlers?

western lands. These lands had previously been set aside for Native Americans. Some of those settlers moved to lands north of the Ohio River, an area that had become known as the Northwest Territory. A **territory** is land that belongs to a national government but is not a state and is not represented in Congress. Over time, thousands of settlers followed the Ohio River west and settled there.

At first, there was no plan in place for how the land should be divided among the settlers. It was difficult to tell where each person's property ended. As a result, many boundary disputes occurred.

In 1785 Congress passed a land **ordinance**, or set of laws, that created a system to survey, or measure, the western lands. The land was divided into squares that were called townships. A township measured 6 miles (10 km) long on each side, and its land was divided into 36 smaller squares, or sections. One of these sections was set aside for public schools. Then the central government sold the rest of the squares for at least one dollar per acre. This system was so successful that most of the land west of the Mississippi River was divided that way. Township and section lines are still used in many parts of the United States today.

Two years later, in 1787, Congress passed the Northwest Ordinance.

Chapter 10 ■ **349**

Members of Congress (above) discussed the possibility of a stronger central government.

This ordinance set up a plan for governing the Northwest Territory and for forming new states from the lands. It said that the Ohio River would form the southern boundary of the Northwest Territory. The ordinance also promised the settlers freedom of religion and it did not allow slavery. It showed that Congress could work to plan the growth of the nation.

REVIEW Which ordinance set up a plan for governing the Northwest Territory?

A Rope of Sand

Some people argued that Congress needed more power. James Madison, who represented Virginia, was the youngest member of Congress in 1780. Madison had studied ways of governing, and saw several weaknesses in the Articles of Confederation. He worried that Congress had become "a rope of sand."

Some others, such as John Adams and Thomas Jefferson, agreed with Madison. They believed that the nation needed a stronger central government. That was the only way, they said, to keep the states from breaking apart.

Others did not agree. Patrick Henry of Virginia was one of many who favored the Articles. Henry, like others, feared a strong central government. A rope made out of sand they said, was better than a rope made out of iron.

REVIEW Why did James Madison and others want a stronger central government?

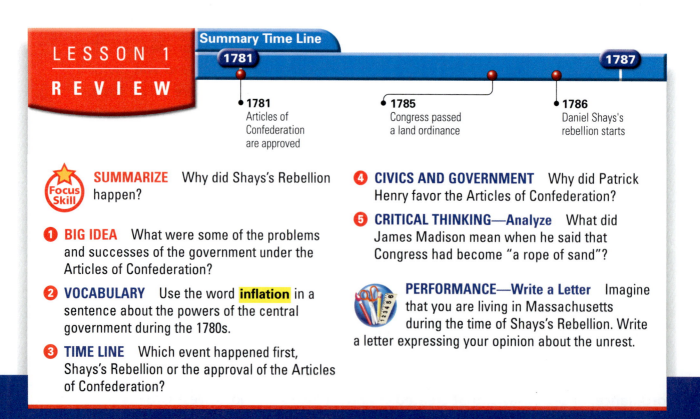

LESSON 1 REVIEW

Summary Time Line
- 1781 Articles of Confederation are approved
- 1785 Congress passed a land ordinance
- 1786 Daniel Shays's rebellion starts
- 1787

SUMMARIZE Why did Shays's Rebellion happen?

1. **BIG IDEA** What were some of the problems and successes of the government under the Articles of Confederation?

2. **VOCABULARY** Use the word **inflation** in a sentence about the powers of the central government during the 1780s.

3. **TIME LINE** Which event happened first, Shays's Rebellion or the approval of the Articles of Confederation?

4. **CIVICS AND GOVERNMENT** Why did Patrick Henry favor the Articles of Confederation?

5. **CRITICAL THINKING—Analyze** What did James Madison mean when he said that Congress had become "a rope of sand"?

PERFORMANCE—Write a Letter Imagine that you are living in Massachusetts during the time of Shays's Rebellion. Write a letter expressing your opinion about the unrest.

The Constitutional Convention

· LESSON ·

2

| 1780 | 1800 | 1820 | 1840 | 1860 |

1786–1787

 SUMMARIZE

As you read, summarize the key events at the Constitutional Convention.

BIG IDEA

Leaders had to work together to decide on a new plan of government.

VOCABULARY

convention
commerce
federal system
bill

Governing the country under the Articles of Confederation became very difficult. In 1786 some leaders called on the states to hold a **convention**, or an important meeting, to discuss trade among the states. It was held at Annapolis, Maryland, in September 1786.

The Annapolis Convention

Only five states—Delaware, New Jersey, New York, Pennsylvania, and Virginia—sent representatives in time to attend the Annapolis Convention. Chief among the delegates' concerns was **commerce**, or trade. Under the Articles, each state had the authority to print its own paper money. However, money from one state was usually not accepted in another state.

The delegates to the convention talked briefly before deciding that a stronger national government was needed in order to regulate commerce.

The Annapolis State House in Maryland is the oldest state capitol still in use. Shown below is an eight-dollar bank note from Massachusetts.

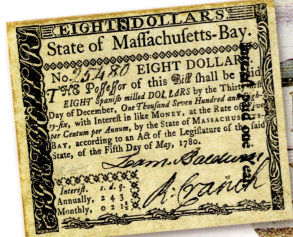

Chapter 10 ■ 351

This meant that the Articles of Confederation had to be changed. To change the Articles, however, all the states had to agree.

The delegates sent a letter to Congress, asking it to call another convention. Representatives from all the states could meet to discuss all their problems. They could also decide whether changing the Articles might help solve those problems.

At first Congress did not want to call a convention, but after Shays's Rebellion it agreed to participate. Each state was asked to send delegates to a convention to be held in Philadelphia in the spring of 1787. Rhode Island was the only state that refused to send a delegate. Its leaders feared a strong national government. They believed that such a government would be a threat to the rights of citizens.

REVIEW What decision did delegates reach at the Annapolis Convention?

The Philadelphia Convention

The delegates to the convention began to gather in Philadelphia in May 1787. One of the first to arrive was George Washington of Virginia. In 1787 Washington was 55 years old and the most highly honored hero of the Revolutionary War. The first action the delegates took was to elect Washington president of the convention.

Benjamin Franklin, representing Pennsylvania, made the most colorful entrance. Franklin was 81 years old, and he was unable to walk far or ride in a bumpy carriage. He arrived in a Chinese sedan chair carried by prisoners from the Philadelphia jail.

In all, 55 delegates from 12 of the states met in the Pennsylvania State House, which later became known as Independence Hall. The delegates were mostly lawyers, planters, and merchants. Some, such as Roger Sherman and

• BIOGRAPHY •

James Madison   1751–1836
Character Trait: Citizenship

James Madison's Virginia Plan provided the basic framework for the Constitution. Because of his efforts in planning the Constitution and winning its final approval, Madison is remembered as the Father of the Constitution. Madison, however, often dismissed this title by saying the Constitution was not "the off-spring of a single brain" but "the work of many heads and many hands." Madison later served as an official in the United States government. In 1808 he was elected fourth President of the United States.

MULTIMEDIA BIOGRAPHIES
Visit The Learning Site at www.harcourtschool.com to learn about other famous people.

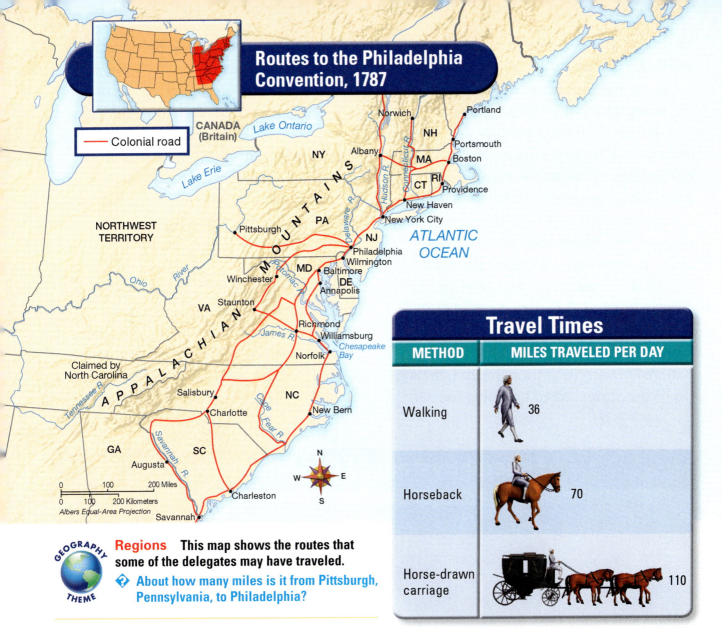

Regions This map shows the routes that some of the delegates may have traveled.

❓ About how many miles is it from Pittsburgh, Pennsylvania, to Philadelphia?

Benjamin Franklin, had been signers of the Declaration of Independence.

Some famous people were not delegates. Thomas Jefferson, who had written the Declaration of Independence, was in Paris as ambassador to France. John Adams was in London as ambassador to Britain. His cousin Samuel Adams was in ill health, and John Hancock was too busy as governor of Massachusetts to attend. Patrick Henry refused to take part because he did not believe that a stronger national government was a good idea.

REVIEW Who was elected president of the convention?

The Work Begins

From the beginning, the delegates agreed to conduct their meetings in secret. They believed that secret meetings would allow them to make the best decisions. Windows in the State House were covered, and guards stood at the doors.

As the convention began, some of the delegates offered ideas that they thought would improve the Articles of Confederation. Almost immediately, however, they reached a surprising decision. An entirely new plan of government—a new constitution—needed to be written.

Chapter 10 • 353

To do this, the delegates worked diligently for the next four months.

One of the first issues discussed by the delegates to the Constitutional Convention, as the Convention in Philadelphia became known, was the relationship between the states and the national government. Some delegates thought there should be a strong national government. Others believed that the state governments should be stronger.

Only a few delegates agreed with George Read of Delaware. He said that the states should be done away with. Even most of those who wanted a strong national government thought that getting rid of the states would be going too far.

Instead, the delegates agreed to create a **federal system**, one in which the right to govern would be shared by the national government and the state governments. The states would keep some rights, and share some rights with the national, or federal, government. The national government would keep all power over matters that affected the nation as a whole.

The states would keep power over their own affairs, set up state and local governments, make state laws, and conduct state and local elections. However, the states would no longer print money, raise armies and navies, or make treaties with other countries, as they had done under the Articles of Confederation.

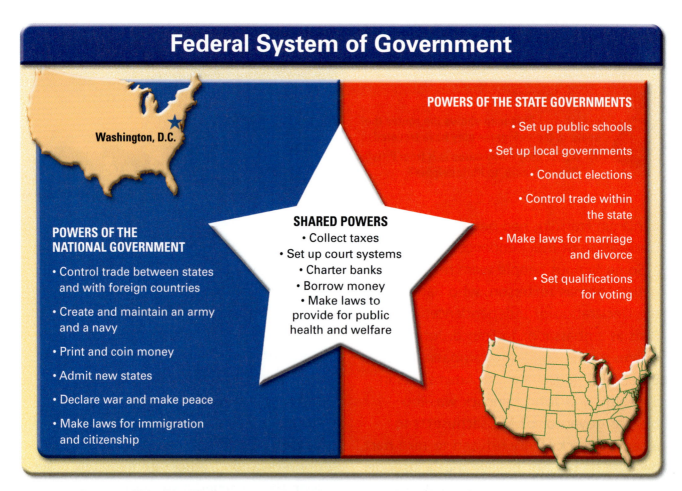

Analyze Charts This chart illustrates the relationship between the national and state governments.

◆ Why do you think state governments need the power to create local governments?

Three delegates to the Constitutional Convention—Edmund Randolph of Virginia, Roger Sherman of Connecticut, and William Paterson of New Jersey—presented ideas for the new government that started great debate and compromise.

Both the states and the national government would be able to set up their own court systems and to raise money by taxing citizens. The delegates made it clear that, under this federal system, the new rules of government would be "the supreme law of the land." They called these new rules the Constitution of the United States of America.

REVIEW How is the power to govern shared in a federal system? **SUMMARIZE**

Debate and Compromise

During their work, the delegates to the convention often failed to agree with one another. The new Constitution came into being only because the delegates were willing to agree to several compromises. The delegates often had to give up some of what they wanted in order to reach an agreement. As compromises were made, decisions were written down and the Constitution took shape.

One important compromise resolved the delegates' differences over how each state would be represented in the new Congress. Some people called this agreement the Great Compromise.

Edmund Randolph and the other Virginia delegates, including James Madison, thought the number of representatives that a state would have in the new Congress should be based on the number of people living in that state. Under this Virginia Plan, as it was called, states with more people would have more representatives and more votes in Congress. This plan would favor the large states of Virginia, Massachusetts, and Pennsylvania, which had many people.

"Not fair!" replied the delegates from the small states. William Paterson of New Jersey said that he would "rather submit to a monarch, to a despot [ruler with unlimited power], than to such a fate." Paterson then offered his own plan.

Chapter 10 ■ 355

The Virginia Plan, supported by Edmund Randolph, called for representation based on population. The New Jersey Plan, offered by William Paterson, favored an equal number of representatives for each state.

Under this plan, called the New Jersey Plan, the new Congress would have one house, in which each state would be equally represented. This plan would give the small states the same number of representatives as the large states.

For weeks the delegates argued about how states should be represented in Congress. "We are now at a full stop," wrote Roger Sherman of Connecticut. The convention decided to set up a committee to work out a compromise.

In a committee meeting, Sherman presented a new plan, which became known as the Great Compromise. It was based on the idea of a two-house Congress. In one house, representation would be based on the population of each state, as in the Virginia Plan. In the other house, each state would be equally represented, as in the New Jersey Plan. Either house could present a **bill**, or an idea for a new law, but both had to approve it before it became a law.

Committee members from the large states did not like the compromise. They believed that it gave too much power to the small states. The committee added another idea.

The house in which representation was based on population would have the sole authority to propose tax bills. In the end, the committee presented its plan to the whole convention. The delegates soon came to understand that if they did not agree to the Great Compromise, there would be no new plan of government.

Another compromise had to do with slavery. Delegates from the northern and southern states argued about whether enslaved African Americans should be counted when figuring each state's population. Population would affect a state's taxes and its representation in Congress.

Because the northern states had fewer enslaved African Americans than the southern states, the northern states did not want slaves to be counted for representation. After all, the delegates argued, slaves were not citizens under the Articles of Confederation and they would not become citizens under the Constitution. For tax purposes, however, the northern states did want slaves to be counted.

Delegates from the southern states wanted slaves to be counted for representation. That way they could count more

This painting by Thomas Coram shows slave quarters on a South Carolina plantation. The issue of slavery sparked heated debates among northern and southern delegates.

people and get more representatives in Congress. For tax purposes the southern states did not want slaves counted.

The delegates finally reached a compromise by counting three-fifths of the total number of slaves. This Three-fifths Compromise moved the delegates closer to forming a new government.

REVIEW What idea was called the Great Compromise?

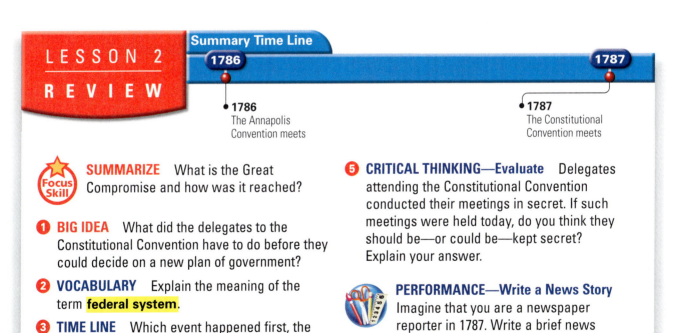

LESSON 2 REVIEW

Summary Time Line
- 1786 The Annapolis Convention meets
- 1787 The Constitutional Convention meets

SUMMARIZE What is the Great Compromise and how was it reached?

1 BIG IDEA What did the delegates to the Constitutional Convention have to do before they could decide on a new plan of government?

2 VOCABULARY Explain the meaning of the term **federal system**.

3 TIME LINE Which event happened first, the Annapolis Convention or the Constitutional Convention?

4 CIVICS AND GOVERNMENT Under the new Constitution, what rights would the states keep?

5 CRITICAL THINKING—Evaluate Delegates attending the Constitutional Convention conducted their meetings in secret. If such meetings were held today, do you think they should be—or could be—kept secret? Explain your answer.

PERFORMANCE—Write a News Story Imagine that you are a newspaper reporter in 1787. Write a brief news story about the Constitutional Convention and the decisions the delegates finally reached. Share your report with classmates.

· LESSON · 3
Three Branches of Government

SUMMARIZE
As you read, summarize the powers of the different branches of government.

BIG IDEA
Delegates created three branches for the United States government.

VOCABULARY
census
electoral college
veto
impeach
justice
checks and balances

Gouverneur Morris (right) was responsible for much of the wording of the Constitution (below).

The delegates to the Constitutional Convention, wrote the Constitution with great care. Gouverneur (guh•ver•NIR) Morris of Pennsylvania spent long hours writing down and polishing each sentence. The delegates gave him the job of recording all the ideas that had been approved during the convention.

The Preamble

In the Preamble to the Constitution, Morris began with the words

> **We the people of the United States . . .**

He had originally written "We the people of the States of New Hampshire, Massachusetts, . . ." Morris changed the words because he wanted the American people to know that the Constitution would make them citizens of a nation first and citizens of separate states second. This change also helped link the Constitution with the idea in the Declaration of Independence that a government should get its power from the consent of the people.

Morris went on to explain in the Preamble that the purpose of the Constitution was to create a better plan of government. This government would work toward fairness and peace. It would allow the nation to defend itself and it would work toward the nation's well-being.

Morris also wrote that the Constitution would provide "the blessings of liberty" for the American people. These words let the citizens of the United States know that the Constitution would make sure that they remained a free people.

REVIEW Why did Gouverneur Morris change the wording in the Preamble to the Constitution?

The Legislative Branch

In Article I of the Constitution, Gouverneur Morris described the law-making, or legislative, branch of the new government. The Congress could make laws, regulate commerce between states and with other countries and Indian tribes, and raise an army and a navy. It would also have power to declare war and coin money.

Congress would have two houses—the House of Representatives and the Senate. Either house could propose most bills, but tax bills could be proposed first only in the House of Representatives. For any bill to become law, the majority of those voting in each house would have to vote for it.

The number of members each state sent to the House of Representatives would depend on the state's population. A census, or population count, would be taken every ten years to find out the number of people in each state. Today the total number of members in the House of Representatives is limited to 435. That number is divided among the states, based on their populations. In the Senate each state has two senators.

For more than 200 years, the United States Capitol building has been home to the legislative branch of the federal government.

James Madison thought that the voters of each state should elect the members of both houses of Congress. Other delegates disagreed. Some felt that most citizens were not informed enough to have a say in government. After a long debate, the delegates agreed that citizens should vote directly for members of the House of Representatives. Senators would be selected by their state legislatures. Today, however, citizens vote directly for members of both houses of Congress.

In Article I, the delegates also outlined other rules for Congress that are still in effect. Members of the House of Representatives are elected to 2-year terms. They must be at least 25 years old, must have been citizens of the United States for at least 7 years, and must live in the state they represent. Senators are elected to 6-year terms. They must be at least 30 years old, must have been citizens of the United States for at least 9 years, and must live in the state they represent.

REVIEW What are the main responsibilities of Congress? **SUMMARIZE**

The Executive Branch

Once Congress makes the laws, it is the job of the executive branch, according to Article II of the Constitution, to carry them out. The delegates had many long arguments about whether this branch should be headed by one person or by a group of people. Some delegates believed that one person should be the chief executive, or leader. Others worried that a single executive would be too much like a monarch.

The delegates finally decided on a single chief executive called the President. The President is elected to a 4-year term. To be elected President, a person must be at least 35 years old and must have been born in the United States, or have parents who are United States citizens.

The President must also have lived in the United States for 14 years.

The delegates decided that citizens would vote for electors, who, in turn, would vote for the President. This group of electors is called the electoral college.

The White House is the official residence of the President of the United States.

Housed in this building since 1935, the Supreme Court is the highest court in the United States.

The delegates also had long debates about how much power the President should have. They eventually decided that the President should be able to **veto**, or reject, bills that are passed by Congress.

The delegates decided that the President would represent the nation in dealing with other countries. The President would also be commander in chief of the military. The President's chief responsibility, however, would be to "take care that the laws be faithfully executed." If these duties were not carried out according to law, Congress could **impeach** the President, or accuse the President of crimes. The President could then be tried by the Senate and removed from office if found guilty.

REVIEW What is the President's main responsibility?

The Judicial Branch

Once laws are made and carried out, the judicial branch, according to Article III of the Constitution, must decide if they are working fairly. The judicial branch is the court system.

The states had always had their own courts. Now the delegates agreed on the need for a federal court system. These courts would decide cases that dealt with the Constitution, treaties, and national laws. They would also decide cases between states and between citizens of different states.

The delegates made most of their decisions about the highest court in the United States, which they called the Supreme Court. The delegates decided that the President would nominate the Supreme Court **justices**, or judges.

Chapter 10 ■ 361

The Senate would vote whether to approve them. It was decided that a Supreme Court justice would stay in office for life. In this way, justices could make decisions without worrying about losing their jobs. No decision was made as to how many justices would be on the Supreme Court. Congress decided on that number later. At first there were six justices on the Supreme Court. Today there are nine.

REVIEW What are the duties of the federal courts?

The Branches Work Together

None of the delegates wanted any one branch of the new government to have too much power. So they gave each branch some ways to check, or limit, the power of the other two branches.

Congress, for example, can check the power of the President if two-thirds of each house votes to override, or cancel, the President's veto. If that happens, a bill

Analyze Diagrams This diagram shows the checks and balances within the three branches of the federal government.

◆ How can the President check the authority of Congress?

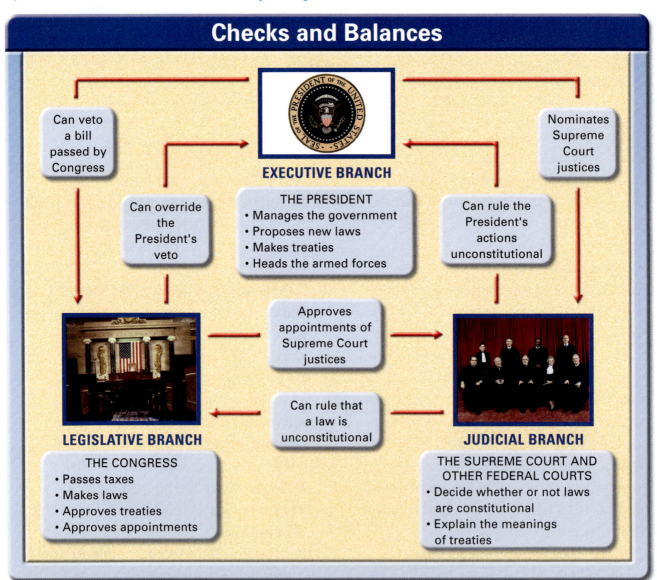

362 • Unit 5

Delegates to the Constitutional Convention set up a system of checks and balances so that no branch of the federal government would have too much power.

becomes a law even if the President objects. The Supreme Court can check the power of Congress by ruling that a law does not follow the Constitution.

The President can check the power of the Supreme Court by nominating its justices, and Congress can check the power of the President by either approving or not approving the President's choices. Congress can check the power of the Supreme Court by suggesting constitutional amendments, by impeaching and convicting justices of wrongdoing, and removing them from the Court.

The delegates set up these checks to keep a balance of authority among the three branches. This system of **checks and balances** keeps any one branch from becoming too powerful or using its authority wrongly. It helps all three branches work together.

REVIEW Why was the system of checks and balances outlined in the Constitution?

LESSON 3 REVIEW

 SUMMARIZE Summarize the powers given to each branch of government.

1. **BIG IDEA** What are the three branches of the United States government?
2. **VOCABULARY** Explain how the terms **veto**, **impeach**, and **checks and balances** are related.
3. **CIVICS AND GOVERNMENT** How can the Supreme Court check the power of Congress?
4. **CRITICAL THINKING—Analyze** Why is the White House a symbol of the United States?

 PERFORMANCE—Draw a Chart Draw a large triangle on a sheet of paper. On each point of the triangle, write the name of one branch of the federal government. Beside each name, write what that branch does and who or what is the head of it. Add a title to your chart, and then compare your chart with those of classmates.

SKILLS · CHART AND GRAPH

Read a Flow Chart

VOCABULARY
flow chart

▶ WHY IT MATTERS

Have you ever read something and had a difficult time understanding its meaning? Sometimes information is better understood when it is presented in a different way—as in a flow chart. A **flow chart** is a drawing that shows the order in which things happen. It uses arrows to help you to read the drawings, or steps, in the correct order.

▶ WHAT YOU NEED TO KNOW

The flow chart on page 365 shows how the federal government makes new laws for the United States. The top box on the flow chart shows the first step in the process of a bill becoming a law. In this step a member of the House of Representatives or Senate introduces a bill. If the bill is a tax bill, however, only members of the House may first introduce it.

In the second step, the bill is sent to a smaller group called a committee, where it is reviewed. This committee is made up of members of either the House of Representatives or the Senate. The committee members study the bill, and if they decide that the bill would make a good law, they tell the rest of the House and Senate. You can find out what happens next by reading the remaining steps shown on the flow chart.

This early gavel was used in the Senate to open and close meetings.

▶ PRACTICE THE SKILL

Use the flow chart on page 365 to answer these questions.

1. What happens after both the House and the Senate approve the bill?
2. What happens if the President signs a bill?
3. Where does a bill go if the President vetoes it?
4. How can a bill become a law if the President vetoes it?

▶ APPLY WHAT YOU LEARNED

With a partner, make a flow chart that explains to your classmates how something works. Write each step on a strip of paper. When you have finished, glue the steps—in order—on a sheet of posterboard. Then connect the strips with arrows. Give your flow chart a title, and present it to your classmates.

364 ▪ Unit 5

How a Bill Becomes a Law

A member of either the House or Senate can introduce a bill, but only a member of the House can introduce a tax bill.

COMMITTEES

The bill is reviewed by committees.

The House and Senate vote to approve the bill.

The bill goes to the President.

SIGN

If the President signs the bill, it becomes a law.

VETO

If the President vetoes the bill, it returns to Congress.

If the bill gets a two-thirds majority vote in both the House and Senate, it becomes a law.

LESSON 4

Approval and the Bill of Rights

1787–1791

 SUMMARIZE

As you read, summarize facts about the Constitution and the Bill of Rights.

BIG IDEA
The Bill of Rights was added to the Constitution to protect the freedoms of people in the United States.

VOCABULARY
ratify
Federalist
Anti-Federalist
amendment
Magna Carta
due process of law
reserved powers

On September 17, 1787, the Constitution was complete. There were 42 delegates still present at the Constitutional Convention, and all but 3 of them—Elbridge Gerry, George Mason, and Edmund Randolph—signed their approval. As delegates were signing the document, Benjamin Franklin spoke of the confidence he felt in the nation's future. During the convention, Franklin had often looked at the chair used by George Washington. Its high back had a carving of a sun on it. Franklin had not been able to decide if the sun shown was supposed to be rising or setting. Afterward, he said, "I have the happiness to know that it is a rising and not a setting sun."

A Struggle to Ratify

Despite Franklin's words, the Constitution that he and the other delegates had approved was not yet the law of the land. According to Article VII, 9 of the 13 states had to **ratify**, or approve, the Constitution before it would go into effect. After the document was signed, the Convention sent it to the Congress of the Confederation. Congress, in turn, sent copies to the states. In each state, voters elected delegates to a state convention.

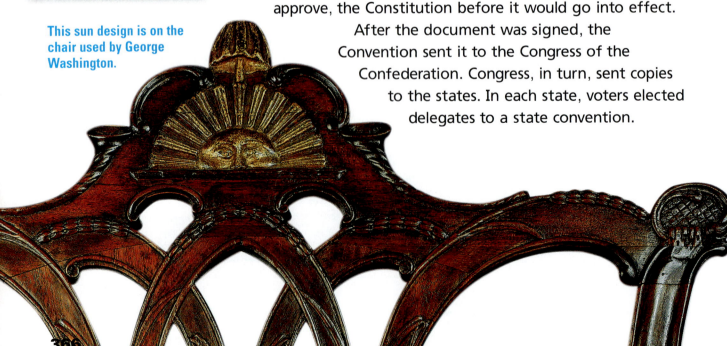
This sun design is on the chair used by George Washington.

This painting shows George Washington (standing at right) addressing the delegates.

These delegates would vote for or against the Constitution.

At the state conventions, arguments began again. Patrick Henry in Virginia and George Clinton in New York told their conventions that the new national government was too strong. Some delegates did not like the way the Preamble began with "We the people." They thought it should say "We the States."

There was one point, however, on which most delegates agreed. They felt the Constitution also should limit the power of the federal government and protect the basic rights of the people. The state delegates wanted to protect the freedoms they had won in the Revolutionary War. They feared unlimited government would have the power to limit freedoms, as the British government had done.

Many delegates to the state conventions said they would be more willing to approve the Constitution if a bill, or list, of rights were to be added. Supporters of the Constitution promised that after the Constitution was ratified, a bill of rights would be added.

REVIEW What would adding a bill of rights to the Constitution do?

The Vote

The first state to call for a vote on the Constitution was Delaware. In December 1787, all the Delaware state delegates voted to ratify the Constitution. Later that month, state delegates in Pennsylvania and New Jersey also voted to approve the Constitution. In January 1788, state delegates in Georgia and Connecticut voted to ratify. Still, eight states had not yet voted. Among those were the states of Virginia and New York. Citizens worried that the new government could not possibly work if some of the nation's largest states voted against it.

From January to June 1788, those who favored the Constitution and those against it both tried to get the backing of people in the states that had not yet voted.

Those citizens who favored the constitution came to be called **Federalists**. Federalists wanted a strong national, or federal, government. Those who did not became known as **Anti-Federalists**. Because the Constitution did not yet contain a bill of rights, the Anti-Federalists feared the document made the national government too strong.

Throughout America the two sides used the newspapers to tell what they thought and why. In New York, Alexander Hamilton, James Madison, and John Jay wrote essays defending the Constitution. These essays were later published as a book called *The Federalist*.

Citizens who could read followed the argument in the newspapers. Others heard the arguments at community meetings and even at church services. Some people saw the Constitution as the work of "lawyers, and men of learning, and moneyed men that talk so finely . . . to make us poor, illiterate people swallow down the pill." Others thought that having a new government was a good idea. They also trusted the promise of a bill of rights.

No one was certain how all the arguing would affect the vote in the state conventions. In Massachusetts, however, the promise of changes to the Constitution

POINTS OF VIEW
For or Against the Bill of Rights

THOMAS JEFFERSON to James Madison—December 20, 1787

66 Let me add that a bill of rights is what the people are entitled to against every government on earth, general or particular, and what no just government should refuse . . . 99

JAMES MADISON to Thomas Jefferson—April 22, 1788

66 Should this [the demand for a bill of rights] be carried in the affirmative, . . . I think the Constitution, and the Union will both be endangered. 99

Analyze the Viewpoints

1. What viewpoint about a bill of rights did each person hold?
2. Why do you think Jefferson and Madison held these views?
3. **Make It Relevant** James Madison eventually changed his view about the need for a bill of rights. Can you think of a time when you changed your view on a subject? Why did you change your view?

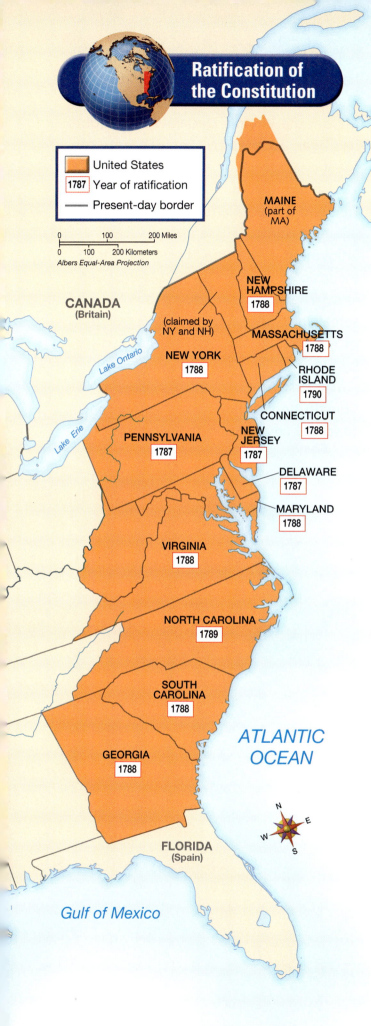

helped change the minds of some very important people. Samuel Adams and John Hancock went to the state convention as Anti-Federalists. They returned home as Federalists. As a result, Massachusetts decided to ratify the Constitution in February 1788.

Maryland and South Carolina followed Massachusetts's example that spring. Then, on June 21, 1788, New Hampshire became the ninth state to ratify the Constitution. That was the number of states needed to put it into effect. Four days later Virginia ratified it, and New York followed in July. By the spring of 1789 the new government was at work.

Place The map and table show when the Constitution was ratified by each of the 13 states. The table also lists the number of votes for and against the Constitution.

❓ In which state was the vote closest to being a tie?

Constitution Ratification Vote

STATE	DATE	VOTES FOR	VOTES AGAINST
Delaware	Dec. 7, 1787	30	0
Pennsylvania	Dec. 12, 1787	46	23
New Jersey	Dec. 18, 1787	38	0
Georgia	Jan. 2, 1788	26	0
Connecticut	Jan. 9, 1788	128	40
Massachusetts	Feb. 6, 1788	187	168
Maryland	April 28, 1788	63	11
South Carolina	May 23, 1788	149	73
New Hampshire	June, 21, 1788	57	47
Virginia	June 25, 1788	89	79
New York	July 26, 1788	30	27
North Carolina	Nov. 21, 1789	194	77
Rhode Island	May 29, 1790	34	32

Later that year North Carolina approved the Constitution. Rhode Island finally gave its approval in 1790.

REVIEW Why did the Federalists favor the Constitution and want a strong national government? **SUMMARIZE**

The Bill of Rights

As promised, not long after the states had ratified the Constitution, ten **amendments**, or changes, were added to protect the rights of the people. These ten amendments, called the Bill of Rights, became part of the Constitution in 1791.

The Bill of Rights was influenced by the Magna Carta and the English Bill of Rights of 1689. The **Magna Carta** was a charter granted by the king of England in the year 1215. It listed the rights of the upper class and limited the power of the king. The English Bill of Rights listed the rights of English citizens.

The Virginia Declaration of Rights also had a major influence on the United States Bill of Rights. Written by George Mason, the Virginia Declaration of Rights had been adopted by Virginia's state constitutional convention in June 1776. It said that "all men are by nature equally free and independent and have certain inherent rights." These rights were "the enjoyment of life and liberty, with the means of acquiring and possessing property." The Declaration also protected some rights by name, including freedom of the press, freedom of religion, and trial by jury.

The First Amendment to the Constitution gives people the freedom to follow any religion they choose.

It also says the government cannot promote or financially support any religion.

Many people believe that the Virginia Statute for Religious Freedom influenced the First Amendment. This statute, written by Thomas Jefferson, supported complete religious freedom. It became law in Virginia in 1786, due in large part to the leadership and support of James Madison.

The First Amendment also protects freedom of speech and freedom of the press. It further says that people can hold meetings to discuss problems and they can petition, or ask, the government to correct the wrongs.

The Second Amendment protects people's right to carry arms or weapons. It says, "A well-regulated militia being necessary to the security of a free State, the right of the people to keep and bear arms shall not be infringed [taken away]."

The Third Amendment says that government cannot force citizens to quarter soldiers in peacetime. Before the Revolutionary War, many colonists had to house and feed British soldiers.

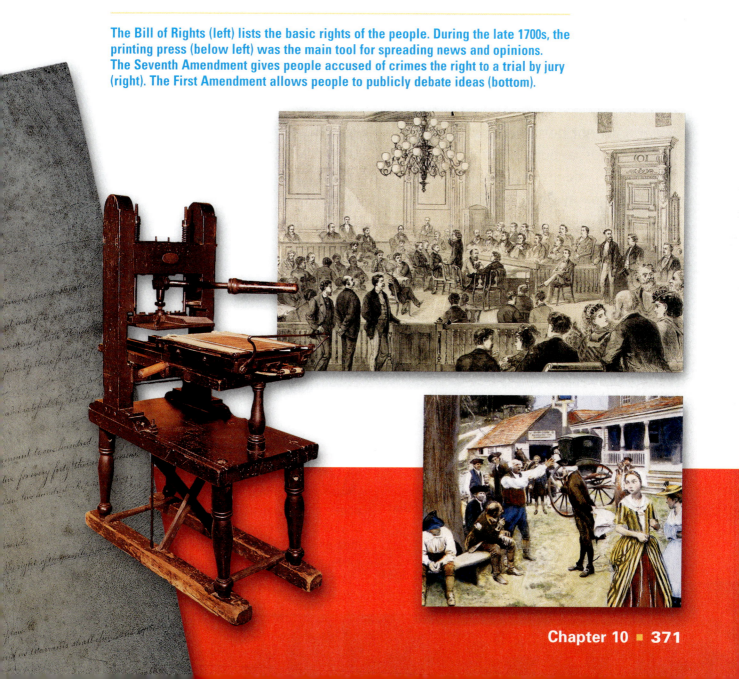

The Bill of Rights (left) lists the basic rights of the people. During the late 1700s, the printing press (below left) was the main tool for spreading news and opinions. The Seventh Amendment gives people accused of crimes the right to a trial by jury (right). The First Amendment allows people to publicly debate ideas (bottom).

The bald eagle became a symbol of the United States in 1782.

Under the Fourth Amendment, the government cannot search a person's home or take his or her property without that person's permission or the approval of a judge.

The Fifth through Eighth Amendments deal with **due process of law**. This means that people have the right to a fair public trial to be decided by a jury. They do not have to testify against themselves in court. They have the right to have a lawyer defend them. If they are found innocent of a crime they cannot be put on trial a second time for that same crime. They also cannot be sentenced to any cruel and unusual punishments.

The Ninth Amendment says that people have many other rights not specifically listed in the Constitution. These include the "unalienable rights" of "Life, Liberty and the pursuit of Happiness" described in the Declaration of Independence.

As a final protection for citizens, the Tenth Amendment says that the national government can do only what is listed in the Constitution. This means that all other authority, called the **reserved powers**, belongs to the states or to the people.

REVIEW Why is the Bill of Rights an important part of the Constitution?

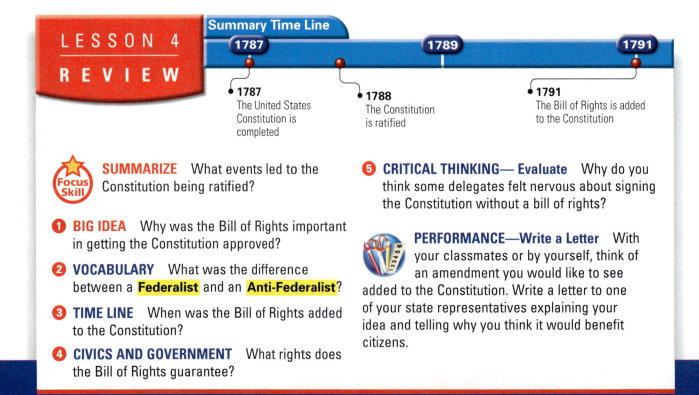

LESSON 4 REVIEW

Summary Time Line

- 1787 — The United States Constitution is completed
- 1788 — The Constitution is ratified
- 1791 — The Bill of Rights is added to the Constitution

SUMMARIZE What events led to the Constitution being ratified?

1 BIG IDEA Why was the Bill of Rights important in getting the Constitution approved?

2 VOCABULARY What was the difference between a **Federalist** and an **Anti-Federalist**?

3 TIME LINE When was the Bill of Rights added to the Constitution?

4 CIVICS AND GOVERNMENT What rights does the Bill of Rights guarantee?

5 CRITICAL THINKING— Evaluate Why do you think some delegates felt nervous about signing the Constitution without a bill of rights?

PERFORMANCE—Write a Letter With your classmates or by yourself, think of an amendment you would like to see added to the Constitution. Write a letter to one of your state representatives explaining your idea and telling why you think it would benefit citizens.

SKILLS

Act as a Responsible Citizen

WHY IT MATTERS

Responsible citizens know what is happening in their country, choose wise leaders, and take part in government. Citizens and leaders must also think about public service.

WHAT YOU NEED TO KNOW

Before the Constitution could be ratified, citizens elected delegates to vote for or against the Constitution. Many of these delegates did not feel they could vote for a plan of government that did not protect the rights of the states and citizens. Here are some steps delegates may have used to act as responsible citizens:

Step 1 They learned about the problem—some of the rights of the states and of individuals might not be protected.

Step 2 They thought about ways to solve the problem that would be good for the whole country.

Step 3 They worked together to bring about change.

PRACTICE THE SKILL

Imagine that you are a delegate to your state convention. Will you vote for the Constitution? Explain your decision and the steps you followed to act as a responsible citizen.

APPLY WHAT YOU LEARNED

Some acts of citizenship, such as voting, can be done only by adults. Others can be done by citizens of almost any age. Use the steps above to decide on ways you might act as a responsible citizen of your school.

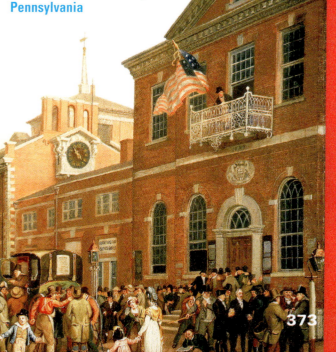

Election day in Philadelphia, Pennsylvania

CITIZENSHIP SKILLS

LESSON 5

The New Government Begins

1780–1800

 SUMMARIZE
As you read, summarize facts about new leaders and the new government.

BIG IDEA
The nation's new leaders worked together despite their growing differences.

VOCABULARY
Cabinet
political party
candidate

The first elections under the new Constitution began in 1788. Voters elected members of the United States House of Representatives. Each state legislature chose two senators for the United States Senate. They also chose people who would serve in the electoral college and elect the first president.

The New Leaders

In 1789 George Washington was elected as the nation's first President. John Adams became the first Vice President. His job was to help President Washington carry out his duties. When

Americans painted pictures and sewed samplers to pay tribute to their new President.

Washington was elected, Congress planned to meet in New York City. On April 30, 1789, George Washington stood on the balcony of Federal Hall in New York City. There he recited the President's oath of office, "I do solemnly swear (or affirm) that I will faithfully execute the office of President of the United States, and will, to the best of my ability, preserve, protect, and defend the Constitution of the United States."

One of Congress's first actions was to pass the Judiciary Act. This act set up the federal judicial branch and decided the number of Supreme Court justices. President Washington named John Jay of New York as the first chief justice.

President Washington also chose advisers to help him carry out the main responsibilities of the executive branch. These people would serve as the secretaries, or heads, of executive departments that included the State Department, the Treasury Department, and the War Department.

The President asked Thomas Jefferson to serve as the nation's first secretary of state. Jefferson helped the President deal with other countries such as Spain, France, and Britain. Washington also asked Alexander Hamilton to serve as secretary of the treasury. Hamilton worked to set up a new banking system and to pass new tax laws.

Henry Knox, who had been a general in the Revolutionary War, served as secretary of war. Knox began building a national army of 1,000 soldiers to defend the nation. Another important adviser was Edmund Randolph. He became the new President's legal adviser, now called the attorney general. He explained the laws and the powers of the Constitution.

Together, Jefferson, Hamilton, Knox, and Randolph became known as the **Cabinet**, a group of the President's most important advisers. Every President since Washington has relied on such a group. Over time, however, the number of Cabinet members has grown.

REVIEW Who were the members of Washington's Cabinet?

The First President

Analyze Primary Sources

This print from 1789 celebrates George Washington and the new nation. Thirteen of the circles around Washington show the 13 state coats of arms. The top circle is the nation's Great Seal.

1. The Great Seal of the United States.
2. State coats of arms.
3. President George Washington.

Why do you think the artist placed the 13 state coats of arms in a circle around President Washington?

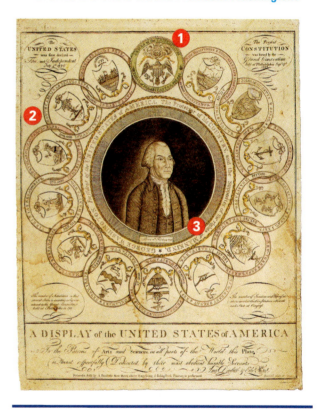

• BIOGRAPHY •

Benjamin Banneker
1731–1806

Character Trait: Inventiveness

Our nation's capital was built by the work of people such as Benjamin Banneker. In 1791 and 1792, he worked with Andrew Ellicott, the chief surveyor, to plan Washington, D.C. Banneker later became famous as the author of his own almanac, and he sent a copy to Thomas Jefferson. Banneker included a letter that asked Jefferson to help work for the rights of African Americans.

Banneker was also successful in other ways. He taught himself astronomy and mathematics. At a time when many African Americans were still enslaved, Banneker became a famous scientist.

MULTIMEDIA BIOGRAPHIES
Visit The Learning Site at www.harcourtschool.com
to learn about other famous people.

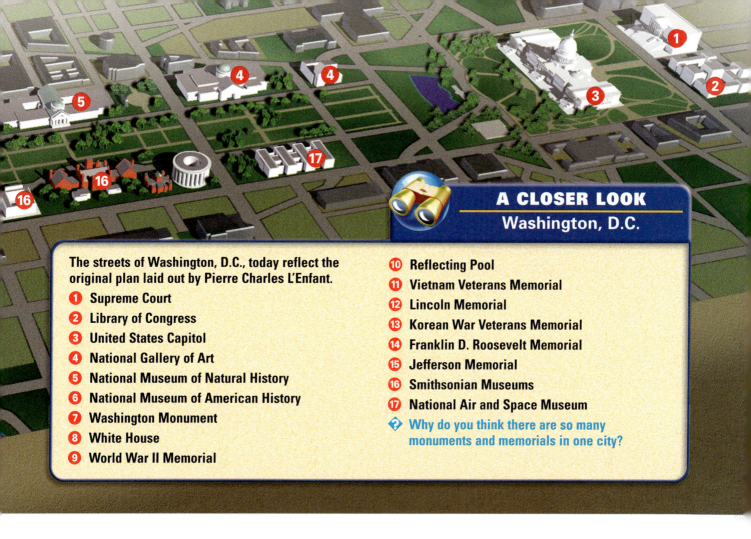

A CLOSER LOOK
Washington, D.C.

The streets of Washington, D.C., today reflect the original plan laid out by Pierre Charles L'Enfant.
1. Supreme Court
2. Library of Congress
3. United States Capitol
4. National Gallery of Art
5. National Museum of Natural History
6. National Museum of American History
7. Washington Monument
8. White House
9. World War II Memorial
10. Reflecting Pool
11. Vietnam Veterans Memorial
12. Lincoln Memorial
13. Korean War Veterans Memorial
14. Franklin D. Roosevelt Memorial
15. Jefferson Memorial
16. Smithsonian Museums
17. National Air and Space Museum

❓ Why do you think there are so many monuments and memorials in one city?

Political Parties

Before long, two of Washington's top advisers, Alexander Hamilton and Thomas Jefferson, began to argue about what was best for the United States. Hamilton wanted to have a strong national government. He favored setting up a national bank to be run by the central government. This bank would be responsible for issuing national money. Hamilton also wanted the United States to become friendly with Britain and to make use of Britain's large trading network.

Jefferson did not agree with these ideas. He thought that there should be as little central government as possible. He also believed that the United States should become friendly with France instead of with Britain. Jefferson argued that France had been an ally of the United States during the Revolutionary War.

From their disagreements, the nation's first political parties were formed. A **political party** is a group whose members try to elect government officials who share the party's point of view about many issues.

Hamilton's followers formed what became known as the Federalist party. It included people who had supported the Constitution during the state ratifying conventions. Like Hamilton, they were in favor of a strong national government. John Adams and Henry Knox became members of the Federalist party.

Chapter 10 ■ 377

Jefferson's supporters, such as James Madison and Patrick Henry formed the Democratic-Republican party. They believed that the powers of the national government should be limited to those listed in the Constitution. Members of the Democratic-Republican party were sometimes called the Jeffersonian Republicans. This political party, however, was not the same as today's Republican party.

In Congress, Jeffersonian Republicans and Federalists often had to compromise so that the laws could be passed. In one compromise, they agreed to build a national capital for the new government. George Washington chose the location for the capital city that came to carry his name. Both Maryland and Virginia agreed to give up some land to create the District of Columbia (D.C.).

REVIEW How can you summarize the disagreements between Alexander Hamilton and Thomas Jefferson? **SUMMARIZE**

A Change in Leadership

George Washington served as President for two terms, each of which was four years long. Many people wanted him to run for a third term, but Washington said that two terms were enough. His decision set an example for future presidents.

By 1796, however, the growth of political parties had changed the way the electoral college chose the President. Instead of making its own list of

George Cooke painted this picture of the nation's capital in 1833. At that time, Washington, D.C., was a much smaller city than it is today.

candidates, or people to choose from, the electoral college was given a list by each political party. In the election of 1796, the Federalist party backed John Adams. The Jeffersonian Republican party backed Thomas Jefferson instead. When the votes were counted, Adams won by three votes. Jefferson became Vice President.

On March 4, 1797, John Adams became the second President of the United States. He took the oath of office at Congress Hall, in Philadelphia. This was an important day in history. It was the first time that the nation had changed leaders by means of a peaceful election.

When John Adams started his term as President, Congress met in Philadelphia. Three years later, in November 1800, the federal government moved to the District of Columbia. When John Adams and his family moved to the new capital city, they lived in a special house built for the President. At first it had many names, including the President's House and the

John Adams was the first President to live in what is now the White House. Abigail Adams, his wife, wrote that the house was "built for ages to come."

Executive Mansion. By the early 1900s, however, this building was known as the White House—the name by which it is known today.

REVIEW Why did John Adams's taking the oath of office mark an important day?

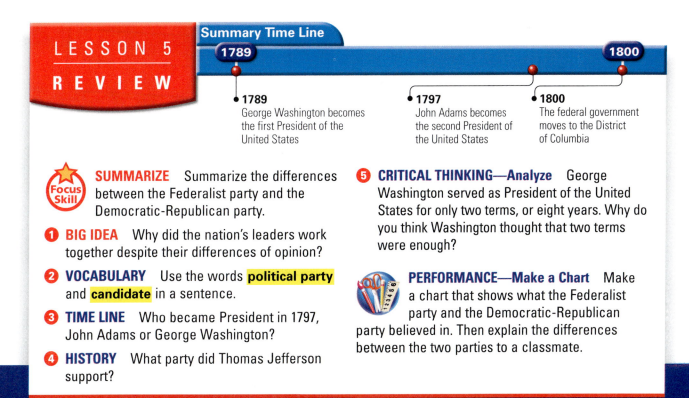

LESSON 5 REVIEW

Summary Time Line

- **1789** George Washington becomes the first President of the United States
- **1797** John Adams becomes the second President of the United States
- **1800** The federal government moves to the District of Columbia

SUMMARIZE Summarize the differences between the Federalist party and the Democratic-Republican party.

1. **BIG IDEA** Why did the nation's leaders work together despite their differences of opinion?
2. **VOCABULARY** Use the words **political party** and **candidate** in a sentence.
3. **TIME LINE** Who became President in 1797, John Adams or George Washington?
4. **HISTORY** What party did Thomas Jefferson support?
5. **CRITICAL THINKING—Analyze** George Washington served as President of the United States for only two terms, or eight years. Why do you think Washington thought that two terms were enough?

PERFORMANCE—Make a Chart Make a chart that shows what the Federalist party and the Democratic-Republican party believed in. Then explain the differences between the two parties to a classmate.

Chapter 10 ■ 379

CHAPTER 10 Review and Test Preparation

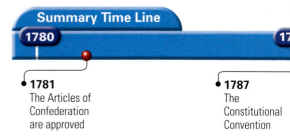

Summary Time Line

- **1781** The Articles of Confederation are approved
- **1787** The Constitutional Convention

Focus Skill: Summarize

Copy the following graphic organizer onto a separate sheet of paper. Use the information you have learned to summarize the facts about the writing and ratification of the United States Constitution.

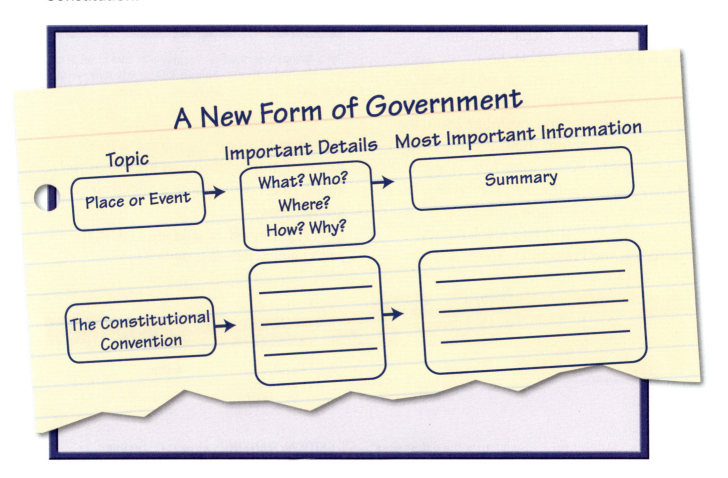

THINK & WRITE

Write a Conversation Write a conversation that could have taken place between James Madison, William Paterson, and Roger Sherman during the Constitutional Convention. The three leaders should discuss the issue of representation.

Write an Explanation The Bill of Rights protects the individual freedoms of all Americans. Many people place a special value on certain rights. Choose one right from the Bill of Rights and explain why it is important to you.

- **1788** The United States Constitution is ratified
- **1789** George Washington is elected the first President of the United States
- **1791** The Bill of Rights is added to the Constitution
- **1797** John Adams is elected the second President of the United States

USE THE TIME LINE

Use the chapter summary time line to answer these questions.

1. When did the Constitutional Convention take place?
2. Was George Washington elected President before or after the Bill of Rights was added to the Constitution?

USE VOCABULARY

For each pair of terms, write a sentence that explains how the terms are related.

3. **veto** (p. 361), **checks and balances** (p. 363)
4. **amendment** (p. 370), **reserved powers** (p. 372)
5. **political party** (p. 377), **candidate** (p. 379)

RECALL FACTS

Answer these questions.

6. How did Roger Sherman contribute to the creation of the Constitution?
7. What is the purpose of the Constitution according to its preamble?

Write the letter of the best choice.

8. The main function of the legislative branch of the federal government is—
   A to carry out laws.
   B to decide whether or not laws follow the Constitution.
   C to make laws.
   D to select members of the Cabinet.

9. George Washington set an example for future American Presidents by—
   F greatly increasing taxes.
   G taking the President's oath of office in Philadelphia.
   H serving only two terms.
   J allowing Congress to select his Cabinet.

THINK CRITICALLY

10. What do you think was James Madison's greatest contribution to the creation of the Constitution?
11. How might representation have been different if African Americans had been counted the same way white citizens were counted?

APPLY SKILLS

Read a Flow Chart
Study the flow chart on page 365. Then answer the following questions.

12. What happens after a bill is introduced?
13. What happens if the President vetoes a bill?
14. What happens if the President signs the bill?

Act as a Responsible Citizen

15. Identify a person who you think is a responsible citizen. Write a paragraph explaining why you think that person is acting responsibly.

CHIMNEY ROCK NATIONAL HISTORIC SITE

For settlers journeying on the Oregon Trail, Chimney Rock was an important landmark. It marked the place where the prairies ended and the ground became more rugged, heading west toward the Rocky Mountains. From 1812 to 1866, nearly half a million settlers passed Chimney Rock on their journey west.

LOCATE IT

NEBRASKA

Chimney Rock National Historic Site

CHAPTER 11

The Nation Grows

" Go west, young man, go west. "
—John B. L. Soule, editorial in the *Terre Haute Express*, 1851

Focus Skill: Draw Conclusions

When you **draw conclusions**, you combine new facts with facts you already know to make a general statement about an idea or event.

As you read this chapter, be sure to do the following.
- Draw conclusions about western expansion and changes in technology during the 1800s.

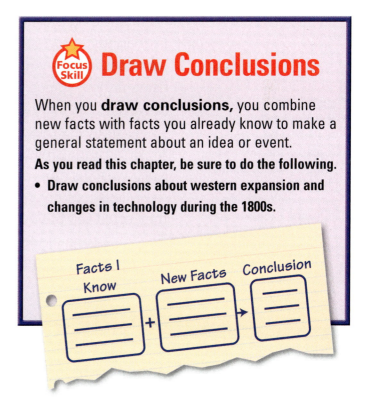

LESSON 1

The Louisiana Purchase

DRAW CONCLUSIONS

As you read, draw conclusions about why the Louisiana Purchase was important to the growth of the United States.

BIG IDEA
The United States grew west of the Mississippi River.

VOCABULARY
inauguration
pathfinder
trespass

1800–1806

By 1800 Vermont, Kentucky, and Tennessee were added to the original 13 states, and the Northwest Territory was divided into the territories of Ohio and Indiana. Americans were moving west in greater numbers. Some Americans even began to look beyond the Mississippi to the land the French had named Louisiana. France had given Spain this huge region after France lost the French and Indian War in 1763. At this time Spain also controlled all the lands along the Gulf coast.

The Louisiana Purchase

On March 4, 1801, Thomas Jefferson became the third President of the United States. At his **inauguration** (ih•naw•gyuh•RAY•shuhn), or taking office, Jefferson spoke of his hopes for the young nation. He called the United States "a rising nation, spread over a wide and fruitful land." He knew, however, that the nation faced some serious problems.

The United States had no ports of its own on the Gulf of Mexico. Farmers who lived in Kentucky, Tennessee, and the Northwest Territory had to ship their goods down the Mississippi River to New Orleans. From there they could sell the goods to ships sailing for ports in Europe or along the Atlantic coast of the United States.

After the Louisiana Purchase, soldiers at the fort at New Orleans replaced the French flag with the United States flag. The French artist, who mistakenly added hills and cactus to the area, had probably never been to New Orleans.

 Place The Louisiana Purchase doubled the size of the United States.
♦ What natural features of the territory made it easy to explore?

Spain once had allowed American farmers to load and unload their goods free of charge at New Orleans. That changed, however, and it became more costly for farmers to sell their products. Jefferson worried that people in the western United States might not stay loyal to the government if they had no way to ship their products to market.

Soon after Jefferson became President, he learned that Spain had given Louisiana back to France. The French leader, Napoleon Bonaparte (nuh•POH•lee•uhn BOH•nuh•part), hoped to once again establish French power in North America. However, Jefferson knew that having the French in control of Louisiana could prevent the United States frontier from moving farther west.

Jefferson sent representatives to France to ask Bonaparte to sell the land along the east bank of the Mississippi River, including New Orleans, to the United States. With this land, the United States would have a port on the Gulf of Mexico.

At this time France was getting ready for war with Britain. People in the French colony of St. Domingue (SAN daw•MANG) in the Caribbean had also rebelled against French rule. Bonaparte needed money to fight two wars. He offered to sell *all* of Louisiana—more than 800,000 square miles (2,071,840 sq km)— to the United States for about $15 million.

The agreement to buy Louisiana was made on April 30, 1803. The sale of this huge territory became known as the Louisiana Purchase.

REVIEW Why did Jefferson want to buy the land along the east bank of the Mississippi?
DRAW CONCLUSIONS

Chapter 11 • 385

Lewis and Clark

Few people in the United States knew much about the Louisiana Purchase. It was a huge region, reaching from the Mississippi River to the Rocky Mountains and from New Orleans north to Canada. Americans had never explored it, so President Jefferson asked Congress for money to pay for an expedition to find out more about it.

Jefferson then chose Meriwether Lewis to lead the expedition. Lewis had been an army officer and had served in the Northwest Territory. Jefferson also chose William Clark, a good friend of Lewis and brother of the Revolutionary War hero George Rogers Clark, to help lead the expedition.

Lewis and Clark put together a group of about 30 soldiers. They called their group the Corps of Discovery. One member of the Corps of Discovery was York, William Clark's African American slave who was skilled in hunting and fishing.

In May 1804 the group left its camp near present-day St. Louis and traveled up the Missouri River by boat. By October the expedition had reached present-day North Dakota. With winter coming on, they built a small camp near a Mandan Indian village. They named their camp Fort Mandan.

At Fort Mandan, Lewis and Clark hired a French fur trader to interpret some Indian languages for them. The fur trader was married to a Shoshone (shoh•SHOH•nee) Indian woman named Sacagawea (sa•kuh•juh•WEE•uh). Sacagawea agreed

William Clark used this compass in the expedition to the Louisiana Purchase.

Meriwether Lewis (far right) and William Clark (right) led the Corps of Discovery through the Louisiana Purchase. The painting shows Sacagawea using sign language to communicate with the Chinooks during the expedition.

to guide the expedition when it reached the land of the Shoshones.

In the spring of 1805, the Lewis and Clark expedition set out again. They moved farther up the Missouri River toward the Rocky Mountains. With Sacagawea's help, the expedition got horses from the Shoshones and continued their journey through the mountain passes of the Rockies. Once over the mountains, the explorers built boats and rowed down the Clearwater, Snake, and Columbia Rivers toward the Pacific coast.

In November 1805, after traveling for more than a year and covering more than 3,000 miles (about 4,800 km), the Lewis and Clark expedition reached the Pacific Ocean. Clark wrote in his journal,

66 Great joy in camp. We are in view of the . . . great Pacific Octean [Ocean], which we have been so long anxious to see, and the roreing [roaring] or noise made by the waves brakeing [breaking] on the rockey [rocky] shores (as I may suppose) may be heard distinctly. 99

In March the Corps of Discovery began the long journey back to St. Louis. They reached the settlement in September 1806. The expedition had collected many facts about the Louisiana Purchase. They brought back seeds, plants, and even living animals. They could tell what the people and the land were like, and they had drawn maps to show where mountain passes and major rivers were. In later years the work of these pathfinders helped American settlers find their way to the Pacific coast. A **pathfinder** is someone who finds a way through an unknown region.

REVIEW Who led the first expedition to the Louisiana Purchase?

The Pike Expedition

As the Lewis and Clark expedition made its way back to St. Louis in 1806, another expedition was exploring the southwestern part of the Louisiana Purchase. This small group of pathfinders was led by Captain Zebulon Pike.

By the winter of 1806, the Pike expedition had reached a huge prairie in present-day Kansas. As the expedition traveled farther west, Pike saw what he described as a "blue mountain" in the distance. Today that blue mountain is called Pikes Peak, for the explorer.

The expedition followed the Rocky Mountains south to what Pike thought was the Red River, one of the rivers that led into the Mississippi River. It was really the northern part of the Rio Grande. The expedition had wandered out of the Louisiana Purchase and into Spanish land.

Spanish soldiers soon reached the small fort that the Americans had built along the river. The soldiers took Pike and the others to Santa Fe, the capital of the Spanish colony of New Mexico. The explorers were put in jail for **trespassing**, or going onto someone else's property without asking. In Santa Fe the Spanish governor asked Zebulon Pike if the United States was getting ready to invade the Spanish lands. Pike answered no.

When the Spanish set him free several months later, Pike reported that the people of Santa Fe needed manufactured goods. Soon American traders were heading for New Mexico.

Zebulon Pike

REVIEW Why did Spanish soldiers put Captain Zebulon Pike and the rest of his explorers in jail?

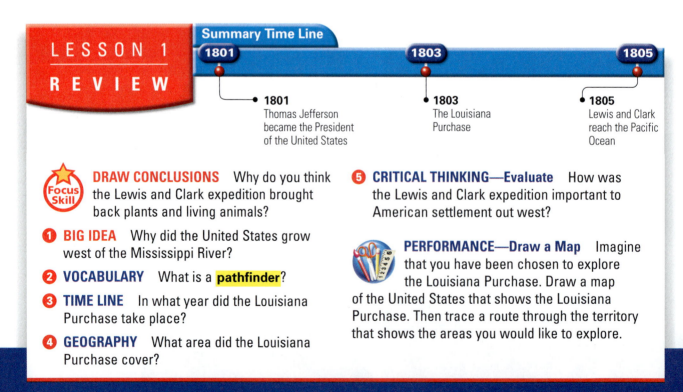

LESSON 1 REVIEW

Summary Time Line

- **1801** Thomas Jefferson became the President of the United States
- **1803** The Louisiana Purchase
- **1805** Lewis and Clark reach the Pacific Ocean

DRAW CONCLUSIONS Why do you think the Lewis and Clark expedition brought back plants and living animals?

1. **BIG IDEA** Why did the United States grow west of the Mississippi River?
2. **VOCABULARY** What is a **pathfinder**?
3. **TIME LINE** In what year did the Louisiana Purchase take place?
4. **GEOGRAPHY** What area did the Louisiana Purchase cover?
5. **CRITICAL THINKING—Evaluate** How was the Lewis and Clark expedition important to American settlement out west?

PERFORMANCE—Draw a Map Imagine that you have been chosen to explore the Louisiana Purchase. Draw a map of the United States that shows the Louisiana Purchase. Then trace a route through the territory that shows the areas you would like to explore.

The War of 1812

1805–1825

As Meriwether Lewis, William Clark, and Zebulon Pike were exploring the Louisiana Purchase, American settlers were pushing the frontier farther and farther west. As settlers moved west, however, they ran into many angry Native Americans who tried to stop them from taking their lands. The Indians were helped by the British in Canada, who sold them guns and encouraged them to fight the Americans. Before long, troubles in the western lands helped push the United States into a second war with Britain—the War of 1812.

War Fever

Americans were angry with the British for other reasons, too. To stop Americans from trading with the French and other Europeans, the British navy stopped American merchant ships at sea. They even forced sailors off American merchant ships and put them to work on British navy ships. Taking workers against their will this way is called **impressment**.

LESSON 2

 **DRAW CONCLUSIONS**
As you read, draw conclusions about events during the War of 1812.

BIG IDEA
The United States once again found itself at war with Britain.

VOCABULARY
impressment
war hawk
national anthem
siege
nationalism
annex
doctrine

This engraving shows impressment of American sailors by the British in Boston.

Members of Congress from Ohio, Kentucky, and Tennessee, as well as the southern states, wanted war with Britain. Those who wanted war became known as **war hawks**. The war hawks thought the way to deal with the British was simple—take over Canada and drive the British out of North America. Many war hawks also believed that the United States should take over Florida, which was held by Spain. Congress member Henry Clay of Kentucky, one of the best-known war hawks, said the United States should "take the whole continent."

The desire for war grew strong in much of the nation. In June 1812 President James Madison of the United States asked Congress to declare war on Britain. Congress quickly voted for war.

As the fighting began, Britain had the strongest navy in the world. Yet the small United States Navy, with only 16 ships, won two important battles early in the war. One was on the Atlantic Ocean and the other on the Great Lakes.

On August 19, 1812, the United States warship *Constitution* fought the British ship *Guerrière* (gair·YAIR) off the coast of Nova Scotia and won. After the two ships had shot cannonballs at each other, the *Guerrière* was in bad shape. Cannonballs, however, could not pierce the hard oak sides of the *Constitution*. Legend has it that a crew member said, "Her sides are made of iron." After that, the *Constitution* was nicknamed Old Ironsides.

On September 10, 1813, the Battle of Lake Erie became an early turning point in the war. Ships commanded by American Captain Oliver Hazard Perry beat the British. This allowed General William Henry Harrison to lead 4,500 soldiers across Lake Erie into Canada. At the Battle of the Thames (TEMZ) on October 5, 1813, the American forces beat the British and their Indian allies. Among the dead was Tecumseh (tuh·KUHM·suh), the Shawnee leader of an Indian group that had tried to stop Americans from taking Indian lands. From that time on, settlers in the Northwest Territory were free of conflicts with Indians.

REVIEW What victory allowed General Harrison to lead his troops into Canada?

The Battle of Lake Erie was a clash between American and British ships that lasted more than three hours.

This engraving shows the White House damaged by fire after the British attack on Washington, D.C., in August 1814.

British Raids

In August 1814 British soldiers marched toward Washington, D.C., a city of only 8,000 people at the time. Just 7 miles (about 11 km) away, American soldiers were fighting to defend the city from the British. As the noise of guns and cannons filled the air, First Lady Dolley Madison waited for news from her husband. President Madison had left the White House the day before to meet with the American soldiers.

With British soldiers quickly advancing, the First Lady gathered up important government papers. Having "pressed as many papers into trunks as to fill one carriage" she also collected valuable items from the White House. One of these items was a life-size portrait of George Washington. Because of the portrait's size, it was secured to the wall. This made it difficult to remove.

With the enemy nearly upon her, the First Lady had the portrait's frame smashed and the canvas rolled up. Only after everything was safe did Dolley Madison finally leave Washington. That evening the British burned many buildings, including the White House, the Capitol, and the Library of Congress.

With Washington in flames, the British sailed up Chesapeake Bay to Baltimore. Baltimore was protected by Fort McHenry. Although British ships bombed the fort for hours, the Americans would not give up. The sight of the huge American flag waving over the fort after the battle made Francis Scott Key very happy. He quickly wrote a poem that became the song "The Star-Spangled Banner." In 1931 it became our national

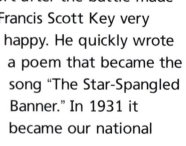

Dolley Madison rescued important items from the White House in the War of 1812.

anthem. A **national anthem** is a song of praise for a country that is recognized as the official song of that country.

When they could not beat the Americans at Baltimore, the British sailed south to New Orleans. American soldiers under the command of General Andrew Jackson were waiting for them there. Earlier that year, with the help of the Cherokees, Jackson had defeated the Creeks at the Battle of Horseshoe Bend in present-day Alabama. The Creeks were allies of the British.

When word came to General Jackson that the British might attack New Orleans, his troops hurried to defend the city. There they lived through a 10-day siege by British soldiers. A **siege** is a long-lasting attack. After fierce fighting, Jackson's soldiers finally forced the British out. Upon learning this, Jackson said, "By the Eternal, they shall not sleep on our soil!"

Americans would later learn that the Battle of New Orleans had not been necessary. On December 24, 1814—two weeks *before* the battle—the British and Americans had signed a peace treaty in Europe. Because news traveled so slowly at that time, word that the war was over had not reached New Orleans in time.

REVIEW Why was Francis Scott Key inspired to write "The Star-Spangled Banner"?
DRAW CONCLUSIONS

• HERITAGE •

"The Star-Spangled Banner"

Originally a poem titled "The Defense of Fort McHenry" the song known today as our national anthem was first performed in October of 1814. Quickly renamed, the song was issued as a handbill, or flyer, and soon became a favorite of American troops. By 1904 American military bases were required to perform the song every time the national flag was raised or lowered. In 1931 Congress voted to officially make "The Star-Spangled Banner" the national anthem of the United States.

Francis Scott Key

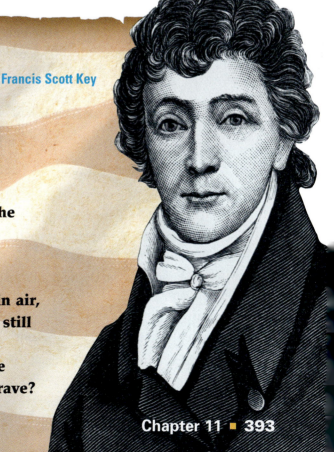

Oh, say can you see by the dawn's early light
What so proudly we hail'd at the twilight's last
 gleaming,
Whose broad stripes and bright stars through the
 perilous fight
O'er the ramparts we watch'd were so gallantly
 streaming?
And the rockets' red glare, the bombs bursting in air,
Gave proof through the night that our flag was still
 there.
Oh, say does that star-spangled banner yet wave
O'er the land of the free and the home of the brave?

The Era of Good Feelings

Neither side was clearly the winner in the War of 1812. However, Americans were proud that the United States had stood up to Britain. After the war a wave of **nationalism**, or pride in the country, swept over the land. For this reason the years from 1817 to 1825 have been called the Era of Good Feelings.

National pride could be seen in the strong way the government acted with other countries. James Monroe, the fifth President of the United States, negotiated a new boundary line between the United States and British Canada. He also got Spain to give up its claims to West Florida, which had been **annexed**, or added on, to the United States earlier. In another treaty, Spain agreed to sell East Florida to the United States, too.

President Monroe knew that if the United States wanted to keep growing, it had to stop the growth of Spanish, French, Russian, and British colonies in the Americas. So on December 2, 1823, President Monroe announced a **doctrine**, or government plan of action. It came to be called the Monroe Doctrine.

In the Monroe Doctrine, President Monroe acknowledged Europe's colonies in the Western Hemisphere. However, the doctrine closed the hemisphere to any future colonization by European countries.

REVIEW What did President Monroe do to stop the growth of European colonies in the Americas?

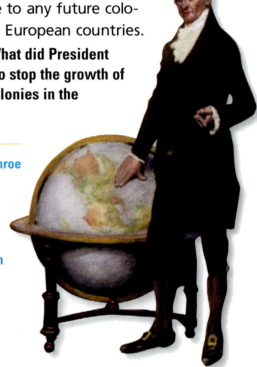

President Monroe sent a strong warning to European nations that had interests in the Western Hemisphere.

LESSON 2 REVIEW

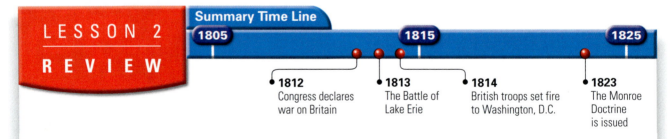

Summary Time Line
- 1812 Congress declares war on Britain
- 1813 The Battle of Lake Erie
- 1814 British troops set fire to Washington, D.C.
- 1823 The Monroe Doctrine is issued

 DRAW CONCLUSIONS Why do you think settlers in the West would support the idea of going to war with Britain?

1 BIG IDEA Why did the United States go to war with Britain?

2 VOCABULARY What clues can you use to remember the meaning of **nationalism**?

3 TIME LINE When was the Battle of Lake Erie?

4 HISTORY Why did President Monroe want to end European colonization in the Americas?

5 CRITICAL THINKING—Evaluate Why do you think that someone who was a war hawk would support the Monroe Doctrine?

 PERFORMANCE—Use the Internet Research the War of 1812 on the Internet to gain more information about it. Then share what you learned with your classmates.

The Age of Jackson

| 1780 | 1800 | 1820 | 1840 | 1860 |

1825–1840

The year 1826 marked the fiftieth anniversary of the Declaration of Independence. In that time the country had grown from the original 13 states to 24 states. Its land area had more than doubled in size. Ideas about democracy also were growing with the nation. In a **democracy** the people rule, and they are free to make choices about their lives and government.

Democracy Grows

In the early days of the country, voting was usually limited to property owners. In most of the new western states, such as Kentucky and Tennessee, this changed. Those states gave the vote to all white men, not just to those who owned property. This practice soon spread to all states. No other country in the world was so democratic, even though women and most free African Americans could not vote and Native Americans were not counted as citizens.

Once all white men could vote, there was a change in the kind of person elected. People elected as public officials were no longer always wealthy, well-educated men who owned property. Some, in fact, had little money or schooling. Davy Crockett, from Tennessee, was an example of this new kind of leader. Many people felt the frontier spirit of the United States was reflected in Davy Crockett's motto.

Davy Crockett started his political career in Lawrence County, Tennessee. The sketch shows the office he had there.

• LESSON •

3

 DRAW CONCLUSIONS
As you read, draw conclusions about how the right of people to make decisions about government changed.

BIG IDEA
Important events took place while Andrew Jackson was President.

VOCABULARY
democracy
ruling

Chapter 11 ■ 395

His motto was "Be always sure you're right—then go ahead!"

Davy Crockett held several local and state offices in Tennessee before winning a seat in the House of Representatives. When Crockett first ran for office, he had to say he knew nothing about government. "I had never read even a newspaper in my life," he said. Crockett learned about government by being part of it.

REVIEW How did government change once all white men could vote?

Andrew Jackson

The Election of Andrew Jackson

In 1828 Andrew Jackson of Tennessee was elected the seventh President of the United States. The six Presidents before him had all come from families from either Massachusetts or Virginia. Now for the first time a person from a western state had been elected. It was also the first election in which all white American men could vote. Many of the new voters liked Jackson because they felt he was a "common man," like them.

Jackson was born in the backcountry of South Carolina to a poor family living in a log cabin. Tough and stubborn, Jackson taught himself law by reading books. In time he became a successful lawyer and later a judge.

While serving in the military, Jackson got the nickname "Old Hickory"—hickory being a very hard wood. "He's tough," said his soldiers, "tough as hickory." As a general during the War of 1812, Jackson

This picture shows the excitement of the crowd outside the White House during President Jackson's inaugural celebration.

became a national hero after his troops beat the British at the Battle of New Orleans.

When Jackson became President on March 4, 1829, his followers were overjoyed. Thousands had streamed into Washington, D.C., for the inauguration. Many of them later showed up at the White House for the party that followed. Rough-and-tumble people from the frontier stood in their muddy boots on the satin-covered chairs to get a look at their hero. To keep from being crushed by the crowd, Jackson had to escape by a back door.

As President, Andrew Jackson continued to be both tough and stubborn. His view of politics soon came to be known as "Jacksonian democracy." According to Jackson, all American citizens needed to play a greater role in government. He did not believe that wealthy landowners should control the actions of the federal government. Many people living in new Western settlements agreed with Jackson's ideas. They believed that men who did not own property should be able to vote. Some wealthy people did not like Andrew Jackson because they feared he would work to end their power.

Andrew Jackson also fought to bring about an end to the Second Bank of the United States. In Jackson's eyes the bank was a "hydra of corruption." A *hydra* is a many-headed monster from Greek mythology. The troubled First Bank of the United States, created while George Washington was President, had closed after the War of 1812. The Second Bank of the United States was started in 1816.

In spite of its success, Jackson believed the bank was too powerful. It controlled one-fifth of all the bank notes in the United States and one-third of all the nation's gold. Jackson argued that the bank put too much money power in the hands of the wealthy bank owners and a few rich customers and did not care about the needs of the general public.

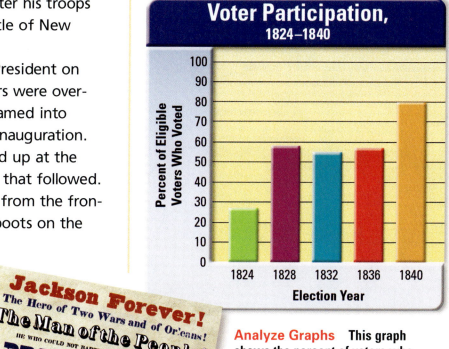

Analyze Graphs This graph shows the percent of voters who voted between 1824 and 1840. The poster (left) helped persuade people to vote for Andrew Jackson.

❖ About what percent of voters voted in the election of 1828?

REVIEW How did Andrew Jackson differ from earlier Presidents of the United States?

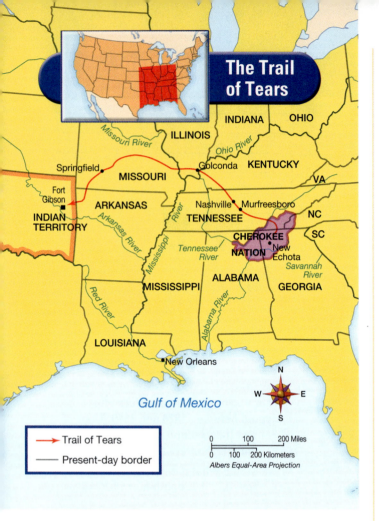

Movement This map shows the route that the Cherokees were forced to take.

To where did the Trail of Tears lead?

Indian Removal

Jackson's toughness also meant harsh and unfair treatment of the Native Americans who lived east of the Mississippi River. In 1830 Congress passed the Indian Removal Act. It had been Jackson's idea. This act said that all Indians east of the Mississippi had to leave their lands and move west to the Indian Territory. This area spread across most of what is now the state of Oklahoma.

Many tribes refused to leave their homelands. Instead, some chose to stay and fight against the soldiers sent to remove them. Led by Chief Black Hawk, the Sauk and Fox Indians in the Great Lakes region fought United States troops and Illinois militia in the Black Hawk War. In the southeastern United States, the Seminoles of Florida, led by Osceola and helped by runaway slaves, also fought United States troops. In both wars, many Native Americans were either killed or forced to leave their homeland.

Instead of fighting on the battlefield, the Cherokee nation chose to fight for its homeland in the United States courts. Led by Chief John Ross, the Cherokees were one of the richest tribes in the United States. They had many towns and villages throughout the Southeast, including New Echota (ih•KOH•tuh), Georgia, the capital of the Cherokee nation.

In a treaty signed in 1791, the United States government had recognized the Cherokee nation's independence. In 1828, however, the state of Georgia said that Cherokee laws were no longer in effect. As a result, when gold was discovered on Cherokee lands a year later, settlers were free to pour in and stake their claims.

By 1832 the Cherokees' case had gone all the way to the United States Supreme Court. There Chief Justice John Marshall gave the Court's **ruling**, or decision. He said that Georgia had no say over the Cherokee lands. The Court's ruling, however, was ignored, and federal troops were ordered to remove the Cherokees.

In late 1838 federal troops forced the last large group of Cherokees to leave their lands. They traveled from North Carolina and Georgia through Tennessee, Kentucky, Illinois, Missouri, and Arkansas—more than 800 miles (about 1,300 km)—to the Indian

This painting by Cherokee artist Troy Anderson shows a group of Cherokees on the Trail of Tears. The Cherokees were forced to walk a great distance to the Indian Territory during the cold winter months.

Territory. By the time their journey ended in March 1839, more than 4,000 Cherokees had died of cold, disease, and lack of food. The Cherokees called their long journey the "Trail Where They Cried." It later became known as the Trail of Tears.

REVIEW How was the way in which the Cherokees fought the loss of their land different from that of other Indian tribes?

LESSON 3 REVIEW

Summary Time Line

1825 — 1830 — 1835 — 1840

- 1828 Andrew Jackson is elected President of the United States
- 1830 Congress passes the Indian Removal Act

Focus Skill
DRAW CONCLUSIONS Why do you think more people in the West might run for a government office once Andrew Jackson became President?

❶ **BIG IDEA** What events took place during Andrew Jackson's presidency?

❷ **VOCABULARY** Write a description of a democracy.

❸ **TIME LINE** When was Andrew Jackson elected as the President of the United States?

❹ **HISTORY** What was the Trail of Tears?

❺ **CRITICAL THINKING—Analyze** How did democracy grow during Jackson's presidency?

PERFORMANCE—Write a Biography Use library or Internet resources to write a biography of Andrew Jackson. Share the biography with a classmate.

Chapter 11 ■ 399

EXAMINE PRIMARY SOURCES

Audubon's Paintings

John James Audubon was a gifted artist born in 1785 in what is now Haiti. During his life, Audubon observed and painted hundreds of pictures of birds and other wildlife. Some, such as those pictured on these pages, are now extinct. Audubon's attention to detail gives people today the opportunity to see animals they can no longer find in North America. Audubon's work inspired George Bird Grinnell to establish the National Audubon Society in 1886. The society works to conserve nature.

FROM THE EWELL SALE STEWART LIBRARY AND THE ACADEMY OF NATURAL SCIENCES

John James Audubon

Carolina Parrot
Because they were used as a source for feathers to decorate hats, Carolina parrots were extinct by 1920.

Pied Duck
The last recorded sighting of a pied, or labrador, duck was in 1878 in Elmira, New York.

Passenger Pigeon
Hunted for food, the last passenger pigeon died in 1914.

Analyze the Primary Source

1. What do the paintings tell you about the environment in which each bird lived? Look at the bills of each of the birds shown here. Why might different birds need bills that are suited for their different environments?

2. Why do you think people chose to use the feathers from the Carolina Parrot?

3. Why do you think people might be interested in studying Audubon's bird paintings?

Audubon kept drawings in this box.

Great Auk
The Great Auk was the last flightless seabird of the Northern Hemisphere. The last two confirmed adults were killed in 1844.

ACTIVITY

Compare and Contrast Keep a journal for one week of the kinds of birds that you notice in your yard or on the schoolgrounds. Write or draw details that are unique to each kind of bird you see. Share your observations with the class. How are your observations alike? How are they different?

RESEARCH

Visit The Learning Site at **www.harcourtschool.com** to research other primary sources.

LESSON 4

From Ocean to Ocean

1820–1850

 **DRAW CONCLUSIONS**

As you read, draw conclusions about why Americans settled new lands.

BIG IDEA
The United States expanded its borders westward in the 1800s.

VOCABULARY
manifest destiny
dictator
cession
gold rush
forty-niner

Americans in the early 1800s began to push beyond the nation's borders. They looked to the Spanish colony of Texas, to the Oregon Country in the Pacific Northwest, and to other western lands. In 1845 the words **manifest destiny** were heard for the first time. These words referred to the belief shared by many Americans that the United States should one day stretch from the Atlantic Ocean to the Pacific Ocean.

Americans in Early Texas

In 1820 a Missouri businessperson named Moses Austin asked Spanish leaders in Mexico to let him start a colony in Texas so that people from the United States could settle there. The Spanish leaders agreed to let Austin start a colony, but he died before he could carry out his plan. Stephen F. Austin, Moses Austin's son, took up his father's plan and started the colony. He chose an area between the Brazos and Colorado Rivers. Americans began to settle there in 1821.

That same year Mexico won its independence from Spain. At first the new Mexican government left the Americans alone. As more Americans arrived in Texas, however, the Mexican government became worried. In 1830 it passed a law stopping more Americans from settling in Texas. Mexican leaders also insisted that settlers already in Texas obey Mexico's laws and pay more taxes. This made the Americans angry.

In 1834 General Antonio López de Santa Anna took over the Mexican government and made himself **dictator**, a leader who has complete control of the government. Santa Anna sent troops to Texas to enforce Mexican laws. The American settlers, called Anglos, and many Tejanos (tay•HAH•nohs)—the

Stephen F. Austin started the first American colony in Texas. In the colony's early years, he served as leader, lawmaker, judge, and commander of the military. Present-day Austin, Texas, was named for him.

settlers from Mexico who lived in Texas—were angered by Santa Anna's actions. As a result, fighting broke out. Both groups living in Texas revolted against the Mexican government.

On November 3, 1835, Texas leaders met to organize a temporary government. They wanted to drive out Santa Anna's army, so they ordered Texas soldiers to attack the Mexican troops at San Antonio on December 5, 1835. After four days of fighting, the Mexican troops gave up. Santa Anna was so angry that he marched to San Antonio himself with thousands of soldiers to take back the city.

Texans in San Antonio took shelter behind the walls of a Spanish mission called the Alamo. Among them were Americans who had come to Texas to help them in their fight for freedom. They included James Bowie, Davy Crockett, and their commander, William B. Travis.

Santa Anna's forces attacked the Alamo on February 23, 1836. When it finally fell on March 6, all 189 Texans and their supporters had been killed. Only women and children survived.

On March 2, as the battle at the Alamo raged on, Texas leaders met to declare their independence and set up the Republic of Texas. They chose David G. Burnet as president of the new nation and Sam Houston as commander of the army.

On April 21, 1836, Houston's army took the Mexicans by surprise at the Battle of San Jacinto (hah•SEEN•toh). With the battle cry "Remember the Alamo!" the Texans beat the Mexican army and captured Santa Anna. In return for their sparing his life, Santa Anna agreed to grant Texas its independence. Texas remained an independent republic until it became part of the United States in 1845.

REVIEW When did Texas become a republic?

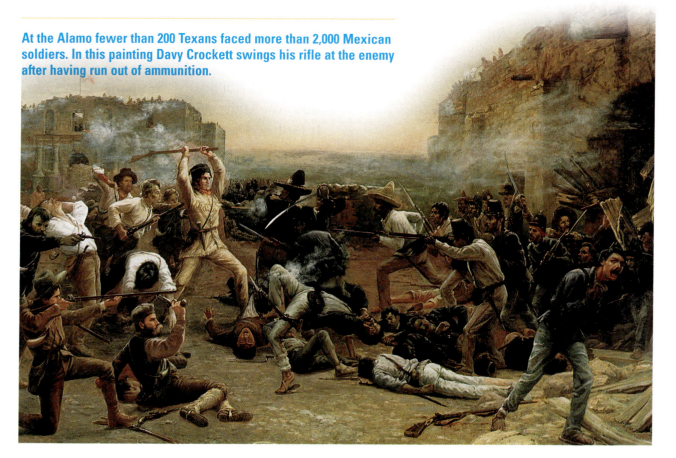

At the Alamo fewer than 200 Texans faced more than 2,000 Mexican soldiers. In this painting Davy Crockett swings his rifle at the enemy after having run out of ammunition.

Place This map shows Austin's original colony and the battles for Texas independence. The Lone Star flag (left) became the flag of the Republic of Texas.

♦ Which battles did the Texans win during their fight for independence?

Trails West

The same year that the first settlers from the United States traveled to Texas, a Missouri trader named William Becknell opened the Santa Fe Trail. This trail ran from Independence, Missouri, to the city of Santa Fe in New Mexico and covered a distance of 780 miles (1,255 km). By the 1850s, many people were using the trail to travel west. A new part of the trail, called the Old Spanish Trail, linked Santa Fe to Los Angeles in California.

In 1834 Christian missionaries pushed into the Oregon Country. This region in the Pacific Northwest was claimed by both the United States and Britain. It included what are now Oregon, Washington, Idaho, western Montana, and western Wyoming.

Travelers in the West wrote about the new lands. One settler named Narcissa Whitman wrote letters about the beautiful valleys and rich soil of the Oregon Country. Her letters were later published, and by 1842 they had attracted a large group of settlers to the region. An explorer named John C. Fremont also wrote about his travels with a guide named Kit Carson. Many people read Fremont's writings about Oregon and California.

404 ■ Unit 5

Travelers to the Oregon Country usually gathered in St. Louis, Missouri. From St. Louis they traveled up the Missouri River to Independence, Missouri. In Independence they joined wagon trains to cross the Great Plains and the Rocky Mountains.

The route they followed came to be called the Oregon Trail. It led northwest from Independence to the Platte River. From the Platte, it cut through the Rocky Mountains and crossed the Continental Divide. Then the trail followed the Snake and Columbia Rivers and ended at the Willamette (wuh•LA•muht) Valley in present-day Oregon.

The Oregon Trail was more than 2,000 miles (about 3,200 km) long. The journey could take as long as six months, and there were many hardships along the way. Yet many reached Oregon, and settlements there grew quickly.

The United States wanted to set up a clear border between itself and British Canada. For a long time, it looked as if arguments over the Oregon Country

This painting shows settlers gathered in St. Louis, Missouri, which came to be called the Gateway to the West.

might cause yet another war between the United States and Britain. Finally, in 1846, President James K. Polk agreed to divide the Oregon Country with Britain and signed a treaty fixing the 49th parallel as the dividing border.

REVIEW Why might settlers have been eager to travel along the Oregon Trail?
DRAW CONCLUSIONS

• BIOGRAPHY •

Narcissa Prentiss Whitman   1808–1847
Character Trait: Courage

Narcissa Whitman was one of the first white women to travel west along what would become the Oregon Trail. While on her travels, she began to write her family a series of letters describing her new life. The letters, covering a span of 11 years, told of Narcissa's adventures—both good and bad—living in the American West. Upon her death these letters were published, inspiring young women across America to make the journey on the Oregon Trail.

MULTIMEDIA BIOGRAPHIES
Visit The Learning Site at www.harcourtschool.com to learn about other famous people.

Chapter 11 • 405

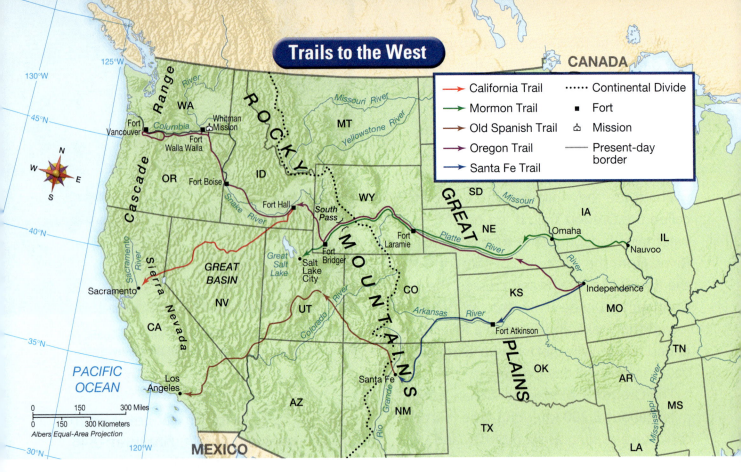

Trails to the West

- California Trail
- Mormon Trail
- Old Spanish Trail
- Oregon Trail
- Santa Fe Trail
- Continental Divide
- Fort
- Mission
- Present-day border

Movement This map shows the trails that settlers followed to the West.

◆ Which trail led to Sacramento, California?

Mormons Settle Utah

In the 1840s the Mormons, or members of the Church of Jesus Christ of Latter-day Saints, joined the many Americans traveling west. The Mormons and their leader, Joseph Smith, had settled in the town of Nauvoo (naw•VOO), Illinois. Their beliefs caused problems with other settlers, however, and in 1844 an angry crowd killed Joseph Smith.

When Brigham Young became the new leader of the Mormons, he decided that they should move to a place where no one would bother them. In 1846 Young and the first group of Mormons set out for the Rocky Mountains. In July 1847 the Mormons reached the Great Salt Lake in the Great Basin. Young said, "This is the place!"

The Great Basin was such a harsh land that Brigham Young thought no other settlers would want it. He used words from the Bible to tell his followers, "We will make this desert blossom as the rose." To do so, one of the first things the Mormons did was build irrigation canals. The canals brought water from the surrounding mountains and made the dry land suitable for farming.

Brigham Young

The Great Salt Lake region grew fast. It soon became known as the Utah Territory. Brigham Young became the territory's first governor.

REVIEW What was one of the first things the Mormons did once they settled in the Great Basin?

War with Mexico

The land the Mormons settled and the rest of the lands west of Texas belonged to Mexico. Only a few months later, most of those places would become part of the United States.

The United States and Mexico did not agree on where the border between Texas and Mexico was. The United States wanted the Rio Grande as the border, but Mexico believed its lands went farther north. When Mexican troops crossed the Rio Grande in April 1846 and fought with an American patrol, President James K. Polk asked Congress to declare war on Mexico.

The United States invaded Mexico in 1847. Federal troops led by General Winfield Scott captured Mexico City. After more than a year of fighting, the United States won the war.

In February 1848 the United States and Mexico formally ended the war by signing the Treaty of Guadalupe Hidalgo (gwah•dah•LOO•pay ee•DAHL•goh). Under the treaty's terms, Mexico had to give up all claims to southern Texas and give the United States a huge region known as the Mexican Cession. A **cession**, or concession, is something given up. The Mexican Cession included all of present-day California, Nevada, and Utah and parts of Arizona, Colorado, New Mexico, and Wyoming. In return, the United States paid Mexico $15 million.

In 1853 James Gadsden, the United States minister to Mexico, arranged to buy more of Arizona and New Mexico. This land became known as the Gadsden Purchase. The Gadsden Purchase brought the continental United States, or the part of the United States between Canada and Mexico, to its present size. It also set the current border between the United States and Mexico.

REVIEW How did the United States benefit from the Treaty of Guadalupe Hidalgo?

During the Mexican-American War, American forces captured the Spanish town of Monterey, California.

GEOGRAPHY

Marshall Gold Discovery State Historic Park

Understanding Places and Regions

While building a sawmill in the winter of 1848, James Marshall discovered gold in a nearby riverbed. By 1849, Marshall's find set off one of the largest migrations in history—the California gold rush of 1849. People came from all over the United States in wagons. Some even sailed around the southern tip of South America to reach California.

In time, people from all over the world knew of Marshall's discovery, moving to California with the hope of striking it rich. Today, the site of Marshall's discovery is located inside the Marshall Gold Discovery State Historic Park in Coloma, California.

The California Gold Rush

In the 1840s California was a land of large ranches and a few small towns, such as Monterey and Los Angeles. By 1847 San Francisco had only 800 people. However, that quickly changed when gold was found.

Gold was found in California not long before the treaty with Mexico was signed. In January 1848 James Marshall and several other workers were building a waterwheel for John Sutter's new sawmill along the American River near present-day Sacramento. Suddenly, something was seen glittering in the water. No one is sure who first laid eyes on or picked up the stone that was half the size of a pea, but James Marshall said that he was the one.

This painting shows people digging for gold during the California gold rush. Looking for gold was hard work.

"It made my heart thump, for I was certain it was gold," he remembered.

The finding of gold in California set off a **gold rush**, a sudden rush of new people to an area where gold has been found. Within a year, more than 80,000 gold seekers arrived in California. They came from Europe and Asia as well as from other parts of the United States.

The gold seekers began calling themselves **forty-niners** because they had arrived in the year 1849. Many forty-niners made their way west on the Oregon Trail, cutting south on the Old Spanish Trail across the Nevada desert and through the passes of the Sierra Nevada. This trip often took three months or longer. Others traveled to California by sailing around Cape Horn at the southern tip of South America and then north along the Pacific coast. That journey often took six to eight months. Clipper ships, the fastest ships of the time, could make the same trip in just three to four months. However, travel by clipper ship cost too much for most forty-niners.

A few lucky forty-niners struck it rich, but most did not. While some returned home empty-handed, many stayed and settled in California. It is estimated that California's population grew by 100,000 people by the end of 1849. In 1850, only two years after Marshall's discovery of gold at Sutter's Mill, California became a state.

The discovery of gold brought many people to California.

REVIEW Why did gold seekers in California call themselves forty-niners?

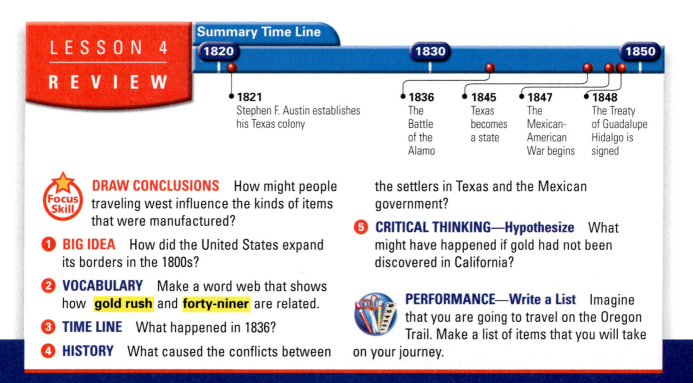

LESSON 4 REVIEW

Summary Time Line

- **1821** Stephen F. Austin establishes his Texas colony
- **1836** The Battle of the Alamo
- **1845** Texas becomes a state
- **1847** The Mexican-American War begins
- **1848** The Treaty of Guadalupe Hidalgo is signed

DRAW CONCLUSIONS How might people traveling west influence the kinds of items that were manufactured?

1. **BIG IDEA** How did the United States expand its borders in the 1800s?
2. **VOCABULARY** Make a word web that shows how **gold rush** and **forty-niner** are related.
3. **TIME LINE** What happened in 1836?
4. **HISTORY** What caused the conflicts between the settlers in Texas and the Mexican government?
5. **CRITICAL THINKING—Hypothesize** What might have happened if gold had not been discovered in California?

PERFORMANCE—Write a List Imagine that you are going to travel on the Oregon Trail. Make a list of items that you will take on your journey.

SKILLS · Identify Changing Borders

▶ WHY IT MATTERS

Historical maps give important information about places as they were in the past. By studying a historical map, you can see how a place and its borders have changed over time. Seeing those changes on a historical map can help you better understand the changes and how they came about.

▶ WHAT YOU NEED TO KNOW

In this chapter you read about the United States and the different countries that have controlled lands west of the Mississippi River. You also read about events that changed borders in the continental United States over time. The map on page 411 uses different colors to show how those borders changed over nearly 70 years. It uses labels to identify the different regions and to give the year in which each one became a part of the United States.

▶ PRACTICE THE SKILL

Use the historical map on page 411 to answer the following questions.

1. What color shows land that was acquired by the United States in 1803?
2. In what year did the United States win control of the Oregon Territory?
3. When did the United States get the land where the states of California and Nevada are now?

The Treaty of Guadalupe Hidalgo ended the Mexican-American War. Mexico agreed to give up the lands that came to be called the Mexican Cession, and, in return, the United States agreed to pay Mexico $15 million.

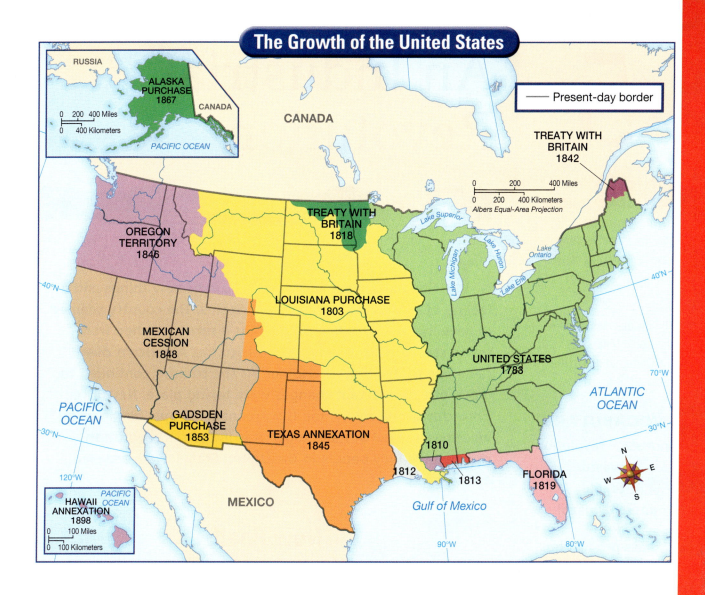

4. What area did the United States get in 1842 as the result of a treaty with Britain?

5. In what year did the Gadsden Purchase become part of the United States?

6. In what year did the Texas Annexation take place?

7. When did Alaska become part of the United States?

APPLY WHAT YOU LEARNED

The map on this page lets you identify the changing borders of the United States. You can also see changes by comparing two maps. On a sheet of paper, draw a map showing the borders of the United States in 1803. Then draw another map showing the borders of the United States in 1848. Find the information in this chapter that explains the difference between the two maps.

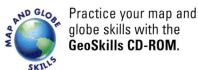

Practice your map and globe skills with the **GeoSkills CD-ROM**.

LESSON 5
An Industrial Revolution

 DRAW CONCLUSIONS

As you read, draw conclusions about how new technologies caused changes.

BIG IDEA
The development of new technology changed life in the United States in the first half of the 1800s.

VOCABULARY
industrial revolution
investor
textile
interchangeable parts
mass production
supply
cotton gin
demand
patent

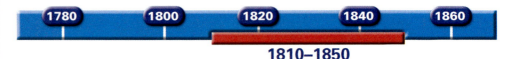

1810–1850

The first half of the 1800s saw a rush of new things and a feeling of confidence in the United States. The country seemed to have met its "manifest destiny," as it now stretched from sea to sea. Nothing seemed too difficult as Americans overcame one problem after another. As the country continued to grow, other important changes were taking place. New inventions changed the way goods were made. People began using machines instead of hand tools. This **industrial revolution** changed the way people in the United States lived, traveled, and worked.

New Roads

Americans badly needed good roads in the early 1800s. Most roads were dirt paths full of tree stumps and holes. When it rained, these roads sometimes turned into "rivers."

Just before Ohio became a state in 1803, Congress voted to build a road to Ohio. The road would be used to transport goods and help settlers reach the new state. This route became known as the National Road. It was the nation's first important highway joining the eastern United States and places west of the Appalachian Mountains.

The National Road was built using the best technology of the day. It was level, and it was paved with stones and tar. The first part of the National Road opened in 1818. It ran from

This mile marker once guided people on the National Road in Maryland.

Maryland to present-day West Virginia. By 1841 the National Road was open through Ohio. It ended in Vandalia, Illinois.

By 1860 there were more than 88,000 miles (about 142,000 km) of roads in the United States. Traveling by road, however, still cost a lot and took a long time. Most wagons could carry only small amounts of goods and travelers often had to make several trips to carry their loads.

REVIEW Why was the National Road important?

Canal Building

Because road travel cost so much and took so much time, people turned to canals. Traveling on canals, boats or barges could carry larger loads at less cost than wagons could on land. One of the most important canals built during these years was the Erie Canal in New York.

People living near the Great Lakes, however, still had to transport products to and from cities in the eastern United States by wagon. Goods could not be moved on boats because the Appalachian Mountains separated rivers flowing into the Great Lakes from rivers flowing into the Atlantic Ocean. Only one river, the St. Lawrence, flowed from the Great Lakes into the Atlantic Ocean. However, rapids and shallows kept boats from sailing its whole length.

In 1817 the state of New York voted to build a "Grand Canal" to Lake Erie.

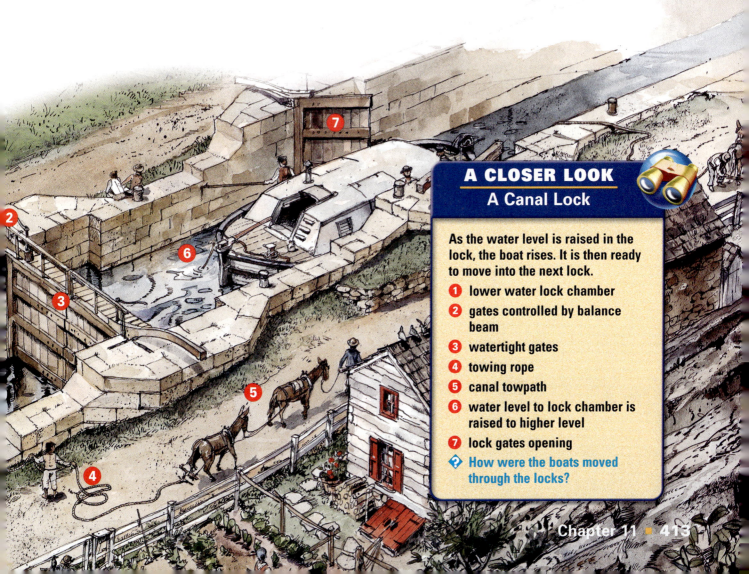

A CLOSER LOOK
A Canal Lock

As the water level is raised in the lock, the boat rises. It is then ready to move into the next lock.

1. lower water lock chamber
2. gates controlled by balance beam
3. watertight gates
4. towing rope
5. canal towpath
6. water level to lock chamber is raised to higher level
7. lock gates opening

◆ How were the boats moved through the locks?

Chapter 11 • 413

It would start at the Hudson River and be 363 miles (584 km) long. To pay for building it, the governor of New York, DeWitt Clinton, asked investors to buy stock in the canal. An **investor** is a person who uses money to buy or make something that will yield a profit. By the summer of 1817, Clinton had enough investors to pay for the digging of the canal.

Most of the Erie Canal was dug by about 3,000 Irish immigrants who used only hand tools. The Irish came to the United States to get jobs working on the canal. Workers were paid 80 cents a day and were given meals and housing. These wages were three times what the immigrants could earn in Ireland.

After eight years of hard work, the Erie Canal opened in 1825. It cut the price of shipping goods between New York City and Buffalo on Lake Erie from $100 a ton to less than $10 a ton. It also helped make New York City the leading center of trade in the United States at the time. The success of the Erie Canal set off a canal-building boom. By the 1830s, canals were being dug all over the country. Pennsylvania developed a system of canals connecting Philadelphia to other parts of the state. Ohio and Indiana built canals joining the Great Lakes and the Ohio River.

This decorative hat box shows a scene on the Erie Canal.

REVIEW Why was the Erie Canal built?

Steamboats and Railroads

Canal building lasted only a short time in the United States. New and faster methods of carrying goods and people soon took over. Steamboats quickly became the main form of river travel, and railroads changed the way people and goods moved on land.

The steam engine was invented in Britain by Thomas Newcomen in the

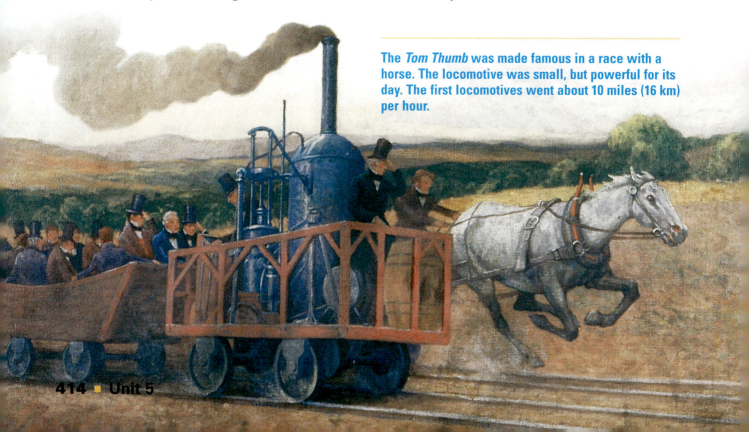

The *Tom Thumb* was made famous in a race with a horse. The locomotive was small, but powerful for its day. The first locomotives went about 10 miles (16 km) per hour.

early 1700s. It used the steam produced by boiling water to power its moving parts. Over the years the steam engine was improved and applied to various uses. Robert Fulton of New York used the steam engine to power a boat. In 1807 Fulton amazed people when his steamboat, the *Clermont*, chugged up the Hudson River from New York City to Albany. It was a 150-mile (241-km) trip, and it took 32 hours. Until this time, boats had not been able to travel easily upstream, or against the flow of the river.

Steamboat builders soon wanted to outdo each other as the new boats grew in popularity. Builders began to build bigger and faster boats. Greater speed meant that more cargo and passengers could be delivered in a shorter amount of time. This meant a bigger profit for cargo companies and their customers.

Soon steamboats were being used in other parts of the country, especially on the Ohio and Mississippi Rivers. By 1860 there were more than 1,000 great paddle-wheel steamboats in the United States. They traveled on most of the country's large rivers and lakes.

About the same time that steam engines were being used to power steamboats, they were also being used to power locomotives, or railroad engines. The first locomotive made in the United States was the *Tom Thumb*. A manufacturer named Peter Cooper built it in 1830 for the Baltimore and Ohio Railroad.

The company had been using railroad cars pulled by horses for its route.

Transportation in the East, 1850

Movement These maps show major transportation links that had been built by 1850.

❖ Why do you think few links had been built west of the Mississippi River?

Chapter 11 • **415**

To prove that a locomotive could pull a heavy load faster than a horse, Cooper raced his *Tom Thumb* against a railroad car pulled by a horse. The locomotive broke down before the finish line and lost the race. Even so, it was clear that the steam-powered locomotive had better pulling power than a horse.

The number of railroads grew quickly after 1830. By 1850 about 9,000 miles (about 14,500 km) of track crossed the nation, mostly joining cities in the East. Railroads made it easier and cheaper to move heavy loads of raw materials and manufactured goods to all regions of the country. As the railroads grew, so did manufacturing in the United States.

REVIEW How did steam engines affect transportation methods in the United States?
DRAW CONCLUSIONS

Growth in Manufacturing

In the late 1700s Britain was the only country in the world that had machines that spun thread and wove textiles, or cloth. People in Britain did not want the rest of the world to find out about these machines. Neither the machines nor the plans for building them were allowed out of the country. Even the textile workers were not allowed to leave. Samuel Slater, however, carefully studied the machines in the British cotton mill where he worked. He memorized how each iron gear and wooden spool worked.

Wearing a disguise and using a different name, Slater left Britain and took what he knew to the United States. With money from an investor named Moses Brown, Slater built from memory machines like the ones he had used in Britain.

In 1790 Slater and Brown started the first American spinning mill in Pawtucket, Rhode Island. This mill marked the beginning of large-scale manufacturing in the United States.

Early mills, like Slater's, were all built next to rushing rivers. These mills used the water to turn waterwheels, which in turn powered the machines connected to them. Later, steam engines were used to power machines. Steam engines were more reliable than water power, so they allowed production to expand. A steam-powered machine called a spinning jenny wove thread into fabric. At textile mills these machines spun up to 120 threads at a time from wool or cotton.

Instead of working at home, as most people had done in the past, more people began to go to work in factories. These workers did not need the same skills as workers who made goods by hand. Factories needed workers who could be trained to run the machines. Many of these workers were women, children, and immigrants. They worked first in the mills and then later in other industries.

Francis Cabot Lowell of Massachusetts developed a new system of organizing factories. Lowell put the entire process of turning cotton into cloth under one roof at his factory in Waltham, Massachusetts. Before that time, factory workers made the thread, but other workers used hand looms in their homes to weave the thread into cloth. Lowell's system, known as the Waltham system, was also different because it provided boardinghouses for its workers. Lowell provided good living conditions for his workers. However, not all factory owners followed his lead.

A CLOSER LOOK
A Textile Mill

Early textile mills used water power to run their machines. The water of a rushing river or waterfall turned the waterwheel. The waterwheel turned gears connected to belts that made the machines run.

① river turns water wheel and gears
② spinning cotton fibers into yarn
③ warping, or lining up side by side, the strands of yarn to prepare them for weaving
④ weaving the yarn into cloth

❓ How does the waterwheel make the machines in the mill run?

Chapter 11 ■ 417

Another idea also had changed American manufacturing. In 1800 Eli Whitney developed a new system of interchangeable parts to make guns. **Interchangeable parts** were parts that were exactly alike. If one part of a gun was damaged, another part of the same kind could be put in its place. In the past, skilled workers were needed to make most products. Now anyone could put together machine-made parts and do it faster than a craftworker.

This idea made **mass production** possible. This is a system of producing large amounts of goods at one time. Over time many goods were made this way.

Because of mass production, the supply of manufactured goods rose sharply. In business, the **supply** is the amount of a good or service available for sale. When the supply of a product is high, prices generally fall. As a result, more expensive handmade goods were quickly replaced by cheaper ones made by machine.

REVIEW How was Lowell's system of organizing factories different from other systems?

Inventions Bring Change

In 1793 Eli Whitney developed a machine called the cotton gin, or engine. The **cotton gin** removed the seeds from cotton fibers much faster than workers could by hand. With the cotton gin, cotton could be prepared for market in less time. This made it possible for plantations to grow more cotton. Because of the cotton gin, more slaves were needed to work in the fields and harvest the cotton. In turn, planters in the southern states could supply more cotton to textile mills in the northern states and in Europe. Worldwide demand for cotton increased.

In business, a **demand** is the need or the want for a good or service by people who are willing to pay for it. When the demand for a product is high, its price usually goes up. When the price of a product goes up, people usually want to use their resources to make more of it. That means the supply of a good usually rises or falls to meet the demand.

Eli Whitney invented the cotton gin (bottom), a machine that removed seeds from cotton fibers.

• SCIENCE AND TECHNOLOGY •

Cast-Steel Plow

As a blacksmith in Grand Detour, Illinois, John Deere was always repairing the wooden and cast-iron plows of farmers. The heavy, damp prairie soil stuck to these plows, and farmers had to stop and clean them every few minutes. Deere and his partner, Major Leonard Andrus, designed a plow that could easily cut through the soil. The blade of the new plow was made of cast steel. The moldboard, or the part of the plow used for lifting and turning the soil, was made of wrought iron. Both parts were then polished so smooth that the damp prairie soil could not stick to them.

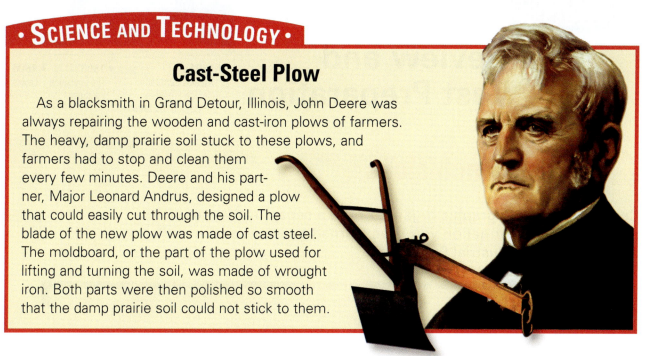

Other useful inventions also made farming on a large scale possible in the United States. In 1831 Cyrus McCormick invented a mechanical reaper for harvesting grain. With this invention farmers could cut as much wheat in one day as they had been able to cut in two weeks using hand tools. In 1837 John Deere developed the first cast-steel plow in the United States. This plow made tilling the soil easier.

As the need for finding new ways of solving problems arose, the number of inventions increased. In 1800 there were 309 **patents**, or licenses to make, use, or sell new inventions, registered with the United States Patent Office. By 1860 there were more than 40,000 patents.

REVIEW How did Cyrus McCormick's mechanical reaper help farmers?

LESSON 5 REVIEW

Summary Time Line

- 1818 The National Road opens
- 1825 The Erie Canal opens
- 1830 The *Tom Thumb* is built
- 1850 Many eastern cities now linked by railroads

Focus Skill — DRAW CONCLUSIONS Do you think the number of inventions has grown or decreased since 1860? Explain.

1. **BIG IDEA** How did new technologies change life in the United States?
2. **VOCABULARY** How are **supply** and **demand** related?
3. **TIME LINE** When did the Erie Canal open?
4. **ECONOMICS** How did the mass production of goods affect the price of many goods?
5. **CRITICAL THINKING—Evaluate** Evaluate the effects of supply and demand on plantations.

PERFORMANCE—Make an Invention Booklet Use information from the lesson and from library sources to make a booklet about the items that were invented in the 1800s. Share your booklet with the class.

Chapter 11 ■ 419

CHAPTER 11
Review and Test Preparation

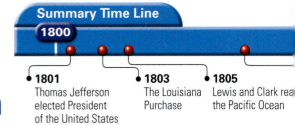

Summary Time Line

- 1800
- 1801 Thomas Jefferson elected President of the United States
- 1803 The Louisiana Purchase
- 1805 Lewis and Clark reach the Pacific Ocean

Focus Skill: Draw Conclusions

Copy the following graphic organizer onto a separate sheet of paper. Use the information you have learned to draw conclusions about the Industrial Revolution.

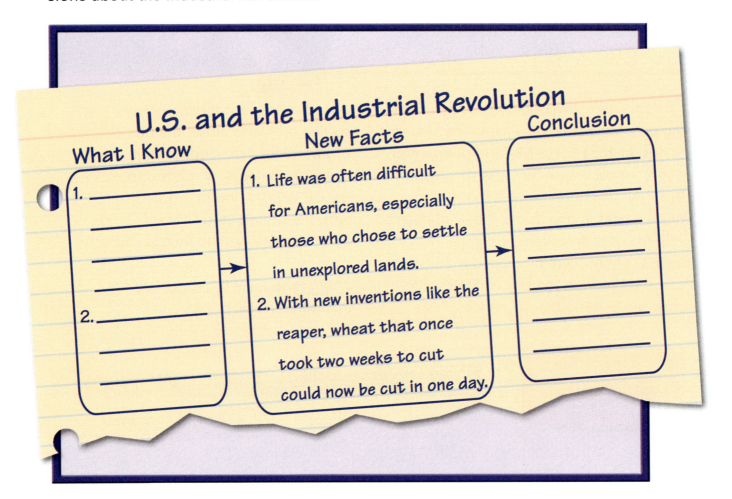

U.S. and the Industrial Revolution

What I Know
1. _____
2. _____

New Facts
1. Life was often difficult for Americans, especially those who chose to settle in unexplored lands.
2. With new inventions like the reaper, wheat that once took two weeks to cut could now be cut in one day.

Conclusion
_____

Think & Write

Write a Journal Entry During the Lewis and Clark expedition, many members of the expedition kept journals. Imagine you are a member of the expedition and are journeying through the Rocky Mountains. Write a journal entry describing your environment.

Write a Persuasive Letter Imagine the year is 1820 and you are trying to raise money to open a textile factory. Write a persuasive letter to a potential investor, explaining why that person should consider investing in your factory.

1812 The War of 1812 begins
1828 Andrew Jackson is elected President of the United States
1830 Congress passes the Indian Removal Act
1836 The Battle of the Alamo
1845 Texas becomes a state
1847 The Mexican-American War

USE THE TIME LINE

Use the chapter summary time line to answer these questions.

1. How many years after the Louisiana Purchase did Lewis and Clark reach the Pacific Ocean?
2. Was Andrew Jackson elected President before or after Texas became a state?

USE VOCABULARY

Use a term from this list to complete each of the sentences that follow.

inaugurated (p. 384)
siege (p. 393)
annexed (p. 394)
dictator (p. 402)
investors (p. 414)

3. After the War of 1812 the United States ____ West Florida.
4. Andrew Jackson's soldiers survived a ten-day ____ during the Battle of New Orleans.
5. To pay for the Erie Canal, DeWitt Clinton brought in ____ from Europe.
6. In 1801 Thomas Jefferson was ____ as President.
7. Antonio López de Santa Anna made himself ____ of Mexico in 1834.

RECALL FACTS

Answer these questions.

8. What event caused the United States to double in size in 1803?
9. Why did many Americans want to go to war with the British in 1812?
10. How did John Deere's cast-steel plow help prairie farmers?

Write the letter of the best choice.

11. The Lewis and Clark expedition was helped by a Shoshone Indian guide named —
    A Dakota.
    B Mandan.
    C Metacomet.
    D Sacagawea.

12. Samuel Slater and Moses Brown helped begin the American—
    F steel industry.
    G railroad industry.
    H textile industry.
    J banking industry.

THINK CRITICALLY

13. Why do you think the United States did not surrender to the British after they invaded Washington, D.C., during the War of 1812?
14. What kind of compromise could Andrew Jackson have negotiated with Native American tribes instead of forcing them to leave their homelands?
15. Do you think many Americans welcomed the changes brought about by the Industrial Revolution? Why or why not?

APPLY SKILLS

Identify Changing Borders
Study the map on page 411. Then answer the following questions.

16. What color shows land that was acquired by the United States in 1846?
17. What present-day states would form the western border of the United States if the nation had not expanded after 1788?

Chapter 11 ■ 421

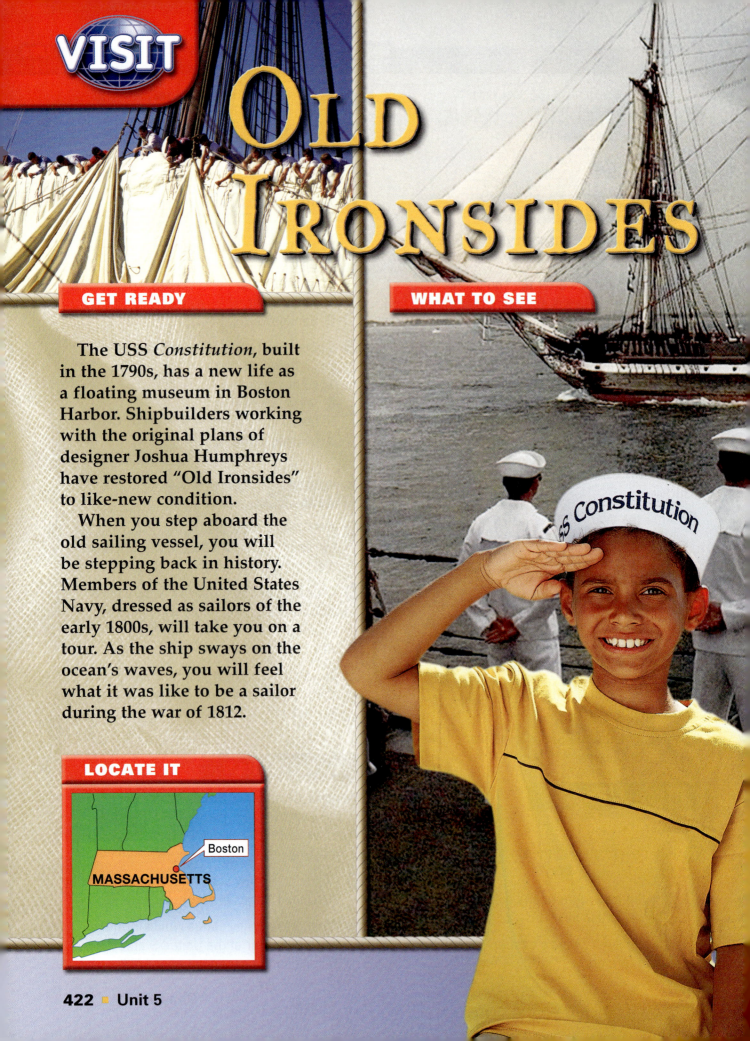

VISIT
OLD IRONSIDES

GET READY

The USS *Constitution*, built in the 1790s, has a new life as a floating museum in Boston Harbor. Shipbuilders working with the original plans of designer Joshua Humphreys have restored "Old Ironsides" to like-new condition.

When you step aboard the old sailing vessel, you will be stepping back in history. Members of the United States Navy, dressed as sailors of the early 1800s, will take you on a tour. As the ship sways on the ocean's waves, you will feel what it was like to be a sailor during the war of 1812.

WHAT TO SEE

LOCATE IT

The USS *Constitution* earned the nickname Old Ironsides during battle. Astonished sailors noticed that cannon balls could not break through the ship's sturdy sides.

Dressed in a historic uniform, the captain of the USS *Constitution* welcomes visitors aboard.

Navy officers aboard the ship slept in beds like these. The beds are attached to the ceiling by ropes so that they move with the swaying of the ship.

TAKE A FIELD TRIP

A VIRTUAL TOUR
Visit The Learning Site at www.harcourtschool.com to take virtual tours of other historical museums.

A VIDEO TOUR
Check your media center or classroom library for a videotape tour of the USS *Constitution*.

UNIT 5 Review and Test Preparation

VISUAL SUMMARY

Write a Paragraph Study the pictures and captions below to help you review Unit 5. Then choose one of the events shown. Write a news story about that event and how it affected the country.

USE VOCABULARY

Identify the term that correctly matches each definition.

arsenal (p. 348)
census (p. 359)
due process of law (p. 372)
doctrine (p. 394)
patent (p. 419)

1. a population count
2. a government plan of action
3. a building used for storing weapons
4. a person's right to a fair public trial
5. a license to make, use, or sell new inventions

RECALL FACTS

Answer these questions.

6. What was Shays's Rebellion?
7. Who was Benjamin Banneker?
8. How did Dolley Madison assist her country during the War of 1812?

Write the letter of the best choice.

9. The Constitutional Convention delegate who actually wrote the Constitution was—
   A Roger Sherman.
   B Benjamin Franklin.
   C Elbridge Gerry.
   D Gouverneur Morris.

10. The term *manifest destiny* referred to a belief that the United States should—
    F stretch from the Atlantic Ocean to the Pacific Ocean.
    G avoid involvement in all foreign conflicts.
    H close the Western Hemisphere.
    J ratify the Constitution.

Visual Summary

1780 — 1800 — 1820

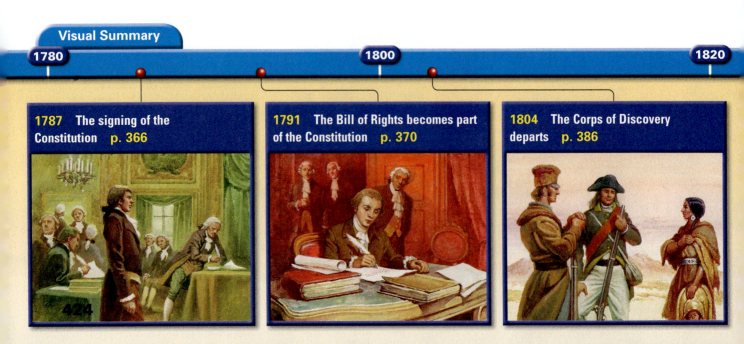

1787 The signing of the Constitution p. 366

1791 The Bill of Rights becomes part of the Constitution p. 370

1804 The Corps of Discovery departs p. 386

424

THINK CRITICALLY

11. What do you think might have happened if the United States had decided to keep the Articles of Confederation?

12. Do you think the United States could have avoided war with Britain in 1812? Explain your answer.

13. How do you think Americans viewed the Monroe Doctrine? How do you think Europeans viewed the Monroe Doctrine?

14. Why do you think the Cherokee nation chose to fight for its homeland in the courts instead of on a battlefield?

15. How do you think the introduction of factory work changed family life in the United States?

APPLY SKILLS

Identify Changing Borders
Use the historical map on this page to answer the following questions.

16. Was Austin's original colony in eastern or western Texas?

17. Was Austin's colony larger or smaller than the Republic of Texas?

18. What river forms part of the western border of the state of Texas?

19. Was the Republic of Texas larger or smaller than the state of Texas today?

20. How did the state border of Texas change from 1845 to the present day?

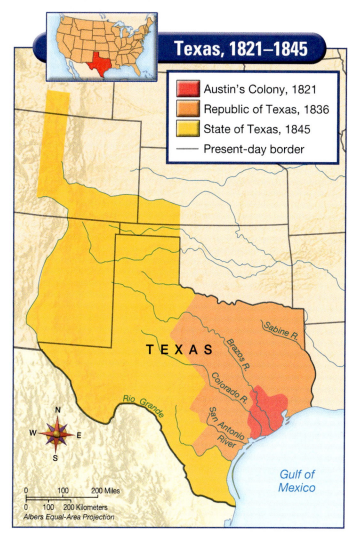

Texas, 1821–1845

- Austin's Colony, 1821
- Republic of Texas, 1836
- State of Texas, 1845
- Present-day border

1836 The Battle of the Alamo p. 403

1847 The Mexican-American War begins p. 407

1849 The California Gold Rush begins p. 409

Unit Activities

Visit The Learning Site at www.harcourtschool.com for additional activities.

Produce a Speech

Work in a group to produce a speech that might have been given by one of these people: James Madison, Benjamin Banneker, Sacagawea, or Davy Crockett. Divide the work of researching, writing, and editing the speech. Then select a member of your group to deliver the completed speech before the class.

Create a Newspaper Front Page

Work in a group to create the front page of a newspaper that will cover one of the following events: the opening of the Erie Canal, the completion of the National Road, Robert Fulton's voyage on the *Clermont*, or the race between the *Tom Thumb* and a horse. First, research and write your story. Then, add pictures. Next, arrange your front page on a posterboard. Finally, present your completed front page to the class.

VISIT YOUR LIBRARY

- **The Santa Fe Trail** by David Lavender. Holiday House.

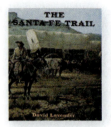

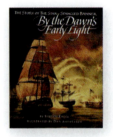

- **By the Dawn's Early Light: The Story of the Star-Spangled Banner** by Steven Kroll. Scholastic.

- **Woman of Independence: The Life of Abigail Adams** by Susan Provost Beller. Shoe Tree Press.

COMPLETE THE UNIT PROJECT

A Growing Nation Time Line Work with a group of classmates to finish the unit project—a time line that shows the economic and territorial growth of the United States through the 1800s. Illustrate the events that appear on your time line by using drawings or pictures printed from the Internet. Present your completed time line to the class. Then explain why your group selected the events that it did.

426 • Unit 5

Civil War Times

GEORGIA CONNECTION

President Abraham Lincoln's Hat

GEORGIA CONNECTION

Georgia in the Civil War

The Union army destroyed the railroad depot (below right) in Atlanta, Georgia. Many Confederate soldiers had to provide their own uniforms.

Along with other Southern states, Georgia fought the states north of Kentucky and West Virginia during the Civil War. The North's plan to defeat the South was to blockade all the South's ports. Georgia's most important port was in Savannah. In 1862, Northern soldiers captured Fort Pulaski, which defended Savannah. The South could no longer ship or receive supplies through Savannah.

The Northern troops then worked to capture Georgia's railroads. Without railroads, the South would not be able to get supplies or move troops. Many of Georgia's important railroads met in Atlanta, so Northern general William T. Sherman wanted to capture the city.

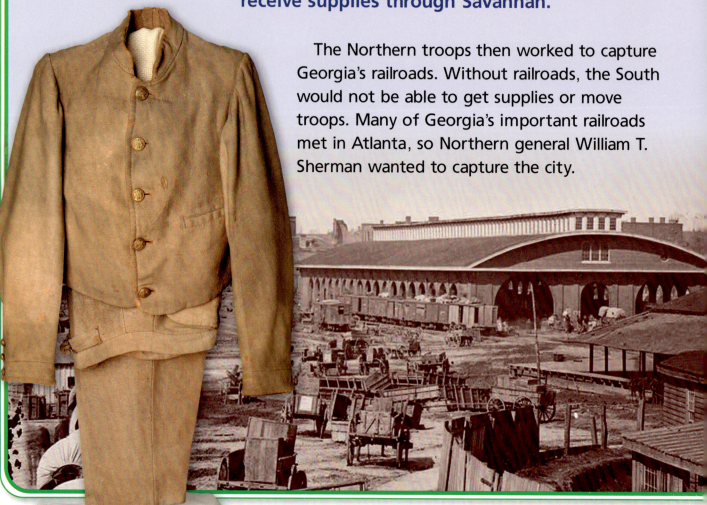

In May 1864, Sherman's troops began marching to Atlanta from Chattanooga, Tennessee. Southern general Joseph Johnston was in charge of the troops protecting Atlanta. Johnston and his troops fought hard to keep Sherman out of the city, but Sherman's army had more soldiers and more supplies. Johnston's army could not hold off Sherman for long.

Sherman captured Atlanta in September 1864. In November, he set fire to the city and began his March to the Sea. As Sherman's troops marched across Georgia from Atlanta to Savannah, they destroyed all factories, mills, public buildings, and railroads. Sherman captured Savannah in December 1864.

The Northern troops now controlled Georgia's railroads, and the Southern army could not get supplies to its troops. Without supplies, the South could not continue fighting. In April 1865, the Southern army surrendered at Appomattox Court House, Virginia.

Confederate General Joseph Johnston graduated from West Point Military Academy.

★ CRCT ★ TEST PREP

❶ During the Civil War, Savannah's port
  A brought in many goods from England.
  B could not ship or receive supplies.
  C had all its ships destroyed.
  D was the only Southern port not under the blockade.

❷ After Sherman captured Atlanta,
  A he set fire to the city.
  B the Civil War ended the next day.
  C Georgia still controlled the railroads.
  D troops from Savannah tried to recapture the city.

❸ The Union wanted to capture Georgia's railroads
  A to use them to take supplies to Union troops.
  B to move building materials into the South.
  C to keep the South from getting supplies or moving troops.
  D because the Union did not have any railroads.

The Lincoln Memorial, Washington, D.C.

Civil War Times

" A house divided against itself cannot stand. "

—Abraham Lincoln, Republican State Convention, Springfield, Illinois, June 16, 1858

Preview the Content

Scan the unit and read the chapter and lesson titles. Use what you have read to make a unit outline. Once you have finished, write down any questions you may have about the Civil War.

Preview the Vocabulary

Compound Words A compound word is a combination of two or more words that form a new word when put together. For each term listed below, use the meanings of the smaller words to figure out the meaning of the compound word. Then look up each word in the Glossary to check its meaning.

SMALLER WORD	SMALLER WORD	COMPOUND WORD	POSSIBLE MEANING
under +	ground =	underground	
rail +	road =	railroad	
share +	cropping =	sharecropping	
carpet +	bagger =	carpetbagger	

Unit 6 ■ 427

UNIT 6 PREVIEW

The Nation Divided, 1861

Legend:
- Union state
- Border state
- Confederate state
- Territory
- ● Major city

Key Events

1820 — The Missouri Compromise p. 438

1850 — Congress passes the Compromise of 1850 p. 439

1854 — The Kansas-Nebraska Act is passed p. 439

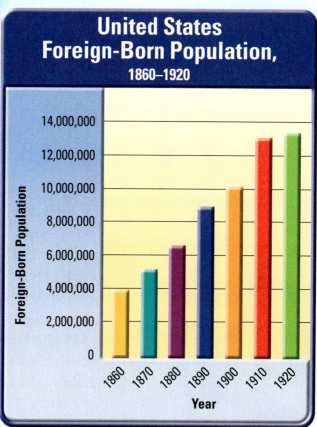

United States Foreign-Born Population, 1860–1920

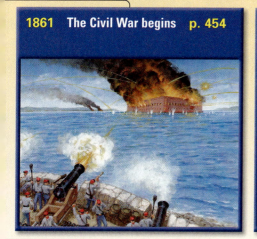

1861 The Civil War begins   p. 454

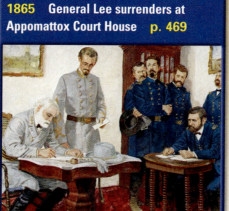

1865 General Lee surrenders at Appomattox Court House   p. 469

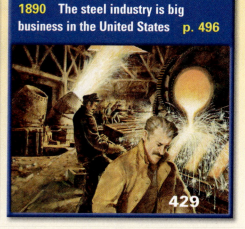

1890 The steel industry is big business in the United States   p. 496

429

START with a JOURNAL

All for the Union

The Civil War Diary and Letters of Elisha Hunt Rhodes

edited by Robert H. Rhodes

By 1863 the United States was no longer a united country. For more than two years, the Northern and Southern states had been fighting each other in a terrible civil war. In July, an important battle took place near the small town of Gettysburg, Pennsylvania. That three-day struggle forever changed our history.

Elisha Hunt Rhodes was a young soldier who fought for the North at the Battle of Gettysburg. As you read his first hand account of the battle, think about how the battlefield looked. Imagine the sights, sounds, and smells the soldiers experienced. Also read to discover whether the Northern army or the Southern army won the battle.

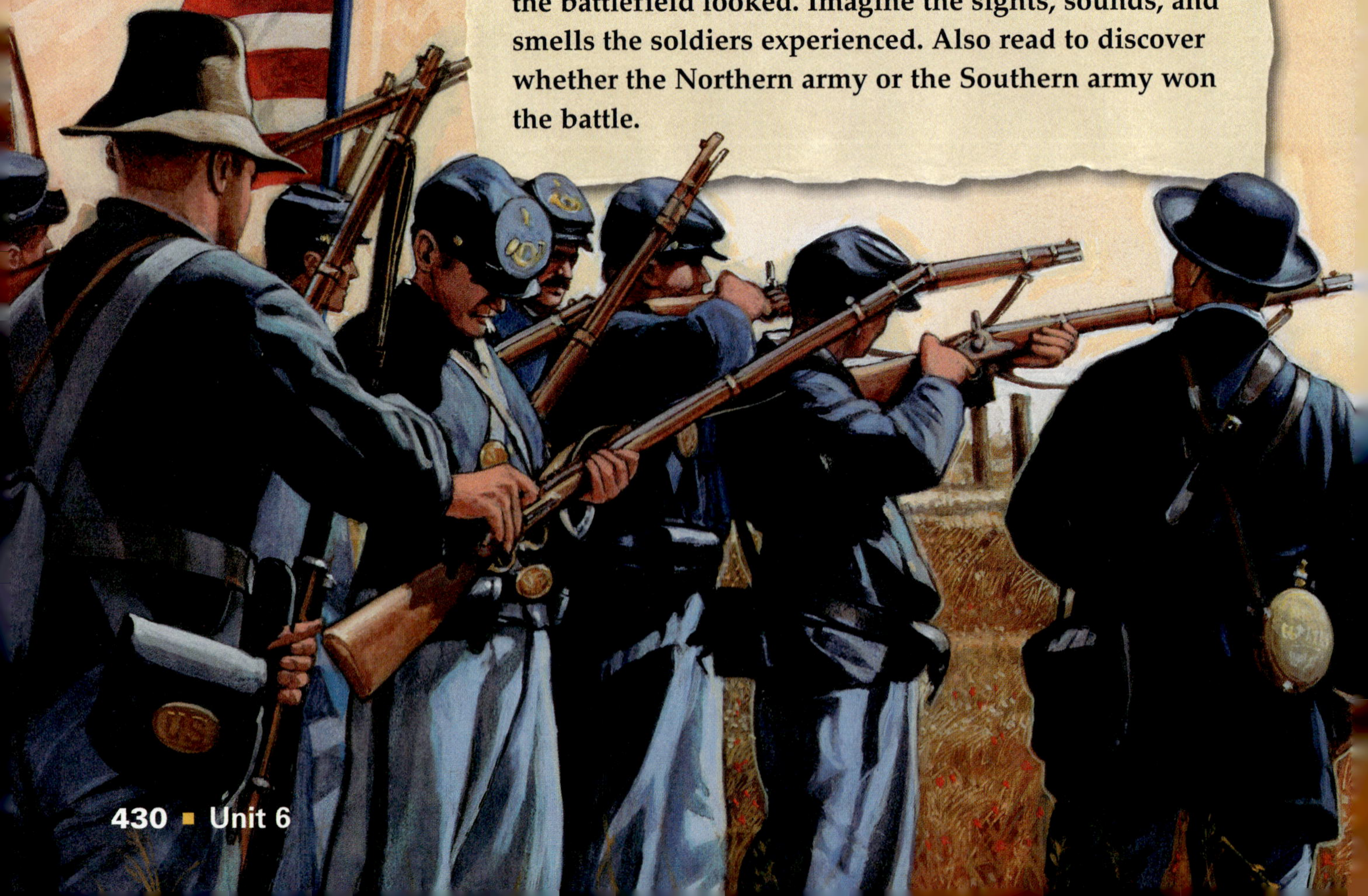

July 3rd 1863—This morning the troops were under arms before light and ready for the great battle that we knew must be fought. The firing began, and our Brigade was hurried to the right of the line to reinforce it. While not in the front line yet we were constantly exposed to the fire of the Rebel Artillery, while bullets fell around us. We moved from point to point, wherever danger to be imminent until noon when we were ordered to report to the line held by Gen. Birney. Our Brigade marched down the road until we reached the house used by General Meade as Headquarters. The road ran between ledges of rocks while the fields were strewn with boulders. To our left was a hill on which we had many batteries posted. Just as we reached Gen. Meade's Headquarters, a shell burst over our heads, and it was immediately followed by showers of iron. More than two hundred guns were belching forth their thunder, and most of the shells that came over the hill struck in the road on which our Brigade was moving. Solid shot would strike the large rocks and split them as if exploded by gunpowder. The flying iron and pieces of stone struck men down in every direction. It is said that this fire continued for about two hours, but I have no idea of the time. We could not see the enemy, and we could only cover ourselves the best we could behind rocks and trees. About 30 men of our Brigade were killed or wounded by this fire. Soon the Rebel yell was heard, and we have found since that the Rebel General Pickett made a charge with his Division and was repulsed after reaching some of our batteries. Our lines of Infantry in front of us rose up and poured in a terrible fire. As we were only a few yards in rear of our lines we saw all the fight. The firing gradually died away, and but for an occasional shot all was still. But what a scene it was. Oh the dead and the dying on this bloody field. The 2nd R.I. lost only one man killed and five wounded. One of the latter belonged to my Co. "B". Again night came upon us and again we slept amid the dead and dying.

Brigade a large body of troops
Rebel the Southern army or a Southern soldier
imminent ready to take place

batteries groupings of big guns
repulsed driven back
R.I. Rhode Island

July 4, 1863— Was ever the Nation's Birthday celebrated in such a way before. This morning the 2nd R.I. was sent out to the front and found that during the night General Lee and his Rebel Army had fallen back. It was impossible to march across the field without stepping upon dead or wounded men, while horses and broken Artillery lay on every side. We advanced to a sunken road (Emmitsburg Road) where we deployed as skirmishers and lay down behind a bank of earth. Berdan's Sharpshooters joined us, and we passed the day in firing upon any Rebels that showed themselves. At 12 M. a National Salute with shotted guns was fired from several of our Batteries, and the shells passed over our heads toward the Rebel lines. At night we were relieved and went to the rear for a little rest and sleep.

skirmishers scouts

July 5th 1863 — Glorious news! We have won the victory, thank God, and the Rebel Army is fleeing to Virginia. We have news that Vicksburg has fallen. We have thousands of prisoners, and they seem to be stupified with the news. This morning our Corps (the 6th) started in pursuit of Lee's Army. We have had rain and the roads are bad, so we move slow. Every house we see is a hospital, and the road is covered with the arms and equipments thrown away by the Rebels.

stupified stunned

Analyze the Literature

1. What brigade did Elisha Hunt Rhodes belong to?
2. Where did the Southern army flee after losing the Battle of Gettysburg?
3. How can reading a first hand account of a historical event help you better understand it?

READ A BOOK

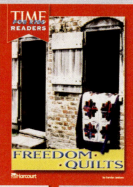

START THE UNIT PROJECT

The Hall of Fame With your classmates, create a Hall of Fame about the key people in the unit. As you read take notes on the contributions key people made. Your notes will help you create your Hall of Fame.

USE TECHNOLOGY

Visit The Learning Site at www.harcourtschool.com for additional activities, primary sources, and other resources to use in this unit.

Unit 6 • 433

ANTIETAM NATIONAL BATTLEFIELD

The Battle of Antietam claimed more American lives in a single day than any other one day battle in United States history. Nearly 4,700 Union and Confederate soldiers were lost on September 17, 1862. Visitors to Antietam National Battlefield can tour over 90 monuments built to honor those fallen soldiers.

LOCATE IT

MARYLAND

Antietam National Battlefield

CHAPTER 12

The Nation Divided

" Yes, we'll rally 'round the flag, boys, we'll rally once again, Shouting the battle cry of freedom. "
—George Frederick Root,
The Battle Cry of Freedom, 1863

Categorize

To **categorize** is to arrange information into similar groups. You can place people or events into categories to make it easier to find facts.

As you read this chapter, do the following.
- Categorize information about regional conflicts and the Civil War.

Chapter 12 ■ 435

LESSON 1

Regional Disagreements

 CATEGORIZE
As you read, categorize the beliefs and actions of Americans by regions.

BIG IDEA
Regional differences caused conflict between Northern and Southern states.

VOCABULARY
sectionalism
tariff
states' rights
free state
slave state

1820 — 1870 — 1920
1820–1860

As the United States expanded its borders in the first half of the 1800s, strong differences developed among the various regions. Because of those differences, it was difficult for Americans to agree on many issues. In Congress, representatives from the North, South, and West often made decisions based on helping their own section, or region, rather than the country as a whole. This regional loyalty is called **sectionalism** (SEK•shuhn•uh•lih•zuhm), and the disagreements it caused threatened to tear the country apart.

Debate over State Authority

Sectionalism in the United States became a serious problem in 1828, when Congress set a high **tariff**, or tax, on some imports. The tariff made goods from Europe cost more than goods made in the United States. This protected factory owners and workers in the United States from foreign competition and made it easier for factories to sell their products.

The tariff helped the North because most of the nation's factories were located there. However, it did little to help the South, which remained mostly an agricultural region. People in the South sold many of their cash crops to businesses in Europe. In return, they bought many European manufactured goods. Southerners generally opposed the tariff because they did not like having to pay higher prices for those goods.

In 1829 Andrew Jackson became President, and John C. Calhoun of South Carolina became Vice President. Calhoun argued against the tariff. He believed in **states' rights**, or the idea that the states, not the federal government, should have the final authority over their own affairs. Calhoun believed

People in the South used money from the cash crops they sold to buy goods from Europe.

that states had the right to refuse to accept a law passed by Congress.

Although President Jackson was known to support states' rights, he still believed that the federal government had the constitutional right to collect the tariff, even if South Carolina thought it was too high. President Jackson made his feelings clear when he spoke at a dinner honoring the memory of former President Thomas Jefferson. Jackson, looking straight at Calhoun, firmly said, "Our Federal Union—It must and shall be preserved!" Calhoun, who was just as determined, answered, "The Union, next to our liberty most dear. May we all remember that it can be preserved only by respecting the rights of the states."

The debate over states' rights continued after Congress passed another tariff in 1832. Sectionalism grew stronger, and it further divided the people of the United States.

REVIEW Why did most people in the South oppose tariffs?

Division over Slavery

Another issue that had long divided the nation was slavery. Northern and Southern states had argued about it since the writing of the Constitution. The Mason-Dixon Line—roughly the border between Pennsylvania and Maryland—was seen as the dividing line between states that allowed slavery and those that did not. As settlers moved west, however, the arguments about slavery flared up again. Many settlers from the South wanted to bring their enslaved workers to the western territories.

Settlers from the North did not want slavery in the new western lands. Most

For political advice Jackson sometimes relied on a group of unofficial advisers, whom many referred to as Jackson's "Kitchen Cabinet."

Northerners thought that slavery should go no farther than where it already was—in the South. Most Southern slave owners believed that they had the right to take their slaves wherever they wanted. As the new western territories grew, settlers there asked to join the Union as new states. In each case, the same question arose. Would the new state be a free state or a slave state? A **free state** did not allow slavery. A **slave state** did.

For a time there were as many free states as slave states. This kept a balance between the North and the South in the Senate. Then, in 1819, settlers in the Missouri Territory, a part of the Louisiana Purchase, asked to join the Union as a slave state. If this happened, slave states would outnumber free states for the first time since the founding of the country.

Regions
The Missouri Compromise line divided lands that could join the Union as free states from lands that could join as slave states.

❓ Which two states were admitted to the Union as part of the compromise?

The Missouri question was debated in Congress for months. Henry Clay, a member of Congress from Kentucky, found himself in the middle of these heated arguments about slavery. Clay himself owned slaves, but he did not want to see the issue of slavery divide the country. He worked day and night to help solve the problem. Finally, in 1820, Clay persuaded Congress to agree to a plan known as the Missouri Compromise.

Under this plan Missouri would be allowed to join the Union as a slave state. Maine, which had also asked to become a state, would join as a free state. This would keep the balance between free states and slave states. Then a line would be drawn on a map of the rest of the lands gained in the Louisiana Purchase. Slavery would be allowed in places south of the line. It would not be allowed in places north of the line.

REVIEW How did the Missouri Compromise keep the balance between free states and slave states? **CATEGORIZE**

Henry Clay became known as the Great Compromiser because of his work to settle differences between the North and the South.

A New Compromise

The Missouri Compromise kept the peace for nearly 30 years. During this time six new states joined the Union. The number of free states and slave states remained equal. Then, in 1848, the United States gained new lands after winning the war with Mexico. Settlers in California, a part of these new lands, asked to join the Union as a free state. Once again arguments about the spread of slavery broke out. The Missouri Compromise did not apply to lands outside of the Louisiana Purchase.

Henry Clay again worked toward a compromise—the Compromise of 1850. Under this compromise, California joined the Union as a free state. The rest of the lands gained from Mexico were divided into two territories—New Mexico and Utah. The people in those territories would decide for themselves whether to allow slavery.

Henry Clay, who became known as the Great Compromiser, died in 1852. He never gave up hope that the country would find a peaceful way to settle its differences. On his grave marker in Lexington, Kentucky, are the words *I know no North—no South—no East—no West*. Two years after Clay's death, however, bad feelings between free states and slave states turned to violence.

REVIEW Who became known as the Great Compromiser?

Bleeding Kansas

In 1854 Congress passed the Kansas–Nebraska Act, which changed the rules of the Missouri Compromise. Under the Missouri Compromise, slavery would not have been allowed in the territories of Kansas and Nebraska. Under the Kansas–Nebraska Act, however, people in those territories were given the opportunity to decide for themselves whether to allow slavery. They would decide by voting.

The Kansas Territory quickly became the center of attention in the nation. People for and against slavery rushed into the territory. They hoped to help decide the outcome by casting their votes.

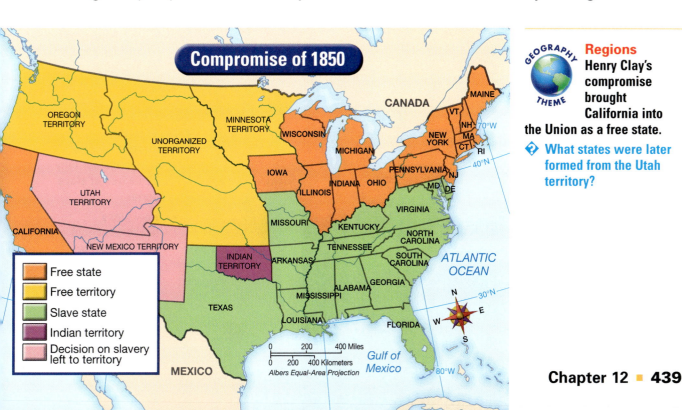

Regions Henry Clay's compromise brought California into the Union as a free state.

◆ What states were later formed from the Utah territory?

Kansas–Nebraska Act

Analyze Primary Sources

This poster was used to announce a meeting of those who supported the Kansas–Nebraska Act.

1. The headline states what type of meeting was being held.
2. The date shows when the meeting was held.
3. The phrase indicates that many people were to attend the meeting.

❖ Why do you think quotations are included on the poster?

It was not long before fighting broke out between the two sides. More than 200 people were killed in the bitter conflict that is known as "Bleeding Kansas."

Kansas eventually joined the Union as a free state, but the bloodshed there was a sign of things to come. Many people on both sides of the slavery issue no longer saw compromise as a possible solution. Some in the South began to speak of leaving the Union.

REVIEW What did the Kansas–Nebraska Act do?

The Dred Scott Decision

In 1857 the United States Supreme Court decided the case of an enslaved African American named Dred Scott. Scott had asked the Court for his freedom. The Court said no.

Scott was the slave of an army doctor. His owner moved often and always took Scott with him. For a time they lived in Illinois, a free state. Then they lived in

Regions The Kansas–Nebraska Act allowed people in the Kansas and Nebraska territories to decide by voting whether they would be free or slave territories.

❖ How many territories could now decide for themselves whether to allow slavery?

Wisconsin, a free territory under the Missouri Compromise.

After his owner died, Scott took his case to court. He argued that he should be free because he had once lived on free land. The case moved up through the federal court system until it reached the Supreme Court. There, Chief Justice Roger B. Taney (TAH•nee) said that because Scott was a slave, he had "none of the rights and privileges" of an American citizen. Having lived in a free territory did not change that.

Taney also declared that Congress had no right to forbid slavery in the Wisconsin Territory. He felt that the United States Constitution protected the right of people to own slaves. Slaves, he wrote, were property. He believed that the Missouri Compromise was keeping people from owning property. This, Taney wrote, was unconstitutional.

In 1857 the Supreme Court decided that Dred Scott should not be given his freedom.

Many people had hoped the Dred Scott decision would finally settle the disagreements among sections of the country over slavery once and for all. Instead, it made the problem worse.

REVIEW Why did the Supreme Court deny freedom to Dred Scott?

LESSON 1 REVIEW

Summary Time Line

- 1820 — Congress passes the Missouri Compromise
- 1854 — Congress passes the Kansas–Nebraska Act
- 1857 — The Dred Scott decision is made

CATEGORIZE What states were affected by the Missouri Compromise?

1. **BIG IDEA** What were some of the regional differences causing conflict between the North and the South?

2. **VOCABULARY** What was the difference between a **slave state** and a **free state**?

3. **TIME LINE** When was the Kansas–Nebraska Act passed?

4. **GEOGRAPHY** In what region of the country were tariffs helpful?

5. **CRITICAL THINKING—Analyze** How was the Missouri Compromise changed by the Kansas–Nebraska Act and the Dred Scott decision?

PERFORMANCE—Write a Plan Imagine that you are Henry Clay and it is 1850. You need to write a plan that will help the country find a peaceful way to settle its differences. Describe in your plan how the country can settle its regional disagreements without tearing itself apart. Share your plan with the rest of the class.

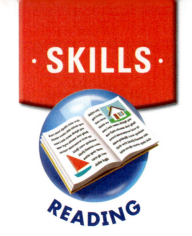

· SKILLS · Identify Frame of Reference

VOCABULARY
frame of reference

▶ WHY IT MATTERS

When you read something that people have written about an event or listen to them tell about it, you need to consider their **frame of reference**—where they were when the event happened or what role they played in it. A person's frame of reference can influence how he or she sees an event or feels about it. It can also influence how a person describes an event. Considering a person's frame of reference as you read or listen can help you better understand what happened.

▶ WHAT YOU NEED TO KNOW

In the 1800s, people's opinions about slavery and other issues were often influenced by where they lived. People who lived in the South, North, and West all had different frames of reference.

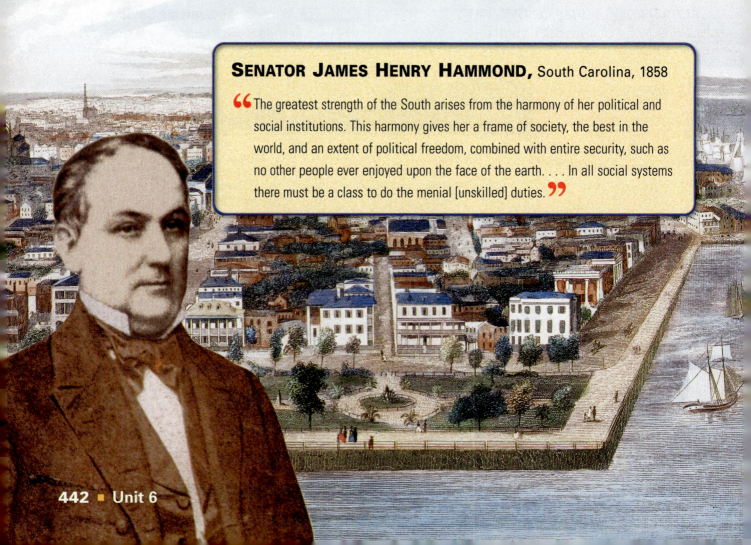

SENATOR JAMES HENRY HAMMOND, South Carolina, 1858

❝The greatest strength of the South arises from the harmony of her political and social institutions. This harmony gives her a frame of society, the best in the world, and an extent of political freedom, combined with entire security, such as no other people ever enjoyed upon the face of the earth. . . . In all social systems there must be a class to do the menial [unskilled] duties.❞

The statements on these pages were made in 1858 by Senator James Henry Hammond of South Carolina and Senator William Seward of New York. Senator Hammond owned a cotton plantation and had served as governor of South Carolina in 1842. Senator Seward was born, raised, and educated in New York State. He served as governor of New York from 1839 to 1843 and established a strong antislavery stand.

As you read the statements, consider how each senator's frame of reference might have affected what he said.

▶ PRACTICE THE SKILL

Answer these questions.

① What was Senator Hammond's position on slavery? How might his frame of reference have affected it?

② How was Senator Seward's position on slavery different from the one held by Senator Hammond? In what way was Seward's frame of reference different?

③ How might a Southerner's opinion of Senator Seward's description of the "slave system" be different from that of a person from the North? of a person from the West?

▶ APPLY WHAT YOU LEARNED

Think about a present-day example of how frames of reference cause differences in opinions and beliefs. Write a paragraph that describes this present-day example and explains why the people involved may think the way they do. Share your paragraph with a classmate.

SENATOR WILLIAM SEWARD, New York, 1858

❝The slave system is one of constant danger, distrust, suspicion, and watchfulness. It debases those whose toil [work] alone can produce wealth and resources for defense to the lowest degree of which human nature is capable . . . and this wastes energies which otherwise might be employed in national development and aggrandizement [the act of making greater].❞

LESSON 2

Slavery and Freedom

1820–1860

CATEGORIZE
As you read, categorize examples of differing views of slavery by regions.

BIG IDEA
Some people worked to try to end slavery.

VOCABULARY
emancipation
resist
code
fugitive
underground
abolitionist
equality

By 1860 there were nearly 4 million slaves in the United States, an increase from 900,000 in 1800. This growth of slavery was due chiefly to the growing importance of cotton as a cash crop in the South. Cotton became such an important part of the Southern economy that it was called "King Cotton." The demand for cotton created a demand for more enslaved workers.

The Slave Economy

Slavery had been a part of American life since colonial days. Some people thought that slavery was wrong. Other people could not make money using enslaved workers. The cost of feeding, clothing, and housing slaves was too great.

In the South, however, slavery continued because owners had come to depend on the work of enslaved people. Slaves were made to work as miners, carpenters, factory workers, and house servants. Some, however, were taken to large plantations. There they raised many acres of cotton and other cash crops, such as rice, tobacco, and sugarcane.

Many slaves had to wear identification badges (above). This scene (right) shows a plantation on the Mississippi River.

444 ■ Unit 6

While wealthy planters owned more than half the slaves in the South, most white Southerners owned no slaves at all. By 1860 one of every four white Southern families owned slaves.

REVIEW In which region of the United States was slavery most important? Why?

Slavery and the Law

Until the 1820s most people in the South thought slavery was wrong but necessary. In 1832, members of the Virginia legislature even debated **emancipation** (ih•man•suh•PAY•shuhn), or the freeing of slaves, in their state.

The debate started because many Virginians had been frightened by a slave rebellion the year before. The rebellion took place in Southampton County, Virginia. A slave named Nat Turner led an attack that killed more than 50 people, among them his owner. In turn, slave owners trying to end the rebellion killed more than 100 slaves.

Most slaves never took part in such rebellions, but they did whatever they could to **resist**, or act against, slavery. They broke tools, pretended to be sick, or acted as if they did not understand what they had been told. Such actions were dangerous, however, and slaves had to be careful to avoid punishment.

The Virginia legislature voted not to end slavery. To prevent future uprisings, Virginia joined with other slave states who had passed laws that put more controls on slaves. These laws were called slave codes. Under these **codes**, or sets of laws, slaves were not allowed to leave their owners' land, to meet in groups, or to buy or sell goods. Most slaves were not allowed to learn to read or write, and speaking against slavery became a crime.

The federal government also passed laws about slavery. One of these laws was called the Fugitive Slave Act. A **fugitive** is a person who is running away from something. Under this law, anyone caught helping a slave escape could be punished. People who found runaway slaves had to return them to the South.

REVIEW What were slave codes?

Analyze Graphs Many people did not own slaves.
◆ What percent of Southerners owned no slaves?

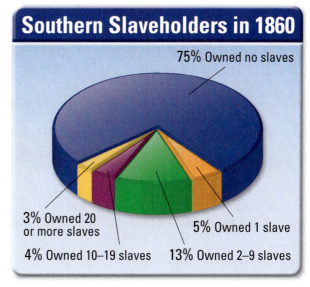

Southern Slaveholders in 1860

75% Owned no slaves
3% Owned 20 or more slaves
4% Owned 10–19 slaves
13% Owned 2–9 slaves
5% Owned 1 slave

Chapter 12 ■ 445

The Underground Railroad

By 1860 there were more than 500,000 free African Americans living in the United States. Some had been born to parents who were free. Some had bought their freedom or had been freed by their owners. Others had escaped slavery by running away.

Over the years thousands of slaves tried to gain their freedom by running away. Some ran away alone. Others tried to escape with their families or friends.

Once away from their owners' land, runaway slaves had to find safe places to hide. Many slaves helped each other along the way. Native American groups helped slaves by giving them shelter. Some slaves hid in forests, swamps, or mountains, sometimes for years.

Many runaway slaves continued moving for months until they reached Canada or Mexico or free states in the North. Some found helpers who led the way—the brave men and women of the Underground Railroad. The word **underground** is often used to describe something done in secret.

The Underground Railroad was a system of secret escape routes leading to free

Movement Lanterns were sometimes used to indicate safe places for runaway slaves. Slave owners sent out posters (below) offering rewards for the return of runaways.

◆ Which rivers may have been used as water routes to free land?

lands. Most routes led from the South to free states in the North or to Canada. Some led to Mexico and to islands in the Caribbean Sea.

Working mostly at night, conductors, or helpers along the Underground Railroad, led runaway slaves from one hiding place to the next along the routes. These hiding places—barns, attics, storage rooms—were called stations. There the runaways could rest and eat, preparing for the journey to the next station.

Most conductors were free African Americans and white Northerners who opposed slavery. Harriet Tubman, an African American who had escaped from slavery herself, was one of the best-known conductors of the Underground Railroad. During the 1850s Tubman returned to the South 20 times and guided about 300 people to freedom. She proudly claimed, "I never lost a single passenger."

REVIEW What was the Underground Railroad? **CATEGORIZE**

Harriet Tubman helped enslaved African Americans escape to free lands.

Women Work for Change

Many of the people who worked to free slaves were themselves not entirely free. White women, many of whom spoke out against slavery, were generally not accepted as men's equals. They could not vote, hold public office, or sit on juries.

In 1840, a group of American women went as delegates to a world anti-slavery convention in London, England. They were denied the right to participate and could only watch the proceedings from the balcony.

One of the women who took part in the convention in London also played an important role at another convention eight years later. Elizabeth Cady Stanton, a defender of the rights of both women and slaves, participated at the first women's rights convention, held in Seneca Falls, New York. Stanton wrote a statement listing women's grievances.

This mural by Hames Michael Newell shows runaway slaves on the Underground Railroad.

Chapter 12 ■ 447

In her statement, she demanded that women "have immediate admission to all the rights and privileges which belong to them as citizens of the United States."

In 1852 Harriet Beecher Stowe worked for change by publishing a novel that turned many people against slavery. The book, *Uncle Tom's Cabin*, told the heart-breaking story of slaves being mistreated by a cruel overseer. The book quickly became a best-seller and was made into a play.

Many of the same people who fought for equal rights for women also fought to end slavery. They often united antislavery and women's rights to form a double crusade for freedom.

REVIEW What book turned many people against slavery?

Abolitionists

People who opposed slavery worked to abolish, or end, it. Those who wanted to abolish slavery were called **abolitionists** (a•buh•LIH•shuhn•ists). Among the first to speak out, as early as the 1680s, were members of the Society of Friends, commonly known as the Quakers. In 1775, Quakers formed the first organized group to work against slavery.

In 1827 two free African Americans, Samuel Cornish and John Russwurm, started a newspaper that called for **equality**, or equal rights, for all Americans. The newspaper, *Freedom's Journal*, was the first to be owned and written by African Americans. In it Cornish and Russwurm wrote, "Too long have others spoken for us."

A few years later another abolitionist, William Lloyd Garrison, a white Northerner, founded a newspaper called *The Liberator*. Garrison called for a complete end to slavery, saying, "On this subject I do not wish to think, or speak, or write with moderation. I am earnest . . . I will not excuse. I will not retreat a single inch—AND I WILL BE HEARD."

In Congress, Horace Mann and others gave speeches against slavery. Other

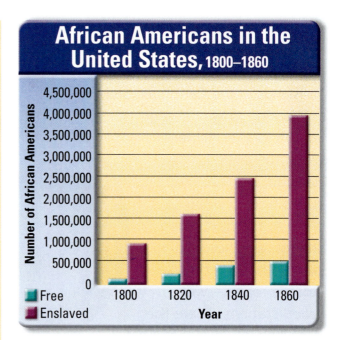

Analyze Graphs This graph shows the numbers of free and enslaved African Americans in the United States.

◆ What trend does this graph show?

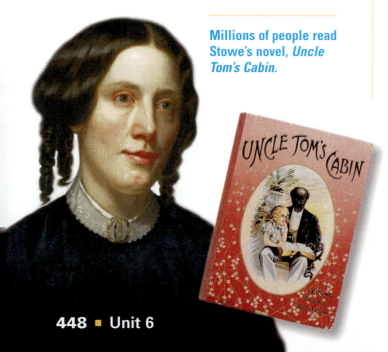

Millions of people read Stowe's novel, *Uncle Tom's Cabin*.

abolitionists gave speeches at crowds. One well-known abolitionist speaker was Frederick Douglass, a runaway slave. In 1841 Douglass attended a convention of the Massachusetts Antislavery Society. He often told his audiences, "I appear this evening as a thief and a robber. I stole this head, these limbs, this body from my master [slave owner], and ran off with them."

Like Douglass, another former slave named Isabella Van Wagener (WAI•guh•nur) traveled the country speaking out against slavery. Van Wagener believed that God had called her to "travel up and down the land" to preach. She changed her name to reflect her path. She chose *Sojourner*, which means "traveler," for her first name and *Truth* as her last name.

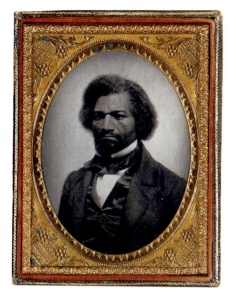

Frederick Douglass was a runaway slave and an abolitionist.

Sojourner Truth believed that slavery could be ended peacefully. On the night of October 16, 1859, John Brown led a group to seize a government storehouse at Harpers Ferry, in what is now West Virginia. The storehouse was filled with guns. Brown planned to give the guns to slaves so they could fight for freedom. He was soon caught, put on trial, and hanged for his actions.

Violence also broke out in Congress. Preston Brooks, a representative from South Carolina, attacked a senator from Massachusetts while he was giving an anti-slavery speech. It was clear that the North and South were going to be divided by civil war.

REVIEW Who were abolitionists?

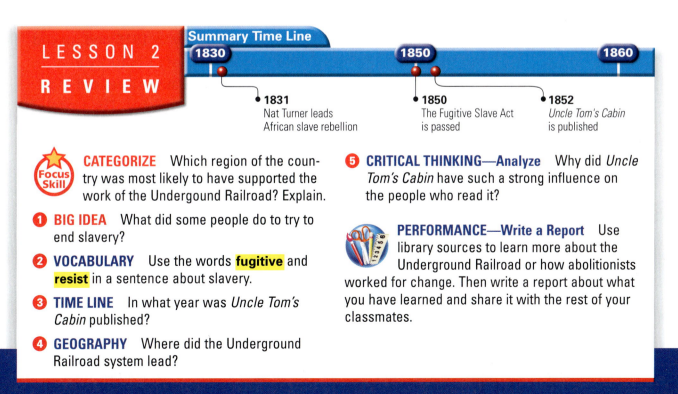

LESSON 2 REVIEW

Summary Time Line
- 1831 Nat Turner leads African slave rebellion
- 1850 The Fugitive Slave Act is passed
- 1852 *Uncle Tom's Cabin* is published

CATEGORIZE Which region of the country was most likely to have supported the work of the Undergound Railroad? Explain.

1. **BIG IDEA** What did some people do to try to end slavery?
2. **VOCABULARY** Use the words **fugitive** and **resist** in a sentence about slavery.
3. **TIME LINE** In what year was *Uncle Tom's Cabin* published?
4. **GEOGRAPHY** Where did the Underground Railroad system lead?
5. **CRITICAL THINKING—Analyze** Why did *Uncle Tom's Cabin* have such a strong influence on the people who read it?

PERFORMANCE—Write a Report Use library sources to learn more about the Underground Railroad or how abolitionists worked for change. Then write a report about what you have learned and share it with the rest of your classmates.

· LESSON ·
3

 CATEGORIZE

As you read, categorize the positions different people took on the issue of slavery.

BIG IDEA
The election of 1860 further divided the United States.

VOCABULARY
secede
Confederacy

The Union Breaks Apart

1855–1865

In the 1850s, new national leaders, such as Abraham Lincoln, began to speak out on the slavery issue. Abraham Lincoln was not an abolitionist, but he was against the spread of slavery. He did not think that the federal government had the right to abolish slavery in the United States. Instead, he hoped that if slavery were not allowed to spread, it would one day die out.

Young Abe Lincoln

Abraham Lincoln was named for his grandfather, who had been a friend of Daniel Boone. Lincoln's grandfather had followed Boone to Kentucky, on the western frontier. He had a son named Thomas, who eventually married Nancy Hanks. They lived in a small log cabin with a dirt floor. Abraham Lincoln was born in that cabin in 1809.

The Lincolns left their home in Kentucky in 1816 and moved to the Indiana Territory. One reason they left Kentucky was that many people there owned slaves. Because slaves did most of the work, there were few paying jobs available. The Lincolns

People today can visit a replica of Abraham Lincoln's boyhood home at the Lincoln Boyhood National Memorial near Little Pigeon Creek, Indiana.

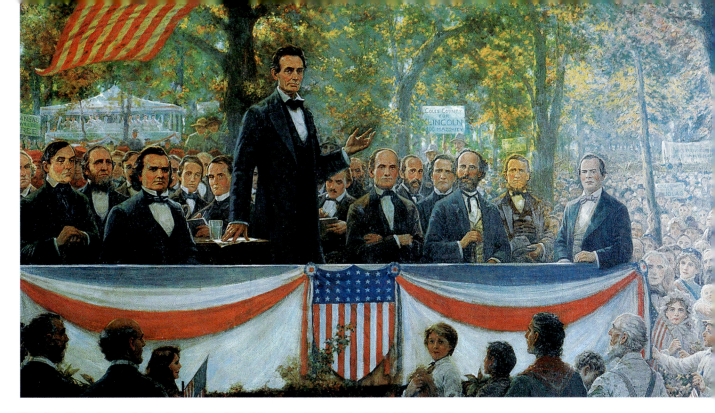

Stephen Douglas and Abraham Lincoln held seven debates in 1858. This painting shows Lincoln (standing) and Douglas (to Lincoln's right) debating in Charleston, Illinois.

lived in Indiana for 14 years. By then, Indiana seemed crowded to them, so they moved to the Illinois Territory.

As a young man, Abraham Lincoln held several jobs. All the while, he studied law. In the 1830s he became a lawyer and opened a law office in Illinois.

In 1834 Abraham Lincoln entered public service. He served first in the Illinois legislature. Later, in 1846, he was elected to the United States Congress, where he served one term in the House of Representatives. After returning to Illinois, Lincoln became concerned about the spread of slavery to the West. He joined a new political party formed to fight the spread of slavery. This party was called the Republican party.

In 1858 Lincoln decided to run again for government office. On June 17, Lincoln was nominated, or chosen, by the Republican party to be its candidate for the United States Senate. In his acceptance speech, Lincoln used words from the Bible to explain his beliefs about the spread of slavery and the future of the United States. He said, "A house divided against itself cannot stand. I believe this government cannot endure permanently half slave and half free." Lincoln hoped that his strong stand would not cost him the election.

REVIEW What newly formed political party did Abraham Lincoln join?

Lincoln and Douglas

Abraham Lincoln ran against Senator Stephen A. Douglas, the person who had written the Kansas–Nebraska Act. Lincoln and Douglas were very different from each other. Abraham Lincoln was very tall and thin, while Stephen Douglas was heavy and a full foot shorter than Lincoln.

Chapter 12 ■ 451

Because Douglas was already serving in the Senate, he was well known across the country. Few people in places other than Illinois had ever heard of Lincoln.

Despite their differences, Lincoln and Douglas were alike in one important way. Both were talented public speakers. In the summer of 1858, the two candidates traveled around the state of Illinois and debated questions that were important to voters. Huge crowds turned out to listen to them, and newspapers printed what each man had to say.

Stephen Douglas argued that each new state should decide the slavery question for itself. That was what the nation's founders had allowed, he said, and that was what the new Kansas–Nebraska Act allowed.

Posters in the North were made to show people's support for the Union.

Abraham Lincoln responded that "the framers of the Constitution intended and expected" slavery to end. The problem, Lincoln pointed out, was more than a question of what each state wanted. It was a question of right and wrong. Slavery should not spread to the West, Lincoln said, because slavery was wrong.

Although Stephen Douglas won reelection to the Senate for another term, people all over the country now knew who Lincoln was. Two years later, in 1860, the two men faced each other in another election. This one would decide the next President of the United States.

REVIEW How were the positions of Lincoln and Douglas on the spread of slavery different?
CATEGORIZE

The Election of 1860

In the 1860 election for the presidency Abraham Lincoln represented the Republican party, which firmly opposed the spread of slavery. The Democratic party was divided in its views. Some members of the party supported Stephen Douglas, who continued to argue that western settlers should decide for themselves whether to allow slavery. Other

The first notice of South Carolina's secession was printed in the *Charleston Mercury*. Jefferson Davis (left) was elected president of the Confederacy.

members, mostly Southerners, backed John Breckinridge of Kentucky. Breckinridge thought that the federal government should allow slavery everywhere in the West.

The division within the Democratic party made Lincoln's election almost certain. Although Lincoln promised not to abolish slavery in the South, he said he hoped it would end there one day. Many Southerners feared that Lincoln was attacking their whole way of life. Some leaders in the South said that their states would **secede** from, or leave, the Union if Lincoln became President. Like most Southerners, they believed that states could freely leave the Union since the states had created the Union in the first place.

On Election Day in November 1860, Lincoln did not win a single state in the South. However, he won enough states in the North and the West to win the presidency. Southern leaders did not wait long before carrying out their threat to secede. On December 20, South Carolina seceded from the Union.

Five other states—Alabama, Florida, Georgia, Louisiana, and Mississippi—soon followed. Together these six states formed their own government at Montgomery, Alabama, early in February 1861. They called themselves the Confederate States of America, or the **Confederacy**. Jefferson Davis, a United States senator from Mississippi, was elected president. Alexander Stephens of Georgia became vice president. That month Texas seceded and later joined the Confederacy.

REVIEW What did seven Southern states do after Lincoln was elected President?

POINTS OF VIEW
Union or Secession

JOHN C. CALHOUN, a senator from South Carolina

❝What is the cause of this discontent? It will be found in the belief in the people of the Southern States . . . that they can not remain, as things are now. . . . If you who represent the stronger portion [the North], can not agree to settle [these differences] on the broad principle of justice and duty, say so; and let the states we both represent agree to separate and part in peace.❞

SAM HOUSTON, the governor of Texas

❝I tell you that, while I believe with you in the doctrine of State's Rights, the North is determined to preserve this Union. They are not a fiery, impulsive people as you are, for they live in colder climates. But when they begin to move in a certain direction. . . they move with the steady momentum and perseverance of a mighty avalanche.❞

Analyze the Viewpoints

1. What views about secession did each Southerner hold?
2. What other viewpoints might Southerners have held on the matter of secession?
3. **Make It Relevant** Look at the Letters to the Editor section of your newspaper. Find two letters that express different viewpoints about the same issue, and summarize the viewpoints of each letter.

A CLOSER LOOK
Fort Sumter Prior to the War

Fort Sumter was one of many forts built by the United States after the War of 1812.

1. stair tower
2. soldiers' barracks
3. officers' quarters
4. wall facing Charleston
5. fort lantern
6. mess hall
7. cannons
8. wharf

❓ Why do you think cannons were placed on nearly every side of the fort?

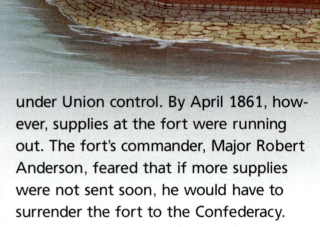

Crisis at Fort Sumter

On March 4, 1861, Abraham Lincoln took the oath of office as President of the United States. In his inauguration speech, he declared, "I have no purpose directly or indirectly to interfere with the institution of slavery in the states where it exists." Yet he firmly stated, "No state, upon its own mere action, can lawfully get out of the Union." Like many Northerners, Lincoln believed the United States could not be divided.

For one month after Lincoln's inauguration, the tension built. Americans everywhere wondered what Lincoln would do about the seceding states. Some people thought he should let them go. Others said that he should accept the Southern position on the slavery question and hope that the Southern states would return. Still others felt that Lincoln should use the army to end the revolt. The country's fate was soon determined at Fort Sumter, which is located on an island off the coast of South Carolina.

When the Southern states seceded, they had taken over post offices, forts, and other federal government property within their borders. Fort Sumter was one of the few forts in the South that remained under Union control. By April 1861, however, supplies at the fort were running out. The fort's commander, Major Robert Anderson, feared that if more supplies were not sent soon, he would have to surrender the fort to the Confederacy.

Lincoln had promised to hold on to all property that belonged to the United States. He sent supply ships to the fort and waited to see how the Confederate leaders would react. On April 12, 1861, Confederate leaders demanded that Union forces surrender. When Major Anderson refused, Confederate troops fired their cannons on the fort. They bombarded the fort for the next 34 hours, until the Union troops surrendered.

Learning of the fall of Fort Sumter, President Lincoln called for 75,000 Americans to join an army to stop the Southern rebellion and preserve the United States. Four more states—Arkansas, North Carolina, Tennessee, and Virginia—seceded and joined the

FAST FACT — Major Robert Anderson and Confederate General P.G.T. Beauregard, the two opposing commanders who fired the first shots of the Civil War, were close friends from their days at West Point Military Academy.

Confederacy. This brought the number of Confederate states to 11. Tensions between the Union and the Confederate States—the North and the South—had reached their breaking point. The Civil War had begun.

REVIEW Who was in command of Fort Sumter when it was fired upon?

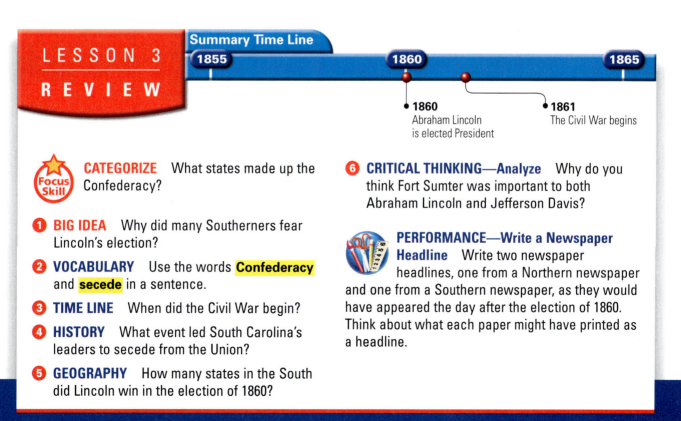

LESSON 3 REVIEW

Summary Time Line
1855 — 1860 — 1865
- 1860 Abraham Lincoln is elected President
- 1861 The Civil War begins

CATEGORIZE What states made up the Confederacy?

1. **BIG IDEA** Why did many Southerners fear Lincoln's election?
2. **VOCABULARY** Use the words **Confederacy** and **secede** in a sentence.
3. **TIME LINE** When did the Civil War begin?
4. **HISTORY** What event led South Carolina's leaders to secede from the Union?
5. **GEOGRAPHY** How many states in the South did Lincoln win in the election of 1860?
6. **CRITICAL THINKING—Analyze** Why do you think Fort Sumter was important to both Abraham Lincoln and Jefferson Davis?

PERFORMANCE—Write a Newspaper Headline Write two newspaper headlines, one from a Northern newspaper and one from a Southern newspaper, as they would have appeared the day after the election of 1860. Think about what each paper might have printed as a headline.

Chapter 12 ■ 455

SKILLS · MAP AND GLOBE

Compare Maps with Different Scales

▶ WHY IT MATTERS

Have you ever helped your family plan a trip? You may have wanted to know how far you had to travel.

A map scale helps you find out how far one place is from another. The map scale compares a distance on a map to a distance in the real world. Map scales are different depending on how much area is shown. This means that different maps are drawn to different scales. Knowing about map scales can help you choose the best map for gathering the information you need.

▶ WHAT YOU NEED TO KNOW

Look at the map below and the map on page 457. They both show Fort Sumter and the surrounding area, but with different scales. On Map A, Fort Sumter looks larger. For that reason the scale is said to be larger. When the map scale is larger, more details can be shown. On Map B, Fort Sumter appears smaller, and the scale is said to be smaller.

Although they have different scales, Maps A and B can both be used to measure the distance between the same two places.

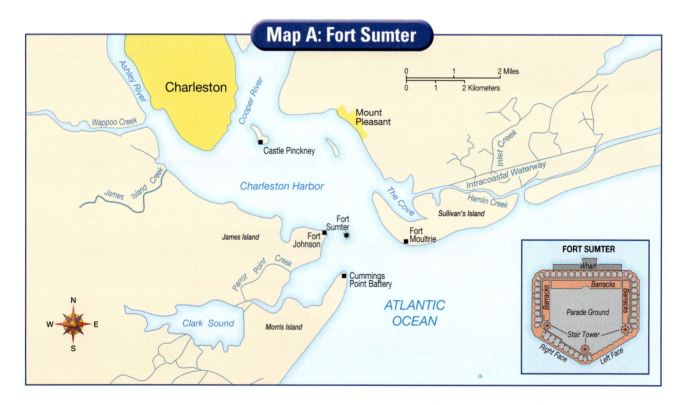

456 • Unit 6

▶ PRACTICE THE SKILL

On April 12, 1861, Confederate troops opened fire on Fort Sumter from Fort Moultrie, Fort Johnson, Castle Pinckney, and various batteries around Charleston Harbor. This act signaled the beginning of the Civil War.

Use the maps below to find the real distance in miles between Fort Sumter and Castle Pinckney.

1. On Map A, use a ruler to measure the exact length of the scale, or use a pencil to mark off the length on a sheet of paper. How long is the line that stands for one mile?

2. Still using Map A, find Fort Sumter and Castle Pinckney. Using the ruler or the sheet of paper you marked, measure the distance between these two places. What is the real distance in miles between Fort Sumter and Castle Pinckney?

3. Now go through the same steps for Map B. How long is the scale length that stands for one mile? Use that scale length to measure the distance between Fort Sumter and Castle Pinckney on the map. What is the real distance in miles? Are the real distances you found on the two maps the same? You should see that even when map scales are different the real distances shown on the maps are the same.

▶ APPLY WHAT YOU LEARNED

Find two maps with different scales—perhaps a map of your state and a map of a large city within your state. Compare the real distances between two places that are on both maps.

Practice your map and globe skills with the **GeoSkills CD-ROM.**

Chapter 12 ▪ 457

· LESSON ·
4

CATEGORIZE

As you read, categorize events that affected the North and South during the Civil War.

BIG IDEA

Several key events happened in the early years of the Civil War.

VOCABULARY

retreat
border state
strategy
casualty

Civil War

1861–1863

After Confederate troops fired on Fort Sumter, hopes for peace between the North and the South ended. Both the Union and the Confederacy prepared for war. Men and boys eagerly joined regiments made up of their neighbors and friends.

The Fighting Begins

The first of the major battles between the Union and the Confederacy was fought in July 1861. The battle took place at Bull Run, a stream near the town of Manassas Junction, Virginia. On the day of the battle, crowds of enthusiastic sightseers came in carriages from nearby Washington, D.C. They brought picnic lunches as if to watch a sporting event. A Union soldier said, "We thought it wasn't a bad idea to have the great men from Washington come out to see us thrash the Rebs [Confederate troops]."

At Bull Run two untrained armies clashed in a confusing battle. At first it appeared that the Union army would win. Then, as the Confederate army started to **retreat**, or fall back, new troops arrived. At their head was Thomas Jackson, a skilled Confederate general from Virginia. Jackson managed to stop the retreat. "There's Jackson standing like a stone wall," shouted another general as the Confederates turned and again

General Thomas Jackson

FAST FACT

The Union named battles after the nearest streams, and the Confederates named battles after the nearest towns. That is why the Battle of Manassas (shown here) is also known as the Battle of Bull Run.

Northern soldiers wore blue uniforms.

Southern soldiers wore gray uniforms.

Advantages in the Civil War

NORTHERN ADVANTAGES
Advanced industry
Advanced railroad system
Strong navy

SOUTHERN ADVANTAGES
Large number of military leaders
Troops experienced in outdoor living
Familiar with the environment of the South

Analyze Graphs This graph compares the advantages of the North and South.

❖ What advantages did the North have?

attacked the Union army. From that day on, General Jackson was known as Stonewall Jackson.

The Confederates won the Battle of Manassas, also called the Battle of Bull Run. The defeat shocked the Union. The South had proved more powerful than most Northerners had expected. Americans came to realize that this war would last far longer than they had first believed.

Most Northerners supported the Union, while most white Southerners supported the Confederacy. For some Americans, however, the choice between the Union and the Confederacy was not an easy one. The war had deeply divided people in all regions. People in the **border states**—Delaware, Kentucky, Maryland, and Missouri—were especially torn between the two sides. These states, which were located between the North and the South, permitted slavery but had not seceded.

REVIEW Where did the first major battle of the Civil War take place? **CATEGORIZE**

Battle Plans

The Union **strategy**, or long-range plan, for winning the war was first to weaken the South and then to invade it. To weaken the South, Lincoln and his advisers came up with a strategy that some people called the Anaconda (a•nuh•KAHN•duh) Plan. An anaconda is a large snake that squeezes its prey to death. The Union would squeeze the South by not letting it ship its cotton or bring in goods. If the South could not sell its cash crops, it would not have the money to buy supplies for its army.

The purpose of the plan was to block all imports from reaching the South. The plan called for winning control of the Mississippi River and for establishing a naval blockade of Confederate ports. Not everyone in the North liked the idea of a blockade, however. Many people thought it would take too long to set up. They wanted the Union army to invade the South. "On to Richmond!" they shouted.

Chapter 12 ■ 459

The Union and the Confederacy

- Union state
- Border state
- Confederate state
- Territory

Regions The Civil War had divided the nation. In western Virginia, feelings for the Union were so strong that the people voted to break away from Virginia. West Virginia joined the Union in 1863.

❓ Which states were border states?

Richmond, Virginia, had become the capital of the Confederacy by this time.

At first the most important strategy of the Confederate states was simply to protect their lands. This strategy was based on the belief that Britain and France would help the South. Both countries depended on Southern cotton to keep their textile mills going. The South also hoped that the North would tire of the war. Many Southerners, however, were impatient. Cries of "On to Washington!" were soon answered with plans to invade the North.

REVIEW How did the battle plans of the North and South differ? **CATEGORIZE**

The Battle at Antietam

As the Civil War dragged on into 1862, the Anaconda Plan seemed to be working. The blockade brought trade in the South to a halt, and supplies there ran

This cannon was used in the Battle of Antietam.

460 ■ Unit 6

very low. This made life increasingly difficult for Southern troops, who became poorly equipped, fed, and clothed. Even so, many Northerners became discouraged by the long lists of war casualties. A casualty is a person who has been killed or wounded in a war.

Then, in September 1862, the Union and the Confederates fought a major battle at Antietam (an•TEE•tuhm) Creek, near Sharpsburg, Maryland. By that time Robert E. Lee was Confederate commander of the Army of Northern Virginia. General Lee had led his army from Virginia into Maryland, intending to reach Harrisburg, Pennsylvania. There, Lee planned to cut off railroad communication between the states in the East and those in the West. Lee also hoped to find in Pennsylvania supplies that his troops badly needed.

At Antietam Creek, Lee's army was stopped by Union troops. The battle that followed resulted in the highest number of casualties in one day of the whole war. Union casualties numbered more than 2,000 killed and 9,500 wounded. Confederate casualties totaled 2,700 killed and over 9,000 wounded. "Never before or after in all the war were so many men shot on one day," historian Bruce Catton wrote. Having lost one-fourth of his army, Lee retreated to Virginia.

Although the battle at Antietam was really a draw, or tie, it had an important result. Five days later, on September 22, 1862, President Lincoln announced his decision to issue an order freeing the slaves in areas that were still fighting against the Union.

REVIEW Why was General Lee leading his army to Pennsylvania?

The Emancipation Proclamation

To President Lincoln, the purpose of the war had been to keep the country together—to save the Union. It had not been to abolish slavery. In 1862 President Lincoln wrote a letter explaining his view to Horace Greeley, publisher of the *New York Tribune*. "My [main] object in this struggle is to save the Union, and is not either to save or destroy slavery.

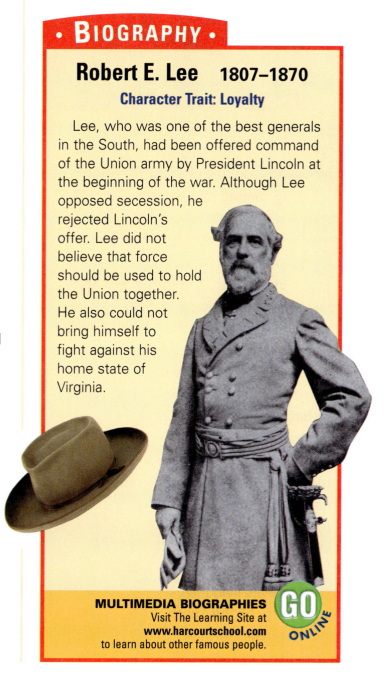

• BIOGRAPHY •

Robert E. Lee 1807–1870
Character Trait: Loyalty

Lee, who was one of the best generals in the South, had been offered command of the Union army by President Lincoln at the beginning of the war. Although Lee opposed secession, he rejected Lincoln's offer. Lee did not believe that force should be used to hold the Union together. He also could not bring himself to fight against his home state of Virginia.

MULTIMEDIA BIOGRAPHIES
Visit The Learning Site at
www.harcourtschool.com
to learn about other famous people.
GO ONLINE

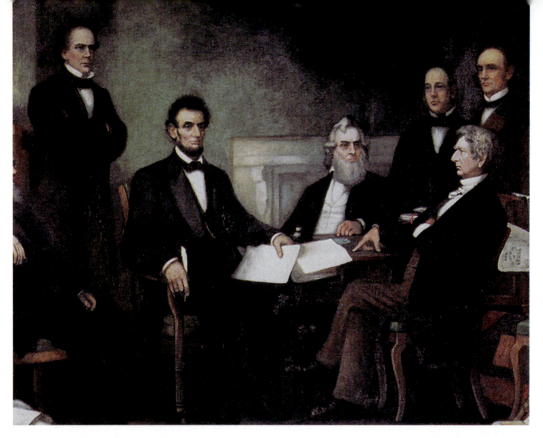

This painting shows Abraham Lincoln meeting with his cabinet to discuss the Emancipation Proclamation.

If I could save the Union without freeing any slave I would do it; and if I could save it by freeing all the slaves I would do it; and if I could save it by freeing some and leaving others alone I would also do that."

Early in the war Lincoln had felt that making emancipation the main goal of the war might divide the North. It might also turn people in the border states against the Union. However, the move to end slavery grew stronger. Finally, after the Battle of Antietam Creek, Lincoln decided the time had come for an emancipation order.

The Emancipation Proclamation, which Lincoln issued on January 1, 1863, said that all slaves living in those parts of the South that were still fighting against the Union would be "then, thenceforward, and forever free." The proclamation did not give all enslaved people instant freedom. The order was meant only for the states that had left the Union, not for the border states or for areas that had already been won back by the Union.

The Emancipation Proclamation hurt the South's hopes of getting help from Britain and France. Now that the war had become a fight against slavery, most British and French citizens, who opposed slavery, gave their support to the Union. Confederate President Jefferson Davis called Lincoln's proclamation "the most execrable [terrible] measure recorded in the history of a guilty man."

To celebrate the proclamation, it was reprinted on this poster.

As the Union troops advanced farther and farther into the Confederacy, they carried out the Emancipation Proclamation. Thousands of enslaved people fled to freedom behind the Northern battle lines, where they worked as laborers or joined the Union army or navy. By allowing freed slaves to serve in the military, the Emancipation Proclamation helped ease the Union army's shortage of soldiers.

REVIEW What was the Emancipation Proclamation?

Contributions from All

In both the North and the South, only men were allowed to join the army. Women, however, found many ways to help. They took over factory, business, and farm jobs that men left behind. They sent food to the troops, made bandages, and collected supplies. Many women, such as Clara Barton and Sally Tompkins, worked as nurses. Dorothea Dix worked as the supervisor of all nurses. A few women served as spies, and some even dressed as men and fought in battles.

About 180,000 African Americans eventually served in the Union army during the Civil War as well. They served in separate regiments, mostly under the command of white officers. At first they were not paid as much as white soldiers. They were also given poor equipment, and they often ran out of supplies. Despite these hardships, African American soldiers proved themselves on the battlefield. They led raids behind Confederate lines, served as spies and scouts, and fought in almost every major battle of the war.

The Union navy was open to African American men when the Civil War began. During the war the Union navy enlisted about 20,000 African American sailors. Among those who served was Robert Smalls. In 1862 Smalls and some other slaves took over a Confederate steamer in Charleston Harbor and surrendered it to Union forces.

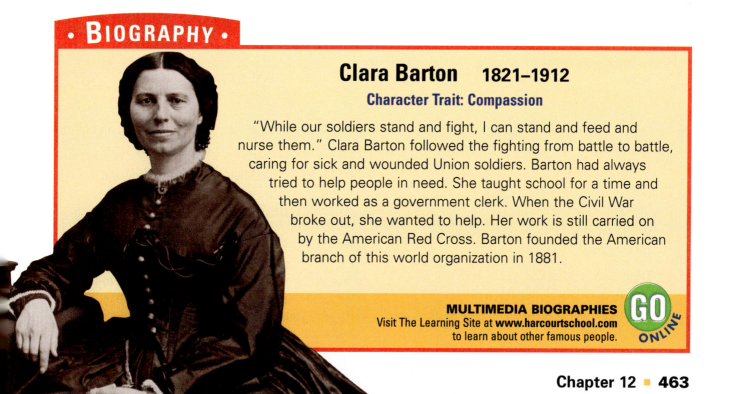

• BIOGRAPHY •

Clara Barton   1821–1912
Character Trait: Compassion

"While our soldiers stand and fight, I can stand and feed and nurse them." Clara Barton followed the fighting from battle to battle, caring for sick and wounded Union soldiers. Barton had always tried to help people in need. She taught school for a time and then worked as a government clerk. When the Civil War broke out, she wanted to help. Her work is still carried on by the American Red Cross. Barton founded the American branch of this world organization in 1881.

MULTIMEDIA BIOGRAPHIES
Visit The Learning Site at www.harcourtschool.com to learn about other famous people.

GO ONLINE

Chapter 12 • 463

African American troops (left) played a key role in support of the Union. Thousands of Hispanic Americans also took part in the war, with some fighting for the Union and others fighting for the Confederacy. Unlike African American soldiers, most Hispanic Americans served in regular army units.

European immigrants who came to this country for a better life marched off to preserve the Union, as well. There were Irishmen in the Fighting 69th, the Irish Zouaves, Irish Volunteers, and St. Patrick Brigade. Italians fought with the Garibaldi Guards and Italian Legion. Germans fought with the Steuben Volunteers, German Rifles, Turner Rifles, and DeKalb Regiment. In fact, the immigrant population in the Northern states helped the Union army replenish itself and eventually wear out a depleted Confederate army.

REVIEW How did African American soldiers help the Union during the war?

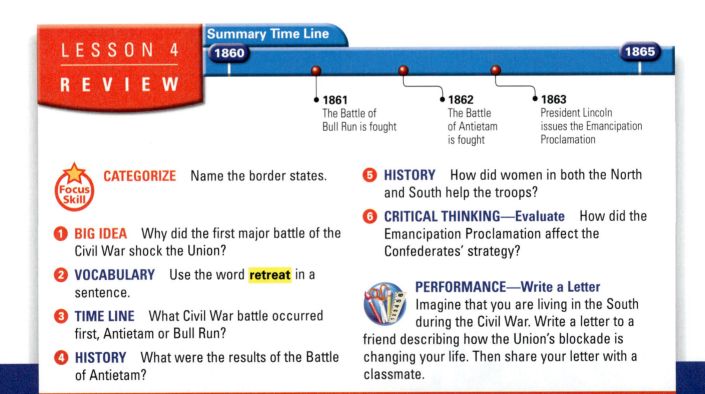

LESSON 4 REVIEW

Summary Time Line
- 1860
- 1861 The Battle of Bull Run is fought
- 1862 The Battle of Antietam is fought
- 1863 President Lincoln issues the Emancipation Proclamation
- 1865

CATEGORIZE Name the border states.

1 BIG IDEA Why did the first major battle of the Civil War shock the Union?

2 VOCABULARY Use the word **retreat** in a sentence.

3 TIME LINE What Civil War battle occurred first, Antietam or Bull Run?

4 HISTORY What were the results of the Battle of Antietam?

5 HISTORY How did women in both the North and South help the troops?

6 CRITICAL THINKING—Evaluate How did the Emancipation Proclamation affect the Confederates' strategy?

PERFORMANCE—Write a Letter Imagine that you are living in the South during the Civil War. Write a letter to a friend describing how the Union's blockade is changing your life. Then share your letter with a classmate.

The Road to Union Victory

1863–1865

· LESSON ·
5

CATEGORIZE
As you read, categorize key events as Union or Confederate victories.

BIG IDEA
Several key battles led to a Union victory.

VOCABULARY
address

The Emancipation Proclamation gave new hope to enslaved people and new spirit to the North. In the months that followed, the Union won several key battles and seemed to be winning the war. Across the South, very young men joined the army to replace soldiers who had been killed or wounded. In southern cities such as Richmond, Virginia, there was so little food that there were bread riots. Huge groups of people ran through the streets demanding bread.

Vicksburg and Chancellorsville

By May 1863 the Union army finally had a general as effective as Confederate General Robert E. Lee. His name was Ulysses S. Grant. One of Grant's first important battles began in May at Vicksburg, Mississippi, the Confederate headquarters on the Mississippi River.

Grant laid siege to the city. The Union guns pounded Vicksburg, and the Union army cut off all supplies to the city. The trapped Confederates, both soldiers and townspeople, soon ran out of food. Conditions were so bad that they had to tear down houses for firewood and dig caves in hillsides for shelter. Yet the people of Vicksburg were determined to endure whatever Grant had in store for them. One Vicksburg woman wrote, "We'll just burrow into these hills and let them batter away as hard as they please."

Ulysses S. Grant (right) used this box to carry his saddle and other field equipment.

• SCIENCE AND TECHNOLOGY •

The *H. L. Hunley*

In 1864 the *H. L. Hunley* became the first submarine to sink an enemy ship during wartime. Measuring just over 39 feet (12 m) long and just under 4 feet (1 m) wide, the *Hunley* was powered by crew members who cranked a propeller by hand. The submarine was built to ram a torpedo into a target and then back away, causing a trip line to set off the explosion. The design of the *Hunley* proved to be successful when it sank the Union warship *Housatonic*.

The diagram (above right) shows the inside of the Hunley (below).

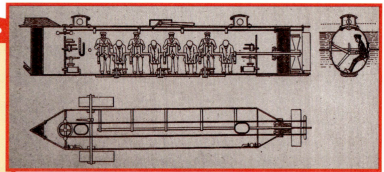

However, by July 4, 1863, the people of Vicksburg could hold out no longer. They finally surrendered.

Vicksburg proved to be a key victory. Its location gave the Union control of the Mississippi River. This, in turn, cut the Confederacy into two parts. The western states of the Confederacy were no longer able to communicate easily with the states to the east or to supply many reinforcements to them.

At about the same time that Grant started to lay siege to Vicksburg, General Lee and his army defeated a Union army at Chancellorsville, Virginia. In winning, however, Lee lost one of the South's best generals. In the confusion of battle, Stonewall Jackson was accidentally shot by one of his own troops and later died.

Despite Jackson's death, the victory at Chancellorsville gave the Confederacy confidence to try again to invade the North. The Confederates' goal was to win a victory on Northern soil.

If they could do so, the Confederates hoped people in the North would demand an end to the war. In June 1863, General Lee's troops headed north. They reached the small town of Gettysburg, Pennsylvania, on July 1.

REVIEW Did the Union or the Confederacy win at Vicksburg? at Chancellorsville?

 **CATEGORIZE**

The Battle of Gettysburg

General Robert E. Lee believed that victory at Gettysburg might turn the war in favor of the Confederacy. However, after two days of fighting, victory did not seem possible. In a final attempt on July 3, 1863, Lee ordered General George Pickett's entire division—15,000 soldiers—to make a direct attack. They were to charge across open country toward a stone fence at the Union army's center.

Marching shoulder to shoulder, Pickett's troops formed a line half a mile (0.8 km) wide. Steadily, the wall of soldiers in what came to be called Pickett's Charge moved forward. As the Confederates moved closer, they were met by the fire of Union guns, which controlled the higher ground of the battlefield. "Men were falling all around us, and cannon and muskets were raining death upon us," remembered a Confederate officer. "Still on and up the slope toward the stone fence our men steadily swept."

Pickett's soldiers reached the fence but were stopped there in fierce fighting. The charge had failed, and Pickett's men retreated, leaving behind half their number dead or wounded.

The Battle of Gettysburg was one of the deadliest battles of the Civil War. In fighting between July 1 and 3, 1863, more than 3,000 Union soldiers and nearly 4,000 Confederates were killed. More than 20,000 on each side were wounded or reported missing.

The fate of the Fourteenth Tennessee Regiment tells the story. When the battle began, there were 365 men in the unit. When the battle ended, there were only 3.

The Union victory at Gettysburg marked a turning point in the war. After the battle, General Lee's army retreated to Virginia. It would never again be able to launch a major attack against the Union.

This pin was worn on the hats of Civil War soldiers to indicate that they were foot soldiers.

REVIEW What was Pickett's Charge?

The Gettysburg Address

On November 19, 1863, President Lincoln went to Gettysburg to dedicate a cemetery for the Union soldiers who had died in the battle. A crowd of nearly 6,000 people gathered for the ceremony.

Lincoln gave a short speech, or **address**, that day. In fact, he spoke for less than three minutes. Lincoln's Gettysburg Address was so short that many people in the crowd were disappointed. Soon, however, people realized that this short speech was one of the most inspiring speeches ever given by a United States President.

In his address, Lincoln spoke to the heart of the war-weary North.

This scene, painted by James Walker, shows the battle at Gettysburg.

The Gettysburg Address

Four score and seven years ago our fathers brought forth on this continent a new nation, conceived in Liberty, and dedicated to the proposition that all men are created equal.

Now we are engaged in a great civil war, testing whether that nation or any nation so conceived and so dedicated, can long endure. We are met on a great battlefield of that war. We have come to dedicate a portion of that field, as a final resting place for those who here gave their lives that that nation might live. It is altogether fitting and proper that we should do this.

But, in a larger sense, we can not dedicate—we can not consecrate—we can not hallow—this ground. The brave men, living and dead, who struggled here, have consecrated it, far above our poor power to add or detract. The world will little note nor long remember what we say here, but it can never forget what they did here. It is for us the living, rather, to be dedicated here to the unfinished work which they who fought here have thus far so nobly advanced. It is rather for us to be here dedicated to the great task remaining before us—that from these honored dead we take increased devotion to that cause for which they gave the last full measure of devotion—that we here highly resolve that these dead shall not have died in vain—that this nation, under God, shall have a new birth of freedom—and that government of the people, by the people, for the people, shall not perish from the earth.

He spoke of the ideals of liberty and equality on which the nation had been founded. He honored the many soldiers who had died defending those ideals. He also called on the people of the Union to try even harder to win the struggle those soldiers had died for—to save the "government of the people, by the people, for the people" so that the Union would be preserved.

REVIEW Why did Lincoln give the Gettysburg Address?

The Road to Appomattox

In March 1864 Lincoln gave command of all the Union armies to General Ulysses S. Grant. Grant soon devised a plan to invade the South and destroy its will to fight. The plan called for an army under Grant's command to march to Richmond, the Confederate capital. At the same time a second army under General William Tecumseh Sherman was to march from Chattanooga, Tennessee, to Atlanta, Georgia.

As Sherman captured Atlanta, much of the city burned to the ground. The destruction of Atlanta, a manufacturing center and junction of several railroads, was a great loss for the Confederacy.

From Atlanta, Sherman's army of 62,000 men headed toward Savannah in a march that has become known as the March to the Sea. The army cut a path of destruction 60 miles (97 km) wide and 300 miles (483 km) long. Union soldiers burned homes and stores, destroyed crops, wrecked bridges, and tore up railroad tracks. When Sherman reached Savannah on December 22, 1864, he sent a message to President Lincoln. He wrote, "I beg to present you as a Christmas gift the city of Savannah."

From Georgia, Sherman turned north and marched through South Carolina, destroying even more than he had in Georgia. At the same time, General Grant moved south into Virginia. In his pursuit of General Lee's army, Grant cut off Lee's supply lines and kept pushing the Confederates in retreat. In early April 1865, Richmond was evacuated and set on fire by retreating Confederates. More than 900 buildings were destroyed and hundreds more were badly damaged. Union troops took control of the city.

General Lee's army moved west, with General Grant in constant pursuit. Lee's men were starving, and they were now outnumbered by 10 to 1. Lee could retreat no farther, nor could he continue to fight. Lee said, "There is nothing left for me to do but to go and see General Grant, and I would rather die a thousand deaths."

On the afternoon of April 9, 1865, Lee surrendered to Grant at Appomattox (a•puh•MA•tuhks) Court House, Virginia.

This painting shows General Lee (seated at left) surrendering to General Grant (seated at right) at the home of Wilmer McLean.

• HERITAGE •

Memorial Day

On May 5, 1866, people in Waterloo, New York, honored those who died in the Civil War. The people closed businesses for the day and decorated soldiers' graves with flowers. This was the beginning of the holiday known as Memorial Day, or Decoration Day. On this day Americans remember those who gave their lives for their country in all wars. Today most states observe Memorial Day on the last Monday in May.

People often celebrate this holiday by holding parades.

In a meeting at the home of Wilmer McLean, the two generals agreed to the terms of the Confederate army's surrender. After signing the surrender, Lee mounted his horse Traveller and rode back to his men.

In the next few weeks, as word of General Lee's surrender reached them, other Confederate generals surrendered, too. After four years of bloodshed the Civil War was over. The Union had been preserved, but at a horrible cost.

More than 600,000 soldiers had died during the war. Many died as a result of battle. Others, however, had died from disease. Thousands of soldiers also returned home wounded, scarred both physically and emotionally from the terrible devastation the war had brought.

REVIEW Why did Lee surrender to Grant?

LESSON 5 REVIEW

Summary Time Line

1863 — The Battle of Gettysburg; President Lincoln delivers his Gettysburg Address

1865 — The Civil War ends

 **CATEGORIZE** On what holiday do Americans remember those who gave their lives for their country in wars?

1 BIG IDEA What key battles led to a Union victory in the Civil War?

2 VOCABULARY Use the word **address** in a sentence about Abraham Lincoln.

3 TIME LINE Did Lincoln give his Gettysburg Address before or after the Civil War ended?

4 HISTORY What was the purpose of General Sherman's March to the Sea?

5 CRITICAL THINKING—Evaluate Why do you think people today still find meaning in the words of Lincoln's Gettysburg Address?

 PERFORMANCE—Make a Diorama
Make a diorama of one of the events described in the lesson. Then share your diorama with your classmates.

Chapter 12 ■ 471

· CHAPTER ·

12 Review and Test Preparation

Summary Time Line
1820

• **1820** Congress passes the Missouri Compromise

 **Categorize**

Copy the following graphic organizer onto a separate sheet of paper. Use the information you have learned to categorize important leaders and battles of the Civil War.

THINK & WRITE

Write a List of Questions Imagine you are a newspaper reporter in 1863. You have the opportunity to interview President Lincoln at the White House. Write a list of questions you would like to ask the President.

Write a Song The Civil War inspired the writing of many patriotic American songs, such as "The Battle Hymn of the Republic." Write a song to honor the soldiers who fought in the Civil War.

Timeline:
- 1845
- 1850 Congress passes the Compromise of 1850
- 1854 Congress passes the Kansas-Nebraska Act
- 1860 Abraham Lincoln is elected President
- 1861 The Civil War begins
- 1863 The Emancipation Proclamation is issued
- 1865 Lee surrenders at Appomattox Court House
- 1870

USE THE TIME LINE

Use the chapter summary time line to answer these questions.

1 In what year did the Civil War end?

2 How many years after the Missouri Compromise did the Civil War begin?

USE VOCABULARY

Use these terms to write a story about life in the United States during the Civil War.

states' rights (p. 436)

abolitionist (p. 448)

equality (p. 448)

secede (p. 453)

Confederacy (p. 453)

RECALL FACTS

Answer these questions.

3 What effect did the Kansas-Nebraska Act have on life in the Kansas Territory?

4 How did Harriet Tubman contribute to the abolitionist cause?

5 What were some of the causes of the Civil War?

Write the letter of the best choice.

6 One effect of the worldwide demand for Southern cotton was that —
  A it made Southern planters want to end slavery.
  B many new public schools were built in the South.
  C it created a need for more enslaved workers.
  D many new factories were built in the South.

7 During the Civil War, many European immigrants helped preserve the Union by—
  F serving as members of Congress.
  G working as Union spies.
  H donating money to the war effort.
  J serving in the Union army.

THINK CRITICALLY

8 How did changes brought about by the Industrial Revolution lead to conflicts between different regions in the United States?

9 Why do you think the North and South were not able to reach a compromise over slavery in 1861?

10 What do you think would have happened if Abraham Lincoln had waited until after the Civil War to issue the Emancipation Proclamation?

APPLY SKILLS

Identify Frame of Reference

11 The debate over states' rights was one of the issues that led to the Civil War. Explain how a Southern politician's view of states' rights might have been different from a Northern politician's.

Compare Maps with Different Scales

Study the two maps of Fort Sumter on pages 456 and 457. Then answer the following question.

12 Which map would you use if you wanted to see a more detailed view of Fort Sumter and the surrounding area? Explain.

DRAYTON HALL

During the Civil War, many of the South's plantation homes were destroyed or badly damaged. Drayton Hall managed to survive the conflict and today serves as a living history museum. Visitors can learn about its various buildings, farming methods, and the daily lives of those who once lived there.

LOCATE IT

· CHAPTER ·

13

The Nation Reunited

" The war is over—the rebels are our countrymen again. "

—Ulysses S. Grant, April 9, 1865, silencing his cheering troops after Robert E. Lee surrendered

 **Point of View**

When you determine someone's **point of view** on a subject, you identify that person's way of looking at it.

As you read this chapter, be sure to do the following.

- Determine different people's points of view about Reconstruction, industrial growth, and immigration.

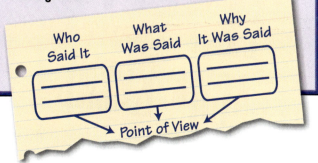

Chapter 13 ■ 475

· LESSON ·

1 Reconstruction

1820 — 1870 — 1920
1865–1870

POINT OF VIEW
As you read, look for different points of view about the rebuilding of the South.

BIG IDEA
The United States government tried to rebuild the South after the Civil War.

VOCABULARY
Reconstruction
assassinate
black codes
acquittal

The end of the Civil War brought the Confederacy to its end. Now it was time to try to bring the country back together. This time of rebuilding, called Reconstruction, had two distinct parts. The first part was the President's plan for Reconstruction. The second part was Congress's Reconstruction plan. Before Reconstruction could begin, however, one more tragedy would add to the country's pain.

One More Tragic Death

Before the Civil War ended, Abraham Lincoln was inaugurated for a second term as President. He realized he would face a challenging task in rebuilding the country. Lincoln, however, believed the South should not be punished for the war. He wanted to bring the country back together peacefully and as quickly as possible. Lincoln spoke of his plans for Reconstruction in his second inaugural address on March 4, 1865.

❝With malice toward none, with charity for all, with firmness in the right as God gives us to see the right, let us strive on to finish the work we are in, to bind up the nation's wounds. . . .❞

This poster announces Lincoln's plans to attend Ford's Theatre. Below are the glasses he wore that night.

FAST FACT
After shooting the President, John Wilkes Booth jumped onto the stage and cried out, "Sic semper tyrannis!," which means "Thus ever for tyrants" in Latin.

476

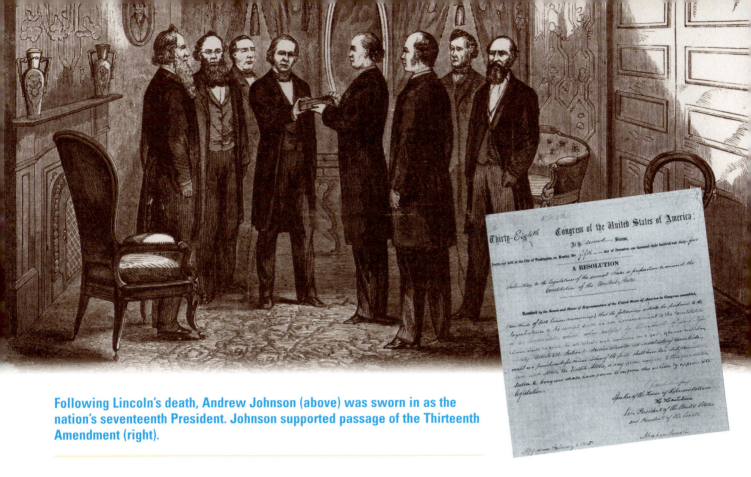

Following Lincoln's death, Andrew Johnson (above) was sworn in as the nation's seventeenth President. Johnson supported passage of the Thirteenth Amendment (right).

The President's plans were tragically cut short. On April 14, 1865, just five days after Lee's surrender, Lincoln went with Mary Todd Lincoln, his wife, to watch a play at Ford's Theatre in Washington, D.C. There he was assassinated—murdered in a sudden or secret attack—by John Wilkes Booth. Booth, an actor at Ford's Theatre, supported the Confederate cause.

Lincoln's death shocked the nation. Northerners had lost the leader who had saved the Union. Southerners had lost the leader who had promised an easy peace between the North and the South. Mary Chesnut, a Southerner, feared the worst. When she learned of Lincoln's death, Chesnut wrote in her diary, "Lincoln—old Abe Lincoln—killed. . . . I know this foul murder will bring down worse miseries on us."

REVIEW Why might many Southerners be upset by Lincoln's death?

The President's Plan

After Lincoln's death, the Vice President, Andrew Johnson, became President. Johnson returned the rights of citizenship to most Confederates who pledged loyalty to the United States. Their states then held elections, and state governments went back to work.

Johnson also said that the former Confederate states had to abolish slavery before they could rejoin the Union. To that end, the Thirteenth Amendment to the Constitution was ratified in December 1865. It ended slavery in the United States and its territories.

Such easy terms for rejoining the Union made many Northerners angry. They felt the Confederates were not being punished for their part in the war. White Southerners were again being elected to office and running state governments.

However, few people talked about the rights of the former slaves.

It was not long before the newly elected state legislatures in the South passed laws to limit the rights of former slaves. These laws, called **black codes**, differed from state to state. In most states, however, former slaves were not allowed to vote. In some they were not allowed to travel freely. They could not own certain kinds of property or work in certain businesses. They could be forced to work without pay if they could not find other jobs.

REVIEW Why was the Thirteenth Amendment to the Constitution ratified?

Congress's Plan

Congress was upset about what was happening in the South. As a result, Congress replaced the President's Reconstruction plan with one of its own.

As part of its plan, Congress did away with the new state governments and put the Southern states under military rule. Union soldiers kept order, and army officers were appointed to be governors. Before any Southern state could reestablish its state government, it had to write a new state constitution giving all men, both black and white, the right to vote.

Under its plan for Reconstruction, Congress sent Union troops to the Southern states. The troops in the photograph below are standing in front of a house in Atlanta, Georgia.

Johnson was the first President to be impeached. His trial in the Senate (above) drew large crowds of people.

BIOGRAPHY

Edmund G. Ross 1826–1907
Character Trait: Courage

Edmund G. Ross moved to Kansas in 1856 to lead the "free state" movement. He started two Kansas newspapers, the *Topeka Tribune* and the *Kansas State Record*, both of which supported this cause. During the Civil War, Ross became a major in the Union army. In 1866 he was appointed to the Senate, where despite pressure from other senators, he voted to acquit President Johnson.

MULTIMEDIA BIOGRAPHIES
Visit The Learning Site at
www.harcourtschool.com
to learn about other famous people.

A state also had to approve the Fourteenth Amendment. The Fourteenth Amendment states that all persons born in the United States, except Native Americans, and those who later become citizens are citizens of the United States and of the state in which they live. The amendment also protects the rights of all citizens.

President Johnson was very angry about this plan and about other laws Congress had passed to limit his authority as President. After Johnson fired a popular member of his cabinet in 1868, the House of Representatives voted to impeach him. The Senate put Johnson on trial. By just one vote, the Senate failed to get the two-thirds majority needed to remove Johnson from office. The final and deciding vote for **acquittal**, or a verdict of not guilty, was cast by Senator Edmund G. Ross of Kansas. Although Andrew Johnson stayed in office, he was no longer respected as a strong leader. In 1868 war hero Ulysses S. Grant was elected President instead.

REVIEW What was Johnson's point of view about Congress's plan? **POINT OF VIEW**

Reconstruction Governments

As the Southern states began to write new state constitutions and approve the Fourteenth Amendment, new elections were held. For the first time African Americans, such as Blanche K. Bruce and Hiram R. Revels of Mississippi, were elected to the United States Congress.

Many African Americans also served in the new Reconstruction governments in the Southern states. Jonathan C. Gibbs became secretary of state in Florida and helped set up Florida's public school system. Before this time, most schools in the South were privately run. Francis L. Cardozo, another African American, was secretary of state and, later, state treasurer in South Carolina.

Most Confederates accepted their defeat and the abolition of slavery.

Chapter 13 ■ 479

This poster (left) celebrates the passage of the Fifteenth Amendment (above).

However, many were against equal rights for African Americans. They did not want African Americans to vote or to hold office, and they opposed the Reconstruction governments.

Congress then proposed the Fifteenth Amendment to the Constitution. It states that no citizen shall be denied the right to vote because of "race, color, or previous condition of servitude." This amendment, which was ratified in 1870, was designed to extend voting rights and to enforce them by law.

REVIEW What is the Fifteenth Amendment?

LESSON 1 REVIEW

Summary Time Line

- **1865** Abraham Lincoln is assassinated; The Thirteenth Amendment is ratified
- **1868** The Fourteenth Amendment is approved
- **1870** The Fifteenth Amendment is ratified

POINT OF VIEW How did President Lincoln think the South should be treated after the Civil War ended?

1. **BIG IDEA** How did the United States government try to rebuild the South after the Civil War?

2. **VOCABULARY** Use the words **Reconstruction** and **black codes** in a sentence about the South after the Civil War.

3. **TIME LINE** When did the Fifteenth Amendment become part of the Constitution?

4. **HISTORY** Which amendment ended slavery in the United States?

5. **CRITICAL THINKING—Evaluate** Why did many white Southerners oppose the new Reconstruction governments?

PERFORMANCE—Conduct an Interview Imagine that you are a news reporter. Write an interview with President Andrew Johnson, a senator who supports Congress's plan for Reconstruction, or an African American elected to serve in a Reconstruction government in the South. Provide both questions and answers. Then share your interview with classmates.

The South After the War

1820 — 1870 — 1920
1865–1877

· LESSON ·
2

 POINT OF VIEW
As you read, determine different points of view held by Southern citizens after the war ended.

BIG IDEA
The South faced many challenges after the war.

VOCABULARY
freedmen
sharecropping
carpetbagger
scalawag
secret ballot
segregation

When the Civil War ended, much of the South was in ruins. The money issued by the Confederacy was worthless, and most Confederate banks were closed. Entire cities had been burned, and many railroads, bridges, plantations, and farms had been destroyed. As one Southerner remembered, "All the talk was of burning homes, houses knocked to pieces, . . . famine, murder, desolation."

The years following the war were hard ones for all people in the South. For the more than 4 million former slaves living there, however, those years also brought new hope.

The Freedmen's Bureau

In March 1865, even before the war ended, the United States Congress set up the Bureau of Refugees, Freedmen, and Abandoned Lands—the Freedmen's Bureau, as it was called. It aided all needy people in the South, although **freedmen**—men, women, and children who had been slaves—were its main concern.

Many former slaves, like those shown outside this Freedmen's Bureau school (below), were eager to learn to read and write. Many of the teachers in those schools were Northern women.

481

Many former slaves were wandering through the country looking for the means to start a new life. The Freedmen's Bureau gave food and supplies to these people. It also helped some white farmers rebuild their farms. The most important work of the Freedmen's Bureau, however, was education. Newly freed slaves were eager to learn to read and write. To help meet this need, the Freedmen's Bureau built more than 4,000 schools and hired thousands of teachers.

The Freedmen's Bureau also wanted to help former slaves earn a living by providing them with land to farm, but this plan did not work. The land was to have come from the plantations taken or abandoned during the war, but the federal government decided to give those plantations back to their original owners. In the end, most former slaves were not given any land. Without money to buy land of their own, they had to find work where they could.

REVIEW Why was the Freedmen's Bureau set up?

This photograph (left) shows people going to an early Juneteenth celebration. Many people, such as those participating in this parade in Austin, Texas (below), celebrate Juneteenth.

• HERITAGE •

Juneteenth

Abraham Lincoln had issued the Emancipation Proclamation on January 1, 1863. But because Union troops did not control Texas at the time, the order had little effect there. On June 19, 1865, Union soldiers landed in Galveston, Texas. On that day Union General Gordon Granger read an order declaring that all slaves in Texas were free. Today people in Texas and across the country celebrate June 19, or Juneteenth, as a day of freedom. It is a holiday marked by picnics, parades, and family gatherings.

Sharecropping

In their search for jobs, many former slaves went back to work on plantations. Planters welcomed them. Fields needed to be plowed, and crops needed to be planted. Now, however, planters had to pay the former slaves for their work.

Because there was not much money available in the years following the war, many landowners paid workers in shares of crops rather than in cash. Under this system, known as **sharecropping**, a landowner gave a worker a cabin, mules, tools, and seed. The worker, called a sharecropper, or tenant farmer, then farmed the land. At harvesttime the landowner took a share of the crops to cover the cost of the worker's housing. What was left was the worker's share.

Sharecropping gave landowners the help they needed to work the fields. It also gave former slaves work for pay. Yet few people got ahead through sharecropping. When crops failed, both landowners and workers suffered. Even in good times, most workers' shares were very little, if anything at all.

REVIEW How were workers paid in a sharecropping system?

Using tools like this plow, many former slaves worked as sharecroppers in the years following the Civil War.

Carpetbaggers and Scalawags

To rebuild bridges, buildings, and railroads, the South's Reconstruction governments had to increase taxes. In Louisiana, for example, taxes almost doubled. Mississippi's taxes were 14 times higher than they had been. White Southerners blamed the higher taxes on African American state legislators and on other state government leaders they called carpetbaggers and scalawags.

Carpetbaggers were people from the North who moved to the South to take part in Reconstruction governments. They were called carpetbaggers because many of them carried their belongings in suitcases made of carpet material. Some of them truly wanted to help. Others were looking for an opportunity for personal gain.

Chapter 13 ■ 483

James Longstreet believed that building factories would help the South rebuild its economy.

A **scalawag** (SKA•lih•wag) is a rascal, someone who supports a cause for his or her own gain. Many scalawags were white Southerners who had opposed the Confederacy. Some were thinking only of themselves. Others felt they were doing what was best for the South.

Among the most famous of the scalawags was James Longstreet, a former Confederate general. Longstreet believed that the South needed to cooperate with the North in order to prosper. He and other leading business people wanted to build factories to lessen the South's dependence on agriculture.

REVIEW Why did Southerners blame higher taxes on state legislators and other state government leaders? **POINT OF VIEW**

Reconstruction Ends

Many white Southerners did not want their way of life to change. Burdened by heavy taxes and a changing society, they began to organize to regain their authority. One way to do so was to control the way people voted.

In the 1860s there was no secret ballot, as there is today. A **secret ballot** is a voting method that does not allow anyone to know how a person has voted. Before the secret ballot was used, the names of voters and how they voted were published in newspapers.

Secret societies were formed to keep African Americans from voting or to make sure they voted only in certain ways. Those who joined the secret societies included white Southerners who resented the fact that African Americans were now considered their equals. Members of one secret society, the Ku Klux Klan, used violence to keep African Americans from voting or to make sure they voted as they were told.

Over time, white Southerners once again took control of their state governments and society. Despite the Fifteenth Amendment, new state laws were passed that made it very difficult, if not impossible, for African Americans to vote. African Americans also were required to go to separate schools and churches and to sit in separate railroad cars. Laws such as these led to **segregation**, or the

Many carpetbaggers who came to the South during Reconstruction carried their belongings in bags made of carpet material.

The Fifteenth Amendment guaranteed African Americans the right to vote, as seen in this illustration. With the end of Reconstruction, however, that right was again denied to most African Americans living in the South.

practice of keeping people in separate groups based on their race or culture.

Reconstruction was over by 1877. In that year the last of the Union troops left the South. The rights and freedoms that African Americans had won were again being taken away in the South. By 1900 African Americans in many of the Southern states were not allowed to vote, and few held public office.

REVIEW How did white Southerners take back control of their state governments and society?

LESSON 2 REVIEW

Summary Time Line

1865 — The Freedmen's Bureau is founded
1877 — Reconstruction ends

POINT OF VIEW How did members of the Ku Klux Klan feel about African Americans being allowed to vote?

1. **BIG IDEA** What challenges did the South face after the Civil War?

2. **VOCABULARY** Use the words **carpetbagger** and **scalawag** in a sentence about the South after the Civil War.

3. **TIME LINE** When did Reconstruction end?

4. **ECONOMICS** Why was it difficult for sharecroppers to get ahead?

5. **CRITICAL THINKING—Analyze** In what ways did the Freedmen's Bureau help African Americans? In what ways did it fail?

PERFORMANCE—Write a List Write a list of things you would have done to help rebuild the South after the Civil War. Be sure to include ways in which you would have helped the newly freed slaves, as well as the economies of the Southern states. Share your list with the rest of the class.

LESSON 3

Settling the Last Frontier

1850–1890

 POINT OF VIEW

As you read, identify the points of view that different settlers and explorers had about the West.

BIG IDEA
Many people decided to move to the West after the Civil War.

VOCABULARY
boom
refinery
prospector
bust
long drive
homesteader
open range
reservation

After the Civil War, many Americans moved to the Great Plains, the Rocky Mountains, and the Great Basin. Among those settlers were soldiers who had fought in the war and freed African Americans. They believed this last frontier would provide them with new opportunities.

Miners

After the California gold rush of 1849, new discoveries of gold and silver brought more miners to the West and supplied new sources of mineral wealth for the nation. Thousands of miners hurried to Colorado after gold was found near Pikes Peak in 1858. The next year, news of huge deposits of silver in the area known as the Comstock Lode drew thousands to what is now Nevada. Between 1862 and 1868, other finds in present-day Arizona, Idaho, Montana, and Alaska added to the West's **boom**, or time of fast economic or population growth.

When gold or silver was discovered in a place, miners moved into the area hoping to strike it rich. They claimed

Many stores in towns that were abandoned in the late 1800s are once again open for business. Stores, such as the one mentioned in this poster (left), were closed.

486 ■ Unit 6

land and set up camps, which often grew into towns. Some towns sprang up almost overnight as people quickly started businesses and farms and built refineries. A **refinery** is a factory where metals, fuels, and other materials are cleaned and made into usable products.

Fights often broke out among the **prospectors**, or those searching for gold, silver, and other mineral resources. The towns had no sheriffs, and law and order did not exist. "Street fights were frequent," one writer reported, "and . . . everyone was on his guard against a random shot." As mining towns grew, families began to arrive. Many mining towns set up governments and started schools, hospitals, and churches.

In most places all of the gold or silver was mined in just a few years. When that happened, the miners left to look for new claims and the mining town was often abandoned. Just as quickly as a boom built a town, a **bust**, or time of fast economic decline, left a town lifeless. Some of these abandoned towns, called ghost towns, can still be seen in the West today.

REVIEW What brought miners to the West?

Ranchers

Settlers had many resources available to them in the West. The Pacific Ocean made trade with China easier. Settlers trapped wild animals for the fur trade and built fisheries along the coast. One of the most plentiful natural resources was the grassland. The West's vast grasslands attracted many ranchers to the region. Large-scale cattle ranching had begun in Texas in the early 1800s. After the Civil War, however, as cities in the East grew, the demand for beef increased. Ranchers could make more money if they could get their cattle to eastern markets.

At first Texas ranchers drove, or herded, their cattle to port cities, such as Galveston, Texas, for shipment to New Orleans and to cities in the East. In the late 1860s, a cheaper, faster method became available as railroads were built out West. Between 1867 and 1890, ranchers drove about 10 million head of cattle north to the railroads on **long drives**.

The long drives followed cattle trails such as the Sedalia Trail, which went from Texas to Sedalia, Missouri.

Chapter 13 • 487

Cattle Trails

Movement This map shows the four major cattle trails used by ranchers in the 1880s.

 Which trail led to both Abilene and Ellsworth?

Other trails—the Chisholm, the Western, and the Goodnight-Loving—led to other "cow towns" along the railroads. Abilene, Kansas; Ogallala, Nebraska; and Cheyenne, Wyoming, were towns that grew at the end of cattle trails. At each town the cattle were loaded onto railroad cars and sent to Chicago. There the animals were prepared for market. The meat was then sent in refrigerated freight cars to markets in the East.

REVIEW How were railroads important to Texas ranchers?

Barbed wire was used to build fences on the Great Plains.

Saddles and hats like these were used by ranchers on long drives.

Homesteaders

In 1862 Congress passed the Homestead Act. This law opened the Great Plains to settlers by giving 160 acres of land to any head of a family who was over 21 years of age and who would live on the land for five years. Thousands of Americans, as well as about 100,000 immigrants from Europe, rushed to claim those plots of land called homesteads. The people who settled them were known as **homesteaders**.

Living on the Great Plains was very difficult. There were few streams for water or trees for wood. Many settlers used sod to build their houses, but sod houses were difficult to keep clean. Dirt often fell from the sod ceiling onto the furniture. Drought, dust storms, and floods were common in the summer, and homesteaders worried about prairie fires. In winter, snow and bitterly cold temperatures froze the region. Insects, too, were a problem. In 1874, grasshoppers came by the millions, turning the sky black and eating anything that was green.

Many homesteaders saw the Great Plains as a "treeless wasteland." They believed that the tough sod and dry soil were unsuited for farming, and they left. Those who stayed used new technologies to solve some of the challenges the land presented. They used an improved steel plow, invented by James Oliver of Indiana, to cut through the thick sod. They used new models of windmills to pump water from the ground. They planted Russian wheat, which needed less water, and used reapers to harvest it.

Relations with ranchers posed another problem for farmers. It was difficult to grow crops in the same area where cattle ranchers kept their herds. To keep the cattle out of their fields, farmers began using wire with steel points, known as barbed wire, to build fences. Some ranchers also built fences to keep their cattle from wandering off the ranches.

Fences often kept farmers from reaching the water they needed for their crops and kept ranchers from reaching the water they needed for their cattle. Fences also blocked some cattle from reaching the millions of acres of government land that ranchers used as **open range**, or free grazing land.

Movement This map shows the areas of the United States that were settled by 1870 and 1890. Among the settlers was this Nebraska family (right), who used sod to build their home.

❓ What happened to the frontier as settlers moved west?

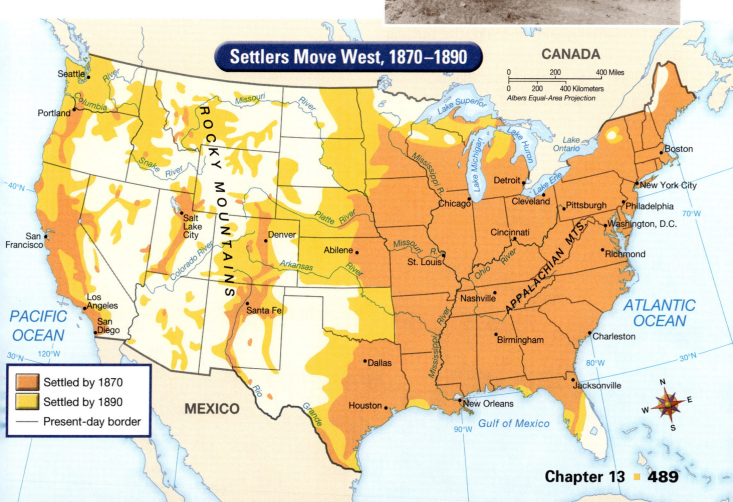

Farmers and ranchers began cutting one another's fences. Some people even started shooting one another. These fights, called range wars, went on through the 1880s until ranchers were told they had to move their cattle off government land.

In spite of these problems, about 5 million homesteaders had migrated to the Great Plains by 1890. So many people had moved there and to lands farther west, in the Rocky Mountains and the Great Basin, that in 1890 the Census Bureau declared the last frontier "closed."

REVIEW How did many homesteaders view the Great Plains? **POINT OF VIEW**

Conflict in the West

Many of the Native American groups on the Great Plains had long depended on the buffalo for their needs. As railroads were built and settlers began using the land for farming and ranching, the buffalo began to die out. By 1880 fewer than 1,000 were left on the Great Plains.

With fewer buffalo and the loss of their hunting lands, many Plains Indian leaders signed treaties with the United States. Those treaties set up reservations for the Indians. A **reservation** is an area of land set aside by the government for use only by Native Americans.

Sometimes Indian groups were forced onto the reservations. In the 1860s members of the Sioux Nation continued to roam the Black Hills region of present-day

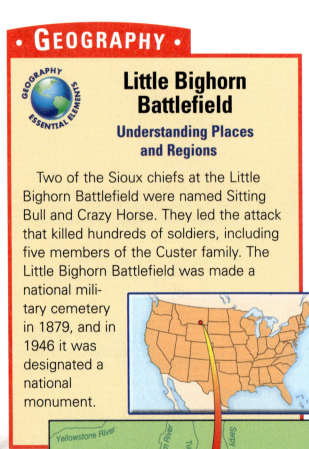

· GEOGRAPHY ·

Little Bighorn Battlefield
Understanding Places and Regions

Two of the Sioux chiefs at the Little Bighorn Battlefield were named Sitting Bull and Crazy Horse. They led the attack that killed hundreds of soldiers, including five members of the Custer family. The Little Bighorn Battlefield was made a national military cemetery in 1879, and in 1946 it was designated a national monument.

South Dakota and Wyoming. After gold was discovered in the Black Hills, the United States sent soldiers to move all the Sioux to reservations.

In June 1876 Lieutenant Colonel George Custer led an attack against the Sioux and their Cheyenne allies at the Little Bighorn River. As many as 2,000 Indian warriors surrounded Custer and his men. In the battle that followed, about 225 soldiers were killed, but the Sioux were later defeated. The fighting ended in 1880 when hundreds of Sioux were killed at the Battle of Wounded Knee in South Dakota.

In 1877 the United States government also ordered the Nez Perce (NES PERS) Indians in Eastern Oregon to move to a reservation in Idaho. The Nez Perce leader, Chief Joseph, led a group of 800 in an attempt to escape to Canada. They were stopped and surrendered without a fight. Chief Joseph told his people, "I am tired of fighting."

Chief Joseph

Other groups did not give up as easily. In the Southwest, an Apache chief named Geronimo led a series of attacks against the United States army. During the 1870s and 1880s Geronimo and his warriors won many battles. In spite of his efforts, though, he was eventually forced to surrender and move to a reservation. By 1880 almost all Native Americans in the United States had been moved onto reservations. In 1924 Congress granted citizenship to all Native Americans. In 1934 it gave Indians on reservations the right to govern themselves.

REVIEW Why did Custer attack the Sioux?

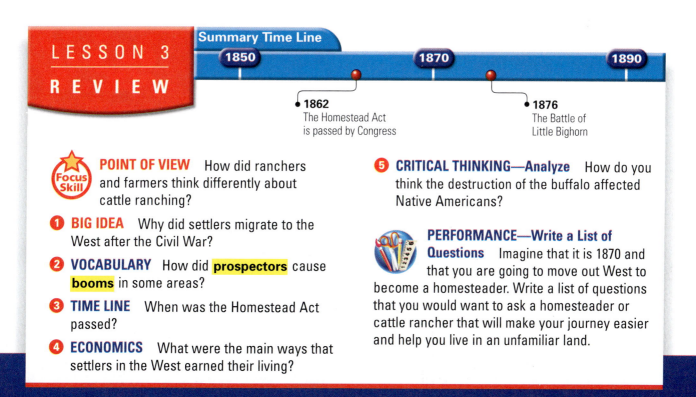

LESSON 3 REVIEW

Summary Time Line
1850 — 1870 — 1890
- 1862 The Homestead Act is passed by Congress
- 1876 The Battle of Little Bighorn

POINT OF VIEW How did ranchers and farmers think differently about cattle ranching?

1 BIG IDEA Why did settlers migrate to the West after the Civil War?

2 VOCABULARY How did **prospectors** cause **booms** in some areas?

3 TIME LINE When was the Homestead Act passed?

4 ECONOMICS What were the main ways that settlers in the West earned their living?

5 CRITICAL THINKING—Analyze How do you think the destruction of the buffalo affected Native Americans?

PERFORMANCE—Write a List of Questions Imagine that it is 1870 and that you are going to move out West to become a homesteader. Write a list of questions that you would want to ask a homesteader or cattle rancher that will make your journey easier and help you live in an unfamiliar land.

SKILLS Use a Climograph

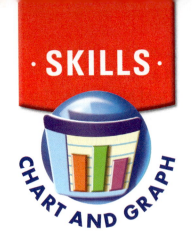

VOCABULARY
climograph

WHY IT MATTERS

In the late 1800s many Americans who moved from eastern cities to the Great Plains were surprised by much of what they found there. However, probably nothing surprised them more than the extremes of temperature and precipitation.

If you and your family were moving to another place, you would want to know more about its climate before you moved there. One way to learn about the climate of a place is to study a climograph, or climate graph. A **climograph** shows on one graph the average monthly temperature and the average monthly precipitation for a place. Comparing climographs can help you understand differences in climates.

WHAT YOU NEED TO KNOW

The climographs on page 493 show the average monthly temperature and precipitation for Omaha, Nebraska, and Philadelphia, Pennsylvania. The temperatures are shown as a line graph. The amounts of precipitation are shown as a bar graph. The months are listed along the bottom of each climograph, from January to December.

Along the left-hand side of each climograph is a Fahrenheit scale for temperature. A point is shown on the climograph for the average temperature for each month. These points are connected with a red line. By studying the line, you can see which months are usually warm and which are usually cold.

Along the right-hand side of each climograph is a scale for precipitation. The average monthly amounts of precipitation are shown in inches. By studying the heights of the blue bars, you can see which months are usually dry and which are usually wet.

Pioneers who settled on the Great Plains sometimes experienced ice storms. These storms covered fences, plants, and the ground with a layer of ice.

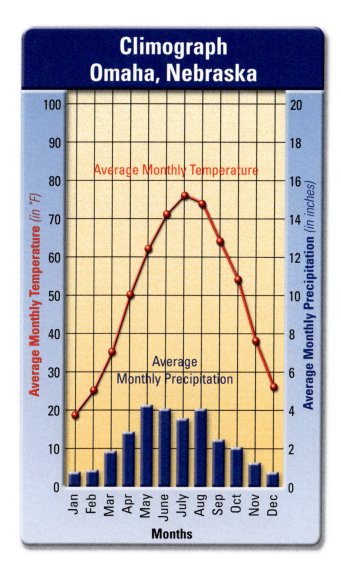

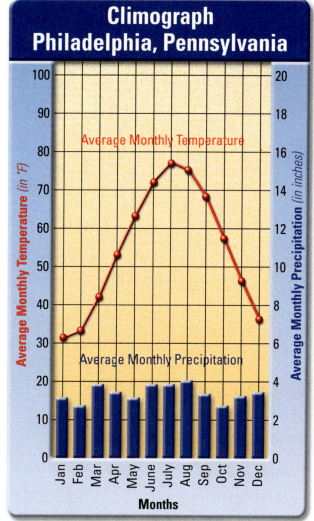

PRACTICE THE SKILL

Use the climographs above to answer the following questions.

1. Which is the warmest month in each of these cities? Which is the coolest?
2. What is the wettest month in each city?
3. What is the driest month in each city?
4. Which city receives more precipitation during the year?
5. What is the average temperature for each place in January?
6. How much precipitation falls during January in each place?

APPLY WHAT YOU LEARNED

Use an almanac, an encyclopedia, or the Internet to create a climograph for your city or for a city close to where you live. Compare your climograph with the ones shown on this page. Which place shows the greatest changes in temperature and precipitation? Share your findings with a family member or friend. Then discuss why people might need to know this kind of information.

CHART AND GRAPH SKILLS

Chapter 13 ■ 493

LESSON 4

The Rise of New Industries

1820 — 1870 — 1920
1860–1900

Focus Skill
POINT OF VIEW
As you read, determine ways in which points of view changed as businesses and cities grew.

BIG IDEA
The United States economy grew and changed in the late 1800s.

VOCABULARY
free enterprise
transcontinental railroad
entrepreneur
petroleum
capital
human resource

After the Civil War great changes took place in the American economy. Inventors developed new technologies that made it easier for people to travel and communicate with one another. It was an important time for **free enterprise**—an economic system in which people are able to start and run businesses with little control by the government.

The Transcontinental Railroad

From 1860 to 1900, the railroad network in the United States grew rapidly. Railroads were used for travel and to move raw materials to factories and finished products to market. The people who owned the railroads made millions of dollars. They became known as tycoons, or powerful businesspeople. By 1900 a **transcontinental railroad** crossed the entire continent of North America. The transcontinental railroad was actually made

FAST FACT
A train trip from New York to California on the transcontinental railroad typically took from 10 to 12 days. For $100, people could sit on plush seats in fancy cars. For $40, they had to sit on hard benches in plain cars.

494

up of a number of different lines, including the Union Pacific Railroad and the Central Pacific Railroad. Together they linked the Atlantic and Pacific coasts and opened the nation's vast interior to people who wanted to settle there. They also made trade between different parts of the country easier, which caused the economy to grow.

One reason for the growth of railroads was the development of new inventions that improved rail transportation. George Westinghouse's air brake made trains safer by stopping not only the locomotive but also each car. Granville T. Woods improved the air brake and also developed a telegraph system that allowed trains and stations to communicate.

The transcontinental railroad crossed both the Rocky Mountains and the Sierra Nevada. Workers had to build bridges across valleys, cut ledges on mountainsides, and blast tunnels through mountains. At Promontory, Utah, on May 10, 1869, workers laid the last of the transcontinental railroad. A ceremonial golden spike was driven into place.

REVIEW How did the transcontinental railroad help the economy grow?

The Steel Industry

Railroads needed strong, long-lasting tracks. At first, iron rails were used. With bigger and heavier locomotives, however, iron rails were no longer strong enough. Steel rails would be harder and last longer than iron, but steel was much more expensive to make.

In 1872 Andrew Carnegie, an entrepreneur (ahn•truh•pruh•NER) from Pittsburgh, Pennsylvania, visited Britain. An **entrepreneur** is a person who sets up and runs a business. In Britain, Carnegie saw a new process for making steel. Invented by Henry Bessemer, this process melted iron ore and other metals and materials together in a new kind of coal-fired furnace, called a blast furnace.

A CLOSER LOOK
Transcontinental Railroad

To complete the transcontinental railroad, workers often worked long hours in dangerous conditions. Most of the workers were Chinese and Irish immigrants.

1. Workers used tools, such as pickaxes and shovels, to clear tunnels.
2. A small locomotive powered machines that hauled dirt and rock to the surface.
3. Explosives were used to blast through rock.
4. Workers stayed behind a protective wall during tunnel blasting.
5. Workers on the transcontinental railroad laid more than 1,776 miles (2,858 km) of track.

 What kinds of work did immigrant workers have to do to build the transcontinental railroad?

It was called a blast furnace because blasts of air were forced through the molten metal to burn out the impurities. This process made the steel stronger.

Back in Pennsylvania, Carnegie found investors to help him build a steel mill. By the early 1870s, Carnegie's steel business was so successful that he built more steel mills and bought coal and iron mines to supply them. Then he bought ships to carry these natural resources to his mills. With his mines and ships, he could make a greater supply of steel at a lower cost than other mills could.

By the 1890s Andrew Carnegie had become one of the wealthiest people in the world. Some people called Carnegie and other rich entrepreneurs "robber barons" because they had become so wealthy from their businesses. However, Carnegie also gave much of his wealth to build libraries and schools.

Other industries quickly discovered new uses for steel. In the 1880s William Jenney used steel frames to build taller buildings. People called these tall buildings skyscrapers because they seemed to scrape the sky.

John Roebling, a German immigrant, used steel cables and beams to build suspended bridges. One of his bridges, the Brooklyn Bridge, still links Manhattan with Brooklyn, in New York City.

As the demand for steel increased, more steel mills were built. In the late 1800s, large deposits of iron ore were discovered in the Mesabi Range, west of Lake Superior. To be nearer to those resources, the steel industry spread to cities along the Great Lakes, such as Cleveland, Ohio, and Chicago, Illinois.

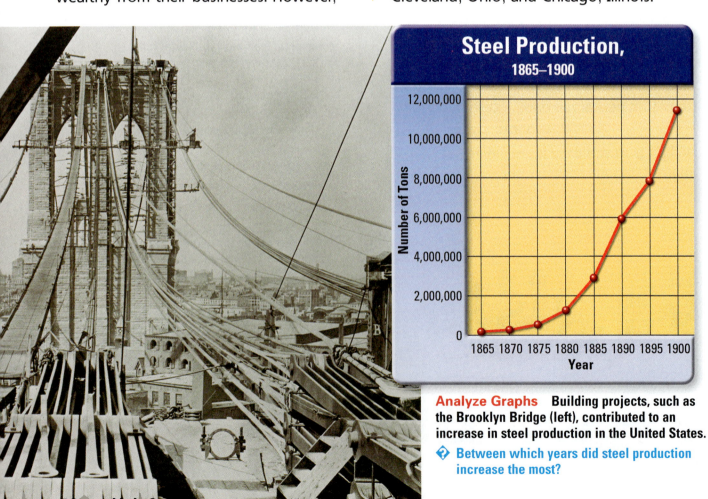

Analyze Graphs Building projects, such as the Brooklyn Bridge (left), contributed to an increase in steel production in the United States.

❖ Between which years did steel production increase the most?

Ships and railroads carried raw materials to steel mills and carried steel to factories and cities across the nation.

REVIEW Why did the steel industry spread to cities along the Great Lakes?

The Oil Industry

For years people had been aware of the petroleum, or oil, that gathered on ponds in western Pennsylvania and other places. Then, in the 1840s, a Canadian scientist named Abraham Gesner discovered that petroleum burned well. When kerosene, a fuel made from petroleum, became widely used for lighting lamps, the demand for petroleum increased. This caused its price to rise.

In 1859 Edwin Drake drilled an oil well in Titusville, Pennsylvania. When the well began producing large amounts of oil, an oil boom took place. Oil towns soon sprang up all over western Pennsylvania and eastern Ohio.

John D. Rockefeller was 23 years old in 1863 when he invested money to build an oil refinery near Cleveland. The money needed to set up or improve a business is called capital. Rockefeller steadily invested more capital, buying up some of the other 30 refineries in the Cleveland area. In 1867 he combined his refineries into one business, which he called the Standard Oil Company.

To cut costs and be more efficient, Rockefeller bought other businesses. His company built its own barrels, pipelines, warehouses, and tank cars. As a result, it could produce and distribute oil products at the lowest prices. Other companies could no longer compete and were driven out of the oil business.

Analyze Graphs Drake's oil well (right) produced large amounts of oil. Such discoveries led to increases in oil production in the United States.

◆ About how many barrels of oil were produced in 1900?

Industry in the United States, 1890s

Regions This map shows industrial areas and resource regions in the United States about 1890.

❓ In which part of the United States were most industrial areas found?

By 1882 the Standard Oil Company controlled almost all of the oil refining and distribution in the United States and much of the world's oil trade as well. After the gasoline engine was invented and automobiles came into use, Rockefeller's oil refineries turned to producing gasoline and engine oil.

REVIEW How did John D. Rockefeller believe he could make his company more profitable?
🎯 **POINT OF VIEW**

Thomas Alva Edison

One of the most important inventors and industrial leaders in the United States was Thomas Alva Edison. Growing up, Edison had learned about the telegraph. Samuel Morse's telegraph, patented in the 1840s, was the nineteenth century's equivalent of the World Wide Web.

While studying the telegraph, Edison learned some of the practical uses of electricity. This knowledge led to his first serious invention in 1869, an electrical vote recorder for the Massachusetts State Legislature. Two years later, in 1871, Edison started a laboratory in Newark, New Jersey. At the time, Newark was known for its many fine machinists. Those machinists were just the kind of **human resources**—the workers and the ideas and skills they bring to their jobs—that Edison needed.

In 1874 Edison's laboratory developed a telegraph system that could send more than one message over a single wire. With the money he earned from selling that telegraph system, Edison opened a laboratory in Menlo Park, New Jersey, in 1876. That laboratory averaged one patented invention every five days. The best known was the first practical electric lightbulb. Among the others was an improved telephone, an invention that Alexander Graham Bell had patented in 1876.

In 1882 Edison set up the first central power station in New York City. It made electricity available to large parts of the city. Less than 10 years later, hundreds of communities all over the United States had Edison power stations. With Edison's help, electricity soon became an important source of power for American homes, offices, and industries.

REVIEW What was Edison's best-known patented invention at Menlo Park?

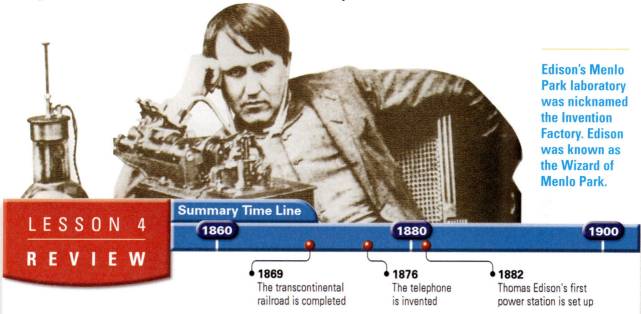

Edison's Menlo Park laboratory was nicknamed the Invention Factory. Edison was known as the Wizard of Menlo Park.

LESSON 4 REVIEW

Summary Time Line

1860 — 1869 The transcontinental railroad is completed — 1876 The telephone is invented — 1880 — 1882 Thomas Edison's first power station is set up — 1900

 POINT OF VIEW How do you think John D. Rockefeller felt about the benefits of the free enterprise system?

1. **BIG IDEA** How did the United States economy change in the years after the Civil War?

2. **VOCABULARY** Use the word **entrepreneur** in a sentence about **free enterprise**.

3. **TIME LINE** When was the transcontinental railroad completed?

4. **ECONOMICS** How did the discovery of oil help the United States economy grow?

5. **CRITICAL THINKING—Analyze** How did Andrew Carnegie contribute to the growth of cities?

PERFORMANCE—Write "Who Am I" Questions Write a list of "Who Am I" questions about some of the people you read about in this lesson. Ask your classmates the "Who Am I" questions and see if they can identify who you are.

EXAMINE PRIMARY SOURCES

Edison's Inventions

In his lifetime, Thomas Edison obtained more than 1,000 patents, the most the United States Patent Office has ever issued to one person. Edison invented items that were just for pleasure, as well as devices to solve problems people faced in their everyday lives. These are some of the inventions Edison and his workers produced.

FROM THE HENRY FORD MUSEUM AND GREENFIELD VILLAGE AND THE SMITHSONIAN INSTITUTION NATIONAL MUSEUM OF AMERICAN HISTORY

The electric lightbulb (left) was invented in 1879. The electric pen (right) was invented in 1874.

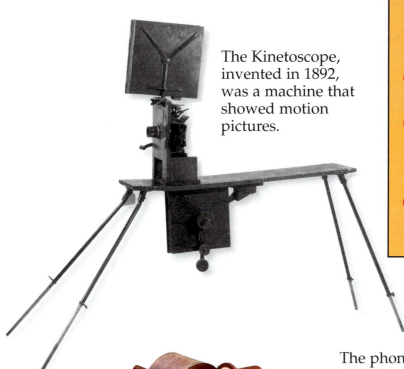

The Kinetoscope, invented in 1892, was a machine that showed motion pictures.

> ### Analyze the Primary Source
>
> 1. Which of these inventions looks familiar to you?
> 2. Identify the purpose of each invention. Which inventions do you think made people's lives easier?
> 3. Explain how one or more of Edison's inventions might work.

The phonograph (left), patented in 1878, is still thought of as Edison's most original invention. The electronic stock ticker (below) was used to print out stock information.

ACTIVITY

Think Critically Make a list of tasks or jobs that you do often. Beside each item on your list, name the tools or appliances that you use to help make the task easier. Do you think you would be able to do the same tasks if the tools or appliances had not been invented?

RESEARCH

 Visit The Learning Site at www.harcourtschool.com to research other primary sources.

Chapter 13 ■ 501

LESSON 5

A Changing People

1820 — 1870 — 1920

1880–1920

 POINT OF VIEW
As you read, determine how points of view about immigration differed.

BIG IDEA
Immigrants to the United States faced problems in the past.

VOCABULARY
old immigration
new immigration
advertisement
tenement
prejudice
regulation

Like its economy, the population of the United States grew and changed after the Civil War. Between 1860 and 1910, about 23 million immigrants arrived on our shores. Those from Europe settled mostly in the cities of the East and Middle West. Those from Asia, Mexico, and parts of Central America and South America settled mostly in the West. Immigrants from all over the world played an important part in the growth of industry and agriculture in the United States.

Immigrants Old and New

European immigrants were by far the largest group to come to the United States. Before 1890 most immigrants from Europe came from northern and western Europe. They were part of the **old immigration**. That is, they came from the same parts of the world as earlier immigrants. The largest groups were from Britain, Germany, and Ireland. Others came from countries such

Between 1890 and 1920, nearly 16 million immigrants from Europe arrived in the United States. The passport below belonged to the Flinck family, from Sweden.

502

Irving Berlin (left) was one of the millions of immigrants who came to the United States. As a result of immigration, many cities, like New York City (above), grew very quickly.

as Denmark, Norway, and Sweden. These were the immigrants who helped build the Erie Canal and transcontinental railroad and who took part in settling the West.

Beginning about 1890, a period of **new immigration** began. People still came from the countries of northern and western Europe, but now most came from countries in southern and eastern Europe and from other parts of the world. Those from Europe came from countries such as Austria, Hungary, Italy, Greece, Poland, and Russia.

Most of the new immigrants from Europe were poor, and they had few opportunities in their homelands. They came to the United States hoping to find a better life. Many of them learned about jobs in the United States through advertisements. An **advertisement** is a public announcement that tells people about a product or an opportunity. Railroad, coal, and steel companies in the United States placed advertisements in other countries to attract new workers.

Most of the new immigrants settled in cities. They tended to live among people from their own country, with whom they shared a common language and familiar customs. Many lived with relatives, crowded together in poorly built apartment buildings called **tenements**. Wages were so low that everyone in the family—even young children—had to work to earn enough money for food.

In spite of the difficult conditions, many new immigrants succeeded. One of these people was Irving Berlin. He and his family moved to New York City from Russia in 1893. While Berlin was a boy, his father died. To help support his family, Berlin performed as a street singer and singing waiter. He began to write song lyrics and published his first song in 1907. During his life, Berlin wrote more than 800 songs, including "God Bless America," perhaps his most famous song.

REVIEW How did many immigrants learn about jobs in the United States?

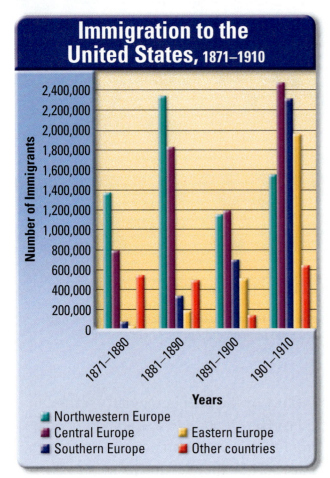

Analyze Graphs This graph compares the number of immigrants for different periods of time.

◆ When did the number of immigrants from central Europe first become larger than the number from northwestern Europe?

Immigrants from Asia

Immigrants from China first came to the United States in large numbers after the California gold rush. By 1852 about 25,000 Chinese were working in the goldfields.

As less and less gold was found, some Chinese immigrants returned home. But most stayed and looked for other kinds of work. They often worked for low wages because above all they wanted to stay in the United States. In the 1860s Chinese workers played an important part in building the transcontinental railroad. Some Chinese immigrants set up businesses in California or other parts of the West.

Immigrants from Japan and other countries in Asia also began to enter the United States and find opportunities in the West. Most found jobs in agriculture, mainly in California. Some bought their own land.

Over time, thousands of immigrants came to the United States from Asia. However, the number of Asian immigrants remained small when compared to the number of immigrants who came from Europe.

REVIEW Why did large numbers of Chinese people first come to the United States?

Reaction to Immigrants

Many people born in the United States reacted harshly to the immigrants. Some Americans felt that because many of the immigrants had little education, they were not qualified to take part in a democracy. Others worried that the newcomers would take jobs away from American workers. As a result, many immigrants faced prejudice. **Prejudice** is an unfair feeling of hate or dislike for

These three children and their families came to the United States from Asia. Most immigrants were searching for new opportunities and a better life.

members of a certain group because of their background, race, or religion.

Immigrants were sometimes taunted and called unkind names. They were denied jobs by many businesses, and certain businesses even posted signs that said things such as "Irish need not apply." Jewish immigrants were denied access to the better universities and often found it difficult to get jobs. Some immigrants also suffered physical attacks, and many were ridiculed for their religious beliefs. These anti-immigrant feelings led to the formation of groups that pressured Congress to pass laws that would limit the number of immigrants who could enter the country.

In the West there had been opposition to Asian immigrants for a long time. Their language, appearance, and customs were unfamiliar to most native-born Americans. As feelings against the Chinese grew, numerous **regulations**, or controls, were set up. Some states in the West passed laws that made life harder for the Chinese. Chinese people could not

· BIOGRAPHY ·

Hiram L. Fong   1906–
Character Trait: Perseverance

Hiram Fong's parents left China to work on sugarcane plantations in Hawaii, where Hiram Fong was born. To earn money, young Hiram shined shoes and sold newspapers. He worked hard to earn enough to attend school. In time he graduated from law school. He dedicated himself to public service and was elected to Hawaii's legislature. Later he served four terms in the United States Congress as the nation's first Chinese American senator.

MULTIMEDIA BIOGRAPHIES
Visit The Learning Site at
www.harcourtschool.com
to learn about other famous people.
GO ONLINE

get state jobs, and their lawsuits would not be heard by state courts.

In 1882 the United States Congress passed the Chinese Exclusion Act. This act excluded, or kept out, all new Chinese workers. It prevented any Chinese workers from coming to the United States for ten years. By the early 1900s many Americans were calling for a stop to all immigration from Asia. Instead of passing such laws, however, the United States government persuaded Asian countries such as Japan to allow only a small number of its people to come to the United States.

REVIEW Why did many Americans react harshly to immigrants? **POINT OF VIEW**

African Americans on the Move

Even as immigrants were moving to the United States from other countries, people within the United States were moving from place to place. This was true of many different groups of Americans, including African Americans. Many African Americans were looking for new places to live and work.

Many African Americans migrated from the South to the West. There they started farms or found job opportunities they did not have in the South. Some African Americans who had fought in the Civil War stayed in the Army and became part of units formed to fight against Native Americans in the West. The Indians gave the African American troops the name buffalo soldiers because they saw the same fighting spirit in the soldiers that they saw in the buffalo.

Most African Americans who did not move after the end of the Civil War found jobs in the South, often as sharecroppers. Few African Americans moved to the cities because they could not find work there. That changed between 1915 and 1930, when many African Americans moved north. This movement of people came to be known as the Great Migration.

One of the main reasons for the Great Migration was that many African Americans working on farms in the South were going through hard times. Floods had damaged many farms, and year after year an insect called the boll weevil had

This painting by artist Jacob Lawrence depicts the Great Migration. In it African Americans are shown leaving the South for cities in the North.

destroyed the cotton crop. At the same time, jobs began to open up in the North.

Many African Americans found factory jobs in large cities such as Boston, Chicago, Cleveland, Detroit, New York, Pittsburgh, Cincinnati, and St. Louis. Newspapers owned by African Americans in those cities actively encouraged this migration. "Get out of the South," advised the *Chicago Defender*. "Come north." As many as 500,000 people did.

Before the early 1900s nearly 90 percent of African Americans lived in the South. Because of the Great Migration, more than half of all African Americans now live in the North and in the Middle West. Most have parents, grandparents, or great-grandparents who were part of the huge movement north.

Jacob Lawrence's parents moved to the North in the early 1900s as part of the Great Migration.

Jacob Lawrence's parents moved north in the early 1900s. Lawrence went to art school in New York City and became a painter. He wrote in his book *The Great Migration*, "Life in the North brought many challenges, but the migrants' lives had changed for the better. The children were able to go to school, and their parents gained the freedom to vote. And the migrants kept coming. Theirs is a story of African-American strength and courage. I share it now as my parents told it to me, because their struggles and triumph ring true today. People all over the world are still on the move, trying to build better lives for themselves and for their families."

REVIEW What was the Great Migration?

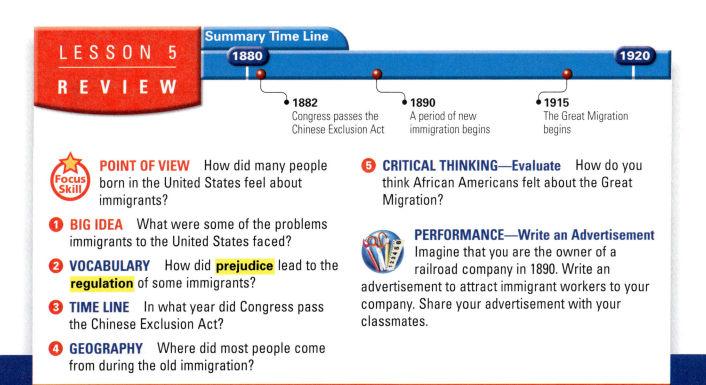

LESSON 5 REVIEW

Summary Time Line
- 1880
- 1882 — Congress passes the Chinese Exclusion Act
- 1890 — A period of new immigration begins
- 1915 — The Great Migration begins
- 1920

POINT OF VIEW How did many people born in the United States feel about immigrants?

1 BIG IDEA What were some of the problems immigrants to the United States faced?

2 VOCABULARY How did **prejudice** lead to the **regulation** of some immigrants?

3 TIME LINE In what year did Congress pass the Chinese Exclusion Act?

4 GEOGRAPHY Where did most people come from during the old immigration?

5 CRITICAL THINKING—Evaluate How do you think African Americans felt about the Great Migration?

PERFORMANCE—Write an Advertisement Imagine that you are the owner of a railroad company in 1890. Write an advertisement to attract immigrant workers to your company. Share your advertisement with your classmates.

Chapter 13 ■ 507

CHAPTER 13 Review and Test Preparation

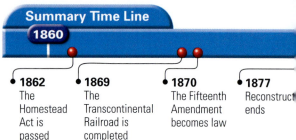

Summary Time Line

- **1862** The Homestead Act is passed
- **1869** The Transcontinental Railroad is completed
- **1870** The Fifteenth Amendment becomes law
- **1877** Reconstruction ends

Focus Skill: Point of View

Copy the following graphic organizer onto a separate sheet of paper. Use the information you have learned to describe different points of view about Abraham Lincoln and Reconstruction.

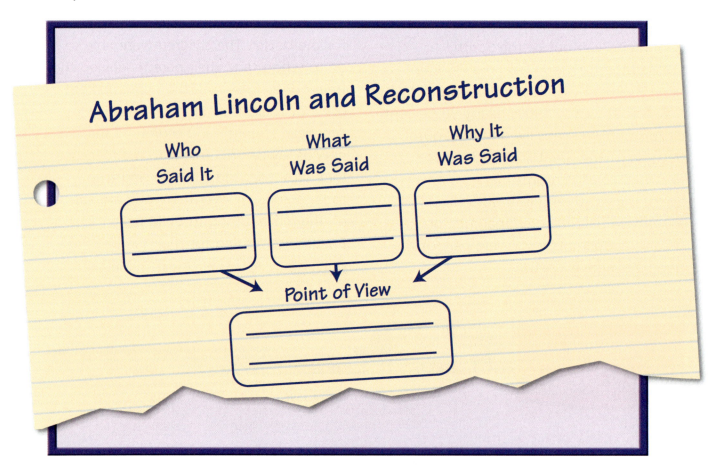

THINK & WRITE

Write a Folktale Many American folktales grew out of the nation's western experience. Imagine you are hiking in the west when you come upon a ghost town. Write a folktale about your discovery and the miners and business owners who once lived there.

Write a Letter Immigrants to the United States have always been presented with both opportunities and challenges. Imagine you are a nineteenth-century immigrant trying to adjust to your new home. Write a letter to a friend describing your situation and hopes for the future.

1915 The Great Migration begins

USE THE TIME LINE

Use the chapter summary time line to answer these questions.

1 When was the Transcontinental Railroad completed?

2 Did Reconstruction end before or after the Fifteenth Amendment was passed?

USE VOCABULARY

For each pair of terms, write a sentence that explains how the terms are related.

3 **freedmen** (p. 481), **segregation** (p. 484)

4 **long drive** (p. 487), **open range** (p. 489)

5 **entrepreneur** (p. 495), **capital** (p. 497)

6 **new immigration** (p. 503), **tenement** (p. 503)

RECALL FACTS

Answer these questions.

7 Why was the Fifteenth Amendment passed?

8 What challenges did Native Americans face in the years after the Civil War?

9 What was the main reason for the Great Migration?

Write the letter of the best choice.

10 The Fourteenth Amendment was passed to—
 A end slavery in the United States.
 B establish the Freedmen's Bureau.
 C give citizenship to all people born in the United States—including former slaves.
 D give every United States citizen the right to vote regardless of his or her race.

11 The most important work of the Freedmen's Bureau was—
 F to ensure voting rights for all African American males.
 G to promote African American political candidates.
 H to decide whether President Johnson should be removed from office.
 J to educate newly freed slaves.

12 The main reason oil production greatly increased in the late ninteenth century was because—
 A ranchers often traded their herds for oil.
 B people used kerosene to light their lamps.
 C homesteaders used petroleum to kill insects.
 D oil was used to fuel trains.

THINK CRITICALLY

13 Why do you think Southern state legislatures passed black codes after the Civil War?

14 How do you think the Great Migration affected the economy of the United States?

15 Why do you think many homesteaders chose to move west despite all the difficulties?

APPLY SKILLS

Use a Climograph
Study the climographs on page 493. Then answer the following questions.

16 What is the average temperature for each city in August?

17 How much precipitation falls during August in each city?

Chapter 13 ■ 509

VISIT

THE GETTYSBURG
NATIONAL MILITARY PARK

GET READY

The largest battle of the Civil War was fought near the town of Gettysburg, Pennsylvania. Today, nearly 6,000 acres of that battlefield have been preserved. On a visit to the Gettysburg National Military Park, a guide can lead you on an informative tour that highlights significant events of the Battle of Gettysburg. At the battlefield you can see more than 1,400 monuments and markers dedicated to the soldiers who fought and lost their lives during the three-day battle.

WHAT TO SEE

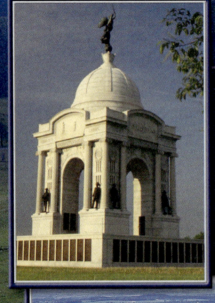

The Pennsylvania Memorial (left) is the largest monument at the Gettysburg National Military Park. It honors the Pennsylvania soldiers who fought at Gettysburg. The Gettysburg National Cemetery (below) was dedicated by President Abraham Lincoln in 1863.

LOCATE IT

Actors dressed as Union and Confederate soldiers reenact Civil War battles at the Gettysburg National Military Park.

TAKE A FIELD TRIP

A VIRTUAL TOUR
Visit The Learning Site at www.harcourtschool.com to find virtual tours of historical sites in the United States.

A VIDEO TOUR
Check your media center or classroom library for a videotape tour of the Gettysburg National Military Park.

Unit 6 ■ 511

UNIT 6

Review and Test Preparation

VISUAL SUMMARY

Write a Letter Study the pictures and captions below to help you review Unit 6. Then choose one of the events shown. Write an informative letter to a friend describing the event and how you think it will change the country.

USE VOCABULARY

Use a term from this list to complete each of the following sentences.

tariffs (p. 436)

acquittal (p. 479)

homesteaders (p. 488)

1 Senator Edmund G. Ross cast the deciding vote for the ____ of Andrew Johnson.

2 Before the Civil War, the North and South disagreed on the issue of ____.

3 Nearly 100,000 European immigrants became ____ on the Great Plains.

RECALL FACTS

Answer these questions.

4 How did enslaved people resist slavery?

5 What is the free enterprise system?

Write the letter of the best choice.

6 The conflict that started the Civil War took place at—
  A Williamsburg, Virginia.
  B Fort Sumter, South Carolina.
  C Gettysburg, Pennsylvania.
  D Antietam Creek, Maryland.

7 One major effect of the Civil War was that—
  F the United States never again admitted a new state to the Union.
  G Northerners were not allowed to settle in the South.
  H Southerners were not allowed to vote.
  J the Southern economy suffered many hardships.

Visual Summary

1820 — 1845 — 1870

1820 The Missouri Compromise p. 438

1850 Congress passes the Compromise of 1850 p. 439

1854 The Kansas–Nebraska Act is passed p. 439

South Carolina Coast, 1861

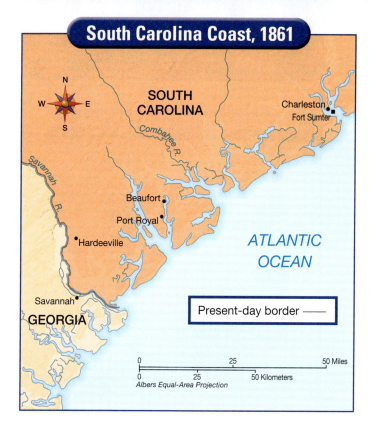

8. During Reconstruction the Southern states were under military rule because—
   A the Fourteenth Amendment to the Constitution allowed Congress to do so.
   B Abraham Lincoln's assassination angered many Northerners.
   C legislators began to pass laws limiting the rights of former slaves.
   D it was a way to return the rights of American citizenship to most Confederates.

Think Critically

9. Lincoln once was called "the miserable tool of traitors and rebels." Today he is thought of as a great leader. Why might someone at the time have been so critical of him?

10. What do you think would have happened if the South had won the Battle of Gettysburg?

11. How did the growth of railroads in the United States play an important role in the growth of the country? Explain your answer.

12. Why did many immigrants come to the United States?

Apply Skills

Compare Maps with Different Scales

Use the map on this page and the maps on pages 456–457 to answer the following questions.

13. Compare the map on this page to Map B on page 457. Which map would you use to find the distance between Fort Sumter and the city of Charleston, South Carolina?

14. Compare the map on this page to Map A on page 456. Which map would you use to find the South Carolina–Georgia border?

1861 The Civil War begins   p. 454

1865 General Lee surrenders at Appomattox Court House   p. 469

1890 The steel industry is a big business in the United States   p. 496

Unit Activities

Visit The Learning Site at www.harcourtschool.com for additional activities.

Draw a Map

Work together to draw a map of the United States at the time of the Civil War. Use different colors for the states of the Union, the states of the Confederacy and the border states. Write the date on which each Southern state seceded. Draw diagonal lines on the border states. Label the capitals of the North and the South and the major battle sites. Use your map to tell your classmates about the Civil War.

Make a Chart

Work together in a group to make a chart titled *How New Laws Affected the Lives of Americans After the Civil War*. The first section of your chart should show how new national and state laws affected African Americans. The second section should show how new laws affected Southerners. The third section should show how new laws affected Northerners. Present your completed chart to your classmates.

VISIT YOUR LIBRARY

- **When Jessie Came Across the Sea** by Amy Hest. Candlewick Press.

- **Tales from the Underground Railroad** by Kate Connell. Steck-Vaughn.

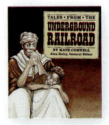

- **Across the Lines** by Carolyn Reeder. Simon & Schuster.

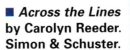

COMPLETE THE UNIT PROJECT

Hall of Fame Work with a group of your classmates to finish the unit project—a hall of fame honoring individuals who showed strength and bravery before, during, or after the Civil War. Your group should choose five people from this unit to include in your hall of fame. Then design a poster that includes short biographies as well as drawings or pictures of the people you have chosen. Display your group's finished poster together with those of your classmates.

From Past to Present

GEORGIA CONNECTION

Apollo 11 mission patch

GEORGIA CONNECTION

FAMOUS GEORGIANS

Many Georgians worked to rebuild their state after Reconstruction. Over time, many people have worked to make Georgia a better place in which to live.

John Emory Bryant worked to get equal rights for freed African Americans. He set up schools, provided African Americans with land, and gave them legal assistance.

Lucille Hegamin was a pioneer African American blues recording artist. She was very popular, and she was often called the "Georgia Peach." Born in Macon, Georgia, Hegamin was the second African American blues singer to record. In 1929, she had her own radio show in New York City, and in 1934, she retired. She worked as a nurse until she returned to recording in 1961 and 1962.

Jimmy Carter grew up in Plains, Georgia, where he worked as a peanut farmer. He later served as a senator and then as governor of the state. In 1976, Carter was elected President. Since he left office, he has worked for peace in the United States and in other parts of the world. In 2002, he received the Nobel Peace Prize.

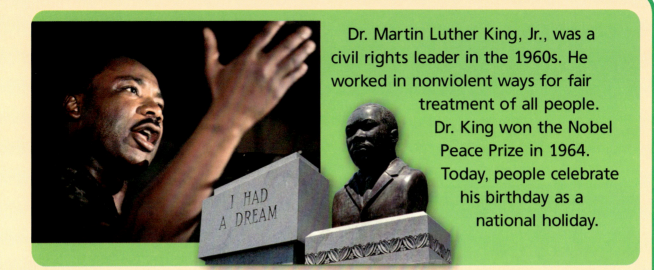

Dr. Martin Luther King, Jr., was a civil rights leader in the 1960s. He worked in nonviolent ways for fair treatment of all people. Dr. King won the Nobel Peace Prize in 1964. Today, people celebrate his birthday as a national holiday.

Margaret Mitchell was born in Atlanta, Georgia. She worked as a journalist until 1926, when she started writing the novel *Gone With the Wind*. This book won the Pulitzer Prize and the National Book Award in 1937. Two years later, the book was made into a movie, and it won eight Academy Awards. Today, *Gone With the Wind* is one of the best-selling books of all time.

★ CRCT TEST PREP

1 Who wrote the novel *Gone With the Wind*?
- A Dr. Martin Luther King, Jr.
- B Jimmy Carter
- C John Emory Bryant
- D Margaret Mitchell

2 Before becoming President, Jimmy Carter worked as
- A a journalist.
- B a peanut farmer.
- C a blues singer.
- D a novelist.

3 Lucille Hegamin did NOT
- A work as a nurse.
- B become the second African American blues singer to record songs.
- C serve as a senator.
- D have her own radio show in New York City.

4 Dr. Martin Luther King, Jr., won
- A the Pulitzer Prize.
- B an Academy Award.
- C the Nobel Peace Prize.
- D the National Book Award.

John F. Kennedy Space Center, Cape Canaveral, Florida

UNIT 7

From Past to Present

> " That's one small step for [a] man, one giant leap for mankind. "
>
> —Neil Armstrong, July 20, 1969, from the *Eagle* moon lander

Preview the Content

Read the lesson titles. Then fill in the first two columns of the chart with information about recent United States history. After you have read the unit, fill in the last column.

K (What I Know)	W (What I Want to Know)	L (What I Have Learned)

Preview the Vocabulary

Related Words Words that are related have meanings that are connected in some way. Using the vocabulary terms **aviation**, **suburb**, **nonviolence**, and **patriotism**, make a chart of words that are related to each vocabulary term.

UNIT 7 PREVIEW

The United States 2001

Key Events

1860 — **1890** — **1920**

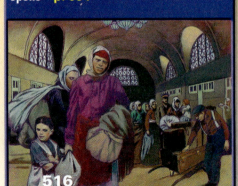

1892 Ellis Island immigrant station opens p. 534

1917 The United States enters World War I p. 577

1941 Japan attacks Pearl Harbor p. 579

START with a STORY

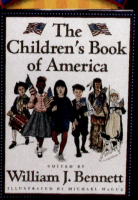

THE EAGLE HAS LANDED

Edited by William J. Bennett
Illustrated by Michael Hague

In 1962 John Glenn became the first American astronaut to orbit Earth. Then a series of explorations called the Apollo program prepared for a moon landing. In 1968 astronauts in *Apollo 8* first circled the moon. By the next year the National Aeronautics and Space Administration, or NASA, was ready to try a moon landing. On July 16, 1969, *Apollo 11* blasted off from Cape Canaveral, Florida. On board were astronauts Neil Armstrong, Edwin "Buzz" Aldrin, Jr., and Michael Collins. Once they were circling the moon, Armstrong and Aldrin climbed into the landing vehicle named the *Eagle*. Michael Collins stayed behind in case he needed to help the other two astronauts. NASA scientists at Mission Control in Houston, Texas, followed their flight closely. Now read the story of the first moon landing.

"*Eagle*, you are go for landing. Go!"

The spacecraft continued downward.

Armstrong turned to the window to look for their landing zone. He did not like what he saw. They were not where they were supposed to be.

The computer was programmed to steer the ship to a flat, smooth place for a landing. But it had overshot its target. They were plunging straight toward an area littered with deadly rocks and craters.

A light blinked on the control panel. They were running out of landing fuel.

There was no time to waste. Armstrong gripped the hand controller and took command from the computer. He had to find a place where they could set down, fast, or they would have to fire their rockets and return to space.

Gently he brought the *Eagle* under his control. The lander hovered as Armstrong searched the ground below for a level spot.

"Sixty seconds," the voice from Mission Control warned.

Sixty seconds of fuel left.

Balanced on a cone of fire, the *Eagle* scooted over rocky ridges and yawning craters.

There was no place to land!

"Thirty seconds!"

Now there was no turning back. If the engines gulped the last of the landing fuel, there would be no time to fire the rockets that could take them back into orbit. They would crash.

The landing craft swooped across boulder fields as its pilot hunted, judged, and committed. Flames shot down as the *Eagle* dropped the last few feet. Dust that had lain still for a billion years flew up and swallowed the craft.

Back on Earth, millions of people held their breaths and waited. They prayed and listened.

Then Neil Armstrong's faint voice came crackling across the gulf of space.

"Houston, Tranquillity Base here. The *Eagle* has landed."

In a short while a hatch on the lander opened. A man in a bulky space suit backed down nine rungs of a ladder and placed his foot on the gray lunar soil. People all over the world watched the fuzzy black-and-white images on their television screens. They leaned toward their sets to catch the first words spoken by Neil Armstrong from the surface of the moon.

"That's one small step for man, one giant leap for mankind."

A few minutes later Buzz Aldrin crawled out of the *Eagle* to join his comrade. Together the astronauts planted a flag. It would never flap in a breeze on the airless moon, so a stiff wire held it out from its pole. Aldrin stepped back and saluted the Stars and Stripes.

America had made the age-old dream come true. When they departed, our astronauts left behind a plaque that will always remain. Its words proclaim:

> HERE MEN FROM THE PLANET EARTH
> FIRST SET FOOT UPON THE MOON
> JULY, 1969 A.D.
> WE CAME IN PEACE FOR ALL MANKIND

Analyze the Literature

1. Why did Neil Armstrong take control of the *Eagle*?
2. What kinds of problems do you think the scientists at NASA had to solve in building a spacecraft to carry people to the moon?

READ A BOOK

START THE UNIT PROJECT

A Class Newspaper With your classmates, create a newspaper about the 20th century. As you read the unit, make a list of key people, places, and events. This list will help you decide which people, places, and events to feature in articles in your newspaper.

USE TECHNOLOGY

 Visit The Learning Site at www.harcourtschool.com for additional activities, primary sources, and other resources to use in this unit.

Unit 7 ■ 521

GOLDEN GATE BRIDGE

The Golden Gate Bridge was built during the 1930s to link San Francisco with the growing cities on the north side of San Francisco Bay. Fog often covered San Francisco, so the bridge designers wanted the Golden Gate to be painted a bright color. They chose reddish orange. The bridge opened in 1937. Almost 2 miles (3 km) long, it was the longest bridge in the world at that time.

LOCATE IT

CALIFORNIA
San Francisco

CHAPTER 14

Changes in the United States

> "Nothing is done in this country as it was done twenty years ago."
> —Woodrow Wilson, *The New Freedom,* 1913

Predict an Outcome

When people make **predictions,** they use information and past experiences to try to determine what will happen next.

As you read this chapter, be sure to do the following.

- Predict likely outcomes for certain historical events.

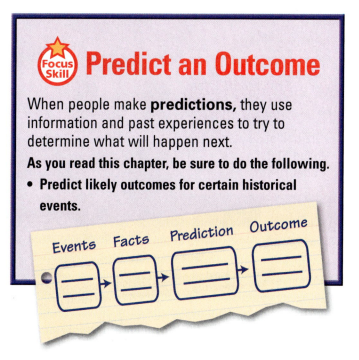

LESSON 1

New Ideas and New Inventions

1900–2000

 PREDICT AN OUTCOME

As you read, predict likely outcomes of the changes that took place during the twentieth century.

BIG IDEA
New ideas and new inventions changed the way people lived during the twentieth century.

VOCABULARY
assembly line
labor union
strike
aviation
satellite
Internet
jazz

In the early 1900s, many people lived and worked on farms. They used horses and buggies for travel, and it was slow and expensive to ship goods across the country. Soon all this changed. The twentieth century transformed life in the United States.

Changing Industries

In 1900 about 60 percent of Americans lived on farms and about 40 percent lived in cities. In cities, people often had to

FAST FACT
The Model T Ford was introduced in 1908 and by 1918 half of all cars in the United States were Model T Fords.

524 • Unit 7

work long hours at home making goods by hand. The average adult worker earned only $15 a week for 58 hours of work. As cities grew, though, more and more people began to work in factories.

Henry Ford, a car maker, changed the way people worked in factories. His company was the first in the United States to use the **assembly line**, a moving belt that took a partly finished product from one worker to the next. This helped people do more work in less time. Soon many factories began using assembly lines. As factories started making more products, workers began spending more time at their jobs.

Henry Ford

During the early 1900s, many companies made their employees work long hours for little pay. As a result many employees joined **labor unions**, or groups of workers who tried to get better wages and working conditions. When companies refused to improve wages or job conditions, the workers went on **strike**, which means they refused to work. Over time millions of workers joined labor unions. By the 1950s about one-third of all American workers belonged to a labor union. People were earning more money, and new industries created new jobs.

One of the century's most important changes in industry started in 1946, when scientists built the first electronic computer.

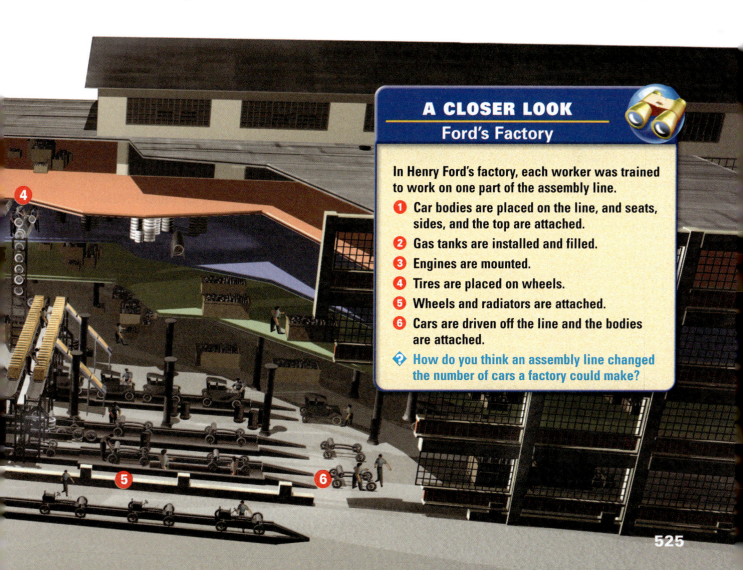

A CLOSER LOOK
Ford's Factory

In Henry Ford's factory, each worker was trained to work on one part of the assembly line.

1. Car bodies are placed on the line, and seats, sides, and the top are attached.
2. Gas tanks are installed and filled.
3. Engines are mounted.
4. Tires are placed on wheels.
5. Wheels and radiators are attached.
6. Cars are driven off the line and the bodies are attached.

? How do you think an assembly line changed the number of cars a factory could make?

The first computer was very different from the computers that people use today. It weighed about 66,000 pounds (29,938 kg) and was larger than a small room. Even though it was difficult to use, scientists were excited because the new computer could calculate numbers 1,000 times faster than humans could.

As computers developed, they made many jobs available in high-tech industries. High-tech businesses invent, build, or use computers or other electronic equipment. One important high-tech industry is the aerospace industry, which builds new planes and spacecraft. During the 1980s, the United States produced more high-tech products than any other country in the world.

By the end of the twentieth century, jobs in the United States had changed a great deal. Very few people lived and worked on farms, and new technologies had made most workplaces safer and more productive.

REVIEW Why did computers help create new kinds of jobs?

PREDICT A LIKELY OUTCOME

Changing Transportation

In 1900 there were almost 20 million horses and mules used for work and travel in the United States. There were only 8,000 automobiles at that time, but their popularity was growing because they were cleaner and safer than horses. In 1908 Henry Ford built the Model T, a car that could go 45 miles (72 km) per hour. His advertisements said that the Model T was "stronger than a horse and easier to maintain." As more people began buying cars, new roads were needed.

At the start of the 1900s there were only 150 miles (241 km) of paved roads and many cars got stuck in the mud on dirt roads. During the Great Depression, the federal government paid thousands of people without jobs to build roads, bridges, and dams. In 1956, Congress passed the Federal-Aid Highway Act to help the states build an interstate highway system. By 1970, there were almost 40,000 miles (64,372 km) of interstate highways across the United States.

Travel changed in other ways, too. In 1903 two brothers, Orville and Wilbur Wright, flew the world's first successful powered airplane at Kitty Hawk, North Carolina. Afterwards, Orville Wright sent a telegram to his father saying, "Success,

Analyze Graphs During the 1920s car prices decreased, which helped increase sales.

◆ About how many cars were sold in 1929?

Automobile Sales, 1920–1929

Year	Sales
1920	🚗🚗🚗🚗
1921	🚗🚗🚗
1922	🚗🚗🚗🚗🚗
1923	🚗🚗🚗🚗🚗🚗🚗
1924	🚗🚗🚗🚗🚗🚗🚗
1925	🚗🚗🚗🚗🚗🚗🚗
1926	🚗🚗🚗🚗🚗🚗🚗
1927	🚗🚗🚗🚗🚗
1928	🚗🚗🚗🚗🚗🚗🚗
1929	🚗🚗🚗🚗🚗🚗🚗🚗

🚗 = 500,000 automobiles

four flights Thursday morning . . . average speed through the air 31 miles [50 km], longest [flight] 57 seconds, inform [the] press." At first, airplanes were slow and difficult to fly. During World War I, the United States Army had only 35 pilots. By the end of World War II, however, fighter pilots were such an important part of the army that the government set up a separate branch of the military for airplanes, called the United States Air Force.

In 1927, Charles Lindbergh flew from New York City to Paris, France, in a plane named the *Spirit of St. Louis*. This was the first transatlantic flight, or flight across the Atlantic Ocean. Five years later, Amelia Earhart became the first woman to make a transatlantic flight alone. Soon people could fly to Europe and other faraway places on passenger planes.

The next major advance in airplane design happened in the 1940s, when engineers built the first jet-powered planes. By the 1970s, most people preferred

Before the Wright brothers made their first flight they experimented with gliders like the one shown here.

traveling on airplanes to using railroads or ships. The making and flying of airplanes, or **aviation**, became an important part of life in the United States.

As the aviation industry grew, people began to think about ways to fly into outer space. In 1958 the United States launched its first satellite into space.

Five years after her transatlantic flight, Amelia Earhart flew across the Pacific Ocean. She left from Hawaii and landed in California.

A <mark>satellite</mark> is a machine that orbits the Earth. Satellites were used to take pictures of the Earth from space. Scientists used those pictures to study weather patterns and other global events.

In 1958, the government also founded the National Aeronautics and Space Administration, or NASA. In 1962, John Glenn, Jr., became the first American astronaut to orbit the Earth. Seven years later, on July 20, 1969, astronaut Neil Armstrong became the first person to walk on the moon.

During the early 1980s, NASA built a space shuttle to launch into outer space. Instead of falling back to Earth in space capsules, astronauts landed the space shuttle like an airplane. Astronauts from many countries recently started work on the International Space Station, where people can live and work in space.

REVIEW How did transportation change during the twentieth century?

The *Apollo 11* spacecraft was launched from Cape Canaveral, Florida, on July 16, 1969.

Technology Changes Daily Life

Today it is hard to imagine life without airplanes, television, or computers. At the beginning of the 1900s, though, these technologies did not even exist. For entertainment, people went to theaters to see plays or concerts. In the 1890s, Thomas Alva Edison introduced motion pictures in the United States. For the first time, people could watch moving pictures of the world around them. By 1920, millions of Americans were going to silent movies.

Movies became even more popular when movie studios learned how to add

• SCIENCE AND TECHNOLOGY •

Early Motion Pictures

In 1893, when movies were introduced in the United States, they were not shown in theaters. Early movie machines did not project pictures onto a large screen. These early machines looked like straight-standing wooden boxes. To see a movie, a person had to look through an eyehole on top. Later, inventors built a projector that could show pictures on a screen. One of the first projectors, the Vitascope, was introduced in 1896.

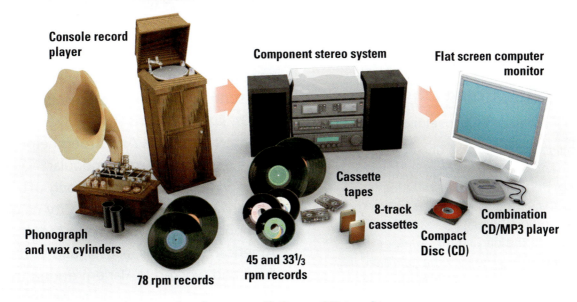

The first sound recordings were made using wax cylinders and listened to on phonographs. Later, music was recorded on records made of vinyl. Today's recording devices can hold hours of music.

sound to moving pictures. Many movie-makers and actors moved to Hollywood, California, where the movie business became a major industry.

The development of television meant that people could see and hear moving images in their own homes. The first national television broadcast was a speech by President Franklin D. Roosevelt in 1939. The first affordable television sets were not available until almost ten years later. By 1962, however, nine out of ten American families owned a television. A decade later people could buy video-cassette recorders, or VCRs, to play tapes of movies at home. Today digital video discs, or DVDs, allow people to watch movies on their television or computer.

Faster, cheaper, and smaller computers also changed the way people lived. By the end of the twentieth century, people could carry small computers called laptops with them wherever they went. Most personal computers today are as powerful as earlier computers that cost millions of dollars. People now use computers to communicate with others around the world.

This communication was made possible by the **Internet**, a system that allows computers to send information by using telephone lines or satellites. By 1999, over 200 million people worldwide used the Internet to do research and talk to each other through electronic mail, or e-mail.

Other new technologies made their way into people's homes as well. Compact disc players let people listen to music at home, at work, and even in their cars. Over the years music-listening devices have changed and improved greatly.

REVIEW How have computers changed people's lives?

Laptop computers allow people to work outside their homes.

· BIOGRAPHY ·

Louis Armstrong 1901–1971
Character Trait: Inventiveness

Louis Armstrong was one of the most important artists in the history of jazz music. Born in 1901 in New Orleans, Louisiana, Armstrong grew up singing on street corners. When he was 13 years old, he started playing the trumpet. In the early 1920s, he joined a jazz band in Chicago. Later, Armstrong started his own band and played a kind of jazz called swing. In 1944, he played in the first jazz concert held at the Metropolitan Opera House in New York City. In later years, Armstrong toured Europe, bringing American jazz to other countries.

MULTIMEDIA BIOGRAPHIES
Visit The Learning Site at
www.harcourtschool.com
to learn about other famous people.
GO ONLINE

Changes in the Arts

As technology changed daily life, there were also changes in the arts. American composers and musicians created new types of music. In the early 1900s, musicians in New Orleans started playing a type of music they made up as they went along. It was called jazz.

Jazz grew out of the African American musical heritage made up of music brought from West Africa and spirituals, or religious songs, that enslaved people had sung in the United States. In the 1920s, jazz musicians such as Duke Ellington and Louis Armstrong helped make this form of music popular.

Both Ellington and Armstrong often performed in the New York City neighborhood of Harlem. So many African American musicians, artists, and writers lived and worked in Harlem during the 1920s that this time came to be known as the Harlem Renaissance.

One of the best-known writers of the Harlem Renaissance was the poet Langston Hughes. He described Harlem during the 1920s as a magnet for African Americans from across the country. Writers such as Claude McKay, Countee Cullen, and Zora Neale Hurston went to Harlem to share their talents.

Another art form that changed greatly over the twentieth century was painting. In the 1920s, the artist Georgia O'Keeffe created paintings about city life. Later, she moved to the Southwest and began making paintings of things in nature. After World War II, New York City became known as the new center of the art world. Many American artists experimented with new ways of painting. Jackson Pollock poured paint right from the can onto his canvases to make lines and splashes of color. Andy Warhol painted colorful pictures of everyday items such as soup cans and soda bottles.

Architecture, or the design of buildings, was also full of changes. At the beginning of the century, American architects built the first skyscrapers. These were buildings with strong steel frames that stood many stories high.

Today, there are skyscrapers in cities all over the United States. Not all American architects built skyscrapers, however. Frank Lloyd Wright designed low buildings that had many angles. His style was inspired by the wide, open spaces of the Midwest. He said that "a good building is one that makes the landscape more beautiful than it was before."

REVIEW What was the Harlem Renaissance?

Frank Lloyd Wright (seated at left) designed this unique house in Oak Park, Illinois.

LESSON 1 REVIEW

Summary Time Line

1900 — 1950 — 2000

- **1908** The first Model T automobile is built
- **1927** Charles Lindbergh flies from New York to Paris
- **1969** United States astronauts land on the moon

 PREDICT AN OUTCOME What do you think might have happened if the government had not built an interstate highway system?

1. **BIG IDEA** How did new ideas and new inventions change the way people lived in the United States?

2. **VOCABULARY** Write a newspaper headline using the words **strike** and **labor union**.

3. **TIME LINE** How many years after Charles Lindbergh's flight did astronauts land on the moon?

4. **CULTURE** What is jazz?

5. **CRITICAL THINKING—Evaluate** Why were labor unions important to workers?

 PERFORMANCE—Interview Interview a grandparent or another older family member about what life was like before computers and the Internet.

Chapter 14 ■ 531

SKILLS · Use a Time Zone Map

VOCABULARY
time zone

▶ WHY IT MATTERS

For centuries people used the sun to determine time. When the sun was at its highest point in the sky, it was noon. However, the sun cannot be at its highest point all around the Earth at the same time. Since Earth rotates on its axis, the sun has already passed its highest point east of where you live. It has not yet reached its highest point west of you.

Whenever people travel by airplane they hope to arrive on time. If you have ever been in an airport, you have seen the large screens that tell when flights are arriving and departing. Understanding the idea of time zones is important to travelers all around the world.

▶ WHAT YOU NEED TO KNOW

In the 1800s, Charles Dowd of the United States and Sandford Fleming of Canada developed the idea of dividing the world into time zones. In a **time zone**, a single time is used for the entire region.

A new time zone begins at every fifteenth meridian, starting at the prime meridian. In each new zone to the west of the prime meridian, the time is one hour earlier than in the zone before it. All parts of a time zone use the same time.

On November 18, 1883, the United States began using six time zones. From east to west, they are called the eastern, central, mountain, Pacific, Alaska, and Hawaii–Aleutian time zones.

Monitors in airports allow travelers to find out when flights are arriving and departing.

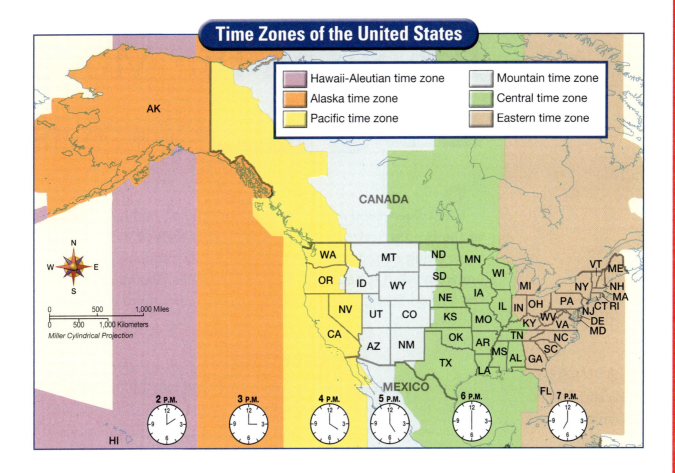

The map on this page shows the time zones in the United States. Find Arkansas, in the central time zone. Now find New York. It is in the eastern time zone, which is just east of the central time zone. The time in the central time zone is one hour earlier than the time in the eastern time zone.

PRACTICE THE SKILL

Use the time zone map of the United States to answer these questions.

1. In which time zone is Virginia?
2. If it is 3:00 P.M. in Virginia, what time is it in Missouri?
3. In which time zone is California?
4. If it is 9:00 A.M. in California, what time is it in Colorado? in Alabama?
5. If it is 9:00 P.M. in Pennsylvania, what time is it in Oregon?
6. Imagine that you are in Hawaii. Is the time earlier or later in South Carolina?

APPLY WHAT YOU LEARNED

Find a world time zone map in an almanac or atlas. Suppose it is 10:00 A.M. where you live. Find the time for each of these cities: Dublin, Ireland; Rome, Italy; and Tokyo, Japan. Explain how you determined the time for each of these cities. Then brainstorm occasions when it would be helpful to know the time in other places.

Practice your map and globe skills with the **GeoSkills CD-ROM**.

Chapter 14 • 533

LESSON 2

People on the Move

1880–2000

PREDICT AN OUTCOME
As you read, predict likely outcomes of the arrival of new immigrants.

BIG IDEA
The addition of new lands and new citizens changed the United States.

VOCABULARY
naturalization
urbanization
suburb
ethnic group

Between 1860 and 1910, about 23 million immigrants came to the United States. As these new people arrived, new states were being added to the Union. Life was becoming very different from what it had been in the early 1800s. The landscape of the United States was changing and becoming more diverse.

The Great Melting Pot

As the nation grew and prospered in the late 1800s, many people from other countries decided that they wanted to begin new lives in the United States. These people were immigrants, or people who leave their native countries to make their homes in a different country.

Before the 1880s most immigrants had come from western and northern Europe, especially from England, Ireland, Germany, and the Scandinavian countries. In the 1880s this changed. Millions of immigrants from Italy, Poland, Hungary, Greece, and Russia came to the United States from eastern and southern Europe. Between 1880 and 1930, more than four and a half million immigrants arrived from Italy alone.

After 1892 most immigrants arrived at Ellis Island, a small island in New York Harbor. Sometimes whole families would travel together to the United States. Other times young men

Ellis Island opened in 1892 and served as the nation's main immigration center until 1924.

An Immigrant Passport

Analyze Primary Sources

When immigrants arrived in the United States, they had to present their passports to be stamped. The immigrant passport shown here belonged to the Flinck family of Sweden.

1. Photograph of the Flinck family
2. Line showing the passport holder's name
3. The date of the passport

> Why do you think most immigrants were very careful with their passports?

came first, hoping to find jobs. Once they had saved enough money, they could pay for their families to come.

Soon, New York City became home to millions of immigrants. The new arrivals from Europe became an important part of the nation's economy. Immigrants from Ireland played important roles in the labor unions that helped American workers. Communities such as Little Italy in New York City brought new foods and customs to the United States. One Jewish immigrant named Israel Zangwill wrote, "America is . . . the great Melting Pot, where all the races of Europe are melting and reforming."

REVIEW How did immigration to the United States change over time?

PREDICT AN OUTCOME

New Immigrants

European immigrants were not the only new Americans to contribute to the nation's growth. By 1880 there were about 75,000 Chinese immigrants in California. These immigrants helped build railroads across the western states.

During the first decade of the 1900s, about 50,000 Japanese immigrants arrived in California and Hawaii. Farmers from Japan brought new ways of farming that helped California grow more farm products than any other state.

By 1900 about 80,000 Mexican immigrants had also arrived. At first most Mexican Americans worked on farms in the Southwest. After 1940, however, many began to work and live in cities.

LOCATE IT — NEW YORK, Ellis Island

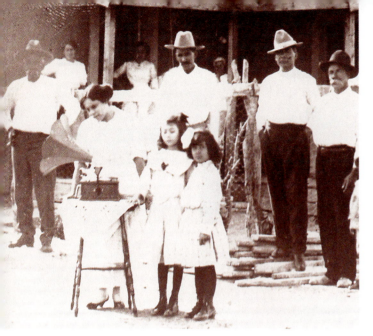

Many Mexican American families have lived in the United States for generations. This 1902 photograph shows several generations of the Aguilar family of Texas.

By the end of the twentieth century, Mexican Americans were one of the fastest-growing groups in the nation.

Not all Americans were happy to see so many new immigrants. Some people worried that there would be too many people living in the United States. They thought that there might not be enough jobs for everyone. These people tried to get laws passed to stop immigrants from coming to the United States.

In 1882 Congress passed the Chinese Exclusion Act, which said that workers from China could not enter the United States for a period of ten years. This ban was later continued and did not end until 1965.

The Immigration Act of 1924 also limited the number of people who were allowed to move to the United States. By 1929 only 150,000 immigrants were allowed each year. New immigrants often faced discrimination, or unfair treatment. They had to work hard to overcome the feelings some people had against them.

Despite these challenges, millions of immigrants wanted to stay and become United States citizens. Citizenship, or membership in the nation, meant that the immigrants would have all the rights and responsibilities of other Americans. These included taking part in the government, voting, and serving on juries.

Each year thousands of immigrants, like these individuals in Seattle, Washington, are sworn in as United States citizens.

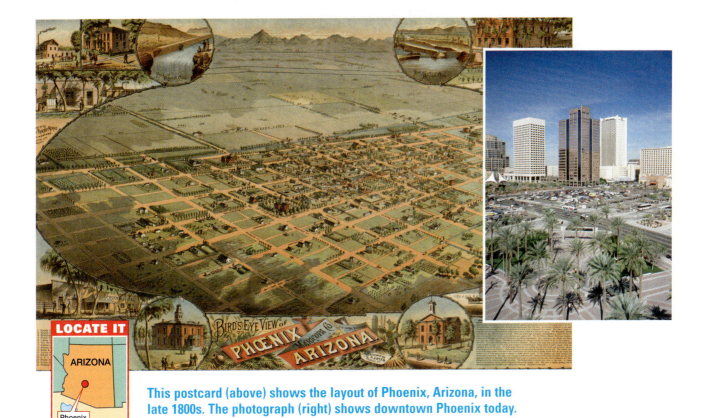

This postcard (above) shows the layout of Phoenix, Arizona, in the late 1800s. The photograph (right) shows downtown Phoenix today.

To become a citizen, an immigrant must go through **naturalization**, or the process of becoming a legal citizen of the United States. To apply for citizenship, an immigrant must be at least 18 years old. He or she must also have lived in the United States for five years or more.

A person applying for citizenship must also pass a test on United States government and history and be able to write and speak English. Those who pass these tests must take an oath promising allegiance, or loyalty, to the United States. Part of the oath says, "I will support and defend the Constitution and laws of the United States of America against all enemies, foreign and domestic . . . I will bear arms on behalf of the United States when required by the law . . ."

REVIEW What must an immigrant do to become a United States citizen?

Territories Become States

In 1880 about 22 percent of Americans lived in areas west of the Mississippi River. By 1900 this number had grown to almost 30 percent. There were 45 states in the United States at that time. Oklahoma, New Mexico, Arizona, and Alaska were still territories waiting for statehood. In 1900 Hawaii was also accepted as a territory.

In 1907 Oklahoma became the forty-sixth state. Before statehood, the territory had been divided into two parts. In the western section, settlers had built homes and farms. In the eastern section, land had been set aside as Indian Territory, and Native Americans from many different groups lived there. When Oklahoma became a state, many Native Americans joined in approving the state constitution, and the two sections united.

Chapter 14 ■ 537

 Regions In 1900 the United States was made up of 45 states and six territories.

❓ In what part of the country were most large cities located in 1900?

Today the state of Oklahoma's cattle and wheat production are an important part of the nation's economy.

In 1912, the last two territories in the contiguous, or joined, United States became states. The first was New Mexico, which some still thought of as part of the "Old West." Even in the new state, some people still traveled by stagecoach and lived in small frontier towns. Today, New Mexico is home to many cultures. During the 1990s, the state had a higher percentage of Hispanic citizens than any other state. About 9 percent of New Mexico's citizens are Native Americans. These cultures add to the state's rich history.

About a month after New Mexico became a state, the territory of Arizona was also granted statehood. Arizona has 22 Native American reservations. It has more reservation land area than any other state. Famous landmarks such as the Grand Canyon bring many tourists to Arizona. In fact, tourism has become one of the most important parts of the state's economy.

In 1959 Alaska was admitted as the forty-ninth state. It is the largest state in

538 ▪ Unit 7

the country, and it increased the nation's size by nearly 20 percent. Today, Alaska leads all other states in fishing and is the second-largest producer of oil in the country.

The fiftieth and last territory to be granted statehood was Hawaii. It was also admitted in 1959. Hawaii, located in the Pacific Ocean, is the nation's only island state. Tourists come from all over the world to see the state's beautiful beaches and mountains.

REVIEW What state had the highest percentage of Hispanic citizens in the 1990s?

The suburb of Medfield, Massachusetts, is located outside of Boston.

From Country to City

In the early 1900s, more than 32 million Americans lived and worked on farms. Cities were often unsafe places because of dirty water and bad living conditions. Soon, however, government regulations made cities cleaner, safer places to live, and the United States began to experience **urbanization**, or the movement of large numbers of people into cities. Changes in transportation helped cities grow, too. Automobiles were used instead of horses, which made city streets cleaner and allowed people to travel faster. Hundreds of thousands of miles of dirt roads were paved so that people could drive from city to city. Railroads and trucking companies brought food and goods from farms to cities. Skyscrapers were built so that many people could work in the same building.

As cities grew larger, many people began to live in **suburbs**, or neighborhoods located on the edges of cities. These suburbs were less crowded than the cities themselves. They were also farther from the pollution caused by factories and automobile traffic.

Over time, however, most suburbs grew so large that they, too, began to look like cities. This growth can be seen around cities such as Los Angeles, California, and Atlanta, Georgia. The suburbs that surround these cities stretch out for miles.

REVIEW What are suburbs?

The Atlanta, Georgia, metropolitan area is home to more than four million people.

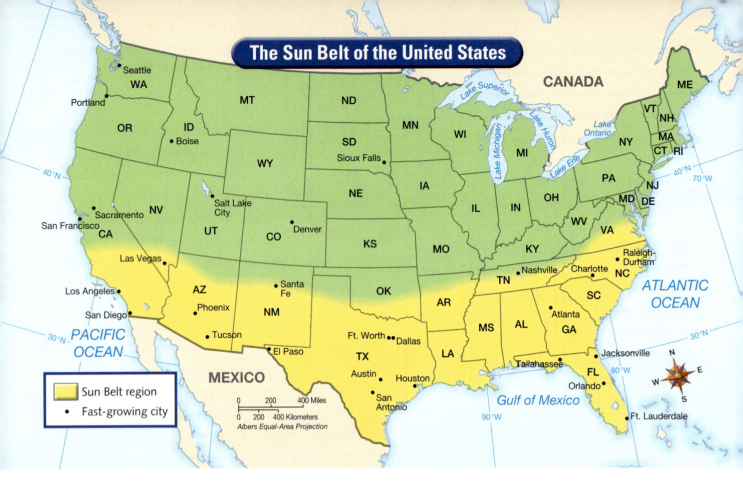

 Regions The Sun Belt stretches across the country from the Atlantic Ocean to the Pacific Ocean.

How many states are included in the Sun Belt?

Americans Today

Today about 290 million people live in the United States. Every ten years, the United States government conducts a census, or a counting of the population. The census counts how many people of all ages live in the United States. It also shows how diverse the population has become. The 2000 census showed that the population had grown by 32.7 million during the 1990s. This was the largest increase in the nation's history.

People from all around the world have made their homes in the United States. In fact, the United States has one of the world's most diverse populations in terms of ancestry. More than 210 million Americans are of European background. Almost 35 million are African Americans, and more than 10 million are of Asian background. Native Americans number close to two and a half million.

Hispanic Americans make up the nation's fastest-growing ethnic group. An **ethnic group** is a group of people from the same country, of the same race, or with a shared culture. More than 1 in 8 Americans, or about 35 million people, are of Hispanic descent.

As a result of the changing population, different regions of the United States are growing at different rates. Most of the

The many neon lights of Las Vegas, Nevada, make it one of the most colorful cities in the country.

nation's population growth is taking place in the "belt" of states that stretches from California to Florida. This region is called the Sun Belt because its weather is usually warm and sunny. California now has the largest population of any state. Nevada is the country's fastest-growing state. One of its cities, Las Vegas, is also the nation's fastest-growing city. The southern region of the United States has the highest regional population, with more than 100 million people.

REVIEW What makes the United States such a diverse nation?

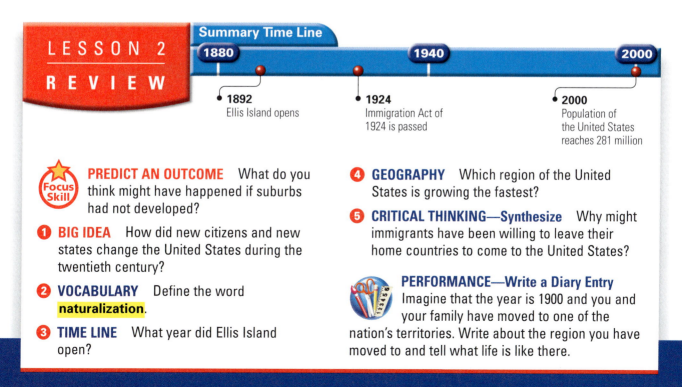

LESSON 2 REVIEW

Summary Time Line

- 1892 Ellis Island opens
- 1924 Immigration Act of 1924 is passed
- 2000 Population of the United States reaches 281 million

PREDICT AN OUTCOME What do you think might have happened if suburbs had not developed?

① **BIG IDEA** How did new citizens and new states change the United States during the twentieth century?

② **VOCABULARY** Define the word naturalization.

③ **TIME LINE** What year did Ellis Island open?

④ **GEOGRAPHY** Which region of the United States is growing the fastest?

⑤ **CRITICAL THINKING—Synthesize** Why might immigrants have been willing to leave their home countries to come to the United States?

PERFORMANCE—Write a Diary Entry Imagine that the year is 1900 and you and your family have moved to one of the nation's territories. Write about the region you have moved to and tell what life is like there.

Chapter 14 ■ 541

SKILLS · CHART AND GRAPH

Use a Cartogram

VOCABULARY
cartogram

▶ WHY IT MATTERS

One way to show population is to use a cartogram. A **cartogram** is a diagram that gives information about places by the size shown for each place. Knowing how to read and understand a cartogram can help you quickly compare information about different places.

▶ WHAT YOU NEED TO KNOW

On most maps of the United States, the size of each state is based on its land area. On a cartogram, the size of a state is based on a geographical statistic. On the cartogram on page 543, the size of each western state is based on its population.

542 ▪ Unit 7

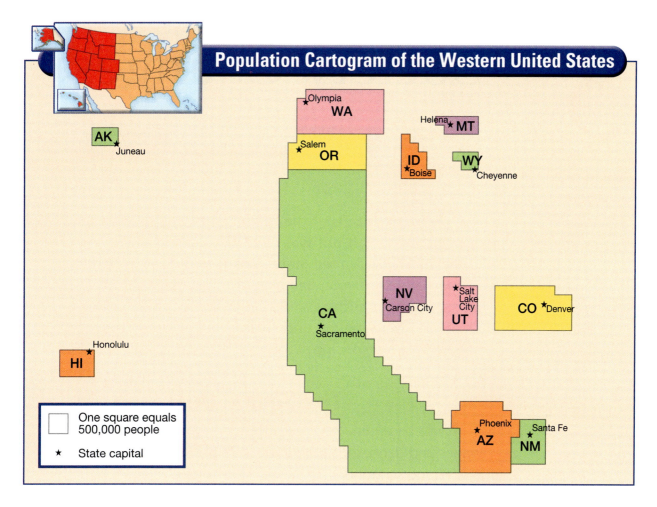

A population cartogram shows the states as their sizes would be if everyone had the same amount of land. A state with many people would be much bigger than a state with few people.

🡆 PRACTICE THE SKILL

The map on page 542 is a political map. The size of each state is based on its land area. Compare the size of Washington with the size of Montana. The cartogram on this page is a population cartogram of the western United States. The size of each state is based on population. Compare the sizes of Washington and Montana again. Although Washington has a smaller land area than Montana, it is shown larger than Montana on the cartogram because it has more people.

Now answer these questions.

1. Which state has more land area, Colorado or Montana?
2. Which of those states is shown larger on the cartogram? Why?

🡆 APPLY WHAT YOU LEARNED

Use atlases, almanacs, and other sources to make a population cartogram of a different region of the United States. Then compare the sizes of the states on your cartogram with their sizes on a political map.

Chapter 14 ■ 543

· LESSON ·

3

Society Changes

1900–2000

 PREDICT AN OUTCOME

As you read, predict a likely outcome for the changes in society.

BIG IDEA
People in the United States worked to gain equal rights and opportunities for all citizens.

VOCABULARY
commission
conservation
primary election
suffrage
migrant worker
nonviolence

Today all citizens of the United States have rights and responsibilities. But this was not always true. At the beginning of the 1900s, the United States was a very different place. Women could not vote, and many places would not hire female workers. Groups such as African Americans and Hispanic Americans were treated unfairly in many places. Across the nation, however, people started working for change.

The Square Deal

At the beginning of the 1900s, many workers faced low wages and dangerous working conditions. Some children could not attend school because they were forced to work in factories. In areas across the country, pollution and population growth were harming the environment. Many citizens felt that changes were needed.

When Theodore Roosevelt became President in 1901, he was 42 years old, making him the youngest person ever to hold the office.

Regions The country's first national park was Yellowstone National Park, which was founded in 1872.

➤ In what part of the country are most national parks located?

Theodore Roosevelt, who became President in 1901, believed it was the job of the federal government to help citizens as much as possible. He started a program called the Square Deal. Under this program, everyone was to be given the same opportunity to succeed.

To make sure that people would receive fair treatment, Roosevelt wanted the federal government to make rules for businesses to follow. He set up or increased the power of special committees called **commissions**. One of these was the Interstate Commerce Commission. Part of its job was to study railroad fares. When the commission decided fares were too high, it made railroad owners lower them.

Roosevelt also asked Congress to give the government the power to see that foods and medicines were safe. In 1906 Congress passed the Pure Food and Drug Act. The act said all foods and medicines had to meet government safety rules.

Roosevelt was also interested in conservation. **Conservation** is the protection and wise use of natural resources. Roosevelt set aside millions of acres of land in different parts of the country as national parks. In 1916 the National Park Service was founded to protect these public lands. Today national parks such as Yosemite in California and Yellowstone in Wyoming have been preserved for people to visit and enjoy.

REVIEW What was the Square Deal?

Chapter 14 • 545

The Progressive Movement

Roosevelt's Square Deal was part of the Progressive movement. Progressives were people who hoped to make life in the United States better. In the early 1900s, people were concerned because political parties often made secret deals with big businesses. Some Americans thought that the principles of democracy were being lost.

Leaders such as Robert M. La Follette (lah faw•LET) of Wisconsin changed the way state governments worked. In the past, state senators had been elected by the state legislature. In Wisconsin La Follette helped change this system by making the state legislature pass a law forcing each party to hold a primary election. A **primary election** is an election in which different people compete to be

Early in the twentieth century there were few laws to protect child workers. By 1910 children between the ages of 10 and 15 made up 18 percent of all workers.

their party's candidate. The winners of the primary elections then run against each other in a general election. La Follette's change meant that the people had more power in choosing their leaders.

In the early 1900s, people were joining groups to protect the rights of workers. Workers were often paid very little. In 1910, for example, women earned about $1.60 for nine hours of work. Early labor unions worked hard to improve the lives of workers. Samuel Gompers and the American Federation of Labor, or AFL, led strikes in order to gain better pay and better working conditions. Soon government laws were passed to enforce fair working conditions. Today, laws protect the health, safety, and welfare of American workers.

REVIEW How did the Progressive movement help change life in the United States?

PREDICT AN OUTCOME

Analyze Graphs This graph shows the number of workers who joined labor unions in the United States from 1898 to 1920.

◆ How did union membership change during this time?

Women's Rights

During the 1800s, women did not have many rights. In some states if a married woman had a job, all the money she earned was given to her husband. Starting in the mid-1800s, American women began to work for equal rights.

At first women tried to change state constitutions to allow voting by women. In 1890 Wyoming became a state, and its constitution was the first to give women the right to vote. By 1900, however, Colorado, Idaho, and Utah were the only other states that allowed voting by women. Many people felt that an amendment to the United States Constitution was needed. This amendment would give women all over the country **suffrage** (SUH•frij), or the right to vote in local, state, and national elections.

Carrie Lane Chapman Catt

Passing this amendment, however, was a difficult task. In 1872 Susan B. Anthony had been arrested for trying to vote in a presidential election in New York. Many years later, Anthony became one of the leaders of a group called the National American Woman Suffrage Association, or NAWSA.

Carrie Lane Chapman Catt was another leader of the suffrage movement. Catt believed that women should be able to vote and take part in government. Soon Catt became famous for her speeches in support of women's suffrage. In 1892 she spoke to Congress and asked its members to grant women the right to vote. In 1915 she became head of NAWSA, and over 40,000 women joined her in Washington, D.C., in a march for suffrage.

This women's suffrage march took place in 1916. Women who took part in such marches were known as suffragettes.

CITIZENSHIP

DEMOCRATIC VALUES
Individual Rights

The movement for women's voting rights began in the early 1800s and continued into the twentieth century. By 1919 Congress had approved a women's suffrage amendment and sent it to the states for ratification. Thirty-six states had to approve the amendment for it to become law. In 1920, the thirty-sixth state, Tennessee, voted for ratification and the Nineteenth Amendment was added to the Constitution.

Analyze the Value

1. What did the Nineteenth Amendment do?
2. **Make It Relevant** Interview an older family member about the first time he or she voted.

The first women's suffrage amendment to the Constitution had been proposed in 1878, but it was defeated. In 1919, however, Congress finally passed the Nineteenth Amendment. The following year, the amendment was ratified by enough states to become part of the Constitution. In 1920, eight million American women voted in the presidential election. It was the first time in the history of the United States that women across the country took part in a national election.

Today women are represented at every level of government. During the 1990s, Janet Reno was appointed as the first female attorney general, and Madeleine Albright was appointed as the first female secretary of state. Women serve as judges on the Supreme Court, and they defend their country in the United States armed forces.

REVIEW How did women work to gain equal rights?

The Civil Rights Movement

African Americans also worked for equal rights. Even though slavery ended after the Civil War, there were still many laws that treated African Americans unfairly. In some areas of the country, segregation, or the separation of people of different races, was common. African American leaders used progressive ideas to try to solve such problems.

One important African American leader of the early twentieth century was W.E.B. Du Bois (doo•BOYS). In 1909 Du Bois and other leaders formed the National Association for the Advancement of Colored People, or NAACP. The goal of the NAACP was to gain political, educational, and civil equality for African Americans. A year later, the National Urban League was founded. It helped the many African Americans who were moving to cities at the time find jobs and homes.

In the early 1950s, Oliver Brown of Topeka, Kansas, wanted his daughter, Linda, to attend a school near their home. But Linda Brown was African American, and state laws said that African American children had to attend schools separate from white students. Linda Brown's family and 12 other African American families decided to try to get these laws

BIOGRAPHY

Booker T. Washington
1856–1915
Character Trait: Citizenship

Booker T. Washington was born into slavery. Freed after the Civil War, he worked his way through school. After graduating he became a teacher. During Reconstruction he had seen how hard it was for African Americans to fight prejudice. He believed that African Americans could get fair treatment only by becoming skilled workers. Washington led an effort to give African Americans more opportunities for education and training. In 1881 he helped found Tuskegee Institute, a trade school for African Americans, in Alabama.

W.E.B. Du Bois
1868–1963
Character Trait: Respect

W.E.B. Du Bois strongly disagreed with Washington's point of view. He wanted African Americans to immediately improve their situation by fighting for equal rights. A gifted speaker, teacher, and writer, he devoted his career to improving life for African Americans. In the later years of his life, Du Bois believed that prejudice in the United States would never be broken down. In 1961 he decided to leave the country and spent the rest of his life in the West African nation of Ghana (GAH•nuh).

GO ONLINE MULTIMEDIA BIOGRAPHIES
Visit The Learning Site at www.harcourtschool.com to learn about other famous people.

---

changed using the court system. Their case, known as *Brown v. Board of Education of Topeka*, went all the way to the United States Supreme Court. In 1954 the Court ruled in favor of the families and ordered an end to segregation in public schools. However, many states were slow to obey that order. Their schools and many other public places remained segregated.

The next step in the civil rights struggle came in Montgomery, Alabama. A law there said that African Americans had to move to the back of a city bus if white passengers wanted the seats in front. In 1955 an African American woman named Rosa Parks was arrested for refusing to give up her seat to a white passenger. African American citizens around the country protested her arrest. For more than a year, Montgomery's African Americans refused to ride the city's buses. Finally the Supreme Court ruled that segregation on public transportation was unconstitutional.

Rosa Parks is fingerprinted after her arrest in Montgomery.

In cities across the country, people joined civil rights marches as a peaceful way to protest segregation. Dr. Martin Luther King, Jr., was an African American leader who led many civil rights marches. In 1963 about 250,000 people gathered for a march in Washington, D.C., to show their support for a new civil rights law. King spoke to the marchers about his hopes for the future. He said,

> **66** I have a dream that one day on the red hills of Georgia the sons of former slaves and the sons of former slaveowners will be able to sit down together at the table of brotherhood. . . . **99**

The Civil Rights movement succeeded in many ways. The year after the Washington, D.C., march, Congress passed the Civil Rights Act of 1964. This act made segregation in public places illegal. It also said that people of all races should have equal job opportunities.

REVIEW How did Martin Luther King, Jr., work for civil rights?

Other Groups Seek Change

In many southwestern states, farmers hired migrant workers to pick crops. A **migrant worker** is someone who moves from place to place with the seasons, harvesting crops. In Texas and California, among other states, many migrant workers were Hispanic. These people often worked in terrible conditions. During the 1930s a Mexican American boy named Cesar Chavez (SAY•zar CHAH•vez) traveled with his family as a migrant worker. The family slept in one-room shacks with no running water. When Chavez grew up, he

In 1963 Martin Luther King, Jr., (shown at center) marched with thousands of other Americans in Washington, D.C., in support of civil rights.

decided to change the way that migrant workers lived. In 1962 Chavez started the National Farm Workers Association. Chavez began leading marches to protest the poor treatment of migrant workers. Like Martin Luther King, Jr., Chavez believed in **nonviolence**, or peaceful ways, to bring about change. In an interview he said,

> [W]e are convinced that non-violence is more powerful than violence. We are convinced that non-violence supports you if you have a just and moral cause.

Native American groups also worked for equal rights. They wanted the rights that the federal government had promised them in treaties. Then, in 1975, Congress passed the Self-Determination and Educational Assistance Act. For the first time, Indian tribes could run their own businesses, hospitals, and schools. They also worked to preserve the constitutions of their different tribal and local governments.

Cesar Chavez speaking in Sacramento, California, in 1973

REVIEW Why did Cesar Chavez believe in nonviolence?

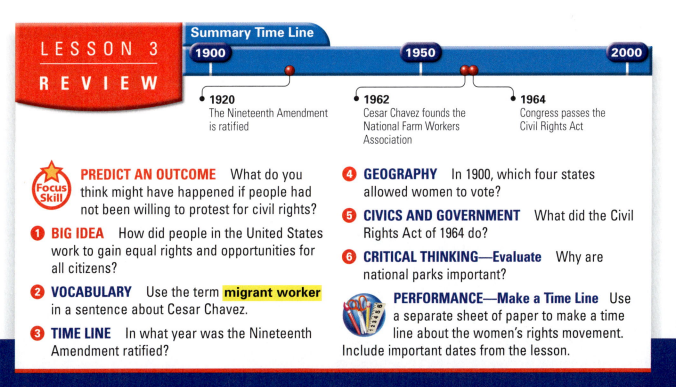

LESSON 3 REVIEW

Summary Time Line

- 1920 — The Nineteenth Amendment is ratified
- 1962 — Cesar Chavez founds the National Farm Workers Association
- 1964 — Congress passes the Civil Rights Act

PREDICT AN OUTCOME What do you think might have happened if people had not been willing to protest for civil rights?

1. **BIG IDEA** How did people in the United States work to gain equal rights and opportunities for all citizens?

2. **VOCABULARY** Use the term **migrant worker** in a sentence about Cesar Chavez.

3. **TIME LINE** In what year was the Nineteenth Amendment ratified?

4. **GEOGRAPHY** In 1900, which four states allowed women to vote?

5. **CIVICS AND GOVERNMENT** What did the Civil Rights Act of 1964 do?

6. **CRITICAL THINKING—Evaluate** Why are national parks important?

PERFORMANCE—Make a Time Line Use a separate sheet of paper to make a time line about the women's rights movement. Include important dates from the lesson.

Chapter 14 ■ 551

LESSON 4

A United Country

1860 — 1935 — Present

1880–2000

PREDICT AN OUTCOME

As you read, predict likely outcomes of the way Americans work together as citizens.

BIG IDEA

Citizens of the United States work together for the good of their country.

VOCABULARY

patriotism
e pluribus unum
recycle

Americans have worked together as citizens since the United States was first formed. People in all areas of the United States are proud of their country. This **patriotism**, or love of country, is an important part of life in the United States. Citizens can show their patriotism in many different ways.

Citizenship Then and Now

In 1920, Woodrow Wilson said that Americans thought of the United States as "a light to the world, as created to lead the world in the assertion [declaration] of the rights of people and the rights of free nations." This feeling of patriotism is one reason that men and women choose to join the country's armed forces. They are citizens who believe in their country so much that they will risk their lives to defend it. During wartime, citizens have worked for the United States in other ways as well. During both World War I and World War II, for example, Americans conserved resources to help the nation's armed forces. Many people

FAST FACT During World War II, Americans planted nearly 20 million victory gardens in backyards and on rooftops across the country.

The photograph below shows children in New York City working on their rooftop victory gardens in 1943. The poster on the right was used to advertise a victory garden contest.

552 ■ Unit 7

This penny (right), Sacagawea gold dollar (far right), and Morgan silver dollar (bottom) all bear the words *e pluribus unum*.

planted gardens, called victory gardens, so they could grow their own vegetables. The government asked people to have "meatless days" once or twice a week so that more meat could be sent to soldiers.

Even in peacetime, Americans work together for the common good. Their belief in democratic values is part of what holds our diverse society together. One way people show this belief is by helping to make life better for others. Citizens have done this throughout the nation's history. In 1889 a woman named Jane Addams opened Hull-House in Chicago, Illinois. Hull-House provided classes in English and civics lessons for workers in the city.

Addams believed it was her duty to help Americans who had little money or education. At Hull-House, immigrant workers learned about American traditions. They learned to be proud of their citizenship. Today, students in the United States can learn about citizenship in school. Public schools teach classes about government and United States history.

Another way that people can show their patriotism is by honoring the American flag. In many schools across the country, children say the Pledge of Allegiance at the start of each school day. "I pledge allegiance to the flag of the United States of America and to the Republic for which it stands, one Nation under God, indivisible, with liberty and justice for all." This pledge shows that Americans honor the flag as a symbol of their freedom.

Other symbols show people's patriotism, too. On the Great Seal of the United States is the Latin saying, *e pluribus unum*. This saying also appears on every coin made in the United States. **E pluribus unum** means "out of many, one."

• HERITAGE •

Flag Day

The national holiday known as Flag Day was first observed in 1877 to mark the one-hundredth anniversary of the selection of the American flag. That year, Congress asked that all public buildings across the country display the flag on June 14. In 1949, President Harry S. Truman officially named June 14 as Flag Day. Today, Flag Day is celebrated with parades and special programs about the history of the flag.

Thomas Jefferson, Benjamin Franklin, and John Adams believed that the saying e *pluribus unum* was important because it pointed out the fact that many individual Americans make up one nation. People are different in many ways, but by working together for the good of the country, Americans show that they are united.

REVIEW Why is it important that Americans show their patriotism?

 PREDICT AN OUTCOME

Rights of Citizens

The Bill of Rights, the first ten amendments to the Constitution, guarantees basic rights to all citizens. The First Amendment to the Constitution guarantees freedom to assemble, or meet in a group. It also protects freedom of speech and freedom of the press. These rights are very important because they say that Americans are free to agree or disagree with what the government says or does. In some countries, people can be arrested for disagreeing with their government's ideas. But in the United States, the right to free speech is protected. The First Amendment also guarantees freedom of religion, which means that citizens can worship in any way they choose.

The Fifth Amendment states that citizens cannot be forced to speak against themselves in a court of law. It also states that no person can be put on trial for the same crime twice. The Seventh Amendment lists people's rights under common law. One of these rights is that citizens who are accused of a crime have the right to a fair trial.

Some amendments were added to the Constitution later to protect civil rights. The Fourteenth Amendment guarantees

Freedom of the press (left) and the right to a fair trial (right) are two rights guaranteed in the Bill of Rights. In 1791 the Bill of Rights was added to the United States Constitution.

Voter Turnout in Presidential Elections, 1952–2000

Analyze Graphs Presidential elections take place every four years, but this graph is divided into eight-year periods.

◆ About what percent of voters voted in the 2000 election?

Responsibilities of Citizens

While citizens of the United States have many rights, they also have important responsibilities. One of these responsibilities is to take part in government. Today, citizens age 18 or older can register to vote for government officials.

Citizens play an important role in government because the United States is a democracy. Americans elect their country's leaders. Every citizen has an individual responsibility to vote. Some citizens also choose to run for public office. If elected, these men and women work as government officials. Their duties include enforcing laws or making new laws to protect people's rights.

that no state can enforce a law that will take away the rights of its citizens. More than 200 years after it was written, the Constitution continues to protect the rights and freedoms of Americans.

REVIEW What is the Bill of Rights?

DEMOCRATIC VALUES
Citizen Participation

On November 7, 2000, the importance of every citizen's vote became clear. That day, more than 100 million Americans cast their votes for the country's next President. Most people voted for either Vice President Al Gore or Texas Governor George W. Bush. Everyone expected that by the next day the winner would be clear. However, the 2000 presidential election proved to be the closest one in history, with its outcome hanging in the balance for five weeks. In the end, Bush's lead of less than 600 votes in Florida, a state with a population of nearly 16 million, helped decide the election in his favor. In his inauguration speech, President Bush said, "The most important tasks of a democracy are done by everyone."

Analyze the Value

1. What did the 2000 presidential election show about the importance of each citizen's vote?
2. **Make It Relevant** Write a paragraph about why it is important to vote.

Chapter 14 ■ 555

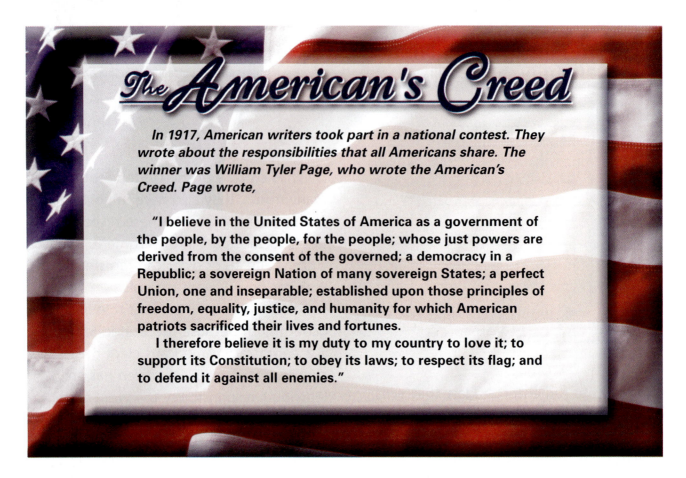

The American's Creed

In 1917, American writers took part in a national contest. They wrote about the responsibilities that all Americans share. The winner was William Tyler Page, who wrote the American's Creed. Page wrote,

"I believe in the United States of America as a government of the people, by the people, for the people; whose just powers are derived from the consent of the governed; a democracy in a Republic; a sovereign Nation of many sovereign States; a perfect Union, one and inseparable; established upon those principles of freedom, equality, justice, and humanity for which American patriots sacrificed their lives and fortunes.

I therefore believe it is my duty to my country to love it; to support its Constitution; to obey its laws; to respect its flag; and to defend it against all enemies."

Laws and regulations influence the economic and social activities of all citizens.

The federal government and the state governments have some of the same powers. These include the rights to tax and to borrow money. Tax money is used to provide many services, such as schools and roadways. Each state also has its own constitution and laws. However, state laws must not conflict with the United States Constitution. In turn, the activities of local governments must not conflict with state and national laws. For example, the mayor of a city does not have as much power as the governor of a state.

All the government offices at the local, state, and federal levels are part of our constitutional democracy. A constitutional democracy depends upon the justice, equality, and honesty of its citizens and leaders.

It is also important for citizens to help their communities. One way people do this is by volunteering, or offering to work without pay. Volunteers help the United States in many ways. During political elections, citizens can give their time to help a candidate run for office. Volunteers might answer phones or distribute flyers telling people why they should vote for that candidate. Many young people are volunteering, too. In the year 2000, almost half of the nation's young adults worked as volunteers.

Some volunteer groups work to help those in need. AmeriCorps is a volunteer program that was started by President Bill Clinton in 1993. Each year, more than 40,000 people work in AmeriCorps. Many young Americans volunteer because they can help their country and receive an education award to help pay for college. Some of these volunteers help tutor schoolchildren. Others serve food and set up shelters for victims of natural disasters.

REVIEW What are two powers shared by the federal government and state governments?

Meeting Challenges at Home

Between 1990 and 2000, the United States census showed a population increase of 32.7 million people. Nine cities in the country have more than 1 million people each. In fact, more than 8 million people live in New York City. Such population growth can cause problems.

A report by the United States Department of Education found that one out of every five schools in the country was overcrowded. One elementary school in Las Vegas, Nevada, had so many students that school officials had to set up 21 portable classrooms on and around the school's playground. Many city and county governments are working hard to raise money to build more schools and to hire more teachers.

Population growth can also bring traffic problems to cities. More people using automobiles means that more roads, highways, bridges, and tunnels must be built. Some cities ask people to use public transportation such as buses, subways, and trains.

Across the United States, millions of city residents have come to depend on public transportation for their travel needs.

Most public transportation systems, like the one shown here in Atlanta, Georgia, have maps at every stop to help direct passengers.

The nation's first subway system was built in Boston, Massachusetts, in 1897. Today subway systems can be found in cities such as Washington, D.C., New York City, and Atlanta, Georgia.

REVIEW What kinds of challenges can population growth bring?

Challenges for the Environment

A growing population creates a greater need for natural resources—soil, water, minerals, plants, and animals. People use natural resources to meet their needs and wants. But a nation must use its resources wisely. In the United States, citizens often work together with the government to stop soil erosion, keep water pure, and prevent pollution.

A large population produces large amounts of trash. One way many communities in the United States are trying to solve their trash problems is by recycling. To **recycle** means to use materials again, instead of just using them once. People sort trash items made of materials such as metal, glass, plastic, and paper that can be used to make new products. Many cities and towns in the United States have recycling centers where people can bring their used materials.

Young people can also help their environment by learning more about it. The National Park Service has started a program called Parks as Classrooms. These programs allow schools to teach classes or join programs in a nearby national park. Children can learn natural science

Plastics recycling plants, such as the one below, turn out plastic that can be used to make new products like this playground slide.

outdoors with the help of park rangers. In Florida's Everglades National Park, for example, teachers of fifth- and sixth-grade classes can take their students to the park for a three-day camping trip. Teachers and rangers lead the class in night walks, geology lessons, and other studies of the environment. Each year, more than 10,000 students travel to the park with their teachers. Students who visit the park learn how national parks help preserve the environment.

REVIEW What kinds of materials can be recycled?

LOCATE IT

Yellowstone National Park, WYOMING

These students are learning from a park ranger in Yellowstone National Park.

LESSON 4 REVIEW

Summary Time Line

1880 — 1940 — 2000

- 1889 Jane Addams opens Hull-House in Chicago
- 2000 George W. Bush is elected President

PREDICT AN OUTCOME What do you think might happen if Americans stopped volunteering?

1 BIG IDEA How do citizens of the United States work together for the good of their country?

2 VOCABULARY Write a letter to the President of the United States, using the vocabulary word **patriotism**.

3 TIME LINE In what year did Jane Addams set up Hull-House?

4 CIVICS AND GOVERNMENT What kinds of things can volunteers do?

5 HISTORY How did Americans help their country during World War I and World War II?

6 CRITICAL THINKING—Hypothesize How might life in the United States be different if the Bill of Rights did not exist?

PERFORMANCE—Make a List Imagine that the year is 1943 and you have chosen to plant a victory garden. Make a list of the things you would like to plant in your garden.

Chapter 14 ■ 559

SKILLS · Identify Political Symbols

▶ WHY IT MATTERS

People often recognize sports teams, clubs, and other organizations by their symbols. The same is true for political parties, the President, Congress, the Supreme Court, and even voters. Being able to identify political symbols and what they stand for can help you better understand news reports, political cartoons, and other sources of information.

▶ WHAT YOU NEED TO KNOW

Two of the country's best-known political symbols are animals. The donkey represents the Democratic party, and the elephant represents the Republican party. The donkey was probably first used to represent President Andrew Jackson, a Democrat, in the 1830s. Later the donkey

Built of white-gray sandstone, the President's home was being called the White House within a few years of its completion in 1801.

became a symbol for the entire party. Cartoonist Thomas Nast introduced the elephant as a symbol of the Republican party in 1874. Both symbols are still used today.

One of the symbols for the national government is Uncle Sam. The bald eagle and the Statue of Liberty are other symbols for our government. Buildings are often used as political symbols. The United States Capitol is a symbol for Congress, and the White House is a symbol for the President.

▶ PRACTICE THE SKILL

When you see a political symbol, answer these questions to help you understand its meaning:

Do you recognize the symbol? Does it stand for the whole national government or for only part of the national government? Does it stand for a person or for a group that is involved in government, such as a political party?

Where do you see the symbol? If it appears in a newspaper or magazine article, does the writer give you any clues about its meaning?

Are there any captions or other words that help explain what the symbol means? For example, the label *To Protect and Serve* might suggest that the symbol stands for the police.

▶ APPLY WHAT YOU LEARNED

Imagine that you have been selected to create a political symbol to represent a new political party. Before you draw the political symbol, decide what you think the political party should stand for. Share your symbol with a classmate, and explain how it represents the new political party.

Uncle Sam owes his name to Samuel Wilson, who stamped *U.S.* on crates of food supplies during the War of 1812. Soldiers joked that *U.S.* meant "Uncle Sam," and he soon became a national symbol.

CHAPTER 14 Review and Test Preparation

Summary Time Line
1860

• 1889 Jane Addams opens Hull-House in Chicago

Predict an Outcome

Copy the following graphic organizer onto a separate sheet of paper. Use the information you have learned to predict likely outcomes about changes in transportation and population.

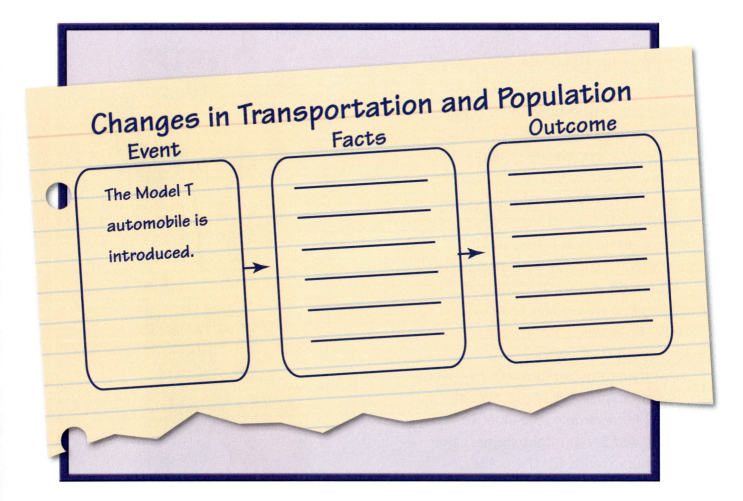

Changes in Transportation and Population

Event: The Model T automobile is introduced. → Facts → Outcome

THINK & WRITE

Write a Journal Entry Imagine you are a witness to the world's first successful airplane flight at Kitty Hawk, North Carolina. Write a journal entry describing the Wright brothers, the weather, and the flight.

Write a Biography Write a biography about an important person mentioned in Chapter 14. Be sure to include in your biography where and when the person was born and why his or her life was important.

1910			1960			Present
• 1920 The Nineteenth Amendment is ratified	• 1927 Charles Lindbergh flies from New York to Paris	• 1959 Alaska and Hawaii become states	• 1964 Congress passes the Civil Rights Act	• 1969 United States astronauts land on the moon	• 2000 George W. Bush is elected President	

USE THE TIME LINE

Use the chapter summary time line to answer these questions.

1. When did Alaska and Hawaii become states?
2. In what year was the Civil Rights Act passed?

USE VOCABULARY

Write a definition for each of these terms.

aviation (p. 527)

conservation (p. 545)

suffrage (p. 547)

recycle (p. 558)

RECALL FACTS

Answer these questions.

3. Why did many working people join labor unions in the early 1900s?
4. What is the Internet?
5. How can a person become a citizen of the United States?
6. Who was Cesar Chavez?

Write the letter of the best choice.

7. The first person to make a transatlantic flight was—
   A Orville Wright
   B Amelia Earhart
   C Charles Lindbergh
   D Wilbur Wright

8. Which of the following amendments gave women the right to vote?
   F the Thirteenth Amendment
   G the Fifteenth Amendment
   H the Nineteenth Amendment
   J the Twenty-second Amendment

THINK CRITICALLY

9. How did the invention of jet-powered airplanes change the airline industry?
10. Why do you think women were willing to work for the right to vote?

APPLY SKILLS

Use a Time Zone Map
Use the map and information on pages 532 and 533 to answer these questions.

11. How is time on Earth measured?
12. If it is 5 P.M. in Los Angeles, California, what time is it in Dallas, Texas?

Use a Cartogram
Use the map and cartogram on pages 542 and 543 to answer these questions.

13. When is it more useful to use a cartogram than another kind of map?
14. What geographical statistic is the cartogram on page 543 based on?

Identify Political Symbols
Use the information on pages 560 and 561 to answer this question.

15. How can understanding political symbols make someone a more informed citizen?

Chapter 14 ■ 563

SAN DIEGO BAY

In 1542 Juan Cabrillo became the first European to sail into what is now San Diego Bay. Today the city of San Diego is the second-largest city in the state of California. The bay itself is 27 miles (43 km) long and is home to hundreds of boats and large ships.

LOCATE IT

CALIFORNIA

San Diego

CHAPTER 15

Becoming a World Power

❝ There never was a country more fabulous than America. She sits bestride [over] the world like a Colossus [giant]. ❞

—Robert Payne, British historian, after visiting the United States in the winter of 1948–1949

Fact and Opinion

A **fact** is a statement that can be proved to be true. An **opinion** is an individual's view that is shaped by that person's feelings.

As you read this chapter, be sure to do the following.
- Separate facts from opinions about the United States.

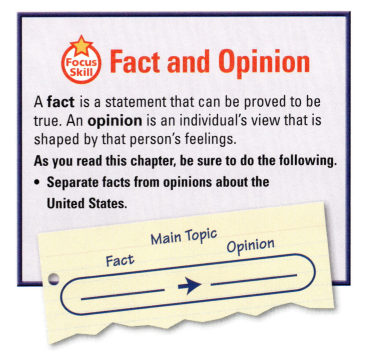

LESSON 1

The United States Grows

1860–2000

 FACT AND OPINION

As you read, look for facts and opinions about how the United States became a world power.

BIG IDEA
The United States added to its land area and increased its power at the end of the 1800s.

VOCABULARY
imperialism
civilian
armistice

By the late 1800s the western frontier had been settled, and the United States had become a world leader in industry and agriculture. Yet many Americans were ready to find new frontiers. They believed that acquiring new territories in other parts of the world would bring the country both new sources of raw materials and new markets for its goods. The United States was on its way to becoming a world power.

Alaska

In 1867, the United States agreed to buy Alaska from Russia for $7.2 million—about two cents an acre! Alaska was so big that its purchase increased the size of the United States by almost 20 percent. Many people, however, thought the government was foolish to purchase such a cold, unknown area. There were large amounts of land that had never been explored, and the climate was harsh.

FAST FACT Alaska is the largest state in the United States. It is 488 times as large as Rhode Island and $2\frac{1}{2}$ times as large as Texas.

The April 1898 cover of the *Klondike News* (right) illustrates the life of Alaskan miners, which included making their way through the Klondike River valley (below).

566 ■ Unit 7

Alaska's Glacier Bay National Park (left) is so isolated it can be reached only by boat or airplane.

At the time the United States bought Alaska, travel there was difficult. For the first ten years after the purchase, there was very little settlement in the new land. The few settlers who did come sometimes found work in the fishing industry.

In 1896, however, many people changed their opinions about Alaska. That year gold was found in the Klondike River valley in Canada, near Alaska. The discovery started a gold rush in the valley. From 1897 to 1899 more than 100,000 people raced to Alaska, hoping to get rich.

Few of those who moved to Alaska found gold. However, Alaska brought new wealth to the nation in other ways. Alaska was rich in natural resources, such as fish, timber, coal, and copper.

As more Americans moved to Alaska, the United States set up a system of government there. By 1884 federal courts were established, and a school system had started. In 1912 Alaska became a territory. By 1940 Alaska had a population of about 72,000 people. During World War II the federal government spent more than $2 billion in Alaska to build military bases and the Alaska Highway. The Alaska Highway connected Alaska with the rest of the United States.

On January 3, 1959, Alaska became the forty-ninth state. Many Americans have moved there, but the state is still known as the nation's last frontier. Today more than half of Alaska's citizens live in and around the city of Anchorage. Commercial fishing is still very important to the economy. Nearly 55 percent of the seafood production of the United States comes from Alaska. Tourism is also an important part of the economy. Every year people from around the world visit parks such as Denali National Park and Glacier Bay National Park.

REVIEW What event caused many Americans to change their opinions about Alaska?

FACT AND OPINION

Salmon fishing is a major industry in Alaska today.

Chapter 15 ■ 567

This photograph shows Waikiki Beach in Honolulu, Hawaii, in the 1890s. In 1900 the state's total population was about 154,000 people.

The Hawaiian Islands

Located in the Pacific Ocean, Hawaii was formed by a chain of volcanoes that rose from the sea floor. The first people to live in Hawaii were travelers from the South Pacific. These Polynesian islanders sailed canoes across the Pacific Ocean to Hawaii about 1,500 years ago. The first Hawaiians fished, raised pigs, and grew crops.

In 1778 Captain James Cook became the first European explorer to arrive in the Hawaiian Islands. Hawaii's location made it a good place for ships to stop when sailing between Asia and the Americas. Trading ships began stopping in Hawaii to get fresh supplies.

This photograph shows Waikiki Beach today. According to the 2000 census, over 1.2 million people now live in Hawaii.

In the early 1800s Christian missionaries were among the first Americans to arrive in Hawaii. Later, American businesspeople started cattle ranches and sugar plantations on the islands. Eventually an American named James Dole organized the Hawaiian Pineapple Company. Soon his workers were producing almost 6 million cases of canned pineapple every year. Over time a modern economy was built from the production of sugar and pineapples for the United States. Although many settlers arrived from Asia, Americans controlled much of the land in Hawaii.

When the Hawaiian king, Kalakaua (kah•lah•KAH•ooh•ah), tried to keep the Americans from taking over the islands in 1887, they decided to take away the king's authority. In 1893 the king's sister, Queen Liliuokalani (lih•lee•uh•woh•kuh•LAH•nee), tried to take back power. But the Americans took over the government and set up a republic.

Hawaii became a territory of the United States in 1898. During the next 40 years, Americans set up national parks, built schools, and farmed the land. On August 20, 1959, Hawaii became the fiftieth state in the United States. The capital city of Honolulu is located about 2,400 miles (3,862 km) from the coast of California. Despite the distance, so many people visit Hawaii today that about 30 percent of Hawaiians work in the tourism industry.

Queen Liliuokalani

• HERITAGE •

Hula Dance

Dancing is one of the best-known arts of the Hawaiian Islands. Hula (HOO•lah) dancing has been practiced by native Hawaiians for centuries. The word *hula* even means "dance" in the Hawaiian language. Hula dancers sway their hips and wave their arms to music. Early Hawaiians had no written language, so they used chants and dances, passed down from generation to generation, to record their history. As a result, every hula dance tells a story. Some of the musical instruments used to accompany the hula include drums, the Hawaiian steel guitar, and the ukulele (yoo•kuh•LAY•lee).

Tourism is a valuable part of Hawaii's economy, but agriculture is still its most important industry. The state is the second-largest sugarcane producer in the nation. It is also the leading producer of pineapples. Some of the many unusual tropical flowers that are grown in Hawaii are also exported. People in the rest of the United States buy orchids, hibiscus, and other colorful Hawaiian flowers.

REVIEW What are Hawaii's two most important industries?

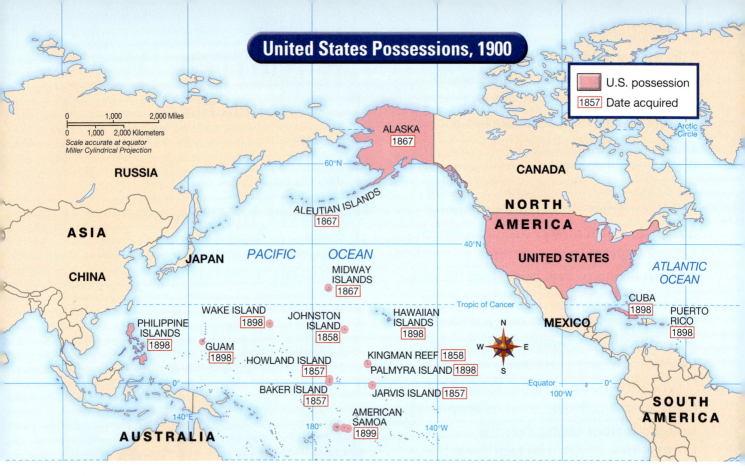

Location In the late 1800s the United States acquired many territories around the world.

 In what part of the world did the United States gain most of its new land in the late 1800s?

War with Spain

As the United States grew in size, some people accused the country's leaders of **imperialism**, or empire building. They believed that adding new lands would cause trouble between the United States and European nations—especially Spain.

For many years there had been trouble in the Spanish colony of Cuba, about 90 miles (145 km) from the coast of Florida. The Cuban people did not want to be under Spanish rule, and many rebellions took place. Some Americans were put in jail for trying to help the rebels. In 1895 another rebellion began. The Spanish army forced many Cuban **civilians**, or people who were not in the military, into guarded camps. Some died there because of poor conditions.

Many Americans, including those who had moved to Cuba to start businesses, supported the Cubans' fight for independence. Newspapers in the United States told exaggerated stories about Spain's harsh rule of Cuba. This practice was known as "yellow journalism."

In 1898 President William McKinley ordered the battleship *Maine* to Havana, Cuba, to protect Americans living there. Just three weeks after the *Maine* arrived, an explosion sank the ship in Havana's harbor. More than 260 sailors were killed. It was not clear why the ship blew up, but the United States blamed Spain. "Remember the *Maine*!" Americans cried. On April 25 the United States declared war on Spain.

The first battles of the Spanish-American War were not fought in Cuba. They took place half a world away—in the Philippine Islands. The Philippines are a chain of islands off the coast of Southeast Asia. Spain had ruled the area for nearly 300 years. Just days after the war began, the United States Navy, led by Commodore George Dewey, defeated the Spanish fleet there. The fighting then shifted to Cuba.

Thousands of Americans fought in the war, including a former Confederate Army general known as "Fighting Joe" Wheeler. A young man named Theodore Roosevelt volunteered to fight in a company made up mostly of cowhands and college athletes. In Cuba the Rough Riders, as they were called, took part in the Battle of San Juan Hill. African American soldiers in the 10th Cavalry, led by John Pershing, fought bravely beside the Rough Riders.

On August 12, 1898, after a number of defeats, Spain signed an armistice (AR•muh•stuhs). An **armistice** is an agreement to stop fighting a war. The Spanish-American War lasted less than four months, but more than 5,000 American soldiers died. Most of them died from diseases such as malaria and yellow fever. As a result of the Spanish-American War, the United States became a world power. Spain agreed to give the United States Cuba, Puerto Rico, Guam, and the Philippines. Cuba and the Philippines later became independent countries, but Puerto Rico and Guam remain part of the United States today.

REVIEW What lands did the United States gain as a result of the Spanish-American War?

This canteen was used by a Rough Rider in Cuba.

Theodore Roosevelt (center, with glasses) is shown here with the 1st Cavalry Volunteers, also known as the Rough Riders.

The Panama Canal

Soon after Theodore Roosevelt returned from Cuba, he was elected governor of New York. Two years later he was elected Vice President of the United States, serving under President McKinley. On September 6, 1901, President McKinley was shot by a person who was opposed to the government. McKinley died eight days later, and Roosevelt became President.

One of President Roosevelt's main goals was to build a canal across the Isthmus of Panama, in Central America. The canal would link the Atlantic Ocean and the Pacific Ocean. This, in turn, would link American ports on the Atlantic coast with those on the Pacific coast. "I wish to see the United States the dominant power on the shores of the Pacific Ocean," Roosevelt said.

In 1902 Congress voted to build the canal. However, the Isthmus of Panama did not belong to the United States. It belonged to the nation of Colombia. The United States offered $10 million to Colombia for the right to build a canal, but Colombia turned down the offer.

Roosevelt then spread the word that he would support a revolution in Panama to end Colombian rule. He sent the United States Navy to protect the isthmus. If a revolution began, the navy was to keep Colombian troops from landing on the shore. Within three months a revolution took place, and the people of Panama formed a new nation. Panama's leaders

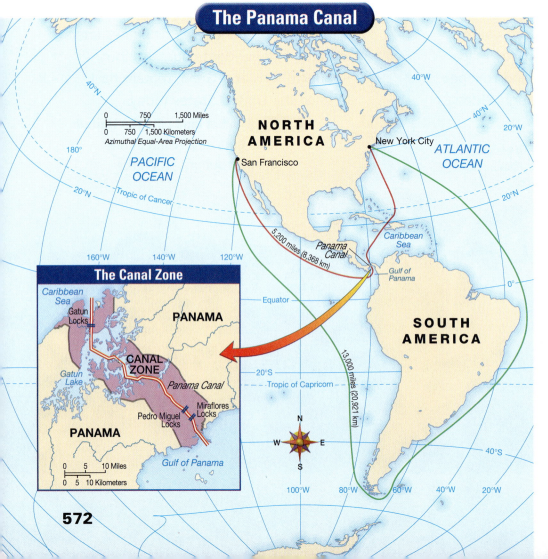

 Human-Environment Interactions The building of the Panama Canal took ten years and involved thousands of workers. It was the largest United States building project since the transcontinental railroad.

➤ What is the length of the Panama Canal?

then gave the United States the right to build the canal. The United States would control the canal and an area 5 miles (8 km) wide on each side of it.

Work on the canal began in 1904. Workers guided huge machines to cut down the trees and thick jungle growth. Engineers designed huge canal locks to help ships move through the waterway.

Unlike the French, who first tried to build a canal in Central America in the 1880s, American workers stayed healthy. Doctors had learned that malaria and yellow fever, the diseases that stopped the French, were carried by mosquitoes. The Americans learned to control the mosquitoes by using poisons and draining the swamps where they lived.

Building the canal took ten years and cost about $380 million. After it opened, goods could be shipped between ports on the Atlantic coast and ports on the Pacific coast in about one month. Today the canal, which is under Panama's control, continues to move people and goods around the world.

Each year nearly 12,000 ships pass through the Panama Canal (above)—an average of about 33 ships per day.

REVIEW Which two bodies of water does the Panama Canal connect?

LESSON 1 REVIEW

Summary Time Line 1860 — 2000

- 1867 The United States purchases Alaska
- 1898 The Spanish-American War begins
- 1959 Alaska and Hawaii become states

FACT AND OPINION Hawaii is located in the Pacific Ocean. Is this statement a fact or an opinion? Explain.

1. **BIG IDEA** How did the United States add to its land area at the end of the 1800s?
2. **VOCABULARY** Use the word armistice in a sentence about the Spanish-American War.
3. **TIME LINE** When did the Spanish-American War begin?
4. **CIVICS AND GOVERNMENT** From which nation did the United States purchase Alaska?
5. **CRITICAL THINKING—Analyze** How did a revolution in Panama benefit the United States?

PERFORMANCE—Write a Newspaper Article Imagine that you are a newspaper reporter who is covering the building of the Panama Canal. Write an article telling people back in the United States about the building process.

Chapter 15 ■ 573

SKILLS · MAP AND GLOBE

Compare Map Projections

VOCABULARY

projections
distortions

▶ WHY IT MATTERS

Because the Earth is round and maps are flat, maps cannot represent the Earth's shape exactly. As a result, cartographers have different ways of showing the Earth on flat paper. These different views are called **projections**. All projections have **distortions**, or areas that are not accurate. But different kinds of projections have different kinds of distortions. Identifying areas on a map that are distorted will help you understand how different maps can best be used.

▶ WHAT YOU NEED TO KNOW

Both Map A and Map B show the same area, but they use different projections. Map A is an azimuthal (a•zuh•MUH•thuhl)

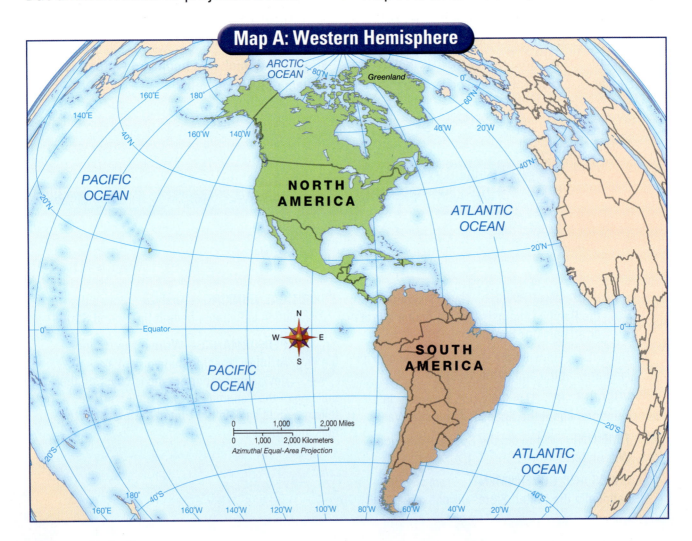

Map A: Western Hemisphere

574 ■ Unit 7

Map B: Western Hemisphere

equal-area projection. Equal-area projections show the sizes of regions in correct relation to one another. However, they distort, or change, the shapes of the areas shown on them.

Map B is a Miller cylindrical projection. It is one example of a conformal projection. Notice that the meridians on Map B are all an equal distance apart. Notice also that the parallels closer to the North and South Poles are farther apart than those near the equator. Conformal projections, like the one used on Map B, show directions correctly, but they distort sizes, especially of the places near the poles.

PRACTICE THE SKILL

Use Maps A and B to answer the following questions.

1. On which map does Greenland appear to be larger?
2. On which map is the size of Greenland more accurate?

APPLY WHAT YOU LEARNED

Write a paragraph explaining when you would use an equal-area projection map. Then write about when you would find a conformal projection more useful.

 Practice your map and globe skills with the **GeoSkills CD-ROM**.

LESSON 2

Defending Democracy

1900–2000

 FACT AND OPINION

As you read, look for facts and opinions about the role the United States played in world events.

BIG IDEA
The United States fought to defend the freedom of people in other nations.

VOCABULARY
military draft
depression
concentration camp
D day
Holocaust
communism
free world
cold war
arms control

The United States entered the twentieth century as a world power. This new role brought new challenges. The leaders of some nations wanted to increase their power by invading other lands. Soon the United States had to defend itself and its allies. During the 1900s and beyond, Americans fought to preserve the rights of people all over the world.

World War I

Because of many years of disagreements, nations across Europe had formed alliances. The members of each alliance promised to help one another if they were attacked. Europeans hoped these alliances would prevent war, but they had the opposite effect.

On June 28, 1914, Austria-Hungary's Archduke Francis Ferdinand and his wife, Sophie, were shot and killed by an assassin from Serbia. By the end of July, Austria-Hungary had declared war on Serbia. When Russia sent troops to help Serbia, Austria-Hungary asked its allies for help. On August 1 Germany declared war on Russia. By the middle of August, almost all of Europe was at war. On one side were the Allied Powers, or Allies. They included Britain, Russia, France, Serbia, and later, Italy. On the other side were the Central Powers, which included Germany, Austria-Hungary, the Ottoman Empire, and Bulgaria.

Most Americans did not want to join the war in Europe. When the war began, President Woodrow Wilson said the United States would

The assassination of Archduke Francis Ferdinand and his wife led to war.

576 • Unit 7

Regions This map shows how World War I divided Europe.

GEOGRAPHY THEME In which European country did the greatest number of major battles take place?

remain neutral. However, in early 1917, German submarines sank three American ships in the Atlantic Ocean. On April 2, 1917, President Wilson asked Congress to declare war on Germany. Four days later the United States joined the Allies.

At the time, the United States Army was small. To make the army larger, Congress passed a new law that set up a **military draft**, a way to bring people into military service. By the war's end, the army had grown from about 300,000 soldiers to over 3 million.

American efforts made an important difference in the war. Working together, the Allies began to push back the German army. Finally, on November 11, 1918, Germany surrendered, and the fighting stopped.

Allied leaders gathered in Paris, France, to make peace terms. However, they disagreed about how Germany should be punished. The Treaty of Versailles (ver•SY) ended the war, but it did not leave Europe fully at peace. The disagreements that came after World War I would soon lead to an even more destructive conflict—World War II.

REVIEW Why were many European countries drawn into World War I?

Worldwide Troubles

In the years after World War I, many Americans enjoyed great prosperity. In the fall of 1929, however, the stock market crashed, and an economic depression gripped the nation and the rest of the world. A **depression** is a time of little economic growth when there are few jobs and people have little money. This depression, which continued through the 1930s, was so serious that it became known as the Great Depression.

Because times were so hard, some countries turned to new types of government. In Germany a World War I veteran named Adolf Hitler became the leader of a political party called the National Socialists, or Nazis (NAHT•seez). The Nazi party took control of Germany in 1933, and Hitler began ruling as a dictator.

The Nazis blamed Jewish people in Germany for the country's problems. In the late 1930s the Nazis set up terrible prisons called **concentration camps**. Millions of Jewish people as well as others who disagreed with the Nazis were sent to these camps. Because of Hitler's power as a dictator, few people in Germany questioned him.

Dictators had risen to power in other countries, too. In Italy, Benito Mussolini (buh•NEE•toh moo•suh•LEE•nee) seized power in 1922. In 1924 Joseph Stalin took control of the Soviet Union, which was formed following a revolution in Russia in 1917. A group of military dictators also ruled Japan.

In the 1930s Japan, Italy, and Germany began taking over other countries. Because of painful memories of World War I, other nations did little to stop these acts. Most people hoped war could be avoided.

REVIEW What countries were ruled by dictators before World War II?

German leader Adolf Hitler addresses thousands of German soldiers at Nuremberg, Germany, in 1937.

German soldiers invaded Poland in 1939 and had taken over Paris, France, by 1940.

World War II Begins

On September 1, 1939, German forces, numbering nearly 2 million, invaded Poland. They attacked with tanks on land and planes in the air, quickly defeating their neighbor. Two days later Poland's allies, Britain and France, responded to this attack by declaring war on Germany. World War II had begun.

German forces stormed across Europe with great speed. By the end of 1941, much of Europe was under German control. The only countries that remained free were Britain, the Soviet Union, and a few small neutral nations. In France, rebel armies fought to weaken Germany's grip. In the skies over Britain, German bombers continued their attacks, but Britain bravely fought on.

Germany's actions shocked and angered most Americans. However, few Americans wanted the United States to become involved in another foreign war. It would not be long, though, before events in the Pacific brought the war home to Americans.

At 7:55 A.M. on Sunday, December 7, 1941, the roar of Japanese planes shattered the early morning calm over the Hawaiian Islands. The planes dropped bombs on American ships docked at Pearl Harbor, an American naval base. World War II had come to the United States.

Americans were outraged by the attack on Pearl Harbor. President Franklin D. Roosevelt called December 7 "a date which will live in infamy." The next day, Congress declared war on Japan.

Three days later, Germany and Italy declared war on the United States, and Congress recognized a state of war with them, too. Germany, Italy, and Japan were known as the Axis Powers. The United States joined with the Allies, which included Britain, France, and the Soviet Union. The Soviet Union had joined the Allies after Germany had invaded it in the summer of 1941.

REVIEW What event caused the United States to enter the war?

Over 1,100 sailors lost their lives when the USS *Arizona* (below) sank at Pearl Harbor. The life preserver (left) is from the *Arizona*.

Chapter 15 ■ 579

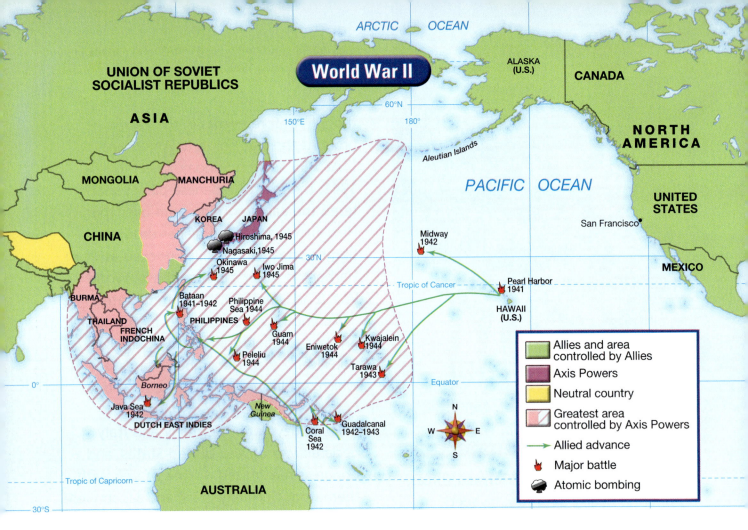

A World at War

At home and overseas, Americans did their part to support the war effort. Across the country, people went to work in factories, steel mills, shipyards, and aircraft plants. Working around the clock, Americans produced huge amounts of war materials at record speed.

More than 15 million Americans served in the armed forces. These men and women defended the Allied cause all around the world. In Europe, General Dwight D. Eisenhower led a massive Allied invasion of the northern coast of France. The date of this invasion, June 6, 1944, was known as D day. The D day operation was the largest water-to-land invasion in history. Many soldiers died, but the invasion was a success. It was a turning point in the war, and in May 1945 Germany surrendered.

Only when the war was over in Europe did people finally understand what Hitler and the Nazis had done. During the war more than 6 million Jewish people were

General Dwight D. Eisenhower speaks with American troops in England, the day before the D day invasion.

Location During the war, almost the whole world was divided between the Allied Powers and the Axis Powers.

◆ Why was the location of the United States helpful in the war?

murdered on Hitler's orders. This terrible mass murder of more than two-thirds of all European Jews came to be known as the **Holocaust** (HOH•luh•kawst). It was a planned attempt to destroy an entire people.

In the Pacific, fierce fighting continued even after Germany's surrender. President Harry S. Truman feared more American lives would be lost if the war did not end quickly. He made the hard decision to try to end the war by using a new weapon called the atom bomb.

On August 6, 1945, American planes dropped an atom bomb on the city of Hiroshima (hir•uh•SHEE•muh), in Japan. About 80,000 Japanese were killed. Still, Japan did not surrender. Three days later the United States dropped a second atom bomb on the city of Nagasaki (nah•guh•SAH•kee). Finally, Japan agreed to surrender, and World War II came to an end.

Afterward, the balance of power in the world was very different than it had been before. New weapons such as the atom bomb now threatened the safety of people everywhere.

REVIEW What was D day and why was it important? **FACT AND OPINION**

Chapter 15 ■ 581

Cold War and Hot Wars

The Soviet Union and the United States had been allies during the war, but that changed once the war ended. The Soviet Union was a communist nation. **Communism** is a political and economic system in which all land and industries are owned by the government. Under communism individuals have few rights and little freedom. When the war ended, the Soviet Union began setting up communist governments in eastern European countries. In China communist forces took control in 1949. The **free world**—the United States and its allies in the fight against communism—saw these actions as threats to freedom.

Hostility, or unfriendliness, soon developed between the free world and communist nations. This hostility became known as the Cold War. A **cold war** is fought mostly with propaganda and money rather than with soldiers and weapons. One early Cold War conflict took place in the Asian nation of Korea.

In June 1950 a Soviet-backed communist army from North Korea invaded the smaller country of South Korea. The United States sent soldiers to defend South Korea. This conflict became known as the Korean War. At first, the United States and its allies wanted to unite North Korea and South Korea as a democracy. But the communist Chinese army joined the North Korean forces. The United States did not want to start a war with China, so the conflict ended without a victory by either side.

In October 1962 the Cuban missile crisis resulted from the Soviet Union's placing missile launch sites in Cuba, just 90 miles (145 km) off the tip of Florida. Fidel Castro had taken control of Cuba in 1959. With the help of the Soviet Union, he had formed a communist government there. United States President John F. Kennedy knew the Soviets could use the missiles in Cuba to attack the United States, so he ordered a naval blockade of Cuba. After 13 tense days the two sides reached an agreement that avoided war.

The Korean War was the first war in which helicopters were regularly used in battle by the United States.

A few years later, though, the United States found itself involved in another war. In 1964 the Asian nation of South Vietnam was attacked by communist forces from North Vietnam. The United States sent troops to help the South Vietnamese. By 1966 about 250,000 United States troops were fighting in Vietnam. The conflict became known as the Vietnam War.

The Vietnam War sharply divided Americans. People disagreed about whether the United States should be involved. In 1973, United States troops left Vietnam. Two years later, South Vietnam surrendered and the war ended.

The Berlin Wall divided East Germany and West Germany for 28 years.

The Cold War changed in the next decade. In 1985, Mikhail Gorbachev (mee•kah•EEL gawr•buh•CHAWF) became leader of the Soviet Union. A year later, President Ronald Reagan met with Gorbachev. The leaders discussed **arms control**, or limiting each nation's number of weapons.

During the 1980s democratic revolutions in eastern Europe led to the fall of a number of communist governments. For many years the Berlin Wall had kept people from leaving communist East Germany. But in 1989 the people of Germany tore down the wall to reunite the nation. In 1991 the Soviet Union broke up into several free countries. The Cold War, which had lasted for almost 50 years, was finally over.

REVIEW How did the Cold War end?

LESSON 2 REVIEW

Summary Time Line

1900 — 1918 World War I ends — 1939 World War II begins — 1950 — 1945 World War II ends — 1991 The Cold War ends — 2000

FACT AND OPINION Identify two facts in this lesson.

1 BIG IDEA How did the United States help defend freedom around the world?

2 VOCABULARY Use the term **cold war** in a sentence.

3 TIME LINE When did World War II end?

4 CRITICAL THINKING—Synthesize Why do you think the Cold War lasted so long?

PERFORMANCE—Create a Time Line Use facts from this lesson to create a time line showing important events that happened after World War II.

Chapter 15 ■ 583

Examine Primary Sources

Editorial Cartoons

Cartoons that express opinions about politics or about government are called editorial cartoons. Since the middle 1700s, editorial cartoons have been appearing in magazines and newspapers. Researchers and students can study editorial cartoons to learn more about historical events. The Vietnam War is an example of an event that stirred the opinions of editorial cartoonists. In the cartoon to the right, cartoonist John Riedell expressed his political opinions about President Lyndon B. Johnson's handling of the war.

AAEC Editorial Cartoon Digital Collection at the University of Southern Mississippi

These editorial cartoons (above and right) drawn by Eddie Germano reflect his views. They reveal the difficulty that President Johnson faced as he worked to resolve the conflict in Vietnam.

584 ◾ Unit 7

Analyze the Primary Source

1. What words or images tell you what the cartoons mean?
2. Describe the actions taking place in the cartoons.
3. In your own words, explain the messages of the cartoons.
4. What groups might agree or disagree with the cartoons' messages?

The photograph below shows Eddie Germano at work in his studio in the late 1960s. His editorial cartoon at left is called *Flicker of Hope*.

ACTIVITY

Express an Opinion Think of an issue on which you have an opinion. Make an editorial cartoon that expresses your opinion. Write a caption to help explain the meaning of your cartoon.

RESEARCH

Visit The Learning Site at www.harcourtschool.com to research other primary sources.

585

LESSON 3

A World Superpower

1945–2005

 FACT AND OPINION

As you read, look for facts and opinions about the way the United States is involved in shaping world affairs.

BIG IDEA
The United States works to maintain its role as a superpower today.

VOCABULARY
superpower
terrorism
refugee
developing country
hijack

During the 1900s, United States military forces fought to defend freedom throughout the world. But there were still other problems to solve. The United States was now a **superpower**, or one of the world's most powerful nations. Its citizens enjoyed many new benefits, but they also had many new responsibilities. The American people would rise to meet these responsibilities as they faced the new challenges of the twenty-first century.

Working Together

After World War II many nations had strong and able government leaders. However, conflicts continued to occur around the world. It became clear that one nation alone could not protect the freedom of all people. Some of the most powerful nations agreed to form a new world organization that would oversee the way that all nations interacted.

Before the end of World War II, the United States, the Soviet Union, and Britain had worked together to design the new organization. President Franklin D. Roosevelt, British Prime

Winston Churchill (left), Franklin D. Roosevelt (center), and Joseph Stalin (right) met in Yalta, Ukraine, in 1945.

Minister Winston Churchill, and Soviet leader Joseph Stalin decided on its structure. On October 24, 1945, the United Nations, or UN, was established. The organization first met in San Francisco. At the first meeting, representatives wrote the UN charter, or contract, which was signed by 51 nations. In 1952 the UN moved to its present headquarters in New York City.

Today almost every nation in the world belongs to the United Nations. More than 185 nations have signed the charter and become members. Under the charter, members agree to a policy of nonviolence. They agree to help other nations settle their disagreements peacefully. The main purpose of the UN is to keep international peace and security. This means that its members must sometimes send people to other countries to help settle conflicts.

Today there are about 35,400 UN peacekeepers working all over the world. These men and women wear blue helmets or hats so they can be identified as peacekeepers. UN peacekeepers serve in many troubled areas around the globe.

The United Nations does much more than peacekeeping, though. Some United Nations agencies give loans to help needy countries build schools and hospitals. Other agencies work to stop **terrorism**, or the use of violence to promote a cause. When natural disasters or wars occur, members of the UN help **refugees**, or people who must leave their homes to seek shelter and safety elsewhere. Since the United Nations was established in 1945, its agencies have been awarded five Nobel Peace Prizes.

The United Nations is not the only group of world powers. After World War II, the North Atlantic Treaty Organization, or NATO, was formed to enforce the North Atlantic Treaty. This treaty, approved in 1949, was signed by ten European nations, the United States, and Canada.

A UN peacekeeper helmet

The UN headquarters building in New York City was designed by a team of architects from 11 countries.

The North Atlantic Treaty was meant to protect western nations from communist forces in Europe. At that time many people were afraid that the Soviet Union would attack other nations. One section of the treaty stated that an armed attack against one member of NATO would be considered an attack against all members. This meant that each member nation agreed to defend any other NATO member from a foreign attack.

After the fall of communism in the Soviet Union, NATO's goals changed. However, the organization continued to safeguard security in Europe. In 1998 a serious new conflict developed when Yugoslavia tried to crush a revolution in the neighboring region of Kosovo. NATO forces moved in and the United States sent troops to help them. After NATO air strikes, Yugoslavia agreed to remove its soldiers from Kosovo.

REVIEW What was the original purpose of the North Atlantic Treaty?

Helping Other Nations

The Great Depression, World War II, and the Cold War taught Americans that to keep the world's economy stable, powerful and wealthy nations should help poorer nations.

During the second half of the twentieth century, the United States spent billions of dollars on foreign aid. The government and private groups sent money, food, and equipment to developing countries. A **developing country** is a country that

Regions In 1949 the United States joined NATO. Not since the Revolutionary War had the United States joined in a peacetime military alliance with Europe.

❖ What are the two westernmost members of NATO?

588

In 1960 John F. Kennedy (above, center) introduced his idea for the Peace Corps in a speech at the University of Michigan. This Peace Corps volunteer (right) is teaching an outdoor class in Africa.

does not have modern conveniences such as good housing, roads, schools, and hospitals. The United States has a long tradition of helping nations that need assistance.

During the Cold War the United States wanted to help its allies. One of its most successful foreign aid programs was the Marshall Plan, which helped rebuild Europe after World War II. Between 1948 and 1952 the United States gave about $13 billion in aid to western European nations. In the 1980s, during the time Ronald Reagan was President, he wanted to provide aid to private businesses in other countries. President Reagan hoped that if the United States helped a nation's business owners, the country's whole economy would grow.

American citizens also volunteered to help people in other countries. In 1961 President John F. Kennedy created the Peace Corps (KAWR). The Peace Corps sends American volunteers to developing countries. These volunteers come from different age groups and backgrounds. Peace Corps volunteers live in another country for two years. Some volunteers teach math and science to children. Others help people start businesses or improve farming methods.

Life in the Peace Corps is usually very different from life in the United States. One volunteer in Africa wrote, "For most people in the developing world, a refrigerator is a luxury item . . . most people here—including me—cannot afford one." Serving in the Peace Corps taught Americans what life was like in developing areas. By the year 2000 more than 150,000 Americans had worked as Peace Corps volunteers in 132 countries.

REVIEW What was the Marshall Plan?

During the Persian Gulf War, General Colin Powell (left) helped lead an international alliance against Iraq. The Iraqi army set many oil fields on fire (center). President George Bush (right) traveled to Saudi Arabia to meet with American troops during the war.

Challenges Abroad

The balance of world power changed after the breakup of the Soviet Union. The United States took the lead in many ways. President George Bush led the transition to what he called a "new world order." By a "new world order," Bush meant a world without the conflicts of the past. Despite his hopes, new conflicts soon developed.

In August 1990 the Middle Eastern nation of Iraq, led by its dictator Saddam Hussein (hoo•SAYN), invaded the small country of Kuwait (koo•WAYT). The Iraqi army quickly took over Kuwait, a major producer of oil in the Middle East. When Iraq refused to withdraw its troops, allied forces from 27 countries, including the United States, attacked Iraq. The United States led this attack, known as Operation Desert Storm, or the Persian Gulf War.

Among President Bush's advisers during the war was General Colin L. Powell. He was chairman of the Joint Chiefs of Staff—the leaders of all the branches of the nation's military. General Powell oversaw the alliance's strategy. By the middle of January 1991, a total of 690,000 troops from the allied nations had arrived in Saudi Arabia. The Persian Gulf War began with a five-week bombing operation against Iraq. On February 24 the allied armies sent in ground forces. After only four days Iraq surrendered. The United States had helped restore the balance of power in the Middle East.

REVIEW What caused the Persian Gulf War?
FACT AND OPINION

Toward a New Century

In 1992 Bill Clinton was elected President. Clinton oversaw one of the greatest periods of economic growth in the nation's history. Businesses created millions of new jobs. Unemployment dropped to its lowest levels in decades.

President Clinton and members of Congress also worked to achieve a balanced budget.

The growing economic success was due partly to the American economic system. In the nation's free enterprise economy, producers offer goods or services that consumers want to buy. Consumers have the right to choose between different goods and services. Then they agree to exchange products for money. The study of this interaction between individuals is called microeconomics.

Much of the economic growth was also caused by trade and the growing role of the United States in the world economy. By the middle of the 1990s, the United States imported more than $600 billion worth of goods each year. The nation's exports totaled about $500 billion. The United States had the world's largest share of global trade. This system of imports and exports led to greater interdependence among nations and regions.

Global trade offered many opportunities, but it could also cause problems. Many businesses in the United States moved their factories to other countries where the labor cost was lower. As a result, some Americans lost their jobs. President Clinton proposed the North American Free Trade Agreement, or NAFTA, to open new markets for businesses. This agreement would allow companies in the United States to form partnerships with companies in

President Bill Clinton worked with Congress to achieve a balanced budget.

Canada and Mexico. These companies would not have to pay tariffs, or import duties, on goods brought in from any of the three nations. Congress approved NAFTA in 1993.

REVIEW What three countries were originally part of NAFTA?

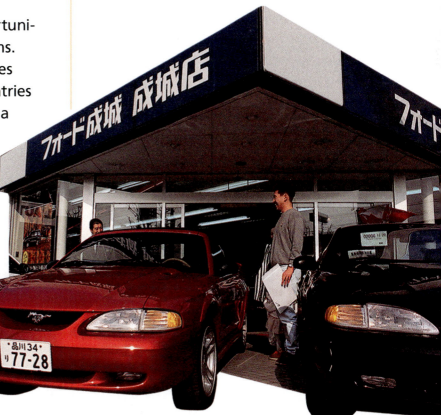

This American car dealership is located in Japan.

Chapter 15 ■ 591

The Oklahoma City Memorial (left) is made up of 168 empty chairs—one for each person whose life was lost.

Facing New Dangers

At the end of the twentieth century, the United States faced new dangers. The nation's military continued to defend democratic values around the world. The nation also experienced acts of terrorism as bombs exploded at two United States embassies in Africa and next to a United States navy ship in the Middle East.

Acts of terrorism occurred inside the United States, too. In the early 1990s, a bomb rocked the World Trade Center in New York City. Then, in 1995, an American citizen who was angry with the government set off a bomb near the federal office building in Oklahoma City, Oklahoma. The blast killed 168 people.

However, the worst act of terrorism in the nation's history occurred on September 11, 2001. That morning, terrorists **hijacked**, or illegally took control of, four American airplanes. Two of the hijacked planes were flown directly into the twin towers of the World Trade Center, both of which collapsed. The third plane was flown into the side of the Pentagon, the nation's military headquarters, near Washington, D.C. The fourth plane crashed in an empty field in Pennsylvania. That tragic day soon became known as 9/11.

President George W. Bush declared that the United States would lead a war

When the World Trade Center in New York City was attacked on September 11, 2001, the city's firefighters and police officers risked their lives to protect others.

After the attacks on September 11, 2001, many Americans gathered in public ceremonies (above). On September 20, President George W. Bush spoke before Congress (right).

against terrorism. The Taliban government in Afghanistan had offered support to terrorists. In 2001, the United States and its allies overthrew the Taliban.

Then, in 2003, the United States and its allies fought against Saddam Hussein, the Iraqi leader. They soon defeated Hussein's government. With the help of many other nations, the Iraqi people are now working to rebuild their country.

REVIEW In what ways has terrorism affected the United States?

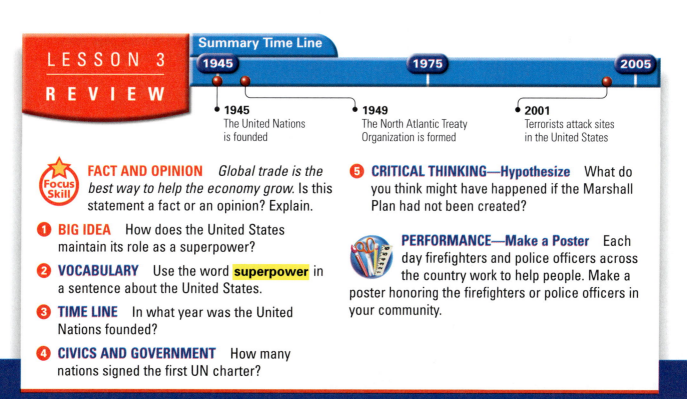

LESSON 3 REVIEW

Summary Time Line

- **1945** The United Nations is founded
- **1949** The North Atlantic Treaty Organization is formed
- **2001** Terrorists attack sites in the United States

FACT AND OPINION *Global trade is the best way to help the economy grow.* Is this statement a fact or an opinion? Explain.

1. **BIG IDEA** How does the United States maintain its role as a superpower?

2. **VOCABULARY** Use the word **superpower** in a sentence about the United States.

3. **TIME LINE** In what year was the United Nations founded?

4. **CIVICS AND GOVERNMENT** How many nations signed the first UN charter?

5. **CRITICAL THINKING—Hypothesize** What do you think might have happened if the Marshall Plan had not been created?

PERFORMANCE—Make a Poster Each day firefighters and police officers across the country work to help people. Make a poster honoring the firefighters or police officers in your community.

Chapter 15 ■ 593

SKILLS · Make Economic Choices

VOCABULARY
trade-off
opportunity cost

▶ WHY IT MATTERS

When you buy something at a store, you are making an economic choice. Choosing how to use your money wisely can be difficult. When you buy something, you are spending money that you cannot use for something else. This giving up of one thing in return for another is called a **trade-off**. What you give up is the **opportunity cost** of what you get. Understanding trade-offs and opportunity costs can help you make thoughtful economic choices.

▶ WHAT YOU NEED TO KNOW

You have read that when people spend money on consumer goods, it helps the United States economy. By helping the economy, Americans can also help themselves economically. On the other hand, people also help themselves economically when they put some of their money in a savings account for things they will need in the future. When they take their money out of the savings account, they also receive interest.

Putting your money into a savings account has its own kind of reward. The bank pays you interest for the use of your money.

594 ■ Unit 7

Spending your extra money helps the economy grow. You also get to enjoy the items you buy.

▶ PRACTICE THE SKILL

Imagine that you work in an office in a big city. At the end of every week, you receive a paycheck. After you pay all of your bills, you have some money left over. You must decide what to do with it. Should you use it to buy something you want now, such as new clothes for work? Or should you save it for things you might need in the future?

1. Think about the trade-off. Decide what is good and what is bad about each possible choice. Consider which of the choices will help you more. What is the trade-off?
2. Think about the opportunity costs. You do not have enough money to buy work clothes and put money in the bank. You must give up one of the choices. If you buy the clothes, you give up the chance to have the money back later, with interest. So the opportunity cost of buying the clothes is that you will not have the money in the bank for later. What is the opportunity cost of putting your money into savings?

▶ APPLY WHAT YOU LEARNED

Suppose you want to buy a book or rent a movie, but you do not have enough money for both. Explain to a partner the trade-off and the opportunity costs of each choice.

CHAPTER 15
Review and Test Preparation

Summary Time Line
1860

• 1867 The United States purchases Alaska

Focus Skill: Fact and Opinion

Copy the following graphic organizer onto a separate sheet of paper. Use the information you have learned to identify facts and opinions about Alaska and Hawaii.

Facts and Opinions About Alaska and Hawaii

Fact	Opinion
The purchase of Alaska increased the size of the United States.	
On August 20, 1959, Hawaii became the fiftieth state.	

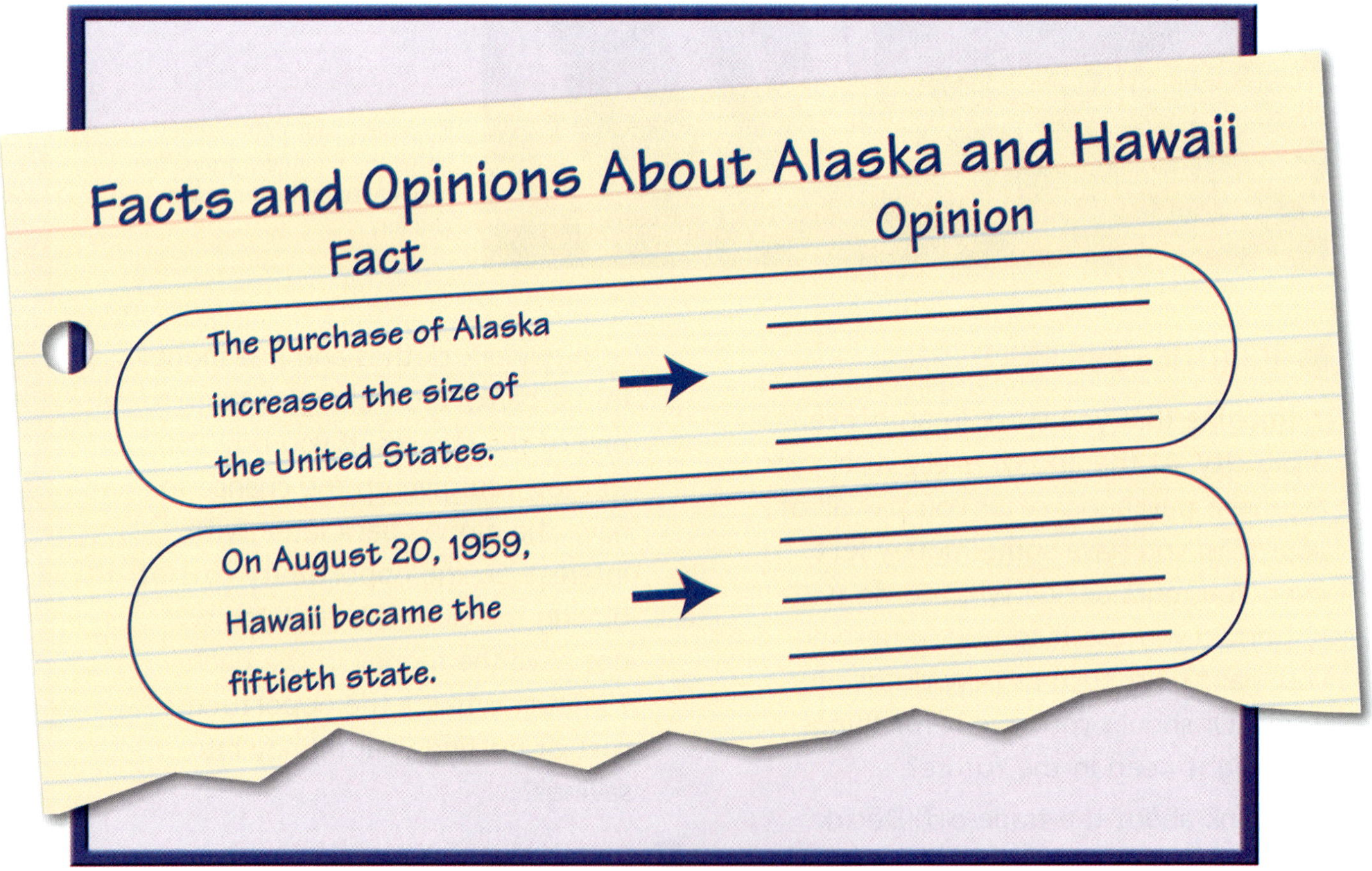

THINK & WRITE

Write a Poem Write a poem about Alaska. Your poem can describe Alaska's landscape, talk about Alaska's gold rush, or explain what Alaska is like today. Draw a picture to go along with your poem.

Write a Compare-and-Contrast Essay Write an essay comparing and contrasting World War I with World War II. Include in your essay why the wars began, who fought in the wars, what weapons were used in the wars, and where the wars took place.

Timeline: 1910 — 1960 — Present
- 1914 World War I begins
- 1939 World War II begins
- 1945 The United Nations is founded
- 1953 The Korean War ends
- 1975 The Vietnam War ends
- 1991 The Persian Gulf War ends
- 2001 Terrorists attack sites in the United States

USE THE TIME LINE

Use the chapter summary time line to answer these questions.

1. When did World War I begin?
2. In what year did the Persian Gulf War end?

USE VOCABULARY

Use each of the following terms in a sentence that will help explain its meaning.

civilians (p. 570)
depression (p. 578)
Holocaust (p. 581)
free world (p. 582)
developing countries (p. 588)

RECALL FACTS

Answer these questions.

3. How much did the United States pay for Alaska?
4. When did Hawaii become a territory of the United States? When did it become a state?
5. What was the Cold War?
6. What is the main purpose of the United Nations (UN)?

Write the letter of the best choice.

7. Which of the following countries were allies during World War I?
  A Germany and Russia
  B United States and Bulgaria
  C Britain and Germany
  D France and Italy

8. The Cuban missile crisis was the result of—
  F the Soviet Union's putting missile launch sites in Cuba.
  G a civil war in Cuba.
  H the Cuban government's placing missiles in the United States.
  J Cuba's selling missiles to communist countries.

THINK CRITICALLY

9. What are the good points and bad points of global trade?
10. How is life in the Peace Corps different from life in the United States?

APPLY SKILLS

Compare Map Projections
Use the maps on pages 574–575 to answer the following questions.

11. On which map, A or B, are the meridians an equal distance apart?
12. On which map, A or B, does the Atlantic Ocean appear to be wider?

Make Economic Choices
You have earned $20 for helping your neighbor plant her garden. You can either buy a new sweatshirt or save the money for your vacation. Answer these questions, using the information on pages 594–595.

13. What is the trade-off in this situation?
14. What is the opportunity cost of buying the sweatshirt?

Chapter 15 ■ 597

VISIT Ellis Island

GET READY

During the period from the late 1800s to the middle 1900s, people came to the United States from all over the world to fulfill their dreams of freedom and opportunity. For many early immigrants, Ellis Island, in New York Harbor, was the first stop on the road to those dreams.

In 1965 Ellis Island became a part of the Statue of Liberty National Monument. Today visitors can tour the three floors of the old immigration building, now a museum. There they can see artifacts, photographs, videos, and displays that tell the story of what it was like to immigrate to the United States so long ago.

WHAT TO SEE

A ferryboat takes visitors to Ellis Island.

Immigrants once waited in the Great Hall to be inspected and registered. Today the Great Hall is a stop on the museum tour.

LOCATE IT

Artifacts such as inspection cards and immigration documents are on display at the immigration museum.

The American Immigrant Wall of Honor features the names of more than 600,000 immigrants.

TAKE A FIELD TRIP

A VIRTUAL TOUR
Visit The Learning Site at **www.harcourtschool.com** to find virtual tours of other historic sites in the United States.

A VIDEO TOUR
Check your media center or classroom library for a videotape tour of Ellis Island.

Unit 7 ■ 599

UNIT 7 Review and Test Preparation

Visual Summary

Write Captions Look at the events on the Visual Summary below. Carefully read the captions that go with each event. Then use what you have learned in your reading to write new captions to go along with each event. As you write, be sure to answer the questions "When?," "Who?," and "Where?"

Use Vocabulary

Identify the correct term that completes each sentence.

strike (p. 525)
aviation (p. 527)
primary election (p. 546)
armistice (p. 571)
refugees (p. 587)

1. The _____ found safety and shelter from the war in a nearby country.
2. If the candidate loses the _____, then she will not be able to run for governor.
3. The workers decided to go on _____ until they got better working conditions.
4. The soldiers cheered when they learned an _____ had been signed, ending the war.
5. The _____ industry involves the making and flying of airplanes.

Recall Facts

Answer these questions.

6. Where did many immigrants to the United States come from in the 1880s?
7. How does the United States government keep track of the nation's population?
8. Who was the first European explorer to arrive in the Hawaiian Islands?
9. Who was President during World War I?
10. What event helped reunite Germany in 1989?
11. A form of government in which the people have power to make choices about their lives and government is called a—
    A democracy.
    B dictatorship.
    C monarchy.
    D empire.

Visual Summary

1860 — 1890 — 1920

1892 Ellis Island immigrant station opens p. 534

1917 The United States enters World War I p. 577

1941 Japan attacks Pearl Harbor p. 579

12. What is the only island state in the United States?
    F Alaska
    G Florida
    H Hawaii
    J Arizona

Think Critically

13. How did cities change during the 1900s?
14. Why are national parks important to the United States?
15. What challenges does the United States face today?

Apply Skills

Use a Time Zone Map
Use the map to answer the following questions.

16. What is the time difference between Sao Paulo and Washington, D.C.?
17. What is the time difference between Mexico City and Honolulu?
18. If it is 9 A.M. in San Francisco, what time is it in Chicago?
19. If it is 11 P.M. in New York City, what time is it in Denver?

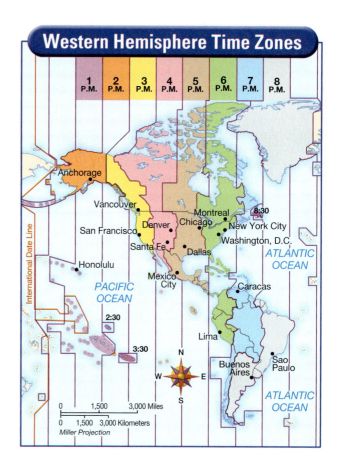

Western Hemisphere Time Zones

1950 — 1980 — Present

1969 United States astronauts land on the moon p. 528

1986 United States and Soviet leaders work to end the Cold War p. 583

2001 George W. Bush becomes the first President of the twenty-first century p. 555

Unit Activities

Visit The Learning Site at www.harcourtschool.com for additional activities.

Make a Pamphlet

Work with a group to make a pamphlet that tells people about the changes in the arts, transportation, and technology that took place in the early 1900s. Before working on the pamphlet, do research to find out more about the early 1900s. The finished pamphlet should tell about important people, places, and events involved in the arts, transportation, and technology in the early 1900s. Illustrate your pamphlet with drawings and graphs.

Invite Guest Speakers

Work in groups to invite several guest speakers to your class. With your teacher's help, choose a date and time for them to come. Then write a letter to a seniors' group in your community, inviting members to talk to your class about life during World War II.

VISIT YOUR LIBRARY

- ***Goin' Someplace Special*** by Patricia C. McKissack. Atheneum.

- ***The Unbreakable Code*** by Sara Hoagland Hunter. Northland Publishing.

- ***The Words of Martin Luther King, Jr.*** Selected by Coretta Scott King. Newmarket Press.

COMPLETE THE UNIT PROJECT

Make a Class Newspaper Work as a class to complete the unit project—a class newspaper. Review the list you made during your reading. Then choose one entry from your list. Write or draw a newpaper item about your entry. Your item could be a news story, an editorial, a letter to the editor, a feature article, a cartoon, or an advertisement. Draw one or two illustrations to go along with your article, or use the Internet to find pictures. Combine your item with your classmates' items to make a newspaper.

For Your Reference

Almanac
R2 Facts About the States
R6 Facts About the Western Hemisphere
R8 Facts About the Presidents

American Documents
R11 The Declaration of Independence
R15 The Constitution of the United States of America
R36 The National Anthem
R37 The Pledge of Allegiance

Biographical Dictionary
R38

Gazetteer
R47

Glossary
R56

Index
R65

Almanac
Facts About the States

State Flag	State	Year of Statehood	Population*	Area (sq. mi.)	Capital	Origin of State Name
	Alabama	1819	4,486,508	50,750	Montgomery	Choctaw, *alba ayamule*, "one who clears land and gathers food from it"
	Alaska	1959	643,786	570,374	Juneau	Aleut, *alayeska*, "great land"
	Arizona	1912	5,456,453	113,642	Phoenix	Papago, *arizonac*, "place of the small spring"
	Arkansas	1836	2,710,079	52,075	Little Rock	Quapaw, "the downstream people"
	California	1850	35,116,033	155,973	Sacramento	Spanish, a fictional island
	Colorado	1876	4,506,542	103,730	Denver	Spanish, "red land" or "red earth"
	Connecticut	1788	3,460,503	4,845	Hartford	Mohican, *quinnitukqut*, "at the long tidal river"
	Delaware	1787	807,385	1,955	Dover	Named for Lord de la Warr
	Florida	1845	16,713,149	54,153	Tallahassee	Spanish, "filled with flowers"
	Georgia	1788	8,560,310	57,919	Atlanta	Named for King George II of England
	Hawaii	1959	1,244,898	6,450	Honolulu	Polynesian, *hawaiki* or *owykee*, "homeland"
	Idaho	1890	1,341,131	82,751	Boise	Invented name with unknown meaning

Reference

State Flag	State	Year of Statehood	Population*	Area (sq. mi.)	Capital	Origin of State Name
	Illinois	1818	12,600,620	55,593	Springfield	Algonquin, *iliniwek*, "men" or "warriors"
	Indiana	1816	6,159,068	35,870	Indianapolis	*Indian + a*, "land of the Indians"
	Iowa	1846	2,936,760	55,875	Des Moines	Dakota, *ayuba*, "beautiful land"
	Kansas	1861	2,715,884	81,823	Topeka	Sioux, "land of the south wind people"
	Kentucky	1792	4,092,891	39,732	Frankfort	Iroquoian, *ken-tah-ten*, "land of tomorrow"
	Louisiana	1812	4,482,646	43,566	Baton Rouge	Named for King Louis XIV of France
	Maine	1820	1,294,464	30,865	Augusta	Named after a French province
	Maryland	1788	5,458,137	9,775	Annapolis	Named for Henrietta Maria, Queen Consort of Charles I of England
	Massachusetts	1788	6,427,801	7,838	Boston	Massachusett tribe of Native Americans, "at the big hill" or "place of the big hill"
	Michigan	1837	10,050,446	56,809	Lansing	Ojibwa, "large lake"
	Minnesota	1858	5,019,720	79,617	St. Paul	Dakota Sioux, "sky-blue water"
	Mississippi	1817	2,871,782	46,914	Jackson	Indian word meaning "great waters" or "father of waters"
	Missouri	1821	5,672,579	68,898	Jefferson City	Named after the Missouri Indian tribe. *Missouri* means "town of the large canoes."

* latest available population figures

Almanac ■ **R3**

State Flag	State	Year of Statehood	Population*	Area (sq. mi.)	Capital	Origin of State Name
	Montana	1889	909,453	145,566	Helena	Spanish, "mountainous"
	Nebraska	1867	1,729,180	76,878	Lincoln	From an Oto Indian word meaning "flat water"
	Nevada	1864	2,173,491	109,806	Carson City	Spanish, "snowy" or "snowed upon"
	New Hampshire	1788	1,275,056	8,969	Concord	Named for Hampshire County, England
	New Jersey	1787	8,590,300	7,419	Trenton	Named for the Isle of Jersey
	New Mexico	1912	1,855,059	121,365	Santa Fe	Named by Spanish explorers from Mexico
	New York	1788	19,157,532	47,224	Albany	Named after the Duke of York
	North Carolina	1789	8,320,146	48,718	Raleigh	Named after King Charles II of England
	North Dakota	1889	634,110	70,704	Bismarck	Sioux, *dakota*, "friend" or "ally"
	Ohio	1803	11,421,267	40,953	Columbus	Iroquois, *oheo*, "great water"
	Oklahoma	1907	3,493,714	68,679	Oklahoma City	Choctaw, "red people"
	Oregon	1859	3,521,515	96,003	Salem	Unknown; generally accepted that it was taken from the writings of Maj. Robert Rogers, an English army officer
	Pennsylvania	1787	12,335,091	44,820	Harrisburg	*Penn* + *sylvania*, meaning "Penn's woods"

State Flag	State	Year of Statehood	Population*	Area (sq. mi.)	Capital	Origin of State Name
	Rhode Island	1790	1,069,725	1,045	Providence	From the Greek island of Rhodes
	South Carolina	1788	4,107,183	30,111	Columbia	Named after King Charles II of England
	South Dakota	1889	761,063	75,898	Pierre	Sioux, *dakota*, "friend" or "ally"
	Tennessee	1796	5,797,289	41,220	Nashville	Name of a Cherokee village
	Texas	1845	21,779,893	261,914	Austin	Native American, *tejas*, "friend" or "ally"
	Utah	1896	2,316,256	82,168	Salt Lake City	From the Ute tribe, meaning "people of the mountains"
	Vermont	1791	616,592	9,249	Montpelier	French, *vert*, "green," and *mont*, "mountain"
	Virginia	1788	7,293,542	39,598	Richmond	Named after Queen Elizabeth I of England
	Washington	1889	6,068,996	66,582	Olympia	Named for George Washington
	West Virginia	1863	1,801,873	24,087	Charleston	From the English-named state of Virginia
	Wisconsin	1848	5,441,196	54,314	Madison	Possibly Algonquian, "the place where we live"
	Wyoming	1890	498,703	97,105	Cheyenne	From Delaware Indian word meaning "land of vast plains"
	District of Columbia		570,898	67		Named after Christopher Columbus

* latest available population figures

Almanac

Facts About the Western Hemisphere

Country	Population*	Area (sq. mi.)	Capital	Origin of Country Name
North America				
Antigua and Barbuda	67,897	171	St. Johns	Named for the Church of Santa María la Antigua in Seville, Spain
Bahamas	297,477	5,382	Nassau	Spanish, *bajamar*, "shallow water"
Barbados	277,264	166	Bridgetown	Means "bearded"—probably referring to the beard like vines early explorers found on its trees
Belize	266,440	8,867	Belmopan	Mayan, "muddy water"
Canada	32,207,113	3,851,788	Ottawa	Huron-Iroquois, *kanata*, "village" or "community"
Costa Rica	3,896,092	19,730	San José	Spanish, "rich coast"
Cuba	11,263,429	42,803	Havana	Origin unknown
Dominica	69,655	291	Roseau	Latin, *dies dominica*, "Day of the Lord"
Dominican Republic	8,715,602	18,815	Santo Domingo	Named after the capital city
El Salvador	6,470,379	8,124	San Salvador	Spanish, "the Savior"
Grenada	89,258	133	St. George's	Origin unknown
Guatemala	13,309,384	42,042	Guatemala City	Indian, "land of trees"
Haiti	7,527,817	10,714	Port-au-Prince	Indian, "land of mountains"
Honduras	6,669,789	43,278	Tegucigalpa	Spanish, "profundities"—probably referring to the depth of offshore waters
Jamaica	2,695,867	4,244	Kingston	Arawak, *xamayca*, "land of wood and water"
Mexico	104,907,991	761,602	Mexico City	Aztec, *mexliapan*, "lake of the moon"
Nicaragua	5,128,517	49,998	Managua	from *Nicarao*, the name of an Indian chief

Country	Population*	Area (sq. mi.)	Capital	Origin of Country Name
Panama	2,960,784	30,193	Panama City	From an Indian village's name
Saint Kitts and Nevis	38,763	101	Basseterre	Named by Christopher Columbus—Kitts for St. Christopher, a Catholic saint; Nevis, for a cloud-topped peak that looked like *las nieves*, "the snows"
Saint Lucia	162,157	239	Castries	Named by Christopher Columbus for a Catholic saint
Saint Vincent and the Grenadines	116,812	150	Kingstown	May have been named by Christopher Columbus for a Catholic saint
Trinidad and Tobago	1,104,209	1,980	Port-of-Spain	Trinidad, from the Spanish word for "trinity"; Tobago, named for tobacco because the island has the shape of a person smoking a pipe
United States of America	290,342,554	3,794,083	Washington, D.C.	Named after the explorer Amerigo Vespucci

South America

Country	Population*	Area (sq. mi.)	Capital	Origin of Country Name
Argentina	38,740,807	1,068,296	Buenos Aires	Latin, *argentum*, "silver"
Bolivia	8,586,443	424,162	La Paz/Sucre	Named after Simón Bolívar, the famed liberator
Brazil	182,032,604	3,286,470	Brasília	Named after a native tree that the Portuguese called "bresel wood"
Chile	15,665,216	292,258	Santiago	Indian, *chilli*, "where the land ends"
Colombia	41,662,073	439,733	Bogotá	Named after Christopher Columbus
Ecuador	13,710,234	109,483	Quito	From the Spanish word for *equator*, referring to the country's location
Guyana	702,100	83,000	Georgetown	Indian, "land of waters"
Paraguay	6,036,900	157,046	Asunción	Named after the Paraguay River, which flows through it
Peru	28,409,897	496,223	Lima	Quechua, "land of abundance"
Suriname	435,449	63,039	Paramaribo	From an Indian word, *surinen*
Uruguay	3,413,329	68,039	Montevideo	Named after the Uruguay River, which flows through it
Venezuela	24,654,694	352,143	Caracas	Spanish, "Little Venice"

* latest available population figures

Almanac
Facts About the Presidents

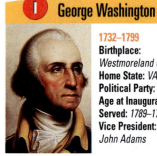
1 George Washington
1732–1799
Birthplace: Westmoreland County, VA
Home State: VA
Political Party: None
Age at Inauguration: 57
Served: 1789–1797
Vice President: John Adams

2 John Adams
1735–1826
Birthplace: Braintree, MA
Home State: MA
Political Party: Federalist
Age at Inauguration: 61
Served: 1797–1801
Vice President: Thomas Jefferson

3 Thomas Jefferson
1743–1826
Birthplace: Albemarle County, VA
Home State: VA
Political Party: Democratic-Republican
Age at Inauguration: 57
Served: 1801–1809
Vice Presidents: Aaron Burr, George Clinton

4 James Madison
1751–1836
Birthplace: Port Conway, VA
Home State: VA
Political Party: Democratic-Republican
Age at Inauguration: 57
Served: 1809–1817
Vice Presidents: George Clinton, Elbridge Gerry

5 James Monroe
1758–1831
Birthplace: Westmoreland County, VA
Home State: VA
Political Party: Democratic-Republican
Age at Inauguration: 58
Served: 1817–1825
Vice President: Daniel D. Tompkins

6 John Quincy Adams
1767–1848
Birthplace: Braintree, MA
Home State: MA
Political Party: Democratic-Republican
Age at Inauguration: 57
Served: 1825–1829
Vice President: John C. Calhoun

7 Andrew Jackson
1767–1845
Birthplace: Waxhaw settlement, SC
Home State: TN
Political Party: Democratic
Age at Inauguration: 61
Served: 1829–1837
Vice Presidents: John C. Calhoun, Martin Van Buren

8 Martin Van Buren
1782–1862
Birthplace: Kinderhook, NY
Home State: NY
Political Party: Democratic
Age at Inauguration: 54
Served: 1837–1841
Vice President: Richard M. Johnson

9 William H. Harrison
1773–1841
Birthplace: Berkeley, VA
Home State: OH
Political Party: Whig
Age at Inauguration: 68
Served: 1841
Vice President: John Tyler

10 John Tyler
1790–1862
Birthplace: Greenway, VA
Home State: VA
Political Party: Whig
Age at Inauguration: 51
Served: 1841–1845
Vice President: none

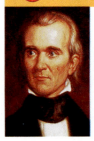
11 James K. Polk
1795–1849
Birthplace: near Pineville, NC
Home State: TN
Political Party: Democratic
Age at Inauguration: 49
Served: 1845–1849
Vice President: George M. Dallas

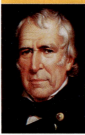
12 Zachary Taylor
1784–1850
Birthplace: Orange County, VA
Home State: LA
Political Party: Whig
Age at Inauguration: 64
Served: 1849–1850
Vice President: Millard Fillmore

13 Millard Fillmore
1800–1874
Birthplace: Locke, NY
Home State: NY
Political Party: Whig
Age at Inauguration: 50
Served: 1850–1853
Vice President: none

Home State refers to the state of residence when elected.

14 Franklin Pierce
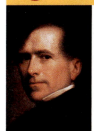
1804–1869
Birthplace: Hillsboro, NH
Home State: NH
Political Party: Democratic
Age at Inauguration: 48
Served: 1853–1857
Vice President: William R. King

15 James Buchanan

1791–1868
Birthplace: near Mercersburg, PA
Home State: PA
Political Party: Democratic
Age at Inauguration: 65
Served: 1857–1861
Vice President: John C. Breckinridge

16 Abraham Lincoln

1809–1865
Birthplace: near Hodgenville, KY
Home State: IL
Political Party: Republican
Age at Inauguration: 52
Served: 1861–1865
Vice Presidents: Hannibal Hamlin, Andrew Johnson

17 Andrew Johnson
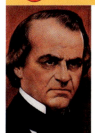
1808–1875
Birthplace: Raleigh, NC
Home State: TN
Political Party: National Union
Age at Inauguration: 56
Served: 1865–1869
Vice President: none

18 Ulysses S. Grant

1822–1885
Birthplace: Point Pleasant, OH
Home State: IL
Political Party: Republican
Age at Inauguration: 46
Served: 1869–1877
Vice Presidents: Schuyler Colfax, Henry Wilson

19 Rutherford B. Hayes
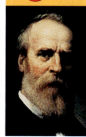
1822–1893
Birthplace: near Delaware, OH
Home State: OH
Political Party: Republican
Age at Inauguration: 54
Served: 1877–1881
Vice President: William A. Wheeler

20 James A. Garfield

1831–1881
Birthplace: Orange, OH
Home State: OH
Political Party: Republican
Age at Inauguration: 49
Served: 1881
Vice President: Chester A. Arthur

21 Chester A. Arthur

1829–1886
Birthplace: Fairfield, VT
Home State: NY
Political Party: Republican
Age at Inauguration: 51
Served: 1881–1885
Vice President: none

22 Grover Cleveland

1837–1908
Birthplace: Caldwell, NJ
Home State: NY
Political Party: Democratic
Age at Inauguration: 47
Served: 1885–1889
Vice President: Thomas A. Hendricks

23 Benjamin Harrison

1833–1901
Birthplace: North Bend, OH
Home State: IN
Political Party: Republican
Age at Inauguration: 55
Served: 1889–1893
Vice President: Levi P. Morton

24 Grover Cleveland

1837–1908
Birthplace: Caldwell, NJ
Home State: NY
Political Party: Democratic
Age at Inauguration: 55
Served: 1893–1897
Vice President: Adlai E. Stevenson

25 William McKinley

1843–1901
Birthplace: Niles, OH
Home State: OH
Political Party: Republican
Age at Inauguration: 54
Served: 1897–1901
Vice Presidents: Garret A. Hobart, Theodore Roosevelt

26 Theodore Roosevelt

1858–1919
Birthplace: New York, NY
Home State: NY
Political Party: Republican
Age at Inauguration: 42
Served: 1901–1909
Vice President: Charles W. Fairbanks

27 William H. Taft

1857–1930
Birthplace: Cincinnati, OH
Home State: OH
Political Party: Republican
Age at Inauguration: 51
Served: 1909–1913
Vice President: James S. Sherman

28 Woodrow Wilson

1856–1924
Birthplace: Staunton, VA
Home State: NJ
Political Party: Democratic
Age at Inauguration: 56
Served: 1913–1921
Vice President: Thomas R. Marshall

29 Warren G. Harding
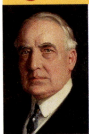
1865–1923
Birthplace: Blooming Grove, OH
Home State: OH
Political Party: Republican
Age at Inauguration: 55
Served: 1921–1923
Vice President: Calvin Coolidge

30 Calvin Coolidge

1872–1933
Birthplace: Plymouth Notch, VT
Home State: MA
Political Party: Republican
Age at Inauguration: 51
Served: 1923–1929
Vice President: Charles G. Dawes

31 Herbert Hoover

1874–1964
Birthplace: West Branch, IA
Home State: CA
Political Party: Republican
Age at Inauguration: 54
Served: 1929–1933
Vice President: Charles Curtis

32 Franklin D. Roosevelt

1882–1945
Birthplace: Hyde Park, NY
Home State: NY
Political Party: Democratic
Age at Inauguration: 51
Served: 1933–1945
Vice Presidents: John N. Garner, Henry A. Wallace, Harry S. Truman

33 Harry S. Truman

1884–1972
Birthplace: Lamar, MO
Home State: MO
Political Party: Democratic
Age at Inauguration: 60
Served: 1945–1953
Vice President: Alben W. Barkley

34 Dwight D. Eisenhower

1890–1969
Birthplace: Denison, TX
Home State: NY
Political Party: Republican
Age at Inauguration: 62
Served: 1953–1961
Vice President: Richard M. Nixon

35 John F. Kennedy

1917–1963
Birthplace: Brookline, MA
Home State: MA
Political Party: Democratic
Age at Inauguration: 43
Served: 1961–1963
Vice President: Lyndon B. Johnson

36 Lyndon B. Johnson

1908–1973
Birthplace: near Stonewall, TX
Home State: TX
Political Party: Democratic
Age at Inauguration: 55
Served: 1963–1969
Vice President: Hubert H. Humphrey

37 Richard M. Nixon

1913–1994
Birthplace: Yorba Linda, CA
Home State: NY
Political Party: Republican
Age at Inauguration: 56
Served: 1969–1974
Vice Presidents: Spiro T. Agnew, Gerald R. Ford

38 Gerald R. Ford

1913–
Birthplace: Omaha, NE
Home State: MI
Political Party: Republican
Age at Inauguration: 61
Served: 1974–1977
Vice President: Nelson A. Rockefeller

39 Jimmy Carter

1924–
Birthplace: Plains, GA
Home State: GA
Political Party: Democratic
Age at Inauguration: 52
Served: 1977–1981
Vice President: Walter F. Mondale

40 Ronald W. Reagan

1911–2004
Birthplace: Tampico, IL
Home State: CA
Political Party: Republican
Age at Inauguration: 69
Served: 1981–1989
Vice President: George Bush

41 George Bush

1924–
Birthplace: Milton, MA
Home State: TX
Political Party: Republican
Age at Inauguration: 64
Served: 1989–1993
Vice President: Dan Quayle

42 William Clinton

1946–
Birthplace: Hope, AR
Home State: AR
Political Party: Democratic
Age at Inauguration: 46
Served: 1993–2001
Vice President: Albert Gore

43 George W. Bush

1946–
Birthplace: New Haven, CT
Home State: TX
Political Party: Republican
Age at Inauguration: 54
Served: 2001–
Vice President: Richard Cheney

American Documents

THE DECLARATION OF INDEPENDENCE

In Congress, July 4, 1776.
The unanimous Declaration of the
thirteen United States of America,

When in the Course of human events it becomes necessary for one people to dissolve the political bands which have connected them with another, and to assume among the powers of the earth, the separate and equal station to which the Laws of Nature and of Nature's God entitle them, a decent respect to the opinions of mankind requires that they should declare the causes which impel them to the separation.

We hold these truths to be self-evident, that all men are created equal, that they are endowed by their Creator with certain unalienable Rights, that among these are Life, Liberty and the pursuit of Happiness.
That to secure these rights, Governments are instituted among Men, deriving their just powers from the consent of the governed,
That whenever any Form of Government becomes destructive of these ends, it is the Right of the People to alter or to abolish it, and to institute new Government, laying its foundation on such principles and organizing its powers in such form, as to them shall seem most likely to effect their Safety and Happiness. Prudence, indeed, will dictate that Governments long established should not be changed for light and transient causes; and accordingly all experience hath shown, that mankind are more disposed to suffer, while evils are sufferable, than to right themselves by abolishing the forms to which they are accustomed. But when a long train of abuses and usurpations, pursuing invariably the same Object evinces a design to reduce them under absolute Despotism, it is their right, it is their duty, to throw off such Government, and to provide new Guards for their future security.

Such has been the patient sufferance of these Colonies; and such is now the necessity which constrains them to alter their former Systems of Government. The history of the present King of Great Britain is a history of repeated injuries and usurpations, all having in direct object the establishment of an absolute Tyranny over these States. To prove this, let Facts be submitted to a candid world.

He has refused his Assent to Laws, the most wholesome and necessary for the public good.
He has forbidden his Governors to pass Laws of immediate and pressing importance, unless suspended in their operation till his Assent should be obtained; and when so suspended, he has utterly neglected to attend to them.

Preamble
The Preamble tells why the Declaration was written. It states that the members of the Continental Congress believed the colonies had the right to break away from Britain and become a free nation.

A Statement of Rights
The opening part of the Declaration tells what rights the members of the Continental Congress believed that all people have. All people are equal in having the rights to life, liberty, and the pursuit of happiness. The main purpose of a government is to protect the rights of the people who consent to be governed by it. These rights cannot be taken away. When a government tries to take these rights away from the people, the people have the right to change the government or do away with it. The people can then form a new government that respects these rights.

Charges Against the King
The Declaration lists more than 25 charges against the king. He was mistreating the colonists, the Declaration says, in order to gain total control over the colonies.

The king rejected many laws passed by colonial legislatures.

Annotation	Text
	He has refused to pass other Laws for the accommodation of large districts of people, unless those people would relinquish the right of Representation in the Legislature, a right inestimable to them and formidable to tyrants only.
The king made the colonial legislatures meet at unusual times and places.	He has called together legislative bodies at places unusual, uncomfortable, and distant from the depository of their public Records, for the sole purpose of fatiguing them into compliance with his measures.
The king and the king's governors often dissolved colonial legislatures for disobeying their orders.	He has dissolved Representative Houses repeatedly, for opposing with manly firmness his invasions on the rights of the people. He has refused for a long time, after such dissolutions, to cause others to be elected; whereby the Legislative powers, incapable of Annihilation, have returned to the People at large for their exercise; the State remaining in the mean time exposed to all the dangers of invasion from without, and convulsions within.
The king stopped people from moving to the colonies and into the western lands.	He has endeavored to prevent the population of these States; for that purpose obstructing the Laws for Naturalization of Foreigners; refusing to pass others to encourage their migrations hither, and raising the conditions of new Appropriations of Lands.
The king prevented the colonists from choosing their own judges. The king chose the judges, and they served only as long as the king was satisfied with them.	He has obstructed the Administration of Justice, by refusing his Assent to Laws for establishing Judiciary powers. He has made Judges dependent on his Will alone, for the tenure of their offices, and the amount and payment of their salaries.
The king hired people to help collect taxes in the colonies.	He has erected a multitude of New Offices, and sent hither swarms of Officers to harass our people, and eat out their substance.
The king appointed General Thomas Gage, commander of Britain's military forces in the Americas, as governor of Massachusetts.	He has kept among us, in times of peace, Standing Armies without the Consent of our legislatures. He has affected to render the Military independent of and superior to the Civil power. He has combined with others to subject us to a jurisdiction foreign to our constitution, and unacknowledged by our laws; giving his Assent to their Acts of pretended Legislation:
The king expected the colonists to provide housing and supplies for the British soldiers in the colonies.	For quartering large bodies of armed troops among us: For protecting them, by a mock Trial, from punishment for any Murders which they should commit on the Inhabitants of these States: For cutting off our Trade with all parts of the world:
The king and Parliament demanded that colonists pay many taxes, even though the colonists did not agree to pay them.	For imposing Taxes on us without our Consent:
Colonists were tried by British naval courts, which had no juries.	For depriving us in many cases, of the benefits of Trial by Jury:
Colonists accused of treason were sent to Britain to be tried.	For transporting us beyond Seas to be tried for pretended offenses: For abolishing the free System of English Laws in a neighboring Province, establishing therein an Arbitrary government, and enlarging its Boundaries so as to render it at once an example and fit instrument for introducing the same absolute rule into these Colonies:

For taking away our Charters, abolishing our most valuable Laws, and altering fundamentally the Forms of our Governments:

For suspending our own Legislatures, and declaring themselves invested with power to legislate for us in all cases whatsoever.

He has abdicated Government here, by declaring us out of his Protection and waging War against us.

He has plundered our seas, ravaged our Coasts, burnt our towns, and destroyed the lives of our people.

He is at this time transporting large Armies of foreign Mercenaries to complete the works of death, desolation and tyranny, already begun with circumstances of Cruelty & perfidy scarcely paralleled in the most barbarous ages, and totally unworthy the Head of a civilized nation.

He has constrained our fellow Citizens taken Captive on the high Seas to bear Arms against their Country, to become the executioners of their friends and Brethren, or to fall themselves by their Hands.

He has excited domestic insurrections amongst us, and has endeavored to bring on the inhabitants of our frontiers, the merciless Indian Savages, whose known rule of warfare, is an undistinguished destruction of all ages, sexes and conditions.

In every stage of these Oppressions We have Petitioned for Redress in the most humble terms: Our repeated Petitions have been answered only by repeated injury. A Prince, whose character is thus marked by every act which may define a Tyrant, is unfit to be the ruler of a free people.

Nor have We been wanting in attentions to our British brethren. We have warned them from time to time of attempts by their legislature to extend an unwarrantable jurisdiction over us. We have reminded them of the circumstances of our emigration and settlement here. We have appealed to their native justice and magnanimity, and we have conjured them by the ties of our common kindred to disavow these usurpations, which, would inevitably interrupt our connections and correspondence. They too have been deaf to the voice of justice and of consanguinity. We must, therefore, acquiesce in the necessity, which denounces our Separation, and hold them, as we hold the rest of mankind, Enemies in War, in Peace Friends.

We, therefore, the Representatives of the united States of America, in General Congress, Assembled, appealing to the Supreme Judge of the world for the rectitude of our intentions, do, in the Name, and by Authority of the good People of these Colonies, solemnly publish and declare, That these United Colonies are, and of Right ought to be Free and Independent States; that they are Absolved from all Allegiance to the British Crown, and that all political connection between them and the State of Great Britain, is and ought to be totally dissolved; and that as Free and Independent States, they have full Power to levy War, conclude Peace, contract Alliances, establish Commerce, and to do all other Acts and Things which Independent States may of right do.

The king allowed General Gage to take military action to enforce British laws in the colonies.

The king hired Hessian mercenaries and sent them to fight the colonists.

The king's governor in Virginia promised freedom to all enslaved people who joined the British forces. The British also planned to use Indians to fight the colonists.

The Declaration explained the efforts of the colonists to avoid separation from Britain. But the colonists said that the king had ignored their protests. Because of the many charges against the king, the writers of the Declaration concluded that he was not fit to rule free people.

A Statement of Independence The writers declared that the colonies were now free and independent states. All ties with Britain were broken. As free and independent states, they had the right to make war and peace, to trade, and to do all the things free countries could do.

> To support the Declaration, the signers promised one another their lives, their fortunes, and their honor.

And for the support of this Declaration, with a firm reliance on the protection of divine Providence, we mutually pledge to each other our Lives, our Fortunes and our sacred Honor.

John Hancock

NEW HAMPSHIRE
Josiah Bartlett
William Whipple
Matthew Thornton

MASSACHUSETTS
John Adams
Samuel Adams
Robert Treat Paine
Elbridge Gerry

NEW YORK
William Floyd
Philip Livingston
Francis Lewis
Lewis Morris

RHODE ISLAND
Stephen Hopkins
William Ellery

NEW JERSEY
Richard Stockton
John Witherspoon
Francis Hopkinson
John Hart
Abraham Clark

PENNSYLVANIA
Robert Morris
Benjamin Rush
Benjamin Franklin
John Morton
George Clymer
James Smith
George Taylor
James Wilson
George Ross

DELAWARE
Caesar Rodney
George Read
Thomas McKean

MARYLAND
Samuel Chase
William Paca
Thomas Stone
Charles Carroll of Carrollton

NORTH CAROLINA
William Hopper
Joseph Hewes
John Penn

VIRGINIA
George Wythe
Richard Henry Lee
Thomas Jefferson
Benjamin Harrison
Thomas Nelson, Jr.
Francis Lightfoot Lee
Carter Braxton

SOUTH CAROLINA
Edward Rutledge
Thomas Heyward, Jr.
Thomas Lynch, Jr.
Arthur Middleton

CONNECTICUT
Roger Sherman
Samuel Huntington
William Williams
Oliver Wolcott

GEORGIA
Button Gwinnett
Lyman Hall
George Walton

> Members of the Continental Congress stated that copies of the Declaration should be sent to all Committees of Correspondence and to commanders of the troops and that it should be read in every state.

Resolved, That copies of the Declaration be sent to the several assemblies, conventions, and committees, or councils of safety, and to the several commanding officers of the continental troops; that it be proclaimed in each of the United States, at the head of the army.

THE CONSTITUTION OF THE UNITED STATES OF AMERICA

Preamble*

We the people of the United States, in order to form a more perfect Union, establish justice, insure domestic tranquillity, provide for the common defense, promote the general welfare, and secure the blessings of liberty to ourselves and our posterity, do ordain and establish this Constitution for the United States of America.

ARTICLE I
THE LEGISLATIVE BRANCH

SECTION 1. CONGRESS

All legislative powers herein granted shall be vested in a Congress of the United States, which shall consist of a Senate and House of Representatives.

SECTION 2. THE HOUSE OF REPRESENTATIVES

(1) The House of Representatives shall be composed of members chosen every second year by the people of the several states, and the electors in each state shall have the qualifications requisite for electors of the most numerous branch of the state legislature.

(2) No person shall be a Representative who shall not have attained to the age of twenty-five years, and been seven years a citizen of the United States, and who shall not, when elected, be an inhabitant of that state in which he shall be chosen.

(3) Representatives [*and direct taxes*]** shall be apportioned among the several states which may be included within this Union, according to their respective numbers [*which shall be determined by adding to the whole number of free persons, including those bound to service for a term of years, and excluding Indians not taxed, three-fifths of all other persons*]. The actual enumeration shall be made within three years after the first meeting of the Congress of the United States, and within every subsequent term of ten years, in such manner as they shall by law direct. The number of Representatives shall not exceed one for every 30,000, but each state shall have at least one Representative [; *and until such enumeration shall be made, the State of New Hampshire shall be entitled to choose three; Massachusetts eight; Rhode Island and Providence Plantations one; Connecticut five; New York six; New Jersey four; Pennsylvania eight; Delaware one; Maryland six; Virginia ten; North Carolina five; South Carolina five; and Georgia three*].

*Titles have been added to make the Constitution easier to read. They did not appear in the original document.

**The parts of the Constitution that no longer apply are printed in italics within brackets [ ]. These portions have been changed or set aside by later amendments.

Preamble
The introduction to the Constitution states the purposes and principles for writing it. The writers wanted to set up a fairer form of government and to secure peace and freedom for themselves and for future generations.

Congress
Congress has the authority to make laws. Congress is made up of two groups of lawmakers: the Senate and the House of Representatives.

(1) Election and Term of Members
Qualified voters are to elect members of the House of Representatives every two years. Each member of the House of Representatives must meet certain requirements.

(2) Qualifications
Members of the House of Representatives must be at least 25 years old. They must have been citizens of the United States for at least seven years. They must live in the state that they will represent.

(3) Determining Apportionment
The number of representatives a state may have depends on the number of people living in each state. Every ten years the federal government must take a census, or count, of the population in every state. Every state will have at least one representative.

(4) Filling Vacancies
If there is a vacancy in representation in Congress, the governor of the state involved must call a special election to fill it.

(5) Special Authority
The House of Representatives chooses a Speaker as its presiding officer. It also chooses other officers as appropriate. The House is the only government branch that may impeach, or charge, an official in the executive branch or a judge of the federal courts for failing to carry out his or her duties. These cases are tried in the Senate.

(1) Number, Term, and Selection of Members
Each state is represented by two senators. Until Amendment 17 was passed, state legislatures chose the senators for their states. Each senator serves a six-year term and has one vote in Congress.

(2) Overlapping Terms and Filling Vacancies
One-third of the senators are elected every two years for a six-year term. This grouping allows at least two-thirds of the experienced senators to remain in the Senate after each election. Amendment 17 permits state governors to appoint a replacement to fill a vacancy until the next election is held.

(3) Qualifications
Senators must be at least 30 years old. They must have been citizens of the United States for at least nine years. They must live in the state that they will represent.

(4) President of the Senate
The Vice President acts as chief officer of the Senate but does not vote unless there is a tie.

(5) Other Officers
The Senate chooses its other officers and a president pro tempore, who serves if the Vice President is not present or if the Vice President becomes President. *Pro tempore* is a Latin term meaning "for the time being."

---

(4) When vacancies happen in the representation from any state, the executive authority thereof shall issue writs of election to fill such vacancies.

(5) The House of Representatives shall choose their Speaker and other officers; and shall have the sole power of impeachment.

SECTION 3. THE SENATE
(1) The Senate of the United States shall be composed of two Senators from each state [*chosen by the legislature thereof*], for six years, and each Senator shall have one vote.

(2) [*Immediately after they shall be assembled in consequence of the first election, they shall be divided as equally as may be into three classes. The seats of the Senators of the first class shall be vacated at the expiration of the second year, of the second class at the expiration of the fourth year, and of the third class at the expiration of the sixth year, so that one-third may be chosen every second year; and if vacancies happen by resignation, or otherwise, during the recess of the legislature of any state, the executive thereof may make temporary appointments until the next meeting of the legislature, which shall then fill such vacancies.*]

(3) No person shall be a Senator who shall not have attained to the age of thirty years, and been nine years a citizen of the United States, and who shall not, when elected, be an inhabitant of that state for which he shall be chosen.

(4) The Vice President of the United States shall be President of the Senate, but shall have no vote, unless they be equally divided.

(5) The Senate shall choose their other officers, and also a President *pro tempore*, in the absence of the Vice President, or when he shall exercise the office of the President of the United States.

(6) The Senate shall have the sole power to try all impeachments. When sitting for that purpose, they shall be on oath or affirmation. When the President of the United States is tried, the Chief Justice shall preside; and no person shall be convicted without the concurrence of two-thirds of the members present.

(7) Judgment in cases of impeachment shall not extend further than to removal from office, and disqualification to hold and enjoy any office of honor, trust, or profit under the United States; but the party convicted shall nevertheless be liable and subject to indictment, trial, judgment and punishment, according to law.

SECTION 4. ELECTIONS AND MEETINGS
(1) The times, places, and manner of holding elections for Senators and Representatives shall be prescribed in each state by the legislature thereof; but the Congress may at any time by law make or alter such regulations, [*except as to the places of choosing Senators*].

(2) The Congress shall assemble at least once in every year, [*and such meeting shall be on the first Monday in December, unless they shall by law appoint a different day*].

SECTION 5. RULES OF PROCEDURE
(1) Each house shall be the judge of the elections, returns and qualifications of its own members, and a majority of each shall constitute a quorum to do business; but a smaller number may adjourn from day to day, and may be authorized to compel the attendance of absent members, in such manner and under such penalties as each house may provide.

(2) Each house may determine the rules of its proceedings, punish its members for disorderly behavior, and, with the concurrence of two-thirds, expel a member.

(3) Each house shall keep a journal of its proceedings, and from time to time publish the same, excepting such parts as may in their judgment require secrecy; and the yeas and nays of the members of either house on any question shall, at the desire of one-fifth of those present, be entered on the journal.

---

(6) Impeachment Trials
If the House of Representatives votes articles of impeachment, the Senate holds a trial. A two-thirds vote is required to convict a person who has been impeached.

(7) Penalty for Conviction
If convicted in an impeachment case, an official is removed from office and may never hold office in the United States government again. The convicted person may also be tried in a regular court of law for any crimes.

(1) Holding Elections
Each state makes its own rules about electing senators and representatives. However, Congress may change these rules at any time. Today congressional elections are held on the Tuesday after the first Monday in November, in even-numbered years.

(2) Meetings
The Constitution requires Congress to meet at least once a year. That day is the first Monday in December, unless Congress sets a different day. Amendment 20 changed this date to January 3.

(1) Organization
Each house of Congress may decide if its members have been elected fairly and are able to hold office. Each house may do business only when a quorum—a majority of its members—is present. By less than a majority vote, each house may compel absent members to attend.

(2) Rules
Each house may decide its own rules for doing business, punish its members, and expel a member from office if two-thirds of the members agree.

(3) Journal
The Constitution requires each house to keep records of its activities and to publish these records from time to time. The House Journal and the Senate Journal are published at the end of each session. How each member voted must be recorded if one-fifth of the members ask for this to be done.

(4) Adjournment
When Congress is in session, neither house may take a recess for more than three days without the consent of the other.

(1) Pay and Privileges
Members of Congress set their own salaries, which are to be paid by the federal government. Members cannot be arrested or sued for anything they say while Congress is in session. This privilege is called congressional immunity. Members of Congress may be arrested while Congress is in session only if they commit a crime.

(2) Restrictions
Members of Congress may not hold any other federal office while serving in Congress. A member may not resign from office and then take a government position created during that member's term of office or for which the pay has been increased during that member's term of office.

(1) Money-Raising Bills
All money-raising bills must be introduced first in the House of Representatives, but the Senate may suggest changes.

(2) How a Bill Becomes a Law
After a bill has been passed by both the House of Representatives and the Senate, it must be sent to the President. If the President approves and signs the bill, it becomes law. The President can also veto, or refuse to sign, the bill. Congress can override a veto by passing the bill again by a two-thirds majority. If the President does not act within ten days, two things may happen. If Congress is still in session, the bill becomes a law. If Congress ends its session within that same ten-day period, the bill does not become a law.

(3) Orders and Resolutions
Congress can pass orders and resolutions, some of which have the same effect as a law. Congress may decide on its own when to end the session. Other such acts must be signed or vetoed by the President.

---

(4) Neither house, during the session of Congress, shall, without the consent of the other, adjourn for more than three days, nor to any other place than that in which the two houses shall be sitting.

SECTION 6. PRIVILEGES AND RESTRICTIONS
(1) The Senators and Representatives shall receive a compensation for their services, to be ascertained by law and paid out of the Treasury of the United States. They shall in all cases, except treason, felony, and breach of the peace, be privileged from arrest during their attendance at the session of their respective houses, and in going to and returning from the same; and for any speech or debate in either house, they shall not be questioned in any other place.

(2) No Senator or Representative shall, during the time for which he was elected, be appointed to any civil office under the authority of the United States, which shall have been created, or the emoluments whereof shall have been increased, during such time; and no person holding any office under the United States shall be a member of either house during his continuance in office.

SECTION 7. MAKING LAWS
(1) All bills for raising revenue shall originate in the House of Representatives; but the Senate may propose or concur with amendments as on other bills.

(2) Every bill which shall have passed the House of Representatives and the Senate shall, before it become a law, be presented to the President of the United States; if he approve, he shall sign it, but if not, he shall return it, with his objections, to that house in which it shall have originated, who shall enter the objections at large on their journal, and proceed to reconsider it. If after such reconsideration two-thirds of that house shall agree to pass the bill, it shall be sent, together with the objections, to the other house, by which it shall likewise be reconsidered, and, if approved by two-thirds of that house, it shall become a law. But in all such cases the votes of both houses shall be determined by yeas and nays, and the names of the persons voting for and against the bill shall be entered on the journal of each house respectively. If any bill shall not be returned by the President within ten days (Sundays excepted) after it shall have been presented to him, the same bill shall be a law, in like manner as if he had signed it, unless the Congress by their adjournment prevent its return, in which case it shall not be a law.

(3) Every order, resolution, or vote to which the concurrence of the Senate and House of Representatives may be necessary (except on a question of adjournment) shall be presented to the President of the United States; and before the same shall take effect, shall be approved by him, or being disapproved by him, shall be repassed by two-thirds of the Senate and House of Representatives, according to the rules and limitations prescribed in the case of a bill.

SECTION 8. POWERS DELEGATED TO CONGRESS

The Congress shall have power

(1) To lay and collect taxes, duties, imposts and excises, to pay the debts and provide for the common defense and general welfare of the United States; but all duties, imposts and excises shall be uniform throughout the United States;

(2) To borrow money on the credit of the United States;

(3) To regulate commerce with foreign nations, and among the several states and with the Indian tribes;

(4) To establish an uniform rule of naturalization, and uniform laws on the subject of bankruptcies throughout the United States;

(5) To coin money, regulate the value thereof, and of foreign coin, and fix the standard of weights and measures;

(6) To provide for the punishment of counterfeiting the securities and current coin of the United States;

(7) To establish post offices and post roads;

(8) To promote the progress of science and useful arts by securing for limited times to authors and inventors the exclusive right to their respective writings and discoveries;

(9) To constitute tribunals inferior to the Supreme Court;

(10) To define and punish piracies and felonies committed on the high seas and offenses against the law of nations;

(1) Taxation
Only Congress has the authority to raise money to pay debts, defend the United States, and provide services for its people by collecting taxes or tariffs on foreign goods. All taxes must be applied equally in all states.

(2) Borrowing Money
Congress may borrow money for national use. This is usually done by selling government bonds.

(3) Commerce
Congress can control trade with other countries and between states.

(4) Naturalization and Bankruptcy
Congress decides what requirements people from other countries must meet to become United States citizens. Congress can also pass laws to protect people who are bankrupt, or cannot pay their debts.

(5) Coins, Weights, and Measures
Congress can coin money and decide its value. Congress also decides on the system of weights and measures to be used throughout the nation.

(6) Counterfeiting
Congress may pass laws to punish people who make fake money, bonds, or stamps.

(7) Postal Service
Congress can build post offices and make rules about the postal system and the roads used for mail delivery.

(8) Copyrights and Patents
Congress can issue patents and copyrights to inventors and authors to protect the ownership of their works.

(9) Federal Courts
Congress can establish a system of federal courts under the Supreme Court.

(10) Crimes at Sea
Congress can pass laws to punish people for crimes committed at sea. Congress may also punish United States citizens for breaking international law.

(11) Declaring War
Only Congress can declare war.

(11) To declare war, grant letters of marque and reprisal, and make rules concerning captures on land and water;

(12) The Army
Congress can establish an army, but it cannot vote enough money to support it for more than two years. This part of the Constitution was written to keep the army under civilian control.

(12) To raise and support armies, but no appropriation of money to that use shall be for a longer term than two years;

(13) The Navy
Congress can establish a navy and vote enough money to support it for as long as necessary. No time limit was set because people thought the navy was less of a threat to people's liberty than the army was.

(13) To provide and maintain a navy;

(14) Military Regulations
Congress makes the rules that guide and govern all the armed forces.

(14) To make rules for the government and regulation of the land and naval forces;

(15) The Militia
Each state has its own militia, now known as the National Guard. The National Guard can be called into federal service by the President, as authorized by Congress, to enforce laws, to stop uprisings against the government, or to protect the people in case of floods, earthquakes, and other disasters.

(15) To provide for calling forth the militia to execute the laws of the Union, suppress insurrections and repel invasions;

(16) Control of the Militia
Congress helps each state support the National Guard. Each state may appoint its own officers and train its own guard according to rules set by Congress.

(16) To provide for organizing, arming, and disciplining the militia, and for governing such part of them as may be employed in the service of the United States, reserving to the states, respectively, the appointment of the officers, and the authority of training the militia according to the discipline prescribed by Congress;

(17) National Capital and Other Property
Congress may pass laws to govern the nation's capital (Washington, D.C.) and any land owned by the government.

(17) To exercise exclusive legislation in all cases whatsoever, over such district (not exceeding ten miles square) as may, by cession of particular states, and the acceptance of Congress, become the seat of government of the United States, and to exercise like authority over all places purchased by the consent of the legislature of the state in which the same shall be, for the erection of forts, magazines, arsenals, dock-yards, and other needful buildings; —and

(18) Other Necessary Laws
The Constitution allows Congress to make laws that are necessary to enforce the powers listed in Article I. This clause has two conflicting interpretations. One is that Congress can only do what is absolutely necessary to carry out the powers listed in Article I. The other is that Congress may stretch its authority in order to carry out these powers, but not beyond limits established by the Constitution.

(18) To make all laws which shall be necessary and proper for carrying into execution the foregoing powers, and all other powers vested by this Constitution in the government of the United States, or in any department or officer thereof.

SECTION 9. POWERS DENIED TO CONGRESS

(1) [*The migration or importation of such persons as any of the states now existing shall think proper to admit shall not be prohibited by the Congress prior to the year 1808; but a tax or duty may be imposed on such importation, not exceeding 10 dollars for each person.*]

(2) The privilege of the writ of habeas corpus shall not be suspended, unless when in cases of rebellion or invasion the public safety may require it.

(3) No bill of attainder or ex post facto law shall be passed.

(4) [*No capitation or other direct tax shall be laid, unless in proportion to the census or enumeration herein before directed to be taken.*]

(5) No tax or duty shall be laid on articles exported from any state.

(6) No preference shall be given by any regulation of commerce or revenue to the ports of one state over those of another; nor shall vessels bound to, or from, one state, be obliged to enter, clear, or pay duties in another.

(7) No money shall be drawn from the Treasury, but in consequence of appropriations made by law; and a regular statement and account of the receipts and expenditures of all public money shall be published from time to time.

---

(1) Slave Trade
Some authority is not given to Congress. Congress could not prevent the slave trade until 1808, but it could put a tax of ten dollars on each slave brought into the United States. After 1808, when a law was passed to stop slaves from being brought into the United States, this section no longer applied.

(2) Habeas Corpus
A writ of habeas corpus is a privilege that entitles a person to a hearing before a judge. The judge must then decide if there is good reason for that person to have been arrested. If not, that person must be released. The government is not allowed to take this privilege away except during a national emergency, such as an invasion or a rebellion.

(3) Special Laws
Congress cannot pass laws that impose punishment on a named individual or group, except in cases of treason. Article III sets limits to punishments for treason. Congress also cannot pass laws that punish a person for an action that was legal when it was done.

(4) Direct Taxes
Congress cannot set a direct tax on people, unless it is in proportion to the total population. Amendment 16, which provides for the income tax, is an exception.

(5) Export Taxes
Congress cannot tax goods sent from one state to another or from a state to another country.

(6) Ports
When making trade laws, Congress cannot favor one state over another. Congress cannot require ships from one state to pay a duty to enter another state.

(7) Public Money
The government cannot spend money from the treasury unless Congress passes a law allowing it to do so. A written record must be kept of all money spent by the government.

(8) Titles of Nobility and Gifts
The United States government cannot grant titles of nobility. Government officials cannot accept gifts from other countries without the permission of Congress. This clause was intended to prevent government officials from being bribed by other nations.

(1) Complete Restrictions
The Constitution does not allow states to act as if they were individual countries. No state government may make a treaty with other countries. No state can print its own money.

(2) Partial Restrictions
No state government can tax imported goods or exported goods without the consent of Congress. States may charge a fee to inspect these goods, but profits must be given to the United States Treasury.

(3) Other Restrictions
No state government may tax ships entering its ports unless Congress approves. No state may keep an army or navy during times of peace other than the National Guard. No state can enter into agreements called compacts with other states without the consent of Congress.

(1) Term of Office
The President has the authority to carry out our nation's laws. The term of office for both the President and the Vice President is four years.

(2) The Electoral College
This group of people is to be chosen by the voters of each state to elect the President and Vice President. The number of electors in each state is equal to the number of senators and representatives that state has in Congress.

(3) Election Process
This clause describes in detail how the electors were to choose the President and Vice President. In 1804 Amendment 12 changed the process for electing the President and the Vice President.

---

(8) No title of nobility shall be granted by the United States; and no person holding any office of profit or trust under them, shall, without the consent of the Congress, accept of any present, emolument, office, or title, of any kind whatever, from any king, prince, or foreign state.

SECTION 10. POWERS DENIED TO THE STATES
(1) No state shall enter into any treaty, alliance, or confederation; grant letters of marque and reprisal; coin money; emit bills of credit; make anything but gold and silver coin a tender in payment of debts; pass any bill of attainder, ex post facto law, or law impairing the obligation of contracts, or grant any title of nobility.

(2) No state shall, without the consent of the Congress, lay any imposts or duties on imports or exports, except what may be absolutely necessary for executing its inspection laws; and the net produce of all duties and imposts, laid by any state on imports or exports, shall be for the use of the Treasury of the United States; and all such laws shall be subject to the revision and control of the Congress.

(3) No state shall, without the consent of Congress, lay any duty of tonnage, keep troops, or ships of war in time of peace, enter into any agreement or compact with another state, or with a foreign power, or engage in war, unless actually invaded, or in such imminent danger as will not admit of delay.

ARTICLE II
THE EXECUTIVE BRANCH
SECTION 1. PRESIDENT AND VICE PRESIDENT
(1) The executive power shall be vested in a President of the United States of America. He shall hold his office during the term of four years, and together with the Vice President, chosen for the same term, be elected as follows:

(2) Each state shall appoint, in such manner as the legislature thereof may direct, a number of electors, equal to the whole number of Senators and Representatives to which the state may be entitled in the Congress; but no Senator or Representative, or person holding an office of trust or profit under the United States, shall be appointed an elector.

(3) [*The electors shall meet in their respective states, and vote by ballot for two persons, of whom one at least shall not be an inhabitant of the same state with themselves. And they shall make a list of all the persons voted for, and of the number of votes for each; which list they shall sign and certify, and transmit sealed to the seat of the government of the United States, directed to the president of the Senate. The president of the Senate shall, in the presence of the Senate and House of Representatives, open all the certificates, and the votes shall then be counted. The person having the greatest number of votes shall be the President, if such number be a majority of the whole number of electors appointed; and if there be more than one who have such majority, and have an equal number of votes, then the House of Representatives shall immediately choose by ballot one of them for President; and if no person have*

a majority, then from the five highest on the list the said House shall in like manner choose the President. But in choosing the President the votes shall be taken by states, the representation from each state having one vote: A quorum for this purpose shall consist of a member or members from two-thirds of the states, and a majority of all the states shall be necessary to a choice. In every case, after the choice of the President, the person having the greatest number of votes of the electors shall be the Vice President. But if there should remain two or more who have equal votes, the Senate shall choose from them by ballot the Vice President.]

(4) The Congress may determine the time of choosing the electors, and the day on which they shall give their votes; which day shall be the same throughout the United States.

(5) No person except a natural-born citizen [*or a citizen of the United States, at the time of the adoption of this Constitution,*] shall be eligible to the office of the President; neither shall any person be eligible to that office who shall not have attained to the age of thirty-five years, and been fourteen years a resident within the United States.

(6) [*In case of the removal of the President from office, or of his death, resignation, or inability to discharge the powers and duties of the said office, the same shall devolve on the Vice President, and the Congress may by law provide for the case of removal, death, resignation or inability, both of the President and Vice President, declaring what officer shall then act as President, and such officer shall act accordingly, until the disability be removed, or a President shall be elected.*]

(7) The President shall, at stated times, receive for his services, a compensation, which shall neither be increased nor diminished during the period for which he shall have been elected, and he shall not receive within that period any other emolument from the United States, or any of them.

(8) Before he enter on the execution of his office, he shall take the following oath or affirmation:—"I do solemnly swear (or affirm) that I will faithfully execute the office of President of the United States, and will to the best of my ability, preserve, protect, and defend the Constitution of the United States."

SECTION 2. POWERS OF THE PRESIDENT

(1) The President shall be Commander in Chief of the Army and Navy of the United States, and of the militia of the several states, when called into the actual service of the United States; he may require the opinion, in writing, of the principal officer in each of the executive departments, upon any subject relating to the duties of their respective offices, and he shall have power to grant reprieves and pardons for offenses against the United States, except in cases of impeachment.

(4) Time of Elections
Congress decides the day the electors are to be elected and the day they are to vote.

(5) Qualifications
The President must be at least 35 years old, be a citizen of the United States by birth, and have been living in the United States for 14 years or more.

(6) Vacancies
If the President dies, resigns, or is removed from office, the Vice President becomes President.

(7) Salary
The President receives a salary that cannot be raised or lowered during a term of office. The President may not be paid any additional salary by the federal government or any state or local government. Today the President's salary is $400,000 a year, plus expenses for things such as housing, travel, and entertainment.

(8) Oath of Office
Before taking office, the President must promise to perform the duties faithfully and to protect the country's form of government. Usually the Chief Justice of the Supreme Court administers the oath of office.

(1) The President's Leadership
The President is the commander of the nation's armed forces and of the National Guard when it is in service of the nation. All government officials of the executive branch must report their actions to the President when asked. The President can excuse people from punishment for crimes committed.

(2) Treaties and Appointments
The President has the authority to make treaties, but they must be approved by a two-thirds vote of the Senate. The President nominates justices to the Supreme Court, ambassadors to other countries, and other federal officials with the Senate's approval.

(3) Filling Vacancies
If a government official's position becomes vacant when Congress is not in session, the President can make a temporary appointment.

Duties
The President must report to Congress on the condition of the country. This report is now presented in the annual State of the Union message.

Impeachment
The President, the Vice President, or any government official will be removed from office if impeached, or accused, and then found guilty of treason, bribery, or other serious crimes. The Constitution protects government officials from being impeached for unimportant reasons.

Federal Courts
The authority to decide legal cases is granted to a Supreme Court and to a system of lower courts established by Congress. The Supreme Court is the highest court in the land. Justices and judges are in their offices for life, subject to good behavior.

(1) General Authority
Federal courts have the authority to decide cases that arise under the Constitution, laws, and treaties of the United States. They also have the authority to settle disagreements among states and among citizens of different states.

---

(2) He shall have power, by and with the advice and consent of the Senate, to make treaties, provided two-thirds of the senators present concur; and he shall nominate, and by and with the advice and consent of the Senate, shall appoint ambassadors, other public ministers and consuls, judges of the Supreme Court, and all other officers of the United States, whose appointments are not herein otherwise provided for, and which shall be established by law; but the Congress may by law vest the appointment of such inferior officers, as they think proper, in the President alone, in the courts of law, or in the heads of departments.

(3) The President shall have power to fill up all vacancies that may happen during the recess of the Senate, by granting commissions which shall expire at the end of their next session.

SECTION 3. DUTIES OF THE PRESIDENT
He shall from time to time give to the Congress information of the state of the Union, and recommend to their consideration such measures as he shall judge necessary and expedient; he may, on extraordinary occasions, convene both houses, or either of them, and in case of disagreement between them, with respect to the time of adjournment, he may adjourn them to such time as he shall think proper; he shall receive ambassadors and other public ministers; he shall take care that the laws be faithfully executed, and shall commission all the officers of the United States.

SECTION 4. IMPEACHMENT
The President, Vice President and all civil officers of the United States, shall be removed from office on impeachment for, and conviction of, treason, bribery, or other high crimes and misdemeanors.

ARTICLE III
THE JUDICIAL BRANCH
SECTION 1. FEDERAL COURTS
The judicial power of the United States shall be vested in one Supreme Court, and in such inferior courts as the Congress may from time to time ordain and establish. The judges, both of the supreme and inferior courts, shall hold their offices during good behavior, and shall, at stated times, receive for their services a compensation, which shall not be diminished during their continuance in office.

SECTION 2. AUTHORITY OF THE FEDERAL COURTS
(1) The judicial power shall extend to all cases, in law and equity, arising under this Constitution, the laws of the United States, and treaties made or which shall be made, under their authority; to all cases affecting ambassadors, other public ministers and consuls; to all cases of admiralty and maritime jurisdiction; to controversies to which the United States shall be a party; to controversies between two or more states; [*between a state and citizens of another state;*] between citizens of different states; —between citizens of the same state claiming lands under grants of different states, [*and between a state or the citizens thereof, and foreign states, citizens, or subjects.*]

(2) In all cases affecting ambassadors, other public ministers and consuls, and those in which a state shall be party, the Supreme Court shall have original jurisdiction. In all the other cases before mentioned, the Supreme Court shall have appellate jurisdiction, both as to law and fact, with such exceptions, and under such regulations as the Congress shall make.

(3) The trial of all crimes, except in cases of impeachment, shall be by jury; and such trial shall be held in the state where the said crimes shall have been committed; but when not committed within any state, the trial shall be at such place or places as the Congress may by law have directed.

SECTION 3. TREASON
(1) Treason against the United States shall consist only in levying war against them, or in adhering to their enemies, giving them aid and comfort. No person shall be convicted of treason unless on the testimony of two witnesses to the same overt act, or on confession in open court.

(2) The Congress shall have power to declare the punishment of treason, but no attainder of treason shall work corruption of blood, or forfeiture except during the life of the person attainted.

ARTICLE IV
RELATIONS AMONG STATES
SECTION 1. OFFICIAL RECORDS
Full faith and credit shall be given in each state to the public acts, records, and judicial proceedings of every other state. And the Congress may by general laws prescribe the manner in which such acts, records, and proceedings shall be proved, and the effect thereof.

SECTION 2. PRIVILEGES OF THE CITIZENS
(1) The citizens of each state shall be entitled to all privileges and immunities of citizens in the several states.

(2) A person charged in any state with treason, felony, or other crime, who shall flee from justice, and be found in another state, shall on demand of the executive authority of the state from which he fled, be delivered up, to be removed to the state having jurisdiction of the crime.

(3) [*No person held to service or labor in one state, under the laws thereof, escaping into another, shall in consequence of any law or regulation therein, be discharged from such service or labor, but shall be delivered up on claim of the party to whom such service or labor may be due.*]

---

(2) Supreme Court
The Supreme Court can decide certain cases being tried for the first time. It can review cases that have already been tried in a lower court if the decision has been appealed, or questioned, by one side.

(3) Trial by Jury
The Constitution guarantees a trial by jury for every person charged with a federal crime. Amendments 5, 6, and 7 extend and clarify a person's right to a trial by jury.

(1) Definition of Treason
Acts that may be considered treason are making war against the United States or helping its enemies. A person cannot be convicted of attempting to overthrow the government unless there are two witnesses to the act or the person confesses in court to treason.

(2) Punishment for Treason
Congress can decide the punishment for treason, within certain limits.

Official Records
Each state must honor the official records and judicial decisions of other states.

(1) Privileges
A citizen moving from one state to another has the same rights as other citizens living in that person's new state of residence. In some cases, such as voting, people may be required to live in their new state for a certain length of time before obtaining the same privileges as citizens there.

(2) Extradition
At the governor's request, a person who is charged with a crime and who tries to escape justice by crossing into another state may be returned to the state in which the crime was committed.

(3) Fugitive Slaves
The original Constitution required that runaway slaves be returned to their owners. Amendment 13 abolished slavery, eliminating the need for this clause.

SECTION 3. NEW STATES AND TERRITORIES

(1) New states may be admitted by the Congress into this Union; but no new state shall be formed or erected within the jurisdiction of any other state; nor any state be formed by the junction of two or more states, or parts of states, without the consent of the legislatures of the states concerned as well as of the Congress.

(2) The Congress shall have power to dispose of and make all needful rules and regulations respecting the territory or other property belonging to the United States; and nothing in this Constitution shall be so construed as to prejudice any claims of the United States, or of any particular state.

SECTION 4. GUARANTEES TO THE STATES

The United States shall guarantee to every state in this Union a republican form of government, and shall protect each of them against invasion; and on application of the legislature, or of the executive (when the legislature cannot be convened) against domestic violence.

ARTICLE V
AMENDING THE CONSTITUTION

The Congress, whenever two-thirds of both houses shall deem it necessary, shall propose amendments to this Constitution, or, on the application of the legislatures of two-thirds of the several states, shall call a convention for proposing amendments, which, in either case, shall be valid to all intents and purposes, as part of this Constitution, when ratified by the legislatures of three-fourths of the several states, or by conventions in three-fourths thereof, as the one or the other mode of ratification may be proposed by the Congress; provided that [*no amendment which may be made prior to the year 1808 shall in any manner affect the first and fourth clauses in the Ninth Section of the First Article; and that*] no state, without its consent, shall be deprived of its equal suffrage in the Senate.

ARTICLE VI
GENERAL PROVISIONS

(1) All debts contracted and engagements entered into, before the adoption of this Constitution, shall be as valid against the United States under this Constitution, as under the Confederation.

(2) This Constitution, and the laws of the United States which shall be made in pursuance thereof, and all treaties made, or which shall be made, under the authority of the United States, shall be the supreme law of the land; and the judges in every state shall be bound thereby, anything in the Constitution or laws of any state to the contrary notwithstanding.

(3) The Senators and Representatives before mentioned, and the members of the several state legislatures, and all executive and judicial officers, both of the United States and of the several states, shall be bound by oath or affirmation, to support this Constitution; but no religious test shall ever be required as a qualification to any office or public trust under the United States.

---

(1) Admission of New States
Congress has the authority to admit new states to the Union. All new states have the same rights as existing states.

(2) Federal Property
The Constitution allows Congress to make or change laws governing federal property. This applies to territories and federally owned land within states, such as national parks.

Guarantees to the States
The federal government guarantees that every state have a republican form of government. The United States must also protect the states against invasion and help the states deal with rebellion or local violence.

Amending the Constitution
Changes to the Constitution may be proposed by a two-thirds vote of both the House of Representatives and the Senate or by a national convention called by Congress when asked by two-thirds of the states. For an amendment to become law, the legislatures or conventions in three-fourths of the states must approve it.

(1) Public Debt
Any debt owed by the United States before the Constitution went into effect was to be honored.

(2) Federal Supremacy
This clause declares that the Constitution and federal laws are the highest in the nation. Whenever a state law and a federal law are found to disagree, the federal law must be obeyed so long as it is constitutional.

(3) Oaths of Office
All federal and state officials must promise to follow and enforce the Constitution. These officials, however, cannot be required to follow a particular religion or satisfy any religious test.

ARTICLE VII
RATIFICATION

The ratification of the conventions of nine states, shall be sufficient for the establishment of this Constitution between the states so ratifying the same.

Done in convention by the unanimous consent of the states present the seventeenth day of September in the year of our Lord one thousand seven hundred and eighty seven and of the independence of the United States of America the Twelfth. In witness whereof we have hereunto subscribed our names.

George Washington—President and deputy from Virginia

DELAWARE
George Read
Gunning Bedford, Jr.
John Dickinson
Richard Bassett
Jacob Broom

MARYLAND
James McHenry
Daniel of St. Thomas Jenifer
Daniel Carroll

VIRGINIA
John Blair
James Madison, Jr.

NORTH CAROLINA
William Blount
Richard Dobbs Spaight
Hugh Williamson

SOUTH CAROLINA
John Rutledge
Charles Cotesworth Pinckney
Charles Pinckney
Pierce Butler

GEORGIA
William Few
Abraham Baldwin

NEW HAMPSHIRE
John Langdon
Nicholas Gilman

MASSACHUSETTS
Nathaniel Gorham
Rufus King

CONNECTICUT
William Samuel Johnson
Roger Sherman

NEW YORK
Alexander Hamilton

NEW JERSEY
William Livingston
David Brearley
William Paterson
Jonathan Dayton

PENNSYLVANIA
Benjamin Franklin
Thomas Mifflin
Robert Morris
George Clymer
Thomas FitzSimons
Jared Ingersoll
James Wilson
Gouverneur Morris

ATTEST: William Jackson, secretary

Ratification
In order for the Constitution to become law, 9 of the 13 states had to approve it. Special conventions were held for this purpose. The process took 9 months to complete.

Basic Freedoms
The Constitution guarantees our five basic freedoms of expression. It provides for the freedoms of religion, speech, the press, peaceable assembly, and petition for redress of grievances.

Weapons and the Militia
This amendment protects the right of the state governments and the people to maintain militias to guard against threats to their public order, safety, and liberty. In connection with that state right, the federal government may not take away the right of the people to have and use weapons.

Housing Soldiers
The federal government cannot force people to house soldiers in their homes during peacetime. However, Congress may pass laws allowing this during wartime.

Searches and Seizures
This amendment protects people's privacy and safety. Subject to certain exceptions, a law officer cannot search a person or a person's home and belongings unless a judge has issued a valid search warrant. There must be good reason for the search. The warrant must describe the place to be searched and the people or things to be seized, or taken.

Rights of Accused Persons
If a person is accused of a crime that is punishable by death or of any other crime that is very serious, a grand jury must decide if there is enough evidence to hold a trial. People cannot be tried twice for the same crime, nor can they be forced to testify against themselves. No person shall be fined, jailed, or executed by the government unless the person has been given a fair trial. The government cannot take a person's property for public use unless fair payment is made.

AMENDMENT 1 (1791)* **
BASIC FREEDOMS

Congress shall make no law respecting an establishment of religion, or prohibiting the free exercise thereof; or abridging the freedom of speech, or of the press; or the right of the people peaceably to assemble, and to petition the government for a redress of grievances.

AMENDMENT 2 (1791)
WEAPONS AND THE MILITIA

A well-regulated militia, being necessary to the security of a free state, the right of the people to keep and bear arms shall not be infringed.

AMENDMENT 3 (1791)
HOUSING SOLDIERS

No soldier shall, in time of peace, be quartered in any house, without the consent of the owner; nor in time of war, but in a manner to be prescribed by law.

AMENDMENT 4 (1791)
SEARCHES AND SEIZURES

The right of the people to be secure in their persons, houses, papers, and effects, against unreasonable searches and seizures, shall not be violated; and no warrants shall issue but upon probable cause, supported by oath or affirmation, and particularly describing the place to be searched, and the persons or things to be seized.

AMENDMENT 5 (1791)
RIGHTS OF ACCUSED PERSONS

No person shall be held to answer for a capital, or otherwise infamous crime, unless on a presentment or indictment of a grand jury, except in cases arising in the land or naval forces, or in the militia, when in actual service in time of war or public danger; nor shall any person be subject for the same offense to be twice put in jeopardy of life or limb; nor shall be compelled in any criminal case to be a witness against himself; nor be deprived of life, liberty, or property, without due process of law; nor shall private property be taken for public use without just compensation.

*** The date beside each amendment is the year that the amendment was ratified and became part of the Constitution.

AMENDMENT 6 (1791)
RIGHT TO A FAIR TRIAL

In all criminal prosecutions, the accused shall enjoy the right to a speedy and public trial, by an impartial jury of the state and district wherein the crime shall have been committed, which district shall have been previously ascertained by law, and to be informed of the nature and cause of the accusation; to be confronted with the witnesses against him; to have compulsory process for obtaining witnesses in his favor, and to have the assistance of counsel for his defense.

AMENDMENT 7 (1791)
JURY TRIAL IN CIVIL CASES

In suits at common law, where the value in controversy shall exceed 20 dollars, the right of trial by jury shall be preserved, and no fact tried by a jury shall be otherwise re-examined in any court of the United States, than according to the rules of the common law.

AMENDMENT 8 (1791)
BAIL AND PUNISHMENT

Excessive bail shall not be required, nor excessive fines imposed, nor cruel and unusual punishments inflicted.

AMENDMENT 9 (1791)
RIGHTS OF THE PEOPLE

The enumeration in the Constitution, of certain rights, shall not be construed to deny or disparage others retained by the people.

AMENDMENT 10 (1791)
POWERS OF THE STATES AND THE PEOPLE

The powers not delegated to the United States by the Constitution, nor prohibited by it to the states, are reserved to the states respectively, or to the people.

AMENDMENT 11 (1798)
SUITS AGAINST STATES

The judicial power of the United States shall not be construed to extend to any suit in law or equity, commenced or prosecuted against one of the United States or citizens of another state, or by citizens or subjects of any foreign state.

Right to a Fair Trial
A person accused of a crime has the right to a public trial by an impartial jury, locally chosen. The trial must be held within a reasonable amount of time. The accused person must be told of all charges and has the right to see, hear, and question any witnesses. The federal government must provide a lawyer free of charge to a person who is accused of a serious crime and who is unable to pay for legal services.

Jury Trial in Civil Cases
In most federal civil cases involving more than 20 dollars, a jury trial is guaranteed. Civil cases are those disputes between two or more people over money, property, personal injury, or legal rights. Usually civil cases are not tried in federal courts unless much larger sums of money are involved or unless federal courts are given the authority to decide a certain type of case.

Bail and Punishment
Courts cannot treat harshly people accused of crimes or punish them in unusual or cruel ways. Bail is money put up as a guarantee that an accused person will appear for trial. In certain cases bail can be denied altogether.

Rights of the People
The federal government must respect all natural rights, whether or not they are listed in the Constitution.

Powers of the States and the People
Any powers not clearly given to the federal government or denied to the states belong to the states or to the people.

Suits Against States
A citizen of one state cannot sue another state in federal court.

Election of President and Vice President
This amendment replaces the part of Article II, Section 1, that originally explained the process of electing the President and Vice President. Amendment 12 was an important step in the development of the two-party system. It allows a party to nominate its own candidates for both President and Vice President.

AMENDMENT 12 (1804)
ELECTION OF PRESIDENT AND VICE PRESIDENT

The electors shall meet in their respective states, and vote by ballot for President and Vice President, one of whom, at least, shall not be an inhabitant of the same state with themselves; they shall name in their ballots the person voted for as President, and in distinct ballots the person voted for as Vice President, and they shall make distinct lists of all persons voted for as President, and of all persons voted for as Vice President, and of the number of votes for each, which lists they shall sign and certify, and transmit, sealed, to the seat of government of the United States, directed to the President of the Senate; the President of the Senate shall, in the presence of the Senate and House of Representatives, open all the certificates, and the votes shall then be counted; the person having the greatest number of votes for President shall be the President, if such a number be a majority of the whole number of electors appointed; and if no person have such majority; then from the persons having the highest numbers not exceeding three on the list of those voted for as President, the House of Representatives shall choose immediately, by ballot, the President. But in choosing the President, the votes shall be taken by states, the representation from each state having one vote; a quorum for this purpose shall consist of a member or members from two thirds of the states, and a majority of all the states shall be necessary to a choice. [An*d if the House of Representatives shall not choose a President whenever the right of choice shall devolve upon them, before the fourth day of March next following, then the Vice President shall act as President, as in the case of the death or other constitutional disability of the President.*] The person having the greatest number of votes as Vice President, shall be the Vice President, if such number be a majority of the whole number of electors appointed, and if no person have a majority, then, from the two highest numbers on the list the Senate shall choose the Vice President; a quorum for the purpose shall consist of two thirds of the whole number of Senators, and a majority of the whole number shall be necessary to a choice. But no person constitutionally ineligible to the office of President shall be eligible to that of Vice President of the United States.

End of Slavery
People cannot be forced to work against their will unless they have been tried for and convicted of a crime for which this means of punishment is ordered. Congress may enforce this by law.

AMENDMENT 13 (1865)
END OF SLAVERY
SECTION 1. ABOLITION
Neither slavery nor involuntary servitude, except as a punishment for crime whereof the party shall have been duly convicted, shall exist within the United States, or any place subject to their jurisdiction.
SECTION 2. ENFORCEMENT
Congress shall have power to enforce this article by appropriate legislation.

Citizenship
All persons born or naturalized in the United States are citizens of the United States and of the state in which they live. State governments may not deny any citizen the full rights of citizenship. This amendment also guarantees due process of law. According to due process of law, no state may take away the rights of a citizen. All citizens must be protected equally under law.

AMENDMENT 14 (1868)
RIGHTS OF CITIZENS
SECTION 1. CITIZENSHIP
All persons born or naturalized in the United States and subject to the jurisdiction thereof, are citizens of the United States and of the state wherein they reside. No state shall make or enforce any law which shall abridge the privileges or immunities of citizens of the United States, nor shall any state deprive any person of life, liberty, or property, without due process of law; nor deny to any person within its jurisdiction the equal protection of the laws.

SECTION 2. NUMBER OF REPRESENTATIVES

Representatives shall be apportioned among the several states according to their respective numbers, counting the whole number of persons in each state, [*excluding Indians not taxed*]. But when the right to vote at any election for the choice of electors for President and Vice President of the United States, representatives in Congress, the executive and judicial officers of a state, or the members of the legislature thereof, is denied to any of the [*male*] inhabitants of such state, being [*twenty-one years of age and*] citizens of the United States, or in any way abridged, except for participation in rebellion or other crime, the basis of representation therein shall be reduced in the proportion which the number of such [*male*] citizens shall bear to the whole number of [*male*] citizens [*twenty-one years of age*] in such state.

Number of Representatives
Each state's representation in Congress is based on its total population. Any state denying eligible citizens the right to vote will have its representation in Congress decreased. This clause abolished the Three-fifths Compromise in Article I, Section 2. Later amendments granted women the right to vote and lowered the voting age to 18.

SECTION 3. PENALTY FOR REBELLION

No person shall be a Senator or Representative in Congress, or elector of President and Vice President, or hold any office, civil or military, under the United States, or under any state, who, having previously taken an oath, as a member of Congress, or as an officer of the United States, or as a member of any state legislature, or as an executive or judicial officer of any state, to support the Constitution of the United States, shall have engaged in insurrection or rebellion against the same, or given aid or comfort to the enemies thereof. But Congress may, by a vote of two thirds of each house, remove such disability.

Penalty for Rebellion
No person who has rebelled against the United States may hold federal office. This clause was originally added to punish the leaders of the Confederacy for failing to support the Constitution of the United States.

SECTION 4. GOVERNMENT DEBT

The validity of the public debt of the United States, authorized by law, including debts incurred for payment of pensions and bounties for services in suppressing insurrection or rebellion, shall not be questioned. But neither the United States nor any state shall assume or pay any debt or obligation incurred in aid of insurrection or rebellion against the United States, [*or any claim for the loss or emancipation of any slave;*] but all such debts, obligations, and claims shall be held illegal and void.

Government Debt
The federal government is responsible for all public debts. It is not responsible, however, for Confederate debts or for debts that result from any rebellion against the United States.

SECTION 5. ENFORCEMENT

The Congress shall have power to enforce, by appropriate legislation, the provisions of this article.

Enforcement
Congress may enforce these provisions by law.

AMENDMENT 15 (1870)
VOTING RIGHTS

SECTION 1. RIGHT TO VOTE

The right of citizens of the United States to vote shall not be denied or abridged by the United States or by any state on account of race, color, or previous condition of servitude.

SECTION 2. ENFORCEMENT

The Congress shall have power to enforce this article by appropriate legislation.

Right to Vote
No state may prevent a citizen from voting simply because of race or color or condition of previous servitude. This amendment was designed to extend voting rights to enforce this by law.

AMENDMENT 16 (1913)
INCOME TAX

The Congress shall have power to lay and collect taxes on incomes, from whatever source derived, without apportionment among the several states, and without regard to any census or enumeration.

Income Tax
Congress has the power to collect taxes on its citizens, based on their personal incomes rather than on the number of people living in a state.

Direct Election of Senators
Originally, state legislatures elected senators. This amendment allows the people of each state to elect their own senators directly. The idea is to make senators more responsible to the people they represent.

Prohibition
This amendment made it illegal to make, sell, or transport liquor within the United States or to transport it out of the United States or its territories. Amendment 18 was the first to include a time limit for approval. If not ratified within seven years, it would be repealed, or canceled. Many later amendments have included similar time limits.

Women's Voting Rights
This amendment protected the right of women throughout the United States to vote.

Terms of Office
The terms of the President and the Vice President begin on January 20, in the year following their election. Members of Congress take office on January 3. Before this amendment newly elected members of Congress did not begin their terms until March 4. This meant that those who had run for reelection and been defeated remained in office for four months.

AMENDMENT 17 (1913)
DIRECT ELECTION OF SENATORS

SECTION 1. METHOD OF ELECTION
The Senate of the United States shall be composed of two Senators from each state, elected by the people thereof, for six years; and each Senator shall have one vote. The electors in each state shall have the qualifications requisite for electors of the most numerous branch of the state legislatures.

SECTION 2. VACANCIES
When vacancies happen in the representation of any state in the Senate, the executive authority of such state shall issue writs of election to fill such vacancies: *Provided*, that the legislature of any state may empower the executive thereof to make temporary appointments until the people fill the vacancies by election as the legislature may direct.

SECTION 3. EXCEPTION
[*This amendment shall not be so construed as to affect the election or term of any Senator chosen before it becomes valid as part of the Constitution.*]

AMENDMENT 18 (1919)
BAN ON ALCOHOLIC DRINKS

SECTION 1. PROHIBITION
[*After one year from the ratification of this article the manufacture, sale, or transportation of intoxicating liquors within, the importation thereof into, or the exportation thereof from the United States and all territory subject to the jurisdiction thereof for beverage purposes is hereby prohibited.*]

SECTION 2. ENFORCEMENT
[*The Congress and the several states shall have concurrent power to enforce this article by appropriate legislation.*]

SECTION 3. RATIFICATION
[*This article shall be inoperative unless it shall have been ratified as an amendment to the Constitution by the legislatures of the several states as provided in the Constitution, within seven years from the date of the submission hereof to the states by the Congress.*]

AMENDMENT 19 (1920)
WOMEN'S VOTING RIGHTS

SECTION 1. RIGHT TO VOTE
The right of citizens of the United States to vote shall not be denied or abridged by the United States or by any state on account of sex.

SECTION 2. ENFORCEMENT
Congress shall have power to enforce this article by appropriate legislation.

AMENDMENT 20 (1933)
TERMS OF OFFICE

SECTION 1. BEGINNING OF TERMS
The terms of the President and Vice President shall end at noon on the 20th day of January, and the terms of Senators and Representatives at noon on the 3rd day of January, of the years in which such terms would have ended if this article had not been ratified; and the terms of their successors shall then begin.

SECTION 2. SESSIONS OF CONGRESS
The Congress shall assemble at least once in every year, and such meeting shall begin at noon on the 3rd day of January, unless they shall by law appoint a different day.

SECTION 3. PRESIDENTIAL SUCCESSION
If, at the time fixed for the beginning of the term of the President, the President-elect shall have died, the Vice President-elect shall become President. If a President shall not have been chosen before the time fixed for the beginning of his term, or if the President-elect shall have failed to qualify, then the Vice President-elect shall act as President until a President shall have qualified; and the Congress may by law provide for the case wherein neither a President-elect nor a Vice President-elect shall have qualified, declaring who shall then act as President, or the manner in which one who is to act shall be selected and such person shall act accordingly until a President or Vice President shall be qualified.

SECTION 4. ELECTIONS DECIDED BY CONGRESS
The Congress may by law provide for the case of the death of any of the persons from whom the House of Representatives may choose a President whenever the right of choice shall have devolved upon them, and for the case of the death of any of the persons from whom the Senate may choose a Vice President whenever the right of choice shall have devolved upon them.

SECTION 5. EFFECTIVE DATE
[Sections 1 and 2 shall take effect on the 15th day of October following the ratification of this article.]

SECTION 6. RATIFICATION
[This article shall be inoperative unless it shall have been ratified as an amendment to the Constitution by the legislatures of three fourths of the several states within seven years from the date of its submission.]

AMENDMENT 21 (1933)
END OF PROHIBITION

SECTION 1. REPEAL OF AMENDMENT 18
The eighteenth article of amendment to the Constitution of the United States is hereby repealed.

SECTION 2. STATE LAWS
The transportation or importation into any state, territory, or possession of the United States for delivery or use therein of intoxicating liquors, in violation of the laws thereof, is hereby prohibited.

SECTION 3. RATIFICATION
[This article shall be inoperative unless it shall have been ratified as an amendment to the Constitution by conventions in the several states, as provided in the Constitution within seven years from the date of the submission hereof to the states by Congress.]

Sessions of Congress
Congress meets at least once a year, beginning at noon on January 3. Congress had previously met at least once a year beginning on the first Monday of December.

Presidential Succession
If the newly elected President dies before January 20, the newly elected Vice President becomes President on that date. If a President has not been chosen by January 20 or does not meet the requirements for being President, the newly elected Vice President becomes President. If neither the newly elected President nor the newly elected Vice President meets the requirements for office, Congress decides who will serve as President until a qualified President or Vice President is chosen.

End of Prohibition
This amendment repealed Amendment 18. This is the only amendment to be ratified by state conventions instead of by state legislatures. Congress felt that this would give people's opinions about prohibition a better chance to be heard.

Two-Term limit for Presidents
A President may not serve more than two full terms in office. Any President who serves less than two years of a previous President's term may be elected for two more terms.

Presidential Electors for District of Columbia
This amendment grants three electoral votes to the national capital.

Ban on Poll Taxes
No United States citizen may be prevented from voting in a federal election because of failing to pay a tax to vote. Poll taxes had been used in some states to prevent African Americans from voting.

Presidential Vacancy
If the President is removed from office or resigns from or dies while in office, the Vice President becomes President.

AMENDMENT 22 (1951)
TWO-TERM LIMIT FOR PRESIDENTS

SECTION 1. TWO-TERM LIMIT

No person shall be elected to the office of the President more than twice, and no person who has held the office of President, or acted as President, for more than two years of a term to which some other person was elected President shall be elected to the office of the President more than once. [*But this article shall not apply to any person holding the office of President when this article was proposed by the Congress, and shall not prevent any person who may be holding the office of President, or acting as President, during the term within which this article becomes operative from holding the office of President, or acting as President, during the remainder of such term.*]

SECTION 2. RATIFICATION

[*This article shall be inoperative unless it shall have been ratified as an amendment to the Constitution by the legislatures of three-fourths of the several states within seven years from the date of its submission to the states by the Congress.*]

AMENDMENT 23 (1961)
PRESIDENTIAL ELECTORS FOR DISTRICT OF COLUMBIA

SECTION 1. NUMBER OF ELECTORS

The District constituting the seat of Government of the United States shall appoint in such manner as Congress may direct:

A number of electors of President and Vice President equal to the whole number of Senators and Representatives in Congress to which the District would be entitled if it were a state, but in no event more than the least populous state; they shall be in addition to those appointed by the states, but they shall be considered, for the purposes of the election of President and Vice President, to be electors appointed by a state, and they shall meet in the District and perform such duties as provided by the twelfth article of amendment.

SECTION 2. ENFORCEMENT

The Congress shall have power to enforce this article by appropriate legislation.

AMENDMENT 24 (1964)
BAN ON POLL TAXES

SECTION 1. POLL TAX ILLEGAL

The right of citizens of the United States to vote in any primary or other election for President or Vice President, for electors for President or Vice President, or for Senator or Representative in Congress, shall not be denied or abridged by the United States or any state by reason of failure to pay any poll tax or other tax.

SECTION 2. ENFORCEMENT

The Congress shall have power to enforce this article by appropriate legislation.

AMENDMENT 25 (1967)
PRESIDENTIAL SUCCESSION

SECTION 1. PRESIDENTIAL VACANCY

In case of the removal of the President from office or of his death or resignation, the Vice President shall become President.

SECTION 2. VICE PRESIDENTIAL VACANCY

Whenever there is a vacancy in the office of the Vice President, the President shall nominate a Vice President who shall take the office upon confirmation by a majority vote of both houses of Congress.

SECTION 3. PRESIDENTIAL DISABILITY

Whenever the President transmits to the President pro tempore of the Senate and the Speaker of the House of Representatives his written declaration that he is unable to discharge the powers and duties of his office, and until he transmits to them a written declaration to the contrary, such powers and duties shall be discharged by the Vice President as Acting President.

SECTION 4. DETERMINING PRESIDENTIAL DISABILITY

Whenever the Vice President and a majority of either the principal officers of the executive departments or of such other body as Congress may by law provide, transmit to the President pro tempore of the Senate and the Speaker of the House of Representatives their written declaration that the President is unable to discharge the powers and duties of his office, the Vice President shall immediately assume the powers and duties of the office as Acting President.

Thereafter, when the President transmits to the President pro tempore of the Senate and the Speaker of the House of Representatives his written declaration that no inability exists, he shall resume the powers and duties of his office unless the Vice President and a majority of either the principal officers of the executive department or of such other body as Congress may by law provide, transmit within four days to the President pro tempore of the Senate and the Speaker of the House of Representatives their written declaration that the President is unable to discharge the powers and duties of his office. Thereupon Congress shall decide the issue, assembling within 48 hours for that purpose if not in session. If the Congress, within 21 days after receipt of the latter written declaration, or, if Congress is not in session, within 21 days after Congress is required to assemble, determines by two-thirds vote of both houses that the President is unable to discharge the powers and duties of his office, the Vice President shall continue to discharge the same as Acting President; otherwise the President shall resume the powers and duties of his office.

AMENDMENT 26 (1971)
VOTING AGE

SECTION 1. RIGHT TO VOTE

The right of citizens of the United States, who are 18 years of age or older, to vote shall not be denied or abridged by the United States or any state on account of age.

SECTION 2. ENFORCEMENT

The Congress shall have the power to enforce this article by appropriate legislation.

AMENDMENT 27 (1992)
CONGRESSIONAL PAY

No law, varying the compensation for the services of the Senators and Representatives, shall take effect, until an election of Representatives shall have intervened.

Vice Presidential Vacancy
If the office of the Vice President becomes open, the President names someone to assume that office and that person becomes Vice President if both houses of Congress approve by a majority vote.

Presidential Disability
This section explains in detail what happens if the President cannot continue in office because of sickness or any other reason. The Vice President takes over as acting President until the President is able to resume office.

Determining Presidential Disability
If the Vice President and a majority of the Cabinet inform the Speaker of the House and the president pro tempore of the Senate that the President cannot carry out his or her duties, the Vice President then serves as acting President. To regain the office, the President has to inform the Speaker and the president pro tempore in writing that he or she is again able to serve. But, if the Vice President and a majority of the Cabinet disagree with the President and inform the Speaker and the president pro tempore that the President is still unable to serve, then Congress decides who will hold the office of President.

Voting Age
All citizens 18 years or older have the right to vote. Formerly, the voting age was 21 in most states.

Congressional Pay
A law raising or lowering the salaries for members of Congress cannot be passed for that session of Congress.

AMERICAN DOCUMENTS

"The Star-Spangled Banner" was written by Francis Scott Key in September 1814 and adopted as the national anthem in March 1931. The army and navy had recognized it as such long before Congress approved it.

During the War of 1812, Francis Scott Key spent a night aboard a British warship in the Chesapeake Bay while trying to arrange for the release of an American prisoner. The battle raged throughout the night, while the Americans were held on the ship. The next morning, when the smoke from the cannons finally cleared, Francis Scott Key was thrilled to see the American flag still waving proudly above Fort McHenry. It symbolized the victory of the Americans.

There are four verses to the national anthem. In these four verses, Key wrote about how he felt when he saw the flag still waving over Fort McHenry. He wrote that the flag was a symbol of the freedom for which the people had fought so hard. Key also told about the pride he had in his country and the great hopes he had for the future of the United States.

THE NATIONAL ANTHEM

The Star-Spangled Banner

(1)
Oh, say can you see by the dawn's early light
What so proudly we hail'd at the twilight's last gleaming,
Whose broad stripes and bright stars through the perilous fight
O'er the ramparts we watch'd were so gallantly streaming?
And the rockets' red glare, the bombs bursting in air,
Gave proof through the night that our flag was still there.
Oh, say does that star-spangled banner yet wave
O'er the land of the free and the home of the brave?

(2)
On the shore dimly seen through the mists of the deep,
Where the foe's haughty host in dread silence reposes,
What is that which the breeze, o'er the towering steep,
As it fitfully blows, half conceals, half discloses?
Now it catches the gleam of the morning's first beam,
In full glory reflected now shines in the stream.
'Tis the star-spangled banner, oh, long may it wave
O'er the land of the free and the home of the brave!

(3)
And where is that band who so vauntingly swore
That the havoc of war and the battle's confusion
A home and a country should leave us no more?
Their blood has wash'd out their foul footstep's pollution.
No refuge could save the hireling and slave
From the terror of flight or the gloom of the grave,
And the star-spangled banner in triumph doth wave
O'er the land of the free and the home of the brave.

(4)
Oh, thus be it ever when freemen shall stand
Between their lov'd home and the war's desolation!
Blest with vict'ry and peace may the heav'n-rescued land
Praise the power that hath made and preserv'd us a nation!
Then conquer we must, when our cause it is just,
And this be our motto, "In God is our Trust,"
And the star-spangled banner in triumph shall wave
O'er the land of the free and the home of the brave.

THE PLEDGE OF ALLEGIANCE

I pledge allegiance to the Flag

of the United States of America,

and to the Republic

for which it stands,

one Nation under God, indivisible,

with liberty and justice for all.

The flag is a symbol of the United States of America. The Pledge of Allegiance says that the people of the United States promise to stand up for the flag, their country, and the basic beliefs of freedom and fairness upon which the country was established.

Biographical Dictionary

The Biographical Dictionary lists many of the important people introduced in this book. The page number tells where the main discussion of each person starts. See the Index for other page references.

A

Adams, Abigail *1744–1818* Patriot who wrote about women's rights in letters to John Adams, her husband. p. 311

Adams, John *1735–1826* 2nd U.S. President and one of the writers of the Declaration of Independence. pp. 303, 306, 353, 377, 379, 554

Adams, Samuel *1722–1803* American Revolutionary leader who set up a Committee of Correspondence in Boston and helped form the Sons of Liberty. pp. 281, 289, 353, 369

Addams, Jane *1860–1935* American reformer who brought the idea of settlement houses from Britain to the United States. She founded Hull House in Chicago. p. 553

Albright, Madeleine K. *1937–* First female secretary of state. p. 548

Ali, Sunni *1400s* Ruler of African empire of Songhay from 1464 to 1492. p. 111

Allen, Ethan *1738–1789* American Patriot from Vermont who led the Green Mountain Boys. p. 318

Anderson, Robert *1805–1871* Union commander of Fort Sumter who was forced to surrender to the Confederacy. p. 454

Anthony, Susan Brownell *1820–1906* Women's suffrage leader who worked to enable women to have the same rights as men. p. 547

Armstrong, Louis *1901–1971* Noted jazz trumpeter who helped make jazz popular in the 1920s. p. 530

Armstrong, Neil *1930–* American astronaut who was the first person to set foot on the moon. p. 528

Arnold, Benedict *1741–1801* Continental Army officer who became a traitor and worked for the British army. p. 323

Atahuallpa (ah•tah•WAHL•pah) *1502?–1533* Inca ruler who was killed in the Spanish conquest of the Incas. p. 133

Attucks, Crispus (A•tuhks) *1723?–1770* Patriot and former slave who was killed during the Boston Massacre. p. 285

Austin, Moses *1761–1821* American pioneer who wanted to start an American colony in Texas. p. 402

Austin, Stephen F. *1793–1836* Moses Austin's son. He carried out his father's dream of starting an American colony in Texas. p. 402

B

Bache, Sarah Franklin *1700s* Daughter of Benjamin Franklin; took over Philadelphia Association when Esther Reed died. p. 311

Balboa, Vasco Núñez de (bahl•BOH•uh, NOON•yays day) *1475–1519* Spanish explorer who, in 1513, became the first European to reach the western coast of the Americas—proving to Europeans that the Americas were separate from Asia. pp. 123, 124

Banneker, Benjamin *1731–1806* African American who helped survey the land for the new capital of the United States. p. 376

Barton, Clara *1821–1912* Civil War nurse and founder of the American Red Cross. p. 463

Bates, Katharine Lee *1859–1929* American educator and poet. p. 17

Becknell, William *1796?–1865* American pioneer from Missouri who opened the Santa Fe Trail. p. 404

Berlin, Irving *1888–1989* American songwriter who moved to New York City from Russia in 1893. p. 503

Bessemer, Henry *1813–1898* British inventor of a way to produce steel more easily and cheaply than before. p. 495

Bienville, Jean-Baptiste Le Moyne, Sieur de (bee•EN•vil, ZHAHN ba•TEEST luh•MWAHN) *1680–1747* French explorer who—with his brother, Pierre Le Moyne, Sieur d'Iberville—started an early settlement at the mouth of the Mississippi River. p. 154

Black Hawk *1767–1838* Leader of Sauk and Fox Indians; led fight against U.S. troops and Illinois militia. p. 398

Bonaparte, Napoleon (BOH•nuh•part, nuh•POH•lee•uhn) *1769–1821* French leader who sold all of the Louisiana region to the United States. p. 385

Boone, Daniel *1734–1820* American who was one of the first pioneers to cross the Appalachians. pp. 225, 276

Booth, John Wilkes *1838–1865* Actor who assassinated President Abraham Lincoln. p. 477

Bowie, James *1796–1836* American soldier killed at the Alamo. p. 403

Braddock, Edward *1695–1755* Commander in chief of British forces in French and Indian War; defeated in surprise attack. p. 271

Bradford, William *1590–1657* Governor of Plymouth Colony. p. 168

Breckinridge, John *1821–1875* Democrat from Kentucky who ran against Abraham Lincoln in the 1860 presidential election. p. 453

Brown, John *1800–1859* American abolitionist who seized a weapons storehouse to help slaves rebel. He was caught and hanged. p. 449

Brown, Linda *1943–* African American student whose family was among a group that challenged public-school segregation. p. 548

Brown, Moses *1738–1836* Textile pioneer who built the first textile mill in the United States, using Samuel Slater's plans. p. 416

Bruce, Blanche K. *1841–1898* Former slave who became U.S. senator from Mississippi. p. 479

Bruchac, Joseph Author of Native American folktales and legends. p. 14

Burgoyne, John (ber•GOYN) *1722–1792* British general who lost a battle to the Continental Army on October 17, 1777, at Saratoga, New York. p. 316

Burnet, David G. *1788–1870* First president of the Republic of Texas, when it was formed in 1836. p. 403

Bush, George *1924–* 41st U.S. President. He was President at the end of the Cold War and during the Gulf War. p. 590

Bush, George W. *1946–* 43rd U.S. President and son of George Bush. In 2000 he won the closest presidential election in United States history. p. 555

C

Cabeza de Vaca, Álvar Núñez (kah•BAY•sah day VAH•kah) *1490?–1560?* Spanish explorer who went to Mexico City and told stories of the Seven Cities of Gold. p. 131

Caboto, Giovanni (kah•BOH•toh) *1450?–1499?* Italian explorer who in 1497 sailed from England and landed in what is now Newfoundland, though he thought he had landed in Asia. The English gave him the name John Cabot. p. 123

Calhoun, John C. *1782–1850* Vice President under John Quincy Adams and Andrew Jackson. He was a strong believer in states' rights. pp. 437, 453

Calvert, Cecilius *1605–1675* First proprietor of the Maryland colony; appointed his brother Leonard Calvert as governor of Maryland. p. 233

Calvert, George *1580?–1632* Member of Virginia Company and the first Lord Baltimore; bought land in Newfoundland, but found it too cold; moved to Chesapeake Bay area; father of Cecilius Calvert. p. 232

Cardozo, Francis L. *1800s* African American who became secretary of state and state treasurer in South Carolina. p. 479

Carnegie, Andrew *1835–1919* Entrepreneur who helped the steel industry grow in the United States. pp. 495, 496

Carteret, Sir George *c.1610–1680* Proprietor with Lord John Berkeley of territory between the Hudson and Delaware Rivers; named the state of New Jersey for his birthplace. p. 213

Cartier, Jacques (kar•TYAY, ZHAHK) *1491–1557* French explorer who sailed up the St. Lawrence River and began a fur-trading business with the Hurons. p. 137

Castro, Fidel *1926–* Leader who took over Cuba in 1959 and made it a communist nation. p. 582

Catt, Carrie Lane Chapman *1859–1947* President of National American Woman Suffrage Association. p. 547

Cavelier, René-Robert (ka•vuhl•YAY) *See* La Salle.

Champlain, Samuel de (sham•PLAYN) *1567?–1635* French explorer who founded the first settlement at Quebec. p. 151

Charles I *1500–1558* King of Spain. p. 145

Charles I *1600–1649* British king who chartered the colonies of Massachusetts and Maryland. pp. 188, 233

Charles II *1630–1685* British king who granted charters for the New Hampshire Colony and the Carolina Colony. Son of Charles I and Henrietta Maria. pp. 197, 234

Chavez, Cesar *1927–1993* Labor leader and organizer of the National Farm Workers Association and, later, the United Farm Workers. pp. 550–551

Churchill, Winston *1874–1965* Prime minister of Britain during World War II; later helped form the United Nations. pp. 586–587

Clark, George Rogers *1752–1818* American Revolutionary frontiersman who helped protect western lands and settlers. p. 319

Clark, William *1770–1838* American explorer who aided Meriwether Lewis in an expedition through the Louisiana Purchase. p. 386

Clay, Henry *1777–1852* Representative from Kentucky who worked for compromises on the slavery issue. pp. 390, 438

Clemens, Samuel Langhorne *1835–1910* American writer and steamboat pilot; he wrote under the pen name Mark Twain. p. 30

Clinton, DeWitt *1769–1828* Governor of New York who found European investors to pay for building of Erie Canal. p. 414

Clinton, George *1739–1812* American politician who helped form the Democratic-Republican party. p. 367

Clinton, William *1946–* 42nd U.S. President. pp. 556, 590–591

Columbus, Christopher *1451–1506* Italian-born Spanish explorer who in 1492 sailed west from Spain and thought he had reached Asia but had actually reached islands near the Americas, lands that were unknown to Europeans. pp. 106, 121

Cook, James *1728–1779* Sea captain who was the first European explorer to land on the Hawaiian Islands. p. 568

Cooper, Peter *1791–1883* American manufacturer who built *Tom Thumb*, one of the first locomotives made in the United States. p. 415

Cornish, Samuel *1795–1858* African American who in 1827 helped John Russwurm found an abolitionist newspaper called *Freedom's Journal*. p. 448

Cornwallis, Charles *1738–1805* British general who surrendered at the Battle of Yorktown, resulting in victory for the Americans in the Revolutionary War. p. 324

Coronado, Francisco Vásquez de (kawr•oh•NAH•doh) *1510?–1554* Spanish explorer who led an expedition from Mexico City into what is now the southwestern United States in search of the Seven Cities of Gold. p. 131

Cortés, Hernando (kawr•TEZ) *1485–1547* Spanish conquistador who conquered the Aztec Empire. pp. 128–130

Crazy Horse *1842?–1877* Sioux leader who fought against General George Custer. p. 490

Crockett, Davy *1786–1836* American pioneer who was killed at the Alamo. pp. 395, 403

Cullen, Countee *1903–1946* African American writer and poet during the Harlem Renaissance. p. 530

Custer, George *1839–1876* U.S. Army general who led an attack against Sioux and Cheyenne Indians. Custer and all of his men were killed in the battle. p. 491

D

da Gama, Vasco (dah GA•muh) *1460?–1524* Portuguese navigator who sailed from Europe, around the southern tip of Africa, and on to Asia between 1497 and 1499. p. 118

Davis, Jefferson *1808–1889* United States senator from Mississippi who became president of the Confederacy. p. 453

Dawes, William *1745–1799* American who, along with Paul Revere, warned the Patriots that the British were marching toward Concord. p. 291

Deere, John *1804–1886* American industrialist who created steel plows for use on the Great Plains. p. 419

Deganawida (deh•gahn•uh•WIH•duh) *1500s* Legendary Iroquois holy man who called for an end to the fighting among the Iroquois, a view that led to the formation of the Iroquois League. p. 90

de Narváez, Pánfilo *1500s* Spanish explorer who hoped to conquer lands along the Gulf of Mexico but failed. p. 130

de Soto, Hernando (day SOH•toh) *1496?–1542* Spanish explorer who led an expedition into what is today the southeastern United States. p. 132

Dewey, George *1837–1917* American naval commander who destroyed the Spanish fleet and captured Manila Bay in the Spanish-American War. p. 571

Dias, Bartolomeu (DEE•ahsh) *1450?–1500* Portuguese navigator who in 1488 became the first European to sail around the southern tip of Africa. p. 118

Dickinson, John *1732–1808* Member of the Continental Congress who wrote most of the Articles of Confederation, adopted in 1781. pp. 283, 293, 306

Dinwiddie, Robert *1693–1770* British Lieutenant Governor of Virginia; sent George Washington to defend Ohio Valley from seizure by the French. p. 269

Dole, James *1877–1958* American businessman who organized the Hawaiian Pineapple Company. p. 569

Douglas, Stephen A. *1813–1861* American legislator who wrote the Kansas-Nebraska Act and debated Abraham Lincoln in a race for a Senate seat from Illinois. p. 452

Douglass, Frederick *1817–1895* Abolitionist speaker and writer who had escaped from slavery. p. 449

Dowd, Charles *1825–1904* American who helped develop the idea of dividing the world into time zones. p. 532

Drake, Edwin *1819–1880* American pioneer in oil industry; became first to tap petroleum at its source. p. 497

Drake, Francis *1543–1596* English explorer who sailed around the world. p. 157

Du Bois, W. E. B. (doo•BOYS) *1868–1963* African American teacher, writer, and leader who helped form the National Association for the Advancement of Colored People (NAACP). pp. 548, 549

E

Earhart, Amelia *1897–1937* Airplane pilot who was the first woman to make a transatlantic flight. p. 527

Edison, Thomas *1847–1931* American who invented the phonograph and the electric lightbulb; he also built the first power station to supply electricity to New York City. pp. 498–499, 500–501, 528

Eisenhower, Dwight D. *1890–1969* 34th U.S. President and, earlier, American general who led the D day invasion. p. 580

Elizabeth I *1533–1603* Queen of England from 1558 to 1603. p. 156

Ellington, Edward Kennedy (Duke) *1899–1974* Band leader who became well-known playing jazz during the 1920s. p. 530

Emerson, Ralph Waldo *1803–1882* American poet who wrote "Concord Hymn." pp. 267, 292

Endecott, John *1588–1665* Member of New England Company who sailed to New England in 1628 and settled at Salem. p. 188

Equiano, Olaudah (ek•wee•AHN•oh, OHL•uh•dah) *1750?–1797* African who was kidnapped from his village and sold into slavery. He later wrote a book describing his experiences. p. 244

Esteban (ehs•TAY•bahn) *1500–1539* African explorer who went with Cabeza de Vaca to Mexico City and told stories of the Seven Cities of Gold. Esteban was killed on a later expedition, the purpose of which was to find out whether the stories were true. p. 131

F

Farragut, Jorge (FAIR•uh•guht, HAWR•hay) *1755–1817* Spanish-born man who fought in the Continental Army and the navy. p. 318

Ferdinand II *1452–1516* King of Spain who—with Queen Isabella, his wife—sent Christopher Columbus on his voyage to find a western route to Asia. p. 121

Finley, John Fur trader who helped Daniel Boone find the way across the Appalachian Mountains to Kentucky. p. 277

Fleming, Sandford *1827–1915* Canadian who helped develop the idea of dividing the world into time zones. p. 532

Fong, Hiram L. *1906–* Chinese immigrant who settled in Hawaii; became first Chinese American senator. p. 505

Ford, Henry *1863–1947* American automobile manufacturer who mass-produced cars at low cost by using assembly lines. pp. 525, 526

Frame, Richard *1600s* Colonist and writer. p. 209

Francis Ferdinand *1863–1914* Archduke of Austria-Hungary who was assassinated by a Serbian, which led to the outbreak of World War I. p. 576

Franklin, Benjamin *1706–1790* American leader who was sent to Britain to ask Parliament for representation. He was a writer of the Declaration of Independence, a delegate to the Constitutional Convention, and a respected scientist and business leader. pp. 221, 271, 283, 303, 318, 352, 366, 554

F

Frontenac, Louis de Buade, Count de (FRAHN•tuh•nak) *1622–1698* French leader who was appointed governor-general of New France. p. 152

Fulton, Robert *1765–1815* American engineer and inventor who created the first commercial steamboat. p. 415

G

Gadsden, James *1788–1858* U.S. minister to Mexico who arranged to buy parts of present-day New Mexico and Arizona from Mexico—known as the Gadsden Purchase. p. 407

Gage, Thomas *1721–1787* Head of the British army in North America and colonial governor. pp. 291, 294

Gálvez, Bernardo de (GAHL•ves) *1746–1786* Spanish governor of Louisiana who sent supplies to the Patriots in the Revolutionary War and led his own soldiers in taking a British fort in Florida. p. 318

Garrison, William Lloyd *1805–1879* American abolitionist who started a newspaper called *The Liberator*. p. 448

Gates, Horatio *1728–1806* American general who defeated the British in 1777 at Saratoga, New York. p. 316

George II *1683–1760* British king who chartered the Georgia Colony. p. 236

George III *1738–1820* King of England during the Revolutionary War. pp. 276, 296

Gerry, Elbridge *1744–1814* Massachusetts delegate to the Constitutional Convention. p. 366

Gibbs, Jonathan C. *1800s* African American who became secretary of state in Florida; helped set up public school system. p. 479

Glenn, John H., Jr. *1921–* Astronaut who was the first American to orbit the Earth. Former U.S. senator. p. 528

Gompers, Samuel *1850–1924* Founder of the American Federation of Labor, or AFL, which led strikes to gain better pay and working conditions for laborers. p. 546

Gorbachev, Mikhail (gawr•buh•CHAWF, mee•kah•EEL) *1931–* Leader of the Soviet Union from 1985 to 1991. He improved relations with the United States and expanded freedom in the Soviet Union. p. 583

Granger, Gordon Union general who read the order declaring all slaves in Texas to be free. p. 482

Grant, Ulysses S. *1822–1885* 18th U.S. President and, earlier, commander of the Union army in the Civil War. pp. 465, 468, 469, 471, 475

Greeley, Horace *1811–1872* American journalist and political leader; publisher of a newspaper called the *New York Tribune*. p. 461

Greene, Nathanael *1742–1786* Commander of the Continental Army in the Southern Colonies; forced British out of Georgia and the Carolinas. p. 322

Grenville, George *1712–1770* British prime minister who passed the Stamp Act in 1765. p. 280

Gutenberg, Johannes *1390–1468* German inventor; invented movable type. p. 109

H

Hale, Nathan *1755–1776* American Revolutionary hero who was hanged by the British for spying for the Patriots. p. 319

Hamilton, Alexander *1755–1804* American leader in calling for the Constitutional Convention and winning support for it. He favored a strong national government. pp. 368, 375, 377

Hammond, James Henry *1807–1864* Senator from South Carolina. p. 442

Hancock, John *1737–1793* Leader of the Sons of Liberty in the Massachusetts Colony. pp. 306, 353, 369

Harrison, William Henry *1773–1841* 9th U.S. President. Earlier he directed U.S. forces against the Indians at the Battle of Tippecanoe and was a commander in the War of 1812. p. 390

He, Zheng *1400s* Chinese admiral who made seven voyages between 1405 and 1433. p. 109

Henrietta Maria *1609–1669* Queen of Charles I of England. The Maryland Colony was named in her honor. p. 233

Henry *1394–1460* Henry the Navigator, prince of Portugal, who set up the first European school for training sailors in navigation. p. 115

Henry IV *1553–1610* King of France. p. 150

Henry, Patrick *1736–1799* American colonist who spoke out in the Virginia legislature against paying British taxes. His views became widely known, and Loyalists accused him of treason. pp. 282, 290, 350, 353, 367, 378

Hiawatha (hy•uh•WAH•thuh) *1500s* Mohawk chief who persuaded other Iroquois tribes to form the Iroquois League. p. 90

Hitler, Adolf *1889–1945* Nazi dictator of Germany. His actions led to World War II and the killing of millions of people. pp. 578, 580, 581

Hooker, Thomas *1586?–1647* Minister who helped form the Connecticut Colony. His democratic ideas were adopted in the Fundamental Orders. p. 196

Houston, Sam *1793–1863* President of the Republic of Texas and, later, governor of the state of Texas. pp. 403, 453

Howard, Martin *1700s* Rhode Island colonist who defended Britain's right to tax the colonists. p. 280

Hudson, Henry *?–1611* Explorer who sailed up the Hudson River, giving the Dutch a claim to the area. p. 138

Hughes, Langston *1902-1967* African American poet and one of the best-known Harlem writers. p. 530

Hurston, Zora Neale *1903-1960* African American novelist and one of the best-known Harlem writers. p. 530

Hussein, Saddam *1937–* Leader of Iraq. p. 590

Hutchinson, Anne Marbury *1591–1643* English-born woman who left Massachusetts because of her religious beliefs. She settled near Providence, which joined with other settlements to form the Rhode Island Colony. p. 195

Iberville, Pierre Le Moyne, Sieur d' (ee•ber•VEEL) *1661–1706* French explorer who—with his brother, Jean-Baptiste Le Moyne, Sieur de Bienville—started an early settlement at the mouth of the Mississippi River. p. 154

Ibn Majid, Ahmad *1432–1500* Great contributor to study of navigation; born in what is today United Arab Emirates. p. 118

Isabella I *1451–1504* Queen of Spain who—with King Ferdinand, her husband—sent Columbus on his voyage to find a western route to Asia. p. 121

Jackson, Andrew *1767–1845* 7th U.S. President and, earlier, commander who won the final battle in the War of 1812. As President he favored a strong Union and ordered the removal of Native Americans from their lands. pp. 393, 396–398, 437

Jackson, Thomas (Stonewall) *1824–1863* Confederate general. pp. 458, 466

James I *1566–1625* King of England in the early 1600s. The James River and Jamestown were named after him. pp. 160, 164

Jay, John *1745–1829* American leader who wrote letters to newspapers, defending the Constitution. He became the first chief justice of the Supreme Court. pp. 368, 375

Jefferson, Thomas *1743–1826* 3rd U.S. President and the main writer of the Declaration of Independence. pp. 303–305, 353, 368, 371, 375, 376, 377, 384

Jenney, William *1832–1907* American engineer who developed the use of steel frames to build tall buildings. p. 496

John I *1357–1433* King of Portugal during a time of great exploration. Father of Prince Henry, who set up a school of navigation. p. 115

Johnson, Andrew *1808–1875* 17th U.S. President. Differences with Congress about Reconstruction led to his being impeached, though he was found not guilty. pp. 477, 479

Johnson, Lyndon B. *1908–1973* 36th U.S. President. He started Great Society programs and expanded U.S. involvement in the Vietnam War. pp. 584–585

Joliet, Louis (zhohl•YAY, loo•EE) *1645–1700* French fur trader who explored lakes and rivers for France, with Jacques Marquette and five others. p. 152

Jones, John Paul *1747–1792* American naval officer who defeated bigger and better-equipped British ships during Revolutionary War. p. 319

Joseph *1840?–1904* Nez Perce chief who tried to lead his people to Canada after they were told to move onto a reservation. p. 491

Josephy, Alvin M., Jr. *1915–* Historian and author of books about Native Americans and the United States westward movement. p. 55

Kalakaua (kah•lah•KAH•ooh•ah) *1836–1891* Hawaiian king who tried but failed to keep Americans from taking over the Hawaiian Islands. p. 569

Kennedy, John F. *1917–1963* 35th U.S. President. He ordered a naval blockade of Cuba during the Cuban missile crisis; he also created the Peace Corps. pp. 582, 589

Key, Francis Scott *1779–1843* American lawyer and poet who wrote the words to "The Star-Spangled Banner." pp. 392–393

King, Martin Luther, Jr. *1929–1968* African American Civil Rights leader who worked for integration in nonviolent ways. King won the Nobel Peace Prize in 1964. p. 550

Knox, Henry *1750–1806* Secretary of war in the first government under the Constitution. pp. 375, 377

Kosciuszko, Thaddeus (kawsh•CHUSH•koh) *1746–1817* Polish officer who helped the Patriots in the Revolutionary War. He later returned to Poland and led a revolution there. p. 317

Kublai Khan (KOO•bluh KAHN) *1215–1294* Ruler of China who was visited by Marco Polo. p. 109

L

La Follette, Robert *1855–1925* Wisconsin governor who began many reforms in his state, including a merit system for government jobs. p. 546

La Salle, René-Robert Cavelier, Sieur de (luh•SAL) *1643–1687* French explorer who found the mouth of the Mississippi River and claimed the whole Mississippi Valley for France. p. 153

Lafayette, Marquis de (lah•fee•ET) *1757–1834* French noble who fought alongside the Americans in the Revolutionary War. p. 317

Las Casas, Bartolomé de (lahs KAH•sahs, bar•toh•loh•MAY day) *1474–1566* Spanish missionary who spent much of his life trying to help Native Americans. p. 145

Law, John *1671–1729* Scottish banker who was appointed proprietor of the Louisiana region in 1717. p. 155

Lawrence, Jacob *1900s* African American artist; his parents took part in The Great Migration. p. 507

Le Moyne, Jean-Baptiste *See* Bienville.

Le Moyne, Pierre *See* Iberville.

Lee, Richard Henry *1732–1794* American Revolutionary leader who said to the Continental Congress that the colonies should become independent from Britain. p. 303

Lee, Robert E. *1807–1870* United States army colonel who gave up his post to become commander of the Confederate army in the Civil War. pp. 461, 466, 471

L'Enfant, Pierre Charles *1754–1825* French-born American engineer who planned the buildings and streets of the new capital of the United States. p. 377

Lewis, Meriwether *1774–1809* American explorer chosen by Thomas Jefferson to be a pathfinder in the territory of the Louisiana Purchase. p. 386

Liliuokalani, Lydia (lih•lee•uh•woh•kuh•LAH•nee) *1838–1917* Hawaiian queen who tried but failed to bring back the Hawaiian monarchy's authority. p. 569

Lincoln, Abraham *1809–1865* 16th U.S. President, leader of the Union in the Civil War, and signer of the Emancipation Proclamation. pp. 450-455, 461, 462, 467, 468, 476-477

Lincoln, Mary Todd *1818–1882* Wife of Abraham Lincoln. p. 477

Lindbergh, Charles *1902–1974* Airplane pilot who was the first to fly solo between the United States and Europe. p. 527

Livingston, Robert R. *1746–1813* One of the writers of the Declaration of Independence. p. 303

Longstreet, James *1821–1904* Former Confederate general who wanted the South to build more factories; considered a scalawag. p. 484

Louis XIV *1638–1715* King of France. pp. 152, 153

Lowell, Francis Cabot *1775–1817* Textile pioneer who set up an American mill in which several processes were completed under one roof. p. 416

M

Madison, Dolley *1768–1849* James Madison's wife and First Lady during the War of 1812. p. 392

Madison, James *1751–1836* 4th U.S. President. He was a leader in calling for the Constitutional Convention, writing the Constitution, and winning support for it. pp. 350, 352, 360, 368, 371, 378, 390

Magellan, Ferdinand (muh•JEH•luhn) *1480?–1521* Portuguese explorer who in 1519 led a fleet of ships from Spain westward to Asia. He died on the voyage, but one of the ships made it back to Spain, completing the first trip around the world. p. 124

Malintzin (mah•LINT•suhn) *1501?–1550* Aztec princess who interpreted for Hernando Cortés and helped him in other ways to conquer Mexico. p. 128

Marion, Francis *1732?–1795* Known as the Swamp Fox, he led Continental soldiers through the swamps of South Carolina on daring raids against the British. p. 319

Marquette, Jacques (mar•KET, ZHAHK) *1637–1675* Catholic missionary who knew several American Indian languages. With Louis Joliet, he explored lakes and rivers for France. p. 152

Marshall, James *1810–1885* Carpenter who found gold at John Sutter's sawmill near Sacramento, California, leading to the California gold rush of 1849. p. 408

Marshall, John *1755–1835* Chief Justice of the Supreme Court in 1832; Marshall ruled that the United States should protect the Cherokees and their lands in Georgia. p. 398

Mason, George *1725–1792* Virginia delegate to the Constitutional Convention who argued for an end to the slave trade. pp. 366, 370

Massasoit (ma•suh•SOYT) *?–1661* Chief of the Wampanoags, who lived in peace with the Pilgrims. p. 169

Mather, Cotton *1663–1728* Member of well-known family of American Congregational clergymen; published over 400 works on religious, historical, scientific, and moral subjects. p. 187

McCauley, Mary Ludwig Hays *1754?–1832* Known as Molly Pitcher, she carried water to American soldiers during the Battle of Monmouth; when her husband fell during the battle, she began firing his cannon. p. 319

McCormick, Cyrus *1809–1884* Inventor of a reaping machine for harvesting wheat. p. 419

McKay, Claude *1890-1948* African American writer during the Harlem Renaissance. p. 530

McKinley, William *1843–1901* 25th U.S. President. The Spanish-American War was fought during his term. pp. 570, 572

Menéndez de Avilés, Pedro (may•NAYN•days day ah•vee•LAYS) *1519–1574* Spanish leader of settlers in St. Augustine, Florida, the first permanent European settlement in what is now the United States. p. 146

Metacomet *1639?–1676* Called King Philip by the English. Son of Massasoit; leader of Wampanoags; made war upon New England settlers—called King Philip's War. p. 198

Minuit, Peter *1580–1638* A director of the New Netherland Colony who purchased Manhattan Island from the Manhattan Indians for $24. p. 211

Mongoulacha (mahn•goo•LAY•chah) *1700s* Indian leader who helped Bienville and Iberville. p. 154

Monroe, James *1758–1831* 5th U.S. President. He established the Monroe Doctrine, which said that the United States would stop any European nation from expanding its American empire. p. 394

Morgan, Daniel *1736–1802* American general who defeated the British at Cowpens in the Revolutionary War. p. 322

Morris, Gouverneur (guh•ver•NIR) *1752–1816* American leader who was in charge of the final wording of the United States Constitution. pp. 358-359

Motecuhzoma (maw•tay•kwah•SOH•mah) *1466–1520* Emperor of the Aztecs when they were conquered by the Spanish. He is also known as Montezuma. p. 129

Muhlenberg, John Peter *1746–1807* Young minister, son of the colonies' Lutheran leader, who became a Patriot militia officer. p. 309

Mussolini, Benito (moo•suh•LEE•nee, buh•NEE•toh) *1883–1945* Ruler of Italy from 1922 until 1943, most of that time as dictator. p. 578

N

Newcomen, Thomas *1663–1729* English blacksmith and inventor who invented the steam engine. p. 414

Niza, Marcos de (day NEE•sah) *1495–1558* Spanish priest who was sent with Esteban to confirm stories of the Seven Cities of Gold. When he returned to Mexico City, he said he had seen a golden city. p. 131

O

Oglethorpe, James *1696–1785* English settler who was given a charter to settle Georgia. He wanted to bring in debtors from England to help settle it. p. 236

O'Keeffe, Georgia *1887–1986* American painter who developed her own style making paintings of objects in nature. p. 530

Osceola *1804–1838* Leader of the Seminoles in Florida. p. 398

Otis, James *1725–1783* Massachusetts colonist who spoke out against British taxes and called for "no taxation without representation." pp. 280, 282, 283

P

Paine, Thomas *1737–1809* Author of a widely read pamphlet called *Common Sense,* in which he attacked King George III and called for a revolution to make the colonies independent. p. 301

Parks, Rosa *1913–* African American woman whose refusal to give up her seat on a Montgomery, Alabama, bus started a year-long bus boycott. p. 549

Paterson, William *1745–1806* Constitutional delegate from New Jersey who submitted the New Jersey Plan, under which each state would have one vote, regardless of population. p. 355

Penn, William *1644–1718* Proprietor of Pennsylvania under a charter from King Charles II of Britain. Penn was a Quaker who made Pennsylvania a refuge for settlers who wanted religious freedom. p. 213

Perry, Oliver Hazard *1785–1819* American naval commander who won an important battle in the War of 1812. p. 390

Philip IV *1605–1665* King of Spain from 1621 to 1665. p. 143

Pickett, George *1825–1875* Confederate general who led the charge at Gettysburg; forced to retreat. p. 466

Pike, Zebulon *1779–1813* American who led an expedition down the Arkansas River to explore the southwestern part of the Louisiana Purchase. pp. 19, 388

Pinckney, Eliza Lucas *1722?–1793* South Carolina settler who experimented with indigo plants. She gave away seeds, and indigo then became an important cash crop in the colonies. p. 236

Pitt, William *1708–1778* British leader of Parliament who helped Britain win battles against the French. p. 273

Pizarro, Francisco (pee•ZAR•oh) *1475?–1541* Spanish conquistador who conquered the Inca Empire. p. 133

Pocahontas (poh•kuh•HAHN•tuhs) *1595–1617* Indian chief Powhatan's daughter. p. 162

Polk, James K. *1795–1849* 11th U.S. President. He gained land for the United States by setting a northern boundary in 1846 and winning a war with Mexico in 1848. pp. 405, 407

Pollock, Jackson *1912–1956* American painter who experimented with new kinds of painting. p. 530

Polo, Maffeo Trader from Venice; uncle of Marco Polo. p. 109

Polo, Marco *1254–1324* Explorer from Venice who spent many years in Asia in the late 1200s. He wrote a book about his travels that gave Europeans information about Asia. pp. 109, 112

Polo, Nicolò Trader from Venice; father of Marco Polo. p. 109

Ponce de León, Juan (POHN•say day lay•OHN) *1460–1521* Spanish explorer who landed on the North American mainland in 1513, near what is now St. Augustine, Florida. p. 127

Pontiac *c.1720–1769* Ottawa Indian chief who led a rebellion against the British to stop the loss of Indian hunting lands. p. 275

Powell, Colin L. *1937–* Chairman of the Joint Chiefs of Staff during the Gulf War; became U.S. secretary of state in 2001. p. 590

Powhatan (pow•uh•TAN) *1550?–1618* Chief of a federation of Indian tribes that lived in the Virginia territory. Pocahontas was his daughter. p. 162

Prescott, Samuel *1751–1777?* American who, along with Paul Revere, warned the Patriots that the British were marching toward Concord. p. 291

Ptolemy, Claudius (TAH•luh•mee) *100s* Astronomer in ancient Egypt. p. 123

Pulaski, Casimir (puh•LAS•kee) *1747–1779* Polish noble who came to the British colonies to help the Patriots in the Revolutionary War. p. 317

Putnam, Israel *1718–1790* American Revolutionary commander who fought at the Battle of Bunker Hill. p. 295

R

Raleigh, Sir Walter (RAH•lee) *1554–1618* English explorer who used his own money to set up England's first colony in North America, on Roanoke Island near North Carolina. p. 158

Randolph, Edmund *1753–1813* Virginia delegate to the Constitutional Convention who wrote the Virginia Plan, which stated that the number of representatives a state would have in Congress should be based on the population of the state. pp. 355, 366, 375

Read, George *1733–1798* Delaware delegate to the Constitutional Convention who thought the states should be done away with in favor of a strong national government. p. 354

Reagan, Ronald *1911–* 40th U.S. President. His meetings with Soviet leader Mikhail Gorbachev led to a thaw in the Cold War and to advances in arms control. pp. 583, 589

Reed, Esther *1700s* American who, in 1780, started the Philadelphia Association to help the Continental Army. p. 311

Reno, Janet *1938–* First woman appointed attorney general of the United States. p. 548

Revels, Hiram R. *1822–1901* First African American elected to U.S. Senate. p. 479

Revere, Paul *1735–1818* American who warned the Patriots that the British were marching toward Concord, where Patriot weapons were stored. pp. 285, 291

Rockefeller, John D. *1839–1937* American oil entrepreneur who joined many refineries into one business, called the Standard Oil Company. pp. 497-498

Roebling, John *1806–1869* Engineer and industrialist who designed suspension bridges. p. 496

Rolfe, John *1585–1622* English colonist of the Jamestown colony whose discovery of a method of drying tobacco led to great profits. p. 163

Roosevelt, Franklin D. *1882–1945* 32nd U.S. President. He began New Deal programs to help the nation out of the Depression, and he was the nation's leader during World War II. pp. 529, 579, 586

Roosevelt, Theodore *1858–1919* 26th U.S. President. He showed the world America's strength, made it possible to build the Panama Canal, and worked for progressive reforms and conservation. pp. 544, 545, 571, 572

Root, George Frederick *1820–1895* American composer and teacher. p. 435

Ross, Edmund G. *1826–1907* Senator from Kansas who voted to acquit President Johnson. p. 479

Ross, John *1790–1866* Chief of the Cherokee nation. He fought in United States courts to prevent the loss of the Cherokees' lands in Georgia. Though he won the legal battle, he still had to lead his people along the Trail of Tears to what is now Oklahoma. p. 398

Russwurm, John *1799–1851* African American who helped Samuel Cornish found an abolitionist newspaper called *Freedom's Journal* in 1827. p. 448

S

Sacagawea (sa•kuh•juh•WEE•uh) *1786?–1812?* Shoshone woman who acted as an interpreter for the Lewis and Clark expedition. p. 386

Salem, Peter *1750?–1816* African who fought with the Minutemen at Concord and at the Battle of Bunker Hill. p. 310

Salomon, Haym *1740–1785* Polish banker who spied for the Patriots and helped fund the Revolution. p. 317

Samoset *1590?–1653?* Native American chief who spoke English and who helped the settlers at Plymouth. p. 169

Santa Anna, Antonio López de *1794–1876* Dictator of Mexico; defeated Texans at the Alamo. pp. 402–403

Scott, Dred *1795?–1858* Enslaved African who took his case for freedom to the Supreme Court and lost. p. 440

Scott, Winfield *1786–1866* American general in the war with Mexico. p. 407

Serra, Junípero *1713–1784* Spanish missionary who helped build a string of missions in California. pp. 148, 174

Seward, William H. *1801–1872* Secretary of state in the cabinet of Abraham Lincoln. p. 443

Shays, Daniel *1747?–1825* Leader of Shays's Rebellion, which showed the weakness of the government under the Articles of Confederation. pp. 347, 352

Sherman, Roger *1721–1793* One of the writers of the Declaration of Independence. Connecticut delegate to the Constitutional Convention who worked out the compromise in which Congress would have two houses—one based on state population and one with two members from each state. pp. 303, 356

Sherman, William Tecumseh *1820–1891* Union general who, after defeating Confederate forces in Atlanta, led the March to the Sea, on which his troops caused great destruction. pp. 468–469

Sitting Bull *1831–1890* Sioux leader who fought against General George Custer. p. 490

Slater, Samuel *1768–1835* Textile pioneer who helped bring the Industrial Revolution to the United States by providing plans for a new spinning machine. p. 416

Slocomb, Mary *1700s* North Carolina colonist who fought in the Revolutionary War. p. 319

Smalls, Robert *1839–1915* African American who delivered a Confederate steamer to the Union forces. p. 463

Smith, John *1580–1631* English explorer who, as leader of the Jamestown settlement, saved its people from starvation. pp. 161, 231

Smith, Joseph *1805–1844* Mormon leader who settled his people in Illinois and was killed there. p. 406

Soule, John B. L. *1815–1891* Editor of the Terre Haute (Indiana) *Express* in the mid-1800s. p. 383

Squanto See Tisquantum.

Stalin, Joseph *1879–1953* Dictator of the Soviet Union from 1924 until his death. pp. 578, 586, 587

Standish, Miles *1584?–1656* Captain who sailed with Pilgrims to America aboard the *Mayflower*. p. 167

Stanton, Elizabeth Cady *1815–1902* American reformer who organized the first convention for women's rights. p. 447

Steuben, Friedrich, Baron von (vahn SHTOY•buhn) *1730–1794* German soldier who helped train Patriot troops in the Revolutionary War. p. 317

Stowe, Harriet Beecher *1811–1896* American abolitionist who in 1852 wrote the book *Uncle Tom's Cabin*. p. 448

Stuyvesant, Peter (STY•vuh•suhnt) *1610?–1672* Last governor of the Dutch colony of New Netherland. p. 212

Sutter, John *1803–1880* American pioneer who owned the sawmill where gold was discovered, leading to the California gold rush. p. 408

T

Taney, Roger B. (TAH•nee) *1777–1864* Supreme Court chief justice who wrote the ruling against Dred Scott. p. 441

Tapahonso, Luci *1953–* Navajo poet and author. p. 72

Tecumseh (tuh•KUHM•suh) *1768–1813* Shawnee leader of Indians in the Northwest Territory. He wanted to stop Americans from settling on Indian lands. p. 390

Thayendanegea (thay•en•da•NEG•ah) *1742–1807* Known as Joseph Brant; Mohawk leader who befriended a British general, became a Christian, and worked as a missionary. p. 312

Tisquantum *1585?–1622* Native American who spoke English and who helped the Plymouth Colony. p. 169

Tompkins, Sally *1833–1916* Civil War nurse who eventually ran her own private hospital in Richmond, Virginia. She was a captain in the Confederate army, the only woman to achieve such an honor. p. 463

Tonti, Henri de (TOHN•tee, ahn•REE duh) *1650–1704* French explorer with La Salle. p. 154

Travis, William B. *1809–1836* Commander of the Texas force at the Alamo, where he was killed. p. 403

Truman, Harry S. *1884–1972* 33rd U.S. President. He ordered the atom bomb to be dropped on Japan to end World War II; he later sent American soldiers to support South Korea in 1950. pp. 553, 581

Truth, Sojourner *1797?–1883* Abolitionist and former slave who became a leading preacher against slavery. p. 449

Tubman, Harriet *1820–1913* Abolitionist and former slave who became a conductor on the Underground Railroad. She led about 300 slaves to freedom. p. 447

Turner, Nat *1800–1831* Enslaved African who led a rebellion against slavery. p. 445

Tuscalusa (tuhs•kuh•LOO•suh) *1500s* Leader of the Mobile people when they battled with Spanish troops led by Hernando de Soto. p. 132

V

Verrazano, Giovanni da (ver•uh•ZAH•noh) *1485?–1528?* Italian navigator who discovered New York Bay while searching for a water route linking the Atlantic and Pacific Oceans. p. 136

Vespucci, Amerigo (veh•SPOO•chee, uh•MAIR•ih•goh) *1454–1512* Italian explorer who made several voyages from Europe to what many people thought was Asia. He determined that he had landed on another continent, which was later called America in his honor. pp. 123–124

W

Waldseemüller, Martin (VAHLT•zay•mool•er) *1470–1518?* German cartographer who published a map in 1507 that first showed a continent named America. p. 123

Warhol, Andy *1928?–1987* American artist who painted colorful pictures of everyday products. p. 530

Warren, Mercy Otis *1728–1814* Massachusetts colonist who wrote poems and plays supporting the Patriot cause. p. 311

Washington, Booker T. *1856–1915* African American who founded Tuskegee Institute in Alabama. p. 549

Washington, George *1732–1799* 1st U.S. President, leader of the Continental army during the Revolutionary War, and president of the Constitutional Convention. pp. 269, 270, 293, 314, 327, 328, 352, 374

Westinghouse, George *1846–1914* American inventor who designed an air brake for stopping trains. p. 495

Wheatley, Phillis *1753?–1784* American poet who wrote poems that praised the Revolution. p. 296

White, John *?–1593?* English painter and cartographer who led the second group that settled on Roanoke Island. p. 158

Whitman, Narcissa *1808–1847* American missionary and pioneer in the Oregon Country. p. 404

Whitney, Eli *1765–1825* American inventor who was most famous for his invention of the cotton gin and his idea of interchangeable parts, which made mass production possible. p. 418

Williams, Roger *1603?–1683* Founder of Providence in what is now Rhode Island. He had been forced to leave Massachusetts because of his views. p. 194

Wilson, Woodrow *1856–1924* 28th U.S. President. He brought the country into World War I after trying to stay neutral. He favored the League of Nations, but the Senate rejected U.S. membership in the league. pp. 552, 576, 577

Winthrop, John *1588–1649* Puritan leader who served several times as governor of the Massachusetts Bay Colony. Helped form confederation among people of New England and served as its first president. p. 189

Woods, Granville T. *1856–1910* African American who improved the air brake and developed a telegraph system for trains. p. 495

Wright, Frank Lloyd *1867–1959* American architect known for producing unusual buildings. p. 531

Wright, Orville *1871–1948* Pioneer in American aviation who—with his brother, Wilbur—made and flew the first successful airplane, at Kitty Hawk, North Carolina. pp. 526, 527

Wright, Wilbur *1867–1912* Pioneer in American aviation who—with his brother, Orville—made and flew the first successful airplane, at Kitty Hawk, North Carolina. pp. 526, 527

Y

York *1800s* Enslaved African whose hunting and fishing skills contributed to the Lewis and Clark expedition. p. 386

Young, Brigham *1801–1877* Mormon leader who came after Joseph Smith. He moved his people west to the Great Salt Lake valley. p. 406

Yzquierdo, Pedro *1400s* Member of Columbus's first expedition to America. p. 105

Gazetteer

The Gazetteer is a geographical dictionary that will help you locate places discussed in this book. The page number tells where each place appears on a map.

A

Abilene A city in central Kansas on the Smoky Hill River; a major railroad town. (39°N, 97°W) p. 488

Adena (uh•DEE•nuh) An ancient settlement of the Mound Builders; located in southern Ohio. (40°N, 81°W) p. 65

Adirondack Mountains (a•duh•RAHN•dak) A mountain range in northeastern New York. p. 89

Africa Second-largest continent on Earth. p. 27

Alamo A mission in San Antonio, Texas; located in the southeastern part of the state; used as a fort during the Texas Revolution. (29°N, 98°W) p. 404

Alaska Range A mountain range in central Alaska. p. 20

Albany The capital of New York; located in the eastern part of the state, on the Hudson River. (43°N, 74°W) p. 212

Aleutian Islands (uh•LOO•shuhn) A chain of volcanic islands, extending west from the Alaska Peninsula; located between the northern Pacific Ocean and the Bering Sea. pp. 20, 570

Alexandria Seaport on the northern coast of Egypt. (31°N, 29°E) p. 108

Allegheny River (a•luh•GAY•nee) A river in the northeastern United States; flows southwest to join the Monongahela River in Pennsylvania, forming the Ohio River. p. 341

Altamaha River (AWL•tuh•muh•haw) A river that begins in southeastern Georgia and flows into the Atlantic Ocean. p. 234

American Samoa (suh•MOH•uh) A United States territory in the Pacific Ocean. p. 570

Annapolis (uh•NA•puh•luhs) The capital of Maryland; located on Chesapeake Bay; home of the United States Naval Academy. (39°N, 76°W) p. 234

Antarctica One of Earth's seven continents. p. 27

Antietam (an•TEE•tuhm) A creek near Sharpsburg in north central Maryland; site of a Civil War battle in 1862. (39°N, 78°W) p. 470

Appalachian Mountains (a•puh•LAY•chuhn) A mountain system of eastern North America; extends from southeastern Quebec, Canada, to central Alabama. pp. 20, 225

Appomattox (a•puh•MA•tuhks) A village in central Virginia; site of the battle that ended the Civil War in 1865; once known as Appomattox Courthouse. (37°N, 79°W) p. 470

Arctic Ocean One of Earth's four oceans; located north of the Arctic Circle. p. 27

Arkansas River A tributary of the Mississippi River, beginning in central Colorado and ending in southeastern Arkansas. pp. 29, 153

Asia Largest continent on Earth. p. 27

Atlanta Georgia's capital and largest city; located in the northwest central part of the state; site of a Civil War battle in 1864. (33°N, 84°W) p. 470

Atlantic Ocean Second-largest ocean; separates North and South America from Europe and Africa. p. 27

Australia A country; smallest continent on Earth. p. 27

B

Baghdad Capital of Iraq; located on the Tigris River in central Iraq. (33°N, 44°E) p. 108

Baltimore A major seaport in Maryland; located on the upper end of Chesapeake Bay. (39°N, 77°W) pp. 47, 234

Baxter Springs A city in the southeastern corner of Kansas. (37°N, 94°W) p. 488

Beaufort Sea (BOH•fert) That part of the Arctic Ocean between northeastern Alaska and the Canadian Arctic Islands. p. 20

Beijing (bay•JING) The capital of China; located on a large plain in northeastern China; once known as Khanbalik. (40°N, 116°E) p. 108

Benin (buh•NEEN) A former kingdom in West Africa; located along the Gulf of Guinea; present-day southern Nigeria. p. 108

Bennington A town in the southwestern corner of Vermont; site of a major Revolutionary War battle in 1777. (43°N, 73°W) p. 323

Bering Strait A narrow strip of water; separates Asia from North America. p. 57

Beringia (buh•RIN•jee•uh) An ancient land bridge that once connected Asia and North America. p. 57

Black Sea A large inland sea between Europe and Asia. p. 113

Bonampak An ancient settlement of the Mayan civilization; located in present-day southeastern Mexico. (16°N, 91°W) p. 65

Boston The capital and largest city of Massachusetts; a port city located on Massachusetts Bay. (42°N, 71°W) p. 291

Boston Harbor The western section of Massachusetts Bay; located in eastern Massachusetts; the city of Boston is located at its western end. p. 291

Brandywine A battlefield on Brandywine Creek in southeastern Pennsylvania; site of a major Revolutionary War battle in 1777. (40°N, 76°W) p. 323

Brazos River (BRAH•zuhs) A river in central Texas; flows southeast into the Gulf of Mexico. p. 404

Brookline A town in eastern Massachusetts; west-southwest of Boston. (42°N, 71°W) p. 291

Brooks Range A mountain range crossing northern Alaska; forms the northwestern end of the Rocky Mountains. p. 20

Bull Run A stream in northeastern Virginia; flows toward the Potomac River; site of Civil War battles in 1861 and in 1862. p. 470

C

Cahokia (kuh•HOH•kee•uh) A village in southwestern Illinois; site of an ancient settlement of the Mound Builders. (39°N, 90°W) pp. 65, 108

Calicut (KA•lih•kuht) A city in southwestern India; located on the Malabar Coast. (11°N, 76°E) p. 108

Cambridge A city in northeastern Massachusetts; located near Boston. (42°N, 71°W) p. 291

Camden A city in north central South Carolina, near the Wateree River; site of a major Revolutionary War battle in 1780. (34°N, 81°W) p. 323

Canal Zone A strip of territory in Panama. p. 572

Canary Islands An island group in the Atlantic Ocean off the northwest coast of Africa. (28°N, 16°W) p. 122

Canton A port city in southeastern China; located on the Canton River; known in China as Guangzhou. (23°N, 113°E) p. 108

Canyon de Chelly (SHAY) An ancient settlement of the Anasazi; located in present-day northeastern Arizona. p. 65

Cape Cod A peninsula of southeastern Massachusetts, extending into the Atlantic Ocean and enclosing Cape Cod Bay. (42°N, 70°W) p. 197

Cape Fear A cape at the southern end of Smith Island; located off the coast of North Carolina, at the mouth of the Cape Fear River. (34°N, 78°W) p. 234

Cape Fear River A river in central and southeastern North Carolina; formed by the Deep and Haw Rivers; flows southeast into the Atlantic Ocean. p. 234

Cape Hatteras (HA•tuh•ruhs) A cape on southeastern Hatteras Island; located off the coast of North Carolina. (35°N, 75°W) p. 234

Cape of Good Hope A cape located on the southernmost tip of Africa. (34°S, 18°E) p. 119

Cape Verde Islands (VERD) A group of volcanic islands off the western coast of Africa. (16°N, 24°W) p. 119

Cascade Range A mountain range in the western United States; a continuation of the Sierra Nevada; extends north from California to Washington. p. 20

Chaco Canyon (CHAH•koh) An ancient settlement of the Anasazi; located in present-day northwestern New Mexico. (37°N, 108°W) p. 65

Chancellorsville (CHAN•suh•lerz•vil) A location in northeastern Virginia, just west of Fredericksburg; site of a Civil War battle in 1863. (38°N, 78°W) p. 470

Charles River A river in eastern Massachusetts; separates Boston from Cambridge; flows into Boston Bay. p. 291

Charleston A city in southeastern South Carolina; a major port on the Atlantic Ocean; once known as Charles Towne. (33°N, 80°W) pp. 234, 249, 323, 470

Charlestown A city in Massachusetts; located on Boston Harbor between the mouths of the Charles and Mystic Rivers. p. 291

Chattanooga (cha•tuh•NOO•guh) A city in southeastern Tennessee; located on the Tennessee River; site of a Civil War battle in 1863. (35°N, 85°W) p. 470

Cherokee Nation (CHAIR•uh•kee) A Native American nation located in present-day northern Georgia, eastern Alabama, southern Tennessee, and western North Carolina. p. 398

Chesapeake Bay An inlet of the Atlantic Ocean; surrounded by Virginia and Maryland. pp. 29, 233

Cheyenne (shy•AN) The capital of Wyoming; located in the southeastern part of the state. (41°N, 105°W) p. 488

Chicago A city in Illinois; located on Lake Michigan; the third-largest city in the United States. (42°N, 88°W) p. 488

Chickamauga (chik•uh•MAW•guh) A city in northwestern Georgia; site of a Civil War battle in 1863. (35°N, 85°W) p. 470

Cincinnati (sin•suh•NA•tee) A large city in southwestern Ohio; located on the Ohio River. (39°N, 84°W) p. 47

Coast Mountains A mountain range in western British Columbia and southern Alaska; a continuation of the Cascade Range. p. 20

Coast Ranges Mountains along the Pacific coast of North America, extending from Alaska to Baja California. p. 20

Coastal Plain Low, mostly flat land that stretches inland from the Atlantic Ocean and the Gulf of Mexico. p. 20

Cold Harbor A location in east central Virginia, north of the Chickahominy River; site of Civil War battles in 1862 and in 1864. (38°N, 77°W) p. 470

Colorado River A river in the southwestern United States; its basin extends from the Rocky Mountains to the Sierra Nevada; flows into the Gulf of California. p. 29

Columbia River A river that begins in the Rocky Mountains in southwestern Canada, forms the Washington–Oregon border, and empties into the Pacific Ocean below Portland; supplies much of that area's hydroelectricity. pp. 29, 385

Compostela (kahm•poh•STEH•lah) A city in west central Mexico. (21°N, 105°W) p. 129

Concord A town in northeastern Massachusetts, near Boston; site of a major Revolutionary War battle in 1775. (42°N, 71°W) pp. 291, 323

Concord River A river in northeastern Massachusetts; formed by the junction of the Sudbury and Assabet Rivers; flows north into the Merrimack River at Lowell. p. 291

Connecticut River The longest river in New England; begins in New Hampshire, and empties into Long Island Sound, New York. p. 197

Constantinople (kahn•stant•uhn•OH•puhl) A port city in northwestern Turkey. (41°N, 29°E) p. 108

Copán (koh•PAHN) An ancient settlement of the Mayan civilization; located in present-day Honduras, in northern Central America. (15°N, 89°W) p. 65

Cowpens A town in northwestern South Carolina; located near the site of a major Revolutionary War battle in 1781. (35°N, 82°W) p. 323

Crab Orchard An ancient settlement of the Mound Builders; located in present-day southern Illinois. (38°N, 89°W) p. 65

Cuba An island country in the Caribbean; the largest island of the West Indies. (22°N, 79°W) pp. 129, 570

Cuzco (KOOS•koh) The ancient capital of the Inca Empire; a city located in present-day Peru, in western South America. (14°S, 72°W) pp. 108, 133

D

Damascus (duh•MAS•kuhs) The capital of Syria; located in southwest Syria. p. 108
Deerfield A town in northwestern Massachusetts. (43°N, 73°W) p. 197
Delaware Bay An inlet of the Atlantic Ocean; located between southern New Jersey and Delaware. p. 212
Delaware River A river in the northeastern United States; begins in southern New York and flows into the Atlantic Ocean at Delaware Bay. p. 89
Denver Colorado's capital and largest city. (40°N, 105°W) p. 488
Des Moines (dih•MOYN) Iowa's capital and largest city. (42°N, 94°W) p. A3
Dickson An ancient settlement of the Mound Builders; located in present-day central Illinois. p. 65
Dodge City A city in southern Kansas; located on the Arkansas River; once a major railroad center on the Santa Fe Trail. (38°N, 100°W) p. 488
Dover (DE) The capital of Delaware; located in the central part of the state. (39°N, 76°W) p. 212
Dover (NH) A city in southeastern New Hampshire. (43°N, 71°W) p. 197

E

Edenton (EE•duhn•tuhn) A town in northeastern North Carolina; located on Albemarle Sound, near the mouth of the Chowan River. (36°N, 77°W) p. 234
Ellsworth A city in central Kansas. p. 488
Emerald Mound An ancient settlement of the Mound Builders; located in present-day southwestern Mississippi. (32°N, 91°W) p. 65
Equator Great circle of Earth that is equal distance from the North and South Poles and divides the surface into Northern and Southern Hemispheres. p. 50
Erie Canal The longest canal in the world; located in New York; connects Buffalo (on Lake Erie) with Troy (on the Hudson River). p. 415
Europe One of Earth's seven continents. p. 27

F

Falmouth (FAL•muhth) A town in southwestern Maine. (44°N, 70°W) p. 197
Fort Atkinson A fort in southern Kansas; located on the Sante Fe Trail. (43°N, 89°W) p. 406
Fort Boise (BOY•zee) A fort in eastern Oregon; located on the Snake River and on the Oregon Trail. p. 406
Fort Bridger A present-day village in southwestern Wyoming; once an important station on the Oregon Trail. (41°N, 110°W) p. 406
Fort Christina A Swedish fort; located in present-day Wilmington, Delaware. p. 211
Fort Crèvecoeur (KREEV•ker) A fort in central Illinois; located on the Illinois River; built by La Salle in 1680. (41°N, 90°W) p. 153
Fort Crown Point A French fort; located in northeastern New York, on the shore of Lake Champlain. p. 274
Fort Cumberland A British fort located in northeastern West Virginia, on its border with Maryland. p. 274
Fort Dearborn A fort in northeastern Illinois; built in 1803; eventually became part of Chicago; site of a major battle in the War of 1812. (42°N, 88°W) p. 391
Fort Donelson A fort located in northwestern Tennessee; site of a major Civil War battle in 1862. p. 470
Fort Duquesne (doo•KAYN) A French fort in present-day Pittsburgh, Pennsylvania; captured by the British and new fort built and named Fort Pitt. (40°N, 80°W) p. 274
Fort Edward A British fort in New York, on the Hudson River; a present-day village. (43°N, 74°W) p. 274
Fort Frontenac (FRAHN•tuh•nak) A French fort once located on the site of present-day Kingston, Ontario, in southeastern Canada; destroyed by the British in 1758. (44°N, 76°W) pp. 153, 274
Fort Gibson A fort in eastern Oklahoma; end of the Trail of Tears. (36°N, 95°W) p. 398
Fort Hall A fort in southeastern Idaho; located on the Snake River, at a junction on the Oregon Trail. p. 406
Fort Laramie A fort in southeastern Wyoming; located on the Oregon Trail. (42°N, 105°W) p. 406
Fort Ligonier (lig•uh•NIR) A British fort; located in southern Pennsylvania near the Ohio River. p. 274
Fort Louisbourg (LOO•is•berg) A French fort; located in eastern Canada on the coast of the Atlantic Ocean. (46°N, 60°W) p. 274
Fort Mackinac A fort located on the tip of present-day northern Michigan; site of a major battle in the War of 1812. (46°N, 85°W) p. 391
Fort Mandan A fort in present-day central North Dakota, on the Missouri River; site of a winter camp for the Lewis and Clark expedition. (48°N, 104°W) p. 385
Fort McHenry A fort in central Maryland; located on the harbor in Baltimore; site of a major battle in the War of 1812. (39°N, 77°W) p. 391
Fort Miamis A French fort located on the southern shore of Lake Michigan, in present-day southwestern Michigan. p. 153
Fort Necessity A British fort located in southwestern Pennsylvania; located in present-day Great Meadows. (38°N, 80°W) p. 274
Fort Niagara A fort located in western New York, at the mouth of the Niagara River. (43°N, 79°W) p. 274
Fort Oswego A British fort; located in western New York, on the coast of Lake Ontario. (43°N, 77°W) p. 274
Fort Sumter A fort on a human-made island, off the coast of South Carolina, in Charleston Harbor; site of the first Civil War battle in 1861. (33°N, 80°W) p. 470
Fort Ticonderoga (ty•kahn•der•OH•gah) A historic fort on Lake Champlain, in northeastern New York. (44°N, 73°W) p. 274
Fort Vancouver A fort in southwestern Washington, on the Columbia River; the western end of the Oregon Trail; present-day Vancouver. (45°N, 123°W) p. 406
Fort Wagner A fort near Charleston, South Carolina; site of a Civil War battle in 1863. p. 470
Fort Walla Walla A fort in southeastern Washington; located on the Oregon Trail. (46°N, 118°W) p. 406

Fort William Henry A British fort located in eastern New York. (43°N, 74°W) p. 274

Fox River Located in southeast central Wisconsin; flows southwest toward the Wisconsin River, and then flows northeast and empties into Green Bay. p. 153

Franklin A city in central Tennessee; site of a major Civil War battle in 1864. (36°N, 87°W) p. 470

Fredericksburg A city in northeastern Virginia; located on the Rappahannock River; site of a Civil War battle in 1862. (38°N, 77°W) p. 470

Frenchtown A town in present-day eastern Michigan; site of a major battle in the War of 1812. (42°N, 83°W) p. 391

G

Gatun Lake (gah•TOON) A lake in Panama; part of the Panama Canal system. p. 572

Germantown A residential section of present-day Philadelphia, on Wissahickon Creek, in southeastern Pennsylvania; site of a major Revolutionary War battle in 1777. (40°N, 75°W) p. 323

Gettysburg A town in southern Pennsylvania; site of a Civil War battle in 1863. (40°N, 77°W) pp. 470, 510

Golconda (gahl•KAHN•duh) A city in the southeastern corner of Illinois; a point on the Trail of Tears. (37°N, 88°W) p. 398

Gonzales (gohn•ZAH•lays) A city in south central Texas; site of the first battle of the Texas Revolution. (30°N, 97°W) p. 404

Great Basin One of the driest parts of the United States; located in Nevada, Utah, California, Idaho, Wyoming, and Oregon; includes the Great Salt Lake Desert, the Mojave Desert, and Death Valley. pp. 20, 406

Great Lakes A chain of five lakes; located in central North America; the largest group of freshwater lakes in the world. p. 29

Great Plains A continental slope in western North America; borders the eastern base of the Rocky Mountains from Canada to New Mexico and Texas. pp. 20, 406

Great Salt Lake The largest lake in the Great Basin; located in northwestern Utah. pp. 29, 406

Great Wagon Road A former route used in the mid-1700s by colonists moving to settle in the backcountry. p. 225

Greenland The largest island on Earth; located in the northern Atlantic Ocean, east of Canada. p. 20

Groton (GRAH•tuhn) A town in southeastern Connecticut; located on Long Island Sound. (41°N, 72°W) p. 197

Guam (GWAHM) United States territory in the Pacific Ocean; largest of the Mariana Islands. p. 570

Guilford Courthouse (GIL•ferd) A location in north central North Carolina, near Greensboro; site of a major Revolutionary War battle in 1781. (36°N, 80°W) p. 323

Gulf of Alaska A northern inlet of the Pacific Ocean; located between the Alaska Peninsula and the southwestern coast of Canada. p. 29

Gulf of California An inlet of the Pacific Ocean; located between Baja California and the northwestern coast of Mexico. p. 20

Gulf of Mexico An inlet of the Atlantic Ocean; located on the southeastern coast of North America; surrounded by the United States, Cuba, and Mexico. pp. 29, 153

Gulf of Panama A large inlet of the Pacific Ocean; located on the southern coast of Panama. p. 572

H

Hampton Roads A channel in southeastern Virginia that flows into Chesapeake Bay; site of a Civil War naval battle in 1862 between two ironclad ships, the *Monitor* and the *Merrimack*. p. 470

Hartford The capital of Connecticut. (42°N, 73°W) p. 197

Havana The capital of Cuba; located on the northwestern coast of the country. (23°N, 82°W) p. 129

Hawaiian Islands A state; a chain of volcanic and coral islands; located in the north central Pacific Ocean. p. 570

Hawikuh (hah•wee•KOO) A former village in southwestern North America; located on the route of the Spanish explorer Coronado in present-day northwestern New Mexico. p. 129

Hiroshima Japanese city upon which first atom bomb was dropped, in World War II. p. 580

Hispaniola (ees•pah•NYOH•lah) An island in the West Indies made up of Haiti and the Dominican Republic; located in the Caribbean Sea between Cuba and Puerto Rico. p. 129

Honolulu (hahn•nuh•LOO•loo) Hawaii's capital and largest city; located on Oahu. (21°N, 158°W) p. 568

Hopewell An ancient settlement of the Mound Builders; located in present-day southern Ohio. (39°N, 83°W) p. 65

Horseshoe Bend A location in eastern Alabama; site of a battle in the War of 1812; a present-day national military park. p. 391

Hudson Bay An inland sea in east central Canada surrounded by the Northwest Territories, Manitoba, Ontario, and Quebec. p. 138

Hudson River A river in the northeastern United States beginning in upper New York and flowing into the Atlantic Ocean; named for the explorer Henry Hudson. p. 89

I

Iceland An island country in the northern Atlantic Ocean; between Greenland and Norway. p. 581

Illinois River A river in western and central Illinois; flows southwest into the Mississippi River. pp. 29, 153

Independence A city in western Missouri; the starting point of the Oregon and Santa Fe Trails. (39°N, 94°W) p. 406

Indian Ocean One of Earth's four oceans; located east of Africa, south of Asia, west of Australia, and north of Antarctica. p. 27

Isthmus of Panama (IS•muhs) A narrow strip of land that connects North America and South America. p. 125

Iwo Jima Japanese island; site of major battle during World War II. p. 580

J

Jamaica (juh•MAY•kuh) An island country in the West Indies; south of Cuba. p. 129

Jamestown The first permanent English settlement in the Americas; located in eastern Virginia, on the shore of the James River. (37°N, 76°W) p. 234

Jerusalem The capital of Israel; located in the central part of the country. (32°N, 35°E) p. 108

K

Kaskaskia (ka•SKAS•kee•uh) A village in southwestern Illinois; site of a major Revolutionary War battle in 1778. (38°N, 90°W) p. 323

Kennebec River (KEN•uh•bek) A river in west central and southern Maine; flows south from Moosehead Lake to the Atlantic Ocean. p. 197

Kennesaw Mountain (KEN•uh•saw) An isolated peak in northwestern Georgia, near Atlanta; site of a Civil War battle in 1864. p. 470

Kings Mountain A ridge in northern South Carolina and southern North Carolina; site of a Revolutionary War battle in 1780. p. 323

L

La Venta An ancient settlement of the Olmecs; located in present-day southern Mexico, on an island near the Tonalá River. (18°N, 94°W) p. 65

Labrador A peninsula in northeastern North America; once known as Markland. p. 20

Labrador Sea Located south of Greenland and northeast of North America. p. 20

Lake Champlain (sham•PLAYN) A lake between New York and Vermont. p. 89

Lake Erie The fourth-largest of the Great Lakes; borders Canada and the United States. p. 29

Lake Huron The second-largest of the Great Lakes; borders Canada and the United States. p. 29

Lake Michigan The third-largest of the Great Lakes; borders Michigan, Illinois, Indiana, and Wisconsin. pp. 29, 153

Lake Okeechobee (oh•kuh•CHOH•bee) A large lake in south Florida. p. 29

Lake Ontario The smallest of the Great Lakes; borders Canada and the United States. pp. 29, 89

Lake Superior The largest of the Great Lakes; borders Canada and the United States. p. 29

Lake Tahoe A lake on the California-Nevada border. p. 29

Lancaster A city in southeastern Pennsylvania. (40°N, 76°W) p. 212

Lexington A town in northeastern Massachusetts; site of the first battle of the Revolutionary War in 1775. (42°N, 71°W) pp. 291, 323

Lisbon The capital of Portugal; a port city located in the western part of the country. (39°N, 9°W) pp. 108, 119

Little Bighorn A location near the Little Bighorn River in southern Montana; site of a fierce battle in 1876 between Sioux and Cheyenne Indians and United States Army soldiers led by General George Armstrong Custer. p. 490

London A city located in the southern part of England; capital of present-day Britain. (52°N, 0°) p. 108

Long Island An island located east of New York City and south of Connecticut; lies between Long Island Sound and the Atlantic Ocean. p. 323

Los Adaes Site of a mission of New Spain; located in present-day eastern Texas. p. 149

Louisiana Purchase A territory in the west central United States; it doubled the size of the nation when it was purchased from France in 1803; extended from the Mississippi River to the Rocky Mountains, and from the Gulf of Mexico to Canada. p. 385

M

Machu Picchu (MAH•choo PEEK•choo) The site of an ancient Inca city on a mountain in the Andes, northwest of Cuzco, Peru. (13°S, 73°W) p. 133

Macon (MAY•kuhn) A city in central Georgia; located on the Ocmulgee River. (33°N, 84°W) p. 415

Madeira (mah•DAIR•uh) An island group in the eastern Atlantic Ocean, off the coast of Morocco. p. 122

Marshall Gold Discovery State Historic Park A park in eastern California located at the site where James Marshall discovered gold in 1848; setting of the California gold rush of 1849. p. 408

Massachusetts Bay An inlet of the Atlantic Ocean; on the eastern coast of Massachusetts; extends from Cape Ann to Cape Cod. p. 189

Mecca A city in western Saudi Arabia; a holy city and chief pilgrimage destination of Islam. p. 108

Medford A city in northeastern Massachusetts, north of Boston. (42°N, 71°W) p. 291

Mediterranean Sea (meh•duh•tuh•RAY•nee•uhn) An inland sea, enclosed by Europe on the west and north, Asia on the east, and Africa on the south. p. 113

Menotomy Located in northeastern Massachusetts. p. 291

Merrimack River A river in southern New Hampshire and northeastern Massachusetts; empties into the Atlantic Ocean. p. 197

Mesa Verde (MAY•suh VAIR•day) An ancient settlement of the Anasazi; located in present-day southwestern Colorado. (37°N, 108°W) p. 65

Midway Islands A United States territory in the central Pacific Ocean. p. 570

Minneapolis The largest city in Minnesota; located in the southeast central part of the state, on the Mississippi River; twin city with St. Paul. (45°N, 93°W) p. 498

Mississippi River The longest river in the United States; located centrally, its source is Lake Itasca in Minnesota; flows south into the Gulf of Mexico. pp. 29, 153

Missouri River A tributary of the Mississippi River; located centrally, it begins in Montana and ends at St. Louis, Missouri. pp. 29, 385

Mobile Bay An inlet of the Gulf of Mexico; located off the coast of southern Alabama; the site of a Civil War naval battle in 1864. p. 470

Mohawk River A river in central New York that flows east to the Hudson River. p. 89

Montreal The second-largest city in present-day Canada; located in southern Quebec, on Montreal Island on the north bank of the St. Lawrence River. (46°N, 73°W) p. 274

Morristown A town in northern New Jersey; located west-northwest of Newark. (41°N, 74°W) p. 212

Moscow The capital and largest city of Russia; located in the western part of the country. (56°N, 38°E) p. 108

Moundville An ancient settlement of the Mound Builders; located in present-day central Alabama. (33°N, 88°W) p. 65

Murfreesboro A city in central Tennessee; located on the west fork of the Stones River; a site on the Trail of Tears. (36°N, 86°W) p. 398

Mystic River A short river rising in the Mystic Lakes; located in northeastern Massachusetts; flows southeast into Boston Harbor north of Charlestown. p. 291

N

Nagasaki Japanese city upon which the second atom bomb was dropped, resulting in an end to World War II. p. 580

Narragansett Bay An inlet of the Atlantic Ocean in southeastern Rhode Island. (41°N, 71°W) p. 197

Nashville The capital of Tennessee; site of a Civil War battle in 1864. (36°N, 87°W) p. 470

Natchitoches (NAH•kuh•tuhsh) The first settlement in present-day Louisiana; located in the northwest central part of the state. (32°N, 93°W) p. 385

Nauvoo (naw•VOO) A city in western Illinois; located on the Mississippi River; beginning of the Mormon Trail. (41°N, 91°W) p. 406

New Amsterdam A Dutch city on Manhattan Island; later became New York City. (41°N, 74°W) p. 211

New Bern A city and port in southeastern North Carolina. (35°N, 77°W) p. 234

New Echota (ih•KOHT•uh) A Native American town in northwestern Georgia; chosen as the capital of the Cherokee Nation in 1819. (34°N, 85°W) p. 398

New France The possessions of France in North America from 1534 to 1763; included Canada, the Great Lakes region, and Louisiana. p. 269

New Guinea (GIH•nee) An island of the eastern Malay Archipelago; located in the western Pacific Ocean, north of Australia. p. 580

New Haven A city in southern Connecticut; located on New Haven Harbor. (41°N, 73°W) p. 197

New London A city in southeastern Connecticut; located on Long Island Sound at the mouth of the Thames River. (41°N, 72°W) p. 247

New Orleans The largest city in Louisiana; a major port located between the Mississippi River and Lake Pontchartrain. (30°N, 90°W) pp. 391, 470

New Spain The former Spanish possessions from 1535 to 1821; included the southwestern United States, Mexico, Central America north of Panama, the West Indies, and the Philippines. p. 269

Newark A port in northeastern New Jersey; located on the Passaic River and Newark Bay. (41°N, 74°W) p. 212

Newport A city on the southern end of Rhode Island; located at the mouth of Narragansett Bay. (41°N, 71°W) p. 197

Newton A city in south central Kansas. (38°N, 97°W) p. 488

Norfolk (NAWR•fawk) A city in southeastern Virginia; located on the Elizabeth River. (37°N, 76°W) p. 234

Normandy Region of northwest France; site of Allied D day invasion on June 6, 1944. p. 581

North America One of Earth's seven continents. p. 27

North Pole The northernmost point on Earth. p. 50

Nova Scotia (NOH•vuh SKOH•shuh) A province of Canada; located in eastern Canada on a peninsula. p. 151

Nueces River (noo•AY•says) A river in southern Texas; flows into Nueces Bay, at the head of Corpus Christi Bay. p. 404

O

Ocmulgee (ohk•MUHL•gee) An ancient settlement of the Mound Builders; located in present-day central Georgia. p. 65

Ocmulgee River (ohk•MUHL•gee) A river in central Georgia; formed by the junction of the Yellow and South Rivers; flows south to join the Altamaha River. p. 234

Oconee River (oh•KOH•nee) A river in central Georgia; flows south and southeast to join the Ocmulgee and form the Altamaha River. p. 234

Ogallala (oh•guh•LAHL•uh) A city in western Nebraska on the South Platte River. (41°N, 102°W) p. 488

Ohio River A tributary of the Mississippi River, beginning in Pittsburgh, Pennsylvania, and ending at Cairo, Illinois. p. 29

Old Spanish Trail Part of the Santa Fe Trail that linked Santa Fe to Los Angeles. p. 406

Omaha (OH•muh•hah) The largest city in Nebraska; located in the eastern part of the state, on the Missouri River. (41°N, 96°W) p. 406

Oregon Country A former region in western North America; located between the Pacific coast and the Rocky Mountains, from the northern border of California to Alaska. p. 385

Oregon Trail A former route to the Oregon Country; extended from the Missouri River northwest to the Columbia River in Oregon. p. 406

P

Pacific Ocean Largest body of water on Earth; extends from Arctic Circle to Antarctic Regions, separating North and South America from Australia and Asia. p. 27

Pagan Ruined Asian town; capital of a powerful dynasty during the 11th–13th centuries. p. 113

Palenque (pah•LENG•kay) An ancient settlement of the Mayan civilization; located in present-day Chiapas, in southern Mexico. (18°N, 92°W) p. 65

Palmyra Island (pal•MY•ruh) One of the northernmost of the Line Islands; located in the central Pacific Ocean. p. 570

Panama Canal A canal across the Isthmus of Panama; extends from the Caribbean Sea to the Gulf of Panama. p. 572

Pecos River (PAY•kohs) A river in eastern New Mexico and western Texas; empties into the Rio Grande. p. 488

Pee Dee River A river in North Carolina and South Carolina; forms where the Yadkin and Uharie Rivers meet; empties into Winyah Bay. p. 234

Perryville A city in east central Kentucky; site of a major Civil War battle in 1862. (38°N, 90°W) p. 470

Perth Amboy A port city in central New Jersey; located on Raritan Bay. (40°N, 74°W) p. 212

Petersburg A port city in southeastern Virginia; located on the Appomattox River; site of a series of Civil War battles from 1864 to 1865. (37°N, 77°W) p. 470

Philadelphia A city in southeastern Pennsylvania, on the Delaware River; a major United States port. (40°N, 75°W) p. 219

Philippine Islands A group of more than 7,000 islands off the coast of southeastern Asia, making up the country of the Philippines. pp. 125, 570

Piedmont Area of high land on the eastern side of the Appalachian Mountains. p. 20

Pikes Peak A mountain in east central Colorado; part of the Rocky Mountains. p. 385

Pittsburgh The second-largest city in Pennsylvania; located in the southwestern part of the state, on the Ohio River. (40°N, 80°W) p. 47

Platte River (PLAT) A river in central Nebraska; flows east into the Missouri River below Omaha. p. 406

Plattsburgh A city in northeastern New York; located on the western shore of Lake Champlain; site of a major battle in the War of 1812. (45°N, 73°W) p. 391

Plymouth A town in southeastern Massachusetts, on Plymouth Bay; site of the first settlement built by the Pilgrims, who sailed on the Mayflower. (42°N, 71°W) p. 189

Port Royal A town in western Nova Scotia, Canada; name changed to Annapolis Royal in honor of Queen Anne; capital of Nova Scotia until 1749. (45°N, 66°W) p. 151

Portland (ME) A port city in southwestern Maine; located on Casco Bay. (44°N, 70°W) p. 353

Portsmouth (NH) (PAWRT•smuhth) A port city in southeastern New Hampshire; located at the mouth of the Piscataqua River. (43°N, 71°W) p. 197

Portsmouth (RI) A town in southeastern Rhode Island; located on the Sakonnet River. (42°N, 71°W) p. 197

Potomac River (puh•TOH•muhk) A river on the Coastal Plain of the United States; begins in West Virginia and flows into Chesapeake Bay; Washington, D.C., is located on this river. p. 233

Princeton A borough in west central New Jersey; site of a major Revolutionary War battle. (40°N, 75°W) p. 323

Providence Rhode Island's capital and largest city; located in the northern part of the state, at the head of the Providence River. (42°N, 71°W) p. 197

Pueblo (PWEH•bloh) A city in Colorado. p. 488

Pueblo Bonito (PWEH•bloh boh•NEE•toh) Largest of the prehistoric pueblo ruins; located in Chaco Canyon National Monument, New Mexico. p. 65

Puerto Rico An island of the West Indies; located southeast of Florida; a commonwealth of the United States. pp. 129, 570

Put-in-Bay A bay on South Bass Island, north of Ohio in Lake Erie; site of a major battle in the War of 1812. (42°N, 83°W) p. 391

Q

Quebec (kwih•BEK) The capital of the province of Quebec, Canada; located on the northern side of the St. Lawrence River; the first successful French settlement in the Americas; established in 1608. (47°N, 71°W) p. 151

R

Red River A tributary of the Mississippi River; rises in eastern New Mexico, flows across Louisiana and into the Mississippi River; forms much of the Texas–Oklahoma border. pp. 29, 385

Richmond The capital of Virginia; a port city located in the east central part of the state, on the James River; capital of the Confederacy. (38°N, 77°W) p. 470

Rio Grande A river in southwestern North America; it begins in Colorado and flows into the Gulf of Mexico; forms the border between Texas and Mexico. pp. 29, 385

Roanoke River A river in southern Virginia and northeastern North Carolina; flows east and southeast across the North Carolina border and into Albemarle Sound. p. 234

Rocky Mountains A range of mountains in the western United States and Canada, extending from Alaska to New Mexico; these mountains divide rivers that flow east from those that flow west. pp. 20, 385

Roxbury A residential district in southern Boston, Massachusetts; formerly a city, but became part of Boston in 1868; founded in 1630. (42°N, 71°W) p. 291

S

Sabine River (suh•BEEN) A river in eastern Texas and western Louisiana; flows southeast to the Gulf of Mexico. p. 404

Sacramento River A river in northwestern California; rises near Mt. Shasta and flows south into Suisun Bay. p. 406

Salem A city on the northeastern coast of Massachusetts. (43°N, 71°W) p. 189

Salt Lake City Utah's capital and largest city; located in the northern part of the state, on the Jordan River. (41°N, 112°W) p. 406

San Antonio A city in south central Texas; located on the San Antonio River; site of the Alamo. (29°N, 98°W) p. 404

San Antonio River A river in southern Texas; flows southeast and empties into San Antonio Bay. p. 404

San Diego A large port city in southern California; located on San Diego Bay. (33°N, 117°W) pp. 149, 174

San Francisco The second-largest city in California; located in the northern part of the state, on San Francisco Bay. (38°N, 123°W) p. 149

San Jacinto (hah•SEEN•toh) A location in southeastern Texas; site of a battle in the Texas Revolution in 1836. (31°N, 95°W) p. 404

San Lorenzo An ancient settlement of the Olmecs; located in present-day southern Mexico. (29°N, 113°W) p. 65

San Salvador One of the islands in the southern Bahamas; Christopher Columbus landed there in 1492. p. 122

Santa Fe (SAN•tah FAY) The capital of New Mexico; located in the north central part of the state. (36°N, 106°W) pp. 149, 406

Santa Fe Trail A former commercial route to the western United States; extended from western Missouri to Santa Fe, in central New Mexico. p. 406

Santee River A river in southeast central South Carolina; formed by the junction of the Congaree and Wateree Rivers; flows southeast into the Atlantic Ocean. p. 234

Saratoga A village on the western bank of the Hudson River in eastern New York; site of a major Revolutionary War battle in 1777; present-day Schuylerville. (43°N, 74°W) p. 323

Savannah The oldest city and a principal seaport in southeast Georgia; located in the southeastern part of the state, at the mouth of the Savannah River. (32°N, 81°W) pp. 234, 470

Savannah River A river that forms the border between Georgia and South Carolina; flows into the Atlantic Ocean at Savannah, Georgia. p. 234

Schenectady (skuh•NEK•tuh•dee) A city in eastern New York; located on the Mohawk River. (43°N, 74°W) p. 212

Sedalia (suh•DAYL•yuh) A city in west central Missouri. (39°N, 93°W) p. 488

Serpent Mound An ancient settlement of the Mound Builders; located in present-day southern Ohio. (39°N, 83°W) p. 65

Shiloh (SHY•loh) A location in southwestern Tennessee; site of a major Civil War battle in 1862; also known as Pittsburg Landing. (35°N, 88°W) p. 470

Sierra Nevada A mountain range in eastern California that runs parallel to the Coast Ranges. p. 20

Snake River A river that begins in the Rocky Mountains and flows west into the Pacific Ocean; part of the Oregon Trail ran along this river. p. 385

South America One of Earth's seven continents. p. 27

South Pass A pass in southwestern Wyoming; crosses the Continental Divide; part of the Oregon Trail. p. 406

South Pole The southernmost point on Earth. p. 50

Spiro An ancient settlement of the Mound Builders; located in eastern Oklahoma. (35°N, 95°W) p. 65

Springfield (MA) A city in southwestern Massachusetts; located on the Connecticut River. (42°N, 73°W) p. 197

Springfield (MO) A city in southwestern Missouri; a point on the Trail of Tears. (37°N, 93°W) p. 398

St. Augustine (AW•guh•steen) A city on the coast of northeastern Florida; the oldest city founded by Europeans in the United States. (30°N, 81°W) pp. 129, 149

St. Croix (KROY) A city on the border of Maine and New Brunswick, Canada. (45°N, 67°W) p. 151

St. Ignace (IG•nuhs) A city in Michigan; located on the southeastern side of Michigan's upper peninsula. (46°N, 85°W) p. 153

St. Joseph A city in northwestern Missouri on the Missouri River. (40°N, 95°W) p. 488

St. Lawrence River A river in northeastern North America; begins at Lake Ontario and flows into the Atlantic Ocean; forms part of the border between the United States and Canada. p. 151

St. Louis A major port city in east central Missouri; known as the Gateway to the West. (38°N, 90°W) pp. 47, 385

St. Marys A village in southern Maryland; the capital until 1694; present-day St. Marys City. (38°N, 76°W) p. 233

St. Paul The capital of Minnesota; located in the eastern part of the state, on the Mississippi River. (45°N, 93°W) p. 498

Strait of Magellan (muh•JEH•luhn) The narrow waterway between the southern tip of South America and Tierra del Fuego; links the Atlantic Ocean with the Pacific Ocean. p. 125

Sudbury River A river in western Massachusetts; connects with the Concord River. p. 291

Susquehanna River (suhs•kwuh•HA•nuh) A river in Maryland, Pennsylvania, and central New York; rises in Otsego Lake, New York, and empties into northern Chesapeake Bay. p. 89

T

Tenochtitlán (tay•nohch•teet•LAHN) The ancient capital of the Aztec Empire, on the islands of Lake Texcoco; location of present-day Mexico City, in southern Mexico. (19°N, 99°W) p. 108

Tikal (tih•KAHL) An ancient settlement of the Mayan civilization; located in present-day Guatemala, in Central America. (17°N, 89°W) p. 65

Timbuktu A town in Mali; located in western Africa, near the Niger River. (17°N, 3°W) p. 108

Toledo (tuh•LEE•doh) A port city in northwestern Ohio located at the southwestern corner of Lake Erie. (42°N, 84°W) p. 498

Trail of Tears A trail that was the result of the Indian Removal Act of 1830; extended from the Cherokee Nation to Fort Gibson, in the Indian Territory. p. 398

Trenton The capital of New Jersey; located in the west central part of the state; site of a major Revolutionary War battle in 1776. (40°N, 75°W) p. 323

Tres Zapotes (TRAYS sah•POH•tays) An ancient settlement of the Olmecs; located in southern Mexico. (18°N, 95°W) p. 65

Turtle Mound An ancient settlement of the Mound Builders; located on the present-day east central coast of Florida. (29°N, 81°W) p. 65

V

Valley Forge A location in southeastern Pennsylvania, on the Schuylkill River; site of General George Washington's winter headquarters during the Revolutionary War. (40°N, 77°W) p. 323

Vandalia (van•DAYL•yuh) A city in south central Illinois. (39°N, 89°W) p. 415

Venice A port city in northeastern Italy; located on 118 islands in the Lagoon of Venice. (45°N, 12°E) pp. 108, 113

Vicksburg A city in western Mississippi; located on the Mississippi River; site of a major Civil War battle in 1863. (32°N, 91°W) p. 470

Vincennes (vihn•SENZ) A town in southwestern Indiana; site of a Revolutionary War battle in 1779. (39°N, 88°W) p. 323

W

Wabash River (WAW•bash) A river in western Ohio and Indiana; flows west and south to the Ohio River, to form part of the Indiana–Illinois border. p. 323

Wake Island A United States territory in the Pacific Ocean. p. 570

Washington, D.C. The capital of the United States; located between Maryland and Virginia, on the Potomac River in a special district that is not part of any state. (39°N, 77°W) pp. 25, 391

West Indies The islands enclosing the Caribbean Sea, stretching from Florida in North America to Venezuela in South America. p. 202

West Point A United States military post since the Revolutionary War; located in southeastern New York on the western bank of the Hudson River. p. 323

Whitman Mission Site of a Native American mission, established in 1836 by Marcus and Narcissa Whitman; located in present-day southeastern Washington. p. 406

Williamsburg A city in southeastern Virginia; located on a peninsula between the James and York Rivers; capital of the Virginia Colony. pp. 234, 254

Wilmington A coastal city in southeastern North Carolina; located along the Cape Fear River. p. 234

Winchester A city in northern Virginia; located in the Shenandoah Valley. (39°N, 78°W) p. 353

Wisconsin River A river located in central Wisconsin that flows south and southeast to the Mississippi River. p. 153

Y

Yellowstone River A river in northwestern Wyoming, southeastern Montana, and northwestern North Dakota; flows northeast to the Missouri River. p. 385

York Former name of Toronto, Canada; located near the northwestern end of Lake Ontario; site of a major battle in the War of 1812. p. 391

Yorktown A small town in southeastern Virginia; located on Chesapeake Bay; site of the last major Revolutionary War battle in 1781. (37°N, 76°W) p. 32

Glossary

The Glossary contains important social studies words and their definitions. Each word is respelled as it would be in a dictionary. When you see this mark ´ after a syllable, pronounce that syllable with more force than the other syllables. The page number at the end of the definition tells where to find the word in your book.

add, āce, câre, pälm; end, ēqual; it, īce; odd, ōpen, ôrder; to͝ok, po͞ol; up, bûrn; yo͞o as u in fuse; oil; pout; ə as a in above, e in sicken, i in possible, o in melon, u in circus; check; ring; thin; this; zh as in vision

A

abolitionist (a•bə•li´shən•ist) A person who wanted to end slavery. p. 448
absolute location (ab´sə•lo͞ot lō•kā´shən) The exact location of a place on Earth, either a postal location or its lines of latitude and longitude. p. 50
acquittal (ə•kwi´təl) A verdict of not guilty. p. 479
adapt (ə•dapt´) To fit ways of living to land and resources. pp. 6, 70
address (ə•dres´) A formal speech. p. 467
advertisement (ad•vər•tīz´mənt) A public announcement that tells people about a product or an opportunity. p. 503
agriculture (a´grə•kul•chər) Farming. p. 64
allegiance (ə•lē´jəns) Loyalty. p. 303
alliance (ə•lī´əns) A formal agreement among nations, states, or individuals to cooperate. p. 270
ally (a´lī) A partner in an alliance; a friend, especially in times of war. p. 270
almanac (ôl´mə•nak) A yearly calendar and weather forecast that helps farmers know when to plant crops. p. 222
amendment (ə•mend´mənt) An addition or change to the Constitution. p. 370
analyze (a´nəl•īz) To look closely at how the parts of an event connect with one another and how the event is connected to other events. p. 3
ancestor (an´ses•tər) An early family member. p. 59
annex (ə•neks´) To add on. p. 394
Anti-Federalist (an´tī•fe´də•rə•list) A citizen who was against ratification of the Constitution. p. 368
apprentice (ə•pren´təs) A person who learns a trade by living with the family of a skilled worker and training for several years. p. 249
archaeologist (är•kē•o´lə•jist) A scientist who studies the culture of people who lived long ago. p. 57
arid (ar´əd) Dry. p. 36
armada (är•mä´də) A Spanish fleet of warships. p. 159
armistice (är´mə•stəs) An agreement to stop fighting a war. p. 571
arms control (ärmz kən•trōl´) A limiting of the number of weapons a nation holds. p. 583
arsenal (är´sə•nəl) A place for storing weapons. p. 348
artifact (är´tə•fakt) An object made by early people. p. 58
assassinate (ə•sa´sən•āt) To murder a leader by sudden or secret attack. p. 477
assembly line (ə•sem´blē līn) A moving belt that takes a partly finished product from one worker to the next. p. 525
astrolabe (as´trə•lāb) An instrument formerly used to calculate one's position compared to the sun, moon, and stars. p. 116
auction (ôk´shən) A public sale. p. 243
authority (ə•thôr´ə•tē) The right to control and make decisions. p. 164
aviation (ā•vē•ā´shən) The making and flying of airplanes. p. 527

B

backcountry (bak´kən•trē) The land between the Coastal Plain and the Appalachian Mountains. p. 224
barter (bär´tər) To exchange goods, usually without using money. p. 77
basin (bā´sən) Low, bowl-shaped land with higher ground all around it. p. 22
bias (bī´əs) An opinion or feeling for or against someone or something. p. 286
bill (bil) An idea for a new law. p. 356
bill of rights (bil uv rīts) A list of freedoms. p. 276
black codes (blak kōdz) Laws limiting the rights of former slaves in the South. p. 478
blockade (blä•kād´) To use warships to prevent other ships from entering or leaving a harbor. p. 289
boom (bo͞om) A time of fast economic growth. p. 486
border state (bôr´dər stāt) During the Civil War, a state—Delaware, Kentucky, Maryland, or Missouri—between the North and the South that was unsure which side to support. p. 459
borderlands (bôr´dər•landz) Areas of land on or near the borders between countries, colonies, or regions that serve as barriers. p. 146
boycott (boi´kät) To refuse to buy or use goods or services. p. 282
broker (brō´kər) A person who is paid to buy and sell for someone else. p. 241
budget (bu´jət) A plan for spending money. p. 280
buffer zone (bu´fər zōn) An area of land that serves as a barrier. p. 146

R56 ■ Reference

burgess (bûr´jəs) A representative in the legislature of colonial Virginia or Maryland. p. 163

bust (bust) A time of quick economic decline. p. 487

C

Cabinet (kab´ə•nit) A group of the President's most important advisers. p. 375

candidate (kan´də•dāt) A person running for office. p. 378

capital (ka´pə•təl) The money needed to set up or improve a business. p. 497

caravel (kar´ə•vel) A ship that used square or triangular sails to travel long distances swiftly. p. 116

cardinal direction (kärd´nəl də•rek´shən) One of the main directions: north, south, east, or west. p. A3

carpetbagger (kär´pət•ba•gər) A Northerner who moved to the South to take part in Reconstruction governments. p. 483

cartogram (kär´tə•gram) A diagram that gives information about places by the size shown for each place. p. 542

cartographer (kär•tä´grə•fər) A person who makes maps. p. 116

cash crop (kash krop) A crop that people raise to sell rather than to use themselves. p. 163

casualty (ka´zhəl•tē) A person who has been killed or wounded in a war. p. 461

cause (kôz) An event or an action that makes something else happen. p. 120

census (sen´səs) An official population count. p. 359

century (sen´chə•rē) A period of 100 years. p. 60

ceremony (ser´ə•mō•nē) A series of actions performed during a special event. p. 72

cession (se´shən) Something given up, such as land. p. 407

charter (chär´tər) An official paper in which certain rights are given by a government to a person, group, or business. p. 188

checks and balances (cheks and ba´lən•səz) A system that gives each branch of government different powers so that each branch can watch over the authority of the others. p. 363

chronology (krə•nä´lə•jē) Time order. p. 2

circle graph (sûr´kəl graf) A round chart that can be divided into pieces, or parts; often referred to as a pie graph. p. 223

city-state (si´tē•stāt) A city and the surrounding area that stands as an independent state. p. 111

civic participation (si´vik pär•ti•sə•pā´shən) Being concerned with and involved in issues related to the community, state, country, or world. p. 9

civics (si´viks) The study of citizenship. p. 9

civil war (si´vəl wôr) A war between two groups in the same country. p. 151

civilian (sə•vil´yən) A person who is not in the military. p. 570

civilization (si•və•lə•zā´shən) A culture that usually has cities and well-developed forms of government, religion, and learning. p. 65

claim (klām) To declare that a person or a country owns something. p. 121

clan (klan) A group of families that are related to one another. p. 78

class (klas) A group of people who are alike in some way. Classes are treated with different amounts of respect in a society. p. 65

classify (kla´sə•fī) To group. p. 175

climograph (klī´mə•graf) A chart that shows the average monthly temperature and the average monthly precipitation for a place. p. 492

code (kōd) A set of laws. p. 445

cold war (kōld wôr) A war fought mostly with propaganda and money rather than with soldiers and weapons. p. 582

colonist (kä´lə•nist) A person who lives in a land ruled by a distant country. p. 144

colony (kä´lə•nē) A land ruled by a distant country. p. 144

commander in chief (kə•man´dər in chēf) A person who is in control of all the armed forces of a nation. p. 294

commerce (kä´mərs) Trade. p. 351

commission (kə•mi´shən) A special committee. p. 545

common (kä´mən) An open area where sheep and cattle graze; village green. p. 190

communism (käm´yə•ni•zəm) A social and economic system in which all land and industries are owned by the government. p. 582

compact (käm´pakt) An agreement. p. 167

company (kum´pə•nē) A business. p. 138

compass (kum´pəs) An instrument used to find direction. p. 109

compass rose (kum´pəs rōz) A circular direction marker on a map. p. A3

compromise (käm´prə•mīz) An agreement in which each side in a conflict gives up some of what it wants in order to get some of what it wants. p. 91

concentration camp (kon•sən•trā´shən kamp) A guarded camp where prisoners are held. p. 578

Confederacy (kən•fe´də•rə•sē) The group of eleven states that left the Union, also called the Confederate States of America. p. 453

confederation (kən•fe•də•rā´shən) A loosely united group of governments working together. p. 89

congress (kän´grəs) A formal meeting of government representatives who have the authority to make laws. p. 270

conquistador (kän•kēs´tə•dôr) Any of the Spanish conquerors in the Americas during the early 1500s. p. 127

consent (kən•sent´) Agreement. p. 195

consequence (kän´sə•kwens) Something that happens because of an action. p. 313
conservation (kän•sər•vā´shən) The protection and wise use of natural resources. p. 545
constitution (kän•stə•tōō´shən) A written plan of government. p. 235
contour line (kän´tōōr līn) A line on a drawing or map that connects all points of equal elevation. p. 24
convention (kən•ven´shən) An important meeting. p. 351
cotton gin (kä´tən jin) A machine that removed seeds and hulls from cotton fibers much more quickly than workers could by hand. p. 418
council (koun´səl) A group that makes laws. p. 90
county (koun´tē) A large part of a colony or a state. p. 250
county seat (koun´tē sēt) The main town of a county. p. 250
crossroads (krôs´rōdz) A place that connects people, goods, and ideas. p. 46
cultural region (kul´chə•rəl rē´jən) An area in which people share some ways of life. p. 45
culture (kul´chər) A way of life. p. 10
current (kûr´ənt) The part of a body of water flowing in a certain direction. p. 26

D

D day (dē dā) June 6, 1944, the day on which Allied Forces began the invasion of northern France in World War II. p. 580
debtor (de´tər) A person who was put in prison for owing money. p. 236
decade (de´kād) A period of ten years. p. 60
declaration (de•klə•rā´shən) An official statement. p. 283
delegate (de´li•gət) A representative. p. 271
demand (di•mand´) The need or want for a product or service by people who are willing to pay for it. p. 418
demarcation (dē•mär•kā´shən) A line that marks a boundary. p. 126
democracy (di•mä´krə•sē) A form of government in which the people have power to make choices about their lives and government. p. 395
depression (di•pre´shən) A time of little economic growth when there are few jobs and people have little money. p. 578
descendant (di•sen´dənt) A person's child, grandchild, and so on. p. 58
desertion (di•zûr´shən) Leaving one's duties, such as military service, without permission. p. 132
developing country (di•ve´lə•ping kun´trē) A country that does not have modern conveniences such as good housing, roads, schools, and hospitals. p. 588
dictator (dik´tā•tər) A leader who has complete control of the government. p. 402
distortion (di•stôr´shən) Something that is not accurate on a map. p. 574
doctrine (däk´trən) A government plan of action. p. 394
drainage basin (drā´nij bā´sən) Land drained by a river system. p. 31
drought (drout) A long period with little or no rain. p. 36
due process of law (dōō prä´ses uv lô) The principle that guarantees the right to a fair public trial. p. 372
dugout (dug´out) A boat made from a large, hollowed-out log. p. 76

E

e pluribus unum (ē plōōr´ə•bəs ōō´nəm) A Latin saying that means "out of many, one." p. 553
earthwork (ûrth´wərk) A wall made of dirt or stone. p. 294
economic region (e•kə•nä´mik rē´jən) An area defined by the kind of work people do or the products they produce. p. 45
economics (e•kə•nä´miks) The study of how people use resources to meet their needs. p. 8
economy (i•kä´nə•mē) The way people of a state, region, or country use resources to meet their needs. p. 8
effect (i•fekt´) The result of an event or action. p. 120
electoral college (i•lek´tə•rəl kä´lij) A group of officials chosen by citizens to vote for the President and Vice President. p. 360
elevation (e•lə•vā´shən) The height of land in relation to sea level. p. 24
emancipation (i•man•sə•pā´shən) The freeing of enslaved peoples. p. 445
empire (em´pīr) The conquered lands of many people and places governed by one ruler. p. 106
encounter (in•koun´tər) A meeting. p. 106
enlist (in•list´) To join. p. 315
entrepreneur (än•trə•prə•nûr´) A person who sets up and runs a business. p. 495
equality (i•kwä´lə•tē) Equal rights. p. 448
erosion (i•rō´zhən) The wearing down of Earth's surface, usually by wind or water. p. 42
estuary (es´chə•wer•ē) The wide mouth of a river where ocean tides flow in. p. 137
ethnic group (eth´nik grōōp) A group of people from the same country, of the same race, or with a shared culture. p. 540
expedition (ek•spə•di´shən) A journey. p. 118
expel (ik•spel´) To force to leave. p. 195
export (ek´spôrt) A product that leaves a country. p. 201
extinct (ik•stingt´) No longer in existence. p. 64

F

fact (fakt) A statement that can be checked and proved to be true. p. 240

fall line (fôl līn) A place where the elevation of the land drops sharply, causing rivers to form waterfalls or rapids. p. 31

farm produce (färm prō´dōōs) Grains, fruits, and vegetables for sale. p. 215

federal system (fe´də•rəl sis´təm) A system of government in which the authority to govern is shared by the central and state governments. p. 364

Federalist (fe´də•rə•list) After the American Revolution, a citizen who wanted a strong national government and was in favor of ratifying the Constitution. p. 368

fertilizer (fûr´təl•ī•zər) Matter added to the soil to make it produce more crops. p. 41

flow chart (flō chärt) A diagram that shows the order in which things happen. p. 364

fork (fôrk) A place in which a river divides. p. 369

forty-niner (fôr•tē•nī´nər) A gold seeker who arrived in California in 1849. p. 409

frame of reference (frām uv ref´rəns) A set of ideas that determine how a person understands something. p. 3

free enterprise (frē en´tər•prīz) An economic system in which people are able to start and run their own businesses with little control by the government. p. 494

free state (frē stāt) A state that did not allow slavery before the Civil War. p. 437

free world (frē wûrld) The United States and its allies in the fight against communism. p. 582

freedmen (frēd´mən) Men, women, and children who had once been slaves. p. 481

frontier (frən•tir´) The land that lies beyond settled areas. p. 199

fugitive (fyōō´jə•tiv) A person who is running away from something. p. 445

fundamental (fən•də•men´təl) Basic. p. 197

G

gap (gap) An opening or a low place between mountains. p. 277

generalization (jen•ə•rə•lə•zā´shən) A statement based on facts, used to summarize groups of facts and to show relationships between them. p. 68

geography (jē•ä´grə•fē) The study of Earth's surface and the way people use it. p. 6

glacier (glā´shər) A huge, slow-moving mass of ice covering land. p. 56

gold rush (gōld rush) A sudden rush of new people to an area where gold has been found. p. 409

government (gu´vərn•mənt) A system by which people of a community, state, or nation use leaders and laws to help people live together. p. 9

grant (grant) A sum of money or other payment given for a particular purpose. p. 127

Great Awakening (grāt ə•wā´kən•ing) A religious movement started by a Dutch minister in the Middle Atlantic Colonies that called for greater freedom of choice in religion. p. 215

grid system (grid sis´təm) An arrangement of lines that divide something, such as a map, into squares. p. A3

grievance (grē´vəns) A complaint. p. 305

H

hacienda (ä•sē•en´dä) A large estate where cattle and sheep are raised. p. 147

harpoon (här•pōōn´) A long spear with a sharp shell point. p. 79

hatch lines (hach līnz) A pattern of stripes used on historical maps to show areas claimed by two or more countries. p. 278

heritage (her´ə•tij) Culture that has come from the past and continues today. p. 10

hijack (hī´jak) To illegally take control of an airplane. p. 592

historical empathy (hi•stôr´i•kəl em´pə•thē) An understanding of the thoughts and feelings people of the past had about events in their time. p. 3

historical map (hi•stôr´i•kəl map) A map that provides information about a place as it was in the past. p. 112

history (hi´stə•rē) Events of the past. p. 2

hogan (hō´gän) A cone-shaped Navajo shelter built by covering a log frame with bark and mud. p. 72

Holocaust (hō´lə•kôst) The mass murder of more than two-thirds of all European Jews. p. 581

homesteader (hōm´sted•ər) A person living on land granted by the government. p. 488

human feature (hyōō´mən fē´chər) Something created by humans, such as a building or road, that alters the land. p. 6

human resource (hyōō´mən rē´sôrs) A worker who brings his or her own ideas and skills to a job. p. 499

humidity (hyōō•mi´də•tē) The amount of moisture in the air. p. 36

I

immigrant (i´mi•grənt) A person who comes into a country to make a new home. p. 219

impeach (im•pēch´) To accuse a government official, such as the President, of "treason, bribery, or other high crimes and misdemeanors." p. 361

imperialism (im•pir´ē•ə•liz´əm) The building of an empire. p. 570

import (im´pôrt) A product brought into a country. p. 201

impressment (im•pres´mənt) The taking of workers against their will. p. 389

inauguration (i•nô´gyə•rā´shən) A ceremony in which a leader takes office. p. 384

indentured servant (in•den´chərd sûr´vənt) A person who agreed to work for another person without pay for a certain length of time in exchange for passage to North America. p. 234

independence (in•də•pen´dəns) The freedom to govern on one's own. p. 302

indigo (in´di•gō) A plant from which a blue dye can be made. p. 235

industrial revolution (in•dus´trē•əl re•və•lōō´shən) The period of time during the 1700s and 1800s in which machines took the place of hand tools to manufacture goods. p. 412

industry (in´dəs•trē) All the businesses that make one kind of product or provide one kind of service. p. 200

inflation (in•flā´shən) An economic condition in which more money is needed to buy goods and services than was needed earlier. p. 347

inlet (in´let) An area of water extending into the land from a larger body of water. p. 27

inset map (in´set map) A smaller map within a larger one. p. A3

interchangeable parts (in•tər•chān´jə•bəl pärts) Identical copies of parts made by machines so that if one part breaks, an identical one can be installed. p. 418

intermediate direction (in•tər•mē´dē•it də•rek´shən) One of the in-between directions: northeast, northwest, southeast, or southwest. p. A3

Internet (in´tər•net) A system that allows computers to send information by using telephone lines or satellites. p. 529

intolerable (in•tä´lər•ə•bəl) Unacceptable. p. 289

investor (in•ves´tər) A person who uses money to buy or make something that will yield a profit. p. 414

irrigation (i•rə•gā´shən) The use of canals, ditches, or pipes to move water to dry areas. p. 41

isthmus (is´məs) A narrow strip of land that connects two larger land areas. p. 123

J

jazz (jaz) A kind of music that grew out of the African American musical heritage. p. 530

justice (jus´təs) A Supreme Court judge. p. 361

justice (jus´təs) Fairness. p. 214

L

labor union (lā´bər yōōn´yən) A group of workers whose goal is to improve wages and working conditions. p. 525

land use (land yōōs) The way in which most of the land in a place is used. p. 43

landform (land´fôrm) A physical feature, such as a plain, mountain, hill, valley, or plateau, on the Earth's surface. p. 18

legislature (le´jəs•lā•chər) The lawmaking branch of government. p. 163

liberty (li´bər•tē) The freedom of people to make their own laws. p. 285

line graph (līn graf) A chart that uses one or more lines to show changes over time. p. 205

lines of latitude (līnz uv la´tə•tōōd) Lines on a map or globe that run east and west; also called parallels. p. 50

lines of longitude (līnz uv lon´jə•tōōd) Lines on a map or globe that run north and south; also called meridians. p. 50

location (lō•kā´shən) The place where something can be found. p. 6

locator (lō´kā•tər) A small map or picture of a globe that shows where an area on the main map is found in a state, on a continent, or in the world. p. A3

lodge (läj) A circular house of the Plains Indians. p. 82

loft (lôft) The part of a house located between the ceiling and the roof. p. 226

long drive (lông drīv) A trip made by ranchers to lead cattle to the market or the railroads. p. 487

longhouse (lông´hous) A long wooden building in which several related Iroquois families lived together. p. 89

Loyalist (loi´ə•list) A person who supported the British government during the American Revolution. p. 308

M

Magna Carta (mag´nə kär´tə) The English charter granted in 1215 by King John. It lists the rights of the royal class and limits the rights of the king. p. 370

majority rule (mə•jôr´ə•tē rōōl) The political idea that the majority of an organized group should have the power to make decisions for the whole group. p. 168

manifest destiny (ma´nə•fest des´tə•nē) The belief, shared by many Americans, that the United States should one day stretch from the Atlantic Ocean to the Pacific Ocean. p. 402

map key (map kē) A part of a map that explains what the symbols on a map stand for. p. A2

map scale (map skāl) A part of a map that compares a distance on the map to a distance in the real world. p. A3

map title (map tī´təl) Words on a map that tell the subject of the map. p. A2

mass production (mas prə•duk´shən) A system of producing large amounts of goods at one time. p. 418

mercenary (mûr´sən•er•ē) A soldier who serves for pay in the military of a foreign nation. p. 296

meridian (mə•ri´dē•ən) A line of longitude that runs from the North Pole to the South Pole. p. 50

metropolitan area (me•trə•pä´lə•tən er´ē•ə) A large city and the suburbs that surround it. p. 47

migrant worker (mī´grənt wûr´kər) A person who moves from place to place with the seasons, harvesting crops. p. 550

migration (mī•grā´shən) The movement of people. p. 57

military draft (mil´ə•ter•ē draft) A way to bring people into military service. p. 577

militia (mə•li´shə) A volunteer army. p. 221

millennium (mə•le´nē•əm) A period of 1,000 years. p. 60

mission (mi´shən) A small religious settlement. p. 148

missionary (mi´shə•ner•ē) A person sent out by a church to spread its religion. p. 148

modify (mä´də•fī) To change. p. 40

monarch (mä´närk) A king or queen. p. 108

monopoly (mə•no´pə•lē) The complete control of a product or service. p. 288

mountain range (moun´tən rānj) A group of connected mountains. p. 19

mutiny (myōō´tə•nē) Rebellion against the leader of one's group. p. 138

N

national anthem (na´shə•nəl an´thəm) A song of praise for a country that is recognized as the official song of that country. p. 393

nationalism (na´shə•nəl•i•zəm) Pride in one's country. p. 394

natural resource (na´chə•rəl rē´sôrs) Something found in nature that people can use. p. 40

natural vegetation (na´chə•rəl ve•jə•tā´shən) The plant life that grows naturally in a place. p. 33

naturalization (na•chə•rə•lə•zā´shən) The process of becoming a legal citizen of the United States. p. 537

naval store (nā´vəl stôr) A product that is used to build and repair a ship. p. 203

navigation (na•və•gā´shən) The method of planning and controlling the course of a ship. p. 115

negotiate (ni•gō´shē•āt) To talk with another to work out an agreement. p. 327

neutral (nōō´trəl) Not taking a side in a disagreement. p. 309

new immigration (nōō i•mə•grā´shən) After 1890, the large group of people who came from southern and central Europe and other parts of the world to settle in North America. p. 503

nomad (nō´mad) A wanderer who has no settled home. p. 63

nonrenewable (nän•ri•nōō´ə•bəl) Not able to be made again quickly by nature or people. p. 41

nonviolence (nän•vī´ə•ləns) The use of peaceful ways to bring about change. p. 551

Northwest Passage (nôrth´west pa´sij) A nonexistent waterway in North America thought to connect the Atlantic Ocean and the Pacific Ocean. p. 136

O

old immigration (ōld i•mə•grā´shən) Before 1890, people who came from northern and western Europe to settle in North America. p. 502

olive branch (ä´liv branch) An ancient symbol of peace. p. 296

open range (ō´pən rānj) Land on which animals can graze freely. p. 489

opinion (ə•pin´yən) A statement that tells what a person thinks or believes. p. 240

opportunity cost (ä•pər•tōō´nə•tē kôst) The value of the thing a person gives up in order to get something else. p. 594

oral history (ôr´əl his´tə•rē) Stories, events, or experiences told aloud by a person who did not have a written language or who did not write down what happened. p. 2

ordinance (ôr´dən•əns) A law or set of laws. p. 349

origin story (ôr´ə•jən stôr´ē) A story or set of stories by Native American people that tell about their beginnings and how the world came to be. p. 59

overseer (ō´vər•sē•ər) A hired person who watched field slaves as they worked. p. 243

P

pacifist (pa´sə•fist) A believer in the peaceful settlement of differences. p. 310

palisade (pa•lə•sād´) A wall made of sharpened tree trunks to protect a village from enemies or wild animals. p. 87

parallel (par´ə•lel) A line of latitude. It is called this because parallels are always the same distance from one another. p. 50

Parliament (pär´lə•mənt) The lawmaking body of the British government. p. 271

patent (pa´tənt) A license to make, use, or sell a new invention. p. 419

pathfinder (path´fīn•dər) Someone who finds a way through an unknown region. p. 387

Patriot (pā´trē•ət) A colonist who was against British rule and supported the rebel cause in the American Colonies. p. 308

patriotism (pā´trē•ə•ti•zəm) Love of one's country. p. 552

permanent (pûr´mə•nənt) Long-lasting. p. 144

petition (pə•ti´shən) A signed request made to an official person or organization. p. 290

petroleum (pə•trō´lē•əm) Oil. p. 497

physical feature (fi´zi•kəl fē´chər) A land feature that has been made by nature. p. 6

piedmont (pēd´mänt) An area at or near the foot of a mountain. p. 19

pilgrim (pil´grəm) A person who makes a journey for religious reasons. p. 166

pioneer (pī•ə•nir´) A person who first settles a new place. p. 276

pit house (pit hous) A house that was partially built over a hole in the earth so some rooms could be underground. p. 78

plantation (plan•tā´shən) A huge farm. p. 155

planter (plan´tər) A plantation owner. p. 241

plateau (pla•tō´) A broad area of high, mostly flat land. p. 21

point of view (point uv vyoō) A person's perspective. p. 3

political party (pə•li´ti•kəl pär´tē) A group whose members seek to elect government officials who share the group's points of view about many issues. p. 377

political region (pə•li´ti•kəl rē´jən) An area that shares a government and leaders. p. 45

population region (po•pyə•lā´shən rē´jən) An area based on where people live. p. 45

potlatch (pät´lach) A special Native American gathering or celebration with feasting and dancing. p. 78

prairie (prâr´ē) An area of flat or rolling land covered mostly by grasses and wildflowers. p. 38

preamble (prē´am•bəl) An introduction; first part. p. 304

prejudice (pre´jə•dəs) An unfair feeling of hate or dislike for members of a certain group because of their background, race, or religion. p. 504

presidio (prā•sē´dē•ō) A Spanish fort. p. 146

primary election (prī´mer•ē i•lek´shən) An election in which different people compete to be their party's candidate. p. 546

primary source (prī´mer•ē sôrs) A record of an event made by a person who saw or took part in it. p. 4

prime meridian (prīm mə•ri´dē•ən) The meridian marked 0 degrees, which runs north and south through Greenwich, England. p. 50

principle (prin´sə•pəl) A rule that is used in deciding how to behave. p. 329

proclamation (prä•klə•mā´shən) An order from a leader to the citizens. p. 276

profit (prä´fət) The money left over after all expenses have been paid. p. 115

projections (prə•jek´shəns) The different kinds of maps cartographers use to show the Earth. p. 574

proprietary colony (prə•prī´ə•ter•ē kä´lə•nē) A colony owned and ruled by one person who was chosen by a king or queen. p. 155

proprietor (prə•prī´ə•tər) An owner. p. 155

prospector (prä´spek•tər) A person who searches for silver, gold, and other mineral resources. p. 487

prosperity (prä•sper´ə•tē) Economic success. p. 162

public office (pub´lik ô´fəs) A job a person is elected to do. p. 192

public opinion (pub´lik ə•pin´yən) The point of view held by the majority of people. p. 302

public service (pub´lik sûr´vəs) A job someone does to help the community or society as a whole. p. 245

pueblo (pwe´blō) A Spanish word for "village." p. 66

Puritan (pyûr´ə•tən) A member of the Church of England who settled in North America to follow Christian beliefs in a more "pure" way. p. 188

Q

quarter (kwôr´tər) To provide or pay for housing at no cost to another person. p. 289

R

rain shadow (rān sha´dō) The drier side of a mountain. p. 35

rapid (ra´pəd) A fast-moving, dangerous place in a river caused by a sudden drop in elevation. p. 138

ratify (ra´tə•fī) To approve. p. 366

raw material (rô mə•tir´ē•əl) A resource that can be used to make a product. p. 158

Reconstruction (rē•kən•struk´shən) The time after the Civil War during which the South was rebuilt. p. 476

recycle (rē•sī´kəl) To use materials again. p. 558

refinery (ri•fī´nə•rē) A factory in which materials, especially fuels, are cleaned and made into usable products. p. 487

refuge (re´fyooj) A safe place. p. 213

refugee (ref´yoo•jē) A person who must leave his or her home to seek shelter and safety elsewhere. p. 587

regiment (re´jə•ment) A large, organized group of soldiers. p. 310

region (rē´jən) An area of Earth in which many features are similar. p. 6

regulation (re•gyə•lā´shən) A rule or an order. p. 505

relative location (re´lə•tiv lō•kā´shən) The position of one place in relation to another. p. 44

Renaissance (re´nə•säns) A French word meaning "rebirth," used to name a time of advances in thought, learning, art, and science. p. 109

renewable (ri•no͞o´ə•bəl) Able to be made or grown again by nature or people. p. 42

repeal (ri•pēl´) To cancel, or undo, a law. p. 283

representation (re•pri•zen•tā´shən) The act of speaking on behalf of someone else. p. 281

republic (ri•pub´lik) A form of government in which people elect representatives to govern the country. p. 346

reservation (re•zər•vā´shən) An area of land set aside by the government for use only by Native Americans. p. 490

reserved powers (ri•zûrvd´ pou´ərz) Authority that belongs to the states or to the people, not to the national government. p. 372

resist (ri•zist´) To act against. p. 445

resolution (re•zə•lo͞o´shən) A formal statement of the feelings of a group of people about an important topic. p. 303

resolve (ri•zälv´) To settle. p. 91

retreat (ri•trēt´) To fall back. p. 458

revolution (re•və•lo͞o´shən) A sudden, great change, such as the overthrow of an established government. p. 268

royal colony (roi´əl kä´lə•nē) A colony ruled directly by a monarch. p. 152

ruling (ro͞o´ling) A decision. p. 398

rural (rûr´əl) Like or having to do with a place away from a city. p. 46

S

satellite (sa´tə•līt) A machine that orbits Earth. p. 528

savanna (sə•va´nə) A kind of grassland that has areas with a few scattered trees. p. 39

scalawag (ska´li•wag) A rascal; someone who supports something for his or her own gain. p. 484

sea dog (sē dôg) A commander of English warships that attacked Spanish ships carrying treasure. p. 156

sea level (sē le´vəl) The level of the surface of the ocean. p. 21

secede (si•sēd´) To leave. p. 453

secondary source (se´kən•der•ē sôrs) A record of an event written by someone who was not there at the time. p. 5

secret ballot (sē´krət ba´lət) A voting method in which no one knows how anyone else voted. p. 484

sectionalism (sek´shən•ə•li•zəm) Regional loyalty. p. 436

sedition (sə•di´shən) Speech or behavior that causes other people to work against a government. p. 196

segregation (se•gri•gā´shən) The practice of keeping people in separate groups based on their race or culture. p. 484

self-rule (self•ro͞ol´) Control of one's own government. p. 168

self-sufficient (self•sə•fi´shənt) Able to provide for one's own needs without help. p. 147

sharecropping (shâr´kräp•ing) A system of working the land in which the worker was paid with a "share" of the crop. p. 483

siege (sēj) A long-lasting attack. p. 393

slash and burn (slash and bûrn) A method of clearing land for farming that includes cutting and burning of trees. p. 87

slave state (slāv stāt) A state that allowed slavery before the Civil War. p. 437

slavery (slā´və•rē) The practice of holding people against their will and making them carry out orders. p. 66

society (sə•sī´ə•tē) A human group. p. 10

sod (sod) Earth cut into blocks or mats, held together by grass and its roots. p. 82

sound (sound) A long inlet often parallel to the coast. p. 28

specialize (spe´shə•līz) To work at one kind of job and do it well. p. 190

spiritual (spir´i•chə•wəl) A religious song based on Bible stories. p. 244

staple (stā´pəl) Something, such as milk or bread, that is always needed and used. p. 71

states' rights (stāts rīts) The idea that the states, rather than the federal government, should have the final authority over their own affairs. p. 436

stock (stäk) A share of ownership in a business. p. 161

strategy (stra´tə•jē) A long-range plan. p. 459

strike (strīk) To refuse to work. p. 525

suburb (su´bərb) A neighborhood located on the edge of a city. p. 539

suburban (sə•bûr´bən) Of or like the area of smaller cities or towns around a large city. p. 46

suffrage (su´frij) The right to vote in local or national elections. p. 547

superpower (so͞o´pər•pou•ər) One of the world's most powerful nations. p. 586

supply (sə•plī´) The amount of a product or service that is available. p. 418

surplus (sûr´pləs) An amount that is more than what is needed. p. 71

T

tariff (tar´əf) A tax on goods brought into a country. p. 436

technology (tek•nä´lə•jē) The use of scientific knowledge or tools to make or do something. p. 63

tenement (tĕ′nə•mənt) A poorly built apartment building. p. 503

tepee (tē′pē) A cone-shaped tent made from wooden poles and buffalo skins. p. 84

territory (tĕr′ə•tôr•ē) Land that belongs to a national government but is not a state. p. 349

terrorism (tĕr′ər•i•zəm) The use of violence to promote a cause. p. 587

textile (tĕk′stīl) Cloth. p. 416

theory (thē′ə•rē) A possible explanation. p. 57

tidewater (tīd′wô•tər) Low-lying land along a coast. p. 241

time line (tīm līn) A diagram that shows events that took place during a certain period of time. p. 60

time zone (tīm zōn) A region in which a single clock time is used. p. 532

totem pole (tō′təm pōl) A tall wooden post that is carved with shapes of animals and people and that represents a family's history and importance. p. 79

town meeting (toun mē′ting) An assembly in the New England Colonies in which male landowners could take part in government. p. 192

township (toun′ship) An area of land. p. 218

trade-off (trād′ôf) A giving up of one thing in return for another. p. 594

traitor (trā′tər) One who works against one's own government. p. 323

transcontinental railroad (trans•kän•tə•nen′təl rāl′rōd) The railway line that crossed North America. p. 494

travois (trə•voi′) A device made of two poles fastened to a dog's harness, used to carry possessions. p. 85

treason (trē′zən) The act of working against one's own government. p. 282

treaty (trē′tē) An agreement between nations about peace, trade, or other matters. p. 126

trespass (tres′pas) To go onto someone else's property without asking permission. p. 388

trial by jury (trī′əl bī jûr′ē) The right of a person accused of a crime to be tried by a jury, or group, of fellow citizens. p. 214

triangular trade route (trī•ang′gyə•lər trād rōōt) A shipping route that linked England, the English colonies in North America, and the west coast of Africa, forming an imaginary triangle in the Atlantic Ocean. p. 202

tribe (trīb) A group of people who share the same language, land, and leaders. p. 64

tributary (tri′byōō•ter•ē) A stream or river that flows into a larger stream or river. p. 30

tundra (tun′drə) A cold, dry region where trees cannot grow. p. 37

turning point (tûr′ning point) A single event that causes important and dramatic change. p. 316

underground (un′dər•ground) Done in secret. p. 446
urban (ûr′bən) Of or like a city. p. 45
urbanization (ûr•bə•nə•zā′shən) The movement of large numbers of people into cities. p. 539

veto (vē′tō) To reject. p. 361
volcano (väl•kā′nō) An opening in the Earth, often on a hill or mountain, through which hot lava, gases, ash, and rocks may pour out. p. 23

wampum (wäm′pəm) Beads made from cut and polished seashells and used to keep records, send messages to other tribes, barter for goods, or give as gifts. p. 88

war hawk (wôr hôk) A member of Congress who wanted war with Britain before the War of 1812. p. 390

wigwam (wig′wäm) A round, bark-covered Native American shelter. p. 88

Index

Page references for illustrations are set in italic type. An italic *m* indicates a map. Page references set in boldface type indicate the pages on which vocabulary terms are defined.

A

Abenaki Indians, 169
Abolitionists, 448–449
Absolute location, 50
Acquittal, 479
A.D., 61
Adams, Abigail, *311*
Adams, John
 and the Boston Massacre, 287
 and the Declaration of Independence, 303, 306
 patriotism of, 554
 President, 379, *379*
 and the Treaty of Paris, 327
 Vice President, 374
 views on government, 350, 377
Adams, Samuel
 biography, 289
 and the Constitution, 369
 in ill health, 353
 and the Revolutionary War, 291
 statue of, *335*
 on taxation, 281
Adapt, 70
Addams, Jane, 553
Address, 467
Adena Indians, 66
Admiral of the Ocean Sea, 122
Admiral of the Sea of India, 119
Adventures of Huckleberry Finn, The (Twain), 30
Adventures of Tom Sawyer, The (Twain), 30
Advertisement, 503
Advisers to the President, 375
Aerospace industry, 526
Afghanistan, 593
Africa, 110–111, 118, 202
African Americans
 See also slavery
 in American Revolution, 310
 art of, *506*
 Civil Rights movement, 548–550
 in Civil War, 463
 leaders
  in civil rights, 548–550
  in the military, 463
  political, 479
 against slavery, 440–441, 445, 448–449
 migration of, 506–507
 rights of, 484–485
 scientists, 376
 soldiers, *464*
 in the United States, 1800–1860, *448*
 women, 296, 447, *447*, 449
 in World War I, 577
Agricultural regions, 45
Agriculture, 64
 changes in, 535
 in the colonies, 193, 215, 235–236
 in Hawaii, 568–569
 of Indians, 64, 71, 82–83, 87
 shipping produce, 385
 slash-and-burn, 87
 working conditions, 550–551
Aid, foreign, 589
Air brake, 495
Alabama, 453
Alamo, 403, *403*
Alaska, 57, 486, 538–539, 566–567
Albany, New York, 270
Albany Congress, 270–271, 283
Albany Plan of Union, 270
Albright, Madeleine, 548
Aldrin, Edwin "Buzz," Jr., 518, 520–521
Alexander VI, Pope, 125
Algonkin Indians, 152
Algonquian Indians, 88, *88*
Ali, Sunni, 111
All for the Union: The Civil War Diary and Letters of Elisha Hunt Rhodes, 430–433
Allegiance, 303
Allen, Ethan, 318
Alliance, 270
Allied Powers, 576–577
Allies, 270, 579
Almanac, **222,** *222*
Alpine tundras, 39
Amadas, Philip, 158
Amendments
 See also Bill of Rights
 American citizenship, 479
 Bill of Rights, 370–372
 ending slavery, 477
 right to vote, 480, 548
America, name of, 123
America the Beautiful, 17–18
American bison. *See* Buffalo
American Federation of Labor (AFL), 546
American Immigrant Wall of Honor, 599
American Indians. *See* Indians, American
American Revolution
 African Americans in, 310

 American Indians in, 296–297, 311–312
 battles of, 294–297, 315–316, 322–326
 beginning of, 308–309
 British soldier, *314*
 and the churches, 309–310
 Continental Army in, 293–294, 310
 Continental Army soldier, *314*
 Continental Army vs. British army, 314–315
 effect of, 328–329
 end of, 326–327
 events leading to, 268
 foreign help, 317–318
 French and, 317–318
 French blockade, 324, *324*
 German mercenaries, 296
 heroes, 318–319
 people in western lands, 311–312
 slavery during, 310
 victory at Yorktown, 324–326
 war in the North, 315–318
 war in the South, 322–326
 women in, 311, 319
American's Creed, The, 556
Americas in 1400s, 106–108
AmeriCorps, 556–557, *556*
Anaconda Plan, 459, 460
Analysis, 308
Analyze, 3
Analyze diagrams
 change of seasons, 35
 checks and balances, 363
 early Spanish structures, 146
 making a dugout, 77
Analyze graphs
 advantages in the Civil War, *459*
 African Americans in the U.S., 1800–1860, *448*
 automobile sales, *526*
 labor union membership, *546*
 oil production, 1865–1900, *497*
 Southern slaveholders, 1860, *445*
 steel production, 1865–1900, *496*
 voter participation; 1824–1840, *397*
 voter turnout in Presidential elections, 1952–2000, *555*

Analyze primary sources
 Audubon's paintings, 400–401
 calendar robe, 84
 conquistador armor, 134–135
 Declaration of Independence, 304
 Edison inventions, 500–501
 editorial cartoons, 584–585
 the first President, 375
 the Great Awakening, 216–217
 an immigrant passport, 535
 Kansas–Nebraska Act, 440
 Native American pottery, 74–75
 Stamp Act protest, 282
 Washington's mess chest, 320–321
Anasazi Indians, 65–67
Ancestors, 59
Ancient Cultures of North America, *m*65
Ancient Indian civilizations, 65–66
Ancient Indians, 62–67
Ancient people, 66
Anderson, Robert, 454
Anderson, Troy, *399*
Andrus, Leonard, 419
Anglicans, 188
Anglos, 402
Annapolis, Maryland, 329
Annapolis Convention, 351–352
Annapolis State House, *351*
Annexed, 394
Anthony, Susan B., 547
Antietam National Battlefield, 434–435
Anti-Federalists, 368
Anti-immigrant feelings, 504–505
Antislavery, 446–449
Apollo 11 (spacecraft), *528*
Apollo program, 518–521
Apostle to the Indians, 145
Appalachian Mountains, 19
Appomattox, Virginia, 468–469
Apprentices, 249
Archaeologists, 57–58, 107
Architecture, 530–531
Arctic, 76, 80
Arctic Ocean, 26
Arctic tundras, 39
Arid, 36
Arid regions, 43
Arikara Indian nation, 83
Arizona
 Four Corners, 72

Index ■ R65

and the Mexican Cession, 407
mines discovered in, 486
missions in, 148
Paria Canyon Vermillion Cliffs National Monument, 10–11
Phoenix, 537
statehood of, 538
Arkansas, 454–455
Armada, 159
Armistead, James, 310
Armistice, 571
Armor, 134–135
Armorers, 134
Arms control, 583
Armstrong, Louis, 530
Armstrong, Neil, 515, 518–521, 528
Arnold, Benedict, 323
Arsenal, 348
Art activities
book illustrations, 258
brochure, 49
collage, 67
create a hall of fame, 433
design a monument, 258
diorama, 471
draw, 149
make an invention booklet, 419
newspaper front page, 426
picture, 215
plan and draw a community, 222
poster, 32, 155, 204, 338, 514, 593
Articles of Confederation, 307, 346–347, 353–354
Artifacts, 58
Art(s)
Benin, *111*
cartoon, *271*
changes in the, 530
Chinese, *110, 114*
drawing, *282*
engraving, *285, 286, 389, 392*
mural, *447*
Native American. *See* Indians, American
poster, *285, 292*
sandpainting, *73*
statue, *111, 113*
story cloth, *486–490*
woodcarvings, *79*
Asia, 56, 109–110
Assassinated, 477
Assassination
of Abraham Lincoln, 477
of Archduke Ferdinand and wife, 576
of William McKinley, 572
Assembly line, 524–525
Astrolabe, 115–117, *117*
Astronauts, 518–521, *520,* 528
Atahuallpa, 133
Atlanta, Georgia, 539
Atlantic Ocean, 26, 121, 202
Atlatl, 63

Atom bomb, 581
Attorney general, 375
Attucks, Crispus, 285, *285*
Auction, 243
Audubon, John James, 400–401, *400*
Audubon's paintings, 400–401
Austin, Stephen F., 402, *402*
Austin, Texas, 402
Austria-Hungary, 576
Authority, 164
Automobile Sales, 526
Automobiles, 524, 526
Aviation
definition of, **527**
development of, 526–528
glider, 527
jet-powered planes, 527
military, 527
transatlantic flight, 527
Avilés, Pedro Menéndez de, 146
Axis Powers, 579
Aztec Indians, 106, *106–107,* 107–108, 128, 129, 130

B

Bache, Sarah Franklin, *311*
Backcountry, 224–225
See also Frontier
Backcountry, life in, 226–227
Balanced budget, 591
Balboa, Routes of, *m*125
Balboa, Vasco Núñez de, 123, *124*
Bald eagle, *372*
Baltimore, Maryland, 250, *250–251*
Banknote, *351*
Banks, 397
Banneker, Benjamin, 376, *376*
Bar graph, 330–331
Barbed wire, *488*
Barlowe, Arthur, 158
Barn raising, 220
Barrels, 202
Barter, 77, 88
Barton, Clara, 463, *463*
Basin, 22
Bates, Katharine Lee, 17, 18
Battle
See also Conflict; War
at the Alamo, 403
of Antietam, 460–461
Boston Massacre, 284–285, *285,* 286–287, *286, 287*
of Bull Run, 458–459
of Bunker Hill, 294–296, *294–295, m*295
of the Civil War, *m*470
at Cowpens, 322, *322*
of Gettysburg, 466–467, *467,* 510–511, *m*510
of Horseshoe Bend, 393
of Lake Erie, 390
of Little Bighorn, 491
of Long Island, 315

of Manassas. *See* Battle, of Bull Run
of Monmouth, 319
of Moores Creek Bridge, 319
of New Orleans, 393
of San Jacinto, 403
of San Juan Hill, 571
of Saratoga, 315, 316
siege of Santiago, 571
of the Thames, 390
of the War of 1812, *m*391
of Yorktown, 324–326, *324–325*
Battle Cry of Freedom, The (Root), 435
Battles of the Revolution (Major), *m*323
Bayonets, 317
Bays, 27–28
B.C., 61
B.C.E., 61
Becknell, William, 404
Belgium, 211
Bell, Alexander Graham, 499
Benefits and Principals of Oceanography, The (Majid), 118
Benin, 111
Bennett, William J., 518–521
Bering Strait, 56
Beringia, 56–57
Berkeley, John, 213
Berlin, Irving, 503, *503*
Berlin Wall, 583, *583*
Bessemer, Henry, 495
Bias, 286
Bienville, 154
Big Sur, California, 23
Bill, 356, **365**
Bill of Rights, 276
See also Amendments
explanation of, 370–372
promise to add, 367
and rights of citizens, 554–555
Bimini, 128
Bingham, George Caleb, 277
Biographies
Ahmad Ibn Majid, 118
Bartolomé de Las Casas, 145
Benjamin Banneker, 376
Booker T. Washington, 549
Clara Barton, 463
Edmund G. Ross, 479
George Washington, 270
Haym Salomon, 317
Hiram L. Fong, 505
James Madison, 352
James Oglethorpe, 237
Louis Armstrong, 530
Luci Tapahonso, 72
Narcissa Prentiss Whitman, 405
Olaudah Equiano, 244
Phillis Wheatley, 296
Robert E. Lee, 461
Samuel Adams, 289
Samuel Langhorne Clemens, 30

Thayendanegea (Joseph Brant), 312
Thomas Jefferson, 303
W.E.B. Du Bois, 549
Bison. *See* Buffalo
Black codes, 478
Black Hawk, 398
Blackfoot people, 59
Blacksmithing, 190
Blast furnace, 495–496
Bleeding Kansas, 439–440
Blockade, 289, 459–460, 582
Bloody Massacre, The, 285
Boats and ships
See also transportation
canoes, 79, 88, 152, *152*
caravel, *116, 116*
of Christopher Columbus, 122
Clermont, 415
clipper ships, 409
colonial ships, 202
Constitution, 390
Dauphine, 136–137, *136*
dugouts, 76–78, *77*
English, 156
ferry, 238
French, 152
Golden Hind, 156
Guerrière, 390
H. L. Hunley (submarine), 466
Half Moon, 138
junks, 110
of Magellan, 124–125
Maine, 570–571
Mayflower, 167
Paddlewheel steamboats, 415
rowboats, 200
scuttled, 325
slavery ships, 202–203
steamboats, 414–416
trading ships, 202
USS *Arizona,* 579
USS *Constitution,* 422–423
warships, 156–157, 159, 213, 390
whaling ships, 201
*Bodies of Water in the United States, m*29
Bombs, 581, 592–593
Bonaparte, Napoleon, 385
Boom, 487
Boone, Daniel, 225, 276–277, *276, 277*
Booth, John Wilkes, 477
Border states, 459
Borderlands, 146
Borderlands, Spanish, 146–147
Borders, changing, 410–411
Boston, Massachusetts, 204, *284, 334, 558*
Boston Latin School, 191
Boston Massacre, 284–287, *285, 286*
Boston Port Bill, 289
Boston Tea Party, 288–289, *288*
Bow and arrow, 64
Bowen, Ashley, *204*

Bowen, Gary, 182–185
Bowie, James, 403
Boycott, 282–283, 288
Braddock, Edward, 271–272, 272
Bradford, William, 168, 170, 170
Branches, 30
Brant, Joseph, 312
Bread riots, 465
Breadbasket colonies, 210–215
Bread riots, 465
Breckinridge, John, 453
Brenner, Barbara, 308
Britain
 coin, 280
 colonies, 268–272
 Parliament of. See British Parliament
 soldier of, 268
 in Treaty of Paris, 275
 in World War II, 579
British army, 314–315
British Colonists Move West, m225
British flag, 308
British Parliament, 271
 Boston Massacre, 284–285
 French and Indian War, 271
 Intolerable Acts, 289
 taxation without representation, 280–283
British raids, 392–393
Broker, 241
Brooklyn Bridge, 496
Brooks, Preston, 449
Brown, John, 449
Brown, Linda, 548–549
Brown, Moses, 416
Brown, Oliver, 548–549
Brown v. Board of Education of Topeka, 549
Bruce, Blanche K., 479
Bruchac, Joseph, 14–15
Budget, 280, 591
Buffalo, 81–84, 82
Buffalo hunt, 81, 83
Buffalo soldiers, 506
Buffer zone, 146
Bunker Hill Monument, 335
Burgess, 163
Burgesses, House of, 163-164, 282
Burgoyne, John, 315, 316
Burnet, David G., 403
Bush, George, 590, 590
Bush, George W., 555, 555
Bust, 486
Byllinge, Edward, 213

C

Cabinet, 375
Cabot, John, 123, 156
Caboto, Giovanni. See Cabot, John
Caboto, Routes of, m125
Cabral, Pedro Álvares, 126
Cahokia Indians, 66, 67

Calendar Robe, 84, 84
Calhoun, John C., 436–437, 453
California
 gold rush, 408–409, 408, 486
 Hollywood, 529
 Mexican Cession, 407
 Mission San Diego de Alcalá, 174–175
 missions in, 148
 population of, 541
 San Diego, 564–565
Calvert, Cecilius, 233
Calvert, George, 232–233, 232, 240
Calvert, Leonard, 233
Camels, 113
Canada, 591
Canadian Shield, 21
Canals, 406, 413–414, 572–573
Candidates, 378
Cannon, 460
Canoes, 79, 88, 152, 152
Cape Cod, 167–168
Cape of Good Hope, 118
Cape of Storms, 118
Cape Route to India, 119
Capital, 497
Capital cities
 of colonies, 211, 213, 238–239
 of the Confederacy, 460
 Cuzco, 107
 of Ghana, 110
 of Portugal, 119
 selection of, 49
 Tenochtitlán, 107–108, 129, 130
Capitol Building, the, 9, 359
Caravel, 116, 116
Cardozo, Francis L., 479
Caribbean Sea, 102
Carnegie, Andrew, 496
Carolina Colony, 235
Carolina Parrot, 400
Carolinas, 234–236
 See also North Carolina; South Carolina
Carpetbaggers, 483–484
Carson, Kit, 404
Carteret, George, 213
Cartier, Jacques, 137–138, 137, 150, 152
Cartier's routes, m138
Cartographers, 115, 150–151
Cash crop, 163, 235–236, 241, 444
Castillo de San Marcos, 146, 147
Castro, Fidel, 582
Cast-steel plow, 419
Casualty, 461
Categorize, 143, 435
Cather, Willa, 1
Catholicism, 121, 125, 148, 152
Catlin, George, 81, 152
Catt, Carrie Chapman, 547, 547
Cattle drives, 487
Cattle Trails, m488
Catton, Bruce, 461
Cause, 120, 267

Cause and effect, 120, 120
Cave paintings, 58
Cavelier, René-Robert, 153
Cayuga Indians, 89
C.E., 61
Celebrations
 Chinooks, 78
 national. See National celebrations
 potlatches, 78
Census, 359, 540
Center of population, 47
Central America, 572–573
Central Plains, 21
Central Powers, 576
Century, 60
Ceremony, 72
 healing, 73
 Hopi Indians, 72, 94, 95
 Navajo, 73
Cession, 407
Champlain, routes of, m151
Champlain, Samuel de, 151
Chancellorsville, Virginia, 466
Changes of seasons, 35
Character Trait
 citizenship, 289, 352
 courage, 244, 405, 479
 individualism, 30, 303
 inventiveness, 118, 376, 530
 kindness, 237, 463
 loyalty, 317, 461
 patriotism, 296
 perseverance, 270, 505
 respect, 145
 self-discipline, 312
Charles I, king of England, 188, 233
Charles I, king of Spain, 145
Charles II, king of England, 197, 212–214, 234
Charles Town, South Carolina, 236, 248–249, 249
Charles Town Harbor, 249
Charleston, South Carolina, 236
Charleston Mercury, 453
Chart activities, 59, 178, 363, 379
 See also Table activities
Chart analysis, 354
Chart and graph skills
 circle graph, 223
 climograph, 492–493
 compare tables to classify information, 171
 graphs comparison, 330
 line graph, 205
 read a flow chart, 364–365, 365
 time lines, 60
Charter, 188, 587
Chavez, Cesar, 550–551, 551
Checks and balances, 362–363, 362
Cherokee nation, 398–399
Chesapeake Bay, 230–234, 232–233, 240
Chesnut, Mary, 477
Cheyenne Indians, 83, 491

Chicago Defender, 507
Chief Colonial Exports, 1790, 331
Chief Joseph, 491
Child labor, 503, 546
Chimney Rock, 382–383
China, 582
Chinese
 bank notes, 114
 containers, 114
 immigrants, 535–536
 inventions, 109
 silk, 114
 vase, 110
 voyages, 109–110
Chinese Exclusion Act, 505, 536
Chinook Indians, 77–78
Chippewa Indians, 88
Chronology, 2
Chronometer, 117
Church, Fredric Edwin, 196
Church of England, 166, 188, 195
Churchill, Winston, 586–587
Circle graph, 223, 229, 330–331
Cities, land use in, 43
Cities of the 1400s, Major, m108
Cities, Southern, 248–251
Citizens
 responsibilities of, 373, 555–556
 rights of, 280, 283, 441, 554–555
Citizenship, 289, 536–537, 552–554
Citizenship skill
 act as a responsible citizen, 373
 conflict resolution, 91
 decision making, 313
 democratic values
  citizen participation, 555
  common good, 89
  individual rights, 548
  justice, 214
  representative government, 163
  right to privacy, 290
 make a decision, 313
 problem solving, 165
City development, 48–49
City locations, 48–49
City-state, 111
Civic virtue, 352
Civics, purpose of, 9
Civil rights, 554–555
Civil Rights Act of 1964, 550
Civil Rights movement, 548–550
Civil War, 151
 advantages in, 459
 African Americans in, 463
 Anaconda Plan, 459, 460
 Appomattox, 468–469
 battle plans, 459–460
 causes of, 452–455
 diary and letters of Elisha Hunt Rhodes, 430–433

Civilians

Emancipation Proclamation, 461–462
French, 151
Gettysburg National Military Park, 510–511, 510–511
major battles of the, m470
march to the sea, 469
road to victory, 465–471
women in, 463
Civilians, 570
Civilization, 65
Civilizations, early, 65–67
Claim, 121
Claim to land, m337
Clan, 78
Clark, George Rogers, *318,* 319, 386
Clark, William, 386–387, *387*
Classes, 65
Classification of information, 171
Classify, 171
Clay, Henry, 390, 438–439, *438, 439*
Clemens, Samuel Langhorne, 30
Clermont, 415
Climate, 33
after Ice Age, 62
changes in North American, 64
climograph, 492–493
desert southwest, 70
factors affecting, 33–34
in Ice Age, 56–57
regions, 35–37
Regions of the United States, m36
Climograph, 492–493
Clinton, Bill, 556–557, 590–591, *591*
Clinton, DeWitt, 414
Clinton, George, 367
Clipper ships, 409
Clovis point, 63
Coastal Plains, 21, 43, 224, 235
Cobs, 144
Codes, 445
Coins, *144,* 280, 553, *553*
Cold War, 582–583
Collins, Michael, 518
Colombia, 572–573
Colonial
advertisements, 220
exports, *205,* 331
farming, *193*
furnace, *246*
imports, 283
leather box, *281*
life, 254–255
merchants, 201–202, 288
products, m247, m257
teapot, *282*
Colonial America, m180–181, m260
Colonial Philadelphia. *See* Philadelphia, Pennsylvania
Colonial Trade Routes, m202
Colonial Williamsburg, 254–255
Colonies
See also Settlements
agriculture in, 193, 215, 235–236
breadbasket, 210–215
British, m238
British colonists, 268–272
Carolina colony, 235
Connecticut, 197
Dutch and Swedish, m211
economic patterns, 201–202, 215
English, 249
French, 268–272, 385
Georgia, 236–237
hardships of, 168
Jamestown, 160–165, *160,* 182–185, 238
Maryland, 240
Massachusetts Bay, 170, 188–198, m189, 190
Middle Atlantic, 210, m212, 215, 219
Minutemen, 291, *291,* 294
New Hampshire, 19
New Netherland, 210–213
Pennsylvania, 213–214
Plymouth, 166–170
Population of the 13 Colonies in 1750, *223*
Providence, 195
rebellion against Britain, 283–285, 288–297
religion
of Jewish people, 211
in Massachusetts Bay Colony, 194–197
of Pilgrims, 166
of Puritans, 188, 191
of Quakers, 213–215
Rhode Island, 195–196
Roanoke Island, 158–159
Spanish, 249
taxation of, 280–284
Thirteen, *181*
Virginia, m162, 238–239
Colonists, 144
Colony, 144
Colony, royal, *152,* 164
Colorado, 72, 407, 486
Columbia River, 76–77
Columbian Exchange, 127
Columbus, Christopher, 99, 103, *121,* 122–124
Columbus, Voyages of, m122
Columbus Day Parade, *123*
Comanche Indians, 83
Commander in chief, 294
Commerce, 351
Commissions, 545
Common, 190
Common Era, 61
Common Sense, 302–303
Communism, 582
Community schools, 191
Compact, 167
Compact discs (CD), 529
Company, 138
Compare, 55
Comparison of tables, 171
Compass, 109, 117, *386*
Compass rose. *See* Map and globe skills
Compassion, 237, 463
Compound word, 427
Compromise, 91, 355–357
Compromise of 1850, m439
Computers, 526, 529
Concentration camps, 578
Concord, 291–292
Concord Hymn, 267
Conestoga wagon, 220, *220*
Confederacy, 453, 455, 481
Confederate soldiers, *459,* 511
Confederate States of America. *See* Confederacy
Confederation, 89, 189, 307, 346–350
Conflict
See also Battle; War
among colonies, 151, 212
among foreign countries, 156–157, 159, 385
between colonists and American Indians, 162, 164, 169, 212, 275
with Colombia, 572–573
farmers and ranchers, 490
with foreign countries, 402
Indian Removal Act, 398–399
Mormons and settlers, 406
Native Americans and Spanish, 132–133
between North and South, 452–455
over fur trade, 151
over slavery, 444–449
Shays's Rebellion, 347–348
within United States, 436–441
in the West, 490–491
Conflict resolution, 91, 93
Congress, 270
Albany, 270–271, 283
under the Articles of Confederation, 346–350
of the Confederation, 307, 366
duties and powers, 359
First Continental, 290, 304
Second Continental, 293–297, 303
Stamp Act, 283–284
two-house, 356
Congress, Albany, 270
Congress's plan for Reconstruction, 478–479
Connecticut, 196–197, *197,* 202
Connecticut Colony, 197
Connecticut River Valley, 197
Conquerors, Spanish, 127–133
Conquest of the Incas, m133
Conquistador armor, 134–135, *134–135*
Conquistadors, 127, m129, 130–133, 144
Consent, 195
Consequence, 313

Cuba

Conservation, 545
Constantinople, 120
Constitution, 235
Constitution of the United States
amendments to, 477, 479, 480, 548
Bill of Rights, 370–372, 554–555
executive branch, 360–361
judicial branch, 361–362, 375
legislative branch, 359–360
oath to protect, 537
picture of, *9*
preamble to, 358–359
ratification of, 366–370, m369
Ratification Vote, *369*
Shh! We're Writing the Constitution (Fritz), 342–343
Constitution (warship), 390
Constitutional Convention, 351–358, *363*
Context clues, 339
Continental Army, 293–294, 310, 314–315
Continental climate, 35
Continental Congress, 290, 293–297, 303, 304
Continental currency, 294
Continental Divide, 32
Continentals *(paper money),* 347
Continents, 26
Continents and Oceans, m27
Contour line, 24
Contrast, 55
Cook, James, 568
Cooper, Peter, 415–416
Coopers, 203
Coquina, 147
Coram, Thomas, 357
Cornish, Samuel, 448
Cornwallis, Charles, 324
Coronado, Francisco Vásquez de, 131
Coronado, route of, m129
Coronado expedition, 132
Corps of Discovery, 386–387, *386–387*
Cortés, Hernando, 128–130, 134
Cortés meeting Motecuhzoma, *128*
Cotton, 444–445
Cotton gin, 418, *418*
Council, 90
County, 250
County seats, 250–251
Courage, 244, 405, 479
Crazy Horse, 490
Creek Indians, 393
Croatoan Indians, 159
Crockett, Davy, 395–396, 403, *403*
Crossroads, 46
Crow Indians, 68, 83
Crowe, Walter, 233
Cuba, 127, 570–571, 582–583

Cuban missile crisis, 582–583
Cultural maps, 68–69, 93
Cultural regions, 45, 68, 86–90
Culture, importance of, 10
Culture, tribe's, 65
Cumberland Gap, 277, 277
Current, 26, 34
Custom houses, 284, 284
Cuzco, 107

D

D day, 580
Da Gama, Routes of, m119
Da Gama, Vasco, 118–119, 118
da Verrazano, Giovanni. See Verrazano, Giovanni da
Dalles, The, 76–77
Dauphine, 136–137, 136
Davis, Jefferson, 453, 462
Dawes, William, 291
de Bienville, Sieur. See Bienville
de León, Juan Ponce, 127–128, 127
de León, routes of, m129
de Narváez, Pánfilo, 130
de Niza, Marcos, 131
de Soto, Hernando, 132–133, 132,
de Soto, Routes of, m129
Death Valley, 22
Debates, 451–452
Debt, 347
Debtors, 236
Decade, 60
Decision making, 313
Declaration, 283
Declaration of Independence, 303–306, 304, 343
Declaration of Rights and Grievances, 283
Deere, John, 419
Deganawida, 90
Delaware, 213–214
Delaware General Assembly, 214
Delaware Indians, 88, 214
Delaware River, 31
Delegates, 271
Demand, 418, 496–497
 See also Supply
Demarcation, 126, m126
Democracy, 395–396, 556
Democratic party, 452
Democratic values
 citizen participation, 555
 common good, 89
 individual rights, 548
 justice, 214
 representative government, 163
 right to privacy, 290
Democratic-Republican party, 378
Denali, 23
Denmark, 211

Depression, 578
Descendant, 58
Description of New England, A (Smith), 166
Desert, 37, 70–73
Desertions, 132
Developing country, 589
Dewey, George, 571
Diagram analysis. See Analyze diagrams
Dias, Bartolomeu, 118–119
Dias, Routes of, m119
Dia's Story Cloth: The Hmong People's Journey of Freedom (Cha), 486–490
Dickinson, John
 and the Declaration of Rights and Grievances, 283
 hope for peace, 293
 in the new government, 306
 portrait of, 307
 quote of, 259
Dictator, 402
Digital video discs (DVD), 529
Dinwiddie, Robert, 269
Disease control, 573
Diseases, 571, 573
Diversity, 67, 86, 218
Dix, Dorothea, 463
Doctrine, 394
Dole, James, 569
Douglas, Stephen, 451–452, 451
Douglass, Frederick, 449, 449
Draft. See Military draft
Drake, Francis, 157, 157
Drake's Route Around the World, m157
Draw conclusions, 3, 383
Drayton Hall, 474–475
Dred Scott decision, The, 440–441
Drought, 36
Drummond, William, 235
Dry climate, 35
Du Bois, W.E.B., 548, 549, 549
Dugout, 76–78
Dugout, making a, 77
Duquesne, Marquis de, 269
Dutch and Swedish Colonies, m211
Dutch East India Company, 138
Dutch West India Company, 211–212

E

E-mail, 529
E pluribus unum, 553–554
Eagle (spacecraft), 518–521, 519, 521
Eagle Has Landed, The (Bennett), 518–521
Earhart, Amelia, 527, 527
Early Americans, 56–58
Early arrival theory, 57–58

Earth Mother, 73
Earth's resources. See Natural resources
Earthworks, 294
Eastern Hemisphere, 51
Eastern Woodlands, 86–90
Eastern Woodlands Indians, 162
Economic, 8
Economic regions, 45
Economy, 8
 depression, 578
 global, 588–589, 591
 growth, 590–591
 national, 347
 New England, 200–204
 plantations, 241–242
 and slavery, 444–445
Edison, Thomas Alva, 498–501, 499, 528
Edison's Menlo Park, 499
Editorial cartoons, 584–585
Education
 environmental programs, 558–559
 Freedmen's Bureau and, 482
 Peace Corps, 589
 plantations, 245
 and population growth, 557
 Puritan law, 190–191
 segregation in, 548–549
Effect, 120, 267
Eisenhower, Dwight D., 580
El Camino Real, 149
El Morro, 143
Elections, first, 374
Electoral college, 360
Electrical vote recorder, 499
Electricity, 40, 221, 499
Electronic systems, 117
Elevation, 34
Elevation maps, 24–25
Elevations of the United States, m25
Elizabeth I, queen of England, 156–158
Ellington, Duke, 530
Ellis Island, 2, 534–535, 534–535, 598–599, 598–599
Emancipation, 445
Emancipation Proclamation, 461–462, 462, 465
Embassies, 592
Emerson, Ralph Waldo, 267, 292
Empire, 106
 African, 110
 Aztec, 107–108, 128–130
 Inca, 107–108, 133
 Mali, 110
 Songhay, 111
Employment, 236, 249, 268–272, 385, 546
Encounter, 106
Endecott, John, 188
England, 108, 194, 202
English Bill of Rights, 276
Enlisted, 315
Entrepreneur, 495

Environment, 7, 40–42, 558–559
Environmental
 adaptations, 80, 226–227, 489
 changes, 56–57, 64
 modifications, 40, 40–42, 41, 46, 406
Equal rights. See Rights
Equality, 448
Equator, 33, 50
Equiano, Olaudah, 244
Era of Good Feelings, 394
Ericson, Leif, 106
Erie Canal, 413
Erosion, 42
Eskimos. See Inuit
Esteban, 131
Estuary, 137
Ethnic group, 540
Europe, 108–109, 171
European immigrants, 534–535
Everglades National Park, 559
Executive branch of federal government, 360–361
Expeditions, 118, 386–388
 See also Exploration
Expel, 195
Exploration
 Asian, 109–110, m113
 Chinese, 109–110
 English, 138–139
 European, 108–109, 114, 121–126
 French, 152–155
 Portuguese, 115–116, 118–119
 space, 528
 Spanish, 121–122, 124–125, 127–133
 of unknown continent, 123–124
 Vikings, 106
Explorers
 Amadas, Philip, 158
 Avilés, Pedro Menéndez de, 146
 Balboa, Vasco Núñez de, 123, 124
 Barlowe, Arthur, 158
 Cabeza de Vaca, Álvar Núñez, 131
 Caboto, Giovanni, 123
 Cartier, Jacques, 137–138
 Cavelier, René-Robert, 153
 Columbus, Christopher, 106, 121, 122–124
 Cook, James, 568
 Coronado, Francisco Vásquez, 131
 d'Iberville, Sieur, 154
 da Gama, Vasco, 118–119
 da Verrazano, Giovanni, 136–137
 de Bienville, Sieur, 154
 de La Salle, Sieur, 153–154
 de León, Juan Ponce, 127–128
 de Narváez, Pánfilo, 130
 Dias, Bartolomeu, 118–119

Drake, Francis, 157
Esteban, 131
first to the Americas, 101
Hudson, Henry, 138–139
Joliet, Louis, 152–153
Marquette, Jacques, 152–153
Polo, Marco, 109, 112, *112*, *m*113
space, 528
Vespucci, Amerigo, 123–124
Zheng He, 109–110
Exports
during American Revolution, *331*
definition of, **201**
products, 219, 246, 248, 250
value of, 205, *205*, 591
Extinct, 64

Fact, 240
Fact and opinion, 240
Factories, 416
Fall line, **31**
Family heritage, 79
Faneuil Hall, *335*
Far East, 114
Farm produce, 215
Farmland, 43
Farragut, Jorge, 318
Father of the Constitution, 352
Federal-Aid Highway Act, 526
Federal government
court system, 361–362
formation of government, 351–357
and state government, 354–355
system, **354**, *354*
Federalist, The, 368
Federalist party, 377–378
Federalists, 368
Ferdinand, Francis, 576
Ferdinand, king of Spain, 121–122
Ferry boats, 238
Fertilizer, **41**
Fifteenth Amendment, 480, *480*
Finley, John, 276
First Continental Congress, 290, 304
Fishing and whaling, 76–79, 200–201, 567
Five Nations, 89
Flag Day, 553
Flag of the United States, 553
Flags over North America in mid-1700s, *278*
Florida, 394, 453, 559
Flow chart, 364–365
Fong, Hiram L., 505, *505*
Ford factory, 524–525
Ford, Henry, 524–526, *525*
Foreign aid, 589

Forest region, 37–38
Forests, 41–43, *86*
Fork, 269
Fort
Christina, 212
Duquesne, 269, 271
Mandan, 386
McHenry, 392
Necessity, *268–269*, 270
at New Orleans, *384*
Sumter, 454–455, *454–455*, *m*456, *m*457
Ticonderoga, *273*, 318
at West Point, 323
Forty-niners, 409
Fountain of Youth, 128
Four Corners, 72
Fourteenth Amendment, 479
Fox Indians, 398
Frame of Government of Pennsylvania, 214
Frame of reference, 3, **442–443**, 473
Frame, Richard, 209
France, 108, 211, 579
Francis I, king of England, 137
Francis I, king of France, 136
Franciscans, 148
Franklin, Benjamin
and the Albany Plan, *270*
in Congress, 271, 303
and his contributions, 221–222
as a leader, 283, 366
negotiating peace treaty, *327*
patriotism of, 554
and the Philadelphia Convention, 352–353
role in war, 317–318
Free enterprise, **494**
Free enterprise economy, 583
Free state, **437**
Free world, **582**
Freedmen, 481
Freedmen's Bureau, 481–482
Freedmen's Bureau school, *481*
Freedom
in other countries, 586–588
of press, 371
of religion. *See* Religion
of speech, 214, 371, 554
of worship, 214, 370–371
Freedom Trail marker, *335*
Freedom Trail, The, 334–335, *334–335*
Freedom's Journal, 448
Fremont, John C., 404
French and Indian War, 268–276, *m*274
French blockade, 324
French colonies, 268–272, 385
French Quarter, The, 155
Fritz, Jean, 342–343
Frontenac, de, Count of New France, 152
Frontier, **199**
See also Backcountry

Frontier Life, 226–227
Frontier, the Last, 486–491
Fugitive, 445
Fugitive Slave Act, 445
Fulton, Robert, 415
Fundamental, **197**
Fundamental Orders, 197
Furnace, colonial, *246*

Gadsden, James, 407
Gadsden Purchase, 407
Gage, General, 294
Gage, Thomas, 291
Gálvez, Bernardo de, 318
Gao, 110
Gap, **277**
Garrison, William Lloyd, 448
Gaspé Peninsula, 137
Gates, Horatio, *315*, 316
Gateway to the West, *405*
General Assembly, 214
Generalization, **68**, 246
Generalize, 231
Geographic factors, 46
Geographic tools. *See* Map and globe skills
Geography
essential elements of, 7
facts about, 13
five themes of, 6
human systems, 47
importance of, **6**
places and regions
Charles Town, 249
conquest of the Incas, 133
Little Bighorn Battlefield, 490
Marshall Gold Discovery Historical Park, 408
St. Mary's City, 233
Geography theme
human-environment interactions, *m*42, *m*572
location. *See* Location
movement. *See* Movement
place. *See* Place
regions. *See* Regions
George II, king of England, 236
George III, king of England, 276, *280*, 283, 296
Georgia
Atlanta, *539*
missions in, 148
Savannah, *237*, 250
secession from U.S., 453
settlements in, 236–237
Georgia Colony, 236–237
German soldiers, *579*
Germano, Eddie, 584, *585*
Germany, 220, 576–581, 583, *583*
Geronimo, 491
Gesner, Abraham, 497

Gettysburg Address, 467–468
Gettysburg National Cemetery, 510
Gettysburg National Military Park, 510–511
Gettysburg, Pennsylvania, 466–467, 510–511
Ghana, 110
Ghost town, 486–487
Gibbs, Jonathan C., 479
Glaciers, 56
Glenn, John, 518, 528
Glider, 527
Global economy, 588–589, 591
God Bless America, 503
Gods, 71–73, 79, 106, 108, 129
Gold
coins, *144*
discovery of, 398, 491
mines, 144–145, 156
nugget, *409*
rush, 408–**409**, 486–487, 567
search for, 144–145, 160–161
Seven Cities of, 131–132
Golden Gate Bridge, *522*
Golden Hind, 156
Gompers, Samuel, 546
Goods, 384–385, 412, 414–415
Goods and services, 220, 347, 418
Gorbachev, Mikhail, 583
Gore, Al, 555
Government
budget deficit, 591
constitution, **235**
foreign, 276
formation of, 306–307
Frame of Government of Pennsylvania, 214
Fundamental Orders, 197
Mayflower Compact, 166–167, *167*
national. *See* National government
Native American, 89–90
purpose of, **9**
reconstruction, 479–480, 483
regulation, 505
representative, 163
self-rule, 168
Spanish, 148–149
Governor's Palace, *239*
Grand Canyon, 22, 538
Grand Teton Mountain Range, *16–17*
Granger, Gordon, 482
Grant, **127**
Grant, Ulysses S.
accepting General Lee's surrender, *469*
quote of, 475
in the Union army, 465–466, *465*, 468–471
President, 479
Graph activities, 493
Graph analysis. *See* Analyze graphs

Graphs

Graphs
  bar, 330–331
  circle, **223**, 229, 330–331
  climograph, **492**–493
  comparisons, 330–331
  line, **205**, 207, 331
  pie. *See* Graphs, circle
Grassland region, 38
Great Auk, *401*
Great Awakening, The, **215**–217
Great Basin, 22, 29, 406
Great Compromise, The, 355–356
Great Compromiser, 439
Great Council, 90
Great Depression, 578
Great Hall, The, *598*
Great Lakes, 28
Great melting pot, **534**–535
Great Migration, 506–507, *506*
Great Plains, 21, *m*97, 488–490, *492*
Great Salt Lake, 29, 407
Great Valley, 238
Greeley, Horace, 461
Green Mountain Boys, 318
Greene, Nathaniel, 322
Grenville, George, 280
Grid system, 48, 50
Grievances, 305
Grinding stone, *64*
Grinnell, George Bird, 400
Ground zero, *592*
Growth in the United States, *m*411
Guam, 571
Guerrière, 390
Guilford Courthouse, 323
Gulf of Alaska, 27
Gulf of Mexico, 27
Gulf Stream, 34
Gulf War, 590
Gulfs, 27–28
Gutenberg, Johannes, 109

H

Haciendas, 147
  See also ranches and haciendas
Hale, Nathan, 319, *319*
Half Moon, 138
Hamilton, Alexander, *324*, 368, 375, 377
Hammond, James Henry, 442, *442*
Hancock, John, 291, 306, 353, 369
Harlem Renaissance, 530
Harpers Ferry, 449
Harpooners, *78*
Harpoons, **79**
Harrison, William Henry, 390
Hartford, Connecticut, *196*, 197
Harvard University, 191

Hatch lines, **278**
Hatteras Indians, 158
Hawaii, 539, 568–569, *568*, 579
Healing ceremonies, 73
Health care, 545
Hemispheres, 50–51
Henrietta Maria, queen of England, 233
Henry, Patrick, 282, 350, 353, 367
Henry IV, king of France, 150
Henry the Navigator, prince of Portugal, 115–116, *115*, 118
Heritage
  Columbus Day, 123
  definition of, **10**
  family heritage, 79
  Flag Day, 553
  French Quarter, The, 155
  Hula Dance, 569
  Independence Day, 306
  Juneteenth, 482
  Memorial Day, 471
  The Star-Spangled Banner, 393
  Thanksgiving Day, 168
Hessian mercenaries, 315
Hiawatha, 90
High-tech industry, 526
Highland climate, 36
Highwater, Jamake, 102
Highway. *See* Road systems
Hijacked, **592**
Hirohito, emperor of Japan, 578
Hiroshima, Japan, 581
Hispanic Americans, 540
Hispaniola, Island of, 127
Historian, 2
Historical empathy, **3**
Historical map, 112–113, 278–279, 410–411
Hitler, Adolf, 578, *578*, 580–581
Hogan, 72
Holidays. *See* National celebrations
Hollywood, California, 529
Holocaust, **581**
Holy People, 73
Homestead Act, 488
Homesteaders, **488**–490
Honolulu, Hawaii, 568, 569
Hooker, Thomas, *196*, 197
Hopewell Indians, 66
Hopi Indians, 70–72, 94–95
Hopi Nation, 94–95
Horizontal time line, 60, *60*
House of Burgesses, 163–164, 282
House of Representatives, 359
House(s)
  hogan, 72
  igloos, 80
  lodges, **82**
  log huts, 226
  pit house, **78**
  pueblo, **67**, 70–71, *71*
  sod, 488, *489*
  tepee, **84**–85, *84–85*
  wigwams, **88**

Houston, Sam, 403, *453*
Howard, Martin, 280–281
Howe, William, 294, 316
Hudson Bay, *139*
Hudson, Henry, 138–139, *139*, 211
Hudson River, 139
Hudson's routes, *m*138
Hughes, Langston, 530
Huguenots, 235
Hula dance, 569
Hull House, 553
Human-environment interactions, *m*42, *m*572
Human features, **6**
Human resources, **499**
Human systems, 7, 47
Humid subtropical climate, 35–36
Humidity, **36**
Humphreys, Joshua, 422
Hunters and gatherers, 62–63
Huron Indians, 59, 138, 150, 151
Hussein, Saddam, 590, 593
Hutchinson, Anne Marbury, 195–196, *195*
Hutchinson, Thomas, 289, *308*
Hydroelectric power, 40

I

Iberville, Sieur d', 154
Ice Ages, 56
Ice storm, *492*
Idaho, 404, 486
If You Were There in 1776 (Brenner), 308
Igloos, 80
Illustration analysis, 106
Immigrants
  anti-immigrant feeling, 504–505
  from Asia, 504
  after Civil War, 502–507
  in Civil War, 464
  colonial, 219–220, 250
  and Ellis Island, 598–599
  great melting pot, **534**–537
  reaction to, 504–505
  and the Transcontinental Railroad, 495
  and the westward movement, 488
Immigration Act of 1924, 536
Impeach, **361**
Impeachment, 479
Imperialism, **570**
Imports, **201**, 219, 248–249, 591
Impressment, **389**
Impressment of American sailors, *389*
Inauguration, **384**
Inca cities, 107
Inca Empire, 133
Inca Indians, 106–107
Indentured servant, **234**, 242–243

Independence, **302**, 327, 334, 403
Independence Hall, *305*, *306*, *340*, 352
India, 118
Indian Ocean, 26
Indian Removal Act, 398–399
Indian Territory, 398–399, 537
Indiana, 384, 451
Indians, American
  agriculture, 64, 71, 82–83
  allies, 270
  ancient Indian civilizations, 62–67
  of the Arctic region, 80
  art of
    baskets, *95*
    jewelry, *95*
    kachinas, *70*
    model, *68*
    painting, 399
    pottery, 74–75, *74–75*
    statue, *65*
  citizenship, 491
  conflict with colonists, 162, 164, 169, 212, 275
  council, 90
  cultural regions, 68–69
  of the desert Southwest, 70–75
  Eastern Woodlands, 162
  gods of, 71–73, 79, 106, 108
  government of, 89–90
  houses of
    igloos, 80
    lodges, 82–84
    pit house, 78
    pueblo, **67**–68, 70–72
    tepees, *84–85*
    wigwams, 88
  hunters, 76–80, 82–83, 87
  hunters and gatherers, 62–63
  Indian Removal Act, 398
  leaders
    chief, 85, 88
    and the English colonies, 169
    medicine people, 73
    missionary, 312
    in war, 199, 390, 398, 491
  Mound Builders, 66
  of the Northwest Coast, 76–79
  origin stories of, 58–**59**
  Plains Indians, 81–85, *82*, 147
  population density, 537–538
  pottery, 74–75, *74–75*
  religion, 71–73, 106, 108, 148–149
  reservations, 491
  rights of, 551
  Samoset, 169
  settlements, 64–67, 70–72, 82–83, 86–90
  Spanish and, 130–133, 144–145
  theories on first, 57–58
  Tisquantum, 169

trade among, 76–77, 83, 88
tribes
  Abenaki, 169
  Adena Indians, 66
  Algonkin, 152
  Algonquian, 88, *88*
  Anasazi, 65–67
  Arikara, 83
  Aztec, 106–108, *107*, 128–130
  Blackfoot, 59
  Cahokia, 66–67
  Cayuga, 89
  Cherokee, 398
  Cheyenne, 83, 491
  Chinook, 77–78
  Chippewa, 88
  Comanche, 83
  Creeks, 393
  Croatoan, 159
  Crow, *68*, 83
  Delaware, 88, 214
  Fox, 398
  Hatteras, 158
  Hopewell, 66
  Hopi, 70–72, 94–95
  Huron, 59, 138, 150, 151
  Inca, 106–107
  Inuit, 80
  Iroquois. *See* Iroquois Indians
  Kiowa, 83
  Kwakiutl, 79
  Lumbees, 159
  Makah, 78–79
  Mandan, 82–83, *83*, 386
  Manhattan, 211
  Maya, 65–66
  Miami, 88
  Mohawk, 89, 90
  Mohegan, 197, 198
  Narragansett, 195, 198
  Navajo, 72–73, 147
  Nez Perce, 491
  Nipmuc, 198
  Olmec, *65*, 65–66
  Oneida, 89
  Onondaga, 89
  Ottawa, 275
  Pawnee, 82
  Pequot, 198
  Podunk, 198
  Powhatan, 88, 164
  Pueblo, 70–72
  Seminole, 398
  Seneca, 89
  Shawnee, 390
  Shoshone, 386–387
  Sioux, 82, 491
  Taensa, 154
  Taino, 102
  Wampanoag, 88, 168–169, 193, 198
  Wichita, 82
  Zuni, 70, 131
and the Underground Railroad, 446
and the westward movement, 490–491
women, 72

Indigo, 235
Individual rights, 548
Individualism, 30, 303
Industrial Revolution, 412–419
Industry, 200
  aerospace, 526
  changing, 524–526
  fishing, 567
  growth in, 494–499
  high-tech, 526
  movie, 528–529
  oil, 497–498
  steel, 495–497
Industry in the United States, 1890s, *m*498
Inference, 209
Inflation, 347
Inlets, 27–28
Interchangeable parts, 418
Interior Plains, 21, 42, 43, 81–84
Intermountain region, 22
International Space Station, 528
Internet, 529
Interstate Commerce Commission, 545
Interstate highways, 526
Intolerable, 289
Intolerable Acts, 289
Inuit, 80
  See also Eskimos
Invention Factory, 499
Inventions
  See also Technological innovations
  air brake, 495
  compass, **109**
  computer, 526
  cotton gin, **418**
  electric lightbulb, *500*
  electric pen, *500*
  electrical vote recorder, 499
  electronic stock ticker, *501*
  gunpowder, 109
  kinetoscope, *501*
  lightning rod, 221
  lightbulb, 499
  mechanical reaper, 419
  phonograph, *501*
  process for making steel, 495
  steam engine, 414–416
  steel plow, 419, 489
  telegraph system, 495, 498
  telephone, 499
Inventiveness, 118, 376, 530
Inventors
  Alexander Graham Bell, 499
  Benjamin Franklin, 221–222
  Cyrus McCormick, 419
  Eli Whitney, 418
  George Westinghouse, 495
  Granville T. Woods, 495
  Henry Bessemer, 495
  James Oliver, 489
  Johannes Gutenberg, 109
  Thomas Alva Edison, 498–499, *499*, 528

  Thomas Newcomen, 414
Investor, 414
Iraq, 590
Iroquois Indians
  and Britain, 270
  of Eastern Woodlands, 87
  and fur trade, 151
  and Jacques Cartier, 138
  life of, 89–90
  nations, *m*89
Iroquois League, 89–90, 91
Iroquois Nation, *m*89
Irrigation, 41
Irrigation canals, 406
Isabella, queen of Spain, 121–122
Isthmus, 123
Isthmus of Panama, 123–124, 572–573
Italy, 211, 578, 579

J

Jackson, Andrew, 393, 396–397, *396*, 436–437
Jackson, Stonewall. *See* Jackson, Thomas
Jackson, Thomas, 458, *458*, 466
Jacksonian Democracy, 397
Jamaica, 127
James, duke of York, 212
James I, king of England, 164, *164*
James River, 161
Jamestown, 160–164, *160–161*, 182–185
Japan, 578, 579
Japanese immigrants, 535
Jay, John, *327*, 368, 375
Jazz, 530
Jazz, American, 530
Jefferson, Thomas
  ambassador to France, 353
  and Declaration of Independence, 303–304
  patriotism of, 554
  picture of, *303*
  President, 384–386
  secretary of state, 375
  Vice President, 379
  views on government, *368*, 371, 377
Jeffersonian Republicans, 378
Jet-powered planes, 527
Jewish people, 122, 211, 578
Job opportunities. *See* Employment
John F. Kennedy Space Center, *514–515*
John I, king of Portugal, 115
John II, king of Portugal, 118
Johnson, Andrew, 477, *477*, 479, *479*
Johnson, Lyndon, 584
Johnson, Oliver, 226
Join or Die cartoon, *271*
Joliet, Louis, 152–153

Joliet's routes, *m*153
Jones, John Paul, *318*, 319
Josephy, Alvin M., Jr., 55
Judicial branch of federal government, 361–362, 375
Judiciary Act, 375
Juneteenth, 482
Junks, *109*, 110
Justice, 214, 214
Justices, 361

K

Kachina dancers, 72, 94
Kachinas, 70, 71–72
Kalakaua, king of Hawaii, 569
Kansas, 388, 439–440
Kansas Territory, 439–440
Kansas–Nebraska Act, 439–440, *m*440, 452
Kebec, 151
Kennedy, John F., 9, 582, 589
Kentucky, 277, 384
Key, Francis Scott, 392–393, *393*
Key, map. *See* Map and globe skills
King, Dr. Martin Luther, Jr., 550, *550*
King Philip's War, 199
King's Chapel Burying Ground, 335
Kiowa Indians, 83
Kitty Hawk, North Carolina, 527
Kivas, 72
Klondike News, 566, 567
Klondike Valley, Alaska, *566*, 567
Knox, Henry, 375, 377
Korea, 582
Korean War, 582
Kosovo, 588
Ku Klux Klan, 484
Kublai Khan, 109
Kumbi Saleh, Ghana, 110
Kuwait, 590
Kwakiutl Indians, 79

L

La Florida, 128
La Follette, Robert M., 546
La Salle, Sieur de, *152,* 153
La Salle's routes, *m*153
Labor unions, 525, 546
Lafayette, Marquis de, 317, *317*
Lake Itasca, 31
Lakes, 28–29
Land bridge story, 56–57, *57*
Land claims, *m*337
Land ordinance, 349
Land use, 40–43
Land Use and Resources of the United States, *m*42

Landform regions, 18–19
Landforms
of America, *m*20
basins, **22**
definition of, **18**
mountain ranges, 19–20, 22–23
plains, 21
plateaus, 21
valleys, 22–23
Landmarks, National
Capitol building, *9, 359*
Liberty Bell, 306
Lincoln Memorial, *426–427*
White House, *360, 379, 392, 396*
Lane, Ralph, 158
Las Casas, Bartolomé de, 145
Las Vegas, Nevada, 541, *541*
Latitude
See also Longitude
and longitude of the United States, *51*
and longitude of the World, *m*50
use of, 50–51
Law, John, 155
Law of the Great Peace, The **(Iroquois)**, 89–90
Lawrence, Jacob, 506, *507*
Laws
civil rights, 548–550
education, 190–191
governing colonies, 280–283, 289
immigration, 536
labor, 546
land, 349
military draft, 577
Le Moyne, Pierre, *See* Iberville, Sieur d'
Leaders
African American, 447
American Indian
chief, 85, 88
medicine people, 73
for peace, 90
Pontiac (chief), 275
colonial, 280, 283, 291
election of, 197
women, 447, 448, 547
Lee, Richard Henry, 303
Lee, Robert E., 461, 466, 469, *469*
Legal adviser, 375
Legend for maps. *See* Map and globe skills
Legends
explanation of, 14
Fountain of Youth, 128
Indian, 106, 214
origin stories, 58–59
Legislative branch of federal government, 359–360
Legislature, 163
Albany Congress, 270–271, 283
Articles of Confederation, 346–350
Assembly of Maryland, 234
First Continental Congress, 290, 304
General Assembly, 214
Second Continental Congress, 293–297, 303
Stamp Act Congress, 283–284
Virginia General Assembly, 238
Lewis, Meriwether, 386–387, *386,*
Lewis and Clark, 386–387
Lexington, 291–292
Lexington and Concord, *m*291
Liberator, The, 448
Liberty, **285**
Liberty Bell, 306
Life on the Mississippi **(Twain)**, 30
Lightbulb, 499
Lightning rod, 221
Liliuokalani, queen of Hawaii, 569
Lincoln, Abraham
assassination, 477
childhood, 450–451
and the Civil War, 427, 454–455
debates with Douglas, 451–452, *451*
and the Emancipation Proclamation, 461–463, *462*
President, 168
in public service, 451
Reconstruction, 476–477
Lincoln Boyhood National Memorial, 450
Lincoln Memorial, *426–427*
Lindbergh, Charles, 527
Line graph, 205, *207*, 330–331
Line of Demarcation, *m*126
Lines of latitude, **50**
Lines of longitude, **50**
Lisbon, Portugal, 119
Literature
All for the Union: The Civil War Diary and Letters of Elisha Hunt Rhodes, 430–433
Dia's Story Cloth: The Hmong People's Journey of Freedom (Cha), 486–490
If We Should Travel (Bruchac), 14–15
Stranded at Plimoth Plantation, 1626 (Bowen), 182–185
The World of 1492 (Highwater), 102–103
Yankee Doodle, 262–265
Little Bighorn Battlefield, 490
Livingston, Robert R., 303
Location
Civil War, *m*470
French and Indian War, *m*274
Great Lakes, *m*29
major cities, *m*108
Massachusetts Bay Colony, *m*189
New England Colonies, *m*197
New France, *m*154
Thirteen English Colonies, *m*238
U.S. possessions, *m*570
World War II, *m*580–581
Location of American cities, 48–49
Location regions, 44
Locomotive, *414, 415*–416
Lodges, 82
Loft, **226**
Log huts, 226
Lone Star flag, *404*
Long drives, 487
Longhouse, **89**
Longitude, 50–51
See also Latitude
Longstreet, James, 484
Lords Proprietors, 234
Lost Colony, The, 158–159, 161
Louis XIV, king of France, 152
Louisiana, 153–155, 275, 384–385, 453
Louisiana Purchase, 384–385, *m*385
Lowell, Francis Cabot, 416
Loyalists, **308**, 327
Loyalty, 317, 461
Lumbees, 159

M

Machu Picchu, 107
Madison, Dolley, 392, *392*
Madison, James
biography of, 352
and the Constitution, 368
leadership in Virginia, 371
member of Congress, 350, 355
President, 390, 392
quote of, *368*
Magellan, Ferdinand, 124–125, 136
Magellan, Routes of, *m*125
Magna Carta, **370**
Main idea, **17**
Maine, 139, 199, 438
Maine **(battleship)**, 570–571
Majid, Ahmad Ibn, 118
Majority rule, **168**
Makah Indians, 78–79
Making a dugout, *77*
Mali, 110
Mammoths, 62–63
Mandan Indians, 82–83, *83*, 386
Manhattan Indians, 211
Manhattan Island, *210*
Manifest destiny, **402**
Mann, Horace, 448
Manufacturing, 43, *43*, 45, 416–418
Map activities
Civil War, 514
cultural map, 68
elevation maps, 25
exploration of Asia, 113
exploration of North America, 103, 178
latitude and longitude, 97
Louisiana Purchase, 388
product map, 251
regions, 23, 98
Spanish expeditions, 133
using different scales, 457
Map and globe skills
comparing different scales, 456–457, 473, 513
cultural maps, 68–69, 93
elevation maps, 24–25
follow routes, 112–113, 141, 177
historical maps, 112–113
identification of changing borders, 425
key, 246–247, 278–279
latitude and longitude, 50–51, 97
reading contour lines, 24, *m*24
scale, 57, *m*57, 456–457
symbols, 246–247, 278
using maps to make generalizations, 68, *m*69
Maps
cultural, *m*65, *m*69, 93
elevation, 24–25, *m*25, 52
geography themes, 6
human-environment interactions, *m*572
location. *See* Location
movement. *See* Movement
place. *See* Place
regions. *See* Regions
historical, 278–279, 410–411
latitude and longitude, *m*51
regional, *m*36, *m*38, *m*45
resource and product, 246–247
March to the Sea, 469
March to Valley Forge, The **(painting)**, *316*
Marine climate, 37
Marine Corps, creation of, 297
Marion, Francis, *318*, 319
Market towns, 215
Marquette, Jacques, 152–153
Marquette's routes, *m*153
Marshall, James, 408
Marshall Gold Discovery State Historic Park, 408

Index ■ R73

Marshall Plan, 589
Maryland, 232–234, 250, *250*, 351
Maryland Assembly, 234
Maryland Colony, 240
Mason-Dixon Line, 437, *438*
Mason, George, 370
Mass production, **418**
Massachusetts, 289, 294, 347–348, 558
Massachusetts Antislavery Society, 449
Massachusetts Bay Colonists, 197
Massachusetts Bay Company, 170, 188–198, *m*189
Massachusetts Bay Company Charter, *188*
Massachusetts Government Act, 289
Massasoit, 169, 199
Mastodons, 62–63
Mather, Cotton, 187
Maya Indians, 65–66
Mayflower, 167
Mayflower Compact, 166–168, *167*
McCauley, Mary Ludwig Hays, 319
McCormick, Cyrus, 419
McKinley, William, 570, 572
Meadowcroft Rock Shelter, 58
Mechanical reaper, 419
Mediterranean climate, 37
Meetinghouse, 191–192, *213*
Melting pot, 534–535
Mercenary, **296**
Merchants, 249, 389
Meridians, **50**
Mesa Verde National Park, *54–55*
Metacomet, *198*, 199
Metropolitan area, **47**
Mexican Americans, 537–538, 550–551
Mexican Cession, 407
Mexican immigrants, 535
Mexican-American War, 407, *407*, 410
Mexicas. *See* Aztec Indians
Mexico, 591
Mexico City, 107–108, 130
 See also Tenochtitlán
Miami Indians, 88
Middle Atlantic Colonies, 210, *m*212, 215, 219
Middle East, 114, 115, 590
Middle passage, 202
Middle West region, 44
Migrant worker, **550**
Migration
 of African Americans, 506–507
 of American Indians, 72
 to cities, 48–49, 539
 immigrants to America, 534–537
 land bridge story, **56**–58
 of slaves, 446–447

Military aviation, 527
Military draft, **577**
Military institutions
 origin of Marine Corps, 297
 origin of Navy, 296
 United States Air Force, 527
 United States Military Academy, 329
 United States Naval Academy, 329
Militia, **221**
Millennium, **60**
Milliners, *255*
Mills, 416–417, 496, 497
Mineral resources, 41
Miners, 486–487
Mines, 144, *145*, 156
Mining, 43
Ministers, 191, 195, 216–217
Minuit, Peter, 211
Minute Man National Historical Park, *266–267*
Minutemen, 291, *291*, 294
Missionary, **148**, 174, 404, 569
Missions, 148–149, 174–175, 403
Missions of New Spain, *m*149
Mississippi, 453, 465–466
Mississippi River, 30–31, *30–31*, 152
Mississippi River valley, 66
Missouri, 438
Missouri Compromise, 438–439, *m*438
Model T Ford, 524, 526
Modifications to environment. *See* Environmental, modifications
Modify, **40**
Mohawk Indians, 89, 90
Mohegan Indians, 197–198
Monarchs, **108**
Mongoulacha, 154
Monk's Mound, 67
Monopoly, **288**
Monroe, James, 394, *394*
Monroe Doctrine, 394
Montana, 404, 486
Montcalm, Marquis de, 273
Montreal, Canada, 275
Morgan, Daniel, 322
Mormons, 406–407
Morris, Gouverneur, 358–359, *358*
Morristown National Historic Park, *300–301*
Motecuhzoma, *128*, 129–130
Mother civilization, 65
Motion pictures, 528
Mound Builders, 66
Mount McKinley, 23
Mountain ranges, 19–20, 22–23
Movement
 cattle trails, *m*488
 conquistadors, *m*129
 expedition routes, *m*125, *m*153

oceans and continents, *m*27
 road systems, *m*149
 routes, *m*119, *m*291
 trade routes, *m*202
 Trail of Tears, *m*398
 Underground Railroad, *m*446
 voyages, *m*122, *m*157
 waterway, *m*151
 westward, *m*225, *m*406, *m*489
Muhlenberg, John Peter, 309, *309*
Multimedia presentation, 98
Multiple meanings, **259**
Music, jazz, 530
Muslims, 122
Mussolini, Benito, 578
Mutiny, **138**

N

NAACP, 548
NAFTA, 591
Nagasaki, Japan, 581
Narragansett Bay, 195–196
Narragansett Indians, 195, 198
NASA, 518, 528
Nassau Hall, *346*
Nation, becoming a, 342–343
National Aeronautics and Space Administration. *See* NASA
National American Woman Suffrage Association (NAWSA), 547
National anthem, 393
National Association for the Advancement of Colored People (NAACP), 548
National Audubon Society, 400
National celebrations
 Columbus Day, 122–123
 Flag Day, 553
 Independence Day, 306
 Thanksgiving Day, 168
National Farm Workers Association (NFWA), 551
National government, 346–350
National Guard, 329
National Landmarks. *See* Landmarks, National
National Park Service, 545, 558–559
National Parks, 510–511
National Road, 412–413
National Socialists. *See* Nazis
National symbols, 372
Nationalism, **394**
Nation's capital. *See* Washington, D.C.
Native Americans. *See* Indians, American
NATO, 588
NATO countries, 2002, *m*588

Natural resources
 in Alaska, 567
 American Indians' use of, 70, 81, 86–88
 in colonies, 210
 protection of, 545, 558–559
 use of, **40**–43
Natural vegetation, **33**
Naturalization, **537**
Navajo Indians, 72–73, 147
Naval stores, 203, 235, 250
Navigation, **115**
Navigational tools, 116, 117
Navy, creation of, 296
Nazis, 578, 580–581
Nebraska, 439–440
Negotiated, **327**
Neutral, **309**
Nevada, 407, 486, 541, *541*
New Amsterdam, 211, *211*, 213
New England, 188
New England church, *186*
New England Company, 188
New England town, *190*
New France, *m*154
New Freedom, The, 523
New Hampshire, 197, 199, *203*
New immigration, **503**
New Jersey, 213, 499
New Jersey Plan, 356, *356*
New Mexico
 Four Corners, 72
 Mexican cession, 407
 and the Pike expedition, 388
 Santa Fe, *48*
 statehood of, 538
New Netherland, 210–213
New Netherland Company, 211
New Orleans, Louisiana, 155
New Sweden, 212
New York, 2, 270
New York City, *46–47*, 557, 592–593
New York Harbor, *46–47*
New York Tribune, 461
Newcomen, Thomas, 414
Newell, Hames Michael, 447
Nez Perce Indians, 491
Niña, 122
Nineteenth Amendment, 548
Nipmuc Indians, 198
Nobel Peace Prize, 587
Nomads, 63, 72, 83–85
Nombre de Dios, 148
Nonrenewable, **41**
Nonviolence, **551**
Norfolk, Virginia, 250
North America
 early European settlements, *m*101
 eastern region, *m*158
 after the French and Indian War, *m*279
 before the French and Indian War, *m*279

in 1754, m269
in 1783, m329
land bridge story, 56
map of, m12
North American Desert, 37
North American Free Trade Agreement (NAFTA), 591
North Atlantic Treaty Organization (NATO), 588
North Carolina, 225, 277, 454–455, 527
   See also Carolinas
North Dakota, 386
North, Frederick (Lord), 289, 296
North Korea, 582
North Pole, 50
North Vietnam, 583
Northeast region, 44, 44
Northern Hemisphere, 50
Northwest Coast, 76–80
Northwest Ordinance, 350
Northwest Passage, **136**–139, 152
Northwest Territory, 349–350, m349, 384, 390

O Pioneers!, 1
Oath of office for President, 375
Ocean currents, 34
Oceans, 26–27
Oceans and continents, m27
Oglethorpe, James, 236–237
Ohio, 384, 496, 497
Ohio Valley, 268–270
Oil
   boom, 497
   Drake's oil well, 497
   industry, 497–498
   in Middle East, 590
   production, 1865–1900, 497
   whale, 200–201
O'Keeffe, Georgia, 530
Oklahoma, 398, 537–538, 592
Old immigration, **502**
"Old Ironsides," 390, 422–423, 422–423
Old Spanish Trail, 404
Olive branch, 296
Olive Branch Petition, 296
Oliver, James, 489
Olmec Indians, 65, 65–66
Oneida Indians, 89
Onondaga Indians, 89
Open range, **489**
Operation Desert Storm, 590
Opinion, **240**
Oral history, 2
Ordinance, **349**
Oregon, 404, 491
Oregon Trail, 405
Origin stories, 58–**59**
Ortiz, Simon, 11
Osceola, 398
Otis, James, 280, 282, 283

Otis, Mercy, 311
Ottawa Indians, 275
Ottoman Empire, 115
Overseers, **243**

Pacific Ocean, 26, 124–125, 157
Pacifists, **310**
Paddlewheel steamboats, 415
Paine, Thomas, 301–302, *302*
Palisade, **87**
Panama Canal, The, 572–573, m572, 573
Parallels, **50**
Paria Canyon Vermillion Cliffs National Monument, 10–11
Parks as Classrooms (PAC), 558–559
Parks, national, 510–511
Parks, Rosa, 549–550, *549*
Parliament, **271**
Passenger pigeon, *401*
Passport, *535*
Patents, *419*
Paterson, William, 355, *355*
Pathfinder, *387*
Patriotic symbols, 372, 553
Patriotism, 296, **552**–554
Patterns of human activity, 45
Patterns of settlement, 46
Paul Revere's house, *335*
Pawnee Indians, 82
Payne, Robert, 565
Peace Corps, 589
Peace treaty, 275, 393
Pearl Harbor, 579
Penn, William, 179, 213–214, *214*, 218–220
Pennsylvania
   and the Boston Tea Party, 288
   colonial Philadelphia, 218–222
   Lancaster County, 209
   and the steel industry, 495–497
   terrorist attacks, 593
   William Penn, founder of, 213–214
Pennsylvania Gazette, 222, 271
Pennsylvania Memorial, *510*
Pennsylvania rifle, 220
Pennsylvania State House, 352–353
Pentagon, 592–593
People and environments, 40–42
Pequot Indians, 198
Pequot War, 198
Performance activities
   conduct an interview, 307, 480
   deliver a speech, 90
   diary entry, 245
   draw a cartoon, 272
   draw a map, 23, 133, 388

   draw a picture, 149, 215
   draw a poster, 32, 204
   interview, 531
   make a brochure, 49
   make a chart, 59, 363, 379
   make a collage, 67
   make a diorama, 471
   make a graphic organizer, 73
   make a list, 559
   make a map, 251
   make a poster, 155, 285, 292, 593
   make a time line, 551
   make an invention booklet, 419
   plan a celebration, 126
   plan a community, 222
   research, 85
   use the Internet, 394
   write a biography, 399
   write a description, 80
   write a dialogue, 312
   write a diary entry, 111, 245, 297, 541
   write a journal entry, 159, 227, 277
   write a letter, 164, 199, 329, 350, 372, 464
   write a list, 409, 485
   write a list of questions, 170, 491
   write a news story, 357
   write a newspaper article, 193, 573
   write a newspaper headline, 455
   write a packing list, 139
   write a paragraph, 43, 239
   write a persuasive letter, 119
   write a plan, 441
   write a poem, 39
   write a report, 449
   write a song, 319
   write an advertisement, 507
   write "Who Am I?" questions, 499
Permanent, **146**
Perry, Oliver Hazard, 390
Perseverance, 270, 505
Pershing, John, 571
Persian Gulf War, 571
Petition, **290**
Petroleum, 497
Philadelphia, *218*, *219*, *340*, *341*
Philadelphia Academy, 222
Philadelphia Convention, 352–353
Philadelphia, Pennsylvania, 218–222
Philip IV, king of Spain, 143
Philippine Islands, 125, 571
Phoenix, Arizona, *537*
Physical features, **6**
Physical systems, **7**
Pickett, George, 466–467
Pickett's Charge, 466–467
Pie graph. *See* Circle graph
Pied duck, *401*

Piedmont, **19**, 224, 238
Pike, Zebulon, *19*, 388, *388*
Pikes Peak, *19*, 388
Pilgrims, **166**, 168, 188, 199
Pinckney, Eliza Lucas, 236
Pinta, 122
Pioneer, **276**
Pirates, 156
Pit house, **78**
Pitcher, Molly, 319
Pitt, William, 273, *273*
Pittsburgh, Pennsylvania, 269
Pizarro, Franciso, 133
Pizarro's route, m133
Place
   Dutch and Swedish colonies, m211
   explanation of, 6
   Louisiana Purchase, m385
   ratification of Constitution, m369
   Southern Colonies, m234
   Texas, m404
Places and regions, 7
Plains, 21, 81–85
Plains Indians, 81–84, *82*, 147
Plantations
   crops, 235–236
   economy, 241–242
   sewing sampler, *245*
   slavery, 236–237, *444*
   Southern, 241–245, *242–243*
   workers, 242–243
Planters, **241**, 249
Planter's life, 245
Plateau, **21**, 22
Pledge of Allegiance, 553
Plymouth Colony, **166**–170, 168–169
Pocahontas, 162, *162*
Podunk Indians, 198
Points of view, 3
   the Battle of Bunker Hill, 295
   Bill of Rights, for or against, 368
   determine, **286**–287, 299
   of explorers, 124
   reading skill, 475
   states' rights, 473
   taxes, 281
   union or secession, 452
Poland, 579
Polar climate, 35
Political parties, **377**–378
Political region, 45
Political symbols, 372
Polk, James K., 405, 407
Pollock, Jackson, 530
Polo, Maffeo, 109
Polo, Marco, 109, 112, m113
Polo, Niccolò, 109
Ponce de León, Juan, 127–128
Ponce de León, Juan, Routes of, m129
Pontiac (chief), 275, *275*
Pontiac's Rebellion, 275–276
Poor Richard's Almanac, 222, *222*
Poor, Salem, 310

Population

Population
  of the 13 Colonies, 223, 261
  Center of, m47
  challenges of growth, 557–559
  density, 47
  diversity, 540
  region, **45**
Ports, trade. *See* Trade ports
Portsmouth, 197
Portugal, 108
Potlatches, **78**, 79
Pottery, 74–75
Powell, Colin L., 590, *590*
Power, hydroelectric, 40
Power station, 499
Powhatan, 162
Powhatan Confederacy, 162, m162, 164
Powhatan Indians, 88, 164
Powhatans' chief, m162
Prairie, 38
Preamble, **304**, 358
Predicting outcomes, 523
Prejudice, 484–485, **504**
Prescott, Samuel, 291
Preservation, environmental, 558–559
President
  advisers to, 375
  assassination of, 477, 572
  creation of office, 360–361
  duties and powers, 361
  oath of office for, 375
Presidential election
  of 1860, 452–453
  of 2000, 555
  voter turnout, 1952–2000, *555*
President's plan for Reconstruction, 477–478
Presidio, **146**, 147
Prevailing winds, 34
Primary election, **546**
Primary sources, 4–5
Primary sources analysis. *See* Analyze primary sources
Prime meridians, **50**
Prince Henry, *115*
Principle, **329**
Problem resolution, 165, 173, 213
Proclamation, **276**
  of 1763, 276
  of 1786, *348*
Profit, **115**
Progressive movement, 546
Progressives, **546**
Projectors, first, 528
Proprietary colony, **155**
Proprietor, **155**
Proprietors, Lords. *See* Lords Proprietors
Prospectors, 487
Prosperity, 162, 169–170, 200–204, 250
Ptolemy, 123
Public office, **192**
Public opinion, 302

Public services, 245
Public transportation, 557, *557*
Pueblo, **66**, 70–71, *71*
Pueblo peoples, 70–72
Pueblo, The (Yue), 70–71
Puerto Rico, 127, 571
Pulaski, Casimir, 317
Pure Food and Drug Act, 545
Puritans, **188**
  farmers, 193
  home life of, 192, *192*
  as immigrants, 189
  meetinghouse of, 191–192
  and religion, 194
  village of, 190–191
Putnam, Israel, 295
Pyramids, 108

Quaker meetinghouse, *213*
Quakers, 213, *213*, 309–310, 448
Quarter, **289**
Quebec, Canada, 151
Quetzalcoatl, 129
Quipus, 107

R

Radar, 117
Raiders, 147, 156
Railroads
  See also Transportation
  building of, 535
  fares, 545
  Transcontinental, 494–495, *494–495*, 504
  tycoons, 494
Rain shadow, **34**, 35
Raleigh, Walter, 158
Ranchers, 487–488
Ranches and haciendas, 147
Randolph, Edmund, 355, *355*, 375
Range wars, 490
Rapids, 138
Ratification of the Constitution, 366–370, m369
Ratify, **366**
Raw materials, **158**
Read, George, 354
Reading skills
  categorize, 143, **435**
  cause and effect, **267**
  compare and contrast, **55**
  draw conclusions, **383**
  fact and opinion, 240, 253, **565**
  generalization, **231**
  inference, **209**
  main idea, **17**
  point of view, 286–287, **475**
  predictions, **523**
  sequence, **301**
  summarize, **187**

supporting details, **17**
Reagan, Ronald, 583, 589
Reconquest, 121–122
Reconquista, 121–122
Reconstruction, **476**–480
Reconstruction government, 479–480, 483
Recording devices, *529*
Recycling, 558
Recycling plant, *558*
Reed, Esther, 311
Refuge, 213
Refugees, 587
Regiment, **310**
Regions, **6**
  ancient cultures, m65
  boundaries, m329
  climate, 35–37, m36
  compromises, m438, m439
  cultural region, **45**
  economic regions, **45**
  industry, m498
  land claims, m269
  landforms, 18–23, m20
  Line of Demarcation, m126
  location, m45, m89, m538
  people's activities, 45–46
  political regions, **45**
  population region, **45**
  relative location, **44**
  routes, 353
  Sun Belt, m540, 541
  territories, m440
  townships, m349
  vegetation, 37–39, m38
  during war, m323, m391, m460
  waterways, m138, m212
Regulations, 505
Related words, 515
Relative location, **44**
Religion
  of American Indians, 71–73, 106, 108, 147–149
  among slaves, 244
  Catholicism, 125, 148, 152
  Church of England, 166, 188
  freedom of
    Bill of Rights, 554
    First Amendment, 370–371
    Jewish people, 211
    in the Massachusetts Bay Colony, 194–197
    in Pennsylvania, 214–215
  Pilgrims, 166
  Puritans, 188, 191
  Toleration Act, 234
  The Great Awakening, **215**, 216–217
  ministers, 191
  Mormons, 406–407
  movement west, 404
  Protestants, 235
  Puritan church service, 191
  Quakers, 213–215, 309, 448
  Society of Friends, 213
  spirituals, **244**
  Toleration Act, 234
Renaissance, **109**, 114

Road systems

Renewable, **42**
Reno, Janet, 548
Repeal, **283**
Representation, **281**, 283, 353, 355–356
Representative government, **163**
Republic, **346**
Republic of Texas, 403
Republican party, 451–452
Research activities, 85
Reservation, **490**
Reserved powers, **372**
Resist, 445
Resolution, **303**, 305
Resolve, **91**
Resolve conflicts, 91, 93
Resource and product map, 246–247, m247
Respect, 145
Retreat, 458
Revels, Hiram R., 479
Revere, Paul, 285, 291, *292*
Revolutionary, **268**
Revolutionary War. *See* American Revolution
Rhode Island, 194, 202, 352
Rhode Island Colony, 196
Rhodes, Elisha Hunt, 430–433
Rhodes, Robert H., 430–433
Rice field, *235*
Richmond, Virginia, 460
Riedell, John, 584
Rights
  of African Americans, 484–485, 548–550
  of American Indians, 551
  Bill of Rights, **276**, 370–372, 554–555
  denial of, 280, 283
  to due process of law, **372**
  equal, 480
  to fair trial, 554
  of immigrants, 504–505
  of Mexican Americans, 550–551
  of people in foreign countries, 586–588
  to privacy, 290
  of slaves, 441
  unalienable, 372
  to vote, 395–396, 478, 480, 547–548
  of women, 447–448, 547–548
Rio Grande, 32
River branches, 30
River systems, 30–32
River traders, 76
Rivers, 30–32
Road systems
  the Alaska Highway, 567
  development of, 526, 539
  El Camino Real, 149
  Great Wagon Road, 224–225
  in Inca Empire, 107
  National Road, 412–413
  Old Spanish Trail, 404–405
  Santa Fe Trail, 404–405
  wagon, 225, 238
  Wilderness Road, 277

R76 ■ Reference

Roanoke Island, 158, *159*, 161
Rockefeller, John D., 497–498
Rocky Mountains, 19–20
Rolfe, John, 163
Roosevelt, Franklin D., 579, 586–587
Roosevelt, Theodore
　and the Panama Canal, 572–573
　President, *544*
　with Rough Riders, *571*
　in Spanish-American War, *571*
　Square Deal, the, 544–545
Root, George Frederick, 435
Rope of sand, 350
Ross, Betsey, 311
Ross, Edmund G., 479
Ross, John, 398
Rough Riders, 571, *571*
Routes
　of Cabeza de Vaca, *m*177
　of Cartier and Hudson, *m*138
　of Champlain, *m*151
　Colonial Trade, *m*202
　of conquistadors in North America, *m*129
　to the Constitutional Convention, *1787*, *m*353
　of Dias and Da Gama, *m*119
　of Drake, *m*157
　of Early People, *m*57
　of Marco Polo, *m*113
　of Marquette and Joliet and La Salle, *m*153
　of Pizarro, *m*133
　of Vespucci, Caboto, Balboa, and Magellan, *m*125
Royal colony, **152**, 164, 237
Royal governor, 164
Ruling, **398**
Runaway slaves, 445–447
Rural, 46
Russia, 576, 579
Russwurm, John, 448

S

Sacagawea, 386–387
Safety of citizens. *See* Citizens
Salem, 188
Salem, Peter, 310
Salmon, 567
Salomon, Haym, 317
Samoset, 169
Sampson, Deborah, 311
Samuel Adams at Faneuil Hall, *335*
San Carlos Borromeo del Rio, *148*
San Diego, California, 174–175, *564–565*
San Diego de Alcalá, 174–175, *174–175*
San Juan Hill, *571*
San Salvador, 102–103, 122
Sandpainting, *73*

Santa Anna, Antonio López de, 402–403
Santa Fe, New Mexico, *48*, 388
Santa Fe Trail, 131, 404
Santa María, 122
Santiago, *571*
Satellite, **528**
Saudi Arabia, 590
Savannah, 38–39
Savannah, Georgia, *237*, 250
Scalawag, **484**
Scale for map. *See* Map and globe skills
Science and Technology. *See* Technological Innovations
Scott, Dred, 440–441, *441*
Scott, Winfield, 407
Scuttled ships, *325*
Sea dogs, 156
Sea level, **21**, 24
Seal of the United States motto, 339
Seasons, 35–37, *35*
Secede, **453**
Seceding states, 453–455
Second Bank of the United States, 397
Second Continental Congress, 293–297, 303
Secondary sources, 4–5, *5*
Secret ballot, **484**
Secret societies, 484
Secretary of state, 375
Secretary of the treasury, 375
Secretary of war, 375
Sectionalism, **436**
Sedition, **196**
Segregation, **484**, 548
Selective Service Act, 577
Self-discipline, **312**
Self-government, **491**
Self-rule, 168
Self-sufficient, **147**
Semiarid climate, 36
Seminole Indians, 398
Senate, 359
Seneca Indians, 89
Separatists, 166
Sequence, **105**, **301**
Sequoias, *37*
Serbia, 576
Serpent Mound, 66
Serra, Junípero, 148, *148*, 174, *175*
Servant, indentured. *See* Indentured servant
Settlements
　See also Colonies
　British Colonies, *m*238
　Carolina Colony, 235
　Dutch, 210–213
　English, 156–164, 166–170, 188–199
　European, *m*101, *171*
　first Americans, 56–59
　French, 150–155
　Georgia Colony, 236–237
　Indian, 64–67, 70–72, 82–85, 86–90
　Maryland Colony, 240

patterns of, 46–47
of the South, 232–239
Spanish, 146–149
Swedish, 212
types of, 47–48
Virginia Colony, *m*162, 238–239
of West, 224–227, 276–277
in the western land, 348–350
Settlers Move West, 1870-1890, *m*489
Settlers' possessions, *166*
Seven Cities of Gold, 131
Seven Years War, 273
Seward, William, 443, *443*
Seward's Folly, 566
Sewing sampler, *245*
Sextant, 117
Shalom, 188
Sharecropping, **483**, *483*, 506
Shawnee Indians, 390
Shays, Daniel, 347–348
Shays's Rebellion, 347–348, *348*, 352
Sherman, Roger, 303, 352, *355*, 356
Sherman, William Tecumseh, 468–469
Shh! We're Writing the Constitution (Fritz), 342–343
Shipbuilding, 203–204, 250
Ships and boats. *See* Boats and ships
Shoshone Indians, 386–387
Shuckburgh, Richard, 263
Siege, **393**
Silent movies, 528
Silk Road, 114, *115*
Silver mines, 144, 156
Sioux Indians, 82, 491
Sioux Nation, 491
Sitting Bull, 491
Skyscrapers, 530–531, 539
Slash-and-burn, **87**
Slater, Samuel, 416
Slave, 203, 236, **437**, 445
Slavery
　See also African Americans
　abolition of, 477
　from Africa, 145, 163, 250
　during American Revolution, 310
　definition of, **66**
　disagreements over, 437–441
　division over, 437–438
　and the economy, 444–445
　and the Emancipation Proclamation, 461–463
　field slaves, 243
　freedom of, 461–462
　house slaves, 244
　identification badges, *444*
　Indians in, 144–145
　and the law, 243–244, 438–440, 445
　life of, 243
　Lincoln on, 452

Lincoln's view, 450
Nat Turner, 445
ownership of slaves, 440–441
plantation workers, 155, 236, 242–244, 245, *444*
representation in Congress, 356–357
and the royal colony, 237
runaway slaves, 445–447
slave quarters, *357*
slave trade and, 118, 202–203
in Spain, 169
and the Underground Railroad, 446–447
and westward movement, 437–438
Slavery ships, 202–203
Slocomb, Mary, 319
Smalls, Robert, 463
Smith, John, 161–162, 165, *165*, 231
Smith, Joseph, 406
Smith, William, 219
Social classes, 65–66
Social studies, definition of, 1–10
Society, importance of, 10
Society of Friends, 213, 309, 448
Sod, 82
Sod houses, 488–489, *489*
Soil, 37, 41
Sojourner Truth. *See* Van Wagener, Isabella
Soldiers
　Confederate, *459*, *511*
　German, *579*
　Union, *459*, *511*
Songhay Empire, 110–111
Sons of Liberty, 289
Soule, John B. L., 383
Sound, 28
South, settlement of, 232–239
South America, 124, 133
South Carolina
　See also Carolinas
　Charles Town, 249, *248–249*,
　Fort Sumter, 454
　and the Great Wagon Road, 225
　plantations in, 236
　secession from U.S., 453
South Dakota, 491
South Korea, 582
South Pole, 50
South region, 44
South Vietnam, 583
Southern Cities, 248–251
Southern Colonies, *m*234
Southern Hemisphere, 50
Southern ports. *See* Trade ports
Southern rebellion, 454–455
Southern Slaveholders, 1860, *445*
Southwest, 70–73
Sovereign states, 343
Soviet Union, 579, 582–583
Space shuttle, 528

Spain, 108, 121–122, 211
Spain, queen of, 147
Spanish-American War, 570–571
Spanish borderlands, 146–147, 174
Spanish conquistadors, 134–135
Spanish mine, 145
Spears, 63
Spear-thrower, 63
Specialize, 190
Speech, freedom of, 214, 371
Spinning Jenny, 416
Spirit of St. Louis, 527
Spirituals, 244
Squanto. *See* Tisquantum
Square Deal, 544–545
St. Augustine, 146
St. Lawrence River, 137
St. Louis, Missouri, 405
St. Mary's City, 233
Stalin, Joseph, 578, 586–587
Stamp Act, 281–282
Stamp Act Congress, 283–284
Stamp Act Protest, 282
Standish, Miles, 167–168
Stanton, Elizabeth Cady, 447
Staple, 71
Star-Spangled Banner, The, 392–393
State and federal government, 354–355
State authority, 436–437
State capitals, 49
State Department, 375
State House, the, 335
States, Confederate, 455
States' rights, 436
States, secession of, 453–455
Statue of Liberty National Monument, 598
Steam engines, 414–416
Steamboats, 414–416
Steel industry, 495–497
Steel Production, 1865-1900, 496
Stephens, Alexander, 453
Steuben, Friedrich von, 317
Stock, 161
Stock market, 578
Stone points, 58
Stories of the past, 58–59
Storyteller, 59
Stowe, Harriet Beecher, 448, 448
Strait of Magellan, 124, 157
Stranded at Plimoth Plantation, 1626 (Bowen), 182–185
Strategy, 459
Strawberry Banke, 197
Strike, 525
Stuyvesant, Peter, 212, 212
Subpolar climate, 35
Subtropical climate, 35–36
Suburban, 46
Suburbs, 539

Suffrage, 547–548
Suffrage march, 547
Sugar Act, 280–281
Summarize, 187, 345
Summary View of the Rights of British America, A (Jefferson), 304
Sun Belt of the United States, m540, 541
Sun god, 73
Superpower, 586
Supply, 418, 496
  See also Demand
Supporting details, 17
Supreme Court, 361–362
Surplus, 71
Sutter, John, 408
Sutter's Mill, California, 409
Swahili, 111
Symbols on maps. *See* Map and globe skills

Table activities, 171, 173
  See also Chart activities
Table comparison, 171
Taensa Indians, 154
Taino Indians, 102
Taliban government, 593
Taney, Roger B., 441
Tangier Island, 232
Tapahonso, Luci, 72
Tariff, 436
Tax collectors, 281
Taxes
  colonies and, 280–284
  points of view, 281
  Reconstruction, 483
  stamps, 281
  state, 347
Tea, 284, 288
Technological innovations
  See also Inventions
  air brake, 495
  cast-steel plow, 419
  changes in daily life, 528–529
  compact discs (CD), 529
  computers, 526
  cotton gin, 418
  digital video discs (DVD), 529
  early motion pictures, 528
  electrical vote recorder, 499
  H. L. Hunley (submarine), 466
  lightbulb, 499
  mechanical reaper, 419
  motion pictures, 528
  navigational tools, 117
  power station, 499
  steam engine, 415
  steel plow, 419
  telegraph system, 495, 498
  televisions, 529

  videocassette recorders (VCR), 529
Technology, 63, 108–109, 117, 412–413
Tecumseh, 390
Tejanos, 402
Telegraph, 495, 498
Telephone, 499
Television, 529
Ten Largest Cities in the United States, 49
Tenements, 503
Tennessee, 384, 454–455
Tenochtitlán, 106–107, 107–108, 129–130
  See also Mexico City
Tepee, 84–85, 84–85
Territory, 349, 537–538
Terrorism, 587, 592–593
Texas
  1821-1845, m425
  independence of, 402–403, m404
  Juneteenth, 482
  migration to, 49
  secession from U.S., 453
Textile mill, 417
Textiles, 416
Thayendanegea, 312
Theory, 57
Thirteen British Colonies, m238
Thirteenth Amendment, 477, 477
Thomson, David, 197
Three-fifths Compromise, 357
Tides, 27
Tidewater, 241
Timbuktu, 110
Time line activities, 338, 343, 426, 551
Time lines, 60–61, 93
Tisquantum, 169
Tobacco, 162–163, 234
Toleration Act, The, 234, 234
Tom Thumb, 414, 415–416
Tompkins, Sally, 463
Tonti, Henri de, 154
Tools, 63–64, 117
Tories. *See* Loyalists
Totem pole, 79, 79
Tourism, 538–539, 567, 569
Town meeting, 192
Towns, 487, 488, 497
Townshend Acts, 283–284, 288
Township, 218–219
Township and section lines, 349
Trade
  African, 110–111, 118, 202–203
  after American Revolution, 328
  among Indians, 76–77, 83, 88
  Asian, 109, 110, 114–115
  in the colonies, 190, 201–203, 211

  between England and colonies, 201, 241–242, 250
  European, 109–110, 114–115, 201
  global, 591
  with Indians, 147, 150
  Portuguese, 115–118
Trade ports, 248–249
Trade routes
  Cape route to India, 119
  from Europe and Asia, 109–110, 114–115, 120
  to India, 118
Trading centers, 109–111
Trading ships, 202
Traditions, 553
Trail of Tears, 398, 398–399, m398
Trails to the West, m406
Traitor, 323
Transatlantic flight, 527
Transcontinental Railroad. *See* Railroads, Transcontinental
Transportation
  See also Boats and ships; Railroads
  automobile, 524, 526
  canals, 413–414
  changes in, 539
  changing, 526–528
  in the colonies, 238
  in the East, 1850, m415
  ferryboat, 598
  locomotive, 415–416
  public, 557, 557
  railroad, 535
  segregation in, 549–550
  steamboats and railroads, 414–416
  subways, 558
  types of, 517
Travels of Marco Polo, The, 109, 112
Travis, William B., 403
Travois, 85
Treason, 282
Treasury Department, 375
Treaty, 126
  of Guadalupe Hidalgo, 407, 410
  of Paris, 275, 326–327
  of Tordesillas, 126
  of Versailles, 577
Trego, William B.T., 316
Trespassing, 388
Trial by jury, 214, 283
Triangular trade routes, 202
Tribe, 64
Tributary, 30
Tropical wet climate, 35
Truman, Harry S., 553, 581
Trumbull, John, 305, 326
Trunk Bay, Virgin Islands, 98–99
Tsosie, Michael, 73
Tubman, Harriet, 447, 447
Tundra, 37, 39
Tundra region, 37, 39

Turks, 115, 120
Turner, Nat, 445
Turning point, 316
Turtle Island, 59
Tuscalusa, 132
Twain, Mark, 30
Types of settlement, 47–48

U

Uncle Tom's Cabin, 448
Underground, 446
Underground Railroad, 446–447, m446, 447
Uniforms, 459
Union and Confederacy, The, m460
Union Fire Company, 221
Union soldiers, 511
Union soldier's uniform, 459
United Nations (UN), 586–587
United States, 1783–1853, m340–341
United States, 1900, m538
United States, 2001, m516–517
United States Air Force, 527
United States Supreme Court
  Brown v. Board of Education of Topeka, 549
  Cherokee lands, 398
  Dred Scott decision, 440–441
  public transportation, 549–550
Urban, 45
Urban League, 548
Urbanization, 539
Uses of geography, 7
USS *Arizona*, 579
USS *Constitution*, 422–423, 422–423
Utah, 72, 406–407
Utah Territory, 407

V

Valley Forge, winter in, 316–317
Valleys, 22–23
Van Wagener, Isabella, 449
Vegetation, natural, 33
Vegetation regions, 37–39, m38
Veracruz, 129
Vermont, 186–187, 384
Verrazano, Giovanni da, 136–137, 136
Vertical time lines, 60–61, 61
Vespucci, Amerigo, 123–124
Vespucci, routes of, m125
Veto, 361
Vicksburg, Mississippi, 465–466
Victory gardens, 552
Videocassette recorders (VCR), 529

Vietnam, 583
Vietnam War, 583
Viewpoints. *See* Points of view
Vikings, 106
Virgin Islands, 98–99
Virginia
  colonies in, 158, 160, 232
  and the Great Wagon Road, 225
  growth of, 238–239, 250
  and slavery, 445
  and the Civil War, 454–455, 466, 469
Virginia Colony, m162, 238–239
Virginia Company, 160–161, 166–167, 232
Virginia Declaration of Rights, 370
Virginia Gazette, 239
Virginia General Assembly, 238
Virginia House of Burgesses, 163–164, 282
Virginia Plan, 355, 356
Vocabulary skills
  compound word, 427
  context clues, 339
  multiple meanings, 259
  related words, 515
  synonyms, 179
Volcano, 23
Volunteers, 556–557, 589
Voter participation, 1824-1840, 397
Voter registration, 555
Voyages of Columbus, m122

W

Waldseemüller, Martin, 123
Walker, James (artist), 467
Waltham system, 416
Wampanoag Indians, 88, 168–169, 193, 198
Wampum, 88
Wampum belt, 214
War
  See also Battle; Conflict
  of 1812, 389–393, m391, 422
  American Revolution. *See* American Revolution
  Civil. *See* Civil War
  Cold, 582–583
  England and Holland, 211–212
  French and Indian, 268–272, 273, m274, 275, 276
  Gulf, 590
  Korean War, 582
  Mexican-American, 407, 407
  Native Americans and the colonies, 198–199
  range, 490
  Revolutionary. *See* American Revolution
  Seven Years, 273

  Spanish-American, 570–571
  against terrorism, 593
  Texas and Mexico, 402–403
  Vietnam, 583
  World War I, 552–553
  World War II, 552–553
War Department, 375
War Hawks, 390
Warhol, Andy, 530
Warren, Mercy Otis, 311
Washington, 404
Washington, Booker T., 549, 549
Washington, D.C.
  in 1833, 378
  becoming the nation's capital, 49, 378
  a closer look, 376–377
  terrorist attacks, 592–593
Washington, George
  addressing delegates, 367
  biography, 270
  farewell to public service, 327–328
  mess chest, 320–321
  military career, 269–272, 293, 314
  in military uniform, 293
  and the Philadelphia Convention, 352
  President, 374, 375
  resigning as commander in chief, 328
  surrender at Yorktown, 326
  views on government, 343, 346
Washington, Martha, 311
Washington's farewell, 327–328
Washington's mess chest, 320–321
Water Cycle, 28
Water, Major Bodies in the United States, m29
Water use, 40
Weapons
  ancient Indian civilizations, 63
  atom bomb, 581
  bayonets, 317
  bombs, 592–593
  torpedo, 466
West, Benjamin, 327
West Indies, 122
West Point, New York, 329
West region, 44
West, settlement of, 224–227, 276–277
West Virginia, 449, 496
Western Hemisphere, 51
Western lands, 348–350
Westinghouse, George, 495
Westward movement, 328, 404–409, m406, 486–491
Whale harpooning, 78
Whale oil, 201
Whaling, 78–79, 200–201
Whaling ships, 201
Whately, Thomas, 281

Wheatley, Phillis, 296
Wheeler, "Fighting Joe," 571
White House, 360, 379, 392, 396
White House fire, 392
White, John, 158–159, 159
Whitefield, George, 216
Whitman, Narcissa Prentiss, 404, 405
Whitney, Eli, 418, 418
Wichita Indians, 82
Wigwams, 88
Wilderness Road, 277
Williams, Roger, 194, 194, 196
Williamsburg, Virginia, 238–239, 254–255, 254–255
Wilmington, North Carolina, 250
Wilson, Woodrow, 523, 552, 577
Winthrop, John, 189, 189, 195
Wisconsin Territory, 441
Wolfe, James, 273
Women
  in American Revolution, 311, 319
  in Civil War, 463
  helping poor, 553
  leaders against slavery, 448–449
  leaders for equal rights, 547–548, 549–550
  leaders in health care, 463
  leaders in westward movement, 405
  political leaders, 548
  rights of, 547–548
  in World War I, 577
Woods, Granville T., 495
World in spatial terms, 7
World of 1492, The **(Highwater)**, 102–103
World Trade Center, 592–593
World War I, 552–553, 576–577, m577
World War II, 552–553, 579–581, m580–581
Wounded Knee, Battle of, 491
Wright brothers, 527
Wright, Frank Lloyd, 531, 531
Wright, Orville, 526–527
Wright, Wilbur, 526–527
Writing activities
  advertisement, 252, 507
  article, 92
  biography, 338, 399, 514
  book, 185, 258
  classroom compact, 172
  compare and contrast, 52
  compare and contrast journal, 401
  conversation, 380
  descriptive letter, 140, 172, 464, 508
  descriptive paragraph, 43, 80, 336
  dialogue, 312

diary entry, 111, 245, 297, 541
explanation, 380
folktale, 206, 508
informative letter, 512
interview, 480
journal entry, 92, 159, 176, 227, 277, 420
letter, 52, 199, 329, 372
letter giving opinions, 164
list, 135, 217, 485
list of questions, 170, 307, 472, 491
news story, 96, 140, 253, 298, 332, 357, 424
newspaper, 521
newspaper article, 193, 573
newspaper front page, 426
newspaper headline, 455
packing list for a journey, 139, 409
paragraph, 217, 239, 279
persuasive letter, 119, 298, 420
plan, 441
play, 256
poem, 39
problem-solving plan, 165
report, 449
script, 338
short story, 98
song, 228, 319, 472
speech, 90, 126, 332, 426
story, 252
travelogue, 206
"Who am I?" questions, 499
wise saying, 228
Writs of Assistance, 283
Wyoming, *16–17*, 404, 407, 491

Y

Yankee Doodle, 262–265
Yellow journalism, 570
Yellowstone National Park, *559*
Yong Le, 109–110

York, 386
Yorktown victory, 324–326
Young, Brigham, 406, *406*
Yue, Charlotte, 70
Yue, David, 70
Yugoslavia, 588
Yzquierdo, Pedro, 105

Z

Zangwill, Israel, 535
Zero degrees, 50
Zheng He, *109*, 109–110
Zuni Indians, 70, 131

For permission to reprint copyrighted material, grateful acknowledgment is made to the following sources:

Atheneum Books for Young Readers, an imprint of Simon & Schuster Children's Publishing Division: Cover illustration from *Anasazi* by Leonard Everett Fisher. Copyright © 1997 by Leonard Everett Fisher. Cover illustration by Ronald Himler from *Squish! A Wetland Walk* by Nancy Luenn. Illustration copyright © 1994 by Ronald Himler.

Candlewick Press, Inc., Cambridge, MA, on behalf of Walker Books Ltd., London: Cover illustration by Kevin Tweddell from *The History News: Explorers* by Michael Johnstone. Illustration copyright © 1997 by Walker Books Ltd.

Jane Feder, on behalf of Julie Downing: Cover illustration by Julie Downing from *If You Were There in 1492* by Barbara Brenner. Illustration copyright © 1991 by Julie Downing.

Harcourt, Inc.: "If We Should Travel" from *Between Earth & Sky* by Joseph Bruchac. Text copyright © 1986 by Joseph Bruchac.

HarperCollins Publishers: Cover illustration by James Watling from *Finding Providence: The Story of Roger Williams* by Avi. Illustration copyright © 1997 by James Watling. From *Stranded at Plimoth Plantation 1626* by Gary Bowen. Copyright © 1994 by Gary Bowen. Cover illustration by Stephen Fieser from *The Silk Route: 7,000 Miles of History* by John S. Major. Illustration copyright © 1995 by Stephen Fieser. Cover illustration by Bert Dodson from *American Adventures: Thomas* by Bonnie Pryor. Illustration copyright © 1998 by Bert Dodson.

Holiday House, Inc.: Cover illustration by Peter Fiore from *The Boston Tea Party* by Steven Kroll. Illustration copyright 1998 by Peter Fiore.

Henry Holt and Company, LLC: From "San Salvador" by Jamake Highwater in *The World in 1492* by Jean Fritz, Katherine Paterson, Patricia and Fredrick McKissack, Margaret Mahy, and Jamake Highwater, cover illustration by Stefano Vitale. Text copyright © 1992 by The Native Land Foundation; cover illustration copyright © 1992 by Stefano Vitale.

Scholastic Inc.: Cover illustration by Mark Summers from *James Printer: A Novel of Rebellion* by Paul Samuel Jacobs. Illustration copyright © 1997 by Mark Summers. Published by Scholastic Press, a division of Scholastic Inc.

Simon & Schuster Books for Young Readers, an imprint of Simon & Schuster Children's Publishing Division: Cover illustration from *The Story of William Penn* by Aliki. Copyright © 1964 by Aliki Brandenberg; copyright renewed © 1992 by Aliki Brandenberg.

ILLUSTRATION CREDITS

Pages A18-A19, Studio Liddell; 12-13, Angus McBride; 13, Steve Weston; 14-15, Leland Klanderman; 28, 34, 35, Sebastian Quigley; 56-57, Tom McNeely; 62-63, Dennis Lyall; 71, Luigi Galante; 77, Inklink; 96-97, Angus McBride; 100-101, Uldis Klavins; 102-103, Dave Hendersch; 107, Steve Weston; 106-107, Studio Liddell; 116-117, Dennis Lyall; 160-161, Mike Lamble; 167, Bill Smith Studio; 176-177, Uldis Klavins; 180-181, Andrew Wheatcroft; 182-185, Nina Martin; 190-191, George Gaadt; 220, 226-227, Yuan Lee; 256-257, Andrew Wheatcroft; 260-261, George Gaadt; 308-309, Vincent Wakerley; 324, Dennis Lyall; 324-325, Sebastian Quigley; 325 Dennis Lyall; 336-337, George Gaadt; 340-341, Gino D'Achille; 355, Vincent Wakerley; 376-377, Chuck Carter; 393, Bill Smith Studio; 412-413, Don Foley; 424-425, Gino D'Achille; 428-429, Cliff Spohn; 430-433, George Gaadt; 454-455, Luigi Galante; 468, Bill Smith Studio; 494-495, Dennis Lyall; 512-513, Cliff Spohn; 516-517, Bill Maughan; 524-525, Chuck Carter; 529, Chuck Carter; 556, Bill Smith Studio; 600-601, Bill Maughan.

All maps by MapQuest.com

PHOTO CREDITS

Cover: Rick Friedman (statue); Mark Sherman/Photo Network (Declaration of Independence); David Stover/Stock South/PictureQuest (soldiers); Pat & Chuck Blackley (powwow).

PLACEMENT KEY: (t) top; (b) bottom; (l) left; (r) right; (c) center; (bg) background; (fg) foreground; (I) inset.

POSTER INSERT

Flag: Don Mason/Corbis Stock Market, Eagle: Minden Pictures

TITLE PAGE AND TABLE OF CONTENTS

(fg) James Lemass; (bg) Doug Armand/Stone; iv, The Detroit Institute of Arts; v, National Maritime Museum Picture Library; vi, Historical Society of Pennsylvania, Silver Gorget, ©1757 Artist: Joseph Richardson, Sr., S-8-120; vii, Lester Lefkowitz/Corbis Stock Market; viii, Independence National Historical Park; ix, Smithsonian Institution; x, NASA.

INTRODUCTION

1(t) James Lemass, (l) Doug Armand/Stone;2 (t) Bob Daemmrich/Stock, Boston/PictureQuest; 2 (b) ChromoSohm/Sohm/Visions of America; 3 (t) Christie Parker/Houserstock, Inc.; 3 (b) Underwood & Underwood/Corbis; 4 National Park Service; 4 National Park Service; 4 National Park Service; 5 (br) John McGrail; 5 (tl) The Granger Collection, New York; 5 (i) National Park Service; 7 (tl) Mattew Borkoski/Stock, Boston Inc./PictureQuest; 7 (tr) Andre Jenny/Focus Group/PictureQuest; 7 (cl) Peter Pearson/Stone; 7 (cr) Jeffrey Muir Hamilton/Stock, Boston Inc./PictureQuest; 7 (bl) Robert Hildebrand; 7 (br) David Young-Wolff/PhotoEdit/PictureQuest; 8 (l) Jeff Lepore/Panoramic Images; 8 (r) David Young-Wolff/PhotoEdit; 9 (bl) Joseph Sohm/Stock, Boston Inc./PictureQuest; 9 (br) Bill Bachman/PhotoEdit; 10 (t) David Young-Wolff/PhotoEdit/PictureQuest; 10 (b) Calumet Regional Archives, Indiana University Northwest.

UNIT 1

Unit Opener; (fg) The Detroit Institute of Arts; (bg) Tom & Susan Bean, Inc.; 11 (t) The Detroit Institute of Arts; (l) Tom & Susan Bean, Inc; 16-17 Robert Hildebrand Photography; 18-19 (b) Russ Finley; 19 (t) David Muench/Corbis; 21 (b) Dave G. Houser; 22 (b) Marc Muench/David Muench Photography, Inc.; 23 (t) David Muench 26 (b) Stocktrek/Corbis Stock Market; 30 (t) Greg Ryan/Sally Beyer/Positive Reflections; 30 (i) Bettmann/Corbis; 31 (br) Stock Barrow; 32 (t) David Muench; 33 (b) Mark E. Gibson Photography; 37 California Stock Photography; 39 Tom & Susan Bean; 40 Ted Streshinsky/Corbis; 41 Mark E. Gibson Photography; 43 (t) Charles Gupton/Corbis Stock Market; 44 Henry T. Kaiser/Stock Connection/PictureQuest; 46-47 (b) Mark E. Gibson Photography; 48 Place Stock Photo; 54-55 David Muench Photography; 58 (b) John Maier, Jr./JB Pictures; 58 (i) Mercyhurst Archaeological Institute; 59 Lawrence Migdale; 63 (t) Courtesy of Arizona State Museum, AZ/Jerry Jacka Photography; 64 (tl) Harald Sund/The Image Bank; 64 (tr) Zion National Park; 65 (br) Werner Forman/Art Resource; 66-67 (t) Michael Hampshire/Cahokia Mounds Historic Site; 67 (tr) Richard A. Cooke/Corbis; 68 American Hurrah; 70 Place Stock Photo; 72-73 (b) James Cowlin/Adstock; 72 (i) Monty Roessel; 73 (t) Fifth Generation Traders, Farmington, N.M./Jerry Jacka Photography; 74 (t) Stephen Trimble; 74 (b) Smithsonian Institution; 75 (t) Aldo Tutino/ Art Resource, NY; 75 (c) John Bigelow Taylor/Art Resource, NY; 75 (b) Gift of Clark Field, The Philbrook Museum of Art, Tulsa, Oklahoma. Photo by Don Wheeler; 76 (b) Canadian Museum of Civilization; 77 (t) Mark E. Gibson; 79 (b) Kevin Fleming/Corbis; 79 (i) The Heard Museum, phoenix, AR./Jerry Jacka Photography; 80 (t) Michael Evan Sewell/Peter Arnold, Inc.; 81 (b) Smithsonian American Art Museum, Gift of Mrs. Joseph Harrison, Jr./Art Resource; 82 (b) Tom & Susan Bean; 82 (inset, l)) Mandan Dress, 1805; Peabody Museum, Harvard; 82 (inset, r) R. Webber/The Bata Shoe Museum; 83 (l) Gift of Enron Art Foundation/Joslyn Art Museum, Omaha, NE; 84 (t) Museum of South Dakota State Historical Society; 84-85 (b) Thomas Gilcrease Museum, Tulsa; 86 (b) Robert Hildebrand Photography; 87 (tl) National Museum of the American Indian/Smithsonian Institution; 87 (tr) New York State Museu; 88 (bl) Granger; 88 (br) Ashmolean Museum, Oxford; 90 (t) Computer generated image of trim longhouses of bent sapling frames covered with bark, used courtesy of Pathways Productions, Inc. All rights reserved. Copyright 1994; 91 (b) Cranbrook Institute of Science; 94 (c) Jerry Jacka Photography; 94-95 (bg) Jerry Jacka Photography; 95 (bl) Russ Finley/Finley-Holiday Film Corp.; 95 (tl) Russ Finley/Finley-Holiday Film Corp.; 95 (tr) Tom Bean/Corbis; 95 (br) Bob Rowan, Progressive Image/Corbis.

UNIT 2

Unit Opener; (fg) National Maritime Museum Picture Library; (bg) Superstock; 99 (t) National Maritime Museum Picture Library; (l) Superstock; 104-105 Heather R. Davidson; 109 (b) The Art Archive/Eileen Tweedy; 109 (i) China Stock Photo Library; 110 (t) The Art Archive; 110 (bc) Werner Forman Archive/Tanzania National Museum, Dares Salaam/Art Resource; 111 (t) Gift of Mrs. Walter B. Ford/Detroit Institute of Arts; 112 (bl) Giraudon/Art Resource; 112 (bc) Erich Lessing Culture and Fine Arts Archives/Art Resource; 113 (b) Genius of China Expedition/The Art Archive; 114 (bc) Werner Forman Archive/Art Resource; 114 (i) The Art Archive; 114 (bg) Genius of Chinese Expedition/The Art Archive; 115 (t) Michael Yamashita; 115 (b) Bibliotheque Nationale, Paris;

117 (b) National Maritime Museum; 118 The Bridgeman Art Library International, Ltd.; 121 Museo Navale de Pegli, Genoa; 123 (b) Kevin Fleming/Corbis; 124 (bc) The Art Archive; 127 (b) Timothy O'Keefe/PictureQuest; 128 (b) American Museum of Natural History; 128 (tc) National Museum of Anthropology, Mexico City/Werner Forman Archive/Art Resource; 130 (tc) John Bigelow Taylor/Art Resource; 131 (b) Hulton Archive; 132 (t) Private Collection/The Bridgeman Art Library; 132 (br) The Granger Collection; 132 (i) Jeffery M. Mitchem; 134 (t) Giraudon/Art Resource, NY; 134 (bl) Don Eaton/Higgins Armory Museum; 134 (br) Don Eaton/Higgins Armory Museum; 135 Royal Armouries; 136 (b) Culver Pictures; 136 (i) Bettmann/Corbis; 137 (b) National Archives of Canada; 137 (i) Virtual Museum of New France; 139 Tate Gallery, London/Art Resource, NY; 142-143 Robert Frerck/Odyssey/Chicago; 144 (bc) Jeffrey L. Rotman/Corbis; 145 (tl) Courtesy of the Hispanic Society of America, New York; 145 (tr) Archivo Fotographico Seville; 146 (c) Victor Boswell/National Geographic Society; 146-147 (b) Morton Kunstler/National Geographic Image Collection; 148 (b) Lowell Georgia/Corbis; 148 (i) The Santa Barbara Mission; 150 (b) Head of Pechaunigum (Rabbit) Rapids Nipigon River, Lake Superior by William Armstrong 1911/Public Archives of Canada C-114494; 150 (i) Minnesota Historical Society; 152 (t) James Swedberg/The Adirondack Museum; 152 (b) National Gallery of Art, Washington D.C.; 154 Texas Department of Transportation; 155 (c) Bob Daemmrich/Stock, Boston; 156 (b) The Art Archive; 157 (bc) Jean-Leon Huens/NGS Image Collection; 158 (b) The Bridgeman Art Library International, Ltd.; 159 (t) The Granger Collection, New York; 162 (t) Crandall Shifflett; 162 (b) National Portrait Gallery, Smithsonian Institute/Art Resource; 163 (b) The Association for the Preservation of Virginia Antiquities; 164 (t) Gianni Dagli Orti/Corbis; 165 (b) The Granger Collection, New York; 166 (b) Courtesy of The Pilgrim Society, Plymouth, Massachusetts; 166 (b) Walter Meayers Edsards/National Geographic Image Collection; 167 (cl) Bettmann/Corbis; 168-169 (b) Kevin Fleming/Corbis; 169 (c) Cary Wolinsky/Stock, Boston/PictureQuest; 169 (r,inset) Catherine Karnow/Corbis; 169 (b,inset) Lee Snider/Corbis; 170 Hulton Archive/Getty Images; 174-175 (bg) David Olsen/Stone; 174 (i) Richard Cummins/Corbis; 175 (t) James L. Amos/Corbis; 175 (c, inset) Lowell Georgia/Corbis; 175 (bl) John ElkIII/Stock, Boston.

UNIT 3

Unit Opener; (fg) Historical Society of Pennsylvania, Silver Gorget, c. 1757 Artist: Joseph Richardson, Sr., S-8-120; (bg) John McGrail Photography; 179 (t) Historical Society of Pennsylvania, Silver Gorget, c. 1757 Artist: Joseph Richardson, Sr., S-8-120; (r) John McGrail Photography; 186-187 Henryk Kaiser/Leo De Wys, Inc.; 188 The Commonwealth of Massachusetts, Archives Division; 189 Bettmann/Corbis; 192 Todd Gipstein/National Geographic Society; 193 Collection of the New-York Historical Society; 194 (bl) Architect of the Capitol; 194 (br) The Granger Collection; 195 The Granger Collection; 196 (t) Burstein Collection/Corbis; 196 (b) Old State House, Hartford, CT; 198 (t) © Shelbourne Museum, Shelbourne, Vermont; 198 (c) Fruitlands Museums; 198-199 (b) Phil Schermeister/Corbis; 199 (t) Smithsonian Institution, Domestic Life Division, Neg. #LIA-83-30016-9; 200 Smithsonian; 201 Kendall Whaling Museum; 202 (t) Peabody Essex Museum, Salem, MA. Photo by Mark Sexton; 203 Claire White-Peterson Photo/Mystic Seaport, Mystic, CT; 204 Photo Courtesy of Marblehead Historical Society, Marblehead, MA; 208-209 H. Mark Weidman; 210-211 (b) Museum of the City of New York; 212 Hulton Archive; 213 (tl) Haverford College Library Quaker Collection; 213 (tr) The Newark Museum/Art Resource, NY; 214 Francis G. Mayer/Corbis; 215 Mary Steinbacher/PhotoEdit; 216 (t) American tract Society; 216 (b) Library of Congress; 217 (tl) Library of Congress; 217 (tc) Princeton University, gift of the Reverend R.J. Nevin, in 1904; 217 (bc) Princeton University. Presented in 1860 by the great grandsons of President Edwards: Photo Credit: Bruce M. White; 217 (br) Library of Congress; 218 (b) Independence National Historical Park; 219 (bl) Historical Society of Pennsylvania; 220 (tl) Stock Montage; 220 (i) The Provost and Fellows of Worcester College Oxford; 220 (i) The Provost and Fellows of Worcester College Oxford; 221 (tr) Courtesy Henry Francis du Pont Winterthur Museum, Joseph Downs Manuscript Collection, NO. 62x33; 221 (i) CIGNA Museum and Art Collection; 222 (t) Gettysburg College; 222 (i) Bettmann/Corbis; 224 Jeff Greenberg/Photo Researchers; 230-231 Tyler Campbell/Mira; 232 Bettmann/Corbis; 233 (t) Courtesy of Historic St. Mary's City; 234 Maryland State Archives; 235 (b) North Wind Picture Archives; 235 (i) PhotoEdit; 236 (t) Alan & Linda Detrick/Photo Researchers; 237 (t) Hulton Archive; 237 (b) Archives and History Center of the United Methodist Church, Madison, New Jersey; 239 Scott Barrow; 240 Gift of Mrs. Robert Bogle/Maryland Historical Society; 241 (bl) Collection of Tender Buttons/BlackStar; 241 (bc) Collection of Tender Buttons/Black Star; 241 (br) Historical Society of Pennsylvania; 244 (tl) EX17082 Negro portrait: Olaudah Equiano by English School, (18th Century) Royal Albert Memorial Museum, Exeter/Bridgeman Art Library, London; 244 (i) Crandall Shifflett; 245 Peabody Essex Museum; 246 (b) Lee Snider/Corbis; 247 (c) PhotoEdit; 247 (b) John Mead/Science Photo Library/Photo Researchers; 248-249 (b) Colonial Williamsburg Foundation; 250 (b) Dorothy Mills (English), George II saucboat, 1748, Silver, 4 3/4 x 5 1/4 x 3 7/8 in., The National Museum of Women in the Arts, Silver collection assembled by Nancy Valentine, purchased with funds; 250-251 (t) Maryland Historical Society; 254-255 (bg) Colonial Williamsburg Foundation; 254-255 (c) Dave G. Houser/Houserstock; 254 (b) Mary Ann Hemphill; 255 (c) David Hiser/PictureQuest; 255 (cr) Colonial Williamsburg; 255 (bl) Mary Ann Hemphill.

UNIT 4

Unit Opener; (fg) Lester Lefkowitz/Corbis Stock Market; (bg) John McGrail Photography; 259 (t) Lester Lefkowitz/Corbis Stock Market; (l) John McGrail Photography; 266-267 Joanne Pearson/Fair Haven Photographs; 268-269 Larry Olsen Photography; 270 (t) Washington-Custis-Lee Collection, Washington and Lee University, Lexington, Va.; 270 (b) Historical Society of Pennsylvania/Bridgeman Art Library International, Ltd., The; 271 (b) The Granger Collection, New York; 272 (tl) State Historical Society of Wisconsin Museum Collections; 272 (tr) The Granger Collection; 273 (b) Phil E. Degginger/Mira; 273 (i) Hulton/Archive; 275 (bl) Hulton Archive/Getty Images; 275 (i) Fort Wayne Historical; 276 Hulton/Archive; 277 George Calieb Bingham, Daniel Boone Escorting Settlers Through The Cumberland Gap, 1851-52, detail. Oil on canvas, 35 1/2 x 50 1/4. Washington University Gallery of Art, St. Louis; 280 (bl) Bettman Archive/Corbis; 280 (bc) Collection of the Boston Athenaeum; 280 (br) Larry Stevens/Nawrocki Stock Photo, Inc. All Rights Reserved; 280 (bl) Smithsonian Institution; 281 (br) Massachusetts Historical Society; 282 (t) Colonial Williamsburg Foundation; 282 (b) The Metropolitan Museum of Art, Bequest of Charles Allen Munn, 1924; 284 (b) Courtesy of the Massachusetts Historical Society; 285 (tr) The Granger Collection, New York; 285 (i) Stock Montage; 286 The Granger Collection; 287 Hulton/Archive; 288 Bettman/Archive/Corbis; 289 (t) Deposited by the City of Boston. Courtesy of The Museum of Fine Arts, Boston; 289 (bc) American Antiquarian Society; 290 (c) NYPL; 290 (b) The Carnegie Institute/Bridgeman Art Library International, Ltd.; 291 (t) Concord Museum, Concord MA; 291 (b) Stanley L. Rowin/Mira; 292 (tl) Eliot Cohen/Janelco Photographers; 293 (b) Yale University Art Gallery, Gift of the Associates in Fine Arts and Mrs. Henry B. Loomis in Memory of Henry B. Loomis, B.A. 1875.; 296 (t) Courtesy of the Massachusetts Historical Society; 297 (c) Peabody Essex Museum, Salem, MA. Photo by Mark Sexton; 297 (tr) Jamestown-Yorktown Foundation; 300-301 Morristown National Park; 302 (bc) Hulton/Archive; 302 The Granger Collection; 303 (b) Smithsonian Institution; 303 (tr) Independence National Historical Park; 305 Francis G. Mayer/Corbis; 306 (br) Lee Snider Photo Images; 306 (bkgd) Scott Barrow; 307 Historical Society of Pennsylvania; 308 (bl) Courtesy of the Massachusetts Historical Society; 309 (br) Martin Art Gallery, Muhlenberg College, Allentown, Pennsylvania; 310 (b) Valentine Museum, Richmond History Center; 310 (i) Tracey W. McGregor Library/University of Virginia; 311 (tl) Bequest of Winslow Warren/Courtesy, Museum of Fine Arts, Boston; 311 (tr) Bettmann/Corbis; 311 (tlc) Detroit Publishing Co. Photograph Collection/Library of Congress; 311 (trc) Richard Walker/New York Historical Association, Cooperstown; 312 Independence National Historical Park; 314 (br) Eliot Cohen/Janelco Photographers; 314 (bl) Russ Finley; 315 (t) Fort Ticonderoga Museum; 315 (bl) Russ Finley; 315 (i) The Granger Collection; 316 (t) The Valley Forge Historical Society; 317 (t) Bettmann/Corbis; 317 (b) Jewish-American Hall of Fame; 318 (b) Bettmann/Corbis; 318 (tl) Hulton/Archive Photos; 318 (tc) Hulton/Archive Photos; 318 (tr) Independence National Historical Park Collection; 319 Edifice/Corbis; 320-321 American Museum of American History/Smithsonian Institution. Trans. no. 76-3259; 322 (b) David Muench Photography; 325 (br) Roy Andersen/National Geographic Society; 326 (b) Yorktown Victory Center; 326 t a detail, John Trumbull "The Surrender of Lord Cornwallis at Yorktown, 19 October 1781", Yale University Art Gallery, Trumbull Collection; 327 (b) Courtesy, Winterthur Museum; 328 (t) Hulton/Archive Photos; 330 (b) Royal Geographical Society, London/The Bridgeman Art Library International; 330 (i) American Antiquarian Society; 334 (t) Peter Southwick/Stock, Boston; 334 (bc) Michael Dwyer/Stock Boston; 334 (bg) Gibson Stock

Photography; 335 (br) Danilo G. donadoni/ Bruce Coleman; 335 (tr) Tibor Bognar/Corbis Stock Market; 335 (tc) Susan Cole Kelly; 335 (cl) Dave G. Houser/Corbis; 335 (tl) Ed Young/Corbis; 335 (bl) Richard Cummins/Corbis; 335 (cr) Dave G. Houser/Corbis.

UNIT 5

Unit Opener; (fg) Independence National Historical Park; (bg) Independence National Historical Park; 339 (t) Independence National Historical Park; (l) Independence National Historical Park; 344-345 Johnathan Wallen Photography; 346 Roman Soumar/Corbis; 347 (tc) From the Robert H. Gore Jr. Numismatic Collection; 347 (tr) American Antiquarian Society; 348 (bl) The Granger Collection; 348 (br) The New-York Historical Society; 350 Library of Congress; 351 (bl) The Granger Collection; 351 (br) The Granger Collection; 352 Bettmann/Corbis; 355 (tl) The Library of Virginia; 355 (tc) Ralph Earl Roger Sherman (1721-1793) M. G. (Hon.) 1786 Yale University Art Gallery/Gift of Roger Sherman White, BA. 1899, L. L. B. 1902; 355 (tr) Princeton University; 356 Emmet Collection, Rare Books and Manuscripts Division, The New York Public Library, Astor, Lennox, and Tilden Foundations; 357 (t) 'Residences and Slave Quarters of Mulberry; Plantation' by Thomas Coram, The Gibbes Museum of Art, Charleston, SC; 358 (b) Joseph Sohm/Stock, Boston/PictureQuest; 358 (i) Northwind Picture Archives; 359 O and J Heaton/Stock, Boston; 360 (b) Dave G. Houser/Houserstock, Inc.; 361 Lee Snider Photo Images; 362 (bl) Dennis Brack/Black Star Publishing/PictureQuest; 362 (br) Richard W. Strauss/Smithsonian Institute/Supreme Court Historical Society; 363 Independence National Historical Park, Phil; 365 (l) James Foote/Photo Researchers; 365 (cr) James Foote/Photo Researchers; 366 Independence National Historical Park; 367 Virginia Museum of Fine Arts, Richmond. Gift of Edgar William and Bernice Chrysler Garbisich. Photo: Ron Jennings@Virginia Museum of Fine Arts.; 368 (bl) New York Historical/The Bridgeman Art Library International; 368 (br) Colonial Williamsburg Foundation; 370 National Archives and Records Administration; 371 (c) Culver Pictures; 371 (bl) Franklin Institute; 371 (br) The Granger Collection, New York; 372 Dover Publications; 373 (b) Courtesy, Winterthur Museum; 374 (b) LM Cooks Salute to General Washington in NY Harbor, Gift of Edgar Williams & Bernice Chrysler Garbisch Board of Trustees/National Gallery of Art, Washington; 374 (i) Museum of the City of New York, Bequest of Mrs. J. Insley Blair in Memory of Mr. and Mrs. J. Insley Blair; 375 Courtesy of the John Carter Brown Library at Brown University; 376 (b) Maryland Historical Society; 378 White House Historical Assoc.; 379 The New-York Historical Society; 382-383 David Muench Photography; 384 C. Jean/Reunion des Musees Nationaux/Art Resource, NY; 386 (t) National Park Service; 386-387 (b) Amon Carter Museum; 386 (bl) Courtesy Independence National Historical Park; 387 (br) Courtesy Independence National Historical Park; 389 Bettmann/Corbis; 390 Bettmann/Corbis; 392 (t) Library of Congress; 392 (b) Collection of the New York Historical Society; 393 (b) Corbis; 394 Bettmann/Corbis; 395 (b) Burstein Collection/Corbis; 395 (i) Lawrence County Historical Society; 396 (t) The Granger Collection, NY; 396 (b) Library of Congress; 397 Collection of The New York Historical Society; 399 Troy Anderson; 400 (bl) National Portrait Gallery/Smithsonian Institution/Art Resource, NY; 400 (br) Academy of Natural Sciences of Philadelphia/Corbis; 401 (t) Academy of Natural Sciences of Philadelphia/Corbis; 401 (c) North Carolina Museum; 401 (br) Academy of Natural Sciences of Philadelphia/Corbis; 401 (cl) Academy of Natural Sciences of Philadelphia/Corbis, Inc.; 402 The State Preservation Board, Austin Texas; 403 (b) Friends of the Governor's Mansion, Austin, Texas; 404 H. K. Barnett/Star of the Republic Museum, Jefferson, Texas; 405 (t) The Saint Louis Art Museum; 405 Whitman Mission National Historic Society; 406 Bettmann/Corbis; 407 The Granger Collection; 408 Smithsonian American Art Museum, Washington DC/Art Resource, NY; 409 Gill C. Kenny/The Image Bank; 410 National Archives; 412 Russ Poole Photography; 414 (t) Cooper Hewitt Museum; 414 B & O Railroad Museum; 418 (tl) Art Resource, NY; 418 (bl) Bettmann/Corbis; 419 (tr) Courtesy of the John Deere Company; 419 (i) John Deere.

UNIT 6

Unit Opener; (fg) Smithsonian Institution; (bg) Peter Gridley/FPG International; 427 (t) Smithsonian Institution; (l) Peter Gridley/FPG International; 430 All for the Union; 434-435 David Muench Photography; 436 The American Clock and Watch Museum; 437 Stock Montage/Hulton Archive/Getty Images; 438 Bettmann/Corbis; 441 Missouri Historical Society; 442 (bl) Courtesy of the South Carolina Library; 442 (br) Courtesy of the South Carolina Library; 443 (br) Hulton-Deutsch Collection/Corbis; 443 (br) Bettmann/Corbis; 444 (br) Scala/Art Resource, NY; 444 (cl) The Charleston Museum; 446 Library of Congress; 447 (t) Hulton/Archive Photos; 447 (b) National Museum of American Art, Washington DC/Art Resource, NY; 448 (bl) National Portrait Gallery, Smithsonian Institution/Art Resource, NY; 448 (i) Book cover slide of "Uncle Tom's Cabin" by Harriet Beecher Stowe. Courtesy of the Charles L. Blockson Afro-American Collection, Temple University; 449 (t) National Portrait Gallery, Smithsonian Institution/Art Resource, NY; 450 (b) Morton Beebe, S.F./Corbis; 451 Courtesy of the Illinois State Historical Library; 452 (bl) National Portrait Gallery, Smithsonian Institution/Art Resource, NY; 452 (bc) Corbis; 453 (t) National Portrait Gallery, Smithsonian Institution/Art Resource, NY; 453 (b) The Granger Collection; 458 (b) Brown Military Collection, Brown University; 458 (bl) National Portrait Gallery, Smithsonian Institution/Art Resource, NY; 460 James P. Rowan Photography; 461 Library of Congress; 462 (t) National Portrait Gallery; 462 (b) Library of Congress; 463 (b) Bettmann/Corbis; 464 Chicago Historical Society; 465 (bc) Salamander Books; 465 (br) National Portrait Gallery, Smithsonian Institution, Washington, D.C.; 466 (t) Courtesy of General Dynamics Corp., Electric Boat Div.; 466 (cl) Richmond, Virginia/Katherine Wetzel; 467 (b) New Hampshire Historical Society; 469 (b) Tom Lovell©National Geographic; 471 Tom Prettyman/PhotoEdit/PictureQuest; 476 (bl) Corbis; 476 (bc) Library of Congress; 477 (t) Hulton Archive/Getty Images; 477 (i) Library of Congress; 478 Corbis; 479 (c) Library of Congress; 479 (tl) The Granger Collection, New York; 480 (tl) American Treasures of the Library of Congress; 480 (tr) Library of Congress; 481 (bl) Corbis; 481 (br) Southern Historical Collection; 482 (br) Bob Daemmrich Photography; 482 (cl) Bob Daemmrich Photography; 483 (t) The Metropolitan Museum of Art, Morris K. Jessup Fund; 483 (i) Smithsonian Institution, Division of Agriculture; 484 (t) Hulton/Archive/Getty Images; 484 (b) Smithsonian Institute; 485 The Granger Collection; 486 (i) The Bancroft Library; 486-487 Joseph Sohm/Visions of America/PictureQuest; 488 (b) Jeff Greenberg/PhotoEdit; 488 (tc) William Manns Photo/Zon International Publishing; 489 Solomon D. Butcher Collection, Nebraska State Historical Society; 490 Corbis; 491 Corbis; 492 Michael Forsberg; 496 Corbis; 497 Corbis; 499 From the Collections of Henry Ford Museum & Greenfield Village; 500 (t) Transfer from the National Museum of American Art; Gift of Dr. Eleanor A. Campbell to the Smithsonian Institution, 1942.; 500 (bl) Henry Ford Museum & Greenfield Village; 500 (br) Henry Ford Museum & Greenfield Village; 501 (t) Henry Ford Museum & Greenfield Village; 501 (c) Science Museum, London, UK/The Bridgeman Art Library International; 501 (br) Alfred Harrell/Smithsonian Institution; 502 (i) "By Courtesy of the Statue of Liberty National Monument"; 503 (tl) Corbis; 504-505 (b) Corbis; 505 (t) Corbis; 506 The Phillips Collection, Washington, DC; 507 (t) Corbis; 510 (c) Andre Jenny/Focus Group/PictureQuest; 510 (b) Thomas R. Fletcher/Stock, Boston; 510-511 (bg) Thomas R. Fletcher/Stock, Boston; 511 (tl) Mark E. Gibson; 511 (tl) Michael DiBella/Words & Pictures/PictureQuest; 511 (br) Andre Jenny/Focus Group/PictureQuest.

UNIT 7

Unit Opener; (fg) NASA; (bg) Superstock; 522-523 Joseph Melanson/Mira; 525 (t) Schenectady Musuem/Hall of Electrical History Foundation/Corbis; 527 (t) Hulton/Archive; 527 (b) Bettmann/Corbis; 528 (t) Ralph Morse/TimePix; 528 (b) Corbis; 529 (b) Curtis Meyers/Stock Connection/PictureQuest; 530 (b) Eliot Elisofon/TimePix; 531 (bg) Peter Menzel/Stock, Boston/PictureQuest; 531 (inset) Bettmann/Corbis; 532 (b) David R. Frazier; 534-535 (b) Paul Thompson/International Stock; 535 (t) Harcourt; 536 (t) The Institute of Texan Cultures, San Antonio, Texas; 536 (b) Chuck Pefley/Stock, Boston; 537 (tl) Library of Congress; 537 (tr) Don Stevenson/Index Stock Imagery/PictureQuest; 539 (t) Rick Fried/Black Star; 539 (b) Tomas Barbudo/Panoramic Images; 541 (t) The Image Bank; 544 (b) Corbis; 546 (t) Hulton/Archive; 547 (t) National Portrait Gallery; 547 (b) Bettmann/Corbis; 548 (l) Brown Brothers; 549 (b) AP/Wide World Photos; 549 (tl) Bettmann/Corbis; 549 (tr) Corbis; 550 (b) Robert W. Kelley/TImePix; 551 (t) Bettmann/Corbis; 552 (b) Bettmann/Corbis; 552 (inset) Minnesota Historical Society/Corbis; 553 (t) Harcourt; 553 (b) Joanne Pearson/Fair Haven Photographs; 554 (bl) Win McNamee/Reuters/TimePix; 554 (br) David R. Frazier; 554 (bg) Bettmann/Corbis; 555 (b) Reuters NewMedia/Corbis; 556 (b) Nancy Richmond/The Image Works; 557 (b) John Elk III; 557 (inset) MARTA; 558 (bl) Tony Freeman/PhotoEdit/PictureQuest; 558 (br) Jim West/Impact Visuals; 559 Jeff Henry/Roche Jaune Pictures; 560 (b) Stone/Getty Images; 564-565 Joseph Melanson/ Mira; 566 (b) Bettmann/Corbis; 566 (inset) Bettmann/Corbis;

567 (t) Alaska Stock Images; 567 (b) Randy Wells; 568 (t) Michael Maslan Historic Photographs/Corbis; 568 (b) Carl Shaneff/Pacific Stock; 569 (t) Greg Vaughn/Tom Stack & Asso.; 569 (b) Bettmann/Corbis; 571 (t) Michael Freeman/Corbis; 571 (b) Hulton/Archive; 573 (t) Superstock; 576 (b) Bettmann/Corbis; 578 (b) Hulton/Archive; 579 (t) Bettmann/ Corbis; 579 (b) Hulton/Archive; 579 (inset) Henry Groskinsky/TimePix; 580 (b) Corbis; 582 (b) Hulton / Archive; 583 (c) AP/Wide World Photos; 586 (b) Hulton-Deutsch Collection/Corbis; 587 (t) Leif Skoogfors/Corbis; 587 (b) Henryk Kaiser/Leo de Wys; National Archives; 589 (tr) Anders Pettersson/Black Star; 590 (t) Dennis Brack/Black Star/TimePix; 590 (ri) Wally McNamee/Corbis; 590 (li) Terry Ashe/TimePix; 591 (t) AFP/Corbis; 591 (b) Tom Wagner/SABA/Corbis; 592 (t) AP Archive; 592 (b) Fabian Falcon/Stock, Boston; 593 (t) Steve Liss/TimePix; 593 (inset) APPhoto RON EDMONDS; 594 (b) Chip Henderson/Stone; 595 (t) AP Photo/Chris Gardner; 598 (inset),(br Todd Gipstein/Corbis; 598-599 Gail Mooney/Corbis; 599 (tl) United States Department of the Interior, National Park Service; 599 (tr) United States Department of the Interior, National Park Service; 599 (bl) Gail Mooney/Corbis.

REFERENCE

R8-R10, All Presidential Portraits courtesy of National Portrait Gallery except page R10, (br) The Image Works.

All other photos from Harcourt School Photo Library and Photographers: Weronica Ankarorn, Ken Kinzie, U. S. Color.